Sealssong

To Rayna

all my Love,

+

"Sealed" with

a Kiss

Love, — Marco Rosato

Sealssong

Marco Rosato

Library of Congress Control Number:		2013908533
ISBN:	Hardcover	978-1-4836-3886-7
	Softcover	978-1-4836-3885-0
	Ebook	978-1-4836-3887-4

Rev. date: 07/05/2013

To order additional copies of this book, contact:
Xlibris LLC
1-888-795-4274
www.Xlibris.com
Orders@Xlibris.com
134503

ACKNOWLEDGMENTS

My thanks must go to a number of people. First of all, I wish to thank my mother, who, no matter what, never stopped believing in me; love you, mom. To James Gardner, for his unending support; David Hoag, for his early encouragement; and my dear friend Laura Siefert, my deepest gratitude remains with you all. Special thanks to Keith Morley, who made me laugh when no one else could, inspiring the *Mad Mum* character in this book; to my buddy—Lutz Wolfram, my darling—Michelle Goewey, and Marc-Albert Vandermeerssche for his many helpful suggestions; my aunt Tina Sandrock; my family; and of course—*the seals*.

DASTARDLY INTENTIONS

Decara sold her soul to the devil many years before. Possessing powers of unimaginable evil, she had never feared or wanted for anything, except for a single magical teardrop—a magnificent power that existed inside a mystifying purple stone. This was a rare and wondrous gem that could either command the purest of evil or the purest of innocence, depending on whoever possessed it.

For many years, both Decara and her sinister lover Dr. Adrias had searched for this supreme of wonders. Adrias, a tall, alluring man of unscrupulous evil, had also traded his soul to the dark side in exchange for certain vile and menacing powers, unspeakable powers that allowed him to command the black arts by ways of diabolical experiments secretly conducted upon an infamous vessel known as the *Tiamat*. Within this grim ship, Adrias and his mistress collected, tortured, and killed female harp seals and their pups; for of all of God's creations on earth, these snow-white beasts, believed to be the most innocent of all creatures, held within their hearts a power most incredible.

The skinning and the successful marketing of the snow-white baby seal pelts served as a cover-up for Decara and her companion, giving them credence upon the seas, just as it did the many other sealing ships that engaged in the slaughtering of these precious beasts. More importantly, and quite sinisterly, it conveniently concealed the true monstrous undertaking of the wicked couple. Through his deplorable experiments of black magic, the evil doctor had discovered a way of creating diamonds out of female seal tears.

The wealth of stolen seal tears made for a legendary treasure that remained well guarded within the dark domain of the *Tiamat*. Still, and even more valuable and far more indomitable than the thousands of gems they had collected was the rare purple stone, known to hold the supreme tear. Once claimed, this revered wonder, believed to be stolen from the heart of the sea herself, would make it possible for Decara and Adrias to utterly corrupt and rule the world, extinguishing the light forever, banishing innocence, bringing eternal darkness upon mankind for all time.

Many days and nights passed in preparation for the momentous voyage needed to claim the powerful tear. Numerous hours and continuous research, both natural and supernatural, continued, executing toward the discovery of such a fantastic revelation. Having the immoral means of locating such an incredible find, nothing would prevent them from stealing it. *Nothing!*

For the time had finally come for Decara and her companion to set out to sea, charting their course exactly where they believed the stone was waiting—a hidden place, there somewhere off in the Arctic, nestled between treacherous waters and secluded ice, amidst the islands brought forth to protect the snow-white harp seals. It was here that the sacred sanctuary slept, in dreamy childlike slumber. There, somewhere, off in the icy wonderment of a place called Sealssong.

ARAYNA

The fantastic garden of ice glistened in the moonlight, shining magically like a faraway star in the cold winter sky. A brilliant moon illuminated the many snow-covered ice floes that seemed to bend and groan, disturbed by the mighty gusts of winds that frequented the islands. Still, in its entire splendor, this seemingly protected wonderland of frosty illusion would not be able to conceal the dark shadows that would once more advance through the frigid night air.

The hour was near.

Towering mountains of crystal, awakening from their wintry beds, monsters of moving transparencies, framed and gyrated over much of the shimmering nursery, becoming death traps for those who would lose themselves to this ill-fated night.

Soon it would begin.

The approaching storm was not far away now. Some would seek refuge in the white caves; others would seek sanctuary between fixed pillars of glass, burying their snouts into the authentic prisms of light breakers, distorting their seal snouts, their frightened eyes searching through the illusive blur, their only conceivable salvation *the sea!* However, concerned over the approaching storm, the sea remained helpless in her power to prevent such tragic happenings, and yet they all belonged to her, and she belonged to them.

A dark cloud snatched the moon from the heavens as the wind shifted to the northwest, intensifying in strength. Unstable and anxious, the sea rose, exploding into a mystical mist of phosphorescent spray, momentarily covering the ice garden and its frightened inhabitants. Inside the watery womb of its murky depths, the arctic tides responded to the building pressures, causing the freezing masses of icebergs to move and come to life. The sound of the wind began to grow ominous, wailing out to the cold night air, mixing with the haunting moans of the ice glaciers as they convulsed and began to call back to one another. The floes were becoming confused and unsettled, swirling and twisting in alternating directions, losing themselves in the obscurity of the black waters.

The moon's rays illuminated Arayna as she pulled herself out from the cold water. Shaking the chunks of ice back into the whirling slush, the out-of-breath and exhausted pregnant harp seal tried to steady upon the ice. She had become separated from her mate while making their way toward the nursery. Nearly certain of his death, the devastated soon-to-be mother looked out through the various moving floes, frightened, desperate. Unfortunately, they came across one of the swimming monsters man floated upon—ships or vessels, the man-beasts called them. They had accidentally ventured upon it while making their way toward the islands. It was as if man's horrible floating device deliberately tried to crush them between the surrounding icebergs. She believed she saw the dreadful vessel run down her mate, but could not be sure. All that remained certain now was that their encounter with the hideous swimming monster was the last she ever saw of him.

Arayna always knew of man's treacherous ways, fearing him from childhood. She felt the tears torch at her eyes as she wriggled on top of the ice, still trying to catch her breath. Looking down at herself, Arayna placed a single flipper against her stomach, remembering her mate while another birth pang broke against her womb.

Her mate's name was Apollo, known by many of the seals of Sealssong. His cleverness and quick perception had protected the herd many times before, but the mighty warrior held no match for the vile thing called man. As long as Arayna could remember, man had always caused disaster and despair wherever he went, and now it would seem that he had also taken away her lifetime companion. The thought of Apollo never returning made Arayna's heart grow weary with unbearable suffering. *Was he gone forever? Would he never see his child?*

Again, the expectant seal felt her heart break with unspeakable anguish as another labor pain sliced into her. Despite man and his treachery, despite the approaching storm that was beginning to increase in strength, Arayna held fast to the blessing that their child was still safe within her. Nothing would ever come between them, ever! This would be her unspoken promise to Apollo. Still safe within her, their child was not yet aware of such things as man or death; it knew nothing of violent winds or the crushing giant monstrosities encompassing the glittering cradle, for the child still remained untouched and protected within her motherly womb.

Like the many other female harps that already ventured to the nursery, Arayna had come to give birth to her child. Year after year, the mother harps came to bring the precious white-coated baby seals to Sealssong. By now, most of the mothers had given birth to their pups and had spent the last several days on the islands of Sealssong either resting or feeding their young ones. Up until now, their retreat upon the sacred nursery had been a most joyous one. However, presently, fear permeated the air itself; Arayna could clearly smell it—*it was everywhere.*

Frightened, she shivered, feeling the winds begin to grow brutal about her, revealing that the ravaging storm was near. The northwest sky seemed to dissolve as one by one the stars relinquished their lights, covering up the ice garden in uncertain midnight twilight. All at once, Arayna could hear the howls of her fellow seals saturate the night. Now restless and panic stricken, the herd cast their frightened glances toward the sea. If they remained on the ice, they would certainly be destroyed. The emanation of danger filled the air as the clouds thickened, tearing open, allowing the snow to debut itself. Ice and snow swept downward on the wings of the cold night; the baby seals began to cry out, wanting refuge from the storm and the moaning ice creatures surrounding them.

Soon the family would remember death once again.

The provocative screams of the pups echoed out toward each mother until their squealing whimpers seemed to become one. The March night filled with a million shrills of despondency, each seal desperate to survive, each wanting to know life a time longer. Regrettably, they had but existed for a short time, and yet still in their infantile stages, their instincts to survive well encompassed their being. Their cries rang out one by one, peeling the fibers of each mother's heart, puncturing their souls, their cries of impending doom saturating the nursery.

Each year, the whitecoats, as, they came to be known, came into existence on the main island of Sealssong, as did the many baby seals before them, but this lot would not be as fortunate as their predecessors. Up until now, they only knew their shining cradle as a peaceful and quiet haven. How could they know of such terror? Their hearts were not yet told of such things. As if deceived and given eternal promises of life and a dazzling world on which to play, the children of Sealssong would soon realize that to exist meant experiencing mere moments of time, there could be no promises.

Only three feet long, and powdered in a pure white coat, the pups, but yesterday, rested contentedly near their mothers, digesting the warm milk they had hungrily extracted before lazily drifting off into a carefree and cozy little sleep.

The howling wind once again intensified, frosting the family with its icy breath as the children raised their little heads upward, shivering and shrieking for their mothers. "*Maaa-Maaa!*" they cried, sounding remarkably like a human child's cry, their pathetic bleats soaring out as their mamas hysterically fought their dubious consideration to enter the sea, each maternal heart instinctively knowing that safety summoned to them from inside the watery chasm before them. Still, they dared not leave the nursery, for their pups had not yet learned how to swim and bringing them into the waters now would surely mean their death.

The sudden earthquake that hit was inconceivable. The watery floors sweltered with a terrifying eruption, setting free the surrounding masses of ice monsters. A million tons of ice and snow forcefully hit each other, scraping and grinding until the gulf cracked and gurgled as if ready to drop. Incredible towering chunks of ice collided with each other, toppling over innumerable times, appearing as if to slow dance before devouring each other. The rigid, misshapen mountains of glass, growing more hostile, continued to strike at each other while the gale winds hurled themselves around the nursery. The mammoth ice giants rode each other and took domination over one another. One submerged and another rose and took its place, another one disappearing into the inky waters as its opponent glided over high above.

Arayna was filled with sheer panic when she felt the nursery begin to shake. If she were to survive, she would have to find shelter, and quickly. There was not a moment to spare. Hurriedly, she began to wriggle toward the many ice castles littering the jeweled wonderland. Another sharp labor pain crippled her, stopping her dead in her tracks. It had all been too much for her. However tired and exhausted, Arayna diligently pushed onward. With another jolt to her body, the pregnant seal closed her eyes and began panting incessantly, hoping to ease the eruption taking place within her. When she opened her eyes, looking through the heavy curtain of blowing snow, she could see a cave not far off in the distance. Regrettably, she would not be able to reach it. For with still another resilient dose of birth pangs, more painful and far more compelling than any of the others, she suddenly lost consciousness, falling onto the icy floor while the nursery continued to rock and the wild winds covered her up.

DARK FORCES

D r. Adrias and Decara had brought along their servant Oreguss. A large man weighing well over three hundred pounds and standing six foot six, he was entirely bald and wore a rude, brutish expression across his permanently unshaven face. His body was covered in a thick coating of fur, and he could have been easily mistaken for a Neanderthal man. In fact, if questioned, Oreguss would admit that it was the case more often than not, assuming he could talk. The strapping hairy man was not only a mute, but he was also illiterate. Aside from grunting and groaning, Oreguss could make little conversation, but his dastardly ways spoke clearly of his crude and unpolished character. Hopelessly devoted to Decara after she found him starving in some remote and desolate village, giving him food and shelter on her vessel in exchange for his muscle and his unquestioning loyalty, the fumbling but powerful Oreguss soon became part of the unholy partnership of Decara and her evil companion.

On this night of shrieking winds and moving floes that carried ice monsters towering above hundreds of feet high, the evil doctor, his mistress, and her servant secretly came upon the principal island of Sealssong—the main nursery. The yelps and barks of the seals continued to fill the bitter cold, dark air, sensing their presence as the unholy trio made their way from the safety of the *Tiamat*, well beyond the borders of the nursery. Decara and her companion came equipped with every conceivable apparatus needed for such a grave undertaking. Having arrived but just a short time before the storm itself, they had at last come to the place that had filled their minds for a long time now. A certain ice mountain that held the precise thing they had come for: the purple stone protecting the all-powerful tear.

Dr. Adrias, who was more than sufficiently stuffed inside a massively bulky and heavy parka, looked up toward the incredible glacier stretching before him. Its endlessness expanded into the blackened skies, disappearing completely into the gripping masses of dark clouds that continued to scratch and claw at the delicate heavens above. The tiny part of his face, still exposed to the harsh elements, remained stationary in his study over the icy mountain while the savage winds blew all about him. The iceberg would be a most definite challenge, but the evil Adrias was not a mere mortal man, nor was the woman he was now impatiently waiting for. Momentarily turning away, he looked out into the blowing storm, watching Decara and her servant make their way toward him and the magnificent ice monstrosity. Even in the wild winds, draped inside her black cape of furling cloth that twisted and snapped, moving like a blur of a hundred tangled bat wings, Decara still personified sheer sensuousness. It was not just her slender figure and chiseled features or her flawless alabaster skin, but her unnatural, yet alluring black eyes also seemed to eat away and devour all that she looked upon that made the doctor lust after her. She was pure sinfulness, and that made the man hungry for her, always wanting to devour every piece of her. Forever needing to feel the press of her perpetually moist scarlet lips or the touch of her long raven hair, Decara remained the most seductive woman he had ever seen. Even the simplest of movements she made looked reprehensible, always resembling that of a slow-moving reptile, making her appear mysterious and unpredictable.

Perhaps it was how she slithered through the air; perhaps it was the way she seemed to crawl over the ground. This aroused and excited the vile doctor, and yet, still, he was most drawn to his companion by her black and shining eyes, eyes so dark they appeared artificial. They never seemed to possess any semblance of pupils, appearing as only a nocturnal shroud infused with a smoldering amber glow that remained inextinguishable. Having a long and slender reptilian neck, those dark eyes were forever in search of unsuspecting prey. Decara's unearthly seductiveness drove Adrias wild, for she was his beautiful and hungry serpent; the rest of the world was just rats and mice, mere snake food for his disarming and sinister mistress. How he delighted in watching her stalk, shred, and, gobble up the miserable and unfortunate ones who dared to cross her path.

Oreguss outstretched his bulky hand, offering it over to Decara, escorting her over the icy rubble that had come across their way. Pulling down the corners of the massive hood attached to her black cloak, Decara further protected her face from the stinging elements of the frosted world that they had come to defile. The storm increased, the wind howled, the island shook, and both Oreguss and Decara made their way over to the place where the anxious doctor stood feverishly waiting. Upon reaching him right there before the towering iceberg that housed the precious tear they had come for, Adrias took Decara into his grasp. Pulling her into himself, with a powerful thrust, he passionately kissed her. Oreguss stood awkwardly by while the doctor and his mistress remained caught up in their wild and frenzied embrace, the maniacal winds covering their bodies in lavish scales of snow.

"This is it, my beloved!" Adrias said through pressed lips. After finishing off their kiss, he slightly pulled away, looking into her black eyes. "Just as I promised you, soon everything will be ours, my dark and sinister darling."

Suddenly, another stray iceberg hit the nursery, nearly causing them to lose their balance.

"We haven't much time," Decara warned, looking up toward the mammoth iceberg. "Are you sure this is the place?"

"Yes," Adrias confirmed. "Look, it is the very place that bears the outline of the seal, look at the crest!"

With this, Decara walked toward the giant monster, her feet careful upon the ice. There, as she had seen it many times in her mystic mirrors, glowing crystal balls, and the endless supernatural paraphernalia she had stashed away inside the *Tiamat*, stood the precise mark that told her that this was indeed the place they were searching for. Despite the veil of stinging snow and ice that scratched against her eyes and face, she could see the definite shape of a vast and soaring seal, its definitive profile engraved deep into the skin of the towering glacier. It was a form like none other, to be mistaken for none other. Even its chiseled flippers were apparent, its shape cutting straight into the ice, appearing as if it could come alive at any moment.

"*Yessss,*" Decara hissed with delight. "You have found it, my love! Come!" She beckoned, kissing him hard against his cracked lips, splitting the bottom open, drawing out some blood by her abrasive touch. Adrias smiled, his tongue quickly lapping at the warm blood, savoring its taste, pasting it against his exposed and bloody teeth, grinning like a ghoulish vampire. Decara smiled evilly, then, motioned to him, waiting for him to reach into the bulging black bag they brought. Pulling out a strange metallic crescent-shaped disc, both ends glistening sharp, Adrias took hold of a ropey cord, probing from its center measuring approximately two inches thick. The rope, as did the disc, shone with an eerie light. There in the darkness of the powerful storm, Decara watched it glow against her lover's gloved hands, the disc vibrating from the icebergs striking against the nursery.

"Let us take it, my darling, let us claim what is ours and be gone from this wretched, worm-infested cesspool!"

Adrias, who was still lapping his lips, tasting the bitterness of his blood, looked once more upon the giant mountain resembling a fantastic seal. He grotesquely smiled, showing off his vampire grimace one last time before looking back to the shining disc in his hand. He pulled out some of the rope and wrapped it around the thick cushion of his glove. With a powerful and thrusting hurl, he cast the disc up onto the glacier, waiting for it to catch somewhere on its jagged corners. Not waiting to see if he was successful, an impatient Decara reached into the black bag and pulled out her own disc, just as Oreguss did the same. Another violent spasm hit and the nursery shook, its, quaking brought on by the sudden arrival of even more pushy ice monsters. With all lines cast, each one secure in its hold, the three dark figures began to crawl up the thick and massive sides of the iceberg, one directly behind the other. Oreguss remained the last in line, carrying along the black bag of goodies while swiftly ascending the glacier, the wind pulling and tugging at him, blowing off his knitted hat, exposing his herculean bald head. He cursed and grunted, trying to catch it, but in doing so, he lost his footing and inadvertently grabbed on to Decara.

"You clumsy fool!" she shrieked, steadying herself, her skeleton-like fingers covered in black gloves. Without hesitation, she kicked back, the heel of her boot slicing into Oreguss's bristly mug. The oafish servant lost his balance, and once again he grabbed on to Decara, knocking her sideways, pushing her hard against the iceberg, scraping her face against its cutting edge. Infuriated, she continued to hold on to the line with one hand. Reaching into her pocket, she pulled out a sharp silver dagger and began cutting the rope Oreguss was grasping.

"Asinine pig, go below! Wait for us there! Fool!" she screamed. With one more slice, Decara severed the line and sent her servant back down the incline of the iceberg, black bag and all, hitting and twisting as he swiftly dropped out of sight, crashing painfully to the very bottom, the bag following, directly hitting hard on his already bruised head. The evil Dr. Adrias never turned to see if his mistress continued behind him. Sheathed in total concentration, he was solely intent upon reaching the top, it now being the only thing filling his mind. He continued to crawl up the side of the iceberg like a menacing spider, Decara not far behind.

ICE GARDEN

Another horrendous crash rocked the island.

The monstrous obstructions of ice graded and crushed the sides of the crumbling ice garden. The collision was near fatal. The glass nursery shook and cracked, splintering, sending trillions of spiderweb tentacles throughout the frozen veins of its icy floors. Now the crazed current, even more forceful than before, churned and pulsated, dissolving the draped snow near the many edges of the ice holes, reducing them into gray deluded slush. In gushes of gurgling mounds, the icy froth spilled, drenching the snow and covering Arayna, spreading itself over her like melted ice cream. The sudden cold wash revived the seal but sent another round of panic-filled chills through her body. Springing open her eyes, Arayna slowly pressed herself away from the slushy sea pulling at her from all sides.

Wanting desperately to remain conscious, she snorted, blinking her eyes. Her frightened heart beat wildly, her sharp nails digging into the solid crust beneath the slush. Clutching tightly, so as not to roll backward into the abyss of the sea, she rested her wet nose on the hardened snowdrifts, her head palpitating deplorably. She gasped heavily then exhaled, her breath battling against the gusts of the assaulting winds determined to steal it from her. She readied herself for the possibility of death, and with her enervated pate still limply gazing into the white nothingness, she slowly rolled her eyes to the corner of her head, closed them, and held on to her haunting memory of Apollo.

Leaving the sea during times past would be suicidal, but Arayna realized that at any given moment, her child would be born. She had to make sure that no matter what, even if their time remained brief upon the jeweled world, she would know her child; she would forever become an inseparable part of it, even if it meant her demise. For, to leave the nursery at this time would sentence the whitecoat to an agonizing death of suffocation, and Arayna would die first before forsaking her unborn pup. She would remain no matter how devastating the circumstances. *Apollo's child would be born!*

Once more, she tried to move toward the sheltering caves, and as before, another more severe birth pang tore through her insides. Once a free and graceful spirit swimming imponderable through the sea, Arayna now became an awkward slithering creature. She listened to the floes grow wild, the sea lashing itself against the nursery, drenching her with its freezing arms. The sea was her home, and Arayna had always answered to its call. However, tonight she would not listen to its compelling demands. With whatever strength that remained, she would battle the stringent stings of the wind and snow continuing to whip against her.

Determined to crawl toward the center of the ice garden in search of the nearest cave, she persisted onward. Ahead, hundreds of other female seals helplessly watched the struggling pregnant harp in her decisive attempt to find shelter. However, their attention quickly diverted when the obstinate ice monsters continued making known their presence. For at that given moment, another substantial hit exploded through the nursery as more icy obstructions wrathfully slashed against the borders of Sealssong. Every harp seal suddenly cried out in complete terror while the storm raged on, their screams blending into a dramatic display of symphonic discordance. This night, even the children's high-pitched squeals would overpower the pealing theatrics of the sea, the night air inflating with an orchestrated eruption of shrilling seal voices.

Arayna, temporarily stunned by the sudden jolt in the ice, found herself losing her grip, overturning in a downward slide back toward the watery depths of the perilous currents. Nearing the edges of the jetting floes, she grabbed on to the ice just in time, digging her nails deep into its frozen skin. She slid a few feet but found that she could swing herself back onto the icy ledge.

She lay trembling attempting to retain her breath, every muscle exploding. Suddenly, the worst of the labor pains thus far shot through her with a crippling grip. She could not possibly hold back much longer. With all her strength, she began to crawl away, desperate to find a niche on the fractured ice so that she could give birth to the wonderment now awakening inside of her. As if even more enraged, the boasting snow further assaulted her with a caustic vengeance, impairing her breathing while she struggled away from the treacherous ice dungeons.

Able to see incredibly clearly underwater, a harp seal's vision is not particularly proficient on land, and the ponderous blanket of snowy chaos before her was impossible to penetrate and easily blotted out a frantic pair of fear-stricken harps swiftly moving toward her. Resembling snow creatures shrouded by the unfailing formations of layered snow and ice on their sleek wet coats, they nervously wriggled up to the pregnant harp. With pain nearly paralyzing her, Arayna's eyes darted upward, immediately recognizing one of the seals. It was her sister Lakannia.

Lakannia was older than the other seals on the island and had surprisingly given birth on the eve of this moment and was enduring the hardships of the tragic storm, as were the rest. However, Lakannia appeared her usual staunch and unfaltering self, strong and brave. It was her way, the only way as far as she believed. She also prided herself on her exceptional obesity and welcomed every added pound of blubber with divine bliss, knowing it to be an extra blessing of protection against the fierce storms and any unkind adversary who just might happen to come along, armed with a couple of sets of long and pointed teeth. For her blubbery figure did not hinder her in the least within the scope of the sea, there, she was weightless and maintained a surprising speed. Her color was that of a dark chocolate, considerably darker than Arayna's silver coat, but it was still soft in color as was Arayna's. However, in the midst of the storm, she now resembled a lost and silly-looking snowman romping about in this winter wonderland filled with danger and cruel uncertainties.

Lakannia excitedly barked before pressing her snout toward the pregnant seal. "Arayna, my dear sister, what has happened?"

Arayna lifted her weak gaze upward. Her body quivering, the violent spasms slicing through her, she tried to remain calm as she spoke. "The time has come, Lakannia. My child is about to be born."

"But, my dear," cried the corpulent seal, "we have been expecting you these past several days. We all promised we would meet here at the same time. What happened?"

"The man-beast!" Arayna cried while another pain ripped at her insides.

"The man-beast?" Lakannia barked.

"Yes," Arayna tried to explain through crippling agony. "We encountered him halfway to Sealssong. He came out of nowhere. Man and his horrible swimming machine! He killed my Apollo."

She began to weep. "I did not know what to do. I kept searching for him . . . I could not find him . . . I . . . could not . . ."

"Never mind that now," Lakannia said. "It's going to be all right, I shall watch over you. However, we must leave the island at once. It is breaking up like a dried-out crab! We haven't much time!" she howled, trying to nudge Arayna along. "Most of the others are carrying their children on their backs or trying to leave by catching rides on broken icebergs, you must do the same."

"No! I cannot leave! I won't leave!"

The chocolate-colored Lakannia shook her head and snorted in disbelief. "Don't be absurd. If you remain, you will die!"

More terrific labor pains shredded her insides. *My baby!*

"Listen to me," Lakannia pleaded, explaining while Arayna convulsed in pain and the storm savagely broke up the island, the wind and snow persisting in covering everyone up. "Your child has not a ghost of a chance in this odious jumble! If you remain, you both will surely be killed."

Just then, Lakannia's traveling companion and its shivering pup abruptly came out of the storm. Interrupting, she barked as loud as possible in order to override the shrieking sirens of the winds. "Head for the sea, Arayna, she is our only refuge!"

Lakannia sharply turned to the other seal, snorting out her words with a firm bark. "Never, you mind about, Arayna, tend to your own child. I should think that it would be your only concern now! Be off with you! There is not much time left for any of us, as it is!"

Upset yet realizing that Lakannia was right, the confused harp wriggled off with her whining pup.

Lakannia slumped down, crunching her large muzzle into Arayna's. "Fools, all of them, listen to me, dear heart. You must leave the nursery! Y toou must hold out for yet a time longer! Once you have given birth, you, like the others, can carry it on your back away somewhere safe. I will help you."

Tears formed once again in Arayna's shining black olivelike eyes. Once more, she begged. "Please, Lakannia, help me away from the floes. I have to move away from the floes!"

Becoming even more alarmed, Lakannia implored once again. "Arayna, you are not listening, dear. You must find safety in the sea. You have got to hold out until then; there simply is no other way."

Arayna coughed, feeling her throat constrict and become extremely dry. "My dear Lakannia, I cannot. Besides, it is impossible now. Apollo's child will be born, and I cannot restrain myself much longer, or we both will perish!"

"You will perish if you remain. Come; let me help you to the sea!"

The defiant pregnant harp shook her head and resisted. Lakannia nudged at her again, pushing her toward the icy waters. Arayna grew more anxious and threw out her flippers, digging them deep into the ice. "Stop, Lakannia. If you will not help me, then just leave me here. Return yourself to your child and try to save both of your lives. Do what you must as I must do as I must."

Lakannia remained silent, the wind shaking her body, as if she had become weightless. The barbaric snow continued to cover her up while she remained frozen, shaking in the thermal jaws of the incredible wind. "My child is gone," Lakannia softly whispered. "He was born sickly, too weak to overcome such a horrible storm. He died about an hour ago."

Although the sounds of the winds were ferocious, Arayna clearly heard Lakannia's sad words. They burned like acid in her brain. Closing her eyes, she began to weep again, daring to question the existence of seal moments and life itself.

How could Lakannia stand the grief?

This would be the second whitecoat she would have lost in three years, and if Arayna could have melted through the halo of snow around the face of her dear sister, she would have witnessed the pain burning in her eyes. The massive seal, having the ability to conceal her emotions when the occasion demanded, succeeded in most cases. However, imprisoned within her were the knowledge and the haunting of her sleepless nights and the tormenting recollection of the many times she had witnessed and smelled death, this she could never hide; it was the reality and the truth of her existence. The time was indeed diminishing, and Lakannia realized that if she did not act quickly, Arayna's life would be forsaken.

Arayna's eyes remained fixed shut, listening to the thunderous crashes of bombarding ice titans abraded and splinter where the currents remained strongest. Determined to stay, she dug her nails further into the surface of the glassy nursery. Jolting forward, she stopped. Her eyes flashed open, and she gasped. The muscles in her beautiful seal face suddenly contorted. She struggled to take another breath. The very walls of her chest began to tremble as if to forewarn of their collapse. Fear struck deep in every fiber of her being, and her rigid body convulsed and pulsated with an uncontrollable rhythm of hysteria. The massive pain within her womb exploded and now seemed to burn her insides, stunning her, making the frozen environment a vague smear of surrealism.

Many of the pups would drown.

In only a short time, their world would vanish and transform into a mutation of darkness: an ambiguous turning point of yesterdays and tomorrows never to be experienced.

The hour was upon them all.

Another wall of solid ice hit the nursery. The impact was fantastic! It split the floe in half, swelling, spilling over the island, bringing with it another million spiderweb lines of fragmented breaks. There was a brief period of unsettling silence before the structure erupted into its final climax of ruin.

Once more, the sacred place called Sealssong would lose another part of itself. Suddenly, the floor shook furiously and started shifting apart, moaning with an agonizing vibration, crumbling and pealing into the raging waters. Gigantic hummocks ruptured from beneath, ascending with savage screams, consuming and destroying parts of the nursery, each claiming their separate territory, towering to thirty feet and more. Baby harp seals went slithering and slipping helplessly along the frozen structures. They cried out in sheer terror, their mothers clawing frantically into the glass floor, desperately claiming their children between their jaws. Instinctively, they wriggled toward the floes, away from the boisterous earthquake rumbling within the ice garden, away from all that was once sacred and safe.

Arayna shivered, her huge walnut-sized eyes swimming in pools of tears, salty and stinging like the waters that would seize many lives this night.

"It is time," Arayna announced. "My child has come!"

THE TEAR

The harsh trembling of the island did not stop Decara and Adrias from proceeding.

Up they crawled, their feet embedded deep in the ice, their hands clutching tightly around the rope that made possible such a bold adventure. The severity of the storm had just broken when finally they reached the tip of the iceberg. Adrias turned and pulled up his dark companion, climbing to the very top of the glacier that took on the shape of a massive seal's head. With a surprised impulse, Decara pushed past the doctor and quickly walked out onto a stretch of ice that led to the frosty nose of the colossal mammal.

"Wait," Adrias called out. "The ice may be weak; we had better check it first!"

"We haven't the time. This whole wretched place is falling apart!"

"Still, I think we had better check it out. This icy beast has sustained some considerable hits."

"Are you getting cold feet, my darling?" Decara asked with a devilish smile.

"I'm serious, Decara, let me test the ice."

"I told you, we haven't the time!" she scoffed, proceeding to walk farther onto the ice.

"Decara, wait!" Adrias warned with a powerful and strained voice.

By now, the dark woman had ventured to the middle of the iceberg. Already halfway across, she stopped and studied the turned head of the engraved seal, its snout pointing directly at her. Without warning, a loud snapping sound broke through the ice. Decara felt the tear in the floor, and her feet began to slide apart from one another.

"It's all right!" she called back to her lover. "You forget who you are dealing with, my precious darling." Proceeding, she began walking on the splintered ice, her feet moving slowly. The wind tore at her, and the ice continued to split and crack in violent retaliation. It was then that she outstretched her long, thin arms and began to levitate. Up she rose, hovering a few inches above the ice. Shrouded in black, appearing ghostlike, Decara continued to float, her cloak savagely whipping itself around her body while her feet shadowed the splintered ice, never touching it for a moment.

Adrias watched with a mischievous grin that plainly told of his ongoing awe for the dark woman that he had come to worship. She still surprised and intrigued him; she still excited him, and that made her all the more desirable. Hopelessly consumed in his lust for her, he continued to grin, watching Decara perform her black magic. His heart raced. Needing to touch her made his flesh ooze with sweat. No degree of cold could ever extinguish the wanting he felt for her.

Decara continued to float over the ice, her hanging feet almost grazing the ground, her black snaky cloak crawling right along with her. When at last she reached the sweep of the giant nose, Decara softly touched down, her feet barely sinking through the crust. Once more, the iceberg shook and another icy titan collided with it. Nearly losing her balance, she stretched out both her arms, grasping on to the frozen formation, pulling herself up to the shaft of the nose. She pressed her body against it, holding on to it, pressing her face against its cold and abrasive skin. Deep within its transparent interior, a small stone holding a seashell necklace began to glow with a spectacular purple blaze. She closed her eyes, listening to the sounds it made.

"I can hear it breathing," she whispered. Then slightly moving away from the curve of the ice, she waved her hand but only once. The ice began to shimmer and shine, moving in and out, wavering and bending just as water does when contained and has nowhere to go. A wicked smile quickly broke out over her face, its evilness squirming from inside the folds of her black hood.

"The tear . . . *the tear*," she chanted slowly, raising her arm toward the penetrable vision before her. With a mighty thrust, she plunged her clenched fist through the ice, breaking off a chunk of the sculpted nose. Her hand dug inside its icy contents, and reaching further still, she came upon the pulsating and glowing purple stone attached to a chain of one hundred tiny white seashells. "At last, at last!" she exclaimed, squeezing it tightly inside her gloved fingers. Then quickly pulling back, she took the stone from the mutilated ice.

Without warning, the rest of the seal nose broke apart, hurling Decara backward, crashing her to the cold splintered floor she had only moments before floated upon. Down she went, hitting the ice hard, the stone coming undone from her gripping hands. She screamed when she felt the ice crack and split across her spine. Flipping over like some wild animal, her eyes frantically began searching for the purple marvel. She came upon it nestled inside a deep crack in the ice not far from her. Adrias was calling to her, but she chose not to listen. She had to get the stone! That was all that mattered now!

Standing up, she felt her feet break through the ice; more zigzagging waves of countless cracks shattered the floor beneath her. Partially falling between the gaping holes and grabbing on to any formation of ice possible, she continued to move toward the stone, the slippery floor breaking up all around her. With outstretched arms and her face taut with madness, she slowly neared the stone, its purple face aglow with wonder, her eyes more frantic and wilder than before. Carefully crouching down, she heard her knees break up more ice while she stretched out her trembling hand. It was nearly hers!

"Just a little farther," she moaned. "I'm almost there! I'm almost—" Just as her fingers touched the powerful treasure, the glacier sustained another hit. Once more, the stone fell, this time escaping by way of a large twisted hole spread across the fractured floor of the trembling iceberg.

On a ledge several feet away, the tear sat a mere half an inch from a drop one hundred feet or more. Decara screamed and cursed at the stone pushing through the chopped-up disorder, crawling toward the icy hole. Losing her balance, she fell, nearly shattering the rest of the roof, almost sending both her lover and her, as well as the entire top of the glacier, to the sea below. Sprawled out, Decara felt a heavy wash of slushy ice hit her from behind, spilling over the stone, nearly sending it down into the plunging cavern. With one hand anchored to the nearest mass of rubble, she reached down toward the partially covered gem with straining fingers, clawing at the air frantically, trying to retrieve it. She could hear the doctor screaming something to her, but she did not turn or even consider his clattering appeals. The only thing that mattered now was the transparent purple stone and the magic tear within, a power she was so close to claiming. Upon doing so, she would quickly put the necklace that came complete with sparkling tiny white seashells over her head before pressing the attached glowing wonderment deep against her dark heart. Fully knowing that she could never remove the stone once she defiled it by daring to wear its omniscient energy, Decara's fingers finally met up with the purple marvel. Slowly wrapping her gloved hand around it, she began to laugh like a madwoman. She had finally captured the sacred teardrop.

"I've got it! It's mine! *It's mine!*" she shrieked, quickly standing up, her right hand still wrapped around the stone as she held it out high in the air, proclaiming her magnificent find.

It would have been well advised for the dark woman to heed the calls of the infamous doctor, for all that while, he had been warning her of a massive crack in the ice that was slowly making its way directly toward her. Not able to wait any longer, he set out on the broken floor trying to get to her before the fatal rip in the ice did, but as Decara looked down at the stone in her hand, drunk with power, she prepared to put the seashell necklace over her head. With a forceful thrust of her neck, she removed the black hood that framed her face and immediately began to slip the stone over her head.

Just then, the fantastic split in the ice sliced itself beneath her, this time sending both the doctor and her through the roof of the glacier, out the side of a cavern that plunged several hundred feet to the ice below. Adrias was the first to go, but Decara quickly followed, her hand still grasping the stone that never made it over her head.

KILLING SASHA

Down the side of the iceberg seal they slid, their hands scratching its slick sides as they continued to fall. Adrias hit a gnarled formation sticking out from the side of the glacier. Panic stricken, he grabbed at it. Decara fell in the same direction, but when her elbow hit the icy limb, the ice shattered, dislodging the purple gem, setting it free and downward once again. In a flash, she kicked out her boot, catching the pearly string of seashells around her foot. The evil woman howled viciously, clutching to the pants leg of her lover, both of them dangling hundreds of feet in the air, the purple stone hanging there, swaying back and forth in the wind, its tangled pearly chain wrapped twice around the tip of her boot. Decara flinched and tried to grab at the stone, but it was impossible. The more she fussed and twisted, attempting to touch her frozen toes, the worse she made matters.

"Stop!" Adrias shouted. "I am losing my grip! We're going to fall!"

The insisting Decara once again paid no attention to his warning. Once more, she was doubling over, straining pathetically, kicking up her heels. It would prove to be another dreadful mistake, for this time she kicked Adrias in a most sensitive spot. Screaming out in bitter pain, he instinctively went for his crotch. He felt his hands slip from the icy limb, and before he could do anything, both he and the crazed woman, who remained stuck to him, went sliding down the rest of the accursed iceberg.

As she fell, Decara continued to bend herself in the air, determined to reach the stone before she hit bottom. Unfortunately for her, just as she nearly managed to grab hold of it, her foot hit against the incline of the ice, tearing it off, sending it down to the cold, snowy ground that was rapidly coming up before her. Fortunately, the snow broke her fall, as it did the doctor, but still, there was plenty of ice to slide on, thus making for yet another escape for the runaway stone.

Decara pulled her face out of the snow, wildly clawing at her eyes, removing the clumps still pasted to her face. She could see the purple thing making its getaway, sliding nonchalantly down a steep embankment.

Dazed, Adrias pulled himself up and tried to catch his breath. Ironically, he had landed next to Oreguss. The oafish servant was sitting on top of the black bag that had landed on him when he fell from the iceberg, compliments of his illustrious boss. Oreguss did not move a muscle to help either one of them. He merely stared at Adrias, comfortably sitting on a block of ice, chomping his stained yellow teeth up and down, eating a banana that he had stashed away in his coat, delighted that the infamous Dr. Adrias got a taste of Decara's rotten medicine just as he did. Adrias dismissed Oreguss's infantile glances, coughing, trying to rid his throat of the remains of ice he had ingested; but all too soon, he realized that Decara had vanished again. She had already ventured out onto the snow, waving her arms insanely, groping the air, the savage winds hurling the cloak about her like an angry mass of killer bees. Without delay, the bruised and aching man began trekking through the snow, panting while making his way toward the unhinged woman.

The purple wonder had come to rest in the middle of a snowy meadow situated a considerable distance from any swirling ice floe or grating ice monsters. Aside from the incessant winds and the shifting of the nursery, Decara saw no further mishaps occurring. The tear at last would be hers!

Slowly, she approached the stone, its shiny face like a speck of moonbeam upon the snow. Once more, she removed the resurfacing shroud of snow from her face. She smiled wickedly, moving toward the stone, her arms never retracting; and just as she went to reclaim it, a most peculiar thing happened. From out of nowhere, a tiny baby harp appeared.

Having seen the stone and becoming extremely fascinated with it, the small pup had disobediently left its mother. While hiding in a nearby cave, the tiny harp wriggled out in order to get a better view of the pretty shining something that was lighting up the snow. Although her mother was wriggling as fast as her flippers could take her so that she could redeem her child, she would never reach her pup before it would do the unthinkable. The pup gobbled up the stone playfully and began swishing it around in her tiny mouth. Although most of the stone stuck out like a weird purple tongue, the pup had a pretty firm hold on the glowing thing. Decara became enraged by the insolent behavior of the brazen slug; she glared down at the small creature with smoldering eyes. The pup, having never seen a human before, smiled. Her adorable round face ridiculously distorted as it continued to half spit out the strange thing.

"Give it to me, give me the tear, you filthy slug!" Decara cursed.

However, the tiny seal merely looked at her with eyes full of confusion. Carefully, it began to back away from the dark woman, the stone still in its mouth. Decara scurried across the ice in mad pursuit, swiping at the air, nearly scratching the pup's eyes out. Instinctively, the baby seal began to whimper, now terrified as the dark woman came forward like a wild beast. Decara started kicking at the pup, grazing it once, but it was enough for the pup to wince out in pain, causing it to spit up, exposing the purple gem, the tiny seashells spilling over both sides of her baby seal face.

"Give it to me, give it to me!" Decara shrieked. Suddenly, she heard a vicious growling sound coming out from the swirls of blowing snow. It was no doubt its mother having come for the deviate slug. Out of the wind and blowing storm she came. She was a humongous seal, nearly five feet long and as robust as they come. Having the typical black harp-shaped marking on its back, the hairs on her hide rose as she plowed through the snow. Wild with terror, she growled viciously, snarling, showing her teeth, ready to strike, her face a mask of rage, her lips twisting like a mad dog.

Surprisingly, Decara just laughed. "Come to save your filthy little worm? Well, think again! You would have been better off dead, crushed beneath one of those sliding ice monsters rather than having come here tonight!"

Undaunted, the growling mother moved toward her pup, but Decara intercepted the seal's move, or at least tried too. Immediately, the mother harp attacked. With a vicious growl, the corpulent beast went for Decara, biting her hard on the tender part of her thigh. Decara fell to the icy floor and felt the blood begin to saturate the heavy clothing under her massive cloak. With the strength of a madwoman, Decara once again went to her feet and once again the seal went for her, but Decara was prepared this time. She pulled the silver dagger from her pocket and struck out at the creature. She managed to tear away a tiny flap of skin from the attacking harpie's side, but certainly not enough to stop her. Once more, the growling mother went for Decara.

Knocking her down, it swung out its head, hitting the wicked woman hard on the side of her face, throwing her senseless into the ice and snow. "Run, Sasha, run!" shouted the mother seal as she and her child, who had once again gobbled up the purple stone, wriggled away frantically. But as the mother harp turned, she suddenly felt a heavy blow to the back of her head. Down she went, as if dead upon the snow. Barely conscious, the seal managed to turn to find that the evil woman that she attacked was also lying in the snow. There must have been another human beast, one she did not see. Dazed, the seal suddenly caught sight of the other assaulting human as he marched past her. However, before she could stop him, the monster known as man, before her eyes, killed her precious little Sasha.

The smoke from the shotgun billowed up into the buzzing snow and wind, its barrel having already cooled from the severe cold snapping all around it. Adrias had secretly secured a small firearm under the lining of his parka, knowing it would undoubtedly come in handy, and this was just the time.

The baby seal was dead. Shot straight through the head, a perfect ending for just such a day. Adrias had enough of shaking islands, collapsing icebergs, and bitter cold. More than ready to return to the *Tiamat,* he knelt beside the dead pup; and with a swift swipe of his hand, he took the stone. The doctor had to chuckle slightly. He had imagined incredible digs and fantastic, supernatural extrapolations made upon the ice, but never did he think for a moment that the claiming of the tear would be as easy as taking candy from a baby—*a dead baby seal, that is.* He simply had to laugh out loud now, and he did.

Throwing up the stone, Adrias aggressively caught it between the many folds of his gloved hand. He turned from the dead pup and began making his way over to Decara, who was now just beginning to come back to life. Aside from the injuries that she had received from the attacking harp, having also sustained a gash on her forehead, she was going to be just fine. Elated, she grimaced, watching her handsome, devilish lover trek through the wind and snow, the glowing purple stone dangling from his hand, a deranged smile of gloating empowerment smudged all over his raw lips.

"You've got it, you have the tear! Give it to me! Give it to me!" Decara furiously implored. With her scrawny long arms stretching out before him, her fingers grabbed at the air as if to tear it apart. All the while Adrias continued to go to her, he tauntingly dangled the stone in front of his rugged face. He began seductively licking it as a devilish grin smudged deliberately across his face, but all too quickly his cocky smile was torn clean from his lips.

In a tremendous rush, the mother seal pounced out of the swirling snow, and with what remained of her strength, she clipped Adrias's knees with her massive head. She heard the man-beast's bones snap when she hurled him to the ice, and before he could defend himself, the uncontrolled harpie finished him off, tearing away at his throat.

TAKEN

The screams, which Decara made, were not remotely human.

In wild madness, she continued to scream out to her dead lover, fleeing to his side. *"Nooooo!"* she ranted, falling on top of him, his blood drenching her frozen cloak. Pulling up his head, she took it into her hands and pressed it against her shivering scarlet lips. Looking down at him, she almost looked as if she would cry, but she did not. Instead, she moved his dead face away from hers. "Don't you dare leave me, I will not let you!" she howled, her voice sounding fiercer than the screaming winds that assaulted her from every side.

Again, she lifted his limp head and kissed his cold, dead lips. Blood soaked and with a darting turn of her head, she looked toward the *Tiamat* and began mumbling some strange words; and while doing this, she turned, gazing down at the dangling head that she unsteadily held. Suddenly, the dead man's jaw slowly opened as if to gasp, but he made no sound. Instead, coming from the dark corners of his open mouth, a white grayish vapor began to form. Gradually, it seeped out like some toxic gas. It swirled and began to evolve into different shapes until it began to take on the ghostly semblance of the dead doctor. As it rose, it began swelling in the blowing winds, its ghostlike shape growing larger and larger, becoming more distorted and grotesque as it moved away floating in the direction of the vessel.

Decara stood up abruptly, dropping the head back to the ice. She remained standing, watching the white grayish mist drift over to the *Tiamat*. It hovered there, thoroughly surrounding the vessel, melting over the ship like dripping ice in a freakish heat wave. Then suddenly, out of nowhere, there was a scream that evoked a name.

"Decaraaaaaaa!" it shrieked, overpowering the wails of the strong winds, giving one final blood-chilling scream before going deathly silent.

Decara stood there with her eyes closed. The wind brutally bombarded her while she finished off the last of her chant. With both arms outstretched, her cloak drenched in her own blood as well as the dead man's, she stood momentarily frozen. Just then, another ice monstrosity hit the island, and she fell to the ice. "Oreguss!" she screamed while positioned on her hands and knees. "Help me find that bloody stone!"

In just a short time, Oreguss was at Decara's side, lifting her up. He looked down at the dead doctor and then cast his glance farther away to the seal that killed him. The large harp was halfway to the secluded ice cave when Oreguss spied her.

"Stop her!" Decara commanded.

The seal was carrying the remains of her destroyed pup in her shivering jaws, wriggling as fast as possible toward the secluded ice cave that had once protected both her and her pup. Faster and faster she wriggled, trying to escape the nightmarish fiends responsible for the death of her precious Sasha, but after having sustained such an attack herself, she was not sure just how long she could remain conscious. Half out of her mind with grief, the large harp found that she could not move fast enough. Once again, she felt another blow to the back of her head, sending the pup clear out of her jaws before she crashed headfirst into the snow and ice.

Steadying her gait upon the rocking island, Decara flew over to where the dead pup lay, its crumpled body now sprawled shamefully on the ice. Sick with mad irrationality, the demented woman picked up the lifeless pup as if it were an old rag, shaking it, waiting for the stone to drop from its mouth; but nothing happened. Turning the dead pup over and holding it by its rear flippers, she continued shaking it as if she were emptying an overcrowded purse. Remembering that the stone was no longer there, she carelessly threw the dead creature aside into a nearby pile of icy rubble.

The wind remained at the peak of savagery when Decara looked once more upon the lifeless body of her beloved. Dropping herself down next to him, she carelessly flipped him over and began combing the snow for the stone. Growing more and more hostile, Decara's hands began digging and scratching into the bloodstained ground, her fingers wide open, sweeping the snow into blurs of chaotic hazy showers. Finding nothing, she grabbed on to the dead body of the doctor and callously rolled him over so she could further investigate. She began wildly digging again, but after more shameful bursts of shooting snow and ice, Decara came up with nothing. The stone was nowhere to be found!

Not giving up, she began crawling on her hands and knees. Her arms outstretched as far as they would go, she swiped at the ground, deplorably crawling along like a mad thing. "Where is it?" she shrieked. *"Where is it?"*

Still finding nothing, she began striking the snow with both fists, screaming obscenities at the top of her voice, shrieking against the island, the snow, the wind, the ice, and the insignificant dead pup responsible for her unthinkable loss. Foremost, she continued shrieking out against the wretched mother seal that had taken away her beloved on this night of countless failures, and failure was something the prince of darkness, her dark lord, would not overlook in the slightest. She would have to pay for her mishaps, one way or another, but she would not think about that now. She had to get back to the ship before the whole place fell apart. She was not about to feel the cold sting of the freezing waters; she knew exactly what they wanted for she could hear them growing more and more aggressive. They wanted to swallow her up; she could almost hear them screaming out, daring her to remain.

Decara stared down at her gloved hands that remained embedded in the wet snow and saw a dark shadow suddenly move over her. Raising her eyes, she saw that it was Oreguss. He had dragged through the snow by her hind flippers the lifeless body of the mother seal who dared to give birth to the despicable stone-snatching slug! A diabolical smile suddenly wired itself around Decara's lips as she asked in a low voice, "Is it alive?"

Oreguss punched at the stomach of the unconscious harpie and stuck his ear next to its belly. It slightly moved. Oreguss grinned and then nodded his head.

"Good!" Decara hissed. "We will take it with us, the miserable slug! I have plans for this one!" she said, drawing closer, glaring hatefully at the lifeless thing in her servant's massive arms. "We must leave this place for now, but we will return! Do you hear that?" Decara shouted, spinning around, hurling out her screams in all directions of Sealssong. "A curse, on your wretched Sealssong—a curse on all of you! For this is far from over! Do you hear me? Oh, I'll be back! You bet I'll be back for every one of you!" she raved. "And sooner than you think! I'll find the tear, all right, and then I'll skin every last wretched worm upon this worm-infested cesspool—once and for all!" And with a dramatic turn, she looked toward the *Tiamat*, her eyes a mass of madness.

Decara never shed a single tear in all her life, but at that moment, would it be possible, she would have, but no tears ever wet those eyes. It was just not possible. "My poor darling, they will pay for what they have done. I swear to you! They will pay!"

Again, the island shook as if to fall apart, knocking down Decara just as she stood up.

Oreguss and the unconscious seal that he was now haphazardly dragging, most of its body bloody and bruised from its brutal haul, extended his massive bicep, and Decara grabbed on tightly. "Come, and take that filthy thing with you!" she wailed, trekking on toward the *Tiamat.*

Every step of the way the wind assaulted her, showing neither she nor her servant any mercy while he strained to pull the unconscious enormous mammal through the raging storm.

As the nursery continued to shake with uncontrolled spasms, the sinister duo disappeared into the wickedly looking vessel, leaving behind the remains of the dead seal and the dead man, taking with them the helpless mother harp that killed him.

THE BIRTH

Lakannia felt another break in the ground.

Losing her balance, she rolled to one side, the wind slapping at her wrathfully. She tried to straighten herself while clawing frantically into the shifting world beneath her before howling into the violent air. Although Lakannia was staunch, she was getting on in years. In fact, the tragedy of her loss on this night would more than likely prove to be her last attempt at procreation.

"Leave me," Arayna told the older seal. "Save yourself, go, it is too late for my child, it is too late for me, but you still have time. Please, go to the sea, go—*now!*"

Lakannia's eyes saddened through the mounds of snow forming over her worried face. She knew Arayna had made up her mind. She would not try to alter it any further. Turning away for but a brief moment, the lamenting Lakannia witnessed the other seals of Sealssong, all of them helpless, the storm raging on with its stifling fury. The haunting pleas of the whitecoats caused the nightmare to expand even further as their little forms soon disappeared beneath incredible sheets of ice, crushing their tiny bodies instantly.

The islands of Sealssong would once again know death.

As their world disassembled around them, both harp seals became tossed and scattered over the ice. Fighting the whipping winds, Lakannia rolled herself into Arayna, their snouts lining up to one another. Lakannia looked long and deep into Arayna's saturated eyes, now only visible as two narrow slits caused by the irritants of the blowing ice and snow. Lakannia then quickly moved forward on the ice, her flippers firmly embedded into the snow. Jerking her head upward and opening her jaws into a fantastic gape, she proceeded to howl. Hearing this, Arayna knew now that Lakannia would remain with her and that she was renouncing the ice monsters, proclaiming the coming of the child, loyally granting a blessing upon her and her unborn pup.

Another crash hit the nursery. The jolt spun Lakannia's head around where she again viewed another part of the doomed ice garden. She witnessed still another harp with her child scrambling on the edge of the floe, holding and protecting the pup within her shaking jaws.

CRASH!

The collision was extreme! The jolt severed the nursery, jarring the child from the harp's mouth. The white orb of fur plunged into the icy blackness, trying desperately to stay afloat, grasping at the cold air, wanting to fill its throbbing lungs. *"Maaa Maaa!"* it cried in a high-pitched voice that quickly turned to a powerless plea only to be swallowed up by the frosted sea. Merely leaving a tiny gurgle behind for it to be remembered by, the baby seal sank into the blackness of the water, its body now forever belonging to the sea. Insane with despair, its mother broke through the inky waters after her destroyed child. Sacrificing her life as well, she became entrapped between the thick ice floes that quickly extinguished the last bit of breath from her pounding lungs.

Lakannia could not venture to look any further. Turning her eyes back to Arayna, she spoke, "I will remain here with you until the child is born, and if I am taken because of it then so be it!"

More labor pains shot through Arayna, rendering her speechless. The time had arrived. The whitecoat would indeed be born! Lakannia scratched at the floor of the dying nursery, pulling herself even closer to the trembling Arayna, shaking her large frame wildly like a wet dog trying to get the rain out of its coat. The snow became temporarily dismissed, but all too quickly, and just as before, Lakannia soon resembled a ridiculous snowman. Arayna screamed out in pain and then stood bleakly silent, her eyes rolling up into their sockets. "Try to straighten out, dear heart!" Lakannia instructed all the while the earth fell apart around them.

Arayna's dark V-shaped nostril slits suddenly flared wide open, and she began to breathe deeply with spastic abruptness. She nodded, slightly complying with Lakannia's request. The older self-appointed midwife shook her head again, trying to avoid the incessant snow and ice and began lightly stroking Arayna's head with her own, comforting her. "I am here, dear heart. I won't leave you. This child will be born. I promise!" Arayna strove for a thin smile, then quickly lost it and bit down hard on her quivering lips. The pain was raw and unbearable. Feeling the bursting spasm in her womb, she began to lose consciousness. It felt as if her insides were grinding against themselves, imitating the ice monsters surrounding her, consuming and devouring one another like cannibals.

The two seals grew even more indistinguishable as the unremitting snowdrifts piled lavishly around them. "We must move farther away from the floes!" Lakannia barked. Not sure if she had the strength left, Arayna obeyed and then fell limp to the ice. Lakannia swung around to the pregnant seal's hindquarters and started dragging her toward the ice caves. Halfway there, Arayna abruptly sat up and let out a most alarming cry. Not quite sure how she managed it, Arayna partially lifted herself up off the ice. Her hind flippers bound together in deep prayer, she grunted and gasped aloud, this time sounding more urgent than ever.

With one tremendous muscular contraction, it happened there, a miraculous moving life-form that came from within her. The miracle of moments saturated the sheer winds themselves, and with a lofty heart, Lakannia threw back her head and, with one final howl, proudly announced the birth of the whitecoat. It was almost too much to comprehend, but somehow, despite everything, the baby seal arrived: the pure innocence of Apollo and Arayna, now and forever embraced.

Arayna slowly gazed down at her child. His beautiful sight was beyond anything the feeble new mother could comprehend. "He is here, Apollo," she weakly murmured, fighting to remain conscious. All at once, the brand-new miracle began to stir, a complete wonderment and vision of purity. As the newborn lay on the ice, still partially enveloped in its luminous caul, he once again began to wiggle. The tiny miracle became stunned by the abrupt and spasmodic temperature drop. All too quickly, it went from a warm and cozy tropical climate of ninety-eight degrees Fahrenheit into a world of ultimate cold. He began to cry, shivering in a frenzy of discomfort. His mother raised her head, never taking her eyes off the pup for a moment, and with a twist of her hindquarters, she severed the umbilical cord. They became separated.

The white-coated miracle, now blessed with his own respected seal moment, shivered in the cold, he now belonging to the family of Sealssong and to the sea herself and they belonging to him.

Lakannia remained excited to the point of absolute exhaustion, wriggling herself near the newborn, wanting to examine it thoroughly. She smiled down at the wonderment, her eyes flooding over with tears, remembering her own lost child. Its innocence overwhelming her, she gazed down toward the weakened, but proud mother. "Danger is somehow forgotten when love is present," Lakannia said, still smiling. "My dear sister, you have a beautiful and healthy baby boy, bless you both!"

Arayna's face temporarily dispersed of worriment, and she sighed. She nuzzled her pup, breaking the fetal membrane still wrapped around his fragile body. Then the weary mother licked at her son's matted fur while Lakannia hovered nervously nearby, continuously trying to block out the inexhaustible blowing wind and snow from carpeting the innocent prodigy of life she had witnessed arriving only moments before. The exclusive scent of Arayna's child replenished the hostile air with momentary calmness. The unique aroma of her pup stimulated and excited her. This distinct scent would forever be recorded in her mind and heart. From that moment on, his scent would only belong to her. No matter how many thousands surrounded him, she would always know her miracle. This was the promise of Sealssong: a covenant that would never be forsaken. Unrelentingly, Arayna breathed in her child's aroma, desperately wanting to preserve this moment for always. She was still terribly conscious of the considerable threats of death that were extremely close at hand, but for a moment, they ceased to be relevant.

The miracle blinked his large dark, resplendent eyes as Arayna continued to lap at his moist yellow-tinted coat still stained by amniotic fluid. In the beginning, the white rarity would suffer the pains of utter cold, the malicious chill penetrating his fur and stinging his body with blind vengeance. If the pup matured, he would sustain the cold, but not now. He did not yet possess the protective blubber required to survive in this gelled terra of glaze. Violently shaking, the tiny miracle became aware of his mother, she who gave him his moment.

Instinctively, the pup, who was now cleaned and snowy white, began to creep closer to Arayna. The howling cruel winds made his feeble attempts nearly impossible, but with a little help from Lakannia, the small pup finally crawled into his mama's embrace.

At last, bliss.

WATERY DISARRAY

Arayna's shape, which disappeared and reappeared in the frenzied swarms, confused the baby seal; yet once again, instinctively, he knew that he would always perceive her as home no matter what. Home would stop the cold burning pain. It would calm his rigid nerves; it would ease his confusion and fill it with love.

As if caught up in the moment themselves, the ice monsters quickly snapped out of their momentary gaze, making their way once again toward the seals and the trembling nursery of Sealssong. Suddenly, a broad shaft of ice pierced the floor but a few inches away from Lakannia. Its impetuous punch shot upward, and Lakannia screamed, losing her balance, rolling toward the treacherous currents now spinning like volatile cyclones through a dark liquid space. The damaged floor shattered beneath her, crumbling apart like the fragile cast of an old worn-out seashell. At that moment, the sea sweltered and yet another gigantic iceberg appeared through the ghostly shadows, colliding and breaking through the nursery, towering above one hundred feet high and coming straight for Lakannia! Terrified, she desperately tried to move out of its path, but she was helpless, her massive weight becoming a hindrance instead of a blessing. It all happened so quickly that all she could do was to bury her snout into the snow and say a final prayer before it was all over.

The powerful wall of ice and water forcibly came down upon her with a thunderous crash, immediately erasing her from sight. Crippled and stunned by the crashing impact, Lakannia was furiously hurled into the raging waters. Before Arayna could call out to her, she also felt the impact of the volatile elements collapsing over both her and her pup, scattering them across the ice.

The small, snow-white miracle suddenly became unnerved when he felthimself begin to spin under the great pressure of the water. He found that he did not like this at all! Why, this was nothing like home! Around and around and upside down he clumsily rolled, his little seal body contorting within the pull of the sea.

When the exploding watery disarray finally settled, the newborn lay still, convulsing. His dazed eyes searched frantically for home but could not find her. In utter despair, he began to crawl toward where he believed his mother remained waiting for him, his small claws hardly breaking through the glasslike surface. Desperately trying to fill his depleted lungs, he found that the more he persisted, the less he could breathe. His shivering body pitifully thumped the ice while he continued to open his shaking jaws.

Driven by total instinct and not knowing where the intensity of her strength came from, Arayna managed to squeeze herself out from the crunch of the binding ice. Gasping, just as her pup was, she wriggled toward him, wanting to protect him from any further disasters about to surprise them. Quickly, she covered up her stunned pup with the heavy weight of her body. The whitecoat attempted to breathe again, feeling and hearing the frantic beating of his mother's heart. It crashed against her chest, sounding as a million raindrops hitting the ice all at the same time. The tiny pup breached a small slit in his quivering lips, fighting the sudden pressure that insisted upon flattening him. He inhaled again, and this time he breathed in the distinctive sweet scent of home, his dear mama.

Still, why couldn't he move? Why was she so stiff? Why wasn't home moving?

Although he was gaining control over his breathing reflexes, he began to feel as if something bad had happened. He started to cry, the weight from his mother increasing, the ground beneath him cracking and shaking. Immobile and trapped inside the folds of home, the whitecoat closed his eyes. Already confused and hurting from the heaviness that pressed down on him, the baby seal cried out when he felt the wounds he had received begin to sting.

From where did all this pain suddenly come?

Regaining consciousness for only a moment, Arayna struggled to bow her head toward her pup. A blast of wind frosted the tiny face of the baby seal as she opened herself up, softly kissing the precious life beneath her. Her tears froze on her beautiful face, gazing upon him one more time before losing all consciousness. She did not hear the screams of the sea or the extreme eruption of the ice monsters or experience the bitter pain of losing Lakannia and her beloved Apollo. At that moment Arayna did not perceive anything, not even the saddened cries of the frightened small one she alone protected.

Then—pitch-black.

ICE CARPET

Darkness so black, so unfriendly, surrounded the small seal, and he was still unable to move. The intense pressure of his mother once again cut short his breathing.

"Maaa Maa!" he cried, whimpering and squealing; the screams of the wind overpowered his pleas. Then unexpectedly, he became aware of his mother's beating heart. He instinctively knew that this sound was good and that somehow home was still with him, and he began to feel less frightened. In some way, the strange drumming noise made him feel safe. This solace, however, would last for a few moments before he would fear that something was wrong. His nose was becoming extremely cold and wet, and this frustrated him thoroughly. Jerking his head upward, he quickly disappeared into the folds of his mother, but that did not help either. The unbearably cold water was rising dramatically, and without warning, the icy floor suddenly split open, cutting into his tender belly, making way for the gushing waters to swiftly swallow up both him and his mother.

The shock of the freezing sea jolted Arayna back to consciousness. Panicking, she watched her baby become entrapped within the suction. Desperately trying to seize the pup, Arayna opened her mouth, attempting to snatch him, but was not quick enough; and in that instant, they were covered with the blast from the sea. Arayna was the first to collide with a nearby iceberg, then her child, his fragile body shoved smack into her stomach. With a powerful jerk, they felt the iceberg ascend with alarming speed. Suddenly, a small portion of the moving hummock made a loud groan before breaking free. Screeching, it cut through the undercurrents with a grinding gurgle, its fast torpedo-like rush gluing both harps together in a bond of ultimate horror.

From the desolate paunch of the sea, the shrieking slab of ice broke off into the dark winter sky, soaring high over the treacherous waters while the magnificent breath of the cold night air blasted both seals. Arayna reached out toward her infant with frantic pursuit, snapping at him just as he was about to slide off. Holding on to her pup with all her strength, they went soaring through the black clouds, zooming on the ghostly ice carpet in the sky. The crazed wind gushed all around the tiny white seal, and he felt terrified. Helplessly gazing up toward his mother, he could feel her mouth tighten around his plump neck, her eyes remaining closed. Daring to see for himself, he looked out into the swirling disorder, finding that he was inside the bellies of the clouds. Flying high above the rumbling nursery, he feared that he would be hurled off, never again to be seen. Sick with dizziness, the small miracle quickly closed his eyes, and both of the seals' mounting fear intensifying as the out-of-control soaring ice carpet began to lose momentum. It would not be long before the incredible soaring sheet of rime would take the seals smashing down into the frigid chaos once more.

It was here that the ice would relinquish its wings, and with one tremendous crash, they disappeared into the open mouth of the sea.

MIRACLE

Morning came and with it came the quietness of daybreak as well as the reality of the small seal's situation.

Where was he? Was it possible that he was still sailing on the ice carpet?

Unsure of everything, and with his eyes still fixed shut, he dug his sharp little claws into the cold and icy world beneath him.

Could he dare to open his eyes?

Just then, he felt something wet and scratchy moving on his furry white head. He still did not open his eyes though; he anxiously fought the curiosity bursting about him. The wet scratchy thing would stop for a brief moment and then start up again. Relentlessly, it continued. Up and down it went; just like the familiar drumming heart sound, it came to comfort the small pup.

Very carefully the baby seal opened his enormous black walnut-sized eyes, cautiously glancing upward. There she was again, his mother with the same silver color, with the loveliest eyes he could have imagined, her scent washing itself over him like a warm and inviting wave. His vision was somewhat blurry, but soon Arayna's beautiful face came into view, and both mother and child beheld one another. It was a moment that both seals would always remember. The pup sighed while gazing at her—she was home, and she was warm and glorious and gave him the sweetest-tasting yellowish milk that was thick and creamy and most delicious.

Within his mother's translucent glimmering eyes, he could see that her heart held many secrets that he could not possibly understand, but it did not matter. Those magical sparkling eyes told of a special love, a love that would forever remain with him;

and it was not long before the pup began to feel weightless, happily floating off into a dreamlike place within the endearing realms of his mother's exquisite dark and radiant eyes.

Somehow, they survived the ice monsters, enduring the night, as did the ice carpet. Well, not all of it, but there was enough of it left to protect them. Regrettably, the once flying sheet of ice had lost most of itself; the impromptu crash-landing it made back to the sea did not help any. Still, an adequate portion had remained, and the baby seal could feel the cold hug under his soft belly, its chilling surface quietly creaking while he nestled further into the warmth of his mother. A soft ray of sunshine quickly snuck out from the morning clouds, and with a steady shaft of filtering light, a warm glow gently spread out from the awakening heavens, eager in its descent to cradle itself over the floating iceberg now carrying two extremely exhausted and wearied harp seals.

Arayna tenderly looked down upon her small child. He was truly a miracle and would always remain that way. She watched him look up at her, his snowy-white face all aglow by the morning rays of sunshine now lighting him up like a heavenly vision, his tiny mouth curving into an enchanting smile. It was at this moment that the pup received his name.

Gazing downward, tears fell from Arayna's shining black eyes, their tiny splashes disappearing almost instantly within her baby's soft snow-white coat. "I will name you Miracle, for that is what you are—my Miracle . . . *my beautiful Miracle.*"

Then all at once, the baby seal heard something strange.

It was a sound that began as a soft murmur in the breeze, turning into a distinct humming noise, thrilling his insides, making him smile, tingling softly against his cheek. This ticklish, humming sound continued to expand, growing louder, etching itself within his mind and heart, just like home. Amazingly, the newborn instinctively knew that this beautiful experience could only happen between a mama and her pup, and it was happening right then for him, and just for him! It was his seal song, his mother's lullaby, the most incredible sound he ever heard! It was wondrous in every way! Its sonnet was a sheer magical experience that would record itself in his heartstrings and would never end. How he loved it, enjoying it as the scratching on his head started up again, his mother lovingly licking at his furry forehead.

Arayna's lullaby played on and on as the tiny ice raft floated in the shimmering silver sea speckled in frothy drifts of snow and ice. Swaddled in his rapturous daydream, the baby Miracle continued to smile. Raising his head further, he thoroughly delighted how his mother's tongue stroked him, easing all his fears, the enticing lullaby singing to him.

In this vision of melodic entrancement, the baby seal began to purr in absolute contentment, all senses of reality ceasing to exist. All he could perceive was her comforting scent, the scratching on his head, her incredible and beautiful dark eyes that sparkled like two mystical pools of wonderment, and above all else, the glory of that beautiful song she adoringly sang to him.

While Arayna's tongue flicked upon Miracle's head, she too felt an awe of separation from reality, serenading him with the music that would play on in both of their hearts for always and forever. And while the small iceboat sailed onward, the heavens lighting their way, from out of the awakening skies, two large white gulls suddenly appeared. Down they flew, wanting to hear more of the song that had enticed them from the clouds. On each side of the raft, they posted themselves—private escorts, maintaining their sail over the blowing winds, each continuing to listen to the magical seal song that filled the sea. *"For I will love you . . . your whole life through,"* she sang, her beautiful voice taking away all the fear, the small seal feeling the sensation of slumber wrapping itself around him like a toasty snuggle of sunlight, his eyes drooping as the lovely song played on joyously.

Arayna continued stroking her son's head, knowing that in a matter of moments she would join her child in the peaceful kingdom of dreams. Yawning contentedly, she closed her eyes and nestled herself around her pup, singing herself back into the quiet world of repose. The glacial mass progressed in its voyage, enabling the two harps to find the rest they so desperately needed, the shimmering rays of the heavens cavorting around and above them. Reality was no longer. There was just the moment of a magical lullaby; that and the soft sweetness of their togetherness.

Almost one week would pass before their togetherness would end.

NIGHTMARE

The monster was the color of the night.

In his nightmare, it moved slowly through the darkened space, its yellow eyes peering through the eternal darkness surrounding it. The monster made moaning sounds. It growled and hissed, disappearing and reappearing in a foreboding shroud of mist that continued to accompany it. Although the monster was far away, Miracle knew that somewhere in its stomach, someone was crying, someone with glowing blue eyes, someone who needed help, someone gobbled up and imprisoned in the thing's bulging belly. He could hear weeping as the terrible monster crawled and slithered with uneasy steadiness, cutting through blackened waters. With its yellow eyes glaring out from the shadows, stalking phantoms screamed and danced in a deranged fashion all around its misshapen face. The monster hissed, this time sounding more maniacal while it crept through the water. The monster was approaching! The monster was close now! The monster was coming! *The monster was coming!*

Miracle's eyes shot open, panic flooding his brain as he abruptly woke from his nightmare. Not sure what to make out of the terrifying experience, the frightened seal forced his head into the soft darkness of his mother, his eyes madly darting in endless circles. His small mouth was open, slightly making a sick wheezing sound. Jerking his head further inward, Miracle desperately took in the sweet, familiar scent he knew to be home. Crunching his tiny body next to hers, he trembled, breathing in home's warmth, wanting protection from the dreadful nightmare.

Becoming aware of his sudden movements, Arayna awoke from her exhaustion. Slightly raising her head, she looked down upon her small pup. She positioned herself in such a way, causing a thin shaft of light to fall directly over him. Sympathetically she smiled.

"Miracle," she softly whispered, "it's all right. It was just a dream . . . Nothing more." Miracle blinked his eyes hard, trying to erase the horrifying menace from his confused and racing mind. His little head was nervously pulsating against the cold slab of floating ice on which they sailed when Arayna gently lowered herself, proceeding to stroke softly the white seal with her tongue.

At first, Miracle was not aware of his mother's caress, but gradually, and with each tender stroke, the vision of the dreadful monster began to fade. The light from above made his eyes sparkle when he slowly lifted his feeble head, wanting to see his mother who now eagerly prepared to return to sleep. She softly turned and nestled down once more, but sleep would not easily return to the small pup. He remained frightened by the vision of the monster, and the recollection of those yellow eyes hauntingly remained with him as well.

In a little while, the tiny seal became restless. Having had enough of remembering his nightmare, he began to push himself further into the warmth and protection of his mama, merely staring out into the abyss of the sea, still trying to forget his dream and the dread it brought to him. Then like before, Miracle began to succumb to sleep, all traces of the dream slowly melting away from him.

TOOTH WALKERS

*T*hump! *Thump!*

The vibration was slight at first, but it was enough to jar the pup from his peaceful slumber. Once more, he sheltered further into his mother. Suddenly, the reverberation came again, and this time it was louder than before. It rocked the tiny ice boat, causing it to totter in the silver waters. Arayna remained unaffected by the disruption, but Miracle was most aroused by this sound that seemed to vibrate directly against his soft belly. *Thump! Bang!* The noise went, convulsing the waters around the floating ice raft.

Crash! Swish!

The ice boat appeared to be exploding.

The baby seal, now confused and alarmed, nervously crawled on top of his sleeping mother who remained decidedly much in repose. Miracle pushed his snout into his mother's belly, but she remained unaffected by his efforts. Crunching his small features together, he squeezed out a perplexed expression on his worried and questioning little muzzle. The water continued to rush and scurry around the ice raft, antagonizing the swirls into a miniature whirlpool, turning the ice cube around and around. He grew dizzy while it pulled both him and his mother in endless circles. Whimpering, he looked at his sleeping mama, alarmed and anxious, not knowing what to make out of any of it. One more time he would nudge her with his tiny muzzle, hoping to gain her attention. Remaining unsuccessful and most annoyed, he tried again wriggling up to her face, pulling on her whiskers with his mouth. Still, she remained fast asleep. Frustrated, he snorted loudly.

The upsetting thud returned, and with more aggression this time, followed by the same swirling disorder of the traversing waters. Compelled by a sudden curiosity, the small seal decided to investigate the strange turbulence.

THUD! SWISH!

Miracle quickly relinquished his short-lived bravery and instinctively shrank down, nearly disappearing within the folds of his mother, his large eyes darting back and forth. All at once, the frightened pup became aware of yet another strange sound. At first, it began as an unusually very high-pitched resonance that quickly dropped to a melodious moan. The queer noise seemed to echo all around the ice boat, crooning, *"Whooo-whooo!"*

Obstinate curiosities overtook Miracle's fear, and he surprisingly left the safety of his mother. Slowly, he crawled toward the edge of the bobbing raft, cautiously approaching the border, careful not to fall over. Timidly lowering his head, he viewed the swirling waters swishing around him. The liquid space below was endless, and within its depths, the baby seal found himself most intrigued by the sheer wonder of it all.

The moving waters mesmerized him, diminishing the rest of his fear. He began to venture further, dropping his vibrating snout down toward the swirling currents. His nose bounced above the sea for a few moments and then suddenly touched on its cold surface. Quickly, he retracted as if having been stung by a bee. He hastily remembered how cold the water was, and it was nipping cold. Once more, he snorted and shook his head disagreeably. Without warning, there was a vast explosion in the sea. An overpowering surge of water forcefully shot out, drenching his entire body, all happening so quickly.

In utter dismay, the small seal gasped, blinking his terror-filled eyes, experiencing yet another startling occurrence. Positioned directly in front of and staring right back at him was another pair of enormous dark eyes, each eye blinking perversely. The big eyes belonged to an enormous head situated steadily on the ridge of the ice boat as if disembodied, and on the lower part of its face, there was a bulbous nose that poked out with a wiggle, precisely touching the tiny nose of the wet and frightened seal. This strange thing suddenly spoke to him with a low nasal inflection. "Pull over, *pull over!"* it groaned.

Alarmed, Miracle quickly pulled away, panting, not having the slightest clue as what to think about the bizarre head that remained floating absurdly over the edges of the raft. Still determined to study this strange visitor, he continued staring at the blubbery face sitting directly before him. He tilted his head, looking at its dark brown nose, a nose surrounded by rubbery cheeks, cheeks that were extremely bloated and puffed out and continued to stay that way as if it were perpetually blowing bubbles. However, there was more, much more! The bloated cheeks possessed long thick whiskers that danced ridiculously as the head steadied itself in proportion to the constant moving waters. Now included in the compilation of oddities was a pair of long white tusks oddly positioned near the mouth of this preposterous creature, each tooth half disappearing into the surrounding waters. Despite the warnings going off in his head, the overall gist of this suspended head somehow made the baby seal want to laugh out loud. The thing before him then protruded its lower lip quite considerably, continuing to bat its colossal eyes, dramatizing its absurd gawk. "Pull over, pull over, I said!"

Suddenly feeling terribly uneasy, Miracle scrambled back toward his mother, hiding behind her curled-up body. The pup waited for the big spooky head to go away, but when he peeked out from behind the sleeping Arayna, he could still see it sitting there, just staring at him with those gigantic blinking eyes, its preposterous head resting upon the ice raft while commencing with its illogical babble.

"Whoody-whooo! I'm pooped! Boop-boop-dee-looped!" it huffed. Then the head stopped for a moment, trying to catch its breath, smacking its lips all the while. It made a heavy wheezing sound, taking in a whopping gulp of air before babbling again. "Gosh, if you can't pull over, MOVE OVER, why don't cha?"

Miracle was about to find out that there was a great deal more to this beast than merely whiskers, tusks, two gigantic blinking eyes, and silly prattle. Suddenly, the ice boat tilted sideways, nearly taking the raft to a dangerous ninety-degree incline while the head exposed more of its rumbling rubbery girth feebly attempting to grasp hold both sides of the screaming raft.

"Oh, poo-coo it all!" the thing grumbled as it fell back into the swelling waters. Miracle went sliding across the ice, colliding right into the moaning big head. The raft appeared to be sinking, and he felt the water wash over him with its biting sting of cold. Panic stricken, the soaking wet pup fought to back away from the head, but all too quickly he slammed back into the ridiculous face, its commodious eyes still blinking crazily. The head tried to wrap itself around the ice for the third time, and that was when Arayna abruptly came back to reality. Her body went hurling into Miracle's, hitting him from behind, sandwiching him against the queer thing, nearly squeezing the breath clean out of his tiny lungs. Once more, the baby seal was grasping for air.

"I said . . . ," cried the big head, "would you PLEASE move over!" With a wide swing of its backside, the thing tried to get onto the raft, failing miserably. The ice abruptly popped from its straddling grip then came crashing back down into the watery turbulence with another tremendous *THUD!* "Oh, double poo-coo it all!" The head sighed, spraying another drawn-out stream of water through its long tusks.

Arayna remained stunned by the jolt and the rushing water. She desperately tried to conceive what was happening, grasping Miracle who remained frozen and embedded against her heaving belly. Both watched the head, not knowing what to expect next. Although she too became thoroughly confused, Arayna was able to recognize the beast. The groaning thing with the big head and flapping eyes was a common marine mammal known as a walrus, a tooth walker as they were sometimes referred to. However, this was the largest tooth walker she had ever seen. Arayna did not remember seeing one quite this size before.

It began once again. First, one flipper grasped the side of the ice flotation and then the other, and once more it pulled it into the water. The floundering walrus was in the process of trying to get its considerably obese self aboard the ice cube while babbling away incessantly. "Not to worry, not to worry, boop-boop-dee-scurry! I think I can lick it this time! Yep 'er-ree! Boop-boop-dee-dee," it said, but just as before, the ice raft pathetically sank this time even further. The walrus continued with its nonsensical adventure, also sinking into the water. "Guess not, boop-boop-dee-snot," it grumbled before disappearing altogether.

Miracle buckled beneath his mother then looked up at her with a nervous shudder.

Arayna continued to study the sea while she stared at the place where the cumbersome creature had dissolved. "That was a walrus," Arayna told her pup, "a rather large and clumsy walrus!"

"Well, that is certainly a snooty thing to say!" the returned walrus said with an extraordinary nasal retort.

Both harps simultaneously jerked around, looking at the opposite side of where they stood, each confronting the annoying tooth walker once again. "A snooty thing, indeed!" exclaimed the insulted creature. Locking both its tusks onto the raft, it continued to glide along, trying to talk out of the corners of its fleshy mouth. "Speaking as a seasoned sister of the sea and as a true Odobenus," the walrus said, "I find your behavior to be most unacceptable. Everybody has an attitude these days! A snooty, moody, att-a-toot-eee!" it exclaimed, grunting unhappily, batting its eyes neurotically.

While Arayna gawked in disbelief, the talking blob maintained its post over the raft, still holding on with its tusks. "I beg your pardon," Arayna barked. "Ms—Ms—Odobe—you must understand that—"

"Odobenus, I believe you meant to say," corrected the walrus, "is a word given to the particular species that I happen to be, deary! I learned that from a very old and wise walrus long since gone, you know. He had actually befriended a man-beast, so he told me, a man-beast that taught him many things . . . as if a man-beast could possibly teach anyone anything—nasty, nasty creatures! Still, he promised me that it was true, boop-boop-dee-doo!"

"Look, miss, whatever your name is, I do not want to appear rude, but what is it that you want? You nearly drowned my son!" Arayna scolded, moving away from the tooth walker, taking Miracle and herself to the center of the raft.

"Touchy, touchy, touchy!"

"Please," Arayna begged, "tell us what it is you want, and then please go away."

"I only wanted to rest for a moment," grunted the spongy sea creature, still talking through the corner of its mouth. "It's my first time, don't you know. Some suitable company would have been nice as well." It annoyingly rolled its eyes.

Arayna's expression reveled anything but amusement. She suddenly felt anger warm at her cheeks. "Suitable company?" she barked, trying to contain herself, continuing from the center of the raft. "Look, what you did could have had very serious consequences. My little one has not yet learned how to swim. If I didn't wake up when I did, he might have . . . never mind," further snapped Arayna. "Besides, someone of your size trying to fit on such a small raft, I mean, *really!* What were you thinking? Go and find your own ice raft, better still, your own island and let us be!"

"But . . . But—"

"Please, just go away and leave before you cause any more trouble!" Arayna called out, looking toward her shivering pup.

The walrus slowly released its grip from the float, its tusks sinking further into the water. The Odobenus snorted, shaking its head, trying desperately to control its quivering lower lip but not succeeding. "But . . . but . . . I only wanted to—"

"I said, please leave!" Arayna sharply retorted, fully turning her back disdainfully on the blubbery vexation.

The large eyes of the walrus opened wide, ushering in a private pool of tears that soon spilled over its swollen cheeks before draining off its relentless vibrating lip. Hurt and humiliated, the giant monstrosity began to cry uncontrollably. In just a few moments, both seals found themselves surrounded by the dramatic and deafening hysterics of the wailing tooth walker.

"Whooo-whooo!" the walrus wept. "I meant no harm, I promise I didn't! Oh, triple poo-coo it all anyway!" It continued bawling while its face melted into a million blubbery wrinkles. Instinctively, Miracle raised his tiny head and strained to focus on the lamenting queer creature, he and his mother observing the pathetic display of unexpected emotions ringing from the crying sea beast. Still, the small seal remained quite intrigued by the curious actions of the walrus and found that he was moving toward the wailing head, almost as if in a trance. The sobbing grew more intense as the walrus tried to speak through its bulbous wiggling lips. "Oh, please do forgive such an outburst, but I find that I'm just a little more sensitive in my present condition. Oh, what to do? What to do? Boop-boop-dee-do!"

Arayna slowly turned toward the ailing beast; with her head cocked to one side, she remained in the center of the raft. "Your condition, now what do you mean by that?"

"Never mind," mourned the walrus, pausing while the rest of its features sadly dissolved into the creases of its rubbery face. "You are right; I'll just have to find another place. Sorry to have troubled you, boop-boop-adieu."

Becoming ashamed of her behavior, Arayna wriggled toward the edge of the raft. The lamenting walrus was already swimming away when she called after it, saying, "Wait, I did not mean to upset you. It's just that—"

"Never mind," the walrus sulked. "Adieu, adieu, and quadruple poo-coo!"

Suddenly, Arayna heard another surprising sound. It was another voice—a tiny voice. *"Poo-Coo!"* the bantam voice imitated with an added blast of gusto to his sudden bark.

Arayna's expression of absolute surprise filled around her face, her eyes enlarging, feeling the reverberation of the small voice coming from the small one now cushioned beneath her. She looked down, somewhat dumbfounded. It could not be. The tiny pup surely could not have formed his first words. Besides from being able to call "mama," as all baby seals do instinctively, he would not have learned how to speak for some time. Carefully looking down and coming directly in contact with his large eyes, Arayna watched Miracle look up at her, his tiny face framed by her shining silver fur. He was smiling, but his smile was that of a brazen smile. He just continued leering up at his bewildered mother, his white eyelashes fluttering over his lovely big dark eyes.

"*Poo-Coo!*" he blurted out again, giggling while repeating the silly words he heard the repetitive walrus recite. Not having the slightest idea what he was saying or what it meant, amused at his own sounds and the way it tickled his throat, Miracle once again reiterated, mimicking the sound *Poo-Coo* over and over again.

Arayna's confused expression surprisingly grew into a grin of utter amazement. Although his words were nothing but nonsense, Miracle was still reciting them most skillfully. Even the buoyant tooth walker remained impressed. She gazed at the chortling pup, swimming back toward the ice raft, clapping her flippers. "Well, I'll be! What a perfectly splendid name! How did you ever think it up, you clever boop-boop-dee-buttercup! Well, that's exactly what I will name him, don't ya know!"

"Name him?" Arayna asked, confusion washing over her face again.

"Yes, indeed!" cried the walrus. "I've been wondering what to call it. That will be a perfect name for my baby! It has a friendly, familiar ring to it! Doesn't it, deary?"

"Your baby?" an even more confused Arayna asked.

Miracle did not allow the walrus to respond for he remained delighted with the vibrating sounds the words made in his throat. "Poo-Coo! Poo-Coo! *Poo-coo!*"

Instantly, the sniffling walrus took on the grand symphony of uncontrolled laughter. The bouncing thing was roaring so heartily, consequently straining its throat, causing it to break out into a coughing fit that it could not control. The tooth walker shifted back and forth, slapping the surrounding waters with both her flippers, coughing and snorting, but most of all, laughing, laughing, and laughing! For never had she heard such a funny sound come out of a creature such as this tiny puff of seal.

Arayna glanced over at the laughing walrus and then looked back at her smug little pup. He was wearing a most defiant grin, obviously very proud of the sounds he could make. Unable to keep from laughing herself, Arayna began to join in with the contagious hilarity. However, as quickly as it began, the laughter suddenly stopped, at least for the walrus. Suddenly, the tooth walker's eyes jolted open, popping out even further than usual. It began to twist and contort its face, indicating some initial stream of discomfort. Relinquishing her laughter as well, Arayna and her pup looked out to the walrus with concerned eyes. "What is wrong?" Arayna questioned.

The blubbery creature did not answer at first. It merely bit down on its lips, creating a noisy, groaning sound. Forced oxygen expelled from its bloated cheeks, making way for large bubbles. They exploded around the walrus's mouth, the impelling water slapping at her. Then all at once, with one notable howl, the walrus spoke out. "It's a-comin'! *It's a-comin'!*"

Arayna became alarmed. "What on earth?"

"Never done this kind of thing before, deary, not sure how it goes, can you help me out here, do ya suppose?" The walrus cringed, continuing to inflate its face with preposterous looks of discomfort.

"But how can I help you when you have not yet told me what the matter is?"

"It's about the baby."

"What baby?"

"The baby I'm going to have."

"You mean here—*now?*"

"Right now, boop-boop—And how!"

Arayna gasped. "A baby, oh my . . . *oh my*, right now, why didn't you say something sooner?"

"Thought I did!"

"Good grief!"

"Boop-boop-dee-dee, boy, howdy, is it ever comin' out of me!"

"This very minute?"

"Well, I ain't talking next spring, honey!"

"Oh my, *oh my*, what can I do to help?" cried Arayna, feeling inadequately prepared. Pacing back and forth on top of the ice raft, she watched the walrus make ridiculous faces within the water. Then another jolt of pain shot through the expectant tooth walker, pulling her further into the water, the sea swallowing her up. Arayna frantically wriggled along the ridge of the ice flotation while Miracle pathetically tried to remain near her side, his devilish smile long since discarded. Without warning, the walrus impetuously emerged, striking the belly of the raft, punching it out of the water. It wavered, tottering in the air; but as before, gravity clutched at it, pulling it back to the watery floor below. This time, the walrus and its partially exposed newborn slammed down on the ice and both seals.

For a brief moment, there was no sign of life; not even the ice raft was visible. However, with a gush of foamy surge, the shaken-up ice vessel returned, somehow managing to carry all its disheveled occupants. Both Arayna and her pup could not be seen, for they remained utterly covered over by the obesity of the tooth walker, her enormous folds crushing them. In her final stages of giving birth, the walrus gave one surprising thrust, and a brand-new baby tooth walker slid out onto the ice.

The exhausted mother walrus looked in awe at the gurgling creature before her, wasting no time in cleaning him up. Then the mama walrus tilted her big head, studying the newborn, not knowing what to make out of it. It looked all funny and wrinkly, but then again, so did she. Still, it looked fake and unreal. A hundred different folds covered its face while it instinctively reached out, smacking its protruding lips, already hungry and wanting to suckle her. Surveying her stimulating accomplishment, she suddenly burst into another fit of uncontrolled laughter. It would seem that the delivering experience had suddenly become just too amusing for her.

Then the laughter abruptly came to a halt, and in a rather blustery voice, the mama walrus shouted, "Happy birthday, Poo-Coo!" Immediately, the mother tooth walker's crazed laughter once more commenced, and this celebrated guffawing went on for some time, eventually wearing off into a wheezing giggle, soon to be followed by more coughing. Then turning her thick walrus head around in endless circles, she began to look for the two seals that had originally occupied the ice raft. "Whoody-whooo-hoe . . . Where d'ya all go?"

As the exhausted walrus lay prostrate on the ice raft, her baby boy still suckling her, she began to feel pushing sensations coming from below. It soon became evident that the movements belonged to the probing snouts of the seals she had mercilessly crushed.

With frustration and determination strongly leading them onward, both Arayna and Miracle squealed and squirmed rambunctiously, pushing with all their strength into the numerous folds of the coarse blubber consuming them. Nonchalantly, the walrus suddenly shifted positions, presenting a quick escape for the two dazed seals.

"First there was one! Now there are two! Lookie, look!" exclaimed the proud mama walrus smilingly. She then extended her flipper, ushering the small seal to look upon her miraculous accomplishment.

Miracle gazed at the newborn walrus that grunted and gurgled happily, suckling away at his mother's spongy belly. The white pup could not help but smile again. It seemed that the funny big head had this effect on him, and now the sight of this latest smaller big head made him smile all the more. Though he could not rationally define his thoughts, Miracle instinctively knew that he was witnessing a sacred and privileged moment.

Arayna's confused thoughts softened, drawing nearer to the sight of the suckling and rather noisy newcomer, her eyes glazing over the infant, her expression sharing the same amazement, imitating her own miracle.

The creaking ice floated onward, and the prostrate mother tooth walker, the once again exhausted Arayna and the smiling Miracle all remained hushed with awe, all except for the baby walrus who continued to grunt and slurp all the while, the streaming shafts of sunlight celebrated happily over them all.

WELCOME TO THE *TIAMAT*

The evil man-beast had killed her beautiful and precious Sasha. Now, why he killed her child, she knew not. However, her baby was dead, this much was certain. Still, the reparation of destroying the man that killed her child somewhat settled her for the time being. She knew in her heart of hearts, however, that this satisfaction would be short-lived, for not even her vindicated act of retribution would bring back her baby.

Sasha was gone—forever.

The harp fought the tears as her eyes searched through the dark shadows that filled the foreboding foul-smelling place she now found herself trapped. Her body ached. Her mouth burned, and the places where the massive ape man had beaten her were throbbing with a merciless persistence.

Ever since the two humans had taken her away from Sealssong, she had refused to give in to any state of mind that would render her weak or obscure; that included the many injuries she had sustained. Fainting or unconsciousness, even sleep, was no longer an option. She would not succumb to these vile monsters, these dreadful murderous man-beasts, not a second time. She had to be alert and prepared at all times no matter what! All too aware that she remained captive inside their floating machine, a dastardly invention allowing man-beasts to float on the water, the seal understood that such monstrosities could hold hundreds of humans at a time; all of them neatly protected inside the belly of a fiendish thing that could defile the waters with its blasphemous impersonation of sacred sea life.

Brought there and thrown into a large and peculiar black enclosure that hurt with its rough and cutting skin, the frightened harp contemplated what her next move might be. One thing was certain—wherever she was, it was not about to let her out. It seemed to be put together with sheets of frozen black bones that were sharp and grating, a trap of some kind. She had seen something like this before, only smaller, when she secretly watched from safe waters as a gathering of less aggressive men caught and housed hundreds of fish in such likely contraptions. She believed the humans referred to them as cages.

Since her abduction, she had only seen the tall, dark devil woman with the evil eyes but once. However, the vile woman would return, of this she was certain, and the seal knew that her actions would certainly not go unpunished. But the brave harpie would never show remorse for what she did. She would kill her child's murderer—all over again if she had the chance.

Floating in the air, the black mesh cage swayed while the vessel pushed through icy waters, causing the seal to slide back and forth. A small separate door that was part of the meshlike contraption wickedly stared at her, defiant, from its squeaking hinges. It taunted her with its closed passageway that undoubtedly led to freedom. For the seal had already savagely chewed against it, and all she could achieve from such resentment was a mouth full of lacerated gums and bloodstained teeth. For the time being, she had to stay put. There was no way out of the black cage with its harsh floors and walls that cut like sharp teeth and jagged bones—not yet. From the moment she opened her eyes, all she could see were shifting shadows and black silhouettes of unfamiliar and grotesque shapes. Several large cables strapped to the ceiling beams of the vessel helped support the mesh monster that imprisoned her. The seal turned, continuing to survey the dismal place, and flinched. Her neck throbbed from the way the nasty Oreguss had manhandled her. Brutally grabbing her, he had thrown her into the black cage. Her flippers, still slashed from its cutting grip, were just beginning to stop from bleeding when she lowered her head, licking at her stinging wounds, trying to ease their burning. Wiping her tongue over her swollen and bruised gums, the seal cleaned the blood from her teeth. She swallowed down its acrid taste and saw a faint yellow glow from inside the monster's belly spill itself over the blackened floors. She tried to remain still, looking through the bottom of the mesh, watching the floor change color, growing brighter with an eerie glow that painted itself over everything as she hung there swaying back and forth against the clawing shadows of the room. It was the evil man-beast with the dark and frightening eyes and her servant! They had returned, just as she expected. With only the movement of the vessel to stir her, the seal stared at the sinister woman.

Slowly, Decara approached the floating black cage, her black and serpentlike shape cutting through the shadows. Her thin, long fingers were clutching and holding out a single red candle embedded firmly inside a holder made of tarnished silver, its base a gnarled claw that looked as if it belonged to a demon that had once crawled on the floors of hell. Oreguss followed close behind, his bald head glowing slightly in the moving shades of flickering light.

"Enjoying, ourselves?" Decara teased, pressing her alabaster cheek against the cold mesh of the cage, her eyes burning with a monstrous fire, terrifying and different from anything the seal had ever encountered. Still, the harp did not recoil. Instead, defiant, she glared back at Decara, growling, her exposed teeth now locked in a maddening snarl.

"Is that supposed to frighten me?" Decara scoffed, bringing the candle still closer to the seal's staunch face. The trapped creature could hear the dark woman's servant making noises with his mouth somewhere in the midst of the black and flickering gloom, but the harp's eyes never left the taunting wicked woman for a single moment. Again, she growled.

"Why, that's no way for a guest to behave, and I assure you that you are a guest, my sweet little slug," Decara chanted before quickly changing her tone to a most sinister discharge.Welcome to the *Tiamat*," she growled her face losing all traces of the slightest smile her voice becoming even more vicious—"the place where you will live out the last days of your miserable life!" She continued with slits for eyes, only the molten evil remotely burning through the narrow openings. "True, your life will not end as swiftly as your precious stone-snatching slug did. Yours will be somewhat drawn out." She chuckled sinisterly. "Just think of it as an extended stay. After all, we have so few visitors, and whenever we do, I can hardly contain myself. Just can't bear to let them go, I guess. A selfish flaw on my part, I'm afraid, but just think of all the fun we'll have."

Decara suddenly shifted into the shadows, allowing Oreguss to find his way to the door of the cage. After fiddling with the lock and getting the key to fit just right, the door hastily sprang openly, exposing the vulnerable creature. Decara's red candle washed all over the seal while she positioned herself directly in front of the snarling beast. "And I guarantee you, we will have fun—lots and lots of fun—starting—*right now!*"

The seal, sensing immediate danger, wriggled backward, growling every wriggle of the way until she could go no further. She had reached the back of the cage and was helpless to the doings of the evil man-beast holding the candle. Pressed up against the cold mesh, the harp listened as the dark woman spoke to her. "We're going to play a little game I invented. You'd like to play, wouldn't you?"

Again, the distressed seal growled furiously, pressing itself pitifully against the cold and biting mesh of the cage.

"It's oodles and oodles of fun! Honest! I call it 'Slugs and Fears and Diamond Tears'! How do you play? Well, I'm glad you asked. First, you need a slug, a despairing mother slug! Why, that would be you, my dear. Then with a little help from sources I'd like to keep confidential, the slug begins to cry oodles and oodles of tears! But that's not the best part! You'd like to hear the best part, wouldn't you? You'll get a real big seal kick out of this, I'm sure! The lucky slug, that's you again, gets to relive over and over and over the murder or death of their precious little baby slug! Confused? Don't be! You see, all the tears you will be shedding because of the untimely demise of your stone-snatching brat will be transformed into diamond chips! Yes, you heard right—sparkling diamond chips! How, you ask? Why, it's simple! 'Tis dark magic that could not possibly work without pathetic slugs like you! Slugs who fortunately witness the death of their own slimy offspring just so I could get appallingly rich while I suck out every last drop of breath from what's left of your tragic and grieving pathetic hearts. Sound fun? Good! Now—let's play!"

The seal remained stationary, slightly teeter-tottering back and forth inside the cage as the dark woman stretched a vile grimace across her ruby red lips, staring back at the seal, opening her dark, fiery eyes, making them flare with a demonic flicker that smoldered with a pale yellow glow. Then turning toward the shadows where Oreguss was hiding, Decara raised the candle, summoning him. While chomping his yellow-stained teeth, up and down, Oreguss grunted, emerging from the gloom. Decara turned to face her servant, causing a streak of light from her odious candle to catch sight of four glaring reflections coming from the faces of four large and shiny portholes, all of them placed neatly in a row positioned against a black wall at the very end of the room.

Each pane of glass was stained a pale yellow color, but to the seal, they appeared to be ice chambers or ice passageways that if broken

would once again take her to the sea. The seal could see them
plainly, but when Decara returned to stand before the cage as before,
they became immediately swallowed up in the darkness. However
vanished, the harp made a permanent mental impression of those
portholes and would certainly not forget where they were.

Decara's mouth twisted again, pulling on itself in a strained
grimace that looked as though it would tear the skin from her
lips. For a moment, the shadows in the room moved about with a
nervous cringe when she gave the light to her servant in exchange
for something else. Now having possession of the candle, Oreguss
held up his arm, scattering away the shadows. The room swam in
the devilish glow of the waxy demon when Decara drew closer to
the cage. The seal could see that she was holding something most
strange and peculiar. Within the squeeze of her long fingers, the
evil woman held out a black chalice. It appeared to be covered in a
substance that made it look shiny and three-dimensional. It danced
and seemed to waver, and on the top of its fluctuating shape, there
was a covering that sealed whatever waited inside.

Once again, Decara spread her monster grimace across her pale
face. "Now the fun really begins," she hissed, removing the lid. The
seal watched it half fall away, the lid still connected to the odd cup
by a small hinge. With a pounding heart, the harp listened as a low
fizzing sound escaped, and with its sputtering gasp, the frightened
creature watched a green metallic vapor crawl out from the strange
chalice. Out it came, swirling, resembling a twisted mass of serpents.
Sinisterly, the creeping mist began to spread out like thousands of
fingers, all of them stretching and fizzing toward the captured seal.
With nowhere to go, the harp watched with terrified eyes as the
hellish mist came toward her, suffocating her. Immediately, the seal
bit down on her tongue and her eyes exploded with pain, more
incredible and unbearable than any suffering ever imagined. She
moaned and wretched in agony, never opening her mouth but only
biting down, her mouth still in the mad-dog snarl, her eyes feeling as
if set on fire.

Then blindness surrounded her; it was darker than the night
and blacker than all nothingness. The seal threw herself hard on the
cutting floor of the mesh cage, her snout grating the jagged edges.
The absolute torment in her eyes ripped at her pupils, and it felt as
if her eyes were being shredded and sliced. Then once again, a small
portion of the seal's sight returned. Crippled within this semiblind
misery, the crawling green mist continued to cover her. It lashed out
at her, burning her, eating away her eyes. From this torment, a vision

materialized. For what she was now forced to look upon made her blood turn to ice. It was her beloved Sasha! She was alive again, but just for the moment. For what seemed like an eternity of living hell, the seal examined over and over again the death of her innocent pup. In horrendous replay, the violated mother watched in helpless torment as the wicked ghost of Dr. Adrias destroyed her child again and again in the longest, cruelest nightmare ever conceived! In floods of grieving torture, the seal began weeping uncontrollably, shedding tears from burning sockets that were once cool and dark, now red, swollen, and ablaze with a hellish inferno that seared her soul. In seconds, the seal's face became drenched in a deluge of tears. She cried and wept until she thought she could weep no more, then, wept again. This ghastly torment went on for what seemed forever. Soon, the harp went limp as if dead, her degraded body left spreading over the cold and cutting floor of the mesh cage.

The seal lay this way for some time until she eventually lifted her weary head. Her eyes still burned with consummate agony, fighting to remain conscious. Gradually, the unbearable burning sensation left her and she could see like before, but as she began to pull herself up, she could feel the tingle and hear the faint clamor of objects that shone like the stars themselves. They were everywhere! They filled up the horrible black cage with an erratic sea of glittering sparkle.

Unable to ponder the shimmering phenomenon further, the disoriented seal became harshly startled when the hairy paw of Oreguss slammed hard against the cage. In an excited frenzy, he continued to slam his fist against the black mesh, all hopped up to see the piles and piles of endless diamond chips, thinking, this slug really paid off! Never had he seen so many tears come out of one slug before, consequently jostling up more fortune than he thought could ever be squeezed out of one grimy beast. Once again, he slammed his fist, chomping on his yellow teeth, jumping up and down as Decara came out of the shadows. "We hit the definitive jackpot with this one, didn't we, Oreguss?" she vaunted, holding out the red candle, the black shining chalice no longer anywhere in sight.

The languishing seal tried to get up again but slipped on thousands of diamond stones from beneath. Both her front flippers went first and she followed, crashing deplorably into the sea of glassy wonders. The dazed creature shook her head with annoyance, then snorted and tried to push herself toward the back of the cage, the front of the mesh prison swinging wide open. The hairy arm of the massive Oreguss came toward her. With nowhere to go, she remained immobile. Terrified, she felt the rough and thick grip of Oreguss wrap itself around her throat.

"Careful, Oreguss, we want this one to last a bit longer," Decara cautioned with a slight chuckle underscoring her words. "Besides, I have something else planned for our honored guest. Bring the slug to me!"

Forcefully pulling the seal along the diamond-covered mesh floor, Oreguss yanked the harp forward, spilling several hundred diamond chips out of the opening of the cage. Decara did not waste any time. Grabbing hold of both sides of the seal's face, she squeezed her fingers around its muzzle, crushing its jaw while she spoke out. "And to show you just how much more fun we're going to have, I have another surprise for you." Releasing her hand from the seal's snout, Decara quickly twisted her fingers around its head. "You took from me the only thing I ever loved, and for that, you will pay! And since you took away something from me—I shall take away something *from you*—your slimly brain!" Decara hissed with madness foaming around her lips. While squeezing the seal's head with her skeleton grip, she continued, her red flaring eyes disappearing up inside her head as her wet lips chanted forth:

> *From this moment on, your mind shall be void!*
> *For it shall only be filled with the one you destroyed!*
> *'Tis his face you shall seek, in all that you see!*
> *In madness, you will dwell, nevermore to be free!*

Decara flung back the seal's head, watching it hit a pile of diamonds, causing the door to slam closed. The evil woman began to walk away, laughing crudely, but then quickly stopped when she saw something shine from the corners of the beast's mouth. The bewitched seal merely stared ahead blankly, a queer, almost comical look stamped across her once intense features. Decara flew over to the door of the cage and threw it open, striking it hard against the cold black netting of itself, and looking into the mesh prison, she glared suspiciously at the seal, her red glowing eyes penetrating into the afflicted creature. "What is it that you have in your dirty mouth?" Decara demanded in a raging outburst.

The dazed seal merely looked at her with a dumfounded look as if not realizing what she had contained inside her own jaws. It would take the weary harpie time to remember things as before, for Decara's wicked spell was most potent and most debilitating.

"Answer me!" Decara shouted.

The mindless seal moved her tongue about the innards of her mouth. Immediately, the object that she had managed to conceal beneath her tongue and along the wide passageways of her cheeks and throat stood exposed and lodged just behind her smirking seal lips. Sucking on it, she flipped it over in her mouth as if savoring its taste then allowed a piece of it to stick out from her munching lips. It was the purple stone!

Decara's eyes flared with unbridled astonishment. *"The tear!"*

The mad harpie crossed her eyes, trying to look down at the glowing object partially peeking out from the folds of its mouth. Satisfied in her recall, the seal slurped up the stone and slammed shut her jaws.

"You've had it the whole time!" cursed the infuriated woman. "Give it to me!" she demanded.

However, the bewitched seal had no intentions of giving it up. For whatever the reason, the glowing thing that she held in her mouth was most relevant to the murdering man-beast. Daft or not, she would always remember what the vicious woman and her dead companion did to her child and therefore she would die before relinquishing anything to her, and that meant the glowing purple stone!

The mad seal smiled, suddenly remembering the moment when she initially took the stone. It somehow came back to her without delay despite her newly accursed madness. It was back in Sealssong when the man-beasts were not looking, that very split second they took their vile eyes off her. That was when she decided to take advantage of their carelessness, and with a quick bend of her head, she swiped her tongue into the snow, slurping up the magical ornament, concealing it deep in her mouth. She knew it was what they had killed her precious Sasha for, and now the precise thing that they would kill for belonged to her—and there was no way she would ever give it up! It would be like watching Sasha die all over again, and after the loss of her mind and the horrific experience of stealing seal tears, she could not bear such a torturous ordeal. No, the stone was hers, and she was keeping it!

Without warning, Decara flew at the seal. She scratched at its lips, trying to pry its mouth open, but the mad beast clenched down tight, growling at her like a vicious dog.

"Give it to me, I said!"

Retreating, the seal only growled louder.

Decara was hardly intimidated. "Open your dirty mouth, slug!" she screamed, grabbing hold of the seal's head, both her skeleton hands clawing at the corners of the mad creature's lips, cutting into them and making them bleed. Still, the seal did not budge.

"Give it to me or I will kill you, right here and now!"

"No, and you can't make me!" stung the seal through clenched lips that had difficulty forming words from the way the stone and its seashell chain remained lodged between them.

A shocked Decara glared at the harp with open and fiery eyes. "Oh, you decided to speak, did you? Didn't know I could understand your pathetic dialect, did you, slug? Well, you better give it to me now and be quick about it!"

The mad seal continued to growl angrily, this time even wilder as if to attack. A small stream of spittle formed around her taut lips while she continued to glare back at the vile woman. Decara became outraged with further frustration. She lunged toward the seal again, ripping at its mouth, wanting to tear it clean off its face.

"Give it to me or I will cut off your filthy head and feed it to the sharks, but not before I take the tear from those dirty lips of yours!" However, no matter how Decara scratched and pulled, the seal would not open its mouth. *"Oreguss,"* Decara shouted, "hold the beast while I remove its head!"

The hairy man was immediately at the side of his insane mistress, both his arms ready to seize the growling beast. The mad seal tried to recoil to the back of the cage, but Oreguss was exceptionally quick and extremely powerful. In seconds, he had the seal between his large apish fingers, his grip tight around her neck. Immersed in the shadows, Decara temporarily disappeared but returned in just a few moments, bursting through the gloom with a long silver sword in her hands.

"Hold the wretched thing steady while I cut off its head!" she shrieked, but the wicked woman did not realize that with madness comes newfound strength, exactly what the cursed seal now possessed.

Upon first sight of the sword, the seal flew into a wild fury, swinging her backside toward the brutal servant, clipping Oreguss against the side of his head, stunning him long enough to pull free from his dastardly grip. Then plunging forward, the harp flipped out from the cage and landed with a harsh slump on the black floor, her stony tears crashing forth in every direction. In a sudden wriggle, the mad beast plowed through the shadows, away from the raving dark woman with the fiery red eyes. Becoming mad herself, Decara began to rake through the darkness. She overturned everything in her path. Tables, chairs, shelves that held countless bottles of potions and lotions holding mystical powers, all of them discarded while clawing her way through the darkness with only one intent—to find and kill the seal with the magic tear!

"You'll never get away, *never!*" threatened Decara. Suddenly tripping over the rubble she had just created, Decara crashed into dozens of strange apparatuses housing glowing colors and swirling mists of unknown origins, all of them pressed inside glass vials, now all crushed and broken beneath her darting feet. "Oreguss, you fool! Bring me the candle!" she hissed. "That tear belongs to me! It is mine! *MINE!*" she ranted, ripping the candle out of her servant's hand, slapping the unsuspecting man across his unshaven face. "Idiot, help me find the wretched thief!" In complete obedience, Oreguss rubbed the sting out of his scruffy face while turning into the shadows, looking for the seal with the purple stone still stuck somewhere inside its mouth.

"Over here!" Decara screamed. "I heard something coming from behind there!"

Oreguss looked through the distinct layers of darkness. He quickly came across a massive cabinet that remained specifically constructed to hold even more vials of potions upon potions. "I must get that stone! No one must wear it but me!" howled the insane, dark woman holding out the candle, dispersing the shadows, so she could see where the mad harpie was hiding. Again, she thought she heard something coming from behind her fancy chiffonier. "There! There, it is again! I am sure it is hiding behind the bloody thing. Move it! Now!" she screamed with an earsplitting yell.

Jumping to her command, Oreguss quickly straddled the large and bulky piece of furniture, positioning his massive feet just right on the dark floor so as not to lose his balance. With encore after encore of loud grunting groans, he slowly moved the cabinet farther away from the wall, but when Decara lowered her candle, expecting to see the cowering seal that she would immediately destroy, only darkness flashed back at her. Wanting to investigate further, she probed the candle into the consuming seam of the gloom made up of a hundred different scary shadows, all of them dancing against the wall behind the chiffonier. Bending forward, sure she would find the accursed seal there, she felt a heavy SMACK against the back of her head. Down she fell, crashing to the floor, dropping the sword, her head hitting the wall behind the cabinet of potions and spells, her candle nearly dropping out of her hand. Then another SMACK!

The mad seal had managed to trick her once again. She may have become recently unhinged, but she was still shrewd enough to grasp between her flippers a piece of one of the broken objects Decara had hurled to the floor, casting it against the opposite side of the room at just the right moment to confuse the vile, dark devil woman.

The crazed harp hurriedly wriggled away, sinking further into the shifting shadows. Clutching the candle with a firm grip, Decara whirled around, losing her balance, nearly falling into the wall again, her head still spinning from the blows she had taken from the mad but cunning harpie. Tromping through the dispersing shadows with her blazing candle, her red eyes burning fiercer than the flame she carried, Decara shrieked, "Give it to me, give me the damn tear, you loathsome stone-stealing worm!"

More cloaks of folding darkness engulfed the wicked woman as she penetrated the room with only blind fury as her guide. The sound of broken glass beneath her feet played havoc with her senses, making it difficult to hear any sudden movements, but through the corner of her wild eyes, she believed that she saw something rush past her. Twirling around, she saw its faint silhouette pasted against the darkness. It was the mad seal; it was pressed against the back wall, and it was trapped! The tear would finally be hers, but not before she tore out the pilfering slug's wretched heart with her own hands.

"Oreguss!" she shrieked in her usual loud and high-strung voice. "I found it! Come here and hold it still, nitwit, and none of your blundering mistakes!" Huffing and puffing from excitement, Decara suddenly smiled a most sinister smile, her breast heaving up and down while standing there watching the faint outline of the seal cowering in the shadows, its back pressed up against the wall. "Time to go bye-bye, slug," Decara sadistically hummed, slowly moving toward the seal, her eyes maniacal and her expression like that of a serpent coming for its prey. The seal remained motionless, continuing to stare on through the shadows while the deranged woman slithered toward her, and just as Decara reached out her clawing fingers, the mad harp took advantage of the glassy openings attached to the wall.

The portholes! They were right behind her!

She could feel their shiny, smooth exteriors pressing against her backside all the while. Instinctively, the seal knew this represented freedom away from this ghastly place and the demon-woman plaguing her. Turning around with a quick flip of her head, she chose her mark, looked back toward Decara, and then smashed the back of her thick head into the glassy pane of the yellow-stained window. The exceptionally wide pothole immediately shattered, most of its glass breaking free from its circular hold. In a rumbling heap, the mad harpie crashed through, flipping over to the other side, some of the seashell chain spilling from her mouth. Slurping it up with a swift gulp and jerking her stare out toward the vast deck of the *Tiamat,* the crazed seal proceeded to flee with an amazingly fast wriggle, away from the already perusing Decara and her servant, both not far behind.

Decara felt some of the remaining broken glass and sharp splintery bite of the once massive porthole rip into her skin while hurling over it. The ragged glass cut her along her arms and legs, but she paid no mind. She had to stop the seal with the purple stone at all cost! "Kill the beast, don't let it get way!" Decara ordered in a mad and boisterous sirenlike scream.

However, Oreguss would never reach the seal.

Unbelievable as it was, once again, the mad creature had outsmarted them both. She did this not only with her mad, shrewd wit but with her expedient wriggle, a fleeting wriggle never before achieved by such a large and cumbersome mammal. Over the icy deck of the *Tiamat,* the seal slid until she finally came to the very end of the despicable floating machine. Then crawling out toward the very borders of its wet and slippery ridge, she grasped both flippers around several thick and wiry ropes that appeared to fence the vessel, closing it off from the rest of the unwary world. The seal had but a moment before the shrieking Decara and her servant would reach the edge of the ship where she was spitefully waiting for them. "One, two, three—you'll never catch me!" she sang, laughing before diving into the sea.

The mad seal could still hear the wild and maniacal screams of the devil woman while plunging further into the freezing waters, her grinning mouth tightly sealed, happily protecting the purple tear with which she had cleverly stolen away.

EMMA

Leukemia was not a pleasant thing to have, especially for a young girl in her early teens. In fact, it hurt Emma almost as much as remembering back to the time when she could do things with her brother Kenyan. She missed the moments they shared—going to the movie shows, laughing, playing, and running through endless meadows, throwing themselves into soft patches of grass while looking up into the passing clouds, something they loved to do. They would talk for hours, watching the clouds change shapes while they spoke of their innermost secret dreams and what they would one day do with their lives.

Emma looked at the hospital's white windowsill and studied how the sun was shining on it. The windowsill ignited in the burst of the sun with a glare that hurt her eyes like the reflection of icy pavements on a bright winter's day. Still, she did not turn away from it. The longer she stared at it, the more her eyes adjusted to its vibrant light, its glow becoming brighter and brighter as she raised her gaze toward the sky where clouds curtsied prettily around a warm and radiant sun. Just as she had done so many times before, Emma could imagine a whole world full of snowy brightness and fantastic castles made of nothing but billowy clouds that could somehow take the pain away forever.

The three minutes were way over due, but Emma did not care. She could hardly remember that the thermometer was still in her mouth or that the nurse had left her side in order to attend to the sick little girl brought into the hospital ward but yesterday. The tiny girl occupied bed D. There were four beds in that room, and only A and D promised the warmth and cheeriness of the sun for they were the only beds sitting next to a window. Emma was extremely grateful for that window. It helped set her mind free from all the reality pressing around her. It made her daydreams possible and supplied a tiny portion of the sky that provided more than enough light for the many drawings she loved to create. For it came complete with sunshine, glittered with imaginary snowy meadows, wispy hills, silly-looking seals and dancing dolphins, all which eventually drifted past the sun. And yet despite her heavenly wonderland, she could not wish away the pain that even now hurt with a mournful, unendurable quality that would undoubtedly go on hurting her indefinitely.

It was nearly one year since both of her parents died in that dreadful fire, for everything they owned, including their treasured dog Peggy, perished in the flames. Not a single day went by that Emma did not think about that tragic night. It was the night that both she and her brother went to Bonnie Blue Mountain near the old creek, just as they had done every summer for as long as she could remember. From their secluded place in the woods, they would watch the July fireworks shoot off into the warm starless summer night sky, an event she relished and looked forward to every year—until that night—the night when everything changed.

Emma had learned of her terminal illness just before the fire, but with the love and guidance of her mother and father, she found the strength and courage to fight the malignancy growing inside her, but all that ended when she left them on that fatal night, never to see them again. How the fire started no one ever knew. Not even the many men and women who came to investigate.

After the funerals, everything changed yet once again, and everything that happened occurred with an unusual and uncanny expediency that still disturbed her immensely. For within several weeks, both she and her twin brother Kenyan, now both nearly fifteen, were residing at a place called the Hudson Boarding School. Their parents had left them enough money through stocks, bonds, and insurance policies that would see them well into the better part of their lives. All of Emma's medical issues remained financially secured and would go on that way for some time. However, there was not one moment that went by that Emma would forgo all the financial security in the world if only she could see her parents again. She missed them more than life itself. Since their demise, everything was difficult. Everything was a challenge. If it were not for her brother who continued to give her strength, she knew she could not find the will to live, nor would she even dare to try. There would be no reason to watch the glaring sun shine on the clean and white hospital ledge, or draw her pictures, or merely daydream. She would be gone—forever, just like her mother and father.

Emma suddenly watched the light on the windowsill shut off as the nurse returned to her bed, temporarily closing off all the brightness moving in front of the window ledge, reaching down toward Emma so she could reclaim the thermometer. "Hmmm . . . running a little high today," the attractive nurse with the deep green eyes and the neatly styled hair tucked beneath her nurse's cap said while studying the mercury-filled glass thermometer in her hand.

"Did I beat yesterday's record?" Emma asked with a crooked smile.

"A trifle," answered the pretty nurse, her green eyes softening, looking at the terribly fragile and petite girl with the curly blond hair and the largest icy blue eyes she had ever seen. "Perhaps you should rest today. Work on your drawings tomorrow," kindly suggested the nurse.

Emma shook her head. "Can't . . . ," she told her, reaching toward the side of the bed taking her drawing pad away from the small table next to her, "promised my brother I'd finish this one today. See . . . ," Emma said, giving the nurse her sketch pad.

The nurse smiled again, taking the drawing, secretly excited to see what the young girl had created. Although the composition was different, as were the many drawings she had fashioned with her pens and pencils and bits and pieces of charcoal, the settings were always the same—a winter wonderland of icy fantasy that consisted of arctic life ranging from penguins to walruses, even whales. But the one creature the young girl with the breathtaking blue eyes consistently drew was a seal—a snowy-white seal. A particularly adorable baby seal, but with the saddest eyes she had ever remembered seeing. As the nurse looked away from the beautiful but somewhat depressing drawing, she realized for the first time that the eyes of the creature resembled the sick young girl before her.

"It's beautiful," the nurse said, losing her smile, a soft shade of sadness washing over her face as she placed the drawing back on the table. "You sure like seals, don't you?"

Emma nodded, glancing toward the small table next to her.

"Have you been drawing them for a long time?"

Emma shrugged. "I guess."

"Any reason?"

Not seriously thinking about it, Emma smirked, saying "Don't really know . . . just like them . . . always have."

The attractive nurse took the liberty of sitting at the corner of Emma's bed. "I like them too, they are so adorable," she said, happily, gently touching her hand. "But why are they always so sad?"

This time Emma did not answer. She merely looked away, keeping her eyes on her sketchpad, shrugging despondently.

Once more, the nurse studied the frail features of the sick girl's wanton face, watching Emma's magnificent blue eyes well up with tears. "More pain?" delicately asked the nurse.

Again Emma remained silent, her eyes still fixed to her sketchpad, shaking her head, looking as if she no longer wanted to talk. Feeling helpless and yet still wishing to remain, the nurse knew her other duties had fallen far behind schedule, so she got up from the side of the bed, drew up the security bar that retracted easily from its side, and stared down compassionately at Emma. "Try to get some rest. I'll be back later to check on you before the doctor examines you." Again, the nurse looked affectionately at Emma, wanting to say anything that would make her smile in return. "I think we're having spaghetti and meatballs for dinner tonight, your favorite. I'll see to it that you get some extra meatballs if you like."

Emma never turned away from her drawing, nor did she answer.

The nurse, feeling defeated and dispirited, managed to grab for one more smile before she left. "I'll see you later, Emma. Please try to rest; it's what you need now."

Emma still did not look away from her drawing, but the nurse saw the tear streak against the side of the sick girl's turned cheek. Saddened, she slowly backed away, leaving the room, saying, "Your drawing is really beautiful, Emma. I know your brother is going to love it."

Emma never saw the pretty green-eyed nurse leave, but she could hear her footsteps gradually fade, disappearing into the long hallway outside her room. Immediately, Emma was reminded of the other sick girls in her room as the respirators and various other medical devices made their beeps and clicks while the little girl in bed D began to cough uncontrollably.

Emma sighed and wiped away her tears, then looked back toward the glaring white light still shining brilliantly against the ledge of the meticulously clean windowsill. She would fall asleep this way with her eyes filled with a scintillating glow and her mind complete with a world of magical snowy wonderment a million daydreams away from her room.

In a little while, Emma was asleep and dreaming, and all the pain and sadness she felt temporarily vanished—at least for a little while.

WHOODY, SCHMOODY, RUDEY!

Miracle was the last to awaken.

He remained silent at first, suckling his mother for a while before he looked up toward the shadowed night sky. The lustrous great yellow ball in the heavens had vanished, and with its departure came a sky filled with shining lights that twinkled and sparkled like the newly fallen snow.

In this shaded dimension of reflecting, flickering lights, the white seal found himself mesmerized. He continued to stargaze, maintaining the awareness of the waves hitting against the ridges of the floating ice boat. The vibration began to drill itself into the very core of his senses, now set against the suckling sounds of the newborn baby walrus. Cloaked within the many rolls of his mother's insulation, the baby tooth walker stirred and whimpered as it continued suckling. Then Miracle heard his mother's voice, but his mother's soft whispers were not meant for him. Curiously, the tiny Miracle moved his head away from the stars and focused on the two adults. Arayna's words remained soft and delicate as she asked the walrus, "Are you asleep?"

The mother walrus immediately responded, pulling in some of her girth that unintentionally spilled over the sides of the struggling ice boat. "Heavens, no!—Goodness me!Boop-boop-dee-dee! Why, I can barely take my eyes off my precious, *precious* Poo-Coo!" The walrus then began to talk in a singsong voice, rubbing her wiggling nose against her noisy suckling child. "Adorable, Poo-Coo, simply adorable!" she sang.

Arayna could not help smiling.

"Can you believe it," boasted the walrus, "I actually did something wonderful for once in my life!"

"I'm sure that isn't true," soothed Arayna.

The walrus became every excited. "Oh, but it is true! Absolutely, without a doubt . . . *ta-haa-RUE!* Why, I didn't even know that my little Poo-Coo was on his merry way until nearly the very end! Imagine, not knowing it was your child's birthday! Could you just die? All that time I thought it was sea gas . . . Go figure!"

Arayna felt her cheeks blush, trying to reserve a forming grin, immediately slipping into another train of thought. "We haven't really met properly, have we?"

"Why no, we haven't, have we? Boop-boop-dee-dee!"

Arayna offered another engaging smile. "Well, my name is—"

"Whoody, schmoody, rudey! Me, me, I'm first! Me, me first!" interrupted the agitated walrus.

Startled by the excited tooth walker, Arayna readily complied.

Once more, the mama tooth walker persevered in the ridiculous batting of her enormous eyes, clearing her throat. "My name is—oh, it just makes me so mirthful just to say it!" She giggled, batting her eyes even more wildly than before. "My name, as was my mother's and her mother's and her mother's before her and so on and so on, was and is and always will be Crumpelteeverella! Beautiful, isn't it?" announced the walrus, delighted at the way her name still rolled off her tongue with such effortless ease. Arayna tried to restrain herself, widening her eyes, simply staring at the simpering creature. "Say it with me now, won't you?" instructed the silly walrus, its eyes still a-fluttering like the blurring wings of a hummingbird.

Arayna gave the strange request a feeble attempt but soon rejected the effort. "Well, I'm afraid that I—"

Interrupting again, the gibbering walrus continued. "Oh, that's all right, deary, no one has ever been able to say it on the first try, but isn't it adorable, simply adorable?" Then the walrus paused for a moment, just staring at Arayna, almost mimicking the perplexed expression on the seal's face. "Not to worry, dear, for short, you can call me Crumpels."

"Crumpels?" Arayna repeated, offering the walrus another nervous smile.

"Yep-er-ree, that's me! That's me, now you, *now you*—boop-boop-dee-doo!"

"Well, my name is Arayna."

"Oh, I like that! I really do . . . It's so . . . so . . . you! Such a lovely name too, and your little white puff . . . what's his name?" the walrus excitedly asked.

"Miracle," Arayna told her.

"Very nice. However, you mentioned that he cannot swim, poor thing."

Arayna shook her head, prepared to educate the walrus about baby seals and not knowing how to swim initially, but was all too quickly cut off.

"Oh, you don't have to be ashamed, deary," stated the smirking walrus. "After all, how can he possibly know how to swim when his own mother can't teach him properly, poor misguided dear."

"I'm not sure I know what you mean," Arayna said.

"Now, now, now, don't get all touchy-touchy again! There is nothing wrong in being a dysfunctional swimmer; why else would you be floating around on this ice cube? Why, I once knew an octopus that wasn't very good at directional swimming either. A real propelling disaster, as I recall. If he was to make a left, he couldn't help but go right, and vicie-versie! Dreadful! It was always the same old story. You both seem to have an awful lot in common, don't you, deary dear?"

"Now see here!"

"Now, now, now, we cannot all be exceptional navigators, can we?" recited the walrus.

By now Arayna was becoming visibly annoyed. "My dear Ms. Crumpels, just what are you insinuating?"

"Well, I don't want to point any flippers, but for starters, let's talk about how you got us lost in the middle of nowhere, dear," the walrus sweetly said, still batting its enormous eyes, "and in my condition!"

"Now just a minute—"

"Well, tell me, do you know where we are, dearest one?"

"Well, no . . . not exactly, but I'm sure—"

"I thought not," insisted the walrus.

"Oh, you're absurd!"

"Well, if you'll forgive me, dearest seal," continued the walrus, inflating its cheeks with more air, "sadly, the only thing absurd is our present situation." She shifted her weight while her baby hung on, continuing with his incessant suckling. Nearly knocking Arayna overboard, Crumpels continued to shift herself around the ice. "Now see what you did, dear, you forced me into a discourtesy."

"What are you talking about?"

"Very well," snorted the walrus. "I'm talking about the fact that you have gotten us lost, and there seems to be no direction in your course. Let's face it, deary, as far as conquering the sea goes, you have most certainly lost the battle—boop-boop-dee-fiddle-faddle!"

Arayna became outraged. "Of all the nerve!"

"Whooo! Still quite the touchy one, aren't we? My, my, my!" blurted the walrus. "I was only sympathizing with your sad lack of judgment in navigational skills, that's all. But if you want to be snooty about the whole thing, then you can just forget I brought up the entire dangerous and foreboding jeopardy you have rendered us unto . . . boop-boop-what-to-do!"

"How dare you imply such a thing!" retorted Arayna. "I've had nothing to do with any of this! Besides, I never forced you to come along in the first place, did I?"

The walrus merely stuck out her tongue and grunted annoyingly.

"Oh, you are impossible!" Arayna barked. "You could never understand just how devastating a situation this entire ordeal has been, not only for me, but my child also."

"Oh poo!" ridiculed the walrus.

"You are infuriating!" growled Arayna. "Both my son and I have had to contend with all sorts of disasters since his birth, namely, you for one! I can't tell you how many times we nearly lost our lives while in the midst of the great storm. We are lucky to have survived! And furthermore—"

The walrus seemed unaffected by the seal's growing frustration. "Oh, do chill out, missy . . . boop-boop-dee-prissy! My goodness, you're going to give yourself a migraine, dear."

"Well, you are most provoking, you must agree!"

"I will not agree . . . boop-boop-dee-dee!"

"Will you please stop that!"

"Stop what?" snorted the walrus.

"That—that—infernal RHYMING!"

The walrus smacked her lips before grunting off in an exasperated voice. "Well, like I said, *touchy-touchy-touchy!*"

The seal tried to control her growing anger and frustration but was failing rapidly. "Oh, this is ridiculous!"

Suddenly, the tooth walker made a loud shrilling sound, frightening the baby walrus and Miracle, as well as Arayna. "And just whooo are you calling ridiculous? Why, you're nothing but a misguided globe-trotter, that's all . . . boop-boop-dee-folderol!"

Arayna's exasperation quickly surfaced in her eyes. The preposterous creature had inadvertently broken the dam of despair that was building since the night of the storm. So many painful emotions suddenly washed themselves over her that she could not hold back any longer. The walrus was right. She was lost. She was scared, and she was no longer able to hide the growing fear grasping within her. She felt alone in this obscure darkness of probing uncertainties, her aching heart still experiencing the hammering memory of her dead mate Apollo, and where was Lakannia, her dear and loyal sister of the sea? Would she never again see her? She quickly shook her head, not wanting to think of it further. However, more tormenting thoughts of Apollo quickly took its place. In complete misery for their tragic separation, Arayna closed her eyes and felt the tears freely wash against her snout. Apollo was the only one who could ever invalidate any affliction she might encounter. She always felt safe when she was with him. If only she could see him, feel his presence, embrace his being, and experience his strength for yet one more time, one more moment.

It was at this particular moment that she felt a gentle snuggling sensation near her side. Arayna looked down and immediately beheld her tiny pup. His dark and shining chromatic eyes looked upward, questioning his mother's sad and misplaced way. She fought the sting of tears, constraining a broken smile down in his direction. It was obvious that her son was not fooled by her pretentious gesture. However, the sight of Miracle comforted and calmed the agony swelling inside her. Despite the unthinkable fact that the world she once knew would never again be the same no matter what, she was truly not alone, not while she had her beloved Miracle. It was now most clear that through the glistening eyes of her baby, Apollo would remain with her unfailingly, right there in the sparkles that radiated from those wondrous eyes of his. Miracle would always be a remarkable confirmation of their undying love, and nothing could ever take that away from her.

"Mama . . . ," softly whimpered the whitecoat, continuing to look up into his mother's eyes, the solace of their union enveloping them. He then licked at his mother's soft belly, shivering, confused, and relentless in his comforting just the same. Arayna suddenly felt the recent torment slowly begin to drain away as she went to her child. In total adoration, both encompassed one another and rubbed seal noses, purring with contented love while the tiresome walrus who had been continuously chattering away, however ignored, disrupted the unification of their private enthrallment.

"Well, boop-boop-dee-crude, there is no need to be so rude!" grumbled Crumpels. "You haven't heard one single solitary word I said!"

"Thank heavens for small favors," retorted Arayna, still joyful with the playful seal game of nose rubbing.

"Well, aren't we an impertinent missy? Boop-boop-dee-prissy!"

Finding strength in the consolation of the whitecoat, Arayna prepared herself once more in an attempt to rationalize with the highly irrational tooth walker. "Do you think it possible, Ms. Crumpels, that you could remain quiet for a moment? I am tired, and I am hungry, and I am—"

"LOST, we mustn't forget that one, mustn't we?" interrupted the sassy walrus.

Arayna tried to control her temper, proceeding with, "No, I am sure you and your insistent ramblings would certainly never allow it."

"Insistent ramblings! Well, I never! Why, you are, a conceited snot, and I have decided that I shall have no more to do with you!" Pulling the bottom part of her lip over its top, the spongy Crumpels started up with a most persistent boohooing wail. Arayna remained somewhat unaffected by the crying beast as Miracle curiously looked upon the queer creature, not sure what to make out of her silly display of claptrap theatrics. "Now," howled the walrus, "you will sail this blasted ice cube over to the nearest part of Sealssong you find! That's if we are even anywhere near Sealssong! I know where I am not wanted, and I am not wanted where there seems to be an overabundance of moody, snooty snot creatures!" With this outrageous outburst, Crumpelteeverella bluntly stuck out her wide tongue.

"Oh please, do calm down," Arayna calmly suggested. "There is no need for all of this. Besides, you are frightening the children."

Just then, Crumpels heard the whimper of her own pup. It was a discomforting cry, a sad cry that momentarily put an end to his incessant suckling sounds. "Well, I hope you are satisfied! Now you've gone and upset my little Poo-Coo!"

"I upset him?"

"Who else? I want to go home immediately, I tell you! You better take me home this very second or I'll smack you!"

Arayna was unable to hold back her outrage any further. "Well, of all the ungrateful—very well, if that is how you feel, then perhaps it would be to both our advantages if you did leave!"

"Fine, I am going home!"

"Fine, it is of no concern to me!"

"Well, I will then! *I will! I will!*" blasted the truly hysterical walrus, throwing a most upsetting glare toward the mother harp.

Miracle sensed the growing tension, and he also began to whimper. Still, Arayna did not flinch. She remained determined, staring off crossly in the opposite direction of the very, most extraordinary, quite contrary, exasperating walrus she had ever come to know.

Crumpels stubbornly turned and began to wobble toward the edge of the ice float, pushing her newborn along with the aid of the abundant slabs of her blubber. The baby walrus stiffened and began wailing out in fear. Crumpels abruptly stopped and looked down at the yelping pup. A flipper full of tears began to sting the tooth walker's eyes. Turning her massive head ever so slowly, she faced Arayna. The distressed walrus's lower lip began to bounce pitifully up and down, grossly imitating the fluctuation of her pompous batting eyes.

"I cannot go," sniffed the walrus. She swallowed hard, looking afraid and pathetic. "You see, we do not have a place to go." Shaking her head slowly with a sad and forlorn swing, she lamented, "We are all alone . . . We are all alone . . . boop-boop-no-home."

Feeling that the situation had gone far enough, Arayna broke the climbing intensity. "Please, we mustn't argue. Right now, like it or not, we're all we got. So please try and understand that I want to be your friend if you'll let me. And most importantly, don't you know that the sea is our refuge and our protector? Within her arms, we are never truly alone. She is our home no matter where she may lead us."

The upset walrus opened her eyes wide, trying to stifle a whimper, sucking in the running flow from her wet nose.

Arayna continued. "You are tired and hungry, and overwrought from the birth of your child, but it will be all right, I promise," said the seal, significantly softening her stare. "Come, rest upon the ice float. For you are welcome, Crumpelteeverella," Arayna said, holding to a warm and inviting seal smile.

The walrus returned a surprised but affectionate grin toward the kind harp. Slowly turning around, she began to wriggle back toward Arayna and Miracle. She pushed along her own child, nearly knocking everyone over, coming mighty close to capsizing the entire slab of ice while still managing to sustain the precious cargo that it carried.

Finally, after an annoying few minutes that seemed to take forever, the walrus and her pup plopped down and there was not an inch to spare. While the tooth walker tried to get comfortable, the ice boat continued to rock unsteadily within the shifting arms of the sea. Eventually, Crumpels and Poo-Coo managed to settle back inside the limited scope of the raft. Stopping only inches away from the velvety face of Arayna, the mama walrus pushed out her bulbous lips and softly kissed the cheek of the forgiving seal.

"You are most kind." The walrus sniffed. "Thank you—boop-boop-dee-doo," she whimpered, her large eyes swimming in the wake of her immeasurable tears. "I shouldn't have said those things to you, dear. It was unkind and deplorable. I am sorry. Sometimes I can be such a hateful ninny ass!"

Arayna blushed again.

"I guess, it's just that . . . well, I guess I'm scared. Never been a mama before."

"It's all right," Arayna promised. "I understand."

"Bless you, my friend," thanked the walrus. "My friend . . . my friend . . ."

"Come," Arayna said smilingly, "let us get some sleep. We are both exhausted, and the children need nourishment."

"Yes," agreed Crumpels, "and I'm hungry too . . . boop-boop-dee-drool!"

Arayna nodded. "I know. So am I. Perhaps soon we can eat, but for now, we should rest. I have a feeling tomorrow holds much for us all."

*　　*　　*

Time passed and soon the wind murmured its expected evening song, but it was Crumpels's constant snoring that would govern the air. Still, the four worn-out mislaid travelers remained unaware of any distracting sounds, cuddling, snuggling, each blending and fitting perfectly into one another as a tight-fitting intricate puzzle.

It would be morning soon, and before the following night would end, there would be no intrepid ice boat. It would have already existed in its final night among the watery environment that created it. Soon, the four lost creatures would forever say goodbye to their silent and remembered crystal savior.

SERPENT HEADS

The *Tiamat* snuck through the shrouded darkness as a silent serpent moving through the soft brush of the summer grass.

A thick fog had surrounded the vessel as it made its way through the sea, its yellow glowing portholes appearing like evil, cruel eyes that could only see with a malignancy of their own.

Deep inside its gullet, within the secret part of her chambers, the dark and vile Decara, mad with rage, slammed the door behind her, angrily entering her laboratory, preparing to practice her wicked spells. Before any plans could be finalized, she would have to consult the three-headed serpent. It was her only way of first knowing where exactly the mad seal was hiding. Upon discovering this, she would then invest in the upcoming voyage back to Sealssong.

The room she now stood in was frightfully dark. In fact, only a small sliver of light just above her head shone down. It was a pale green color, and its faded streak only made Decara's face look ghoulish, turning the dark of her hair into strange fragments of twisted bends like wet seaweed. Proceeding out of the shadows, she suddenly raised her arms, and an unusual light began to mist and, from this glowing emanation, a large transparent sphere appeared.

A massive glowing ball made up of gooey globs of a metallic watery substance now floated ghostlike inside the middle of the room. It pulsated with a green radiation, igniting its eerie afflictions over the walls and immediate surroundings. Decara outstretched her arms, allowing the shadows to crawl about her, littering her presence into the gloom of the room like festering decay.

Cloaked within her raven-colored cape, she slowly approached the green shining blare hovering before her, its see-through form beating like some monstrous heart muscle. As if to embrace it, Decara placed both arms around the globular pulsation. Instantly, her eager hold broke into its liquid form. Screaming out, she felt her flesh sink and flung her head back, undoing her intricately braided coiffure with one abrupt thrust. A thick wad of whipping black hair, long and unconfined, fiercely blew about her bloodless face, her arms still clutching the glowing ball, her mouth openly gaping. She gave out another loud, guttural moan. From her gaping eye sockets, spurting green flames shot out, causing both of her eyes to explode, the same hellish flares billowing from her mouth. Resembling a loathsome dragon, Decara continued to breathe out the demonic fires. Instantly, they spread over her and yet never consuming her. She lowered her head, waiting for the flames to dissipate before backing away from the liquid orb that had ignited the smoldering sorceress within her.

Deep inside the glowing gooey ball, a tiny red spot materialized. Appearing like a small drop of blood, it began to grow. Spiderwebbing into wafer-thin veins, the bloody extensions soon covered the shining green sphere with a menacing fungus. As the growing gore twisted itself around the globe, it began to rupture. Instantaneously, three veiny strings began to wiggle, widening, fighting to separate from one another; and while they divided, their ghastly forms began to alter into something even more sinister. Convulsing, the three oozing lines transformed into three beastly serpent heads, each head permanently dripping with a crimson color matching their long necks and coiled snake trunk, one singularly scaly stem in which they remained attached. The three snake heads continued to pull away from one another. Drenched in the color of blood, one slithered to the top of the globe, the other settling near the bottom, the final squirming nearest the middle, their connected trunk flapping grotesquely about, oozing wet with the foul trickling of dread. The serpent closest to the pinnacle of the floating orb was the first to shoot open its wild eyes, the remaining two serpent heads immediately following her awakening.

Three sets of intense and glowing yellow eyes now stared out through transparent eyelids, each one just as malignant as the other. In vile unison, the scale-ridden serpent heads opened their jaws, bearing elongated yellow fangs. With one unsettling slurp, the heads began sipping up the revolting slime in which they floated. The three monstrosities seemed to enjoy their ghoulish feast, their wiggling throats expanding, preparing to speak. A distorted raspy breath escaped from each serpent head's open mouth, a garbled gurgle foaming around their reptilian jaws. "*Sss*-salutations, dark mistress-*sss*," hissed Sin. She was the largest head of the three connected abominations.

Decara, now restored to her usual self, looked back at the talking beasts with her cold black eyes, all traces of the burning flames long since removed. If it were not for her disheveled hair that lay wildlike against her long thin neck, one would have never imagined she had only recently been doused in the fires of hell. "Alas! You have heeded my evocation and have come from the black of night so that you may serve me," Decara gloated, her eyes ablaze with the vilest of wonders.

"*Sss*-speak . . . and ask what it is-*sss* you wish to know . . . ," requested the serpent named Sin.

"Tell me, my clairvoyant viper, where can I find the filthy, mad, thieving seal that has stolen the precious tear?"

Sin twisted herself before the dark woman, her mouth opening grotesquely. "The seal you have filled with madness has fled back to the islands of *sss* . . . Sealssong. However, by the time you find her, she will not be the one that you will need to reckon with."

Her patience already wearing thin, Decara's voice began to rise. "What do you mean she will not be the one? What kind of absurdity are you going on about, snake?"

The second serpent head suddenly spoke up. Its head was not as large as her sister Sin's was. Her name was Sadness, but the cruel way that the curled-up grimace on her red snaky lips stretched about her wicked face made her appear anything but sad. "When you come upon the mad creature, she will have already offered the tear to another—the white *sss*-seal of Sealssong.

"All harp seals are born white, fool!"

"He is different—the very creature the ancient prophecies have spoken of."

"Careful! You should not speak of things that are blasphemous to your scaly lips!" Decara warned, bellowing.

"We are able, dark mistress-*sss*. The dark master has given his permission to speak of this. To you, he has granted this consideration of being exalted over the powers of darkness in the final days of light upon this miserable planet," Sadness evilly divulged, wrapping her snake lips contemptibly around her wicked grimace.

"My reign over darkness is not a mere consideration! Don't rile me, viper!" Decara screamed. "I have already been promised domain over the earth after the Night of Screams has come upon us!"

The talking serpent coiled itself into a circular pile of scaly loops while all three of its crimson heads rested smugly on top of its twisted self. "Things have changed, oh dark one, since the loss of the sacred teardrop that *you* so carelessly allowed to be taken," Sadness explained. "Because of your reckless blunder, you are, once more, a mere consideration for such greatness, oh magnificent evil one."

"How dare you!" raved the vile woman cloaked in black.

"Now, now," warned Sadness, "if you continue with such rage, I shan't be able to disclose the rest to you."

"That would be ill advised, I assure you, cocky viper!"

"There is no reason to fret," Sadness replied. "The dark master still considers you his foremost choice in bestowing upon you his darkest of treasures, only there are a few modifications in regard to the stolen tear."

"Tell me plainly, and spare me your reptilian riddles!" Decara shrieked.

The third head then spoke up. This connected abomination was the smallest of all three. Her name was Suffering. "Since you have lost the powerful teardrop to the seals of Sealssong, you naturally must take it back. However, it shall not be a simple task, as it was before."

"Continue!" ordered the infuriated woman.

"Such tidings may not please you," cautioned the third serpent head.

"I warn you," smoldered Decara. "Don't antagonize my temper further with your exasperating prattle! Explain, provoking serpent!"

"You must force innocence to destroy itself," Suffering hissed.

"Yes yes, go on, rambling reptile!"

It was then all three of the connecting serpent heads began to speak out in one tongue, each malevolent voice blending into the other. "The dark lord requests that you destroy his greatest adversary, namely, *innocence*. It is far more crucial than ever since the tear now belongs to the seals of *sss*-Sealssong, the most innocent of all creatures! Again, your error, I believe."

"Spare me your swaggering tongue, or I will rip all three of them out by the roots! Now tell me, vicious viper, by what means shall I achieve this?"

The fiendish serpent began to grow more excited as all three of its heads began to swarm incessantly around each other. "This shall be done by allowing innocence to destroy the white seal, of course."

"The white seal, the white seal, enough about this wretched white seal!" Decara raved, her eyes growing wide with unnerving displacement.

"We assure you, dark mistress-*sss*, what we say is not to be dis-*sss*-carded. The innocent power of the beast must not be underestimated. You, above all, should know this for it is in this purest form of innocence that you are able to extract the precious diamonds from the tears of their mothers, is it not?"

"Yes, but what has one pathetic seal slug have to do with any of this?"

"Alas," the blood-colored serpent explained, "it is not just any pathetic seal. He possesses the true essence of this contemptible and hazardous gift, an attribute that in itself is capable of destroying evil—every last bit of it!" warned the talking snake. "The white seal is the epitome of all that is pure. Such authority was initially given to man, but fortunately a progressive mankind grew to despise such a gift. Except for a very few, this powerful force have long since been given to the meekest and purest of all creatures: the seals of Sealssong, to be exact, and the ones who possess-*sss* the greatest of this innocence are the children, the baby harp seals. Their power is extreme, as you know, but the white seal that will come to wear the tear will hold the most dangerous power of all, far greater than yours will ever be."

"Lies," Decara swore.

"There is more."

"Unmask your ambivalence and be quick about it, my patience is at an end, and you might as well know it! Reveal this prophetic proposal that you shamelessly claim to understand!"

"Our words are *sss*-simple," went on to say the three-headed serpent, its twisting form slithering aimlessly about the floating globe. "The mad seal shall place around the whitecoat's neck the mighty tear, and once worn, it can never be removed or both the seal and the power it holds will die."

"You blundering senile serpent, you infuriate me with what I already know! That is why I must find the thieving mad beast in the first place, clod poll! I must be the first to wear the tear! Why do you think I summoned you here in the first place? Fools! All three of you! I should kick your bloody mutant skulls back to the slimy sea you crawled out of—*imbeciles!*"

"Do not be so quick to dismiss us-*sss*," cautioned the demonic snake heads. "You can still claim the tear, destroy innocence, and return the one you have placed inside the walls of this accursed vessel. Together, you and your murdered companion can still reign with the dark lord for all of eternity."

"How dare you speak of my beloved!" shrieked Decara.

"The only way to claim and forever change the power of the tear into pure evil is to kill the white seal while he still wears the sacred teardrop, but here is the rub, oh vile mistress. This cannot be done by your hand, but by yet another one who also has the gift of absolute, pure innocence," continued the scarlet-painted serpent. "Thus—, *innocence destroying innocence.*"

In a rage, Decara flew toward the floating green ball as if to strike at it. "You have thirty seconds to explain, or you will find yourself splattered and dripping all over these godforsaken walls, prophecy or no prophecy! Do you understand me?"

"The answer lies-*sss* in the sick girl . . . ," the snake quickly replied with a trio of gulps and hollow groans.

"Girl? What sick girl?"

"Have you forgotten your own kin?" bravely ridiculed the probing serpent.

"You are pushing your luck, viper! I have no kin! My sister is dead! She refused to serve the dark side, and she and her waste of a husband were dealt with accordingly. I toasted them, remember?"

The serpent waited for all three of its crawling heads to grin. "Yes, the fire was indeed delightful, but have you forgotten about the surviving *sss*-siblings? There are two that remain."

A discomforting look of surprise inadvertently shadowed over the dark woman's face while she glared harshly into the transparent sphere before her. *"The twins . . . ,"* she murmured, remembering, the heads plainly hearing what she said.

"Yes-*sss*," excitedly hissed the snake. "Your dead sister's children—the sick girl is your ticket! She is gifted and unlike any other . . . a misfit that was born from creation's mistakes. You can right this wrong by using the power she holds. Like you, she is not without certain . . . talents-*sss*. After all, she is of your blood."

"Silence, insolent serpent, I have long since forgotten my feeble sister and her sniveling brats! They are of no importance to me! Besides, the last I heard about the girl was that she was terminally ill. How do you know the girl isn't dead? She may be already a wasted corpse for all I know!"

"She still lives-*sss*," the serpent hissed.

"So, what can a dying girl offer me?"

"Like the white seal, she is one of the very rare creatures-*sss* that has managed to keep this powerful gift of innocence alive," the titillating snake exposed its fork tongues shooting out in every direction. "This next part will please you, I am sure, for it reeks-*sss* of the ultimate poetic justice! It should be plain to see, evil one, that your niece is the 'innocence' that will destroy itself! Behold!" marveled the serpent as the swirling mist inside its suspended orb began to glow brightly, revealing a vision of its own.

Decara found herself drawn to the transparent sphere, nearly pressing her face through its transparent surface. As the globe continued to be engulfed in thick mists, Decara was no longer able to see the serpent. Instead, she watched a burning image play before her. The vision was that of her long forgotten niece. Hearing the three voices of the snake spew out words, she listened while they explained, her sick niece's image staring at her, a mist of green smoke framing the girl's small doll-like face.

"Go to the place of the great city," hissed the red snake. "There, you will find her in a place that mends the sick. You will be guided by the dark powers that be. Seek both offspring—the girl alone will not be easily convinced. The boy will allow you to control your niece, influence her. In time, you will come to know this influence, and when you do, it will bring you insurmountable powers. Steal them both away. Bring them here and persuade the girl, your kin and blood of your blood, to destroy the white seal: *innocence destroying innocence*, thus bringing about the Night of Screams, the night that will proclaim you as its dark goddess for all time!"

Decara continued to stare at the vision before her, the face of the ill girl fluctuating like a ghostly apparition. It had been a long time since she laid eyes on her sister's kid. The image of the girl lying in that hospital bed was quite the stranger to her. She studied the wanton face of her dead sister's child and then watched it fade away, the three-headed serpent, including the glowing globe, disappearing, as well. "We have revealed all we have been commanded to reveal . . . ," hissed the snake." The rest is up to you. Find the girl. Force her to kill the white seal! Claim the tear and be seated next to the dark lord for all eternity!"

"Wait!" Decara ordered. "I am not finished with you! I still have more to ask!"

By the time Decara had finished her words, the floating ball of green glow, along with the irritating but the revealing soothsaying serpent, had vanished. Only scouring dark shadows remained before her, all of them hideously worming themselves over her, covering her up in a flash.

Decara furled her long black cape, snapping it like a whip. Storming across the floor, her brain curdling with millions of uncertainties, she went for the door. Grabbing the handle with a powerful and ripping turn, she hurled it open; and with one furious swing, she slammed it shut, nearly tearing it off its creaking hinges, scaring the shadows away that quickly jumped into the pores of the walls of the breathing *Tiamat* as if never to show themselves again.

HUNGRY

The next morning there was no sun.

Arayna was the first to awaken.

Hundreds of dark clouds filled the sky, pushing and shoving, soaking up the heavens until not another could possibly squeeze itself into the already gloomy confusion. The mother seal had been up for hours, having been awakened by her perpetual hunger pains. Wriggling over to the edge of the ice boat, she gazed out into the sea. She would need to eat soon, but she procrastinated, not wanting to leave Miracle while he slept. However, she was not sure if she could hold out much longer. She needed to replenish herself for the sake of her tiny pup that remained ever constant in his pursuit for fresh and tasty seal milk.

"Mama . . . ," Miracle whimpered with a timely yawn. Stretching out his tiny joints, he began to shake. "Maa-aaa," he cried out again, wriggling himself over the spilling blubber of the walruses who took up most of the ice boat. His tiny flippers pitifully slipped out before him like a small dog with broken forelegs as he persistently crawled toward his seemingly deserting mother. With a quick turn, Arayna scooped up her pup in her gentle jaws, returning him to his spot on the ice. She reassured him with a smile.

"No, little one, you must stay. Mother is hungry. I need food, but I won't be gone long," she promised. The tiny Miracle looked up at her, as if he had just been scolded, shivering with uncertainty. Once more, Arayna smiled down at him, her heart aching, wanting never to leave his side but knowing she must if she wanted to survive. The tiny pup cried out again, this time sounding frantic, determined to go to her, but Arayna stopped him with a gentle nuzzle of her head.

"Hush now, and listen to Mama. You must not move from this place, keep close to the walruses, and I promise I'll be back in no time, my sweet baby." And with a quick kiss on top of his white furry head, Arayna removed herself from the ice boat, dove into the water, and in a flash disappeared.

The confused and disheartened pup remained still at first, tears welling up in his large dark eyes. Determined to be with his mother again, he began pushing his way through more of the snoring walrus's blubber, edging his way carefully toward the ridge of the ice float. Upon reaching it, the tiny pup looked deep into the water, but he could not find his mother. All he could see was a thick silvery color that hurt his eyes. He then turned and looked at the walrus, hoping to find consolation, but the snoring Crumpelteeverella and her noisy suckling son remained unaffected by his believed abandonment.

Heartsick, the baby harp unhappily turned his head from the two slumbering but deafening creatures, returning his teary eyes out into the direction where he last saw his mother. There he would wait, shivering and sorrowfully whimpering until she at long last returned to him.

KENYAN

It had already been several hours that Kenyan had been impatiently waiting in that dreadful hospital waiting room.

His sister had taken a turn for the worse, or so he was told. A member of staff from the Hudson Boarding School had escorted him to the hospital sometime after lunch. He was just putting the finishing touches on the wooden frame that he had so cleverly assembled in wood shop class when the news reached him. From that moment on, everything else appeared a blur. He had intended to frame the drawing Emma had made for him, wanting to surprise her with it on his visit to her after school, but instead it appeared that she had plans of surprising him.

It wasn't the first time the hospital had brought him such grave tidings. In fact, it was the second time this month that he had to leave school after learning that his sister might not last through the night, but he knew otherwise. He would never give in to their wishy-washy prognoses and dim-witted last calls for Emma's existence. She was going to be just fine; she always was. She was a fighter, and then some. No matter how small or frail, Emma certainly was no lightweight when it came to challenges. After all, who would know better than he? Nope, there was nothing ordinary about Emma. In fact, there were countless times Emma's abilities surprised even him.

He remembered how she licked that big bully in their neighborhood one day. It was after the stout ruffian had called him a sissy for having played hopscotch with Emma. In truth, Kenyan had taken all the obvious precautions to make sure that they remained unseen. Why, they even went behind old Mrs. Potter's dairy barn way off in the woods, far behind the old schoolyard, just so none of the kids would see them, but that stupid bully was already there long before he and Emma arrived. They were all twelve years old back then, as he recalled.

In a real big hurry to grow up, the neighborhood tyrant, Matt Fisher, a self-appointed brawler, was copying every bad habit that came his way. That included smoking. The mean overweight kid had stolen a pack of smokes from his dad and thought he would inhale the whole bundle to show off just how much of a man he was. He even went so far as to invite two of his buddies to watch the impressive wonder. Kenyan remembered he was not particularly excited about playing the game with Emma that day, but he was a sucker for whatever his sister asked of him. It was before Emma was dreadfully sick, when she could still do things, play games, run and swim like everyone else. In fact, she beat him at both on many occasions, but that was something he would always keep to himself. Just as he intended to keep the action of playing hopscotch a hush-a-bye secret. However, that would suddenly change after the fifth toss of the stone, after landing on the scraggly chalk drawing he had scratched deep into the dirt beneath a towering evergreen.

It was Emma's turn. The stone had landed on the number 7, and she was already off and jumping when they heard a loud voice, hoarse and gruff, coming out of nowhere. It was Matt Fisher, and he and his mean-spirited buddies had been watching from the side of the barn, having hidden inside the dense trees that ran rampant in that part of the wood. Emma finished her jump, returning to the start of the game, successfully having regained the stone in her tiny hand after hearing Fisher's smoke-irritated voice. As did Kenyan, she turned and looked to see the bully and his two buddies approaching. The arrogant Matt Fisher was dead center between the other kids, taking his last draw on the cigarette before throwing it carelessly on the ground while all three bullies walked toward them just as tough as they could be. After several rounds of choking fits, Matt Fisher fought to catch his breath resolved not to let the other kids see how the smoke made his eyes and throat burn. He quickly wiped the stinging wetness away, streaking a black dirty smudge down his cheek while calling out to them.

"Hey, little girlie girl," Matt Fisher shouted over to Kenyan blatantly spitting out a wad of mucus from his burning throat, "you and your freaky sister going to play dollhouse after you're done playing your little sissy game?"

"Get lost, Fisher! Go light up another smoke! Maybe you'll light yourself on fire and do us all a favor," Kenyan yelled determined not to let the boy intimidate him.

"Kenyan," Emma said in a hushed voice. "We best go. It's getting late. Mama will be worried."

"Yeah," teased Fisher. "Mama will be worried."

"It's my turn," Kenyan insisted, holding out his hand, waiting for his sister to give him the tiny stone.

"Please," Emma begged, her face growing pale watching the three boys draw closer and closer. "You don't have to do this. I want to go home now."

"Give me the stone," he said, taking it from her hand.

"But, Kenyan—" Emma pleaded, unable to finish her words.

"Oh yes, little girlie girl," Fisher said, spitting again, nearly dousing Emma's black shoes with his slimy discharge. "Better listen to your creepy sister before she puts one of her voodoo spells on you."

"I said get lost, Fisher! You're such a loser!" Kenyan yelled, not looking at the bully, tossing the stone, watching it land on the number 10, not aware that Fisher was coming up fast directly behind him.

Kenyan felt the sting of the rocky earth bite at his face as he went down. The blood spouted from his lower lip, and he quickly jumped to his feet, ready to attack the dirty rotten bully. He punched Matt Fisher right on the nose as he recalled, but he would not get a second chance to swing. Like clockwork, Fisher's two derelict buddies were on top of him. Despite Kenyan's small frame and thin stature, he gave them a decent fight, but he was no match for all three, especially when Fisher hit him hard in the belly while the other two kids held him down. Kenyan got the wind knocked clean out of him. As he pulled himself up from the ground and got up on one knee, gasping for air, Fisher kicked him down, hitting him a second time square in the stomach. Kenyan saw the lights go out before falling to the ground. He could hear Emma screaming while he fought to put air back in his lungs.

"Go away, you horrible boy! Leave him alone!" Emma cried, running to her brother, but as she ran toward him, Fisher put out his foot and tripped her. Down she fell, scraping both her knees.

"Have a nice trip, freak!" Fisher laughed.

"What is your problem? Why did you do that?" Emma asked, the tears flooding in her blue eyes.

"'Cause you're a freak! Everybody knows it!" Fisher said as the other boys laughed. "You're some kind of spooky retard, talking to animals and trees. Kids around here say you're a witch or something! Isn't that true, *Freak-O?*"

"Leave her alone!" Kenyan attempted to shout, but his words were barely understandable, still not having enough wind left inside.

Emma wiped her tears and got up. Covered in the leaves and small stones that stuck to the bloody parts of her skinned knees, she went to her brother. Kenyan was sitting up, half of his lungs replenished, but hurting badly. "You'll pay for this, Fisher!" Kenyan promised, sucking in the air.

"Kenyan, are you okay?" Emma asked, taking a handkerchief from her pocket, wiping away the blood from his lip.

"Yeah, sissy girlie girl, you okay?" Fisher teased.

Emma turned her head with an unexpected jerk and looked directly at the bully, her eyes burning with rage. "You best go home, Matt Fisher. You've caused enough trouble for one day."

However, Matt Fisher just kept right on laughing. He was all venom now, his stout face now bright red. "Shut up, creep, think I'm afraid of you? What are you going to do, turn me into a bug or something?"

"I'm warning you, Matt Fisher," Emma said, her eyes never leaving the bully. "You leave us alone, or you'll be sorry."

"Hey, I don't like threats—*Freak-O!*"

"Just go away," Emma warned, turning her eyes back to her brother.

However, Emma's defiance seemed to peeve Fisher all over again. He was not going to let her get away with threatening him, not in front of the other kids. He was going to make her pay. Girl or not, nobody talked to Matt Fisher like that and got away with it. No one! With a sudden rumble added to his clumsy stride, he went for Emma. Seeing this, Kenyan stood up and didn't waste any time plowing into the bully, tackling him to the ground. Both boys went hurling into a sticker bush, Kenyan slamming hard on top of Fisher, the other two boys running toward them.

While Kenyan punched away at the bully, Fisher pulled up his knee, clipping Kenyan in the groin, proceeding to throw him into a nearby pile of stony rubble. The bully's eyes remained wild, wanting to kick Kenyan on the side of his face. However, that was when he heard the loud growling noise. With a quick turn, Fisher looked toward Emma for that was where the sound seemed to be coming from, and it was filling the forest. Still, all he could see was the strange weirdo girl, her back turned to him, her gaze looking somewhere into the dense forest. She seemed to be calling or chanting words that sounded all singsonglike and devilishly peculiar. Unfortunately for him, he wasn't able to study the girl for long because Kenyan wasn't staying down for the count. He was already halfway up on his knees, crawling toward the bully, ready for the next round, but even he had to stop when the next horrific blast blared out from the wood.

The two derelict kids were the first to see it. In unison of one magnificent and cowardly gasp, the two boys grabbed on to each other, screaming before taking off like two bucks after the sound of a gunshot. In a flash, they vanished. Fisher watched them run, their legs moving faster than the spokes of racing bicycles. He went to call out some obscenities after them but never got the chance. He never knew what hit him. Well, not until he opened his eyes. He was lying on his back and looking straight into the black eyes of the biggest grizzly bear imaginable. The monster bear was as large as an elephant, which was how it appeared as it furiously loomed over him, its hot breath barreling down over his face. Matt Fisher could hear Kenyan yelling something to his sister, but soon the only sounds he could hear was heavy breathing mixed with angry sniffs and growls.

The massive hulking grizzly pushed his black snout forcefully in the bully's face, opening its jaws, blasting out a growl that sounded like a freight train. Fisher immediately felt the wetness squirt out all over his brand-new denim jeans, the one's he picked out himself, thinking it made him look real tough. However, the more that the bear roared over him, the more his pants became saturated, some of it trickling out, forming a yellow puddle on the rocky ground below. With another irascible growl, the monstrous grizzly pushed his long muzzle into his face and then moved slowly down toward the bully's chest. Matt Fisher tried to scream but found that he was unable. Instead, he started to cry as even more wetness came out of him. The bear bit down, ripping into the boy's breast pocket, tearing up the material along with the crumbled, half-puffed pack of cigarettes. With one massive crunch, the bear chewed up the remaining cigarettes and, not liking the taste one bit, spit them into Fisher's face with a powerful and earsplitting howl.

"Mama!" Matt Fisher cried as the bear raised his incredible paw, its endless mass spanning before his face. Below, the glare of the sun shone dangerously above nails that were sharp enough to rip through steel, ready to tear him to shreds. Closing his eyes, Fisher started to scream and cry all over again. That was when Emma thought that he had been sufficiently taught a proper lesson. She

smiled, looking at the huge grizzly, his massive head turning to meet with her pretty blue eyes. Partially moving off the bully's body, the magnificent grizzly looked toward Emma as an unusual bearish smile curled across his giant and intimidating snout.

"Good bear!" Emma said, bending down, kissing the tremendous grizzly directly on his black and furry head. "That will be all, and thank you."

The bear nestled his head affectionately against Emma's soft cheek, his eyes closing, but for a moment. With a savage turn of his head, he looked back down at the bully and ripped his teeth into the boy's pants belt, severing it with one bite. Sniffing him angrily, he grunted, growled, and barreled off the boy's chubby heaving belly, then rumbled back into the wood.

"Okay, fat Matt," an out-of-breath Kenyan said while nonchalantly joining his sister, "I think it's time to go home and change our *pee-pee* undies, don't ya think?"

Carefully, Fisher turned his head, his face covered in bear drool, mixed with a heavy dose of his own black streaked tears, his open pants soaked in urine, his pride equally as washed up. He could not utter a word, but merely stared at them as if seeing a couple of ghosts. He didn't even bother to try and pull up his sopping pants. He just bolted upward and started running as fast as his chubby legs could take him, his soggy pants occasionally falling down around his ankles, tripping him twice as Kenyan so vividly recalled.

They watched the boy run away, each trying to hold back the smile determined to show itself on both of their faces. Finally giving in, Kenyan looked toward his sister and laughed out loud, Emma doing the same. "I have to admit the bear was good! Just the right touch," he said, still trying to catch his breath. "He scared even me. I guess Fisher will think twice before he goes after little girls again, won't he?"

Emma smiled back at her brother. His lip was still bleeding, and he managed to acquire a few more bruises and cuts over his boyish face. There were some stripes of smeared blood that had gotten washed into his curly golden blond hair. Emma did not waste any time in cleaning up his face with her trusty handkerchief, fussing over him as she so often did. "Are you sure you're okay?" Emma softly asked, wiping away at the blood.

Kenyan felt his face smart and grabbed for another needed smile. "Let's just say, I'm a lot better than Fisher is right now, no doubt, never thought fat Matt could ever run that fast."

"Serves him right," insisted Emma, still cleaning out the scratches and cuts over Kenyan's face. "He's a dreadful boy. He could have hurt you."

Kenyan reached out and took hold of his sister's busy hand, holding it gently in his own. "Your knees are bleeding."

"I'll be okay," Emma insisted.

Kenyan smiled impishly, his twinkling eyes melting into hers. "You never cease to amaze me, little sister."

Emma graciously smiled back, taking her hand from his, returning it to his face. After a few more wipes, she looked at him and sighed, the same smile still lingering about her lips. "There," she said. "Good as new . . . Well . . . almost." They both laughed again as Kenyan put his arm around her tiny shoulders.

"Come on, let's go home and get you cleaned up."

"Okay," Emma agreed, falling into the same walk as her strolling brother, his arm wrapped close around her. "But promise you won't tell Mama about the bear. You know how those things always seem to upset her."

Kenyan nodded, rolled his eyes, grinned slyly, and promised he would think of something, just as he always did. They would walk the rest of the way, arm in arm, laughing and talking as if nothing ever happened. If it were not for the bruises and traces of scratches and dried-up blood, no one would have been the wiser. Why should they be? There would be no mention of bullies and bears, but only a day of vigorous and somewhat aggressive hopscotch playing somewhere off in the wood near old Mrs. Potter's barn on a warm spring afternoon—nothing more.

Kenyan would forever remember that day, a day like many others that would always remind him of just how different his sister was. So if she could take care of mean bullies and summon up humongous grizzly bears, she surely could beat this disease cluttering up her blood. She was Emma, and she was going to lick this thing, one way or another. He would not accept anything less. He knew his sister, and no matter how long he remained in that dreadful hospital waiting room, watching the doctors and nurses pass him by with their concerned looks and worried glances, he would not show them the slightest shadow of doubt or concern. Emma was going to be just fine. She just had to be.

BLACKFISH

Beneath the surface of the sea, Arayna glided skillfully through the icy waters, her body slipping wondrously in the semidarkness of dark blue and green.

The revitalized harp, no longer clumsy and awkward as she was on land, exulted in her dexterous mobility, swiftly wafting and twirling in an ultimate form of linear grace and beauty. The tactile hairs on her nose, which remained dormant above the sea, now became a crucial red light, recognizing and alerting her to any sudden changes in movement or temperatures of water. The sensitive nerves would aid the harp toward the nearness of floes, other seals, or any other creatures.

Arayna rejoiced in her long sought-after agility. Her eyes grew large and incredibly light sensitive in the darkened environment, here, in this shadowed existence where a seal's vision becomes an instrumental phenomenon. Circular muscle bands contract the pupils, revealing only hair-thin slits, making visible a once nearly obscure, unrealistic world into a crystal-clear reality of magnificent colors and shapes. Unfortunately, this vision would be drastically reduced when Arayna would again return to the ice floes, for the light there would scatter images, and her world would once more be transformed into a soft and cloudy place of perception. However, in this watery arena of adventure, she was a mere revelation of perfection. The changing colors in the water told her that food was plentiful, and she knew that she had hit the jackpot; the abundance of plankton quickly surrounded her. Churning inside the liquid space, she eagerly fed, gorging on the floating substance, inhaling up as many small fish that happened to be mixed up within this most welcomed infinitesimally feeding ground.

It was not long before Arayna found herself splendidly hemmed in a dense patch of shrimp. Happily consumed in this unexpected delicacy, the hungry seal opened her mouth and swallowed. While filling herself, the color of the sea suddenly and drastically changed into a dark and odious contrast, its moving blackness quickly consuming her, signifying immediate and present danger.

Abruptly, she retracted her front flippers and began cautiously gliding through the unexpected shadow, her heart racing as if to explode. All at once, she found herself filled with terror! She could taste the foreboding, infusing the water with its dread. From all around her, she immediately became aware of the shifting currents closing in on her. It was then she saw it. Directly above her, coming out of nowhere was a monstrous shadow. She felt the panic burn at the back of her head while she nervously submerged deeper. Feeling her heart drum faster and faster, she saw a black silhouette of a dorsal fin cut across her torso. Panic stricken, she was suddenly face-to-face, looking into the black eyes of a twenty-six-foot-long blackfish, better known as a killer whale. Besides man, the aggressive grampus was one of the greatest enemies of the harp seal.

In absolute terror, Arayna darted ahead, crashing through a dense galaxy of seaweed, their spider-veined stems shattering into a green blur as the roar of the killer whale followed her. The shriek of the beast was ravenous with menace and filled her with a million shivers. She could not believe that she had been so careless as to allow herself to be this vulnerable. Having seen the delectable smorgasbord, she had momentarily let down her guard, and now she would have to pay for it. She had to act quickly, for the whale had certainly seen her. It had already smelled her scrumptious odor, and in all its ravenous glory, it would settle for nothing less than to have her for its breakfast. Although his size far surpassed hers, the killer whale's underwater propulsion promoted a strict agile mobility, and he was rapidly gaining on her. Driven further by mad instinct, the fleeing seal submerged deeper still, hoping to lose the beast within the darkened caverns of the ice floes that stretched far beneath the vague regions of this secluded underwater universe. Turning to see just how far her determined assassin was, she found that the whale was not there. For some strange reason, the whale had suddenly changed course and was now heading toward the surface of the sea where multitudes of light summoned him . . . and perhaps something else—*her child!*

In wild pursuit of reaching Miracle before the killer whale did, Arayna abruptly swam toward the soaring beast, successfully cutting him off, confusing him, at least for a short while. Somersaulting and then jolting sideways, the disheveled harp began to swim up toward her son, the killer now following dangerously behind her. Inexorably darting through the freezing waters, she became aware of another shocking vulnerability—if she continued; she would be leading the hungry creature directly to her pup and the two walruses. This she could not dare chance. She had to lose this pursuing demon through yet another alternative route. Dramatically shifting her place in the sea, she deliberately began to lead the whale in the opposite direction of the ice boat; and in her attempted flight, she was aware, every inch of the way, that the monstrous grampus was only several feet from gobbling her up with one big crunch!

Perversely seizing the moment, the killer whale jolted open his mouth revealing an endless and admonishing array of spiny flesh-tearing teeth, wrathfully preparing to devour his wearied game. The antagonizing beast wasted no time in slamming down its jaws, and although Arayna's swift maneuvers saved her from becoming severed in two, she was not quick enough to extricate herself from total injury. The teeth penetrated the tip of her back flipper, causing her to lose her equilibrium.

Pain exploded over her.

Relentlessly, she fought to continue to pull herself forward, tearing a small part of her rear flipper. Another unspeakable twinge slashed through her pumping veins. Fleeing from the hounding beast, the immediate passing of blood temporarily stained the crossing waters as she shot her body toward the surface of the sea. Crashing upward, the gasping seal remained suspended in the air for a brief terrifying moment, hovering helplessly above the ocean, oxygen filling her pounding lungs. Plunging down, the horrendous fiend surfaced from below, his wide and open jaws expecting the juicy taste of his already bloody and disabled victim. Arayna's body came down hard, forcefully striking the side of the whale's mouth, and once again fate would protect her for when she hit, she was miraculously able to throw herself forward, once more impelling herself from his chomping mouth. Infuriating the hungry beast, but successfully breaking away, Arayna descended back down into the sea, submerging farther than she had ever dared.

Although it was the nature of a harp seal to dive into extreme depths, she was now entering the danger zone of watery descent, but she had no choice. She had to lure her assassin away from not only herself but from her tiny pup that was waiting for her above. However, Arayna soon found the increasing pressure of the sea to be too much. Within the unbelievable dimensions of the ocean's internal density and molecular weight, she would soon render herself to complete obliteration if she continued downward. Her outer skull would not be able to withstand the incredible pressure, her entire cranium would rupture, and she would die. Thinking that she had already gone too far, the frantic harp leveled out and pressed forward in the darkness, hoping to discourage the ravenous thing that had caused her to come this far.

Drifting wearily along within the impossible stress of the sea, weakened with fatigue, she closed her eyes tight, trying to fight the throbbing water pressure. The probing thoughts of the whale remained with her, fearing he had somehow managed to sustain himself from the force of the sea; and this time, he would find her, shred her to pieces, chew her up, and she would never again be seen. Arayna, not knowing where the courage came from, half mad with fear, quickly jerked her head around, ready to confront her hungry stalker. However, when she looked, the giant killer grampus had vanished! Only dark shadows now stared back at her from a place so black, so desolate . . . so still. She remained motionless, her heart racing, droning louder and louder against her inner eardrums, becoming the lone sound while the blood hammered against her brain, booming as if ready to burst into a million unrecognizable slivers. She was gradually losing consciousness when visions of Miracle began to adhere themselves to her fading cognizance. Fortunately, with each new image, the consummate nothingness gradually began to lose its hold over her, and within that moment, she found the strength to call out his name.

"Miracle!" she reverberated into the soundless emptiness. Then an even greater revelation sparked through her, ripping at her just as viciously as if the teeth of the menacing grampus had sliced her in two. Her body began to convulse, determined to ascend from the black desolation possessing her. *Could it be possible?* She thought. Were Miracle and the others revealed when she and the beast surfaced? These thoughts slashed through Arayna's heart, leaving the feeling as if the whale had indeed torn through her chest. "My child, my Miracle, no!" she cried. Her mind sparked again, this time catching fire and exploding, giving her the initial jump start she needed to free herself from the compelling shadows of death.

Frantically, Arayna continued to surface, her hind quarters throbbing in sheer agony. Her mind ignited with desperation and horror, speeding toward the pinnacle of the sea, the recent injury expelling blood, staining her trail, stinging all the way, this physical affliction paling considerably in comparison to the bitter anguish she felt deep within the bowels of her sick stomach. Had she inadvertently sentenced her child and the walruses to a certain and tragic death?

"No!" she screamed. "It cannot be!" She would not accept this! Never! The whale's sudden absence was due to her skillful maneuvering aquatics, nothing more! Surely, the pressures of the vast deep were too much for the gluttonous grampus and he simply retreated, or better still, he had perished from the incredible depth and at that hellish moment was floating upside down, silent, crushed and dead inside the stomach of the nothingness. Yes, she had to believe this! She had to!

The seal pierced the water, cranking up her speed, wild, never faltering from her designated pathway, always in the same direction of where she had last seen her beloved Miracle—always in the same direction where her maternal instincts savagely compelled her to go. Whirling and twirling, slicing through the currents as if to be nothing more than the fragments of weightless plankton only recently gorged on, the desperate harp speared onward up toward the light at the ceiling in the ocean. Her eyes wildly darted back and forth, unable to dismiss the hungry thing away that had nearly destroyed her. However, there was still no sign of the creature. The ocean remained impassive to the perilous eating machine, as if he had never actually existed at all. However, he did exist! He did, and she could not pretend him away, no matter how much she begged.

Wildly soaring toward the light, she watched it grow brighter and brighter before her. With every last remainder of nerve she still managed to hold on to, she reached out into the radiance, praying, pleading, racing toward the fantastic paths of shooting lights. A multitude of illuminated shafts of soft transparent floating lines showered down around her.

"I am almost there, my beloved child! I am almost there!" she wailed through salty waters. Breaking through the watery stage floor of the sea, Arayna crashed through it as if it were a pane of glass. In the crazed despondency for oxygen, the debilitated seal hungrily replenished her nearly flattened lungs, her eyes madly trying to focus on what was now in front of her. Having just returned from the sea, Arayna's eyesight reverted back to viewing the world as a hazy and fragmented place of delicate blurs and wispy shadows. Still, despite her impairment, she was suddenly aware that located only a few inches away was a dark shape moving toward her. She closed her eyes, not knowing if she would ever again open them. Her heart skipped several beats, and her insides went into spasms. This time she waited for the teeth monster to finish her off, her eyes tightly screwed shut. She waited and waited and waited, but there was no attack. There was no tearing of seal flesh. There was no assault to stain the waters a muddy crimson pallor. There was no dreadful grampus teeth monster. The shadow must have come from the dark passing clouds that were still gathering above her. She was free and safe; she had made it, and by all that was holy, she desperately prayed the same for her child and the walruses.

Arayna frantically searched for the ice boat that held her precious baby, her large tearful eyes pathetically seeking him out. She thrust her head back and forth in every possible position, but in answer to her unyielding quest, there came no resolution—the ice boat, her child, and the walruses were nowhere in sight. Refusing to accept this tragic discovery, she began to swim against the swell of the sea. Crazed from grief, she remained desperate to find the ice boat, the place she should have never left just so she might feast upon the sea. She would never forgive herself. No, she could not allow herself to think this way. Perhaps she had just miscalculated. That had to be it. After all, she had suffered a serious and utterly devastating trauma. Surely, this was the reason. She had to remain calm. She was going to find him. Despite the shrouds of fog that were now pouring in around her, she was going to find him! "Miracle, where are you?"

However, no answer came to her.

"Miracle, it is Mother, where are you, darling?"

Still, no word followed.

Unable to hold back any longer, the devastated seal broke down, sobbing loudly, losing her breath while barking out into the growing fogginess. "Please, Miracle, call out to me, I am here! *I am here!*" Once more, the emptiness of her child's voiceless call pierced her heart. "No!" she cried. She would not believe it! She could not believe it! "Miracle, where are you, baby?" Arayna barked in a hoarse and frenzied voice. "Please call out to Mama! Call out to Mama!" she begged. The tears in her burning eyes made for an impossible task of deciphering any real shapes or contrasts in colors. With the forming shroud of fog insistent on plaguing her, she felt overwhelmed. Still, she did not give up. "Where are you?" she wept. "It is Mother! Miracle, answer me!" Regretfully, just as before, there came no answer but only the continuous and agonizing sound of the ocean slapping against her soft pelt of light brown and silver.

Swaying helpless in the swell of the waves, Arayna's eyes unbearably burned from tears, and her stomach constricted and exploded with a fiery sensation while she circled the designated mark in the sea. Not daring to relinquish her last compelling moments of hope, the seal was not ready to give up. She would call out repeatedly, "Crumpels! Can you hear me? It is Arayna! I have gotten myself lost . . . *again!* Please tell me where you are! Are you all right? Is my child with you?"

Again, there was no answer—only the despairing sound of the sea.

"Please," Arayna wept, sobbing on her words, "won't someone answer me? Where are you, my baby! *Where are you?*"

Barely persevering in the waiting of absolute desperation for some kind of response, she suddenly became startled by something creeping toward her out of the chilling fog. It was a fragmented piece of ice—ice that of itself would have never given the seal cause to think, but this sudden ice drift would horrify her.

In pure hysterics, she pounced on the floating chunk. With an uncontrolled pursuit, the seal instinctively pressed her snout deep into the surface of the shattered icy remains, inhaling deeply. She thoroughly saturated herself with its essence. Then with one powerful exhale, Arayna screamed out in agony. The ultimate of fears had suffocated her cause quickly and monstrously putting an end to any hope she may have prayed for.

She had smelled her child!

Once again, in utter suffering, the devastated harp howled out in broken torment. Traces of her son's blood, along with his indisputable and haunting scent, remained on the fragmented piece of ice floating before her. It was all that remained of the once intrepid ice boat—all that remained of the two walruses, all, that she had left of her beloved and destroyed Miracle. His unforgettable aroma ulcerated itself within the very core of her heart, and she once again wailed out her child's name. "Miracle, my baby, no—*no, please—No!*"

On that day, her pitiable cries echoed sadly and profoundly throughout the sea, drenching the engulfing fog with uncompromising sorrow. For a brief moment, even the sea became momentarily inarticulate, retribution of respected silence for having ever allowed for such casualties of grief.

The winds no longer differentiated themselves from the cries of the lamenting and brokenhearted mother. For soon, both became one voice: a feeble voice that morosely began to sink into a desolate whimper, altering the sea for but a brief moment, and in that moment, the ocean no longer consisted of plankton, seaweed, or other extremities. For today, the sea consisted of a salty fullness not of water, but of tears.

SPECIAL LIGHT

Days came and days went, and Kenyan missed not one of them, each of them spent waiting in that dreadful hospital waiting room.

Because of her deteriorating condition, he was not able to see Emma regularly, and when he was able, she never even knew he was there.

He had brought her the picture that she had drawn him, now dramatically bordered in a wooden frame that he created, painted over with a glossy gold color chosen for such a delicate piece of artwork. How proud he was of that frame. He never used such precision cuts before. He knew Emma would notice every single curve that he made against the wood, just as she noticed everything and everyone around her. She would undoubtedly appreciate his unique genius for creative carpentry, certainly noticing how he was improving at his craft.

It would not be long before he would create something incredible for her, something that would certainly make those fantastic eyes of hers sparkle, but first, she had to open her eyes. She had not yet seen his golden masterpiece that so gallantly celebrated her drawing, for it remained near her bed, unseen and waiting for her approval. She had slipped into a gripping unconsciousness and things were as uncertain as they could get, but as always, he would not lose faith. He knew that she would return. No matter how dark things appeared, Emma would not relinquish that special light living inside her. For he had seen this light himself so many times, and he knew deep down in his heart that she would soon turn it on as she had done the many times before. He would sit there and wait and wait and wait forever if that's what it took.

As it would turn out, he would not have to wait much longer. Although he did not know it at the time while expecting to get the okay to visit with his comatose sister, Emma had just opened her eyes, and that special light in her heart was beginning to glow.

LOST

Black-and-white-colored auks momentarily covered the skies, leaving no room for the familiar clouds that claimed such frigid surroundings. These small, plump narrow-billed diving birds slowly uncluttered themselves from the skies, settling down on the spotted foundation below. From a distance way above, the gathering of the seals below appeared to belong to an imaginary and prehistoric canine, consisting of various dots and spots, not unlike some mythical Dalmatian. Consisting within its many spotted shapes formulated

a seemingly unaesthetic design from its aerial perspective. Here,
upon this nursery of Sealssong, herds of seals assembled; it was a
perfectly pearly cradle of dazzle. For many reasons, this particular
island was unique, for storms and sudden attacks of man were not
as easily executed in this place, mainly because it remained nestled
within the numerous surrounding islands protecting it, sparing
it from the typical ongoing casualties many of the encompassing
nurseries sustained. Situated here was a glassy playroom filled with
hundreds upon hundreds of mother harp seals, some having already
given birth, others still eagerly waiting for that incredible moment to
arrive.

It was not long before the hungry black-and-white seabirds came
to merge into the dotty surroundings below. Although small, having
short and stubby bills and dwarfed wings, they remained proficient
at diving in search for food. However, what would be better than
having your lunch served without having to do any work? And that's
just what the plump little auks anticipated for it was here they would
hope to catch an easy meal, swiping fish from unsuspecting jaws. It
was within these floes that the seals would swim and feed, but the
auks offered jolly little competition for the harps. In their feeble
attempts to monopolize the feeding passages, these twittering and
cackling short-neck diving birds with the stubby wings were always
good for a moment of impromptu fun. Whenever a seal would
suddenly emerge from the inky waters, they would deliberately
startle the shrieking birds, propelling them frantically back into the
sky. Seals loved to do this. They all rejoiced in their harmless seal
pranks, always welcoming the comic relief provided by such obstinate
creatures, and obstinate they were. In only a matter of moments,
another unsuspecting diehard would venture down, and once
again the fun would start all over again. Such were the joys of this
day—carefree and lackadaisical, or so it would seem.

Enraptured within this celebrated wintry bliss where the seals
came every year, migrating, meeting and greeting, and most
singularly giving birth to their miraculous purities of splendor, this
would prove to be an extraordinary day, especially for one particular
seal. For somewhere in the midst of the twilight consciousness
captured in this venerated seclusion of whiteness and shine, there
was a tiny and truly lost baby seal named Miracle.

I Was Dreaming

Emma was sitting up when he finally was allowed in her room.

Kenyan could tell by the surprised faces of the doctors, nurses, orderlies, and whoever that Emma once again fooled them. She had pulled through yet once more, just as he knew she would do. He would be instructed, just as he had been the countless times before, not to talk and overexcite her. It was the same *blah-blah-blah-blah* song every time. He could sing it in his sleep, but they didn't have a clue. He knew exactly how to handle his sister, far better than any of them ever could, no doubt. However, just to move things along, he always pretended to listen to their purposeless fuss, nodding his head, making his way over to his sister's bed. Although her face remained covered in ashy grays and unsettling shades of pallor, Emma's magnificent blue eyes shone out as a blazing beacon, offering him safety from the chaotic storm buzzing around him.

"Emma," Kenyan called out to his sister, moving near her, taking hold of her hand while standing beside her. "Welcome back, kiddo, now tell me, what fantastic places have you been visiting?" he playfully asked while looking down at her incredibly small and frail hand.

"I was dreaming," she softly replied, trying to squeeze her brother's hand but unable to find the strength. "It's beautiful," she said, her hand hopelessly falling into his.

Kenyan's smile widened, knowing precisely what she was referring to. "Oh, so you finally got around to seeing it, huh?"

"Ahh-haa," Emma hummed. "It's the best ever. They said they would hang it on the wall for me to look at whenever I wish."

"You'll be able to hang it in your own room soon. I'm breaking you out of here."

"How long has it been?" she asked softly, her magnificent eyes never leaving him.

Again, Kenyan looked down at her extraordinarily tiny and pale hand. "Not that long," he answered.

"The truth."

Kenyan's smile faded a notch but refused to give it up entirely. "A month, maybe, not even that."

Emma's face became quiet and sad. "I'm sorry."

"For what?" her brother asked, momentarily releasing her hand long enough to pull up a chair in order that he could sit next to her. "I knew you wouldn't make me wait too long. You never do."

"Kenyan," Emma said through dry lips, "they said that I wasn't getting any better and that the treatments aren't working like they hoped."

"They don't know what they're talking about. None of them do. Besides, those treatments are a waste of time they only make you sick. I don't think there is a doctor in this whole place that knows what he is doing."

"Kenyan," Emma begged, "you mustn't say such things. They are doing the best they can."

"Well, I think they can do a heck of a lot better! If you ask me, the whole lot needs to go back to med school! There is not one—"

Emma stopped him, reaching over, taking his hand in hers this time. "It's okay," she whispered in a voice mixed with weariness and fortitude. "I'm scared too."

"What makes you think I'm scared? I'm not scared."

"Shhh . . . ," she hushed, swallowing hard before quickly retrieving her smile, never wanting to lose it now. It was what was giving her the courage to continue, and she did. "Kenyan—"

"Yeah?" he answered, wiping a few sudden tears away, hoping to catch them in time before she saw them.

"Don't think me silly, but will you hold me?"

Drawing closer, he nodded, not having to consider such a request. "Yeah . . . I think that would be okay." Lifting himself out of the chair, he quickly slid it away from the bed. He reached over to disengage the hand railing and waited for Emma to move over slightly. Since she was unable to, he immediately helped her, never considering the ever-mindful nurses and attendants who were carefully watching him, not one of them daring to stop him. Scooping up his sister's frail body into his arms, he carefully moved her over. Then sitting on the bed, he lay next to her, embracing her with both of his arms, her face neatly folded into his chest, relieved that she was not able to see his face or the tears that freely washed over him. "It's going to be okay, Emma. We're going to beat this thing. I promise."

Neither one would speak for the duration of the time that he would remain with her. The nurses would wait, watching Emma gradually drift off into another exhausted sleep. Kenyan would patiently wait until the hospital people would once more come to take him away, but for the time being, he was content to be with her. He looked down at Emma's beautiful and innocent face, holding her in his arms while he protected her from the rest of the world, feeling her heart as it peacefully beat next to his.

ALL ALONE

The dream was not like anything Miracle had experienced thus far. There were bubbles, thousands of them, everywhere, and all of them twirling about him like a small tornado. They popped and exploded until he awoke with a gasp.

Whatever the reason, Miracle had survived, and when he awoke, he found that he was utterly confused and entirely alone. None of the events that had occurred made any sense to him, and that included his queer dream. However, the pup would soon come to realize that his recent daydream was the least of his problems. His head hurt with such intensity that it sent a thousand shocks of pain into his entire body. Once more, the whitecoat was near the zone of unconsciousness though he fought desperately to overcome this. His belly hurt and felt unusually swollen. His bruised flippers hurt. His bottom hurt, his mouth and tongue hurt, and it even felt like every single white hair that covered him hurt.

What had happened to him? Had his world suddenly ended, and if so, what was all this blaring white stuff in front of him? He tried to move, but then suddenly winced out in pain. Slowly relinquishing his stare from the icy floor, the tiny pup began to weep, finding that it hurt to cry, so much so that in just a short while, he had to try to stop himself. Then there came a slightly buzzing sound. At first, the dazed seal believed it to be coming from inside his throbbing head, but with each passing second, the sound continued to grow, revealing itself in such a way that he realized that the noise was coming from outside himself, far away in the distance.

Dizzily contemplating the buzzing sound, the noise grew distinguishable, and it soon became apparent that the vibrations were actual echoes of faraway voices, somehow all fused together in an unrelenting jumble of hisses and mutters somewhere beyond. Perhaps he was not alone. It was then that his tiny mind began slowly registering backward. His memory of his extraordinary experience was beginning to unfold itself. He was beginning to remember! It was slowly playing back to him, and as it continued to reveal itself, the small pup yelped out in sudden fear. This time his cry was loud and filled with despair. *"Maaa-maaa! Maaa-maaa!"* he wailed, his absolute panic cutting through the very fiber of the surrounding winds, stifling them almost to a complete and utter halt.

CODE BLUE

Emma woke with a gasp sometime the following morning, and Kenyan was no longer with her.

The side rails of her bed remained in their upright position, and she was still in intensive care. Her throat was dry. She wanted to call out to the pretty nurse with the green eyes, but she too was no longer in that room. In fact, there was no one in that room when Emma opened her eyes.

From somewhere off in the distance, she could hear the hustle and bustle of busy footsteps sounding as if they were running toward something that was not good. *Code Blue! Code Blue!* That is what she heard repeatedly, and the way the nurse screamed it out was most upsetting. For a moment, Emma thought that they were referring to her, and perhaps they were; she was not sure about anything anymore. Perhaps she had died and didn't realize it yet. Still, if she did, then why did she feel so much pain? Wasn't all the pain supposed to go away when you went to heaven? Maybe she wasn't in heaven. She began to cry when the nurse's calls grew more urgent, the sounds of the frantic hospital becoming a noisy vibration of shouts and commands. It took her breath away, and just when she could not take it anymore, she looked up and saw it. It was her framed drawing. Her devoted nurse had undoubtedly hung it up on the wall for her to see.

Emma closed her eyes, praying to herself that Kenyan would return to her while the nurse's voice went on and on and on, calling out a warning that meant that someone was hurting badly—perhaps just as badly as she was.

MAAA-MAAA!

For Miracle, his remembered wannabe assassin would remain nameless, only having dark eyes, being extraordinarily large, and having a hundred pointed teeth, all of them just waiting to crush him. It seemed to have no other bodily characteristics but for these three menacing recollections, but somehow, some way, the baby seal had managed to survive the dreadful Teeth Monster. But how?

What of his mother, where was she?

As his tiny brain searched for answers, he began to cry again. How could she leave him? Where did she go? Was she ever coming back? "Maaa-maaaa!" Miracle cried out, breaking down into another pathetic and desolate whimper. The pain inside him hurt far more than the physical casualties he was enduring. Overcome with more fear and anxiousness, he began to withdraw into himself, feeling terribly alone, tottering in his strange twilight world of aimless trance. He remained motionless, and soon his cries dissolved into sporadic whimpers. Coiling himself into a tiny white ball, he disappeared into the encompassing rolls of billowy softness that covered him. He would stay this way, not daring to move, his trembling flippers pressed intensely into his sides, his dark eyes wide and open.

As the shivering pup lay there appearing artificial as if he were a sewn together stuffed toy, he was once again made aware of the ice and snow surrounding him, still shadowed by the constant background sounds coming from somewhere off in the distance. The nearby wailing of a lone seagull filled his senses and chilled his heart. However, while listening to several other passing seagulls, the small seal realized that there were actually other creatures living in this dazzling world. He was not alone, and more importantly, he was alive. The horrible Teeth Monster did not eat him. He could still breathe. He could still think. He could still feel. Perhaps somewhere out there in all that white dazzle, possibly his mother was alive too unless the Teeth Monster ate her? And if he did the horrible thing, he most assuredly gobbled up the two walruses as well!

With another despondent cry, the baby seal began to shake uncontrollably. Ignited by his fearful premonitions, he widened his teary eyes, turning his plump head, desperate to see both the walruses and his mother once again, but all that reflected back to him was the same empty new world of white dazzle. There was no mother. There was no Crumpels, and there was no Poo-Coo. It was as if they had never existed at all.

Finding Nikki

The many faraway sounds continued, and the tiny seal became less afraid, finding himself more intrigued than anything else.

Somehow these new sounds seemed to warrant a sliver of hope. His small inner ears listened carefully while he gathered up his courage. Stretching out his puffy neck, he pushed down on his front flippers, supporting his weight. Pausing, he continued listening to the many new sounds around him, making up his mind that he was going to find out just where they were coming from and what they meant. With each growing vibration, the pup steadied his flippers against the snow, pressing down ready to wriggle off. Driven by this uncanny curiosity, Miracle pulled himself onward, dragging his injured body in the direction toward the unknown callings in the distance.

He squeaked and wheezed pathetically, pulling his plump form across the icy floor, determined not to stop until he found what those peculiar sounds were. Soon his body ached with fatigue, but he was not giving up no matter what! Then something strange happened. The situation began to intensify. It no longer was a mere curiosity of consideration for what was beyond the dazzle of white. It was apparent his venture was now to become a definite quest, a crusade fueled by the constant hypnotic summons of sounds and the incredible possibility that there, somewhere, among the melodic chanting, he would find Home. This time she would not leave him ever, ever again! She would have forgiven him for whatever he may have done to deserve this terrible separation. With his mouth fully opened, the baby harp once more called out excitedly to her.

"Maaa-maaa!" At last! At last, he was on his way to find Home! He would focus on nothing else but the constant callings reaching out to him, convinced that she would be there waiting for him.

His wheezing growing worse, he boldly pushed onward, allowing that nothing would stop him. Out of breath and brimming with exhaustion, Miracle cried out again, "Maaa-maaa!" The burning fatigue in his limbs was swiftly seeping into his quivering joints. Still, the brave little seal squirmed and trekked onward, and although every part of him ached, he somehow found the strength to continue dragging and pulling himself across the grounds that magnified before him. The pup shook and vibrated above the ice and snow, never hesitating, never unfocused, always in the same direction, always with the same urgent burning in his eyes, always looking out into the blurring white nothingness, desperately searching for Home!

Too weary now and unable to call out, the extremely tired harp began to moan miserably. Trudging forward, awkward, feeble, and feeling unsteady, he suddenly gripped the snow with his tiny front claws, listening. The sounds began growing louder, and the glaring whiteness in front of him gradually took on the semblance of luminous shapes. The great fireball in the sky was now directly over him, and the entire wonderland burst forth with an even grander splendor, showing off its outrageous display of brilliance. Still, the splendid exhibition did singularly little to impress the pup. Eager to find Home, he humped and wriggled forward, moaning from the stings that came from his rear quarters from where the Teeth Monster sliced into him. He did not know how much longer he could withstand this torture, for he feared soon his tiny body would crumble and break apart all over the strange white world he had mysteriously come upon. That was when it happened!

He saw it! It was there, right in front of him, all around him! Suddenly, all the sounds he had been listening for all came together in a bursting surprise, here among the articulations of such sounds where his journey would truly begin.

Seals!

There were seals—*everywhere!*

"Maa-maaa!" he cried out, wriggling excitedly. Once again fueled with newly found strength, he ventured forth with a hurried stride, merging further into the intoxicating sights and sounds. With the bright and shining phenomenon shimmering all about him, the scene filled with even more seals—hundreds and hundreds of them!

Beneath his weight, the snow crunched and cracked, but he did not notice. He remained mesmerized by the sights and sounds. It was fantastic! It was more than fantastic! It was a fantastic seal's playground! As far as he could tell, there seemed to be an unending spotted sea of harp seals happily displayed in all colors, mostly snowy white, just like him! However, there were many mama seals too, all shaded in the most splendid browns, grays, and golden colors ever imagined! They came in every shape and size, all of them stretching out amazingly like a magical field of velvety seal carpet. From the sacred seal code preserving such miracles of miracles, the lost pup instinctively knew that his mama would be able to smell his distinct aroma among the multitudes of countless other harps. If she was there, and she just had to be, she would find him! He also would do as she would—smell the wind. It would take him to her!

Immediately, he went to work. *Sniff! Push! Pull!* At last, he was nearing the remarkable gathering of chortling mammals, their stimulating sounds and vibrant scents intensifying with every single *Sniff! Push! Pull!* He was almost there! Just a little further—don't stop, don't think, don't do anything, just keep on moving! You're almost there! You are almost with Home again!

Finally, the baby seal reached his destination—and stopped.

There he was, among the crowd, the many inhabitants of Sealssong. He cocked his head and looked at all of them with a puzzling baby seal stare. For a moment, the harps appeared dreamlike, looking as if they were only two-dimensional. Could this be a dream? he thought. No, it just had to be real!

The pup watched the other seals before him, strangely captured in flowing strokes of shimmering lights, each one lying exquisitely upon a ghostly canvas of delusive sheets of whiteness. Their unique imagery quickly excited Miracle, and before he realized what had happened, he too was contributing to the echoes and whimsical sights surrounding him, pouncing forward like a leapfrog wriggling as fast as possible, determined to join in the dazzling scenery.

Abruptly giving out a high-pitched bark, he charged onward. He barked repeatedly, slicing through the snow. *Did that come out of me?* He thought, smiling delightfully. He truly liked this new sensation that tickled his throat, especially since it somehow made him a part of this newfound wonderland. *Bark! Chirp!* And *Arff!* He went, sounding out the alarm. He was going to let them all know that he had come looking for his mama. So once more, he cleared his throat, pulled his neck forward away from the pillow of fur collaring him, opened wide his mouth, and blasted out another string of barks, chirps, and arffs zooming out toward them. "I am here! *I am here!*" he chirped and growled, scrambling through the snow, turning his head back and forth while he continued to peep, squeak, bark, and chirp, most insistent on his extremely necessary introduction. On and on he went, expecting that at any moment, the entire seal congregation would embrace him with open flippers. Slowing in his wriggle, he became quiet, suspiciously surveying the situation.

It would appear that all but for a few nosy mother harps that had just returned from nearby slushy ice holes, each seal nonchalantly shaking the freezing droplets of water off their coats, his decided acclamations remained virtually unnoticed. Stubborn with determination, the obstinate pup continued to bark, chirp, and squeak, popping furiously up and down on the snowy ground, most upset that no one would acknowledge him, so much so that his bark suddenly took on another high-pitched ear-splitting squeal. All but for a few turned heads; most of the seals continued, completely engrossed in their own world, sunning themselves, feeding their young ones, or just downright relaxing.

Now Miracle was seriously perturbed.

One way or another, he was going to get their attention. Wriggling forward onto a rather steep and hilly mass of ice, he stood firm, sticking out his tiny chest, blasting them all with another noisy round of ear-piercing, high-pitched, rather annoying squeaks and chirps, but it still did not manage to accomplish what he had hoped. In fact, all it did was jar him from his spot on the hill, causing him to lose his balance. In one embarrassing tumble, Miracle slid down the slippery glade, hitting his head on a rocky pile of broken ice. After gaining his bearings, he shook his head and abruptly snorted. He was slowly getting the point that no one was actually listening, and if they were, they were not interested. He was growing more and more agitated, and yet he was not giving up. Once more, he belted out what he believed to be his loudest rip-roaring blast yet. Still, no one seemed to be impressed in the slightest.

Frustrated and mustering up all the energy he possibly could, he cleared out his parched throat and prepared to begin his tenacious yip-yapping again. This time, in his wild excitement, he jumped several octave scales, considerably higher than before, sounding more ridiculous than ever. Immediately regretting the absurd squeak, he quickly recoiled back with burning humiliation. He lowered his head and twitched his large black eyes back and forth, waiting to be ridiculed; and yet despite his silly squeak, no one seemed to care. He waited a moment before his brazen determination would return. All too soon, the baby seal was back at it, popping and squirming on the ice and snow, wholeheartedly believing that he would find a place in this new world made up of other twittering seals, all of them neatly assembled on a soft, blurry backdrop of billowy illumination. However, just as before, *NOTHING!*

Steamed up more than ever and ready to bite someone if he had to, Miracle started up again. He did not care. He would keep it up all day if necessary, but someone was going to notice him! After wearing out his vocal cords and draining his reserved strength, the exhausted pup began to grow tired and dizzy. When he was finally able to catch his breath, Miracle grunted, shook his head, and looked about, huffing and puffing, trying not to faint. It was at this moment he realized he was in an extraordinary place. He had come to the nucleus of the seal nursery, for the many other baby seals made him aware of this. At first, they just looked at him as if to show their annoyance of his offensive unseal-like squeaks. However, eventually, the tiny whitecoats pensively softened their stare. Watching him, their eyes questioned him in such a way that Miracle could not help wondering, had they lost their mamas too, just as he had?

The shadowy blue-colored nursery, pieced together by the snowcapped runners and starlit stairs of icy steps, entirely surrounded Miracle. *Chirp, cheep, squeak!* he cried, approaching them, hopping excitedly toward the other whitecoats, their angelic faces and huge black eyes filled with anxiousness. These newborns seemed to possess the unexplainable ability to transpire into semblances of unearthly creatures. Dancing along in the snow, Miracle found himself surrounded by their sudden whimpers and cries. He continued studying their animated faces and rippling snouts, their whimpers intensifying. They crinkled up their noses and bunched their muzzles into furry baby seal expressions, indicating that the highly expected moment of moments was at hand. For at last, it was feeding time in the nursery of Sealssong, and these little guys were indeed hungry!

Just about this time every day their mothers would feed them, and because it was morning, the decidedly welcomed breakfast was eagerly awaited. It was not long before they were all crying out in high-pitched tongues, all zealously anticipating the taste of their mother's warm and pearly seal milk. With deafening cries, the craving baby seals of Sealssong suddenly pealed out at the same time, unexpectedly alarming Miracle. Cautiously, he observed and slowly approached the buzzing herd. With one tiny wiggle at a time, Miracle steadily merged with the other whining infants, watching their soulful faces exhibit their immediate urgencies, all of them slurping their mouths, ready for the succulent and scrumptious morning meal. Despite the chorus of bawls, most mothers of the whitecoats seem to remain in a half sleep, oblivious to the crying and feisty assembly. Some mothers quickly woke, going directly to their pups, cradling them, and tucking them neatly into their sides. However, at this time, most of the pups were alone and consequently fretful. Instantaneously, Miracle identified with the seemingly abandoned pups and began to chirp and yelp right along with them, making a much nosier racket than an entire bunch of them put together. On and on his loud chirping continued with nonstop persistence, but again, no one seemed to notice. His full-tongued squeaks merely remained unexceptional along with the murmur of the others. Angry and still determined to defy away neglect, the yelping Miracle continued to sound off his own personal interpretation of urgent and immediate woes.

Eventually and quite by accident, he suddenly zeroed in on one particular pup that was whimpering out most upset, reminding him much of himself. Feeling the immediate camaraderie toward the pup, he quickly bumped and thumped forward. The squalling stopped as Miracle approached the trembling whitecoat. She was a tiny one, almost as small as he was. She looked at him with her beautiful black saucer-shaped eyes, both of which were swimming in tears. Slowly and almost too cautiously, Miracle lowered his head and slightly sniffed out loud, making a silly grunting sound, his nose touching upon hers. They remained transfixed that way momentarily, staring, smelling, both their wet twitching noses rubbing and investigating each other. In his exploration and somewhat confused consolation of the pup, a dramatic occurrence took place. Abruptly, the sky above became dark. The air itself took on an alternate aroma of uncertainty and danger, and out of these probing shadows appeared a large black shape. It fell toward him, positioning itself directly on top of him.

Startled and with an instinctive urge to pull away, Miracle recoiled into a white ball of fur. Only his eyes continued to move in a rather frantic manner. Pressing through the illusive bleakness, he became aware of a large pair of black eyes just glaring down at him. The eyes remained masqueraded within a silhouette of images set against the bright ball of light in the sky that always seemed to make this world ablaze with bedazzle and flash. Uneasiness quickly swallowed him whole. In fact, it made him regurgitate a little, wetting the entire bib of his white and furry neck. He swiftly felt his heart drum just as it had when he first came in contact with that dreadful and horrible Teeth Monster, right before it tried to eat him up. Trembling with fear, he shuddered while the silhouetted thing with the glaring eyes drew closer to him. If Miracle could have screamed out he would have, but he found that he could not utter a sound, not even a single squeak—he was that scared! At once, all of Miracle's senses heightened. There was something strange about the thing with the piercing black eyes, something familiar, yet drastically unsettling. The wavering form was most ornate amidst the glitter of the morning sky, drawing closer still as his gape remained unaltered, some of the sun filling up his eyes.

Although terrified, the white pup intriguingly widened his eyes and dared to look up toward this extraordinary specter. Not prepared for what was to take place, he desperately tried to penetrate the blurring of this alarming presence still pressing down from above. His pondering would last but for a moment, for the alien encounter would soon reveal itself as it adjusted its towering position over him. More bursts of sunshine exploded around the figure while hosts of shattering shafts of sunbeams enraptured it. With a sudden chill, the baby seal found himself in a peculiar state of awe. Then he thought of something wonderful. Was it she? Was this his mother? Had she at last found him?

"Maa-maaa, is it you?" Miracle exclaimed in his unusual striking high-pitched squeal, excitedly pushing away the glare of the sun with his tiny flippers, pulling back staring up toward the welcomed and embellished shape of his beloved mother. The watcher, now cloaked in the sun's glorious rays, proceeded to lower its head, the light continuing to play havoc with a trillion different shafts of glares, all of them cascading over its form. It remained decided that his hopes would be confirmed. It was she! It was Home!

Ecstatic, Miracle squeaked and tweaked unmanageably. "Maaa-maaaa," he pleaded, continuing to press himself upward, unraveling himself like a ball of yarn, reaching up toward her, now utterly irrational and almost hysterical with joyfulness. His heart and mind were racing so rapidly that he began to pant and cough, causing his gasps to drown out into wisps of higher-pitched squeaks and tweaks.

"*Maaa! Chirp! Squeak! Chirp!*" he cried, wholeheartedly embracing the vision of ultimate happiness. But as quickly as the joyous reunion of unbelievable bliss happened, it was all suddenly and unbelievably extinguished with one swift and painful *WHACK!* The unknown mother harp deciding to put an end to this irritating display of mistaken identity had struck the baby Miracle promptly on his behind with one of her front flippers, dazing the pup, sending the little guy tumbling across the icy nursery floor. At first, Miracle remained stunned, motionless, for a long time before slowly unwrapping himself from the contorted position that he was hurled into. His little aching body slumped forward, dropping onto a pile of broken ice and snow. He could not logically justify the obscene action that had just occurred. What went wrong? How could she do such a thing? How could she not love him anymore? What terrible thing had he done?

As he lay there trembling and benumbed, his eyes stung unbearably with tears while he coughed and whimpered, once again calling out to her, this time in a meeker voice. "Maaa-maaa?" he choked, his failing voice closing up, his heart breaking.

"I don't think so, *Squeaky!*" the irritated mother growled.

Miracle trembled, desolated as a new set of agonizing doubts swallowed up his hopes with one painful and despairing blow. Was this truly happening? Was this yet another terrible nightmare? How could this happen? Something must have gone terribly wrong!

Once again, his tearing eyes flashed upward toward his uncertain assailant. The baby seal blinked some of his burning tears away as well as the rest of the sun that was still filling up his eyes. There could be no acceptable or rational behavior for Home to behave in such a way.

Unless . . . Then it happened! The mournful awakening came pouncing down over him, unyielding as the onslaught that swelled from the abyss of the sea herself. Alas, this was not HOME!

Miracle sobbed, blinking his eyes, blurring the image. Although she was indeed a mother harp, she certainly was not his. This mama was not colored silver and did not have the beautiful and kind eyes his mama had. No, this was not Home. Once again, he was alone. The tiny and confused baby seal looked at the erroneous mother harp repeatedly, trying to understand. Slowly relinquishing the rest of his hopefulness, he let out a painful sigh, taking in the stranger's scent. It most certainly did not belong to Home. The brokenhearted Miracle grunted and blew out the mother seal's wrongful scent, mentally storing it within his distraught consciousness, making sure he would never make such a mistake again. Very sad and discouraged, the heavyhearted pup's eyes glazed over further with more tears glancing toward the little harp that he had initially spied. There could be no doubt. This mistaken mother whom he had thought belonged to him belonged to her instead. Miracle listened as the pup's mother called to her.

"Nikki," she barked. "Come away from him!"

The tiny pup named Nikki reluctantly stopped in her tracks while her insistent mother tried to push her along. Miracle lowered his head. Once again crunching himself up into a white fur ball, unable to control his quivering jaw, he remembered the beautiful lullaby his mother sang to him, how far away it sounded now. He began to cry, clinging to the irredeemable melody she alone gave to him, playing somewhere within the deepest part of his lamenting heart. Nikki, who had also been watching Miracle ever so carefully since the unforeseen arrival of her mother, reluctantly removed her stare from him just as her most assertive mama beckoned her with another firm push. "Come along, let us be on our way," the mother harp said, but the tiny pup was once again fixated on the forlorn creature that remained staring teary-eyed at her. Though Nikki could not possibly understand the lost seal's dilemma, she suddenly became overtaken by a plunging sensation of Miracle's terminal grief, and she began to cry again.

Nikki's mother was growing more impatient by the moment. Agitated and planting a queer expression on her rather chunky seal lips, the mother harp spoke out to her pup once more. "Nikki, stop that! I said we have to go—*now!* Come along!" she barked, sharply looking toward the whimpering Miracle. Then slowly squinting shut her eyes, she added, "Sorry, Squeaky, you best be on your way. I am sure your mother is very upset with you. Best go and find her and leave us be."

Miracle remained hushed, his tears staining his cheeks a dull yellow tinge. A pencil-thin slit covered the mother harp's stare while she continued to narrow her eyes, suspiciously surveying the downcast seal. "Look, I am truly sorry, but it is not my fault your mother cannot supervise your whereabouts! Why not try that deplorable squeak of yours again? That will surely get her attention! But for goodness sake, please wait until we've gone," she scoffed, taking hold of her own pup. "That screechy yelp of yours is most deplorable!" the mistaken mother harp barked. Pushing Nikki along by the thick folds of her neck, she moved both her and her child away from the disturbing creature. Miracle did not stir or even try to make a sound. He just remained motionless, losing himself in the fractured snow beneath him.

As Nikki continued to be pulled along, she crinkled her nose and sniffed the air, lessening her cries, still most intrigued by the pup that did not have a mama. Once more, Nikki continued to resist. Again her mother reiterated with a most reprimanding request of her flipper, "Nikki! I said let's go!" Nikki's mother remained unquestionably peeved. "Now that will be all! He'll eventually find his way back to his mother!" With a huff, she cleared her throat. "After all," she said with exasperation smearing itself messily over her eyes, "I cannot be expected to take in every stray we find. Besides"—she once again steered her pup away from the lost Miracle—"I have my own two flippers full just taking care of you!"

The tiny Nikki looked up toward her mother for a moment, but then suddenly shot her gaze back over to Miracle, wanting to stay with him. Her eyes softened and seemed to sparkle just for him, as she once again felt her mother's front flipper sharply smack her sternly on her behind. *"Enough!"* Nikki's mother barked annoyingly, jerking her pup away from the lost and disheveled wanderer. However, Nikki was not giving up, not this time. She began hastily barking frantically toward the lost pup. One more time, Nikki's mother forcefully, perhaps a little too forceful than she had expected, shoved her stubborn and disagreeable pup away from

Miracle. "Now, I am warning you," she snapped, "this is the last time I am going to ask you. Leave that stray alone!" SMACK!

This sharp whack hurt, and she knew that her mother meant business. Instantly, the tiny Nikki felt the tears blister up in her eyes, but she repressed the expected response. Reluctantly, she eventually, but certainly not approvingly, surrendered to her mother's bossy orders while being gruffly taken away from the tiny Miracle, her eyes never leaving him for an instant.

The curious Nikki continued to feel the sadness surrounding the orphan and fought the restraint pull, resolved to keep her stare positioned directly upon him. Although her mother continued to yank her across the ice, she rebelliously corkscrewed and jolted up her head, struggling to keep Miracle in sight. She rocked back and forth, attempting to dodge her mother's rather aggressive shoves while she continued to be whisked away in a hasty manner. Miracle maintained his teary stare, his eyes locked onto the tiny female pup, all the while her mother begrudgingly dragging her along the icy patches of snowy pavements, listening to the pup yelp out against her mother's commands; their visual embrace would last but for a few more moments before disappearing. As with all seals, their moments would be short-lived, but they would always remain significant and always remembered. It was not long before Nikki disappeared into the crowds of the other scrambling and craving pups.

Left only with the sounds of his own congested sniffles, the lost seal remained stationary, feeling terribly alone and afraid. "Now what shall I do?" Miracle groaned aloud, still thinking of his mother. She just had to be somewhere out there. She had to be! She would never leave him! He could not for a moment believe this. Surely, there was a chance that she was in the midst of all those other seals. Tired and hungry, his back flippers aching with a constant throbbing, he fought to find the strength and the courage to endure until he could be with her again. The dreadful and painfully empty feeling in his tummy burned and hurt, but unbearable as the pain was, he would continue onward. No matter what, he was not ready to end this most prestigious crusade; and just as before, the brave little seal found the inner strength to unveil one last measure of hope left inside, as emptied and exhausted as he was.

Carefully, he embraced the ice, rising, uncurling from his usual rolled-up protective ball of fur. Placing his weight evenly forward, balancing with his tiny front flippers, the small Miracle was on his way once again—one baby seal wiggle at a time.

ONE! TWO! THREE! CHARGE!

In a desultory fashion, the lost pup crept onward over the different interlocking passageways of ice, over the floes, onto fresh veneers of frosted pearls of mountainous snow, still certain he would soon find Home.

These incredible ice drifts froze together into fantastic shapes, some of them frightening the pup, appearing like grotesque monsters. The very tips of the icy entrails remained broken up from the savage storms that came to this place, often terminally altering them in appearances. However, they were usually pasted back in some prevailing manner, christened over by the blowing winds that painted them with a brand-new coat of glistening snowy wonder work. In this world of guarded allurement, the ice itself remained animated with a maturing and constant motion of uncertainty. At times, the ice of Sealssong could advance an inch or more in only a twenty-four-hour period, but of its exact accuracy, one could never be certain. For always on duty were the ever-present artistic winds, everlastingly elated to landscape every nook and glassy cranny of the growing paths of ice with a spectacular radiance, a constant glowing, both night and day.

Miracle pressed on over the spectacular nursery, encountering numerous dark and translucent areas having been blown clean of snow. He haphazardly studied his face in unending stretches of icy reflections, wriggling forward, his tears falling to the opaquely shining surface of the ground while dauntlessly searching for his lost mama. It was not long before he reached the point of sheer exhaustion. Although his mind continued to spark with only one determined quest, his weary little body was rapidly losing endurance. He grappled for consciousness, his head spinning in a whirl, and his stomach boldly reminding him of his precarious condition. At any cost, he instinctively realized that he desperately needed food or he would simply stop being. Randomly, he surveyed his immediate surroundings and quickly came upon another mother harp, sunning herself on one of the nearby floes. Having given birth only several days before, she was lying on her back, her belly undoubtedly just packed full of delicious seal juice, her sleepy face pushed up toward the warm embrace of the sun just snoring away with heavy breaths of deep contentment.

Here was just the opportunity he needed! It was perfect! Once again, the exhausted but seriously voracious Miracle instinctively reacted. He was not going to make any mistakes or waste any time in getting the job finished. Made wild with hunger pains, and even more crazed with irrationality, the famished pup zeroed in on the sunning mother's exposed teats. They were still glistening with the delectable yellow seal milk he desperately needed. He smacked his lips hard.

Do it really fast and she will never notice! I am sure she will have plenty left over, won't she? It's not as though I'm going to take it all, he thought, the hunger pangs swallowing up his rationality. Casually, he approached the snoozing seal, still licking his dry and quivering baby seal lips. Just a smidgen, he reassured himself, sneakily wriggling toward her. She won't notice that I was even there, he promised, saliva dripping from both corners of his twitching mouth. Delirious, and with remarkably little caution for any major repercussions, the starving pup made his fearless move, the stinging feeling inside his empty belly taking total control over his senses. He had suddenly become an instrument of his own bodily impulses, utterly fueled by the ravenous drive to simply feast! He just had to eat! That's all that mattered now. It was as simple as that! He needed food, and that mother harp seal had it, and he wanted it *now!*

Devilishly biting down on his tongue, the baby seal counted down for the attack. *One! Two! Three! Charge!* Like he had never moved before, he sprang on the unsuspecting mother just like a coiled rattlesnake, utterly surprising and startling the snoozing seal. Not once had he imagined that he held such a disguised punch of robust running in his veins as he did just then. Hastily, he bit down on one of her exposed teats, nicking the acutely sensitive tip. He immediately went to work, sucking out the needed nourishment but was quickly met with an unexpected and rather resentful and most smarting indifference.

"Ouch!" cried the baby harp, feeling a sturdy kick to the side of his head. With an unsightly expression of sheer unpleasantness, Miracle looked directly into the face of the mother seal right before he went suckling for more. Astonishingly holding on, he continued this way, pushing and yanking in a frenzied state, absorbing the pallid substance, drawing it sloppily and hurriedly from her swollen and extremely irritated mammary gland.

However, her mammary gland was not all that remained intolerantly bent out of shape. Incensed by the nerving gall of the whitecoat, the violated mother harp responded further with an even more defiant outrage. Furiously, she snapped at Miracle, clipping him behind his neck. Snarling, she arched her back, coiled in her hindquarters, and began kicking at the baby seal, deplorably bouncing him while he remained shamelessly and most painfully connected to her.

"Get off of me, you horrible thing, you!" she howled, still bouncing him up and down. Miracle felt himself jerk ridiculously above the bucking harp. With his tiny mouth stuck to her aching nipple, he kept on suckling, losing all control. For some unknown reason, he was not letting go, or so he thought.

Once more, the infuriated mother seal punted and snapped with even more resilience. "How dare you!" she raved over the tiny seal's unthinkable behavior. Feeling the unbearable sting rip at her private area, she found that she would have to attempt one final blow toward the intractable and offensive youngster. This time, her sharp teeth penetrated the skin just beneath his neck, staining his coat red with several spots of blood. It would not prove to be serious, but it would certainly put a stop to all this unexpected insanity.

The bite startled more than hurt the baby seal, and he quickly released his grip, allowing the enraged mother to gain further leverage over him. She kicked at him again, knocking him off. She then quickly inclined her massive body, and with one sharp slam from her backside, she slapped the pup across the ice. He twirled aimlessly and circled several times before colliding into the trunk of a considerable ice formation. Once more, Miracle felt immeasurable pain double him into a crumbled-up ball of fur.

"Now," barked the furious mother seal, "that will teach you, you dastardly thing! The audacity!" she howled, licking at her swollen and throbbing teat. "You best get away from here before I really lose my temper, you—you—insufferable leech! Why, I've never seen such disgraceful conduct in all my years! You should be ashamed of yourself! You horrible little vagrant, you better never come near me again!" With this outburst, she screeched one last time at the defiling whitecoat. "Don't think I'm not going to tell everyone to be on the lookout for you! Disgraceful urchin, most dastardly, indeed!" she barked, scurrying away, eager to divulge to the entire herd all about her most unpleasant encounter with the crazy, barbaric, dastardly baby seal, her aching nipples bouncing and aching every wriggle of the way.

Miracle suddenly felt the raw shame flush across his face. What could make him do such a thing? It was just that his stomach hurt so much, and now on top of that, his side and his neck stung painfully. However, despite his pugnacious action, the burning in his stomach was beginning to cease, and for the time being, he was content with the amount of nourishment he shamelessly stole from the unsuspecting and most unhappy mother harp he luckily chanced upon. Then quite unexpectedly, the pup suddenly belched, quite loud, in fact. He momentarily stamped an insidious grin on his wet and scruffy mouth, giving way to an even louder belch followed by a high-pitched hiccup. He could not help giving out a silly seal giggle, but that was when he felt the pain beneath his chin start to hurt. All too quickly, his little grin of satisfaction ran away from his snout. He tried to lick at the aching wound, but his tongue would not reach the spot. With an unusually slow wriggle to his stride, he made his way over to a tiny hill of snow, soothing his burning neck wound on the cold and refreshing mound. It took away the pain, but the shame of his behavior would not fade so easily. Satisfied, believing that the hurting had subsided, Miracle prepared to straighten up. He was still bleeding in several areas, but his extinguished hunger pains made up for his small battle wounds. Slowly, he began to crawl across the snow in a dizzy, wobbly kind of way, still cooling his aching cuts and scrapes on the icy banks that came up unexpectedly, gliding gently beneath him.

Soon the aching baby seal found a semisecluded spot near a slushy ice floe. For the time being, this would be the place he would nestle down and adjust for a much needed snooze, especially after such a fiery breakfast. Promptly, the pup felt sleep begin to overtake him. The constant slapping sounds that the slushy water made washing up around the open floes made for a relaxing diversion for the tiny and bruised-up, extremely sleepy little fellow.

A screaming pink and orange cloud filled with the glow of the sun finally came to blanket the jeweled world, lavishly inflaming the cold atmosphere with hues of unimaginable colors, all which vibrantly cascaded ever so delicately over the seal nursery, tucking in its inhabitants as a billowy quilt made of snowy dreams.

It was not long before Miracle's eyes closed and absolute fatigue swiftly weaved its somber oblivion lazily about him. There among the multicolored twilight of the iridescence of Sealssong, the tiny seal was at last fast asleep.

SEEING GHOSTS

Emma was transferred to another room, a private room in the intensive care unit of the hospital, until her vital signs had improved. However, they were not going to improve. In fact, she was becoming worse with each passing hour.

It had been a long time since she picked up a pencil or charcoal to create one of her drawings; she was just too weak. This upset her considerably. It certainly was not because of the time she was missing at school or the yearning for her classmates. In truth, most of the other students seemed to be afraid of her. They made fun of her, shunning her like she was a rare and contaminated space alien from another dimension filled with trillions of hungry mutant maggots all ready to explode if they came too close. However, such ignorance did not seem to matter that much anymore, or so she pretended. She had gotten used to the absence of friends, losing herself in her artwork. Besides, she had her devoted brother Kenyan. She smiled tearfully, fully recognizing that he had not missed one single day to be with her. Ironically, this did not make her happy. In fact, she felt rather badly about it.

Although she cherished every moment she spent with him, she knew that she was tearing a large hole in his life, and it seemed to be getting bigger and bigger with each passing day and there was not anything she could do about it. This filled her with more sadness than she could endure. She could bear anything, but no longer this prolonged stripping of what remained of his youthful spirit. It had gone on long enough. Right then and there she made her decision. It would not take long, not really. She was going to let go. Yes, simply drift away . . . go out like a light, or fade into the horizon just like the sun does when it leaves the world at the end of the day. If she did this, and she had made up her mind that she was going to, even if it would initially hurt her brother, she knew that he would eventually heal and, in time, he would be made whole again.

The large rip that she created would be gone and she would at last be able to repay him for his devotion and his unselfish love all these painful years. She would give him back his life. Without her to consume his every waking moment, he could once again rejoin the human race. Even though she never felt as though she belonged herself, she knew with all her heart that her brother had a place among the many that would one day benefit from all the special gifts that he had to offer the world. As these compulsive thoughts swirled around her mind, Emma's eyes filled with more tears while gazing toward the window in her room.

It was dark outside.

Fall had come again, and the days were short-lived. It looked as though a storm was brewing somewhere off in the west, for she could hear the faint grumble of thunder in the distance. Continuing to look toward the window with its dark blue drapes pushed fully open, just as she had insisted they would always remain, something terribly strange happened.

Although she was several stories up from the vast grounds surrounding the hospital and there was no outside ledge against her window, she could have sworn that she saw someone, or something, move inside the shadows of the night. There, directly against the glass, outside that hospital window! "Oh, surely not!" she whispered, dismissing the idea, thinking the whole thing preposterous. It was just the medication and all the endless stream of drugs saturating her blood; it was just her frail body playing tricks on her mind again. That was all and nothing more, but then it happened again. This time, she saw it plainly—someone, or something, was staring at her from outside her window. It was just floating there like a ghost, a most ghastly white-faced thing with bloodred eyes!

Emma recoiled into the covers, afraid, sure that it was the damaging results of the countless drugs invading her body, but just the same still very much afraid. A sudden chill sliced through her. She blinked her eyes and dared to look back toward the window, but this time, there was nothing there. A sigh of relief escaped from her dry lips as her eyes remained stationary toward the window with its pulled-open drapes that once let in the beautiful sunshine, only to now usher in such darkness that seemed to grant admission for things going bump in the night.

While the dark world outside poured into her room, a cold, unsettling feeling further came over her. However, she quickly dismissed it, not wanting to dwell on it further. *A bird must have lost its way. That must be what I saw. Poor thing,* Emma thought, no longer believing it for a moment, straining her eyes through the glare of the window that inadvertently caught bits and pieces of reflections from various hospital apparatuses inside the room. Uneasily, she looked again. Not actually wanting to see a bird or anything else as far as she was concerned, Emma curiously stared back out into the darkness of the night. That was when the sudden reflection of the pretty green-eyed nurse filled up the glassy window frame, chasing away whatever had been lurking on the ledgeless hospital window.

"There's someone who wants to see you," kindly said the nurse, nearing Emma's bed while holding to a brown clipboard with a ton of pink and pale blue papers attached to it. "Told him that you needed your rest, but he just would not take no for an answer. A most insistent young man," the attractive nurse said with a full and beautifully enchanting smile. "But you must keep it short. You have a busy day tomorrow, and you'll need all the rest you can get tonight."

"More tests?" Emma dryly murmured.

"Afraid so," confessed the nurse. "But the doctor has hopes for this next treatment. Something different, I'm told. It has already achieved some incredible results."

"Just more guinea pig experiments, that's all."

A sad frown shadowed over the young woman's face. "You mustn't think that way, Emma. No matter what, there is always hope."

Emma turned and looked blankly at the woman then back toward the blackness of the window, still able to see the nurse's reflection along with the rest of the usual hospital backdrop. It appeared transparent, somehow trapped inside the queer pane of the glass, all of it looking like one gigantic ghost. Then Emma slowly turned away and looked back at the nurse. Emma's stare returned a most changed and altered one, alarming the woman, for it seemed to be void of any real emotion, something the nurse had never experienced from the sick girl—until now.

"Please don't do that, don't make promises of hope. We both know better than that," Emma quietly mumbled. "Besides, it doesn't really matter anymore."

If the nurse heard what she had just said, she was not sure. If she did and had responded, Emma was not aware of that either. In truth, she did not actually care anymore. Her thoughts were of other things, magic things, faraway things that existed only in the guarded corners of her mind. For in that protected haven she had created for herself, she imagined a magical and quite extraordinary balloon. A huge fantastic balloon filled with breath that came straight from the lungs of the most powerful angel in all of heaven, one unusually large and wondrous angel with wings that would cover the earth. That was where her balloon would come from, and it would be her balloon and hers alone. It would be a beautiful purple one, and securely tied around it would be a shining purple string, the color matching the wings of the magnificent angel, and while holding on to such a remarkable object, inside that wonderful balloon, the angel would place her very spirit. Then when no one was watching, she would simply let go. That was how it would happen. She would free it so it could sail up to the stars themselves. She would watch it slowly flying, higher and higher, up and up and up into the blue of the endless sky. She would do it tomorrow. By then the darkness of the night would have gone, and the beautiful glow of the sunshine would have returned one final time to paint itself gloriously and brilliantly over her, streaking her with millions of rainbows, each fantastic burst of color sent down just for her, filling up the entire room, there inside that secluded and sterile place where she would have spent the last day of her life. Yes, she would wait until tomorrow. Then she would release her unusual purple balloon, happy to have been able to free it. She would go on watching it float higher and higher and higher still, until it ran out of sky, passing the universe, until it, just like her, would simply melt into the glow of whatever lies beyond the lights that the world called stars. It was not until Emma felt Kenyan's hand stroking her arm that she temporarily left the image of the purple balloon unattended, knowing fully that she would soon return to it.

"Hey, kiddo, what's going on? The nurse tells me that you're not yourself tonight. You okay?" her brother asked, leaning toward her, his face not far from hers.

Emma surprisingly smiled as if her regular spirited self suddenly returned. She tried to reach out and hug him but found that she could not. Not waiting for her to try again, Kenyan scooped her up in his arms and kissed her on the forehead. She was so small and frail he felt as if she would suddenly break in his hold. "What's the matter, tiring, yourself out drawing all those pretty masterpieces of yours?" Kenyan jokingly asked, turning, seeing her sketchpad abandoned, untouched, and turned aside, facing the opposite post of her bed.

The pretty green-eyed nurse about to leave the room prepared to remind Kenyan to keep his visit brief but thought against it, deciding to forget the matter. The devoted nurse clasped the brown clipboard to her breast, filling up with unexpected woe while looking toward the two siblings. It felt as if it would be the last time she would ever see them again. However, as a professional woman of medicine, she could not allow such sentiment to preclude her judgment, but this time it would not be easy. She had come to love the terribly sick and tiny girl named Emma, and although she had dealt with many terminally ill youths, Emma was different, and she found that she could not shake this feeling plaguing her. However, there were other patients to see and attend to, and besides, Emma's visit with her brother had already seemed to improve the ailing girl's mood significantly. She would check back in just a little while. Meanwhile, she would leave the room as quietly as possible without a single word, hoping that when she returned, Emma would smile at her with renewed faith shining in those magnificent blue eyes of hers. The nurse found that she needed to believe in this renewed faith, almost if not even more than Emma herself. Closing the door, not wanting to be heard, the nurse looked toward Emma once more, her eyes teary-eyed, her clipboard still pressed tight against her heart. Then in a moment, she left, shutting the door without making a sound.

"I saw a ghost," Emma said nonchalantly.

"A—what?" Kenyan asked, pulling up a chair, seating himself next to her bed as he had done a hundred times before.

"I did. I promise," Emma said, looking toward the dark shadows of the window, able to see her brother's reflection, he too now appearing like a ghost inside the transparent walls of her hospital window.

"What are you going on about, Emma?"

"It's true."

"Come on now."

Emma shrugged as if she didn't care if he believed her or not. "It's true," she insisted, looking at the dark clouds filling up her hospital window, a quizzical mask showing on her face. "At first I pretended it might be a bird, but I knew it wasn't. Then I thought it might be an angel come to take me."

"Emma, stop it."

"But then I realized it couldn't be. It was an ugly thing, perhaps a demon, maybe the devil himself come to take me away."

Kenyan's face flushed, and he scratched away nervously at his chin where a nonexistent itch suddenly sprang out of nervousness. Determined to remain composed, he gave her a small smirk. "It's not funny, Emma."

"It wasn't meant to be."

"What has gotten into you tonight? Is it the treatments? If it is, we'll stop them. We'll find another way . . . another doctor!"

Emma shrugged her shoulders, never taking her eyes from the dark window. "It's not the treatments." She sighed with a defeated moan.

"Then what is it?"

"I just told you."

"Told me what?"

"About the ghost."

"Oh, Emma, please don't start that again."

"Does it scare you?" she asked with remarkably little breath left in her lungs, her eyes burning as if she had gritty sand under her lids, still never taking away her indiscreet stare from the window.

Kenyan shook his head, not liking where the conversation was heading. "No, of course not."

"Why, doesn't it?"

Kenyan rolled his eyes and began to show his annoyance; or maybe it was fear, he was not sure. If it was fear, it certainly was not for fear of ghosts. "Because there are no such things, that's why!" he told her, thunder underscoring his words.

"Maybe you're right," Emma agreed with a dry throttle to her voice, her eyes still glued to the dark window. "Just like there aren't any such things as miracles or cures."

With considerable caution, Kenyan moved from his chair and stood up, looking directly down at his sister, her eyes still not meeting his. "Look at me," he gently asked her. Emma looked up at him, her eyes tearing over with a million questions. Finding the strength, she slowly wiped at her eyes but said not a word. "What is happening here? Are you giving up?" Kenyan asked, his hand slipping into hers, a tiny hand that felt like the most delicate and purest of English porcelain, her skin as white as snow. His heart began to beat faster with more urgency. "Is that what this is all about, Emma?" He waited for her answer, his breaking heart beating through his voice, never actually wanting to hear her answer. However, what she said not only confused him, but it truly frightened him as well.

"I just saw it again! It's out there, Kenyan! I think it wants us both!"

"What?"

"Yes! It wants to come in and take us away!" Emma cried, her voice stronger, her eyes frozen, staring intensely toward the dark glass of the hospital window, its pane vibrating with an even louder shudder from the storm now directly over them.

"I'm going to call the nurse!" Kenyan warned. It was something he never did before—losing his cool, and now he suddenly felt frightened.

"Why won't you believe me?" she pleaded, stumbling over her words that forced their way from a voice somewhere between heavy breathing and a peculiar rattle that suddenly appeared out of nowhere.

"I believe you. I believe you!" he indulged her, not wanting to upset her further.

"No, you don't!" she wheezed, her throat filling up with mucus. "I can tell. You're much too practical . . . always have been." She waited for Kenyan to hand her a tissue.

"You're wrong, Emma, I do believe you," he said, offering her a few white sheets from the square paisley-colored box on the small table next to her bed while more lightning and thunder lit up the room with a most disturbing and reckless *KAaaaBoooOOOM!* The rain drummed against the window, and the water came gushing down wildlike against the glass before it went crashing to the gullies below, filling up the places between the walls of the hospital and the pavements beyond with a growing flood that showed no intent of stopping. More thunder rattled the room; the window bent and shook as if ready to come loose.

Emma frowned, her glistening blue eyes falling into two puzzling pools of wonder, her soiled tissue disappearing somewhere under her covers. "I didn't believe it at first either. Imagine, me pretending it was a bird, as if a bird could possible look so frightening."

"I'm sure that's exactly what it was," Kenyan readily agreed. Standing above her, this time squeezing her hand, his eyes flooding over with aggressive tears that he wished he could have kept from her. She was still looking at the dark window before her. "Would you feel better if I go to the window and see what exactly you think is out there?" he asked, clearing his throat.

"No!" Emma answered quickly, her voice trailing off into a wheezing hiss. She had seemed to run out of air and could no longer speak. All she could do was to point toward the window, her eyes suddenly bulging with terror as if witnessing the end of the world. A huge crack of thunder rumbled through the room, discharging itself violently from the beating storm. It began to rain with even more combativeness while Kenyan shouted to override its maddening rush.

"It's all right! It's gone! Whatever it was, I'm certain it's gone. I won't let it hurt you. I promise! No one is going to hurt you, Emma!" His eyes started to fill up with more militant tears and he wiped annoyingly at his face, but once more Emma did not see. She only kept pointing toward the dark window, its dark sheet of glass catching the streams of drenching rain that poured down. The deluge took on unsettling shapes, looking like weird squiggles, all gooey and snakelike against the glass, appearing as if to be massive tears cried out of fantastic eyes—eyes that never belonged to anything human.

Another flash of lightning lit up the outside world followed by another boisterous scream of thunder, this time causing Emma to find the strength to gasp, her wide and dilated, crazed blue eyes filling with more terror than before. Panicking, Kenyan abruptly moved away from her, crashing into the chair behind him, knocking it over sideways on the floor. Quickly racing toward the window to prove that there was nothing outside for her to be afraid of; he extended his arm into the reflected dark shadows of the glass. Kenyan could see his own transparent and ghostly reflection and proceeded with both excitement and apprehension.

"It's just the storm, Emma! You see, everything is all right," he called before looking back out into the raging storm. The rain continued its savage downpour, coming down in enormous sheets, not comparable to anything he had ever remembered seeing before. From not too far away, where the trees had grown around the courtyard, he could see that most of their leaves remained discarded. The once pretty colored ones that had only recently changed their dress for the fall season were blowing like deranged birds, whirling aimlessly inside the gusts of wind and rain that carried them. Some of the leaves occasionally stuck to the glass like dead things, all limp and tattered, their formerly vibrant colors drained and bruised. Looking out toward the enraged storm, he could not help wonder if a tornado would appear from this angry torrent, ready to tear apart the town, eager to rip out trees and gobble away rooftops in a flash, scattering them into heaps of messes that would take forever to clean. However, even when he turned away from the clamoring storm that was throwing its inexorable tantrum, Kenyan never allowed Emma to see the anxiety burning in his eyes. "It's not going to last much longer. It already looks as if it's beginning to settle down," he overtly lied as another explosion of thunder rattled the entire hospital as if it were about to be ripped from its sheer foundation, hurled off somewhere into the sky, never to be found again.

"It's there! It's there! Can't you see it? It's right behind you!" Emma screamed in a depleted gasp.

"What is?"

"That face, that horrible white face!"

"What face? What is it? What do you see out there, Emma?" he yelled back, this time with a voice packed with his own share of mounting excitement.

"Get away from the window!"

"What?"

"Just stop talking and get away from the window!" Emma cried through a mouth full of mucus, frantically fighting her shortness of breath.

Kenyan was not able to hear what his sister was saying, for the roar of the storm with its constant thunder and lightning had totally taken over the room with incredible roars and flashes of greenish explosions. The pretty green-eyed nurse was already running toward Emma's room when the lights went out. Feeling the immediate need to be with the sick girl, the nurse could not help jumping when another violent explosion of thunder rocked the walls.

She began to tremble when she heard Emma start to scream.

The scream was loud and hair-raising, one that the nurse would never forget.

Fumbling ridiculously with the handle of the door before finally throwing it open, she heard the second terrifying sound. It was a shattering of glass, loud and earsplitting. It was not until the door struck the other side of the wall, revealing what was left or what was not left that prompted the nurse to let out her own shrilling scream. It was almost as loud and as terrifying as Emma's had been.

Rain drenched the room, battering the hospital's equipment, most of it overturned and demolished, Emma's bed having also been flipped over. Much of its contents, including half of the mattress and sheets, which remained flattened and drenched, protruded from the massive frame of the turned-over iron bed, horribly thrown there, just showing a piece of the blue pillow where Emma's tiny head had once rested. It now sadistically poked out from underneath the strapping bed that flattened and squashed everything in a mangled wet heap, including some of the shattered and splintered remains of the wooden frame Kenyan had made, it as well as Emma's drawing utterly destroyed.

In a desperate, insane pursuit to find the sick girl, the nurse began flipping machines and tables over. She even tried to lift up the impossible iron bed but could not budge it. She tried to rationalize that no one could survive its crushing impact, especially a sick and dying young girl. If Emma was lying under the bed, she would be in the same condition as the wooden frame that morosely lay there crumbled before her. Unable to accept such a morbid possibility, the frantic woman quickly discarded her despondent thought, refusing to believe that the girl could have ever ended in such a devastating way. Daring to carry out her hunt, she frantically continued. Consumed with a wild determination, she overturned more tables, chairs, and machinery, anything she could lift, frantic and mad, desperate to find Emma. She kept calling out Emma's name, but the thunder and the torrential rainfall took the sounds from her screaming mouth. While the destroyed room continued to be drenched with blasts of wind and rain, the crazed nurse gave out another scream when she looked toward the window, it having been utterly ripped clean from the wall, most of the drapes ripped away as well and what remained just stuck to the walls slowly dripping down like molasses to the already flooded floor. She knew then that no matter what, no matter how long or how involved was her search, neither Emma nor her brother would ever be found. They were both gone, taken away, as if the horrible storm had eaten them alive.

More of the hospital's panic-filled attendants inundated the room, and the green-eyed nurse suddenly stopped screaming Emma's name when she impulsively came across the missing girl's sketch pad. Like the draperies, it remained torn and saturated. Slowly, she crunched through the broken glass and splintered shambles of what snapped and exploded beneath her soaked sneakers. Reaching it, she pulled it away from the drenched wall. Carefully, she bent forward, standing upright, holding the sketch pad against her breast, the remains of the graphite and charcoal pressed tight, bleeding down all over her once white uniform, appearing like blood, the black porous carbon dripping from her as if she had just been shot, her heart having burst.

These ghastly recollections would remain with the nurse until the remainder of her days. Nevertheless, as time went on, she would learn to dismiss it all as traumatic aftermath. Still, the thing that would undoubtedly haunt the pretty green-eyed nurse the most would be what she saw or thought she saw while standing in that mutilated hospital room, looking at the place where the giant window had been ripped out. As hard as she would forever try to forget and rationalize it through years of counseling and endless therapy, she would recall the night that she watched a dying girl and her brother fly through the sky just like two tiny helpless birds. She would never forget how they were pulled by their necks through the gloomy night sky by a most horrible thing! A thing wearing a black shroud, its skeleton hands gripped tight around their necks, having a white face, but worst of all, having the red burning eyes that belong to the devil himself!

She would go on seeing those eyes for a frightfully long time to come; they had looked at her from way up in the night sky, straight down, and right through her! She would shudder, remembering how the horrible thing flew through the storm as if being part

of it, dragging the two young siblings through the black clouds.
No quantity of therapy would erase that. For just as she would go
on seeing those eyes, she would go on forever hearing it, its jaws
fully opened just like its red glowing devil eyes, its crimson mouth
laughing at her as it sailed Emma, Kenyan, and its horrible self
into the night. Up into the stormy sky they flew, toward a thing that
looked like a massive sailing ship, merely floating there, waiting for
them, high atop the blackest clouds ever imagined, clouds that could
have never been created out of atmospheric changes or natural
forces. No, these ghostlike shapes had to be spawned from the
most dismal of places that only lived in the deepest, darkest parts of
madness, where monsters, with white faces and red eyes and ghostly
sea ships, would ever dare to think to haunt.

MUM'S THE WORD!

The next day, when the blazing ball of fire came to the sky,
the nursery once again erupted into its usual bursts of colors. With
these flashes of dazzle, there also came the usual snorts, barks, yaps,
and infant squeaks accompanying the everyday existence in this
unparalleled world of Sealssong.

Yawning, little whitecoats smacked their lips, crying out for their
breakfast, their mothers trying to deal with their persistent whining,
the cold blistering winds whistling out their songs while sunshine
hugged the day with an extra blanket of sparkle. Yes, things seemed
to be no different from any other day in Sealssong until, and
quite suddenly, a frantic bark pierced through the nursery. The
bark quickly turned into a screeching shrill, growing louder and
louder, each scream mounting with an alarming call of hysteria,
its cries bouncing off the glacier backdrops. Then from out of the
white glare, a frantic mother harp appeared, her snout covered in
drool, her eyes large and wildlike. She was pathetically dragging her
swollen teats over the snow, feverishly wriggling toward the watching
crowd.

"Help me!" she frantically bellowed. "It's attacking! The mad
suckling beast is attacking again!" With a hurried and urgent push
to her wriggle, the terrified seal headed toward an open floe. Her
wet mouth had already frozen over into a twisted sneer, covered
with a glazed and icy frost by the time she finally reached the floe.

Before diving in, she looked back with crazed eyes before frantically plunging into the circle of icy water, disappearing into its rift.

It was only a matter of seconds after she vanished that the dreadful fiend happened upon the ice, its high-pitched squeal showing up way before it did. *"Chirp . . . cheep . . . sniff . . . squeak!"* the terrifying chaser blasted, his tiny body wiggling like a spastic worm on the glittering snow, barking out his request for yet another delectable breakfast. It seemed that he had once more lost his senses, compulsively driven by the overpowering instinct to feed. Indeed, the orphaned baby Miracle was at it again. Although he had promised himself that he must refrain from aggressively going after such demanding requests, he found that with the start of each morning, those same commanding bellyaches of hunger quickly persuaded him otherwise. However, maintaining a promise of politely asking before merely helping himself, Miracle found that it was just as difficult to find a willing candidate. The baby seal was quickly learning that going without food made him do the most bizarre things, no matter how much he tried to control himself.

"Sniff . . . Squeak!" Miracle continued, then abruptly stopped, tilting his furry white head, gazing at the place where the antagonized female had vanished. All he wanted was a little breakfast, and after all, he did ask before he simply was forced to help himself again. He just did not see what the big deal was. It was not like they didn't have plenty of the tasty stuff. Why, those enormous mamas were packed tight with all that delicious seal juice! Why shouldn't he have some too?

"Oh well," he sighed, touching the tip of his quivering nose into the icy lid of the freezing water hole, upset that it had swallowed the rest of his breakfast. He suddenly sneezed and shook himself, watching his peculiar image change as it fluctuated in the water. Soon he became aware of another figure swaying within the reflection of the slush pool. Someone else was watching him. It was another mother harp. She was blatantly spying on him, her face arranged in the same shocking and irritated manner as the many others before her. She didn't waste any time in showing her disapproval, shaking her head and clucking her seal tongue. Slapping a mischievous grin to his snout, Miracle wet his lips with a quick swipe of his tongue. Slowly, he turned his head to face her and then slyly advanced in a stalking fashion, his tiny tongue peeking out of his mouth.

The brazen pup was already considered a persistent annoyance, and this mother harpie, like the others, was not about to have her private areas violated. She slowly backed away, partially covering her mammary glands with her flippers. "Now see here!" she nervously growled. "You stay where you are, you indecent creature!" Despite her warning, Miracle appeared quite undaunted. He just kept on licking his lips, giggling to himself and wriggling toward her. The older seal suddenly lost her balance on the ice and rolled over to one side, sliding over a glassy glade. Miracle immediately seized the opportunity. Instantly, he found himself stuck tight to one of her exposed teats. This defiled harp screamed louder than all the other mothers he had degraded. She flopped back and forth, hoping to dislodge the white leech, bucking and bouncing ridiculously through the icy grounds, yelping all the while as Miracle bounced along with her, suckling crazily.

With this quite facetious parade of amusement, the other seals could not help but chuckle, relieved they were not the intended victims. Finally, when Miracle felt his belly to be somewhat satisfied with the delicious seal juice, he abruptly released his grip on the creature's sore and swollen nipples. Directly, the enraged harp swatted him on the behind, sending him airborne. The entertained seal crowds continued surveying the little pup twist in the air before he crashed down, landing headfirst into a pile of snow. Many had already seen this expected conclusion several times before, but it was always good for another jolly seal laugh.

The violated harp glared at the horrid white pup, unashamedly rubbing her aching nipples with her front flippers, growling reprehensibly at him. "This is inexcusable! Do you hear me? Inexcusable!" She then tried to clear her throat from the anger and embarrassment clinging to her, looking around at the gawking seal gathering, all of them roaring with laughter. Humiliated, the sore and aching mama quickly disappeared behind a misshapen slab of towering ice, her outrageous sobs of defiance echoing after her.

It was at this moment that the self-esteeming baby seal felt a part of the whole, but typically, his presumed assumption took an equivocal plunge for the worse. For as the lost pup began to move toward the pack, their frivolity suddenly became clouded by a general concern. Abruptly, their mindless chortling stopped. Now that the little white suckling beast was fancy-free and on the prowl again, the crowd hastily realized the obvious. Almost in absolute unison, and as if previously rehearsed, the nervous clan began systematically covering their private parts with their floppy flippers. In a rather embarrassing compromise, each one held to their very own personal vigil, concealing themselves. Some even began to puff air into their cheeks, vibrating the inner skin, sounding as if they were nervously whistling. Notwithstanding their apprehension, Miracle proceeded to move toward them. However, in his approach, he quickly noticed that they were rapidly dispersing from the scene. Picking up the beat, they began barking and yapping, scattering in all different directions, each still holding on to their personal constituents, deliberately not removing their hold until they were safely out of the danger zone.

Soon all vanished, and once again the baby seal remained behind, perplexed and miserably alone with his familiar share of depression, its hopelessness swallowing him whole. Turning down the corners of his small furry mouth still stained from seal milk he stole, he sadly sighed.

He shook his head, just looking out into the emptiness of the surrounding ice, wishing the seals would come back, but he knew better. Would he always be alone? Would it always be this way?

Just then, Miracle experienced a firm thwack on his left shoulder, nearly toppling him over. A loud and gruff tongue strongly accompanied the startling gesture. "*Are you the Docta?*" the noisy tongue bellowed. Dazed, Miracle hastily twirled his head around, not knowing what to expect. He had to gasp when he looked upon a whopping seal, the biggest that he had seen thus far. Its eyes were irregular, crazed, just floating there inside its wide and silly head, a colossal head that held to a most peculiar and demented expression. The grating voice spoke out once more.

"Aren't we the feisty little *Love-ya?*"

Miracle remained stunned, merely staring wide-eyed at the loud newcomer positioned directly in front of him. "Oh, I like you!" It continued with a raspy voice, sounding very much as if suffering from an extraordinarily bad cold. "And do you know why?" the demented-looking seal asked. Miracle remained silent, not knowing how to respond. "'Cause you've got spunk, that's why!" It started to giggle, smacking its flippers together in a fanatical clap that never seemed to finish. "*Hahaha!*" it laughed, pulling its flippers apart long enough to smack the little seal again. Not waiting for Miracle to finish his abrasive slide across the ice, the outlandish jumbo seal continued. "Mum's the name; Clap-Clap's the game! Happy to make your acquaintance, I say!"

Finally coming to a skidding stop, Miracle shook his head, thinking the crazy thing a queer hallucination. However, as he lay there sprawled shamelessly across the ice, he turned his head around and found that it was still there. "I got spunk, too, *Love-ya!*" the enormous harpie stated smilingly. "What are you doing way over there? Come and snuggle down next to me!" Prostrate upon the ice,

Miracle most assuredly knew this seal was not like the others. Perhaps it was her massive size or the way her eyes continued to float inside her head in a disturbing, unnatural way or the harsh and weird sound of her voice, he could not be sure. No matter, this one was not your average harpie. This would be confirmed all the more as it wriggled unsteadily toward him.

Quickly sitting up on the ice, Miracle watched it swiftly approach with an unsettling charge. Feeling his heart begin to flutter, he felt the ground tremble as the colossal seal clumsily bounced on the ice. He could not help but cringe as it towered over him. Again, possibly it was the fact that her floating eyes stuck out much farther than they should have or the way her fat, shaky nose ran with a constant discharge of pale yellow mucus of which she incisively slurped and sniffed. Perhaps, last but certainly not least, for some unknown reason this particular seal wore a strange covering on top of its head, in short—*a bonnet!* It was quite extensive in size and style and possessed a wide brim that circled her head. Its color looked as though it was once painted a deep pink coral color but had long since faded. Although threadbare, it remained faintly detailed with tiny roses that ran almost endlessly along the marginal borders of its tattered and shabby fabric. Two long, transparent sheers hung on each side of the bonnet, each one loosely dangling around the demented-looking seal's huge expressive face. She winked her eye and clucked her tongue.

"*I'm-mmm . . . hot!* Sassy hot!" she bizarrely and conceitedly bragged with a deep nasal twang, fussing with the bonnet, thinking herself and her bonnet to be absolute eye-catching knockouts. "Simply . . . hot!" she absurdly exclaimed. "That is the hackneyed expression for boasting one's undeniable magnificence, is it not, *Love-ya?* Yes! I'm magnificently, unequivocally, undeniably, most decidedly *red-hot!*"

The tiny pup could only gawk at her in disbelief.

"And so is my hat! Don't you think? Isn't it a beaut?" she excitedly asked him. "Found it in me recent travels, I did! I suppose it must have once belonged to one of those nasty two-footed female man-beasts, filthy lip-lump things. It looks so much better on me, don't ya think?"

Miracle timidly stretched out his neck, investigating the thing on top of her head, sniffing at it, but recoiling when she shouted, "Well, you can't have it! It's mine!" the large seal rattled. "I've become rather attached to it! I can even catch fish with it! If you don't believe me, I'll show you, I will! Are you sure you're not the Docta?"

With a jerky tilt of his head, Miracle looked most queerly at the seal, not knowing what she was going on about, thinking to himself how utterly peculiar she was. Then the peculiar seal did something even more peculiar. She suddenly swung her head around, twisting it, until it was completely upside down, quickly dropping it further still, plopping it hard into the many folds of her enormous belly, her silly bonnet crushed beneath her. "You cannot be the Docta? He is dead, is he not? I killed him, . . . did I not? Still, I am forced to ask—are you the Docta? The face I am cursed to see over and over again, the one I cannot seem to take from my destroyed mind because of her!" With its head still sitting unnaturally upside down in its lap, it continued.

"*Her* . . . the one that takes tears from heartbroken mother seals, the one whose evil companion I took away because he took away my precious Sasha." All at once, for no apparent reason, the queer seal began to giggle again, sounding as mad as ever. "Oh, she may have taken my mind away," it snickered, "but I have taken away something as well! Something I know she wanted even more than her fiendish pup-killing companion! Do you like playing Clap-Clap? 'Tis is my only weakness," the upside-down head of the seal briskly asked, its mad laughter having stopped, its eyes batting ecstatically, still viewing the white seal and the rest of the nursery from a bottom-side-up perspective. Then once more, without warning, the mad beast twisted around, her head returning it to its upright position, the bonnet nearly falling off her head. Commencing with a forceful push from her rear flippers, she threw herself backward. Landing in the snow with a harsh and rumbling thud, her enormous eyes staring straight into the sky, she began madly clapping her front flippers back and forth, startling the baby seal.

"Clap, clap, clap, how I love to love my clap, clap, clap," snorted the seal, "'tis my only weakness, *Love-ya!*" Despite her outrageousness and not having any inkling as to what the mad seal had said to him, Miracle found that he remained strangely amused by the delightful seal game she played. Clap-Clap was a special game that all seals loved to play, and until then he had not had the desire to play it.

Carefully, Miracle wriggled toward the clapping beast. He noticed that she wore an even more demented face while her flippers danced crazily above her plump belly. The bonnet, now crumbled to one side, was quickly scrunched between her flippers in a wasted attempt to wipe some of the drool running down the side of her snout. Smacking away made her appear more unbalanced than before; still, Miracle proceeded. He cautiously smelled the air nearing the applauding oddity. Finally reaching her, he jumped, startled, when the mad harpie flipped over, nearly crushing him in the process.

"Hungry?" the crazed seal shouted her bonnet and mucus dripping from her face. "Bet you are! Tell you what, how would you like the best gosh darn breakfast you ever had, little *Love-ya?*" Miracle's front flipper remained accidentally trapped beneath the girth of the creature, and he began to panic. He tried to pull himself away but could not. He started to cry, unable to get away, scratching the snow beneath him.

"Well?" asked the Mad Mum of Sealssong. "Yes or no? What's it to be? Would you or would you not? 'Tis a simple request." Miracle whimpered, still trying to pull his flipper from under her spilled-over weight. "A bit peaked, are we? Well, no matter, don't you know it is considered most inconsiderate not to answer when spoken to? Furthermore, I must tell you, save for the sea, herself, and even she sometimes gets on me last nerve, I have zero tolerance for rudeness, lovey love! It really peeves the living seal snot out of me, it does!"

After a few more frantic attempts, Miracle managed to free himself, making a sizeable wet popping sound as he fell backward. "Yes, spunk, that's what you got! I just loved how you stirred up those old biddies, *Love-ya*! Bet that was the most excitement they had in years!" roared the mad mammal. Miracle watched the seal with added curiosity, rubbing his throbbing little flipper while the crazy beast wearing the crushed bonnet continued. "Well, you won't have to do that anymore! Even though I have to admit that I will most certainly miss watching you plague those stuffy, snooty ninnies." Mum chuckled, nonchalantly wiping the leaking mucus from her nose. "Besides, those boorish snots can't begin to serve anything close to what your old mum can dish up!" She queerly chuckled again, this time even more crazily than before, if that were even possible, dramatically pasting a fully asinine expression on her lips, slurping in some excess drool. "Come on, how about trying some, *Love-ya?*"

Miracle slowly began to back away, filling with uneasiness. However, this did not stop the mad harpie from wriggling her massive self toward him. "Don't be afraid, I won't bite. Well, that is if you don't peeve me off!" she said, snarling, her bonnet dangling from her chin before dropping to the snowy ground. She then paused for a moment, and almost sounding rational, she proceeded to say, "Many are gone now . . . so, so very many . . . But I am still alive and you're still here, but poor Sasha . . . she never even—*are you the Docta?*"

This time, for some odd reason, Miracle was not frightened. He suddenly felt a growing pity for the peculiar beast. "Well, what are you waiting for?" insisted the mum, popping out one of her motherly filled teats just overflowing with delicious seal juice. Smacking her lips together, she crudely displayed herself toward the baby seal's tiny mouth.

Miracle could not begin to understand the content of what was happening. However, he began to feel a peculiar calmness slowly settle over him. Perhaps it was that this particular seal, as queer as she was, had remained with him and did not wriggle away as the others did. Maybe it was because of the silly bonnet that she wore or perhaps it was because she was willing to give of herself. With her, things appeared to be quite different, very different. He would not have to resort to aggressiveness with the other mother harps, for she so generously rendered to him the nourishment that he so desperately needed to survive and she did it with the biggest, the most preposterous smile that he had ever seen. He could not help giggling to himself, looking at her waving her swollen teat, holding fast to her silly-looking grin. It was too good to be true. He was still hungry, and there she was offering him the delectable seal juice.

Licking his lips, he proceeded to go to her and then stopped, remembering his mother. How he wished that it were she who was offering him this food. He began to feel strange, no longer wishing to go to the peculiar seal. However, after thinking it over, he decided that it was the right thing to do. His days of wriggling after and attacking innocent mothers were over. For the time being, this queer harpie would substitute for *Home* until he could once again be with his rightful mama. Apprehensively, he approached, nearing the tip of her exposed teat, and then stopped again.

"Come on, *Love-ya*, it's fresh and ever so filled with tasty love!" exclaimed the mum seal.

Miracle stared at the inviting seal for the longest time before reapplying his wriggle, and gradually, he gently began to suckle her. He ate and ate, filling himself up to the brim. It was marvelous, and in a short time, the tiny pup felt himself begin to sink into a decidedly welcomed slumber. It would be the first truly substantial sleep he would experience since the tragic separation from his beloved mama. He had at last found a friend, someone who would not wriggle away from him, someone who would stay with him, a guardian to shelter him and give him sustenance. Still, as delightful and comforting as it all appeared, the baby seal could have no way of knowing about the unstable curator that he had indeed and all too easily surrendered upon.

WHAT DID YOU DO TO ME?

The next morning, the sky stopped looking for the stars that have long vanished.

Only thick fearful clouds surrounded the seal nursery, clouds holding tremendous amounts of snow, snow that would not let up for some time. It began at the very break of dawn. Tediously falling from the graylike heavens, its many star-shaped configurations danced with a serious stride, covering the climatic surroundings of one small ice cave now sheltering the baby Miracle and his newfound benefactor.

Many, many weeks had passed since the mad and enormous seal brought the baby seal into her private sanctuary. She had found this small cave all on her own, and as far as she knew, few, if any, knew of its existence. It was a remote place nestled deep in the crevasses of the seal nursery of Sealssong, a place filled with sapphire shadows, all glued together by isolated colors of peerless blues and shadowy grays. Inside this concealed grotto, the two harps slept, ate, and managed to survive. Miracle began to learn and understand seal life and its basic principles. He remained consequently fed and looked after morning, noon, and night, all of this exclusively provided by the seal who made all this possible—the Mad Mum seal of Sealssong. She made sure his tummy stayed properly filled with seal juice while she proceeded to fill his head with outrageous theories, stories, and reasoning she alone perceived. The mad harpie's methods of educating the small pup were extremely unconventional and downright questionable; nonetheless, they remained enforced daily and played out to the fullest. Miracle never questioned these proceedings, for he was only too eager to learn and experience any feasible knowledge of sea life. Well, that is, when he was able. Separating Mum's bursts of madness from reality was not easy for the small pup, but he was gradually beginning to adjust to her erratic behavior.

Although gaining knowledge of the outside world was most imperative, idling time away with games and nonsensical chitchat filled their days. Mum's constant recitations and verbal gibberish were not always a rewarding settlement for the youngster, but it was who she was; and no matter how absurd her methods, he was learning how to communicate and rationalize at a most exceeding rate. This exclusive sequence of moments spent together was beginning to form a special bond among the extraordinary mammals. Miracle was truly finding that he was not alone and that there was someone who would not judge or depart from his destitution no matter what. However, despite the esteemed gratification of safety found there in that small and secluded icy grotto, Miracle could not help the melancholic certainty that he would continuously ache for his lost mother and would at times find himself desperately concentrating on her and nothing else. This snowy morning was just such an occasion.

The wispy snow tickled the end of Miracle's nose while he lay lazily in front of the grotto's opening. His dark eyes aimlessly searched through the hazy congestion before him when the hefty mum waddled herself over to him. The big seal, still situated awkwardly inside her preposterous crumpled-up bonnet, surveyed the solemn pup before she emphatically spoke out. "Wishin' ain't gettin', *Love-ya.*"

"What?" he quietly questioned, turning to face her.

The large seal tried to move in closer, but the concave surface of the grotto strongly suggested otherwise. "I know what you were doing. You were wishin' for your mama, weren't ya?"

Miracle merely offered the big harp a simple smile and then sighed.

"And you were wishin' she was here right about now, weren't ya, *Love-ya?*"

"Well . . . ," Miracle softy answered, "it's just that—"

"It's okay, I understand, I'm sure. I miss my Sasha too," Mum said, putting a flipper around the seal, moving closer still, almost pushing the pup straight through the slippery opening of the cave. Chunks of ice immediately broke and fell down from the ceiling, shattering randomly on top of Mum's head, crushing and thoroughly flattening her tattered bonnet. She became agitated and suddenly grew most annoyed.

"*Back off!*" she barked, utterly peeved at the snow and ice, shaking her head and dusting herself off, rattling the entire grotto with her massive girth. Miracle watched while Mum persisted in shaking her huge self, rumbling the icy house, wondering how she ever managed to get in and out without completely destroying the grotto, but always somehow succeeding. It was not easy to watch, and there were times she nearly took off the entire roof. However, despite her numerous clumsy bangs and bumps of preposterous penetrations and nerve-racking twists and turns, she was always able to make remarkable exits and entrances into the trembling grotto, and quite frequently too.

Miracle looked up into the silly face of the mad seal, shaking off his own pile of snow that had come upon him. Continuing to stare into her humongous face, the wet and tattered sheers of her bonnet relentlessly fingered the top of his head. It was annoying, but Miracle kindly endured. "Not to worry, *Love-ya*, you will find her one day," Mum promised. "I know you will, love." Miracle politely smiled at her before turning his oppressed glance toward the crest-filled planking, never answering her. Mum suddenly softened her face and looked tenderly at the white pup, keeping her fleshy flipper tight around him. "You must believe, little one. Believe that you will be together again."

"I try to believe that every day."

"And you must go on believing. You must! But as for me, I cannot. My Sasha is gone. I am still alive, but she is gone, taken away by the evil of the man-beast, gone and taken, taken and gone. Oh, my poor little Sasha, what did they do to you?" Mum whimpered, the tears filling up her eyes. "I'm still alive, but Sasha never even . . ." Then, with a quick and startling flip, Mum flopped over on her back, this time almost taking down the grotto with her. It shook and moaned violently as parts of the outside fell away from its trembling structure. *"Clap, clap, clap!"* Mum sang while smacking her flippers crazily together in a blurring frenzy. While she lay on her back, she suddenly stopped her fitful clapping, and twisting her head sideways, she looked blankly at the white seal. "Are you the Docta?" she madly asked, more tears filling up her eyes.

Unable to understand these sudden fits of madness; Miracle grew exceedingly concerned for the seal. Whatever happened to her certainly was just as bad, if not worse than what had happened to him. Although he pondered over it quite often, thinking at first that she too had a run-in with the terrible Teeth Monster, he would always come to the same conclusion. Whatever was wrong with Mum had nothing to do with Teeth Monsters. For whatever it was, it was something worse, much worse, and much more frightening than he ever wanted to ponder. The tiny seal wriggled over to the demented harp. Stretching out his neck, he gently kissed her. "Poor Mum, poor, poor Mum."

Mum quietly looked at Miracle, her eyes and nose dripping wetness. Then, without any warning, she suddenly jumped, nearly squashing him, taking more of the grotto with her, shaking it uncontrollably. "Well, gracious me! I almost forgot! I have something for you! Been saving it for just the right moment! I just bet it will help you find your mama, my little love!"

At first, the pup believed her to be having another one of her fits. The way she waddled aimlessly around the grotto, throwing out her neck, opening her mouth as if she were gasping for air, slamming herself against the icy floor only confirmed his unsettling suspicions. Then she proceeded to do something even more bizarre, even for her! The massive harpie abruptly stopped, and plopping down with an uncalled-for and nerve-rattling crash, she disturbingly began to choke and gag, deliberately attempting to regurgitate something from inside her mouth. Alarmed and utterly frightened, Miracle began to bark. He whined and yelped, not knowing how to help the suffocating creature that now appeared to be choking. He nervously circled her around and around, yelping and barking out his confusion and fear. Could she be dying? This thought terrified him. Should she be, he certainly did not know how to, save her. All that the tiny pup managed to do again was to bark and bark and bark!

Then suddenly, he stopped barking as Mum surprisingly hit herself in the gut, blowing up her cheeks, filling them up with some unknown substance. A wide, almost frightening grin spread across her wet and drooling muzzle. Keeping to her lunatic smile, she proceeded to pull out from her throat a long string of tiny white seashells, every single shell heavily coated in mucus and spittle. On and on she retrieved it from her open mouth, its rosary of slime-covered shells finally ending where a rather large glassy stone resided. This stone although thoroughly covered up in stomach and mouth excretions remained purple and had a strange glow to it.

"I swiped it from the witch!" Mum boasted, swallowing hard, soothing the burning irritation in her throat. "Had it tucked away for safekeeping!"

Miracle continued to stare at the dripping object that Mum now dangled from one of her fleshy flippers. "What . . . what is it, Mum?" he nervously asked, sniffing the air, intrigued, yet apprehensive of its mysterious glow. He wondered how in the world she had kept it in her throat all this time, but considering it was Mum, he was not surprised.

"Come closer, *Love-ya*!" Mum instructed in a robust voice.

Miracle nervously shook his head, afraid to come any nearer.

"Oh, don't be such a scare baby, it won't bite!" Mum belted, holding up the string of tiny seashells attached to the strange and sparkling transparent purple stone.

Immediately, the entire grotto flooded over with an unusual purple wash, accompanied by detached sounds of faraway chimes and whimsical voices. The sounds permeated themselves over every part of the grotto as the stone's awareness of wonder immersed itself entirely over the two creatures. A soft, warm breeze was suddenly felt. It seemed to be coming directly from the stone itself. It began to breathe as if it were alive, saturating the frozen place with its omnipotent life force. Instinctively, Miracle quickly dashed away from the stone, retreating behind the enormous backside of the mum. He did not fully know the reason, but this unexpected spectacle put a razor-sharp chill down the center of his back while he cowered near her. Cautiously, he looked upward, staring at the composed face of the large harp. He waited for her to speak, and she did. "Around your heart forever keep this stone . . . For in its protecting light, there you will find your Home."

Miracle momentarily remained still but found that he could not keep his eyes off the shining purple wonder. Lifting his head, he courageously sniffed the air, allowing the stone's light to wash over him. He felt as if he was sitting under the glow of the sun as its light covered him in a cozy blanket of warmth. "You're not afraid any longer, are ya, *Love-ya?*" Mum tenderly asked, her voice sounding almost rational. "Come and look at it for it is yours."

"Mine? But . . . but I don't understand."

"It is very rare. There is some kind of magical teardrop inside that holds many powers that can help you. It will take you to your mama, I'm sure!"

"But how?"

"Don't rightly know," the mad creature uttered. "But I know that it is all-powerful. The witch would not want it so badly if it were not. She had my Sasha killed for it, she did!"

Miracle did not understand any of what was happening, but something unseen compelled him to return to investigate the glowing purple stone hanging from the beautiful seashell necklace. The mum seal did not stir. She remained still, just holding up the stone for the small pup to see. When at last he approached it again, he timidly looked up, his heart drumming in his ears. The magic wonder seemed to intensify in color while he looked upon it, its glowing purple light still filling the grotto. From its core, an even deeper purple encounter pulsated steadily, conforming to the same beating of his heart, its haunting presence palpitating systematically. Whatever was in the stone was indeed alive!

Once again, the white seal felt fear overcome him, and once again he was finding refuge behind the bloated backside of the deranged harpie. She appeared to find the pup's apprehension nothing less than amusing. However, after a few loud sniffles and slurps from sucking up the drool, she placed the stone under her chin and began rubbing it profusely up and down her huge bosom, trying to clean up the rest of the spittle. Satisfied, she reached over to the small seal and pulled him up toward her.

"Lift and love," she dementedly sang to the frightened but ever-so-curious pup. "Up, we go-go!" she grunted, struggling to lift him further to her bust, "up, where I can see the love better!" Miracle looked at her, shivering with apprehension, his eyes full of wonder. Swallowing deeply as if to dislodge his fear the small seal slipped out of Mum's embrace. He quickly wriggled away, his eyes remaining on the shining stone the entire time. It swayed slightly while Mum held on to the string of seashells, wrapping them firmly around one of her flippers. All at once, the mad beast dropped toward him, forcefully pushing the seashell necklace and the purple stone over his head. "Done!" she exclaimed, smacking both flippers together, throwing herself backward entertaining herself with another round of Clap-Clap.

Not knowing what hit him, Miracle felt dazed. Suddenly, a tingling sensation danced over him while a distinct and uncomfortable shock rattled his entire body. His breath stilled, and he felt as if it was he, this time, who was suffocating. His sight became impaired, and his head swam in a dizzy delirium of semiconsciousness. He felt faint, but somehow remained stationary for a few seconds before tilting over to his side, Mum's broad backside preventing his complete fall.

It was at that instant the grotto suddenly ignited further into the same deep hue that continued to pulsate inside the prism of this purple prodigy. Mum proceeded to talk, clapping madly away, her eyes wildly blinking. "There!" she sang. "That should do the trick!"

Miracle tried to call out to her, but he could not speak. His entire body burned, and he felt as if he were being cooked alive, every last piece of him, especially his eyes. Mum momentarily stopped her Clap-Clap game, for what happened next intrigued even her. Flipping herself right side up, she watched the baby seal's eyes begin to change coloring. She continued to watch as the dark color of brown began to drain from the iris, only to fill up with the same intense purple shade. His fur changed as well, clearly imitating the vibrant glow of the stone he now wore.

Miracle began to feel panic stricken when another occurrence took place. His heart started to beat faster and faster until he felt it would surely burst! His tiny body trembled with incredible jerks and painful spasms. Paralyzed with fear, he stared at Mum, looking horrified, but the crazy seal just smiled at him with a ridiculous grin, her battered bonnet drooping to one side of her wide head. He still could not call out to her. With all his terror mounting, there also came an incredible high elation the pup would never forget. He felt as if to be suddenly flying! His aura drastically became altered, the light of the stone freely washing over him, soaking itself thoroughly over his entire being. Then as hurriedly as the whole metamorphism happened, in a flash, it suddenly ended.

The sounds, the whispering voices, the sudden breeze that came out of nowhere, the copious colors of purple, the burning, the pain, the inconceivable elation, the changing of his eyes and fur, the crashing of his heart, all quickly came to an abrupt halt, neutralizing back to their original states. Miracle's mouth felt dry, and he tasted a sour, metallic flavor. He swallowed, quickly washing it deep into his throat. The whole shocking incident left the young seal with a curious sense of unreality. Hoping that the ordeal was over, Miracle looked toward Mum and then gasped. He began to experience something else. Apparently, there was going to be a definite aftermath to this incredible event. All at once, an emotional deluge of bewilderment flooded his veins, and he began to drown in a bursting wave of absolute sadness and desperation. At the same time, he could also feel a pulsing transfusion of new and strange awareness of conviction and hope. This overwhelming consciousness would prove to be too much for the small seal, leaving him light-headed and feeling faint again.

Forcing the sounds from his still opened mouth, the tiny pup gasped. "What has happened? What did you do to me?"

Mum jerked her head and looked at him with open eyes, her expression a mask of madness. "A present of love from the sassy hot mum!" she said happily.

"But I feel so strange."

"Oh, don't be such a scare baby!" Mum jeered with a hardy laugh, smacking the seal on the back of the head, toppling him over, causing him to fall headfirst into the icy floor of the grotto. Flipping herself about again, she wriggled her gargantuan self up to him, picking him straight up with one of her flippers, immediately dusting the snow and ice from his dazed face. "The magic will guide you home back to your mama. It's what you want, is it not?"

"Well yes, but-but . . ."

Mum smiled, sucked up some more drool, not bothering to wipe her nose clean, and then dropped harshly back to the icy floor, crashing on her backside, clapping her flippers together in a crazed fashion again. "Happy, *Love-ya?*" asked Mum, flapping about madly.

"I'm not sure," the bewildered pup answered, his head still swimming in dizziness and confusion. "But how does it work? What do I do now?"

"How should I know? I just know that it's a magic thingamajig, that's all!"

"But if we don't know how it works, how can it help?"

"Don't rightly know that either . . . Oh, but there is one thing," she said, stopping her ridiculous clapping long enough for the pup to hear her plan. "Don't think you're supposed to ever take it off though."

"What!" popped Miracle, his heart racing, waiting for her to answer, most definitely not having a good feeling about any of this.

"Yes," she replied. "I'm not really sure how I know that either. Maybe the witch mentioned it." Mum nonchalantly shrugged.

"Please tell me," the white seal begged, his voice trembling with a squeaking pitch. "Why mustn't I ever remove it? Will something bad happen?"

Mum began to laugh, commencing wildly with her Clap-Clap game. "Yep, yep, let's see, what was it again? Oh yes," she said with more nonchalance. "The power of the stone is great when worn, but when removed, death is reborn—*blah, blah, blah* something like that, I say. Not sure how I knew that either, oh well."

Miracle felt his stomach flip, his head throb, and his eyes grow large as his breath quickened. "You mean I'm going to die?" he managed to gurgle out.

"No! Well yes, if you take the blasted thing off, that is."

"But-but-but—"

"Oh, don't be such an annoying little scare baby! Just don't take the garsh darn thingamajig off, for crying out loud!" Mum snorted, her head tilting to one side as the drool ran from her face, and she stopped clapping. "Now, do be a love and scratch your mum's back. Besides, I think it's a beautiful addition to your white and furry ensemble, little *Love-ya,* I say!"

"But I don't want to die!"

Mum shrugged her shoulders. "Well, you should have thought of that before you put it on."

"What!"

"Oh, stop your bellyaching! Like I told you, don't take the codswalloping thing off, that's all! Great balls of icebergs, you're dense!" Mum bellowed, scratching her back against the icy wall.

Catching a glimpse of her reflection on the side of the glassy grotto, Mum abruptly sprang up and began to stare at herself, fixing the preposterous bonnet around her silly face. She continued to view herself in the ice mirror, now utterly oblivious of the tiny white seal. She drew closer toward the smooth surface of the grotto and proceeded to press her thick seal lips together, smacking them loud with a vulgar whacking sound, her rubbery expression entertaining her. She began giggling, thoroughly enjoying the reflected funny faces she was making. She then shifted her head from side to side, striving to center the disarranged bonnet while smacking her lips, admiring herself. *"I'mmmm—hot!"* she flagrantly boasted with the same nasal twang as before, forever sounding as she had a most persistent cold.

Miracle nervously squirmed over to her side, and trying to catch her vacant attention, he jumped and clamped his jaws down, tugging at one of the dangling tassels of her disheveled hat. "Mum, please look at me! You must explain these things to me, please! You're scaring me," he confessed, releasing his grip from the bonnet.

"Oh my *Love-ya*, don't tell me that you really *are* a scare baby!"

"Please," Miracle begged. "What have you done to me?"

"You have the power now to find Home. Boy, howdy, are you ever annoying! Now I don't want to talk about it anymore! I have to rest! I'm pooped! All that choking and spitting up was tiresome and dastardly, and besides, all your tedious questions have bored me into a sickening weariness!"

"But-but-but—"

Abrasively, Mum proceeded to snatch on to a wide and extensive yawn, making all sorts of noises as her mouth squirted out spurts of spittle over the pup's questioning and worried face. She circled like a tired dog before finding just the right place, crashing her immense self down, ready and eager to take a well-deserved nap. Miracle wriggled up to her excitedly, shaking his head, the glowing medallion swaying back and forth. He looked down at the purple stone again with a puzzling stare. He did not understand any of it, but he knew that for the first time since Mum brought him to the ice grotto, he was afraid—very much afraid.

BROKEN GROTTO

The snow remained ever constant in its rushing descent from the cloudy sky.

Miracle had watched it multiply the entire time Mum slept, her powerful snores vibrating the grotto. However, neither the snow nor Mum's incessant crude sounds could distract the small seal from thinking about the purpose and the unknown power of the stone he now wore over his trembling heart. While contemplating his curious dilemma, the blast from the blowing snow assaulted him, filling the grotto's entrance. Sinking into the snow, he wondered if it would ever stop. If it continued, both he and Mum just might be trapped inside. Immediately, he decided to wake the snoring seal. She had slept long enough, and he needed her assistance in this matter. Once more, wriggling over to her, he began pushing on her enormous belly.

"Mum! Mum! Wake up! The snow is coming in!"

Mum merely grumbled, turned over on her other side, striking the grotto, cracking a portion of it while clumsily rearranging herself comfortably on the ice. Frustrated, Miracle snorted and wriggled around to the other side. Again, he pushed on her spongy belly. "Mum! Please get up! The storm has gotten worse!"

"Bugger off!" Mum groggily grumbled, pushing the baby seal away with one of her back flippers.

"Mum!" demanded the white harp, defiantly pushing himself back toward her. "WAKE UP!"

With a wild and sudden jump, the mad harpie sprang up from the ice. However, when she did, she was in such a position that most of her girth struck the side of the grotto, seriously damaging it, her bulbous fat breaking clean through its icy wall. Miracle yelped, shivering and listening as the grotto cracked and creaked, some of the ceiling falling down on top of them as more of Mum's rump broke through the ice. This time it took a considerable chunk out of the rear of the grotto. Her spillage of plumpness quickly sank into the snow outside, and the blustering winds did not waste any time in frosting themselves over her spilled blubber.

"Now you did it!" Miracle yelped. "You've gone and broke our house!"

"Codswallop," Mum spit. "'Tis a sturdy hut and steadfast as the sea herself! A bit chilly, I say, isn't it, *Love-ya?*"

Exasperated, Miracle shook his head. "That's because you have fallen through—*look!* Most of you is outside, *see!*"

Mum slapped another daft grin to her lips. "Well, I'll be a Klip Kloppen' Klutz! How'd that happen?"

"Can you get back inside?"

"Don't rightly know."

"Well, try!" the white seal suggested aggressively, his face reddening from his growing frustration and fear.

"Yes, I'll do that, *Love-ya*," Mum complied, trying to pull herself back inside, but it was impossible; she just was not able to move. All she did was break off more of the grotto, sending more of the ceiling down. As the small pup shook his coat to attempt to clear the falling debris, even more toppling bits and pieces promptly fell on him. He did not know what to do at this point. Discouraged and sporting a whopper of a headache, Miracle looked at Mum, waiting for some kind of solution. It was at that very moment the crazed Mum pressed her slimy snout into Miracle's small face, her greenish drool sullying the outer frame of his white fur, belching loud before she spoke.

"*Are you the Docta?*" she asked, belching once more.

Miracle had reached his limit. After all, even little seals had their breaking point. He immediately gave out a loud, ear-piercing howl, completely overwhelmed by her unending insanity. His growling scream went on as if never to stop. Mum simply looked at him, just waiting for him to finish; and when he finally did, she sucked in some more drool, licked her lips, and puckered out a sour expression. "Aren't we the sassy, love?"

"Will you stop that!" Miracle demanded. "Our house is falling apart! We've got to do something before the entire place caves in!"

"And that's exactly what your old mum is going to do," she promised, trying once again to pull in her girth from the hole she had created. Yanking mercilessly on the ice grotto, it began shaking violently.

"I don't think that is such a good idea, Mum," warned the white pup.

"Never you, mind, *Love-ya*, you're my little worrier! Now just hush and your old mum will fix everything!" She laughed, giving one final yank, and that was enough to cause the entire grotto to come tumbling down with an enormous crash!

It did not take long for the icy rubble to clear, for the incessant winds quickly took care of dusting off the place, leaving behind the incredible mess of destruction the mad harpie had caused. For in a blink of a seal's eyes, both remained dumbfounded and stunned in the middle of a heaping pile of ice and snow, ice and snow that once made up their home. It was all destroyed—every last piece of it! Crawling out from under a slab of broken ice that once made up part of the ceiling, Miracle coughed, choking on the snow. He shook himself then glared angrily at the mad seal. Mum did not look that pleased either. She smirked, slugging around the smashed-up ice grotto. Smacking her lips and shaking her head while surveying the icy mess, she shouted, "Look what you did to my house!"

Outraged, the white seal screamed out again, "Look what *I* did!"

"Now don't be a lippy, love," Mum scolded. "I just won't have it!"

Coughing some more, Miracle tried to catch his breath while the snow and wind whirled around him. "Now what are we going to do? There is nothing left! What will happen to us now?" He began to shiver, the snow attacking him from all angles.

"Oh, my little fretting *Love-ya*." Mum sighed, exposing her disappointment, clucking her tongue. "We are finished here anyway, time to move on, I say!"

"Move on . . . what are you talking about? Move on . . . in the middle of a blizzard? I never understand anything you're talking about!"

"Well!" the insulted mum seal huffed.

"It's true! I never know what you mean!" Miracle cried. "I don't know if you're good for me . . . ," he paused dramatically, softening his voice, his eyes filling with burning tears, "or bad for me." He quickly wiped his eyes with his tiny flippers before looking up toward the crazy seal. "I'm sorry, Mum. I didn't really mean it . . . It's just that . . . well . . . I'm . . ." He swallowed hard before continuing. "Well, I'm scared and sometimes, well, it is you that scares me the most."

Mum surprisingly smiled as her own explicit set of tears surfaced in her large eyes. "I know. I know. And for this, I am sincerely sorry, sorrier than you will ever know, *Love-ya*, for I am aware of what I have become and I know what she did to me, I cannot pretend. Although I only have a few occasional moments of sanity, I realize just how truly ridiculous I am. For you see," she moaned, pausing as the building emotion lodged in her throat, followed by more tears and more drool, "I am quite mad, you know." Groaning, she affectionately patted Miracle on top of his head. Trying to comfort the once again homeless seal, she smiled through her tears. "Magnificently sassy hot, but quite mad, I'm afraid. How I wish it were not so, but it is what it is, and remember, wishin' ain't gettin', *Love-ya*!" She sighed, and it was drawn out and heartfelt. Slurping up more of her runny discharge, she proceeded to blow out the mucus, christening the snowy rubble beneath both her and the shivering pup.

Miracle tried to calm himself. "It's okay about the ice house, Mum, we'll find another," he said while he cleaned some of her sticky discharge off his whiskers.

"You bet we will, my brave little *Love-ya!*" she shouted, scattering more of the broken grotto in all directions and quickly snatching up the pup with both flippers. While sipping on her drool, she pledged, "Mum will not let any bad come to you! *Ever!* I promise. Come on!" she barked, the madness suddenly returning in her eyes. Squeezing the seal ever so tight against her voluptuous bosom, she howled, "Let's go find your mama!"

And holding fast to the tiny pup with one flipper while somehow holding on to the tattered ties of the drooping bonnet, Mum robustly pushed forward, barreling through the smashed-up grotto, the snowy whistling winds covering them up with one sweeping swallow.

My Darling White Puff!

One afternoon, a few weeks later, they found that it was time to rest again.

Managing only to rest near ice floes or in unusually small caves that they accidentally come upon, they did not find Miracle's mother nor did Mum find any permanent place of lodging. Her madness was well out of control, and when she was not feeding herself or feeding Miracle, she was busy playing Clap-Clap, reciting nonsensical phrases that made absolutely no sense whatsoever.

Miracle remained exhausted and disheartened. Still, he tried to conceal most of his thoughts from Mum; he did not want to hurt her feelings or upset her in any way. She was quite unbalanced, and he never knew how she would react to any given situation. However, despite the odds that stacked heavily against him, he found that with each passing day, he was learning more and more about seal life. Still, he tried his best from keeping himself and Mum as far away as possible from the harps of Sealssong, for the other seals continued to survey them both with suspicious and mistrusting eyes. Both he and Mum had, unfortunately, made quite the sordid reputation around these parts, and Miracle found that it was best if they remained out of sight whenever possible.

In the late afternoon on this one particular day, a rather perfidious fog slowly rolled in from the northwest. Its ghostly shroud made for a haunting backdrop for the two nomadic seals now trekking slowly through the frozen wilderness of Sealssong. Each hummock and every fantastic ice sculpture they passed suddenly began to change into a sinister and oppressive shape as the fog continued to squirm its way around the island. Despite the foreboding scenery, Mum remained unaffected by it. In fact, her movements suddenly changed over to a more aggressive stride. She began galloping, plowing through the fog and snow, making Miracle all that more apprehensive.

It had been quite some time since his last feeding, and he was hungry. Although he now was old enough to eat on his own, he still relied on the seal juice that Mum provided; in fact, she insisted on it. However, on this particular day, it did not appear that she was going to serve lunch any time soon. She was on a quest. It was a secret quest, one that she had not yet shared with the white seal, and that made it all the more frustrating. Miracle tried keeping up with her rushing paces, her expression not remotely affected by the impermanent circumstances.

"Wait, Mum, wait for me!" he shouted, out of breath and not having a clue as to the purpose of her sudden and fanatical expedition. Once more, he hoarsely barked out to her, continuing to scurry along, hoping to catch up, frightened that he might lose her in the shrouded fog. "Mum, please slow down, where are you going?" he puffed out, trying to catch his breath again. He waited for the mum to turn around, but she did not. She just kept on a-plowing through the fog and snow. "Mum," Miracle growled through pounding lungs, "where are you taking us! What is the matter with you?"

It appeared that no question posed at this time would be worthy of any response. The only rebuttal that he could hear was her traditional grunts and groans that she would randomly produce due to her massiveness, as well as the slurps and gurgles she made. In his hurried pursuit, he could not help watching his shining purple stone swing from the seashell chain placed about his furry throat. Looking down toward its faint glow, he accidentally noticed the tattered bonnet dragging mercilessly in the snow before him. Even in her madness, Mum would not relinquish it. She always seemed to keep the tie strings wrapped around some part of her body.

Striving to keep up with her, he began to feel dizzy, the burning sensation in his belly intensifying. He was not only hungry, but he was also extremely tired, much too tired to keep this ridiculous pace up. Once more, the out-of-breath pup zeroed in on the traipsing bonnet before him, watching as if fascinated. Then cleverly seizing the moment, he jumped forward. It was now or never. *PLOP!* He was in the bonnet! He had successfully connected a ride with the zooming headpiece, remaining perfectly oblivious to its illogical operator. He would ride this way for some time, his small form not quite fitting inside, bouncing unmercifully up and down as the Mad Mum scraped over countless broken segments of ice and snow. Rebounding absurdly, the white seal tried to hang on, striving to maintain his awkward position while his furry rump twisted and pivoted in all sorts of contortions while he feebly squealed out preposterous bouncing yelps—*hi-yi-yi-ying!* Every bump of the way!

In the distance, a thunderous rumble sounded. An immeasurable iceberg began to split apart, crashing into the sea. Segments of it blasted off into the surrounding waters, exploding into a frothy fury of icy blur. Miracle shuddered while the desolate timbre penetrated his senses, unnerving and upsetting him considerably. However, Mum continued on her merry way, dashing through the ice and snow, completely indifferent as the sea crashed all around them.

The wild currents hugged the serrated shores of Sealssong with icy fingers. Incarcerated slushy fields squeezed themselves against the rigid banks while the graylike fog pursued their haunts, rolling in continuously from nowhere places, ponderously devouring anything and everything in its shrouding wake until the visibility became utterly impenetrable. The fog had swallowed them both up. Right then and there, Miracle decided to close out the foggy sea ghosts as only he knew how. He would quickly shut his eyes tight with a deliberate determination of overcoming the thick mist, his tiny body still popping up and down unsympathetically upon the hard ice beneath him. This rushing condition through the fog would continue for some time and would show no sign of settling, for the mum's seemingly senseless travels would take the two seals vast distances. They would cross the northern tips of many of the islands and would continue north, the deranged seal fixed straight in mad pursuit of some unexplainable quest. Ranting, starving, and exhausted, babbling words and phrases indistinguishable from reason, the obsessed harpie continued slugging forward, never stopping to eat or rest. She would remain in this disturbing state until at last the irrational expedition came to a sudden and complete halt. With a huff and a mighty puff, the large seal began listening exceedingly carefully as the waters brushed against the ice floes she stood before.

Miracle peeked out from inside the wet and tattered bonnet. More fear seized tightly over him, for it was obvious to see that Mum's unpredictable madness continued to defame her damp and twisted snout. He would remain still, the determined mum continuing to listen, but what she was listening for he knew not—but Mum knew. She knew all too well, and she went on listening, not moving a muscle, as if she suddenly turned to stone. The pallid winds tantalized the twirling foggy vapors that seemed to follow her every wriggle, when quite suddenly, the awaited sound came to her. Someone or something was out there hiding inside the mist. Mum cocked her head sideways and listened some more. Her expression was not what Miracle would have expected, for her face suddenly became perplexed and uncertain. Once again, the noise came, this time revealing itself as a voice that sounded like a loud whistle.

"Whooo-whooo!" went the hooting, disembodied voice. The sound circled them both with a pressing urgency, and although Mum continued to hold to her peculiar expression of uncertainty, a quick chill ran down the spine of the white seal. Sitting up and attentively listening, he stirred uncomfortably inside his flimsy habitat. What was that sound? Why did it suddenly sound familiar?

When the voice returned this time even louder than before, Miracle jumped out from the ragged bonnet, sniffing the air profusely. Listening, he shook his head, believing that he was under the influence of some kind of strange dream for the voice continued to tickle his consciousness with added familiarity. Again, the voice flew at him with defiance. *"Whooody! Whooo! Whooo!"*

With a disgusted smack to her lips, Mum jerked her thick neck around, snorting and sniffing the air, attempting to smell out the proprietor possessing such an annoying whistling, her expression remaining less than pleased. "Oh, botherdash it all," Mum barked. "Show yourself before I tear you to shreds! It was not you who I was looking for! You ruined everything for now I have lost my concentration! Blast, blast, blast it all!"

"Mum, please!" Miracle begged, scurrying up to her. "I know that sound!"

"Preposterous!"

"I do! I promise!"

Mum looked down through the fog at the small pup beneath her, and smacking her floppy lips again and twitching her head back and forth, she began to hyperventilate. She went on to make funny wheezing sounds, her eyes popping out of their watery sockets, and sniffed the air, determined to locate the annoying, yet mysterious voice coming from within the fog. The voice suddenly went silent, but Mum knew it was still there; she could hear it breathing. "You might as well show yourself. I know you are there! I can hear, and I can smell your most foul odor, transgressor!"

Then without warning, from out of the fog, both seals saw something immense coming straight for them. Mum instinctively assumed an aggressive position, nearly crushing Miracle with her rump. Not waiting for any further provocation from the irritating voice, she instantly seized the thing that was still in the process of nearing her. Opening her jaws, the mad harpie grasped on to a rather rough and spongy shape. With a heavy grunt, she flipped the perpetrator over, smacking the thing hard with her backside, sending it off spinning across the icy floor, right into a large ice mountain.

"Whoooeeee!" went the whistling voice as it hit the rocky formation. The crashing pitch was sharp and so was the infuriation it felt. "What's the matter with you, are you crazy! Boop-boop-dee-daffy-daisy! What ya wanna do that for?" it belted before it started to cry extremely loud.

Miracle quickly went out toward the voice, his fear oddly draining from him. Following close behind, Mum snorted and sniffed again, crunching her nose upward, looking piglike as she barreled toward the annoying whimpers.

It was at that precise moment another form came out of nowhere. This one was smaller than the first and in an awful big hurry to reach the crying voice. "You leave my mama alone! You hurt her, ya big bully! Keep away from her or you'll be sorry!"

This inquisitive display amused Mum. Partially squinting shut her eyes, she glared at what appeared to be a young walrus. Miracle stood nearby, spellbound, filled with the riveting hopefulness that uncorked his mind with a startling *whoosh!* Could it be possible? Was it true?

Mum did not waste any time in bringing down her giant head, slicing it through the swirling mist, colliding it into the large nose of the irritating and whining thing. Smacking her lips, the mad seal snorted when coming snout to snout with the creature hiding in the fog. She paused, just glaring at it with an ugly smirk stuck to her muzzle. "Oh, I don't believe it! I don't believe it! All this fuss over a codswalloping walrus and a rather stupid-looking one at that! And she has her stupid-looking kid with her to boot!" Immediately, Mum prepared on ripping into the walruses again, when all at once she felt a sudden sharp pain sting at the bottom of her drooping abdomen. With eyes glaring and nostrils flaring, she swiftly checked out the folding blubber of her stomach. It hurt. It hurt badly. The stupid-looking kid had bitten her!

"Back off, ya short stumpie ass!" Mum bellowed through a gnarled lip, butting the baby walrus from her aching flesh, hitting him with a walloping *bing-bang-boom* with her full-figured hips. Flipping around, Mum's glare was vicious and remained that way as she snarled at the younger, more aggressive walrus, having absolutely no intention of having it react further. "Just keep your grimy gums off me merchandise, punk, or I'll give you something to really growl about!"

"Good gosh almighty, he's just a baby, goodness me! Boop-boop-dee-dee!" the mother walrus howled, pressing into her pup. "What kind of vicious thing are you, anyway?"

"The kind that will smack you the side of your fat head if you let that brat near me again!"

"Well, I never!" grumbled the mother walrus, totally taken back by the aggressive seal, looking down toward her large and wrinkled pup, neurotically kissing the top of his head. "Whoody-rudey-dismay, they certainly are snotty in this neck of the ice, aren't they?" she bellowed, shaking her head in disgust, rolling up her huge eyes in absolute disapproval.

"Back off, blubbo, don't make me have to smack you!"

Having seen and heard enough, Miracle wriggled forward. "Stop it, stop it, I know who they are!" With his unexpected outburst, a sudden quiet encompassed itself over everyone while he swiftly made his way over to both tooth walkers. Upon reaching them, he felt his eyes burn with unexpected emotion. He sniffed the air and tried to bark, but his throat constricted and froze. All that he could manage was to produce another of his annoying high-pitched squeaks. Not giving up, he repeated his squeaky yap, his tiny form popping up and down on the ice, his heart pounding. His eyes were now full and saturated with an uncanny sparkle of familiar reassurance, looking at the baby walrus that remained shadowed deep under the flipper of its mother, its face scrunched up and still growling. Miracle dared to wriggle even closer, sniffing deep into the fog, remembering their scent. This time, his bark came through, and he was able to call to them in a pleading voice.

"Crumpels, Poo-Coo, is that you? Is that really you?"

"My darling White Puff," Crumpels blasted. "We have found you! We have found you! Boop-boop-it's TRUE!"

Defiant, Mum interjected, as usual, "Oh, don't waste your time on such codswallop!"

"You don't understand, Mum," Miracle assured her. "I know who they are!" His voice was building, and he reiterated his unbelievable find. "I know who they are!" Overwhelmed by this discovery, the entire recollection of his friends astonishingly played back to him. There could be no mistake; it was indeed the walrus Crumpelteeverella and her son Poo-Coo! Mum had miraculously stumbled upon them! The mighty Teeth Monster had not swallowed them up! They were wonderfully both still alive! He had at last found someone from his brief but traumatic past. For it was someone that knew of his mother; it was not a dream or some cruel form of nightmare. They were there, and they were real! Instantly, he snuggled into Crumpels's eager embrace, the exact elation spilling itself over her as well. Miracle pushed himself further into her spongy folds, panting and breathing in her familiar scent again as if it were the last breath that he would ever take. He could scarcely believe his own eyes—and nose. Unfolding between the fleshy borders of his newly discovered friends, he knew in the deepest regions of his heart without even asking that they held the answers for what truly happened to his mama. They just had to!

Beautiful, sanguine images of his beloved mother flooded his soul.

Maybe, just maybe, he thought, engaged in holding on to the lumpy forms of the wrinkly tooth walkers, just maybe she was still alive! Arayna, his lost mama, just had to be somewhere out there, there in the shrouded midst of the sea ghosts, still searching, still calling out, still singing her beautiful seal lullaby just for him. Yes, with the kindness of some wondrous miracle, maybe she was truly alive, just like the walruses were, and she was searching for him as he was still searching for her.

Maybe . . . Oh please, *maybe* . . .

BACK OFF, BLUBBO!

Crumpels could hardly believe her eyes. She had been searching for the small white seal and had just about given up on ever finding him again when at last, there he was! "Whooo-whoooing," she stoutly squeezed him, moaning out all kinds of affectionate walrus tones. "We have found you!" she sang. "Just like the whale said we would!" Finally relinquishing her overzealous embrace, both creatures wept in the spirit of remembrance.

"Crumpels, I never thought I would see you again," the white seal cried. "Please, you must tell me where is my—"

It was at this precise moment that the walrus's son, Poo-Coo, pushed himself further into the excited harp, waiting for his mother to reintroduce him, and she did. Fastening an overdressed grin upon her wiggling snout, she told her son, "Poo-Coo, we have found him! The very one we have been searching for!"

Miracle smiled at the young walrus before saying, "Wow, you sure have grown!"

"Guess so," the younger tooth walker replied. Holding to a perplexed expression, he said, "Bro, you sure turned out small and scrawny, didn't ya? Not walruslike at all."

"Never you mind," scolded his mama. "Brothers of the sea often do not resemble one another. It is the stuff inside that really counts—that is our bond."

Poo-Coo merely shrugged his shoulders, commencing to sniff dramatically at the tiny seal. Feeling somewhat uncomfortable, Miracle tried to sit still while the walrus snorted and probed him further with his bouncing nose and whiskers. Mum had remained silent long enough. "Well now," she grunted, barreling forward, "I really do hate to interrupt this auspicious moment, but do tell me, *Love-ya,* who exactly are these clowns?"

Miracle explained. "Mum, you must listen to me. A wonderful thing has happened! This is Crumpels and her son, the ones I have told you about!"

"Yes! The name is Crumpelteeverella, to be exact," announced the mama walrus. "We've been with White Puff from the beginning. You see, boop-boop-dee-dee, we practically birthed him right there in the middle of the sea, we did!"

Mum stared at her appallingly. "You're *who?* You *did what? Where? When?*" she asked, all sassy-mouthed, her eyes burning with mistrust.

"They're okay, Mum, honest," Miracle reassured her.

After a few more moments, Mum closed in on the baby seal, her blazing eyes disappearing into two dark slits. "Do they know the Docta?" she distrustfully whispered.

"No, Mum," Miracle nervously replied, already tense from her continued insanity. "These are the walruses I told you all about, remember? They are my friends."

"Codswallop, they don't look friendly to me! They just look stupid!"

Immediately, Crumpels took offense. "I assure you, my good seal that we are not! Boop-boop-dee snot!" Grunting, the rhyming beast, whose massive bulk weighed in a tad over two thousand pounds, brazenly headed toward the mad harpie.

A piercing roar came from Mum, demanding that the walrus come to an immediate halt. Holding out both flippers, she warned, "You best stay where you are, you melodious moron! Besides, how do we know that you were not sent here by the witch? Why, you could be products of her evil sorcery! Back off, blubbo!" she growled, showing her sharp and grinding teeth, popping her head up and down then cocking it sideways, staring suspiciously at the walrus, drool pouring down her snout, not in the least intimidated by the walrus's size.

Frustrated, Miracle tried to change Mum's perspective by quickly jumping in with an ungainly smile that did not fit right upon his muzzle. "That isn't so, Mum. I promise! Here, let me introduce you properly."

"I couldn't be bothered!"

"Mum, please!" implored Miracle. "I'm trying to tell you that the walruses were with me and my mother!"

"Nonsense!"

"It's true!" Miracle barked. Turning to the walrus, he asked, "You must tell me, Ms. Crumpels"—his eyes filled with promise—"where is she? Where is my mother?"

Crumpels did not answer but only smiled. It was a thin, strained smile, one that certainly was not filled with promise. Remorsefully, the walrus's face melted into the repressed sadness of despair that unfortunately did not require an explanation of any kind. Reluctantly, and most unhappily, she instead returned to him a question. "Oh my poor little White Puff, she is not with you?"

Miracle just looked at her, his heart sinking, his eyes filling with tears.

"Dear heart, the fact of the matter is that I simply do not know. I was so hoping she would have found you by now," sadly whooo-whooed the walrus.

If it were possible, the devastated pup wished that he could somehow dissolve right into the ice and snow, disappearing forever, never again to feel or experience the painful world around him. It felt as if something forcefully snapped away from his heart, rendering him permanently hopeless. All he could do was cry, his naked heart breaking there in front of the three onlookers.

Poo-Coo was surprisingly the first to voice his thoughts. "Why is he crying, Mama? Did that nasty, fat seal with the ugly old lady face do something dreadful to him?" Right away, Mum snarled at the young walrus, exposing her jagged teeth again ready to pounce on him right then and there.

"Oh no, dear," sobbed Crumpels. "He's crying because he has lost his mama and he is very sad."

Turning with a sad look of his own, the young walrus approached Miracle. "Don't worry, White Puff, it will be all right. If you like, you can share my mama, I don't mind. Besides," he chuckled, "it's not like there isn't plenty of her to go around, little bro."

"I don't need another mama," Miracle snapped. "I already have my own." He moved away from his spectators, proceeding toward the icy ridges nearing the spitting floes, his brilliant purple medallion swaying from his white chest. Upon seeing the shining stone, Poo-Coo wriggled over to Miracle again, pushing his head toward the purple glow. "Cool beads! Can I see?" Miracle pulled away and faced the opposite direction, merely looking out into the fog that still crawled over the icy floor.

"Poo-Coo, leave him be, boop-boop-dee-dee," Crumpels scolded, attempting to retrieve her son with a swish of her flipper.

"But, Mama, he has a really cool stone around his neck. It glows and everything!"

"Never mind, come here," Crumpels insisted, her flipper still outstretched.

Mum was quick to snap. "Yes, and keep that probing little brat away from him from now on!" Then flopping toward the forlorn pup, Mum's face saddened when she saw Miracle just sitting there, staring out into the frozen domain all covered up in fog, his poor little heart breaking while his tears dissolved into the graylike slush folding beneath him.

"Mama," the young walrus asked his mother, "what happens now?"

Again Mum snapped. "I'll tell you what happens now!" she roared out, madness gushing over her as she slid into a highly disgruntled state. "The first thing is you two slobs need to get lost before I kill you both!"

"See here, my discourteous seal, you have no right to boss us around like this!" Crumpels cried.

"I have every right! I am his guardian!" Mum hissed.

"Of all the nerve, why, we saw him first, so there," the walrus spit, sticking out her tongue.

"You also lost him and haven't been any help to him whatsoever!"

"I don't think I like you very much," Crumpels told the mad harpie. "Nor do I like the way you talk. I wish not to converse with you any longer! Now, since he rightfully belongs with us, you will render him over so that we may take him back to the blue whale. Thank you very much for your time, but we best be on our way. We wouldn't think of detaining you any further."

"Over my dead body," Mum growled.

"Goody-goody!" howled Poo-Coo. "Can we kill the ugly seal with the old lady face, Mama?"

"Be still!" Crumpels barked.

"Yeah," Mum finally agreed. "Be still and back off, slimy codswallop!"

Crumpels shook her head vehemently. "Not until we have the white seal. For you see, it is he that we were looking for and him we have fond! Now, we appreciate all you have done for him, but I must insist on taking custody of White Puff this very instant!"

"You're not taking *Love-ya* anywhere! What's more, if you two twits aren't gone by the time I count three," Mum warned, smacking her flippers, drool running down her snout, "I'll chew you up so fine that the gulls will be picking up pieces of your greasy carcasses for the next six months!"

"Stop it, stop it," Miracle shouted, having heard enough. "My name is not White Puff, and it is not *Love-ya*! My name is Miracle! Miracle! Do you hear me? *Miracle!* My mama calls me that name! She calls me—" The shouting pup suddenly choked up, turning away again, isolating himself from the others.

Mum's madness left her momentarily, and she relaxed the taut muscles in her twisted snout and snarling lip. At first, she said nothing but only stared at the distressed pup, watching him cry while looking out into the sea. Feeling ashamed, her heart, though she tried to control it, became heavier than even she could withstand. However, with authority still coating her persona, she once again threw her angry glance toward the walruses. "You see what you did? Now you really upset him, stupid codswalloping trash!" Then, turning her snout toward the weeping pup, her expression drastically changed into a soft and inviting look of sincere compassion. "I am sorry, little one, please, won't you forgive me?" she asked, wrapping a flipper about him. "What is it that Mum can do to help, baby love?"

"I want my mama!" cried the white seal.

Mum smiled, saying, "Yes, I know, *Love-ya*, and I will find her for you, I promise." She blasted out a blob of mucus from her quivering nostrils. Naturally, it shot out to the precise spot where the two walruses remained situated.

"You shouldn't promise things you might not be able to deliver," Crumpels cautioned, utterly annoyed while shaking some of the slime from her cheek.

"You dare to believe otherwise?" Mum blasted with a disturbing scowl wired across her distorted muzzle.

"Well, no . . . I only meant that—"

"Then be still!" Mum warned.

Clearing his tears away with a quick swipe of his flipper, Miracle turned to face the mad seal, asking, "Then you will truly find her for me, Mum?"

"Yes, my love, of course I will, and the two stupid-looking walruses will help, won't you?" Viciously growling, Mum glared at both tooth walkers with burning eyes and a mouth dripping with slimy drool, exposing her sharp teeth again, just daring them to refuse.

Feeling most uncomfortable, Crumpels pulled her eyes away from the mad harpie, not wanting to look upon her anymore. She then adjusted her stare over toward Miracle. She nervously smiled. "Of course, we will. It was always our sole intention."

"Now," Mum demanded, facing the walruses, "tell me about this whale you spoke of."

"You mean the whale Kishk?"

"So it is Kishk, how splendid!" Mum hummed, happily clapping her flippers together.

Crumpels was quick to say, "You couldn't possibly know him, deary dear!"

"Just go on!" Mum barked.

"Well, we met him only recently. He saved us, he did! And if anyone can find Miracle's mama, I just know he can!" Turning, Miracle wriggled toward the gathering, his eyebrows raised a glimmer of hope returning to his heart. With eyelashes convulsing in a habitual rapid dance, Crumpels continued in an unusually excited manner. "You see, ever since that nasty business on the ice when that awful killer whale with all those nasty teeth came to us, we were nearly—"

"Killer whale," Miracle interrupted. "You mean the terrible Teeth Monster?"

Crumpels paused, tilting her head, thinking about it before she spoke. "Well, yes yes, I guess you could call him the terrible Teeth Monster, he sure had enough teeth to be ordained such a beast."

"Oh, do go on!" Mum growled cuttingly.

"Well, I'm trying to do just that if you will let me, boop-boop-dee-dee! For you see, we would have been gobbled up if it were not for the blue whale. For out of nowhere he came, and he saved us and has been our blessed friend ever since."

Miracle was all ears, asking, "Did the whale save me too?"

"Yes!" explained Crumpels. "You see, when the beast—I mean, the terrible Teeth Monster began to attack us, your mama, bless her soul, had already surfaced below. She was not on the raft and was spared. However, on that frightful day, one would have certainly considered us real goners! Just as the terrible Teeth Monster began to open his foul mouth, the marvelous and amazing Kishk saved the day! He just burst out of the water like some fantastic explosion, saving us from being gobbled up alive!"

"How nice for you!" sarcastically enticed Mum, "now, can you PLEASE get on with it, tubby?"

"Well, I will*! I will!*" spouted the enthusiastic wound-up creature. "I had already fainted straightaway, right after I saw the despicable thing and its chomping teeth. This was no doubt brought on by my merciless dizzy spells, simply ghastly, you know!"

"All I know," Mum snapped, "is that I'm starting to think that you're making the whole thing up!"

Poo-Coo immediately snarled at the mad seal. "No, she's not, old lady face! Maybe you would find out what really happened if you stopped interrupting all the time and let Mama finish!" Growling, he quickly gave her an offensive tongue gesture, spitting, *"Pppllttwwthpttth!"* in her direction.

Crumpels hurriedly continued. "Now, where was I?" she asked aloud. "Oh, yes . . . yes," she said, clearing her throat in a most dramatic fashion. *"Ahem!"* she went, preparing to unfold the rest of her story. "As the giant Teeth Monster was about to chow down on us, our intrepid and valiant savior appeared!"

Miracle listened attentively, drawing closer to the excited tooth walker, his eyes lighting up with a full burst of wonder. "Was the whale very big?"

"Big? That's hardly the word, dear! He was fantastic, and he had the most enchanting violet eyes I have ever seen! They absolutely without a doubt made me swoon, they did!" Crumpels told, sighing over the memory of the whale while her enormous walrus eyes batted frantically.

"Calm down, big girl!" Mum spit. "You don't know anything about the color of his eyes or what happened at all. Did you forget, you had apparently— *'sa-wooned'* yourself right into a cowardly blackout? Back off with your codswalloping bull!"

Poo-Coo quickly blasted her. "But it is true, every word, you crazy old lady face biddy! It's just like Mama said! We would have been done for if it hadn't been for Kishk! And before that stupid Teeth Monster knew what hit him, Kishk smashed the big dope straight in the kisser, knocking him clear across the ocean floor he did! So there!" spit the baby walrus, once again sticking out his tongue at the mad seal.

"And can he sing!" Crumpels babbled. "What a voice, it is such a wondrous, melodious voice! He sang to us today all the while we rode upon his head while searching for you, way up top, where no one could see us!"

"Liar!" roared the mad seal. "You're making the whole thing up, stupid walrus!"

"I am not!" protested Crumpels.

"*Pppllttwwthpttttth!*" spit her feisty offspring.

"Yes," continued Crumpels. "He sang to us while he carried us along like a whimsical cloud while we told him all about the white seal."

"Can you get on with it?" Mum growled, rapidly losing her ability to endure the walrus's laborious storytelling. "Tell, me, halfwit, what exactly happened to the white seal? How was he separated from you? He obviously did not remain with you."

"Nay, nay, nay," Crumpels excitedly explained. "As you already know, after the dreadful attack, we were rendered unconscious for some time. And while we moaned and tossed within our delirium, the whale knew that he must first attend to the abandoned baby harp. Not knowing exactly who the pup rightfully belonged, he surmised the only place White Puff had a real chance of finding his mother was on the ice of Sealssong."

Miracle spoke up. "Then it was he who brought me here?"

"Yes, dear, and by the time Poo-Coo and me awoke from our rather debilitating exhaustion, Kishk had already dropped you off. We were heretofore a considerable distance from the islands when we immediately explained that we were not going anywhere without you. We told the friendly giant that we considered ourselves ever so simpatico with you and that we needed to know if you and your mama were all right. So without further ado, Kishk directly turned around, bringing us promptly back to Sealssong, eventually to this very place, keeping us safe and sound, way a top his shiny blue head, the magnificent darling!"

"Then you have been looking for me all this time?" asked Miracle.

"Yes! Yep! Yep!" chirped Crumpels.

Miracle directly took his stare away from the walrus, looking into the fog that was slowly beginning to fade. "Where is he now?"

"Oh, he is here," Crumpels promised. "Somewhere out there, not far away, I should imagine."

"Yes," smartly added Poo-Coo. "He told us that whenever we needed him, all we had to do is call out his name."

Miracle's penetrating stare attempted to cut through the diminishing veils of fog, hoping for a glimpse of the mysterious giant who saved his life, as well as both walruses, but he saw nothing. Turning from the shrouds of mist, he wriggled back toward Crumpels, pulling himself close next to her side, asking, "Then the whale was never able to save my mama, was he?"

Crumpels sadly shook her head. "I'm sorry, little one."

Mum gave a sudden and abrupt snort, plowing away from the others. Turning to face the floes, she stared through the lifting curtain of haze now exposing a mist-covered silver sea. Holding to a determined look of discernment, she, once again, just as before, was back searching for what had initially taken her there in the first place. It was the whale she had come for, her mad senses leading her every wriggle of the way, but she never suspected that her search for the gigantic beast would include two cumbersome tooth walkers. However, beggars can't be choosy. She would have to accept the walruses for the time being. Finding the blue whale was all that mattered now.

"What is it, Mum?" Miracle asked.

Mum sniffed the air incessantly. "Well, I'll be a washed-up jellyfish! The stupid walruses have spoken the truth. I was really beginning to think that their story was mere codswallop just like them, but even walruses have purposes, and their purpose was to find us so we could find the blue giant. It is he who can find the answers, for it is he I have come to find!"

Miracle turned up his nose, scratching the side of his head with his tiny flipper. "You truly know of the one called Kishk?"

Mum nodded, continuing to smell the air. "Of course, his name is not a stranger to my ears." Suddenly becoming as still as a statue, the mad harpie stopped sniffing and became extremely quiet.

"How did you know to find him here, Mum?"

"By smelling the wind," she answered. "The chanters have a sweet fragrance that fills the air and sea around them. Can you not smell it?"

Miracle turned and began to sniff hard at the air, but he could smell nothing but the salty mist that surrounded him. "Can the blue whale really find Mama?"

"I would not have come to this place if I believed otherwise," she said, sneezing violently, shooting wetness all over her snout while continuing to stare out into the fog.

The spongy mama tooth walker, who had also been studying the mad seal, spoke out while rumbling toward Miracle. However, before speaking, she took the pup into her grasp, pulling him away from the offensive mad thing and closer to where she was situated. "That's a really strange one that one is. Where on earth did you find her?"

"She found me."

"She sure is a queer nut, boop-boop-dee-butt! What exactly is her problem?"

"Not really sure. Her daughter was killed, and it all has to do with the evil man-beasts."

Crumpels immediately shivered with fear. "Man-beasts, oh nasty, nasty creatures, they are! Nasty! Nasty! Nasty! They are nothing but trouble. You must always steer clear of those nasty, horrible things!"

"Yes, I know. Mum has told me this repeatedly. Still, I would like to see one someday."

"Oh no . . . that would be the sorriest day of your life if you ever do, believes you, me, little one. Tell me, White Puff, what is that preposterous thing that dastardly doofus wears on her head?"

"Not sure, Mum said it was something she found. I think it may have belonged to some unknown human."

Crumpels squealed, quivering. "Oh, how can she even touch it?"

"I don't know, but she has become rather attached to it."

"And what is that thing you wear around your neck, dear?"

"Don't rightly know that either."

"Did she give it to you?"

"Yes."

"Then you best get rid of it at once! You know it has to be some queer trinket from the land of the humans. It can bring you nothing but misfortune. Here, let me take it away from you," Crumpels said, moving in toward the white seal, her spongy flipper reaching out toward his neck.

"No!" Miracle barked. "You mustn't do that."

Crumpels looked both offended and confused. "Why in icy seas not?"

Miracle moved away from her, shaking his head. "Just don't touch it, that's all!"

The walrus's face slowly melted into a frown, and thinking for a moment before she spoke, she lifted her face and reached for a quick smile. "Very well, White Puff, I won't bully you any further. It's just that whatever it is she has given you seems odd and most unsuitable, just like her, a most peculiar creature filled with unnerving gall with the most deplorable hygienic exhibition I have ever had the misfortune of looking upon. She gives me the willies, she does!"

Just then, both she and Miracle became startled by a most serious and angry growl. Apparently, while they remained engaged in conversation, Mum and Poo-Coo had somehow gotten into another disturbing confrontation. Stuck within the depths of her blubber, Poo-Coo was once again biting into Mum's rumpling flesh, growling savagely all the while.

"Oh no, you didn't!" the Mad Mum shrieked, trying to shake him off. Madness unreservedly taking over, with her open jaws the insane seal grabbed hold of the feisty baby tooth walker by the neck. Prying him off, she growled, "Back off, jackass," throwing him smack into the spongy face of its gawking mother, thrusting them both backward into the slush pool where they were both swallowed up indecently.

Miracle quickly rushed to the ridges of the pool, panicking, anxiety flashing over his face. Casting his cutting examination over to the crazy harpie, he shook his head disapprovingly. Mum, who so very nonchalantly looked back at the seal with a gloating grin stuck to her wet and dripping lips, merely commenced with loud, obscene sounds sucking up her drool. Deliberately pausing to play with her idiotic smirk, she crooned, *"I'mmmm—hot!"* quaintly, offering her asinine phrase as her absurd rebuttal, her eyes all cockeyed.

Angry, the white seal shouted, "Mum, how could you?"

Before any further turbulent feelings could gather between the two seals, out from the slush pool both mother and child emerged, both spitting spurts of water directly into the face of the mad harpie. With a roaring howl of utter discontent, the walruses grabbed at the air, filling up their pounding lungs while Miracle scurried over to them, wanting to help but not knowing how.

Then all at once, Miracle froze, breathlessly watching both tooth walkers as they began to float effortlessly on top of the water, their hulking forms weightless, neither one sinking into the slushy abyss below. It appeared as if they were levitating upon the waters, and that was just for starters for the incomprehensible phenomenon quickly expanded into the outer limits of the fantastic. As the walruses continued to ascend, Miracle realized that they were not achieving this spectacular feat on their own; some unknown entity was pushing them both out of the water, up into the fading mist. Frightened, he slowly began to back away, fear gripping him as a very shiny dark-colored object emerged. It came up astonishingly fast from beneath the sea. Roaring, tons of water poured from its outlandish scaffolding, all of which rushed downward while the thing continued with its levitation of the still wheezing mother walrus and her extremely upset offspring.

Higher and higher still went the two creatures, both nearly disappearing into the shrouded clouds of the morning sky. Miracle's neck strained from attempting to view the spectacle while the shiny dark object continued to rise. The mounting thing's enormous embodiment began to crack the ridges of the slush pool, opening the path for an immediate flooding to take place near the spot where both Miracle and Mum stood transfixed. Startled, both harps simultaneously jumped backward, making way for the tremendous pressure of the waters filling up the grounds, each seal never taking their eyes from the shining thing that persisted in its thunderous climb that continued to carry the two walruses up and up and up! Finally, the shiny thing stopped; and when it did, everything seemed to still, all except for the rushing waters that continued to cover the corrugations of the slush pool, its heavy weight snapping and crushing the floor it swathed upon. Then the startling scene commenced further as the dark shiny thing came to life. Suddenly, two large violet-colored eyes sprang open from both sides of the thing's shining dark blue head. The large violet eyes blinked a few times as it stared down toward the mum and the extremely terrified pup that remained crouched behind Mum's rump, looking up cowardly at the creature's stratospheric form towering before him. The gigantic beast seemed to struggle to keep its balance within the borders of the surrounding slush pools, keeping silent while it continued to stare down from way above.

BLUE IN THE FACE

The dark blue thing possessed a remarkably elongated snout, prehistoric and most intimidating, stretching outward, rounding off to a peak.

It appeared that the actual color of the creature was an unusual deep metallic blue. The rest of its enormous shape was unseen and hidden beneath the dark depths of the icy waters. Toward the bottom of its shiny dark head was a crease that spread across its fantastic face, indicating the outline of its tremendous mouth, a mouth that surprisingly opened to present a tame and kindly smile.

Without hesitating, the Mad Mum waddled over to the shiny creature, not showing any fear in the least. Approaching, she proceeded to sniff at it. Only inches away from its unbelievable large mouth that pathetically dwarfed her, she sniffed some more, then sniffed again. Too frightened to remain at her side, Miracle took refuge behind a convenient block of ice, his heart pounding in his ears, his eyes still stretched with wonder. He suddenly jumped when he heard Mum's loud blasting voice. Throwing back her head, the mad seal briskly howled out a rip-roaring yowl! Spanking down her thick rear, she hit the ice hard. Icy droplets shot out everywhere as her backside came down upon the engulfed stretch. She bounced forward with a stupendous grin bursting from her snout.

"Well, shiver me igloos! It's about time! What took you so long, been looking for you for nearly a week now?"

From high above, sitting comfortably upon the head of the thing with the large violet eyes, Poo-Coo shouted down to the mad seal with a loud voice. "Hey, old lady face, I'd like to introduce you to our friend. This is Kishk!" Spitting out water, aiming to hit Mum, the young tooth walker chuckled. "Kishk, this is the nasty, mad old lady seal face. Quite savage, you know. If you wish, you may eat it now."

"Poo-Coo!" scolded Crumpels, a warm flush stinging at her bloated cheeks, also looking down adoringly at the creature suspending her in midair. "What will our dear Captain Kishk think? Whooo-whooo!" she crooned, blushing ashamedly.

The large blue thing with the sparkling violet eyes then spoke. "Greetings, I am Kishk." His voice was both melodic and soothing as it was majestic, wise, and most kind. "Please, do not be afraid. Blue whales are large, but I assure you, so are our hearts. We mean you no harm. I promise."

"I know that!" Mum belted out, smacking her rump against the ice again. "Didn't you hear me? I know all about you! Been living in the sea for some time now, I guess I should know!"

The whale merely tilted his head and widened his violet eyes.

"Oh, don't be a coy, love," Mum roared, sniffing in the sweet fragrance of his being. "You are the one, the only one who can help us!" she barked.

"I am?" questioned the mammoth blue whale.

"Yes, fishy, do you see me talking to any other big galoot around here?"

Suddenly, and quite unexpectedly, from out of nowhere, another voice consolidated with the extraordinary gathering. This voice was unique in every aspect—meaner, gruffer, and yet at the same time high-pitched, sounding singsong, and highly impish. "Aaeeeeeeeee!" it screeched. "Stop that inappropriate display of insolence, you dreadful thing, you're making me sick!"

Mum quickly twirled around, wanting to see the owner of such a peculiar and irritating creature. She watched it descend the long and massive snout of the whale until she was at last face-to-face with it. Immediately, she sniffed rudely about its private parts, something the owner of the irritating voice hardly appreciated. "Get *a-waaay!*" it screeched out.

Mum quietly backed off, staring at the annoying thing suspiciously.

It was a penguin—a highly aggravated, impatient, and supremely irritated penguin.

Once again, Mum began to sniff at it, her eyes shrinking into two interrogating slits of distrust. With his dark and deep-set shining eyes, the squatting penguin quickly returned the taut gesture with his own cross-examination of suspicion. This particular penguin, although short, plump, and stubby, was not to be reckoned with, she would soon discover. He was feisty and ready for a fight at any given moment. The penguin was small, standing less than a foot from the ice, possessing defiant arrogance as it showed off its colorful markings. Its breast remained dusted with a soft white shade, as its black lapel embellishments painted his body entirely from the tip of his beak to the end of his tiny buttocks. An incandescent yellow collar fictitiously embroidered itself brilliantly around his neck while a whimsical shade of bright orange stained the underside of his bill.

Most defiant, Mum continued in her sniffing, pushing her snout up against the marine bird's tiny head. "Are you the Docta?" she asked.

CRUNCH! The penguin straightaway pecked her hard on the snout.

SMACK! The mad seal belted the impertinent bird directly in the belly, hurling him high in the air where he sailed through the air until he eventually plopped down on a pile of sharp and icy rubble. All at once, the enraged bird started hopping up and down on its golden-colored webbed feet as if it were standing on a pile of burning coals.

"*Aeeeeeeee!*" it screamed, approaching the mad seal, continuing to bounce angrily. Undaunted in the least, the mum seal belched in the penguin's face and tried to swing at him, but this time the hopping bird was ready for her punch. With a quick flip, the bird jumped, bouncing higher and higher all around her, propelling itself off her blubbery sides. "*Kitch, me, kitch me*—if you can!" it taunted in a flustered state, running and bouncing in circles about the mad seal who kept snapping at him with her drooling jaws. "*Aeeeeeeeee!*" screamed the fatuous penguin with the bright yellow dickey.

Mum found that she could not keep up with the blasted thing. This impossible penguin was incredibly fast. However, she would not desist in her attempts to pulverize this pestilent dwarf. One way or another, she was going to get him. All at once, the popping penguin jumped unusually high, spinning, and landed right in front of the small white seal that was still partially hidden behind the ice block.

On seeing the pup, the penguin deliberately came to a halt, saying, "Hey, pretty little collar there!" Mesmerized by the shining stone around Miracle's neck, the bird went on to say, "I must have it! I simply must!" It squawked before bringing the stone into its mouth, making crunching wet sounds with its garish beak. It twirled it around over and over again, tasting it with its tongue as if to eat the purple curiosity. Miracle nervously pulled away, hoping somehow to discourage it, continuing with his backward retreat. Watching the whole thing and waiting for the exact moment, Mum anxiously made her move, delighting in getting a second chance to squash the pesky little deviant. The penguin, which was still in the process of yanking the stone from Miracle's throat, never saw the seal coming. With one enormous shift of her enormous rump, Mum nonchalantly plopped herself firmly down on the obstinate bird dressed in the indelible tuxedo sporting the outrageously colored dickey, silencing and covering him up with one swift squat.

Although grateful for her help, Miracle shot Mum another of his disappointed glares, wishing she would have used an alternative method of discouraging the bird's persistence. He cautiously wriggled up to the mad seal's backside, listening to the maniacal screams coming from beneath the many folds of her enormous weight.

Realizing that the time had come to salvage the situation, the blue whale began with a humble request of his own. "I beg your pardon, madam, but I would most assuredly be indebted to anything you wish if you would find it in your consideration to allow my friend his freedom. I do apologize for his inexcusable conduct."

With a lopsided smirk across her snout, Mum looked at the tremendous whale towering before her. "And if I do, you will help the white seal find his mother?"

The whale nodded his enormous head approvingly. "I will do my best in doing so. Perhaps that is the reason our paths have crossed. For reasons unclear to me, I can almost remember dreaming about this moment, déjà vu; I believe it is called, all having to do with lost seals and faraway places."

"How nice for you," Mum answered with a silly smile stamped on her messed-up snout.

"It is odd, but for many years now I have dreamed of a baby seal that wore a purple stone and yet never fully understood why. Curious, isn't it?"

"Of course it isn't, especially when you have the sassy hot mum to guide you! You see, the white seal has lost his mama. We must travel to the heart of the sea. The magical horned creature that lives there can provide us with the means and knowledge of finding her. And I know that only blue chanters such as yourself have the eye and the ear to find just such a place, and just such a creature. You will take us there, and we will find the answers to what we need to know, simple, aye, fishy!"

"Madame, surely you are not referring to the very creature that the chanters have named *Kellis?*"

"Why, yes yes, I am! Smart fishy!"

"But-but . . . I am not sure if I can do such a thing. Such an undertaking could prove to be very dangerous for everyone involved," explained the blue whale. "Besides, how is it that you know of such things?"

Mum smacked her lips and started to play Clap-Clap, wriggling on top of the squirming penguin, his muffled shrieks filling the air. "Don't you think I know everything that goes on in this ocean? Best make up your mind—and be quick about it, or your cranky little traveling imp won't be fit for traveling anymore, if you know what I mean, fishy love."

"Oh please, I must ask you to reconsider such an act."

"Why should I let him go if you will not help us?"

"But I did not say I would not."

"Then you will take us to the Kellis?"

The whale thought for a moment before answering. "First you must release my little friend."

"But he bit me, the bloody little twit!"

"He meant no harm, I assure you. Please allow him to go free, or he will surely suffocate," begged the gentle giant.

Mum looked deep into the whale's mysterious and sparkling violet eyes. Overwhelmed with the sudden urge to comply, she plainly smiled. There was something quite soothing and yet commanding about the shiny dark blue creature whom even she could not find it in herself to defy.

Pulling her rump across the snow, still dragging the bird, the mum leaned in toward the enormous whale's massive lips and gave it a hard smacking kiss. "There!" she barked, *"sealed with a kiss!"* Then lowering her head to the place where the smothered shrieks were rattling against the walls of her blubber, she smirked. "The bloody pinhead's whinny cries were getting on me last nerves anyways!" Pausing, she addressed the shrieking bird covered beneath her girth. "Go on, get out, ya codswalloping bloomin' crybaby!" With another shift of her back end, Mum bilked a large spongy part of her hanging blubber. It made a loud popping noise, snapping and fizzing as if she were expelling something obscene deep inside her bowels.

Instantly, the penguin scooted out from his horrendous imprisonment of sweaty seal flesh, consisting of offensive pungency and slimy excretions. *"Get it a-waaaaaaay!"* wailed the bird, desperate to catch his breath. "Did you see that? She tried to kill me! She tried to kill me that stupid, fat hump-pig—tried to kill me, and she made a nasty stink right in my face!"

"Now, Mulgrew," calmed the whale, "control yourself, mate. As your captain, I must ask you to conduct yourself in an honorable and seaworthy fashion."

"But she sat on me and stunk! Fat sea cow, she nearly squashed me!"

"Yes but only after you provoked her."

"But she tried to kill me!"

The blue whale tilted his head, apparently not buying into the penguin's excuse for his behavior, and this upset the penguin considerably. "Oh, here it comes! I knew it! I knew it!" he squawked. "It's always Mulgrew's fault, isn't it! Almost ten years of sailing the silver sea together, and I am still the patsy for everything that goes wrong! It's always my fault, my fault, *my fault!*"

From a distance, Mum kept right on glaring at the seething penguin that was wiping all the disgusting slime from his soiled penguin suit. *"Mulgrew . . . ,"* Mum scoffed. "What kind of name is *Mulgrew?*"

"Get it a-waaaaaay!" snapped the bird, scooting farther from the mad seal.

"Madam," calmly said the whale, "I am extremely privileged to introduce to you my sailing comrade and friend, Mr. Mickey Millie Mugsy Mulgrew, first mate."

Immediately, Mum busted out loud with laughter, smacking her backside on the ice. *"Millie?* You've got to be kidding!"

"It's Mulgrew to you! Fat head!" the bird sneered from a considerable distance, just fuming with contempt.

"That's not what the whale said!" Mum jeered. "There was a *Millie* somewhere in there! And I must say it fits you to a tee! *Hahaha!"* she roared.

"Millie just happens to be my mother's name, for your simpleminded information!" squawked the infuriated bird. "Every self-respecting penguin has his mother's name incorporated into his official title. It is mandatory, not that it's any of your smelly business! Captain!" screamed the bird, redirecting his words to the gigantic whale. "Can we leave this place now? We have kept our part of the bargain. We have reunited the walruses with the seal! Our job here is done! Now, can we ship ahoy, do ya suppose?"

"I'm afraid it's not as simple as that. Things have changed for us, dear friend."

The penguin glanced toward the mad seal then toward Miracle, who was still cowering behind the ice block. "Oh, you don't really mean that we are stuck with these clowns, do you?"

"I have given my word," Kishk answered, "and yet, it is not the only reason I am compelled to do this. Somehow, some way, I know that it is my destiny—our destiny."

"Here we go again!" scoffed the bird. "Captain Kishk, the naive philanthropist, why is it that whenever you decide to save the world, I always end up paying for it? Will you tell me that, please, will you? Thank you very much!"

"This is very different, Mulgrew—very different."

Just then, and for reasons unknown to him, Miracle wriggled away from the ice block, rendering himself thoroughly vulnerable before the behemoth before him. The white seal could now plainly see that the giant with the violet eyes possessed a most unusual coating beneath his massive self. His underside was much lighter in color and was striped perfectly within the borders of milky and blue horizontal markings, making him appear three-dimensional while slowly dancing within the depths of the chilly currents. The whale looked at the tiny whitecoat and smiled gently. Miracle looked at the fantastic creature and offered a rather nervous smile back. It was then that Kishk began an unhurried decline, lowering his head, preparing to allow the walrus duo the opportunity to slip off and return to the icy ground below.

Anxious to be near the floes again, the assertive young tooth walker shimmied over to the slippery sliding zone of the whale's magnificent head, thoroughly enjoying the ride down, cascading freely and wonderfully toward the sea, splashing playfully into a shimmering slush pool of his own. *"Weeee!"* he sang, hitting the slushy waters, creating a massive explosion, disappearing inside its frothy burst.

Crumpels did not fare as well, for as she made her descent from the whale's head, aiming for a departure filled with elegance and poise, she only floundered into an absurd tumble, crashing down sideways, smashing foolhardy into an open ice hole, hitting her head on its ridge before going under. She did not, however, stay under for very long, for in a flash, she resurfaced, gasping for air, squirting spurts of lengthy shafts of ice water from her whiskered face. Further humiliation prevented her from looking toward the mad seal, which of course had seen her untimely mishap and remained preoccupied with howls of laughter. Poo-Coo merely growled in Mum's direction, exposing his still growing tusks. Miracle watched Crumpels grasp the sides of the icy lip of the crest with her tusks, wooing soft whistles of nervousness while hoisting out from the slush hole. Relieved that she was once again on solid land, Miracle moved his eyes back toward the blue whale. He found that when he looked upon the giant creature, most of his apprehension toward the great leviathan had vanished, for the whale's kind words had comforted him.

Presently, the white seal found himself wriggling bravely toward the blue chanter, making sure that before he dared speak, he would clear his throat so as not to squeak. In his continuous gaze up toward the whale spanning endlessly above, Miracle nearly fell backward, trying to take in the unbelievable scope of things. Soon, all became acutely still, all except for the unwavering sounds of the waters slapping against the folds of the scattered ice pools. "Hello, sir," the tiny white seal managed to utter with a constrained and nervous tone. "You were with me the day that I lost my mama?" he courageously asked.

"Yes," replied the whale with a deep, velvety voice. "Yes, I was."

"Thank you for saving me," Miracle meekly said, lowering his furry white head, bending the plumpness that cushioned there. Swallowing, he prepared to ask the ultimate question that he knew he must. His heart began to stir with a steady and intense beat. "Can you truly find her?"

"I'm certainly going to give it a whale of a try," Kishk vowed, furthering the broadening of his already massive smile, this time looking toward the Mad Mum seal, his mouth tightening with a nervous twitch. "Besides, I don't think your faithful guardian would have it any other way," he confessed, whispering, quickly losing the twitch, replacing it fully with his fantastic smile again conveying his true sincerity. "If your mama is out there, I will find her, small one. I promise."

For the first time, Miracle genuinely believed it. If anyone could find his mother, it would certainly be the shiny blue giant named Kishk. He just knew it.

Mum noisily rumbled up toward the whale, and Poo-Coo recoiled when she passed him, throwing her another cutting glare, waiting for his mother to join him. Mum stared long and hard at the gigantic whale, her head barely coming up to the bottom of his incredible mouth. "It is not by chance but fate that has brought us together, fishy. I have known this from the moment I first laid eyes on you, as you must have known, judging from the dreams you were given, love."

Mulgrew rolled his eyes. "Now, what is she going on about?" he squawked from afar, his voice barely audible.

"Hush," the whale commanded. "She speaks the truth. I have had dreams . . . many dreams."

Mum readily smiled. "Then we have much to do, Mr. Jumbo Fishy, much to do!"

Miracle faintly smiled and wriggled over to the mad harpie, rubbing the soft white pelt of his head against her cheek. Mum joyfully snuggled next to him, drawing him close. Once again, the penguin dared to make his way over to them both. He was back for another look at the mysterious stone around the pup's neck. Finding and claiming the precious jewels of the sea was a constant compulsive obsession of the penguin. He could not help himself. His disorder would often render him helpless to the surrounding dangers of the deep, remaining oblivious to them when it came to any new shiny discovery uncovered from the sea. Zeroing in on the purple medallion, Mulgrew suddenly caught a quick glimpse of the mad seal that was glaring most dastardly in his direction, her teeth exposed, ready to strike. Startled, he abruptly gained his senses. For now, he would merely stare at the pretty purple stone and the irresistible white seashells surrounding it. He would have to admire it from afar until the time presented itself when he would snatch it away, forever to be his, where he would add it to his many cherished and hidden treasures.

Kishk looked down at the white seal from his towering place in the misty sky, his eyes directly rendering over their own share of questions. "Tell me, this odd stone that you wear, it is filled with many secret wonders, is it not?"

Taking over as she usually did, Mum answered for the pup, knowing fully that she only had a few more moments to communicate to the gentle giant before her madness fully returned. She told him of the evil man-beast that killed her child and of the wicked woman who cursed her with eternal madness for destroying her mate. "But I fooled her!" Mum giggled. "I took the sacred tear from her!"

The whale was suddenly filed with anxiousness and trepidation. "Then the legend is true? The first tear ever shed upon the earth . . . the tear of Her Majesty . . . the very tear of the sea herself?"

"Yep yep yep, you got it, bub!"

"But-but—"

"Oh, do stop fumbling, it is most unbecoming."

"But the sacred tear is believed to be the most cherished and sought-after force in the entire world. Its powers are beyond anything imagined!"

"Right again, fishy!"

"But . . . but . . . the tear has been lost for many, many years. How in the world—"

"It was the man-beasts," Mum explained. "They rediscovered it. I merely swiped it when they were not looking, stupid lip-lumps!"

"But-but-but—"

"Oh, there you go again! Clownfish, your stammering has grown tiresome. Now, we haven't much time. The evil man-beast will continue to search for the tear. She will be returning to Sealssong. That is why we must find the seal's mother as soon as possible. That is why you must take us to the Kellis!"

"But no one has ever seen this creature, not really. Many chanters have tried, but most, if not all, have failed. At least none has ever returned to tell about it."

"Oh, do stop being such a scare baby! We will find her, and she will tell us all about the tear, but more importantly, she will tell us where to find the white seal's mother. She is all-knowing, this Kellis person, is she not?"

"Well yes, that is what has been said of her, but like I said, I am not sure if the creature even exists."

"Enough! I say she exists, and that is final!" Mum barked. "Listen, Sasquatch, you're really starting to irk me, you know that?" She slumped down in an awkward squat, the madness returning full strength.

From not so far away, protected by the sharp edges of a nearby ice block, the penguin, Mulgrew, became outraged. "Hey, don't talk to the captain like that!" he chirped, quickly scooting back toward the whale, screeching, hopping in front of his commander in chief. "I must confess that stone certainly intrigued me at first, far more than most, but that is one little trinket we best steer clear of now that we know its true origin! And besides, sir, if we agree to help this—this whacked-out hump-pig find the kid's mother, we'll be stuck with the whole freaky bunch of them for who knows how long! I say we set out for sea at once before this thing goes any further. Sorry, folks! Nothing personal," Mulgrew said, addressing the listening crowd before him. "But it's bye-bye time! Best of luck to you all! May the winds be at your back, may the sun shine on your snoots and snouts and whiskers and mouths and your tusks, husks and flippers, and whatever else it is you have, and may you prosper and live long! Etcetera, etcetera, etcetera! Now, our goodbyes having been said, Sir Captain Kishk, I recommend strongly that we be on our way!"

"Mulgrew," sternly called the whale, "we agreed to help them, no convenient justifications please!"

"You agreed! I never even—"

"Mulgrew—"

"What's this really all about, sir, I ask you?" Mulgrew shrilled. "It goes against everything we believe, everything we promised to leave behind. Isn't that why we took up sailing in the first place? Removing ourselves from the norm of everyday living, wasn't that it? We are nomads! Free spirits! We answer to no one! We have no boundaries to confine us. At least that is what I thought!" puffed the shrieking penguin, proceeding to rant and rave, his tiny face turning sour with further vexation. "A sailor's life is a life of noncommitment and independence! 'Come and see the world, Mulgrew, come with me, come and journey on the very wings of the winds themselves! Let us belong to no one but the sea herself, Mulgrew!' That's what you said! That's what you said! Isn't that what you said?"

"Yes," reluctantly agreed the whale.

"Then what are you doing? Why do we always have to play the good Samaritans? Consistently stopping to help some poor good-for-nothing slob! We are sailors, not nursemaids for lost pups, walruses, and crazy, mad things!"

"We are servants of Her Majesty the Sea, and these are her subjects, I suggest that you remember that."

"But why us, tell me, why always us?"

"Because that is the way of the blue chanter, and as a member of my crew, I would have hoped by now you would have adopted such a philosophy. There is more to the sea than collecting trinkets, stones, and seashells, my friend."

"I know that! Why did you have to go and say that?"

"Because perhaps you had forgotten that helping those less fortunate than ourselves is what we are all about! That is the way of the chanters, it has been this way since the beginning, and it will remain so for always."

The uncontrolled penguin wearing the flashy dickey went on with his incessant protest. "But if we agree to help these—*these*—strange individuals, and I do mean strange," Mulgrew spit, addressing the mum seal with a nasty glare, "I just know it will be our downfall! They admitted to having stolen the sacred tear, for crying out loud! You know it has some kind of terrible curse on it! We'll be doomed—*doomed!*"

Once again, the whale's expression saddened into an even more remorseful sight. "You are free to leave, old friend, I will understand, but as for me, I shall try to help the white seal find his mother."

"*Aaeeeeeeeee!*" screamed the penguin. "Stop it, stop it—stop it! Just don't say anymore! I'm only going to give in anyways, so save the lectures, the philosophies, and the rest of your guilt trips for another time. I give up! You win! But for the record, just know that I was against it from the beginning! You'll see that only tragedy will come of this! Tragedy and doom! Doom and tragedy! You just wait and see!"

ORIGIN OF LIGHTS

Tension was building, and it would go on this way indefinitely, so it would appear.

Mum belched again and then slumped forward while wearing a ridiculous expression on her drool-dripping face. She smacked her lips and looked half cocked at the bird. "Edgy little thing, isn't it?"

"Listen, hump-pig, let's get one thing straight right from the start! You stay as far away from me as possible, and I'll do likewise! Do you understand? Am I making myself perfectly clear—*whack-O?*"

"Indubitably," Mum scoffed, slurping up more disgusting drool right before she lay backward, clapping ridiculously all the while.

Kishk spoke up without delay, placing his violet gaze on the clapping seal before him, speaking louder than normal to override her clip-clapping ruckus. "My dear madam, what my friend is trying to say, in his own humble way, is that we would both be honored to help you and the white pup."

"Yeah, that's just what I was trying to say!" the peeved penguin sarcastically growled, quickly turning his indelible tuxedo body, shunning the whale and the others, once more scampering hurriedly over to the nearest ice crest. *"Whatever!"* he sassed, thoroughly disgusted with the entire situation, kicking about fragmented ice chips into the slush pool, making an extremely loud screeching sound each time his webbed foot struck the broken chunks.

Now it was about this time Crumpels was beginning to feel left out from the whale's undivided attention. Feeling a sting of jealousy ripple down her spine, she decided to wriggle over toward the incredibly massive creature, her face carrying an overexaggerated look of vulnerability. "My dear Captain Kishk, what shall happen to us now? Where do we go from here, boop-boop-dee-dear?"

As usual, Mum answered boldly, directing the sequence of events that would soon take place. With an unequivocal and exclusive purpose in mind, she began informing her diverse audience. "Again, nitwit, I'll tell you what happens now. First of all, we are to return to the populated portion of Sealssong, the main nursery, itself. You, Ms. Crumpels, will remain there to watch over the white seal and your annoying snot-nose brat."

"How dare you," Crumpels roared, "and how dare you tell me what to do and what not to do! I am perfectly capable of—"

"Look," Mum spit, "we all know that you got the hots for the big guy, but I'm afraid your pathetic little crush will just have to wait. We have more important things to do than worry about your embarrassing nonexistent love affair!"

"You insufferable lunatic pig, boop-boop-dee-dig, why, I have a good mind to—"

"Clog it up, fool!" Mum barked, not in the least bit interested in what the walrus had to say. "When you all have been safely returned to the nursery, the whale, his sidekick and I will set off for the channel of tunnels. From there, we will continue toward our destination—the Origin of Lights."

All at once, the whale became unusually quiet, his enormous face taking on the semblance of solemnity. His voice was exceedingly strange now, almost fearful. *"Ahem* . . . you know of such a place?"

"Of course."

An even more intense shadow of awe quickly transpired over his incredible features. "But how? Such things were never told to your kind. They could have never been understood. It is against the sacred decree of the sea for anyone but the blue chanters to know of this." He continued with a whispered voice, "We alone are granted such knowledge. I do not understand. You could not possibly fathom such things. They are forbidden to you."

"And so was the sacred tear, but I managed to swipe it, didn't I, fishy love?" bragged the mad seal. "Guess after carrying it around in me mouth, some of its secrets rubbed off, aye, Jumbo?" She laughed, clapping her flippers. "Besides, after having a wicked spell put on me by an incredibly evil devil woman, where most of my brains were sucked out and substituted for seaweed, anything is possible . . . *N'est ce pas?*"

"Then you truly are bewitched," marveled the whale.

"Guilty!" sang the mum. "I am also well aware that you chanters can see things others cannot, such as the *Origin of Lights.*"

"Yes, but such a region is very dangerous, and there is no guarantee that I will be able to take us through its portal or take us out again."

"You really are a pain in the seal butt, you know that, fishy? *Enough!*"

From over near the ice crest, the penguin spoke up. "I'm telling you, sir, you best reconsider. She's a nut case, a real nut case! Besides, that tear or whatever it is, has a curse on it and it is bad news, just like her! Why, even if we do find this creature, this Kellis, after she finds that we have the tear, she might strike us all down dead! With the curse and all, I'm surprised the puny pup ever put the accursed thing around his neck in the first place!"

"I put it there, tweedy!" Mum brazenly admitted, squirting a streak of nose mucus over toward the bird. "And for your information, *Millie,* the seal will be just fine just as long as he keeps the bloomin' thing on!"

"And if he takes it off, what then, whack-O?"

"Boy, howdy, that shows how much you know! It's no big deal, daffy duck!"

"No big deal, then what is it?"

Mum growled. "He will simply die a horrible traitorous, unthinkable death, that's all, so do sashay—away, little twit," she spat again, sticking out her wiggling tongue, turning around, shaking her plump rump in his direction. "You're beginning to really bore me, tweedy."

Miracle felt a sharp tingle split down his spine while wriggling over toward the whale. Gulping down his fear, he said, "She speaks the truth. Something inside me knows that I must never ever remove the stone no matter what."

The penguin glared at the mad harpie and then quickly scampered over to Miracle. "There! Now you know just what a freaking lunatic your snot-slurping nursemaid is! She knew that she would sentence you to a horrible death if she placed that thing about you, and yet she still went ahead and did it! What kind of demented hump-pig does a thing like that?"

Mum snarled. "You need to step away, little bird."

"She did it to help me. She did it because she loves me," Miracle cried.

"*Loves you?*" screeched the seabird. "She killed you! Can't you see that?"

All at once, Mum slammed herself down upon the ice and pulled tight on the silly bonnet's tie strings. She scrunched her features into a disturbing mass of wrinkles and determinedly went toward the white seal, looking straight up toward the whale, her eyes rolling back in her head, her madness consuming her. "I'mmmmm—*hot-tah!* Simply hot!" she seductively teased, her voice all congested, still sounding as she had a dreadful cold, and she shook her rump again, bucking against the ice. "Now let us stop all this gibberish and be on our way!" she commanded, no longer holding to a smile, but only a dripping snout of mucus, spittle, and drool.

The whale, which was still contemplating the entire bizarre situation, suddenly rose from within the waters, coming closer to shore, bringing another sudden flood with him. Eventually, the water returned to the slushy pools, and the walruses, seals, and the tiny seabird soon found themselves all gazing up toward the mammoth creature.

"Come," Kishk announced. "I have decided that it is time for us to depart." Lowering his massive head, he waited for the mad seal to wriggle before him. "You shall be the first to board, my gracious lady," he gallantly offered. "In your madness, you have once more reminded me of the sacred truths I had forgotten." He sighed before laughing to himself, his mighty head bent before Mum. "I am not certain how you have achieved this miraculous capacity, be it through the unintentional mistakes of those irreparable monsters that nearly destroyed you, or if in truth you are some lunatic destined to take us to our demise, I cannot say . . . but I believe you. Heaven help me," the whale confessed smilingly. "I may be in my dotage, but I believe you." Clearing his throat before addressing the mad seal one more time, the whale went on to say, "Welcome, astonishing creature. Come upon me and sit at the very pinnacle of all the others."

Mum giggled, now playing Clap-Clap, glancing around at the walruses and the penguin. Save for Miracle, all wore a sick face of utter contempt. Mum stuck her tongue at the young walrus, snubbing its mother, showing her sharp teeth at the seething bird right before kissing the white seal on his head before preparing to be the first to make her way up the mammoth face of the bowing blue chanter. Positively glowing in the limelight, she only glanced back once, thoroughly enjoying her prestigious wriggle up the slippery snout of the whale, her head thrown back with pride and arrogance.

Poo-Coo could not hold back any longer. *"Ppppllttwthppwtthh!"* he jealously spat, his long, stringy walrus spittle just about reaching the climbing mad thing.

Kishk waited while the mum situated herself on top of his head before addressing her once more. "Are you comfortable, dear lady?"

"Oh yes, I can see everything from up here, fishy love!"

"It's the best seat in the house. However, in all fairness, there are still so many questions I too must ask if I truly am to be of help."

"Codswallop, you know all you need to know!" Mum barked. "You'll have to find out whatever it is you want after we have departed. Now stop annoying me with your bloody uncertainties, fish!"

The whale stood silently corrected and then took a few moments to collect his thoughts before addressing the others. He began with another of his massive, but warm smiles.

"My dear friends, as it was told to me by my father and his father, and so on and so on, the Origin of Lights speaks of the beginning of the end of time, or time as we believe it to be. For it is said that one day a chanter will go to the Origin of Lights for the greatest challenge of his life and the lives of all who dwell in this snowy land called Sealssong. He will change it for the good or forever lose it to the darkness. For many years ago, far too many for any of us possibly to conceive, sacred wonders were left here by strange beings from another world. Wonders left in order that a great prophecy would be recognized. These wonders were hidden in the stones, in the waters, in the trees, in the wind, and in the hearts of the chosen ones themselves, the very harp seals of Sealssong—the purest of all!" The violet eyes of the whale suddenly grew wide, filling with misty emotion and awe. "So you see, perhaps, just perhaps, the world may actually end . . . or begin . . . with the likes of one innocent and very small white seal pup."

"Asinine poppycock!" tweaked the penguin.

Mum had heard enough by this time. She wriggled as far as she could before nearly falling off the bridge of the whale's nose. Looking down at him, she snorted, "Let's get this show on the road, shall we?"

Kishk remained smiling, loving the seal's unique tenacity for saucy determination.

"Wait an icy dicey minute, hump-pig!" protested the penguin. "What did I tell you? Just where do you get off giving orders like that!"

"Oh, do shut up with your gobbledygook chirping, wimpy pansy!" Mum yelped from way atop the whale's head. "Go and make yourself useful by gathering the others in order that we can begin our journey!" With this, the mad seal fell backward and started up a quick game of Clap-Clap, her flippers beating a mile a minute.

The penguin glared at the mad harpie from way below, barely visible on the icy ground; he was that small. "I hate that fat, crazy seal!" he growled, rounding up the others, aggressively motioning his tiny flippers toward the direction of the whale's incredible mouth. "This is absolutely, without a doubt, unquestionably, emphatically, positively the lamest, stupidest thing I have ever been asked to do!" All at once, Kishk, who was still only partially exposed from inside the great regions of the sculptures of drifting ice formations, proceeded to rise further, exhibiting even more of his massive proportions that of which were not yet halfway realized.

Overwhelmed by the whale's unimaginable size, Miracle found that the rapid beating of his heart had returned, and with it came the overpowering sense of complete amazement. The blue chanter's incredible size and weight remained only moments on the surrounding ice ridges before instantly crushing the icy lips bordering the slush pools, giving way from the pressure of his enormousness, splitting them apart. The many half-moon shapes of the ice unlocked, enlarging the slushy terrain further still. The walruses, the penguin, and Miracle quickly picked up the beat, all nervously moving toward their enormous friend who patiently waited, bobbing excessively while vast amounts of water rushed past him, flooding the immediate grounds.

Eventually, both Crumpels and Poo-Coo made it to the top despite their awkwardness and clumsiness. Selecting their chosen area, they began to circle around the way sleepy puppies do just before they settle down for sleep, Poo-Coo nestling in the many folds of his mother. Once again, the whale smiled down on the tiny white seal.

"It begins now, young friend," he said, his voice encased in its familiar authoritative tone. "Are you ready for what awaits us both? I imagine it is far greater than either one of us suspects," Kishk declared.

Miracle felt another tingle wiggle down his spine. "I 'spect," he uttered smilingly, still looking up into the gigantic face of the fantastic blue beast before him. Nearly slipping off the tiny chunk of ice he managed to come by, the brave white seal struggled to stay afloat. Mulgrew, who also remained situated on his own floating iceberg, swiftly hopped onto the whale's lip and turned to look at the white seal floating before him. He spoke to the whale, suspiciously looking at the tiny seal with the pretty purple stone wrapped around his furry neck. "We're doomed. You do know that, don't you?"

Unaffected by the indignant penguin, Kishk rolled his eyes. "Best get aboard, Mulgrew, and see that the others are comfortable. I'll see to our young friend here," the whale promised.

"Well, excuse me for worrying!" snapped the sarcastic seabird. Turning around and jumping forward and sliding on his round soft belly, he angrily shot himself up the snout of the whale. Mum was waiting for him when he reached the top, and she was gawking at him with a most moronic expression, drool still running down her nose. Sucking it up but hardly succeeding, she began to make obscene gestures with her lips again, smacking them hard, pretending to blow kisses toward the irritating penguin gliding past her.

"Aaaaeeee! Get it—a-waaaaay!" Mulgrew screeched, scooting himself as far away as he possibly could from the horrible, mad, drooling thing. With one propelling spring, the projecting seabird effortlessly landed toward the rear of the great whale, there in a secluded spot where he had gathered an assortment of barnacles. Flopping himself on top of the pile, the bird immediately began chewing on his private stash of marine crustaceans, trying to calm his fury.

Miracle once again struggled to look directly into the vast universe of the hulking whale. He felt himself become dizzy and faint and nearly fell off the floating iceberg again.

"Please, do not be afraid," quickly interjected Kishk. "I will not let you fall."

Miracle nervously nodded, still feeling the dizziness fall around him. Slowly, he nestled down on the iceberg, knowing that if he fell into the sea he would drown. Carefully, he placed one single flipper into the icy water and began paddling himself closer to the awaiting chanter. All the while he paddled, he could only ponder just how incredibly large this creature was. Continuing to strain his taut neck muscles while attempting to take in some of the whale's dinosaurian cranium, to the dwarfed seal, Kishk appeared bigger than all Sealssong.

Trying extra hard not to sink the raft and the seal, Kishk asked, "You're not afraid now, are you?"

Miracle realized that he was trembling uncontrollably, but strived to remain brave. Now situated smack in front of the whale's humongous lips, he could no longer take in any reasonable amount of the whale's form. Kishk was just too tremendous to begin with, let alone at this close range. So for the time being, Miracle would just have to settle with conversing with the whale's extremely vast, particularly fleshy, and endless wobbly lips.

"Would you like to know a very special secret?" Kishk's lips asked.

Miracle shyly nodded.

"Being a chanter, I am somewhat of a connoisseur of music. I have sung every concerto conceived, from the gentlest of lullabies and sweetest euphonious works, to the boldest of grandiose and flamboyant operas, right down to the most fragile and intricate of arias ever imagined. Furthermore, with this gift of song, I can also sing and hear music others cannot, from faraway places, as well as regions and things normally not believed to hold such astounding resonance."

As the white seal continued to maintain his balance on the iceberg, he cocked his head sideways, unsure as to what the whale was saying to him.

Kishk widened his shining violet eyes, crossing them, staring down upon the purple stone gracing the white seal's neck. "I can hear it," softly disclosed the whale.

Miracle quickly stared down at the stone resting against his chest. A small glow was beginning to come from its center. He felt it warm against him.

"Did you know it was singing?" Kishk's lips asked.

Miracle shook his head, his huge black eyes opening wide as his reasoning prepared for almost anything.

Kishk cordially granted the white seal another of his famous and overwhelming grins. "You see," spoke the talking, truly incredibly prodigious lips, "the magic of the tear must have taken on the spirit of your heart, for I can presently hear its intricate and most delicate musical modulations singing out quite clearly now." The lips paused for a moment, listening. "Quite delicate, I should say." Momentarily the lips stopped moving, delighting in listening some more. Then just like before, they commenced with their wobbly movement. "Yes . . . ," the dancing lips rejoiced, "Most delicate, indeed."

Miracle looked at the stone again. Although he could not hear it, he felt the glow tickle his heart, and he knew that whatever the tear was doing, it sure felt as if it were singing. A confirmation of acknowledgment and pride beamed from the small white seal's angelic face. Pumping up his furry chest, this time, Miracle took pleasure in showing off his unprecedented embellishment.

Again, the lips spoke. "There are other secrets I will share with you, but we will leave them for another time. Right now I must make sure that you and the walruses are taken safely to the borders of Sealssong, back to the nursery. Come!" commanded the fantastic giant.

Miracle shyly nodded; he waited as the lips drew even closer to him, their stretching blue flesh almost touching him. He nervously held on to the iceberg, waiting for the whale to bow his head. Opening his tremendous mouth, Kishk allowed his tongue to unravel and carpet forth in front of the young seal. An elongated form coated with an opaque pasty film of sputum outstretched itself on the iceberg while the blue chanter tried to verbalize as best as possible. "Ahhl-a-ord!" muttered the lips.

Miracle quickly braced himself with his front flippers, lifting himself off the tiny iceberg. At last he was on the surface of the giant's fleshy drawbridge. Once on board of the sticky tongue, the seal shivered, having never felt anything like it before. Truth be known, he did not like the experience of this slimy, wet thing at all, not in the least. Being the whale's tongue remained painted with an oily overcoat, his grip and position were considerably decisive and unsteady, but before he could change his mind and retreat, Miracle realized that the creature was elevating him to the very brim of its widespread lips. Without any coaxing or further assistance, the white seal hastily took the initiative in scurrying himself up the brink of the whale's mouth, slipping several times because of the clinging oily residue from the icky tongue. After repetitive shakes from his rear flippers so that he could somewhat remove the slippery substance, Miracle finally reached the top.

Finally, the unequaled gathering on top of the whale's roomy head was complete and ready for departure. Discerningly, Miracle joined the already snoozing Crumpels and Poo-Coo. Although his first impulse was to reunite himself with the mad seal, he soon reconsidered finding that she was tottering dangerously near the extreme edges of the whale's extended forehead. Not wishing to jeopardize his well-being any further by chancing any kind of *"seal overboard!"* casualty, and because he was most anxious to leave the isolated region of slushy ridges and fading misty phantoms, he decided to stay put.

Nevertheless, Kishk still attempted to caution the mad seal of the apparent dangers in which she placed herself while stationing herself so near the borders of his slick confines, but she belligerently scoffed at him. "Back off, slimy!" she snarled. "You're gonna certainly need somebody up here to help you navigate this bloomin' expedition, sugar cakes! So stop with the codswalloping blabber, jumbo lips, and let's have at it already!"

Not wishing to provoke her further, the whale raised his beautifully painted violet eyes in silent prayer, imploring good thoughts for Mum as well as him and all the other passengers he presently carried above.

Alas . . . it was time to go.

Ice gurgled and sizzled everywhere, shifting and abrading while he backed himself out from the icy port. Soon the ridges became entirely flooded over from the whale's sensational movements. Continuing to break free from the confines of the frigid ports, the governing sea did not procrastinate. In only moments, she devoured the remaining ice, covering and pulling it under the currents, drowning and claiming it all for herself.

SLEEPY BUBBLES

It was dawn when the sailing menagerie finally made their way well out of the sinking ice port. The sky had turned from a misty yellow to a reddish orange haze, and it would seem that the ghostly vapors had ended, now raining shafts of lights from above, shining brightly over the whale.

They were at last on their way back to the nursery.

The walruses remained persistent in their slumbering, uproariously snoring, sleeping straight through any further disturbances brought on by the unexpected actions of the mad seal. Meanwhile, Mulgrew remained far removed from the others. Deliberately alienating himself near the tail end of the sailing giant, the small seabird eventually dozed off among the gathering of his guarded and collected variations of tasty barnacles. Engaged within a well-accepted sleep, the, penguin was more than gracious of having been temporarily spared the bothersome task of being plagued with bumbling walruses, mad seals, cursed stones, and ancient prophecies. As for the Mad Mum seal of Sealssong, she had righteously remained at the hull of the whale and was in the middle of one of her rambling sessions, barking out directional commands while Miracle engaged in the excitement of the voyage.

It seemed much longer to get to the nursery than anyone suspected, but the whale remained steady in his course. Mum gradually gave way to sleep, however determined to keep to her post. It was quite apparent that she would eventually lose her balance, making for an unpleasant and shocking visit with the cold passing waters, but no one, even if they were watching, would dare wake her.

Miracle began to feel queasy from the ride, and despite his unsettled tummy, he wanted to speak further with the spectacular blue chanter. He would not be able to converse with him after returning to the nursery, so now would be his only chance. He would wait until Kishk's movements in the water subsided before daring to make his way toward the whale's spacious forehead. However, the ride continued with its choppiness, so the seal decided not to procrastinate further. Making his way to the front of the whale, he nearly toppled inside a peculiar-looking hole. Not wanting to investigate, he quickly humped away from the curious site, and it was not long before he found the place he wished to be. Slowly, he stretched out his neck, careful not to wriggle too far, terrified of falling overboard. The whale quickly recognized the tiny seal's presence and spoke up immediately.

"Is everything all right, my little sailor?" Miracle did not speak at first, for he suddenly found himself in awe of the whale's tremendousness all over again. "Can't sleep, huh?" Kishk asked.

Miracle shook his head.

"Are you feeling a little seasick?"

"A little," he said with an anxious tone.

Kishk laughed. "Not to worry, it won't be much farther now."

"Oh, that's all right," Miracle quickly answered. "I don't mind. Guess I thought about what you said before, you know, about the secrets."

Kishk could not help but delight in the small harpie's enthusiasm. "I did mention that there were more secrets, didn't I?"

Miracle eagerly nodded.

The chanter's voice seemed to come from nowhere and yet from everywhere. From where Miracle was sitting, he was no longer able to see the whale's wobbly lips; nonetheless, Kishk's voice perfectly encompassed him. "Well, let's see now, where shall I begin?" the whale thought aloud, clearing his throat. "Let me begin by telling you how blue chanters initially received their name and why."

Miracle listened, totally enthralled within the sounds of the whale's distinguished voice.

"Blue chanters received their name because of two very simple facts. One, we are painted the most spectacular shade of ultramarine, if I must say so myself. Secondly, we are blessed with the prolific ability to serenade God's entire kingdom, be they big or small, bird, fish, mammal, or even man himself; wind or rain; sea, land, or sky. Our voice was made to sing to all who wish to listen to our melodious whale song."

Miracle tried to steady himself upon the whale's head, trying not to slide around too much while he asked, "Who is it that named you, your mama?"

Kishk chuckled. "Not exactly," he said lightheartedly. "We call them Alula. Wondrous creatures from faraway places, places we could never imagine. And it would seem that this very phenomenal, quite bewildering, and extraordinary race of beings would eventually find favor with the blue giants of the sea. Legend has it that they were drawn to our sensitive nature and kindly ways. I personally think it was our grand voices, but then again, I may be just a little biased. Nonetheless, for whatever the reason, we were indeed chosen, just as you and all the other children of Sealssong were chosen. For yours is the purest and most innocent of hearts—a heart you must always allow to guide you, no matter how difficult the journey."

"But who are they . . . these . . . Alula?"

"Angelic creatures, so I'm told," Kishk answered. "Creatures having been around way before we were even a twinkle in the brainwork of the universe. Until now, I really have not given the matter much thought or maybe I just stopped believing in them, not sure. However, it is said that they are rare and mystical creatures, and they are quite ancient with incredible birdlike wings, far too magnificent for you or me to understand. Practically, it is said that they are what all goodness and love are made of. Angels, I believe the humans call them."

"This . . . Kellis you talk of," Miracle asked, "is it one of these . . . angels?"

The whale tilted his fantastic head, rolling the pup forward, nearly toppling him over the edge. "Don't rightly know that either. Perhaps she is. She may be the only one of her kind still around."

"Will she help me find my mama?"

"Hope so, at least that's what the mum seal is counting on."

"I want to thank you again," Miracle said, swaying upon the whale's extensive brow. "I mean, for saving my life and all."

"You bet. Can you remember any of it?"

Miracle crunched up his black wet nose and wiggled his long, dark whiskers, thinking over the whale's question. "Yes, I believe I almost can. It's strange, but besides the terrible Teeth Monster, I can remember something else now, but I don't know quite how to explain it. You'll think me silly."

"Go on, no matter how silly it seems."

"Well," the seal said, "I can almost remember, like in a dream, one you can almost recall, hearing singing or humming and clicking and what looked like a sea of bubbles, only they were floating in the air, not in the sea."

"Go on," the whale said, trying to contain his growing smile.

"Well, it's just that I suddenly felt very peaceful, almost happy. And then all at once, I fell asleep. At least that is how I almost remember it."

Immediately, the whale burst into a hardy laugh.

"I knew you would think me silly."

"No no! Not, at all, my sagacious chum. That was just another one of my secrets, a rather unique ability!" boasted the whale.

"I don't understand."

"Yes, my astute harpie," sang the whale. "Besides being a remarkable crooner who possesses a fine and amazing alto, making dreamy bubbles just happens to be among my other hidden talents!"

"Dreamy bubbles?"

"Yes, that is what I refer to them as, and they are not just ordinary bubbles either!"

Miracle was about to say something else, when all at once he stopped. From out of nowhere and quite unexpected, an amazing sensation, along with the familiar clicking and beautiful humming he had only recently recalled, suddenly occurred. There, before him, appeared an army of twirling bubbles, all of them coming straight from the hole in the whale's head, the same hole that he had almost slipped into.

Hundreds and hundreds of rainbow-colored bubbles surrounded him, all of them wrapped up in one melodious, marvelous, magical, musical display, all of them bouncing and wafting effervescently. Their many iridescent and whirling forms blew out from the whale's blowhole, their transparent outlines dancing happily around him, each popping in a sparkling delight of sheer wonder. Then as quickly as they appeared, the dancing bubbles vanished, as did the musical accompaniment that they floated upon.

"Sorry," Kishk uttered in a slow, dying giggle. "I had to stop, otherwise I would not be able to finish telling you about the other part of their delightful secret," he garishly boasted.

"Then it was you, you and your bubbles! I wasn't dreaming, was I? It was you! You did it, the music, the humming, and all those hundreds and hundreds of rainbow-painted bubbles! I remember now! And they do something else besides tickle your nose, don't they!"

"Right you are again, my wise comrade!" the amused whale happily chuckled.

All at once, Miracle began to yawn uncontrollably. The whole bubbling encounter had indeed, as it had once before, left him in such a sleepy daydream state; and as strange as it seemed, just as previously, despite his attempts, the white seal could not stop yawning. No matter how he tried to restrain his wide open-mouthed gapes, he just could not stop. His uncontrolled yawns kept coming, one right after the other.

"Not to worry, little fellow," the, whale reassured. "Their sleepy inducement is just another part of their charm. You are simply experiencing more effects of the secret."

"Just like I did before, the day you saved me?" the small seal expressed with a fading voice, finishing off with another irresistible yawn.

"Yes, as you can tell, just a small dosage can result in a most delectable delirium of debilitation."

"In other words, whoever the bubble's touch can't help falling fast asleep, right?"

"Such a bright young pup!" hailed the whale. "You see, when I saw what was about to happen to you and your friends, I immediately went to your aid. I had to do something to stop that overbearing hooligan from harming you. Instinctively, I headed toward the big bully's side, striking him directly, knocking him off course, certain that my endeavor would discourage any further attacks on his part. However, my attempts failed miserably. If anything, I succeeded in only infuriating the beast further. He was determined to go in for the kill. So I quickly called upon my melodious gift of bubbles and song, and within moments, before the appalling tyrant knew what hit him, that vicious ruffian was sleeping like a baby!"

"Gosh," Miracle yawned, "you can even make Teeth Monsters go straight to sleep!"

"Well yes," bragged the whale. "The ability is unique, a compilation of many high frequencies, you know. Only the blue chanters are able to produce them. The simulated humming sounds consist of thrums and clicking pitches that when combined with our pumped-out whale saliva, via the blowhole, augmented by our melodious voice, produces the most penetrating effervescence that promptly affects the nervous system, thus, ultimately rendering anyone and everyone asleep! The bubbles also add a touch of flamboyant flair, most theatrical, wouldn't you agree?"

"Yes, oh yes!" Miracle exclaimed, concluding with another round of stray yawns. All this, along with all the excitement of the remarkable day, definitely made for one singularly, extremely sleepy little seal pup.

"Don't fight it," warned the whale. "Go with it, now hurry, off with you to join the others while you can."

"But I want to . . . [yawn, yawn, yawn] . . . hear more about secrets and . . . [yawn, yawn, yawn] hear more about . . . [YAWN!)"

"Hurry!" urged Kishk.

"But I'm not in the least bit sleepy," assured the white seal, now hardly able to keep his glazed eyes open for another minute.

"Go on," instructed the whale.

"But I'm much too excited to sleep," Miracle promised, starting up with another slew of spit-shooting yawns.

"We'll save our talk for another time. Now hurry along, there's a good little fellow."

Agreeing, Miracle groggily nodded, but before leaving, as exhausted as he was, the seal found that he would once more ask the whale, "You will find her, my mama?" he said, all sleepily, another yawn bursting across his face.

Smiling, the whale answered, "With designs of a pure and innocent heart, little mate, anything is possible."

Miracle smiled back, his eyes almost closed.

"Now off you go. Pleasant dreams, little one," Kishk offered in a singsong voice.

Lethargically nodding his head, unable to speak, his eyes remaining slitlike, the seal turned and slowly wriggled drunkenly toward the still-snoring Crumpels and Poo-Coo. Continuing on his sleepy way, he once again came upon the whale's dorsal blowhole. In a drowsy state of slumber, he listlessly dropped his head into the opening, groggily wondering if there were any more bubbles left inside. Abruptly, and without warning, the small seal was blasted with a spray of cold mist, stunning him, causing him to hurriedly retreat over toward the sleeping walruses. There, he proceeded to nestle himself inside their circle of spilling blubber. Miracle sneezed several times, coughing and shaking his head, dripping with a heavy dose of sea mist and sleepiness, and it was not long before sleep quickly wrapped itself around the pup. With eyelids drooping pathetically, he tried to pry them open, attempting to gaze over to the place Mum occupied.

Resembling some odd nautical boat decor, the mad seal continued to keep her position at the bow of the gliding whale vessel. Her eyes were closed; however, a nearly unconscious Miracle could still make out that she remained engaged in some kind of sleep-talking jibber-jabber. Rambling incessantly, she went on and on, all the while the crashing currents brushed against the sides of the whale drowning out any nonsensical gibberish that she may have remotely demonstrated.

As Kishk moved through the icy dark waters, the exhausted pup found himself lost in twilight consciousness. He managed to look out into the passing shrouds of mist insisting on dampening his snowy pelt, contributing to the miniature beads of moisture that rapidly formed along the shafts of his black whiskers. He lazily twitched at his nose, forcing the condensation to dribble off his thin bristles, continuing to be hypnotically drawn into the swirling pinks and yellows displaying themselves faraway, somewhere out where the sea kissed the sky.

The whale carried on, making his way swiftly through the rapid freezing currents, breaking off occasional edges of protruding ice drifts, dissecting them as he sliced by hurriedly. Crystal-like phantoms stared back at the chanter as he cut through the sea, each mirrored image stained with an intense turquoise glow, others consisted of reflected yellows and pinks as if consumed in fire. The ice appeared to burn steadily until precipitously pushed under the massive sides of the whale. With one sudden thrust, the glaring formations shattered into spectacular bursts of fluorescent explosions. They disappeared one by one, and Miracle found himself disappearing into nothingness, fading rapidly into a dreamlike state that he dare not pull himself away from, unable to, even if he wanted. However, before falling into that all-consuming sleep, he believed he had once again heard the tender lullaby of his mother's seal song, graciously delivered to his ears by the winds that penetrated his pure spirit. The heavenly lullaby played on, documenting its blessing firmly in his heart, all the while the winds continued to embrace him from the very tip of his furry snowy head to the bottom of his woolly back flippers. From that moment, just as the whale told him, the seal would search for his beloved mother with the designs of a pure and innocent heart. There, within the comfort and safety of Arayna's sweet seal song, the tiny pup would finally fall into an exceptionally deep and overdue sleep.

*   *   *

In what would seem like moments, Miracle would find himself back at the seal nursery, and this time what he would find there would change the course of his life for always. Not even the tender retreat to his mother's lullaby could prepare him for what he would eventually witness. For what finally does await him back at the peaceful nursery of Sealssong will attempt to destroy him. It will savagely replace all songs of love and hope with a dark underscoring of foreboding that will haunt him for the rest of his existence.

The hour of the monsters was soon to fall upon him, and this time the heinous beasts were terribly hungry and would not stop until they ate him alive—they, the greatest of all monsters—*the ones they called man.*

COLD DARKNESS

Since the moment that she was spirited away, Emma consistently fought Decara and her evil advances. In her heart of hearts, Emma knew that no matter what outrageous proposes her aunt promised, she would never surrender to the dark side. She could not for a moment consider it. Save for the few times she pretended to mull over such sinful influences only to protect her brother, she would never use her powers to harm anyone. She and Kenyan would simply keep on trying over and over again to escape from the malevolent ship where they remained prisoners.

*   *   *

The accursed vessel eventually found its way back to the freezing seas.

Decara hired the same man, Captain Thorne, along with his usual gathering of seal-killing brutes, to sail the *Tiamat*, rugged men in their twenties and thirties, to oversee the demands of such a massive ship while she concentrated on locating the mad seal that had stolen the sacred tear. That thieving harpie would be the first to die, and it would die horribly. In retaliation for this, and for the death of her lover, Decara would also have every seal that lived in Sealssong slaughtered; old and young, it did not matter. They all were going to die. She would take exceptional delight in the killing of the pups, the ones that held all that festering innocence. As told by the three-headed serpent, the children of the ice did not realize that they posed a definite threat to her having powers far greater than her own. She would not rest until she had destroyed every last one of them! All except for one particular seal—the one that now wore the omnipotent purple stone: *the seal that would ultimately be sacrificed.* For just as the serpent explained, Decara could not destroy this specific seal, she must first corrupt the soul of the one chosen for just such a deed, someone who possessed strange and fantastic powers, but above all else, one who remained filled with the deplorable essence of innocence. That person naturally was none other than Emma. It was perfect! Emma was of her own kin; she too was gifted with alarming powers, filled with what was required—the putrid and sickening infirmity of innocence. Despising having to admit it, the serpent was not as stupid as it appeared, imparting her with the perfect solution.

Decara had used her powers to take away Emma's illness with hopes of tricking her, but it did not work. For whenever she was able, Emma continuously tried to escape. That is why Decara continually plagued her, forever taunting to kill her brother if she did not stop trying to flee. Despite her niece's rebellion, she fed Emma properly, sometimes extravagantly, but only when she obeyed. She went on tempting her by clothing her in garish displays of royal garments, all which Emma refused and discarded with disgust. It seemed that this pure and wholesome niece of hers would not be happy until the brother was set free from his cell. Of course, that was something Decara would never do. Emma and her brother would never be free. Never! Eventually, she would kill the boy, but not before she would have Emma destroy the white seal. Decara would keep the boy alive as a definite incentive for her niece to obey. This would be only until Emma fulfilled the prophecy of *innocence destroying innocence.* Then she would have no further use for either one of them. She would claim the tear, and hers would be the greatest power in the world. She would resurrect the evil doctor, and both would torment the heavens and reign as one over a planet offering a permanent hell of sorrows. Decara would be the ultimate queen of the damned, but before anything could transpire, she would first have to find the wretched pup, the one who now wore the tear, and then, on *The Night of Screams,* Emma would kill the beast!

Forcing the girl to do her bidding was not an easy task. The little brat and the boy had already managed to leave their cells three times this week. It was fortunate that none of the crew or Captain Thorne witnessed their feeble attempts. It would only be a matter of time before someone would discover them if such deviant and obstinate behavior continued. It had to stop! She could not run the risk of having her secret exposed, not yet. True, she would kill the captain and all his men after she obtained the tear. However, not until they had sailed to Sealssong, and not before she found and destroyed the white seal, and most certainly, not before she watched those dirty swilers, which is why she had them there in the first place—butcher every last one of those bloody slugs and the miserable mothers who spawn them. It was settled! She would have to use more drastic methods of restraining her niece, as well as utilizing the many other dark and secluded places for the boy.

Since their abduction, Decara kept Emma and her brother hidden in the deep and secluded passages of the ship, passages not known to any of the men nor the captain for they were places forbidden to venture, places of darkness and foreboding.

It was just such a place that both siblings now found themselves trapped.This was, of course, because Emma, who used her powers for such a cause, had once again dared to escape and tried to free her brother from his wretched rat-infested cell. However, sadly she failed—again. It was all because of that lofty oaf Oreguss. The hairy brute had caught her just as she reached Kenyan's merciless prison. Oreguss had grabbed her with his massive ape paws, holding her in midair, fumbling for the key, throwing her inside with her brother, laughing all the while slamming and locking the door, chuckling while he lingered on the other side of the stony entrapment, grunting and groaning in a most treacherous manner. She had already been there for what surely seemed an eternity. She did not recall how long of a time she wept or how long she slept. She did remember, however, waking once to see the sun come filtering in through a small crack in the ceiling. Where it came from, she knew not, but she was glad that it found its way to this most dismal of all places.

On this particular day, Kenyan was asleep when the stray light streaked into the stony prison cell. Seeing its yellow glow was almost like revisiting an old friend, seeing something that was familiar, unblemished from evil and despair. The reflective sun continued to bathe the cell with a warm light, turning the cold stony wall next to her a muted gold color. She rested her head against the palm of her hand, feeling the warmth of the sunlight wash against her cold but delicate cheeks. If she closed her eyes and concentrated, she could almost pretend herself away from this horrid place, magically finding herself somewhere beautiful and peaceful. Somewhere warm and spacious, where there were no prisons or cold standing upright walls or floorboards that groaned and seemed to come alive in the dark. Someplace, where there were open skies holding multitudes of endless stars and warm summer night breezes.

When she awoke for the second time, the sun had vanished, and cold darkness took its place. Another day had passed, and her exhausted and tortured brother was still sleeping. Decara had provided a small cot for him to lie on, but after their latest attempt at escaping, Emma feared what monstrous substitute for sleeping accommodations her malevolent aunt would offer her brother this time around—a bed of nails perhaps? She would not put it past the evil woman.

Emma's stomach growled and she felt the hunger pangs sting against the burning lining of her belly. It had been a while since Oreguss had brought them anything to eat. As far as she was concerned, she would rather starve than eat the deplorable slop that the apishly looking man brought. Just the thought of eating hardtack again made her want to vomit. How she loathed, hated, and positively despised the taste of the repelling thing called "hardtack"—stale bread camouflaged heavily in a slimy sea of brown muck! Still, whether she wanted to accept it or not, if she were to survive and beat this evil woman, she needed to eat. It was true that her wicked aunt had used sorcery to make her well, but it was entirely for the evil woman's own selfish purposes, Emma knew this. Decara had not a drop of pity or kindness in her entire body. She was ruthless and filled with pure sin. If only she could have been quicker. Faster! If only she could be like her brother, skillful, cunning, swift! Then perhaps, they would not have to be made to suffer these intolerable torments. For soon, she would leave the monstrous cell only to return to the room Decara had initially prepared for her; the room Decara would continue to bribe and evilly try to persuade her to accept the dark side while Kenyan's cruel circumstances would remain. He would never be made comfortable; he would go on to be thrown into one horrible cell after another, each one to be worse than the last. That is why she had to escape over and over again, with the hopes of this time freeing him. Nothing would stop her.

However, this time Decara would unquestionably be watching her.
Soon Oreguss would come for her and take her back to her room.

Her designated quarters were large, consisting of an enormous
bed, the kind that filled up the place, set against walls that were dark
and strange and went endlessly upright, going off into a charcoal
shadowed universe of morbid obscurity. There was a washbasin and
a small desk and chair situated near the bed as well as many wooden
shelves, each anchored into the walls, each one bulging with rows
and rows of books, most in unsatisfactory condition, much of the
typing watered away into inky blurs. There was also a tiny cupboard
next to the bed where she was able to retrieve fresh linen, next to
a small wooden tub, and when she was not being punished, she
received three delicious meals a day. However, she would never eat
them, not if Kenyan would still be given that dreadful slop. It just was
not right, and until her aunt supplied Kenyan with the same food
that she was given, she was not touching a morsel. As horrific as it
appeared, she would just have to live off the rotting guts and slime of
dead fish.

She would endure these hardships; however, there was
something else that disturbed her and remained unendurable. It
was the ship itself, especially its walls. This was one of the hundred
and one reasons she despised going back to her designated room. It
was those disturbing walls, walls constructed out of unfamiliar dark
planks. They seemed to bend then jitter when one turned away from
looking at them, catching them move just for a moment out of the
corner of your eye. These boards that intricately weaved themselves
into the very structure of the *Tiamat* were not ordinary. Emma
knew it in her gut. They remained bewitched by the precise thing
that held the dreadful ship together, and it was pure evil. The walls
were always cold to the touch and consistently sent a chill through
her body. Once, when she dared to run her hand over their frigid
surface, her skin immediately broke and blistered even though her
touch had only grazed it lightly. She knew from that moment on that
it was not advisable to touch or go near the walls, not unless she was
prepared to leave a telltale mark of bloody fingerprints that would
hauntingly stare back at her until they would eventually be sucked
up into whatever lurked inside the walls.

The unusually small desk that remained situated near the
spacious bed carried a silver-cased lantern upon its chipped and
blemished surface. Besides the light that would occasionally filter
through the cracks beneath the bolted door, this lantern was
secondary to the only source of light in the room. For this chamber

had but one small window, and when darkness fell, the room also fell into swarms of ghostly shadows, eerie shadows that remained locked inside with her; but Emma knew if she concentrated hard enough, she could always unbolt the door and release the lock. However, it always gave her incredible headaches and made her extremely exhausted for hours, sometimes days. Emma only saw her brother when she disobeyed, using her powers while trying to escape. She continued to be caught and then thrown into the same cell as Kenyan, forced to witness Oreguss beat him. Aside from being deplorably pitched into her brother's cell from time to time, she had not seen much of the ship, but she knew that they remained hidden somewhere deep inside its ghastly belly. Forbidden to venture forth to investigate, and especially forbidden to go near Decara's chambers, the evil woman told her niece that if she was found there, she would be dissected an inch at a time, beginning with her toes. So for the time being, this was enough to keep her curiosity at bay, at least for a while.

When she was first abducted, Emma could see her brother at frequent intervals, but ever since their first unsuccessful attempt at escaping, Kenyan stayed banished into the dark cells of the ship. She remained constantly plagued by her evil aunt who tirelessly threatened that she would kill Kenyan if she continued to disobey. Decara kept Emma as far away from her brother as possible, separating them both by long, uncertain corridors, corridors that stretched far away from one another. This would be the only alliance that they would share, the cold silence of their rooms and the constant creaking of the moving vessel breaking through the freezing, unseen waters. How things had changed for them during the dismal days upon the ship, and they had changed for the ultimate worst. The wonderment of her rarefied gift now seemed a curse instead of a blessing, and whenever subjected to these cruel rituals of punishment, time seemed suspended. It was when her brother eventually passed out from sheer exhaustion that she felt the most alone in that horrid cell, for this and this alone was precisely why Decara would arrange for such painful gatherings.

As her brother lay there, his hands and legs bound with chains, his body crunched up on that dreadful cot, Emma felt her heart break seeing him, shivering, still wearing the same clothes that he arrived with, clothes that were now ripped and shredded. She continued watching her brother sleep, not wanting to disturb him, knowing that it was the only time he could find peace. Staring at him, she pretended the endless cold night away and all that had happened to them. It was all a dream; they were back at the Hudson house, and she was merely watching him sleep, preparing to wake him for supper. However, sleep did not come easily to the young girl. In fact, Emma found that she could sleep but very little whenever the punishment factor was in progress. The cell was so small, so cold, so utterly lonely, and of course, the smell of rot and waste intensified her repulsion for the horrible place. Nevertheless, sleep would eventually overtake Emma, and for a short time inside that disturbing darkness, she would sleep. And she would dream.

SWEET BOY

"Emma, wake up!" her brother implored, bent over her, supporting her limp neck within his trembling hands, his chains coiling around her tiny face. "Wake up!"

Emma hardly stirred, and her disturbing stillness made her appear as if dead.

Panic stricken, Kenyan continued to try to revive her. Relieved, he watched his sister take in a sudden deep breath; her chest heaved outwardly, and her mouth slightly broke open, her clouded blue eyes slowly opening. Realizing that she was awake, he exhaled another sigh, slowly releasing his sister back to the cold floor of the cell. Peeling her squalid oily strings of her yellow hair away from his cheek and mouth, he spoke to her. "Emma, you scared me . . . I thought you were—are you okay?"

Emma nodded, not wanting to upset her brother further, smiling, taking in the putrid air while adjusting her place on the damp and freezing floor, the dizziness still all around her. Suddenly, a drafty gust of wind began to moan through the cracks and crevasses of the lonely cold cell, lessening the smells, making her recovery back into the nightmare's domain less nauseating. Eagerly, she took in what she could of the fresh air, filling up her lungs before staring upward, suspiciously listening while the ship rocked back and forth. "I was dreaming," she plainly said, determined to keep her smug, but enchanting smile.

"Dreaming?"

"Yes, it was a wonderful dream," she said, stretching her arms, arching her back from the stiffness that had set in.

"Emma, how could you even speak of anything wonderful when this place is one big freaking nightmare?"

"But it had nothing to do with this place. I dreamed of the beautiful white seal again."

"Oh, Emma . . ."

"Yes, and we were flying through the skies, right through all the stars, and I remember laughing and being happy."

"There is nothing to laugh at or be happy about in this filthy hellhole!"

"But it was so real . . . so beautiful."

"Emma," Kenyan warned. "Please get a grip. Remember where you are?"

"I haven't forgotten. How could I?"

"Then no more talk about beautiful dreams and flying white seals. My god, I thought you were dead!" he sternly yelled, his eyes filling with unwanted tears.

The idling smile quickly ran away from Emma's face while she quietly waited for the cell to stop its customary rotation, something that always followed after awaking from one of her dreams. Reaching out, she took her brother's face, cradling it within her tiny palms. "I've upset you. I'm sorry," she said softly.

Surprisingly, her brother coldly withdrew from her touch, his eyes burning with newfound anger. "Emma, this is no dream. This is real! This is really happening to us!"

"I know that. I'm sorry for scaring you, but I'm all right. I promise."

It was not long before a solemn look washed over Kenyan's features. Feeling utterly ashamed for his outburst, he moved toward his sister, taking both her hands, tangling them both up with his chains. "No, I'm the one who is sorry. I didn't mean to talk to you that way, not after everything you've been through, it's just that—" He stopped, the same stubborn unsightly tears returning. "I just don't want anything ever to happen to you," he said, embracing her, further tangling both of them with the string of chains that held him captive.

Emma quickly took up with the same enchanting but haunting smile that never seemed far away. "You mustn't worry about me," she said, precluding her brother from objecting. "Decara wants me. Alive! She needs me for some diabolical plot, and she's not about to get rid of me, not just yet."

An encore of further intensity rattled in Kenyan's voice while he released his grip from his sister, both sitting on the floor facing each other, his hands still holding hers. "But how much more can you take?"

"I'll be all right. Besides, you know she healed me. I'm better now, at least for the time being."

"But at what price and for how long?"

"I don't know, but I am sure she will tell us when she is ready."

"But that's just it! I don't want to wait until she is ready! We've got to get out of here and now!"

"I know. I know. I am trying, Kenyan. I promise. I feel so responsible for everything."

"Now don't start that again."

"But if it wasn't for me, you wouldn't be here in this dreadful place. She wouldn't be able to do these awful things to you."

"It's not your fault, Emma."

"But it is! Whatever Decara wants of me has implicated you, and for that, I can never forgive myself."

"Emma," Kenyan said, squeezing tight, emphasizing his feelings. "Look, you have got to believe me when I tell you that you are not responsible for any of this. She is mad, an insane monster who feeds off our fear. You have nothing to do with this!"

"But I do!" she insisted, her tears now surfacing. "She wants to use me, my power, for evil."

"But you won't let her, will you?"

She looked at him with wide glistening eyes of dread. "No—never!"

Kenyan nodded, finding strength in her words. "We will find a way out of here, I swear we will!"

This time, Emma embraced her brother, a burning chill stinging at her body. "Oh, Kenyan, what in heaven's name could she want?"

"I don't know," he said, closing his eyes, deliberately shutting out the darkness surrounding him. "Whatever it is, you can bet heaven has nothing to do with it."

Emma did not flinch. She only pulled away slightly so that she could see past the shadows before her, shadows that insisted upon covering up her brother's face. "I'm afraid, Kenyan," she whispered softly, not wanting to hear her own words, their confirmation indicative of her fearfulness.

"Shhh," he comforted his sister's face only inches from his, the darkness still thick around them. "It's going to be okay." The cold air created miniature clouds around his lips every time he let out a breath. "We're going to get that vile witch! I promise. She isn't going to hurt you anymore. I won't let her."

Emma squeezed her tiny hands around Kenyan's fingers and felt the cold bite of the chains numb her delicate flesh. "How can I tell you how sorry I am? If I was normal like everyone else, none of this would be happening to us."

"Emma, please stop."

"You sacrificed your whole life for me, and now you're made to suffer intolerable indignities and it's all because of me!"

"Emma, you have got to stop this! Now, I mean it!" Kenyan insisted. "You are my sister, and I love you, and nothing will ever change that. *Nothing!* You mustn't waste your time thinking such things!"

"Why can't I be strong like you?" she asked, her tears freely falling down her pale cheeks.

Her brother looked at her carefully, his eyes pushing through the darkness, his fingers feeling her face as if trying to remember what she looked like. "Though you may not know it, you are braver than me. Emma, I mean this when I say that you are the bravest person I know."

Emma smiled. Reaching for her brother's hand, she brought it to her lips and gently kissed it. "I'll try again. I know that I can work the locks. It doesn't matter where I am. If I concentrate hard enough, I can make them all unlock themselves. It just takes so much time."

"I know," Kenyan said. "And time is the one thing we haven't got, but there is no reason we won't be able to escape this time. Not if we're careful and you do exactly as I say. You just have to trust me, and above all, don't let the darkness inside the ship trick you."

"I won't," she answered. "I hate this ship and all its darkness and dreadful stench! It tricks and teases us every chance it gets!"

"We will conquer it, but we have to outsmart it and the demon witch!"

Emma nodded and wiped away her tears and then jumped when she heard the disturbing thud sound. Both youths remained astonishingly still, each wrapped in a frozen grasp, both holding their breath like two lifeless statues both acknowledging the disturbance at the same moment. It had come many times before, but with each new occurrence came an additional jolt of horrific panic and uncertainty, for there was no way for them ever to prepare for what would take place. One thing was certain: the monsters had come back, and they had come for them. In only a matter of moments, the monsters would be inside the cell—alone with them.

Once more, that unsettling and jingling sound came, this time accompanied with a loud rattling thump striking directly against the wood bolted sentinel that unjustly constrained them. "They're back!" Kenyan warned in a strained whisper. The frequent clanking of the rattling keys that sounded like lightning always came first. Then the thunderous clattering followed, giving immediate forewarning to the imminent presence of the evil that lurked directly within the shadows beyond the locked door. Slowly it screeched open, snapping and splintering, screaming all the way as if in despotic agony. A faint yellow flicker of light tore through the immediate shadows, slicing them, scattering them, scaring them. The yellow light seemed to glow brighter as the door opened further, shrieking out as before, but this time with more harrowing pain in its coarse, splintery throat, striking forcefully against the dark wall and the stubborn shadows shrewdly watching. Emma closed her eyes. Kenyan did not. He remained fixed on the yellow light that was now slowly moving toward him. Like a ghost having been summoned from the cold grave, it fluctuated there hauntingly, dancing in the darkness. Its ghastly illumination reached out to them as if to chastise them for disturbing its rest. However, this was not a ghost, and they most assuredly had never invoked it. They would not dare.

All at once, the light appeared to detonate everywhere, saturating the entire cell, staining the morbid place with grotesque and villainous profiles. Kenyan could see that the yellow light burned indignantly before him, a fire that remained confined to its own cell just as he was. The flame permanently raged on inside a transparent partition made of glass, a glass fastened to a strange silver lantern. He knew that it was she who was holding it high above, her evil face causing the room to ignite even further into hundreds of shadowy slivers that crawled blindly over the ghastly black walls and floor.

Just then, Emma's eyes flashed open, and she watched in terror as Decara's crawling silhouette flooded the room. She had returned, just as Emma knew she would, once again taking her wicked manservant with her.

"Take the boy first," Decara's cruel but seductive voice decreed. "He will visit another cell, a smaller one. This next place just might make him ponder over his disobedience with a little more reverence. I will visit with him later. Perhaps we can have another of our friendly little chats. After all, we do have so much to catch up on, don't we, *sweet boy?*" Her abrading hollow laughter followed, lasting only a few moments before the agile lantern was in an upward swing again.

Deciding that she could no longer look upon the evil woman, Emma closed her eyes again, burying her face into her brother's chest. Down came the sinister lamp securely held by the devil woman's skeleton-like fingers, obscene fingers that wrapped tight around the base of the burning lantern now positioned only inches away from Kenyan's face.

"Get that away from me, *witch!*" the boy snapped, feeling his hatred for her swelling, simultaneously experiencing the heat from the flame begin to burn his skin, blinding him as it devilishly blazed only inches in front of him, silently laughing at him, just as he knew she was.

Despite its unsettling position, Kenyan did not cower as the lamp's incandescence intensified. He would not give her the satisfaction of showing his fear. He obstinately continued to stare back into the flame, his eyes and skin feeling its bite. It burned unbearably, as did his seething abhorrence for Decara. She was currently inspecting him as if he were some strange bug caught in some sticky spiderweb. Daringly, he continued to stare rebelliously into the flame, still refusing to give into its contemptuous glare.

"*Sweet boy,*" taunted Decara, "you look so thin and pale. Now, we can't have that, can we? Your cheeks are so white . . . so bloodless." Kenyan did not utter a sound but only continued to appear unaffected, refusing to surrender to the sparking panic that was rupturing inside him.

"However, I must confess that you really hurt my feelings this time." There was a moment of silence before the blaring light blazed up all around him. "*Tsk, tsk, tsk,*" Decara clucked. "I'm so crushed. Can't imagine why you are always trying to leave our merry little establishment without as much as an itsy-bitsy thank you or a teeny-weenie goodbye, especially after all we've come to mean to each other. Why, I'm simply devastated, sweet boy."

Kenyan felt his anger flare, imitating the scorching heat jailed inside the glass lantern, the devil flame burning ever so close to his face. As it leaped before him, he watched the flame draw nearer, singeing his eyebrows and his blond eyelashes. If the lamp remained where it was, his skin would soon begin to blister. Utterly consumed with terror, he suddenly felt violently ill, the lamp remaining exactly where its possessor intended it to be. Just when he could no longer stand the intolerable pain, Decara's hand did the unthinkable. With a devilish pleasure, she pressed the fiery glass lantern against his face, instantly searing his cheek.

Emma's eyes jolted open upon hearing her brother scream.

Kenyan immutably threw himself to the floor, his hands covering up his injured face. Up went Decara's torturous lantern, and more shredded shadows invaded the cell, each one descending and scattering monstrously all around her. Enraged and in excruciating pain, Kenyan instinctively struck out, kicking, aiming straight for the belly of the diabolical woman holding the burning lamp.

"Oreguss," Decara shrieked, "get him out of here, he's flopping around like one of those damn slimy seals right before we skin it!"

"Keep your filthy hands off me!" Kenyan screamed.

The brutish servant quickly went for him, paying no mind to the boy's idle threats, never flinching even when Kenyan back-kicked him straight in the groin. With a smack to the back of the boy's head, Oreguss stunned him, catching his foot in midair, readily preventing the attacking youth from repeating another determined blow. Resembling some broken marionette suspended in midair wrapped up in its own strings, Kenyan hung there, helpless, vulnerable to the abrasive hands that would savagely play with him. He could not help crying out in complete misery while the barbaric ape-man tightened his grip. Oreguss laughed, holding him upside down, the excess of the chains clashing over all around the boy's face. Firmly twisting the chains around Kenyan's legs, Oreguss chuckled some more, this time most sinisterly turning them around and around as if to squeeze his limbs clean off. Hurting and nearly unconscious, Kenyan was unable to fight back. Regrettably, he surrendered. The black cell twisted frantically around him while Oreguss toyed with him some more, grunting and laughing, spinning him around and around, in and out of the swarming blackness.

"Stop it, *stop it!*" Emma screamed, lunging forward. Clenching her fists, she began punching away with all her strength, right into the bulging belly of the abusive servant. "Leave him alone, you horrid man!" she screamed and kept right on punching.

It would seem that Emma's feeble attempts had temporarily gotten the attention of Decara's cruel servant. Oreguss just stared at her, unsure as to what she was trying to do. Surely the puny kid didn't think for a moment he minded or even felt her inconsequential blows. Still, she did intrigue him, enough so that he stopped spinning Kenyan. A moronic expression covered his stubbly face while looking out through the shifting shadows that stretched over Emma's curious form. Yes, he was certainly intrigued by her. In fact, her little performance amused him. He never remembered seeing the girl bursting with that much pizzazz before. He always thought of her as a mealymouthed weak and pathetic little sewer rat—a small scrawny mouse, a mere pipsqueak, nothing more; and now there she was, taking him on, her tiny fists quivering with fatigue, aching from her repeated blows. The hulking bear of a man allowed Emma to continue but however soon grew weary. A bored-looking frown smudged itself across his face, and opening wide his bristly covered mouth, he yawned, exaggerating his obvious boredom. Then while still suspending her brother with one hand, Oreguss swung his free hand toward Emma, and with one quick and sudden push, he shoved her off into the darkness. She hit the wall and fell down in silence, the shadows swallowing her up.

Barley conscious, Kenyan saw what the monster bully had done. He fought to remain conscious, silently swearing vengeance on the savage servant who now looked out into the shadows with an imbecilic expression pasted all over his brutish face, hoping that he had not seriously hurt the scrawny sewer rat. For Oreguss knew that the scrawny kid was extremely valuable to Decara, and if anything happened to her, he would certainly pay for it with his life.

"Oreguss," Decara shouted, "you stupid fool!"

Nervously turning to confront his mistress, the then not-so-tough man waited for his mistress to go ballistic on him. However, he was quite surprised when Kenyan seized the moment instead. Up went the boy's foot, kicking it high and hard, clipping Oreguss below his dark eyes, breaking his bulbous nose with one swift crunch! Blood shot out everywhere, but the strapping Oreguss did not flinch. He merely grabbed for that same moronic grimace as before. This time it spread itself insidiously across the giant's gruff features, preparing to even up the score. Without the slightest warning, he wrenched down on the boy's leg, snapping it, slamming the insolent youth's body against the icy wooden floor. Kenyan screamed out in agony, knowing fully that his cries would only be eaten alive by the cold and hungry blackness miserably enclosing around him. It was shortly thereafter that he joined his unconscious sister within the gullet of this ravenous darkness, darkness that for once offered refuge against the two monsters inside that dreadful cell.

"Enjoying, yourself?" Decara sneered, looking evilly at her servant.

Oreguss laughed and grunted, clapping his hands together, proud of what he had just done.

"You better wipe that brainless grin off your face and be quick about it!" Decara stung, kneeling next to her unconscious niece, her enormous black cape flowing all around her, settling there among the watching shadows. The wicked woman quickly picked up Emma's lifeless hand then dropped it, letting it smack down hard against the cold floor, not wanting to hold it any longer, waiting for Oreguss to come and pick up the girl.

More shadows prowled aimlessly around Emma's face while she lay there in Oreguss's arms, the evil woman's flickering lamp leaping out against the blackness, making the girl's face dance chaotically inside the shadows. Clutching the lamp, Decara stared out through the flickering gloom, becoming part of the darkness. Then when satisfied, knowing that her niece remained unharmed, she smiled. The fractions of light continued to invade the dismal surroundings, the sorceress's long fingers reaching out slowly, touching the soft skin of Emma's brow.

"Sleep, little dreamer, while you can," she hummed. "Soon, your eyes will remain open until they burn and beg for sleep . . . sleep I will not give them until you surrender all that I want from you," she growled in a harsh whisper, dementedly glaring at Emma, another wicked grimace splitting across her disarming face as the howling wind outside chanted a hellish lullaby.

Decara commenced with watchful eyes, mysteriously fluctuating in the dancing shadows, keeping her leer upon the girl, those black eyes examining her with such wickedness; not even the faltering gloom could conceal her harmful gaze. She appeared to become less human, more animalistic, simulating a wild beast stalking its prey just before it savagely tore into its flesh. However, such ravishment would have to wait until a later time. For now, Decara had a definite need for the once sickly girl with the iridescent blue eyes, a need that would soon have to be fulfilled. Mechanically bringing out her arms, scraping her fingers against the silky blue cobalt lining of her black flowing garment, she abruptly flared her cape, dismissing more of the shadows, resembling a giant bat, her illustrious cloak shooting out around her. With her hand securely wrapped around the lantern, she began swiftly maneuvering its burning light up into the ceiling, motioning after her manservant. Oreguss immediately complied, nodding his head; but instead of going directly to Decara, he could not help taking one last peek at the unconscious boy, his strewn body lying lifeless on the cold floor with only the shadows there to lie with him.

"*Enough,*" Decara shouted, lunging toward Oreguss, striking him hard across the face. "Leave the boy alone and attend to the girl, then come back and remove him, idiot!"

Again, Oreguss complied with an even quicker bounce to his walk, his forehead now coated in a clammy film of sweat, his dirty fingers just begging to run themselves over his whisker-covered cheek to rub out the sting. He would have to be more careful with the sewer rat. If he was, and did exactly as instructed, Decara promised that there would come a time when he could take immense satisfaction in disposing of the cocky-mouthed brother. Still, he had to be extra careful in not angering his mistress. For he knew all too well of her volatile temper and its forbidden limits, limits he did not wish ever to cross.

With Emma buried deep in his grasp, Oreguss waited for his mistress to open the door of the cell. In an instant, both he and Emma vanished. Decara remained. She just stood there, motionless, the black garment rendering her invisible among the eternal night that forever corrupted this dreary place. Suddenly, the lantern flared and then mysteriously went out, turning the room pitch-black.

DEVIL EYES

Kenyan lay there in his semiconscious state, moaning. Quietly, he opened his eyes, the complete darkness flooding over him. At first, he remained intensely still, confused and disoriented, not fully knowing where he was or what happened to him. It was not until he tried to move his injured leg that the entire horror all pounced back. "That filthy ape broke my leg!" he cried out while the tears freely drenched his contorted face. Instinctively, he reached out through the darkness, feeling up toward his face where the witch had burned him. He silently cursed Decara as more shocks of jagged pain shot through his flesh when touching the area of raw skin. The burn throbbed and cut into his nerves, causing him to bite down on his tongue, desperately trying not to scream out in agony.

As he lay there cringing in the gruesome darkness, he became aware that he was still not quite alone. Not daring to move his head but darting his blind vision to the corner of the cell, he could see an outline of someone watching him, its silhouette just barely glowing there in the shadows. It was she! She was standing there in the dark, just staring at him! He could see her eyes! Black like the shadows but glowing an eerie color that sparked like the embers from a fire right before going out, eyes that shone in the night, appearing like the eyes of a cat when the light hits them just right. They shone as burning coals stained in a color so red, so deep it consumed him with unexpected terror, terror that mounted when he began to hear the unmistakable murmur of her evil laughter. She was watching him, taunting him, letting him know that she would never allow him to leave, always there, always watching.

Slowly, the glowing eyes slipped across the room, moving, unattached to any human form, merely floating amidst the black space they drifted within. Closing his eyes, he tried to remain exceptionally still, knowing that he just did not have enough strength left to deal with the dreadful dragon lady, not again. He could barely remain conscious, as it was. Then without a moment's delay, Kenyan felt the sickening warm breath of Decara sweep lightly across his forehead then move down toward his ear. He wanted to scream out, not in fear, but in absolute disgust. If he had ever longed to be free from this horrible nightmare, it was never stronger than that moment. How he desperately wanted to run and continue running, never stopping to look back. Shattered leg or no shattered leg, he would keep on running. For this time, these evil red eyes and the foul breath that carried them truly terrified him. He hated himself for being afraid, but he was . . . terribly afraid. Ashamedly, he could do precisely nothing. He could only lay there pretending, morbidly playing possum, beaten, torn up, bleeding, and just waiting for the witch to finish him off once and for all.

How he loathed this pretentious vulnerability, it would prove to be more painful than his existing injuries. Nevertheless, with extreme precision, he continued to remain still. With eyes pressed securely against their burning sockets, he attempted to block out the thing with the bloody red glowing orbs and the putrid breath, its foulness stirring all about him while he quietly prayed that she would not suspect he was still awake. However, the suspended red eyes continued to hover above his ear, floating in a sea of breath, retching somewhere from Decara's scarlet lips.

Then something most sinister happened, filling Kenyan's blood with icy panic. Repulsed, he felt Decara's wet, obscene tongue dart into his ear. Slowly, it insidiously slithered itself into the opening then moved itself down toward his earlobe. Kenyan quaked with added disgust, fear sparking wildly through his already frozen veins. Still, amazingly, he did not stir. He did not dare move. If he could have stopped breathing, he would have. If she believed him to be unconscious she might leave, but the shining red eyes had no such intentions. His aversion was about to expand even further when he felt Decara sharply bite his earlobe. He felt as if he wet himself, his wild fear numbing every part of him.

The repressed grunt that followed must have surely given him away; still, he did not move. He could only lie there saturated in his fears, his tears burning against the wound on his face. He would intentionally suffer from the crippling pains that racked through him twice over rather than have Decara aware of his tears, and yet somehow, she seemed to know everything always no matter what. This time was undoubtedly no exception. More warm breath probed inside his ear while the wet lips spoke to him.

"Just wanted to make sure that you were listening, *sweet boy*," Decara whispered, blowing into the bleeding ear that she had just defiled. "This will be the last time you engage in one of your theatrical disappearing acts, won't it? Because I warn you, and take heed for it is a solemn warning, if it is not the last, my darling little sweet boy, I promise you, you will no longer have ears to hear with or eyes to see with for I will take them from you and feed them to the sea. Remember, sweet boy, I am never far away from you. I am always watching . . . *always!*" At this point, Kenyan realized that his body had involuntarily begun to quiver. However, not once did he ever open his eyes. He would not dare.

"How sad it would be if you no longer had ears for me to whisper my sweet nothings into," Decara's warm and sour breath told, clashing against the violent ringing in his ear. "You have such small delicate ears. It would be a real shame if anything should happen to them." She once again audaciously darted her vile tongue back into his ear, slurping up the tiny stream of blood that oozed there.

At that moment, something snapped in Kenyan. Demonic red eyes or not, he had ultimately been driven beyond his breaking point. He could no longer hold back the crazed hostility that he felt for this obscene dark and odious woman. Not caring what happened to him any longer, with one sudden jolt, he bolted upright, striking out into the blackness with both fists, fully intending to deliver a substantial blow directly into the witch's face, determined to knock shut those devil eyes and punch out those sharp teeth that had just torn skin off his lower earlobe. Insanely, Kenyan struck out into the shadows, his chains screaming all the way as he punched into the nothingness in front of him, his hands slicing through the putrid air. He punched to the right of him, to the left of him, then behind him, slumping sideways, dragging his injured leg. Regrettably, all his pounding fists confronted were more of the swishing cold black air that whistled past his clenched white knuckles. Decara was nowhere to be seen. She and her sinful red eyes had mysteriously vanished.

The last thing Kenyan would remember right before the unconscious world would reclaim him was the sound of his drumming temples slashing against the sides of his brain and the severe throbbing pain in his twisted leg, all this and the vile strain of Decara's maniacal laughter dominating the walls of the ship. He would never hear the sound of the clanking noise of the raucous key turn and twist, leaving him alone inside that dreaded prison that housed so many unforgivable horrors. He had once again fallen insensibly to the confines of the unspeakable darkness that greedily closed in on him from every side. With open mouths of unqualified gluttony, the blackness silently began to feed upon him.

Burning Curiosity

In times past, as indeed these were, most sealing ships were stoutly built, but they were often no match for the holding strength of the ice. For most, to reach the "main patch," the place where the greatest concentration of seals could be found, was the sheer heart of their aim.

Many seal hunters forced their way through dense miles of endless fields of jagged ice, having to blast their way through with cans of explosive powders when their ships became pressed within the stringent folds of the icy blockades. Some used large and dangerous saws, hoping to break through the strips of ice, sometimes cutting off fingers and hands just to do so. The venture was often brutal and at times fatal, and yet for the *Tiamat*, these serious risks seemed to be minimized. Of course, the men never suspected it was because of Decara, but in due time, and unfortunately for them, they would soon find out.

It took a unique individual to become a seal hunter. The hunt hardened the men. They were indifferent and inured to its savage harshness. Although more than four hundred sealing ships were abandoned or destroyed because of the unbelievable travesties caused by the ice during the early nineteenth century, every single spring, more and more sealing ships gathered, wishing to conquer the vast ice in search for the white seals of Sealssong. Still, the worst of the worst tragedies that ever occurred upon such sealing ships would forever pale in comparison to the misery Decara was about to unleash.

Although Decara could have well afforded to provide superior considerations for Captain Thorne and his men, she simply chose not to do so. She told the captain that it would serve in making the men too soft. They would live and work as did other swilers, and they did just that. The conditions they were forced to endure while sailing the *Tiamat* was indeed grim. Although Decara's ship had stoves and maintained a large galley, the men remained, forbidden to go near or partake of any of these conveniences. Sleeping conditions were unthinkable; the permitted rooms offered were small and usually accommodated more men than should have been allowed. For the most part, the men slept on malodorous seal pelts. They slept in their clothes day and night. If men fell overboard as they sometimes did, they would have to sleep in wet and freezing clothes, for more than likely there was no place to dry off, none that Decara would allow.

Many of the sealers not only willingly endured such hardships, but also took pride in their indomitable defiance over the devastating elements they encountered. The ice was their constant adversary, challenging their wits and courage, turning them into harder, stronger, manly men. The filth they ate, the reeking seal pelts they slept on, the limbs that were frozen beyond repair only to be cut away mattered not. It was the thrill of the hunt that urged the men to continue, this and the incredible amount of money Decara had promised each of them. For more often than not, most swilers were poor and uneducated. They spent most of their time away from their families, but now Decara offered them so much more, enough money to take care of themselves and their families for the rest of their lives.

Some of the men now on board had at one time worked for Decara before, each fully knowing of their employer's crude and barbaric ways. However, they were used to the crude and barbaric in dealing with the icy hazards they constantly were up against. She compensated their efforts with the highest rate of salary ever considered for sealing in its entire history, and that was all the incentive required as far as they were concerned. They were merely there to do a job, and while they did as Decara asked of them, they were paid quite handsomely as promised, but only after they had returned from the islands of Sealssong. She did not know their names or who they were, nor did she care to know them. Their lone significance was how skilful they were at spotting, collecting, slaughtering, and scalping and eventually returning to the *Tiamat* with more than their fair share of scalloped whitecoats. Aside from the usual excretions collected from the slaughtered seal victims, Decara utilized fluids and used them for products that she manufactured, such as oil to burn in lanterns and other miscellaneous heating or lighting devices. Nonetheless, she profoundly prospered from the seal coats that she sold to the many, numerous vendors, all eagerly willing to pay the outrageous prices she charged, for Decara's coats were impeccable and considered exotic and highly fashionable. To own a seal coat tagged with the name of Decara embroidered onto its precious lining clearly boasted of how wealthy the owner was. Each coat remained deliberated as a unique work of art and could only be furnished to those who could afford such luxuries. Decara's coats were in demand and always sought after worldwide. The executions taken were both intricate and complex; all her coats remained snow white. One drop of blood would tarnish the purity of the coat and would reduce its value considerably, but Decara's secret methods never showed a trace of such an unforgivable blemish. Her seal fashions had come to represent perfectibility in a product, thus making her an extremely wealthy woman.

However, as far as the village folk were concerned, she and her evil doctor companion were regarded as charlatans and, even worse, practitioners of witchcraft who did unspeakable things within the confines of that dreadful ship they sailed upon. Others thought Decara as highly inappropriate but in a different light. Aside from the usual clucking of tongues and shaking of heads, many locals considered her entailment with the sealing ships most inordinately suspicious. After all, the sealing business was an occupation consisting exclusively of men—unpolished, crude, rugged men—existing solely within pitted conditions, most often hazardous conditions, and yet such a woman had chosen to place herself in such dangerous waters repeatedly. Yes, to many people, Decara was quite a strange and bizarre businessperson. The thought of any female partaking of such rigorous trades were positively unheard of—that is, until Decara showed up. In any case, it would all become irrelevant, for soon she would no longer have the need to sell her fur because in a little while there would not be anyone left to sell anything to ever again. She had already shut down half of her factories, and many began to suspect that this incredible pioneer of the ice was about to give up her self-appointed profession altogether. Despite the continued gossip, those merchants acquainted with Decara and her refined seal coats renounced such a scheme in fear that such stories would reflect poorly upon their own businesses. Despite the convenient denials, the stories of demons and witches continued, never having been proven and yet never been disproved. This only inflated the haunting legend of *Decara,* making it a constant and maturing ghost story reserved for innocuous folklore, purposely created for dreary nights when the sky was dark and the wind and wolves howled fiendishly. However, she was far more evil and dangerous than any of them could ever suspect. Like the unsuspecting seal hunters, they too would soon find out just how monstrous she truly was. Regrettably, none of them would ever live long enough to tell about it.

As for the thirty-three men who currently embarked upon the *Tiamat* now sailing toward the islands of Sealssong, these sordid tales once again surfaced back into their minds and seemed interlaced with even more desolation than ever before, for the premonition of woe within the *Tiamat* was ever constant now. Captain Thorne was no stranger to this feeling; it had remained with him ever since he first set foot on the accursed ship.

Captain Harrison Thorne was a dedicated man of the sea. He was highly skilled and well accomplished in his trade. Now in his late forties, he stood six feet three inches tall, had long, thinning blond hair, and wore a black patch over his right eye. His left eye was a dazzling royal blue color, and whenever his eye brushed across another, his powerful and dominating individuality remained obvious. His rugged handsome looks easily intimidated those he came in contact with, for one could never dispute that this man was a man of few words. His demeanor was powerful and virile, and like the other men who now sailed upon the *Tiamat*, Thorne's exterior, as well as interior, was hardened and impenetrable to any emotional tendencies connected to the slaughtering of the whitecoats of Sealssong. It was what he did. It was what his father did and his father before him, and nothing could change his fate. He neither liked nor disliked the whitecoats he killed for they had long since become financial commodities to him, nothing more. The whitecoats merely existed as a segment of his trade, allowing him to make a living the only way that he knew how, and he made a grand living working off Decara Enterprises. But the price he paid was steep.

At first, Decara's exotic and rare beauty aroused hidden desires, which he could not define. There was something mismatched and unprecedented about this mysterious benefactor. For she not only evoked a passion that had long since been omitted from his emotional chemistry, she was somehow able to bewitch him in a way no other woman ever could before. With this enthralling potency, she also brought to him a sudden and calculating fear, a fear that would eventually turn his blood to ice and his heart to pure loathing. Still, what Thorne came to loathe the most, even more than his irreverent employer, was the ever-constant and unnerving feeling that he always felt whenever he sailed the *Tiamat*. It was something he could never shake no matter how hard he tried, and yet he remained, but solely for the incredible and outrageous amount of money he was paid.

Decara had commissioned him for nearly two years now. She had picked him from hundreds of capable men, for he and his crew had impressed her with their known reputation for finding and skinning the most whitecoats in the shortest number of times. His ability to conquer the frozen sea as many times as he did, seeking out and finding the obscure seal nurseries of Sealssong, excited her. However, she had made it known to him that before given the opportunity to sail the *Tiamat*, he would have to follow her exact instructions always and obey every decision and wish she conjured up.

He acquired his own quarters near his men, making sure that it was as far away from any place she inhabited. Most of all, besides his immediate duties, she insisted that he remain unattached and uninvolved in anything other than what she instructed him and his men to do. He was to concentrate primarily on getting to Sealssong, slaughtering the seals, skinning them, and returning their pelts back to the ship—and that was all! Aside from his regular and necessary commands upon the vessel, she also made it known that she was the one who was in command, and he was never to forget it. She made sure that he never did. He was forbidden ever to concern himself with her affairs. Aside from navigating the *Tiamat* as well as keeping his men under control, seeing to their needs and being responsible for their whereabouts, above all else, he was never to explore the lower decks of the ship for any reason. He was especially forbidden to seek her out after sunset or go probing into the corridors below the galley. For this discretion, she would pay him plentifully. Agreeing, he eventually became quite prosperous, nonetheless always feeling, no matter how he rationalized or dissected it, he had ultimately sold his soul to the devil.

Many a night inside his cabin, he had heard the intolerable howls of animals that Decara and her hairy henchman brought aboard the ship. They were always female harp seals, some of them still pregnant. He had heard all the gossip about the demonic deeds that she and her strange lover were said to be involved in, having something to do with black magic and the experimentation of harp seals. However, he never gave it much thought, at least not until the night he heard the seals' imploring screams, for their agonizing cries persisted in morbidly filling his long nights, as well as permeating the walls that surrounded him. He would be a liar if he denied the fact that there were times his curiosity got the best of him, nearly forcing him to leave his room in order to see just what that beastly, vile woman was up to; and once, he did just that.

One night, around the time he was first commissioned, nearly a day and a half after they had set out for sea, he was asleep in his quarters when he suddenly awoke and heard strange cries coming from somewhere below the ship's galley. Unable to conquer his burning curiosity, he set out to investigate, ignoring Decara's warning, thinking he would be exceptionally careful never to be discovered. After submerging himself further into the belly of the *Tiamat*, he continued listening, looking carefully about his surroundings. Entranced, he found himself following the cries and squeals assaulting him, leading him deeper into the forbidden areas Decara had warned him against. There, near the very entrance of a large red-stained door, a door that took him several minutes to reach because of a shadowed and elongated corridor that seemed to curve and bend ridiculously, he carefully looked around once more, checking to make sure no one was watching. Placing his ear against the wooden door of this eerie and secluded room, he stood there, just listening. At that precise moment, the cries stopped and the wooden door was suddenly unbolted, swinging partially open with disturbing abruptness. He could only stand there thunderstruck, as a child caught with his hands in the proverbial cookie jar. Preparing to allow for some absurd explanation, he became harshly interrupted.

Out of the shadows, from behind the door, Decara emerged. She was wearing her usual black cloak, her hair tightly coiled up on top her head, her face a mask of hostility and raw wickedness, the likes of which he had never seen before. He again tried to make up some lame excuse for his disobedience, but again he was harshly stopped. Decara abrasively pushed herself up against the startled man, and with a twisted smile on her face, she quickly withdrew a silver hand pistol out of nowhere. Aiming its barrel directly into his face, she pressed it hard against his lips telling him that the only reason she was allowing him to live was because she needed his services, at least for the time being. She also went on to say that should he ever dare to defy her again, she would not think twice about blowing off his face, and as quickly as she appeared, she hastily disappeared, slamming the wooden door shut, forcibly pulling the door's bolt against the steel bracket inside.

Captain Thorne would never speak of this night again. He would never discuss it or even speak to his crew about the way he abhorred the vile woman inside the black cloak who paid astronomical amounts of money for his services. As far as he was concerned, it never happened. He would close his eyes, his ears, and ignore it all—well, all except the money. From that moment on, he decided that the consistent monetary gain he had grown accustomed to would become his one and only reality. He would no longer concern himself with Decara or her screaming seals. After all, sooner or later he would end up skinning the damn beasts anyway, so what did it matter? Besides, he had conquered tempests much worse than her, and under all that mystery and foreboding, she was still just a woman, a conniving, untrustworthy, self-absorbed, shallow, opportunity-seeking woman. As long as she kept right on paying him all that money, he didn't care what she did. Besides, it would never directly affect him, *would it?*

OUT OF THE DIRTY SHADOWS

Now, on this particular midnight, a wild wind came out of nowhere and surrounded the ship.

Despite the exaggerated moans it made, Thorne and many of the men were asleep or passed out with the stench of drunkenness still smeared over their hastened breaths. The constant lulls of snoring swilers, as well as the howling wind that mixed with the foulness of the ship, purposely muffled another distant sound echoing from someplace down in the black bowels of the *Tiamat*.

It was a distinct noise that of something being dragged across the *Tiamat*'s floors.

Suddenly, a splintering and snapping sound of a warped door screamed out a morbid moan somewhere in the distance. From out of the dirty shadows that forever clung to him, Oreguss appeared, his large frame dripping wet from perspiration and seawater. He remained hunched over, tugging and pulling something long and wide, something alive and wiggling, something wrapped and tied inside a sizeable brown burlap sack. Quickly, he made straight for the large wooden door leading into Decara's laboratory, continuing to drag the jerking sack, dragging his own lumbering feet as well. Upon reaching the door, he stopped and turned his head from side to side, releasing the bundle that he had pulled through the black corridors. Whatever was inside continued to move. It twitched and flopped noisily about, pushing itself against the heavy fabric of its prison. Oreguss angrily kicked the sack, stunning the thing inside.

Clumsily searching through his ragged pockets for the key that unlocked the door, he dug aggressively, annoyed that he could not find it quick enough. However, he soon came upon it, but his huge anxious fingers clumsily dropped the key to the floor. As he bent to pick it up, he watched the sack begin to squirm and twist all over again, this time making a high, shrill whining sound while it wiggled frantically.

Again, Oreguss kicked at the sack with his large feet. *"Sha-up!"* he crudely grunted. However, the thing inside remained undaunted in its struggle, conjuring up more resistance, pulsating and rocking back and forth, the dark folds of the scabrous material crumpling into peculiar shapes as it continued to move. Oreguss annoyingly looked down in disgust, clinching his fist into a hairy ball. He had enough. Once again, he struck at the stirring burlap sack, and the thing inside stopped moving. Then he began to fumble with the ties of the sack. Unable to untie the knotted drawstrings, he began to curse and grunt at the aggravating mass that he had created; he was not about to waste any more of his time on it. From somewhere in the rankness of his torn breast pocket, he hastily pulled out a small sharp-edged knife. Impatiently, he cut into the hard entangled knot, and the sack abruptly unfastened. As it unfurled, a shining head appeared, the head of the thing trapped inside suddenly revealed. There, it was—a female harp seal, about three years old, thin and sickly, shaking with fear, her bulging black eyes tearing profusely. The dazed harp simply stared up toward her abductor, her breath quick and short, her eyes blinking crazily while attempting to focus on her surroundings.

Becoming aggravated at just looking at the thing, Oreguss savagely took hold of her head and shoved it forcefully back into the sack. "Down!" he grunted, totally oblivious to the pitiable cry that the creature was making. After all, as far as he was concerned, it was only another one of those stupid, noisy seals, not unlike any of the others he had abused, tormented, and skinned before. It was just another slimy thing void of any feelings, consisting of slimy hide, sharp teeth, and whiskers that danced annoyingly about its face. It was just another turd ball that resembled some fat, ugly dog, and Oreguss hated dogs. In fact, Oreguss hated almost everything except money, food, and whiskey; sailing; and the excitement he experienced whenever he slaughtered and skinned the fat, ugly dog-faced creatures with the annoying whiskers. It was clear that these beasts held no consequence for him whatsoever, and this one did not look like it had long before it croaked. Still, he just bet that it was stuffed full of crybaby seal tears just a-begging to be wrung out. Best of all, he would get to skin it all by himself! No one else would help. It was his find, and his alone, and Decara would reward him for it. Of course, he would never tell her that his find was purely accidental, certainly not attributed to any skillfulness in trapping, or that when he first saw it drifting lifelessly in the water, he thought it to be merely seaweed or some heap of floating garbage discarded by another vessel. Rather that when he finally realized it was indeed a harp seal, amazingly a female harpie, he was able to capture it easily and with the utmost of ease by simply lowering the convenient nets located on the side of the ship, dropping it over his find without the slightest opposition from the captured beast. Instead, he would tell Decara that he alone spotted the beast and that he recognized it immediately as a female harp. Knowing how pleased she would be, he bravely fought the savage thing with the help of his trusty spear and net. In his own neanderthal fashion, he would go on to tell her that when he finally captured the thing, it ferociously tried to chew away his hand and arm. However, being the strong and virile he-man that he was, he fiercely thrashed it good, taking it prisoner inside a sack that he carried all the way to the laboratory—all by himself and all just for her!

Once again, the confused and sickly harp seal stirred, and once again Oreguss struck it. Sadistically, he waited for it to snap at him with its sharp teeth, just as all the rest did right before he bludgeoned them into senselessness—or worse. However, this time would prove to be different.

The dazed seal slowly stretched out its quivering head over the opening of the sack. Her huge black walnut-shaped eyes remained immersed in tears, merely looking upon him sadly, questioning.

"Stupid," Oreguss professed in anger, irritated by her submissiveness, once again grabbing her head and shoving it back down deep into the sack, tightly squeezing the lip of its opening so that the seal could not peek out again. While holding the heavy sack up toward his saturated chest, he turned to face the door while fumbling with the key again, pushing it gruffly into the keyhole. Entering the room, Oreguss did not bother finding a light source, he knew this room inside and out; he needed no assistance. The black meshed cage that he would lock the seal in was not far from the threshold, and the small quantity of light that snuck in after him was sufficient. Finding the unlocked door of the cage, and while still holding the burlap sack in his grasp, Oreguss pulled open its mesh door. Taking the sack, he swung it high and dumped its contents ruthlessly into the narrow opening. He laughed when he saw the seal's head strike the cold black mesh of the cage. It appeared that the thing was knocked silly.

However, it didn't matter, as long as it wasn't dead—that would come soon enough. With his hand blindly reaching for the cage's door, he slammed it shut; locking it, never realizing that this find was grander and more valuable than all the others put together, but it wasn't his fault. How could he possibly know that this was not just any seal and that this was a creature Decara would rejoice in having? Still, would his treatment of the seal be any different? It might be, if he knew how happy it would make his mistress. For it would mean all that much more of a reward for him. Nevertheless, would it actually cause a change in his savagery toward this unique mother harp? Hardly, for what possible difference would it make to him if this particular mother seal had given birth to one truly remarkable whitecoat? A child she believed to be destroyed left forever to turn and spin in the swell of a billion whitecaps that would become a part of the vast frozen monuments belonging to the very sea herself.

What difference could it possibly make to him if she had allowed herself to become ensnared within his horrid nets? How could it matter if she suffered from no ordinary surrender, but sustained something far more excruciating such as a broken heart and that she was sick and dying from hunger and grief, something she now readily accepted? What difference would it make if he knew that seals, like men, had feelings, surprisingly far more intense than his own? Would he even care to know that seals had names? Could he possibly concern himself with such things that happened among the other living creatures of the sea? Would he care to know that this seal's mother had once blessed her with a name that honored the stars and heavens themselves? Once upon happier times not so long ago when she was christened Arayna.

No, he would not care and could not begin to concern himself about such things. What could it matter if he knew of the absolute despair she carried in her afflicted heart? Could the devastation that left her broken and utterly alone and no longer possessing the will to live ever matter to him? Certainly not, how could it? How could anything matter now that she could no longer feel? Never again would she experience her child's tenderness, sing to him her lullaby, or breathe in his wonder while gazing upon the innocence of his beautiful baby seal eyes, her beloved son, her only child, now forever gone. The one she once called her beloved *Miracle*.

SLEEP WELL?

Emma slowly opened her eyes. Her head hurt, so she began massaging the place that was aching, remembering Oreguss and his barbaric shove. The second realization was the absence of the horrible smell of decay and rot of dead fish.

Sitting up much too fast for her own good, she tried to control her anxiousness, waiting for the room to stop its spinning before looking at the softness pressing in all around her. She reached down and felt the warm and gentle garment adorning her, her previous clothes having been discarded. This new pink negligee Decara had embellished her with was the most exquisite yet.

Slowly, she ran her tiny hands down its velvety smoothness, touching the supple material that covered up her arms with a sparkling color of pink. The fit was more than a trifle big for her, but it was exquisite just the same. She continued running both of her hands over the dangling sleeves, her fragile fingers delicately tracing themselves over the rose-colored lace that accented the garment as well as the bodice of the gown. Following the intricate lacing, Emma's glance fell upon the silky covers of the magnificent bed that she slept on. Immediately, she felt the heartache of separation from her brother, and with a heavy downcast sigh, she flopped backward, looking straight up into the blackness staring down at her. A half-dozen enormous pillows, each stained a color much deeper than the pink nightdress, circled her, each arranged perfectly as if wanting to converse with her. Emma turned from side to side and looked at her wall of pillows, then reached out and touched the one closest to her. Taking it in to her hands, she threw it across the room, rolling her eyes in disgust before grabbing for the bedsheet crushed beneath her. It felt as if she had just placed her hand through a mysterious red cloud made of the gentleness of dreams, but she knew better.

Freeing herself from the silken sheets, she kicked out one leg, the other following. She scooted herself toward the edge, looking down at the floor and the oversized garment hanging there, just missing the floorboards beneath by a hair. She moaned, amazed at Decara's appalling tenacity. Then with a slight push against the bedspread and the overzealous sleeves of her nightgown, Emma plopped herself down on the floor. She impetuously felt the warmth the dark floorboards gave off while she squatted above it, just before she lost her balance and fell sideways. Quickly straightening upright, she knelt comfortably on the black floor, her pink nightdress spilling endlessly around her. Picking up some of the material, she remained determined to feel the warm floor with her bare hands; she had been cold for so long she had almost forgotten what warmth felt like. Not wasting one more minute, Emma directly prostrated herself, and pressing her cheek against the floor, she felt her face begin to glow as all traces of coldness left her. She stood this way for a while and then suddenly swooped up her hand, gathering more of her dress. It was far bigger than she initially thought. All at once, she felt as if to be drowning in her own private pool of pink, framed within rose-colored borders of entwined lace. Pressing the drape of the dress against her nose, she breathed in its sweet smell. The outcome was not what she expected. Abruptly, she pushed the softness away, remembering her brother. Immediately, she felt the wash of guilt shadow over her for having been spared the putridity of the ship, knowing that at that precise moment, he was being made to suffer its filth and degradation.

Suddenly, something flashed bright in the corner of the room, catching Emma's attention. Reaching and holding on to the velvety red covers that draped over the side of the bed, she pulled herself upright. Nearly slipping on some of the nightdress that had snuck beneath her toes, she pulled away just in time to stand properly. Turning, she carefully walked away from the bed, her bare feet remaining extremely warm from the heated floor. Once again, she nearly tripped. Having had enough, she gruffly grabbed at the flowing material, folding it around her fingers and began begrudgingly carrying her pink train, continuing to walk, studying the strange room. Although she had been in this room many times before, each time she returned there was always something different about it. It was as if the room was changing into some unusual attire just for her. Hardly impressed, she walked into a puddle of shimmering light, a queer, unnatural light, and the room began to flicker. Awakened by her inquisitive presence, the room further came to life with even more radiance. All at once, Emma found herself surrounded by bursts of dozens and dozens of red-colored candlesticks, each anchored inside wooden, gnarled, and carved-out black candelabras. These dark fixtures stretched out from the walls, glowing with clawing and crooked fingers, each holding on to scarlet wax sticks that burned and wavered with an eerie and mysterious wonder. Each candelabrum held six candles. By themselves, the holders were monstrous works of art, each carved and designed with the same distinctive markings that covered the wooden headboard of the bed on which she slept. The color of the walls began to turn a deep crimson color, its surface flickering profusely within the fiery dance of the flames. Emma distinctly made sure that she distanced herself far enough from the candelabras blistering through the scarlet walls, unintentionally dropping her pink train onto the floor. Bringing her oversized sleeve up to her lips, she nervously began chewing on the soft lace that bordered the edges there. Her heart raced, looking upon the flames that stared back at her from a room now covered in a veil of bleeding reds and flickering tangerine aberrations, all devilishly dancing and tonguing out their crimson settings inside a room that was expanding before her.

Whatever was happening within this chamber made her tremble with fear. The hair on the back of her neck stood erect, and the muscles in her throat tightened. Sudden and growing terror filled itself within her. Something was wrong. Something was dangerously wrong! It was those lurid walls again. Above all, as before, it was the walls that scared her the most. They drastically continued to turn dark shades of red while every part of her being cautioned her to turn away; still, she could not for these were no mere reflections of ordinary things. These walls were alive and had begun to breathe, all on their own. She suddenly stopped dead in her tracks, dazed. All this time, she had been gradually approaching the walls, unable to resist, as if in a trance, as if they were calling to her, summoning her to become a part of them. Emma quickly shook her head, shaking its consuming effect from her thoughts. She rubbed at her eyes with her dripping sleeves still twisted around her fingers. She blinked her eyes then squinted, trying to decipher it a dream or a hallucination, watching the wood expand in and out, snapping and moaning as it inhaled.

Not knowing what possessed her to do such a thing, she slowly pointed one finger out toward the haunting phenomenon now only inches away from her touch. It was then that the fantastic event drastically matured. As boiling bubbles gathering in a cauldron, a thousand floating eyes sprang up and began pulsating over the walls, infesting it with red hues of thumping horror. There also appeared lips that moved and at the same time held no real substance, just disembodied mouths that were both repulsive and diabolical. They pressed out from within the walls, hideously protruding themselves with foul and offensive gestures, swallowing whole the misshapen candelabra while whispering her name in tormenting unison. *"EMMAaaaaaa . . . ,"* they gurgled with distorted sighs, calling out to her while a thousand contorted red mouths and eyes blazed wickedly before her.

The walls began to jerk and vibrate with more excitement in their breath. Walls that should have never moved *moved!* Walls that could have never spoken *spoke!* Walls that should have never watched her, the way they did, continued to consume her. With fiery eyes and appalling red lips, they dared to whisper out her name again. *"EMMAaaaaaa . . . ,"* they moaned, as still more and more blood-filled eyes and mouths rapidly pervaded the room, drenching the walls with ghastly peculiarities belonging only to what real nightmares were made of. Possessed by a haunting trance, she slowly proceeded to press her finger toward the grotesque display of bloody lips and scarlet-colored eyes. Preparing to touch them, she took a deep breath, steadying her trembling fingers, a thousand shivers slicing up and down her spine. Just when she was about to touch the breathing wall, she suddenly gasped, then jolted backward.

SLAM!

She flashed her terror-filled eyes about the room, turning to look back at the door, its sudden slam snapping her out of her trance. Someone had entered before hurling the door shut with startling fury. However, when she looked to see who it was, she found no one there, or so she thought. Cautiously turning her eyes back toward the wall that only moments ago housed such horrors, she shuddered with added surprise, for once again, she was merely staring at a dark wall. Aside from the hanging grotesque candelabras, the red candles having been blown out or perhaps never having been lit in the first place, appeared to be like any other wall. The breathing had stopped; the floating eyes and lips were no more, and all was as if she had merely dreamed the entire thing. Then from out of the shadows, Emma felt a cold hand wrap itself around hers. Gasping aloud, Emma tried to pull away, retreating toward the strange and frightening wall, her back just briefly touching its surface. Too terrified to scream, Emma stood frozen, staring directly into the shining black eyes of Decara.

"Sleep well?" Decara questioned in a low and breathy voice.

Emma did not move nor utter a sound, or show any indication of answering.

Decara remained holding her niece's hand, pulling her even closer. "Answer me, child, I asked if you slept well."

Emma glared at her. That was all.

Decara glared back, losing her make-believe smile, looking as if she wanted to strike the girl. Instead, she quickly changed gears, desperately grasping for her fake smile again, her dark eyes showing the exaggerated concentration needed to do so. "I still frighten you, don't I, dear?"

Emma continued to stare at her with contempt. "What have you done to my brother?"

"Come, let us sit and be comfortable, shall we? I wish to talk to you," Decara said, trying pathetically to keep her voice sweet and nonintrusive. Emma stiffened her arm while Decara tried to steer her toward the bed again. "I assure you, child, your fears are unavailing. I only want to help you," Decara uttered, squeezing out another of her ruby red-lipped fake smiles.

Emma remained as stiff as a statue, her eyes glaring, fully exposing the contempt she held inside. "Yes, I know all about your help, just like you helped my brother—*liar!*"

Abruptly, Decara jerked Emma's rigid arm with an aggressive tug, pulling her further toward her. "Sit on the bed, you will be more comfortable there," she commanded. Ushered crudely toward the bed, Emma could not help notice that whenever Decara moved, she did not walk; she merely floated, her formidable cape sprouting all around her like some terrible dragon with wings made up of bad dreams. Pulling her sternly, Decara stood the girl before the bed. Lifting her up high, she plopped her down like a doll. "Comfy-cozy?" she asked with an insidious smile smeared to her glistening red lips.

Sitting on the edge of the bed, her tiny feet left to dangle there, Emma remained covered up by the oversized nightdress. She tried to straighten the overflowing material while defiantly glaring at her evil aunt. Even standing, Decara seemed to float. She never appeared stationary. Perhaps she was a ghost. No, she could not allow herself to think that this woman was made up of mystical vapors and misty mummy dust. Decara was a real flesh-and-blood woman, all right, yet she could not stop herself from feeling that at any given moment, Decara would simply glide off somewhere like some restless spirit. *Who is she?* Emma thought to herself. *What is it that she wants from me?* She quickly closed her eyes, wishing to dismiss the devil woman away from her.

"I already told you that I only want to help you," Decara surprisingly answered, her smile turning into a maniacal grimace. "You see, you're not the only one who can read minds and probe the soul, my dear."

When Emma could no longer avoid the inevitable, she lifted her eyes; but when she did, expecting her eyes to meet Decara's, Emma's gaze merely fell on a hazy glow of emptiness. The evil woman had once again vanished. Then Emma gasped again. For now, positioned on the bed sitting next to her was the dark woman who once more forcibly reclaimed her small hand. Emma tried to pull away, but to no avail.

"Do you like it?" Decara zealously asked.

"I wish you would stop doing that disappearing act, it's quite annoying."

Decara merely grinned.

Knowing fully as to what her evil aunt was referring to, Emma decided to play confused. "I don't know what you are talking about," she answered, trying to pry her hand away, still unable.

"Why, of course, you do!" Decara over exclaimed.

Ending her pretense, Emma answered sternly, "I hate it. It's too big."

"Nonsense, child, it fits you to perfection, or I should say, it soon will. You'll be surprised to see how quickly you will blossom into a beautiful woman, with my help, of course," Decara boasted, lifting a piece of Emma's nightdress off the bed, holding it in one hand, continuing to squeeze Emma's fingers together. Appalled at her aunt's incredible indifference, Emma rolled her eyes in revulsion while again attempting to pull her hand away, but she only confronted more forceful resistance. "Be still!" Decara warned with an evil voice. Then throwing down her niece's hand forcibly on the bed, she glared at her. "Is this how you repay my generosity? I give you beautiful things, and you scoff at them."

"I never asked for them, and I don't want them!" Emma said loudly, rubbing her hand, trying to take the burning and pinching feeling away from her irritated skin. "I don't want anything from you!"

"Nonsense, child, now let's be sensible about this. A fantastic future bows before you. A future I alone can give you. Soon, you will be set apart from the low and desolate. I am offering you something beyond your wildest dream!"

"Thanks, but no thanks. I just want to go home!"

"*Home* . . . you call that dreadful rundown institution that I redeemed you from, *home?*" Decara laughed.

"Yes, and I want you to take Kenyan back there!"

Decara wickedly smiled. "My, such colossal demands for one so small."

"Do what you want with me, but let my brother go!"

Again, Decara smiled evilly. "Now that's what I like to see—a true penitent."

"Then you will set him free?"

"All in good time, all in good time."

"You're lying!"

"Why, Emma, what could ever make you say such a thing? I thought that we were friends."

"Friends?" she snapped, looking at her aunt in sheer amazement. "I hate you! I hate everything about you! Don't you see that? Are you that incredibly dense?" Unable to help the tears, Emma turned, dropping her head into her hands, covering her eyes, letting her elbows rest upon the many folds of her oversized nightdress. "Oh god, please let me wake up from this nightmare!"

Decara uncomfortably squeezed out another one of her phony smiles, taking hold of Emma's face, pushing her niece's hands away so that she could look directly at her. Then surprisingly, Decara removed her black hood that forever framed her face. It melted off her shoulders, disappearing, boldly exposing her striking features. Immediately, Emma realized that it was the first time she had actually seen Decara's hair. It was as dark as night as were her eyes, both having a sinister fire all their own. She looked upon her aunt's hair, watching it change from black to an exceptionally shimmering color that reminded her of the feathers of a raven she once saw. Decara had arranged it in a rather impressive upsweep, creating a most elaborate fashion for it remained tediously braided in a twist, rising up and disappearing into her crown, leaving her slender swanlike neck delicately exposed. Emma had never imagined her aunt to possess any kind of beauty, but she had to admit it, like it or not, Decara was an uncommonly striking woman, and for a little while, her aunt almost seemed approachable.

"Look," Emma pleaded, taking her eyes off Decara's hair and face, looking straight in her eyes. "I know that you want something from me, so just take it and let's get this over with."

"No no, child," argued Decara. "I don't want to take anything from you. Honestly, I don't," she said in a soft voice. "This is about what I want to give you."

"All right," Emma answered with a frustrated tone. "What is it, tell me then?"

"Patience, my dear," Decara said playfully. "First, I would like to look at you for a moment." Her eyes widened, her mouth turning inward while she devoured Emma with looks that seemed to penetrate down to her very bones. "You're rather pretty, aren't you? Pretty in a dwarflike, dollish kind of way and such incredibly beautiful and innocent eyes you have, and such lovely curly blond hair. Yes, in just a short time, your auntie Decara will turn you into a real looker," she said, taking a lock of Emma's hair in her hands, rolling it around her long fingers.

"Stop it; I don't like you touching me."

A pretentious hurt expression forced its way over Decara's face. "I'm sorry. I meant no harm."

"No harm!" Emma objected. "All you do is harm people and you do the same to animals, I know!"

"My dear, if you are referring to your precious brother, he had it coming to him, the sassy, sweet boy."

"And what about the seals, do they have it coming to them as well?"

"Why, whatever do you mean, child?"

"Oh, just stop it already! You know exactly what I mean. I can hear them. You know I can hear them crying at night. They are in such pain! Surely, you must know I can understand their misery."

"I suspected as much," Decara finally admitted.

"What monstrous thing are you doing to them?"

The raven-haired woman merely stared at Emma, angered at her blatant interrogation. "For a child once so weak and sickly, you sure have become bold and cocky!"

"Answer me!" Emma demanded.

"Careful, whippersnapper, I should be very cautious if I were you. Your ill-fated health could easily return as quickly as it vanished, and this time, I don't think we'll be in any real hurry for such a profound display of remission."

"Why do you hurt them? What could they have possibly done to you? They are beautiful, innocent animals!"

Decara started to laugh insanely. "Innocent! Of course, you would know all about that, wouldn't you?"

"Whatever you are doing to them is unforgivable. I can feel their pain. You are draining them, taking something from them, something sacred!"

Decara excruciatingly grabbed for another half smile. She then reached out, taking hold of Emma's hair again, frolicking with the curled-up ends while she spoke. "Like cattle and swine, they exist for our advantage, something to slap between our bread before we eat, precious child. They are merely commodities, nothing more."

"Don't lie to me, Decara! Don't you know I can see right through you, or did you forget that I too have certain abilities?"

"No, I did not forget."

"Like my brother Kenyan, seals can feel pain. You not only kill and skin them, you do something else to them, something even more diabolical!"

"I think your imaginative mental gifts are working overtime, child. I simply run a business, and my business happens to deal in seal goods and their advantageous wares. Surely you have seen some of my beautiful seal coats."

"No, I have not and I never want to, I think it is horrible! I think you're horrible!"

"That's because you do not understand."

"I never will, never!"

"You will. You'll see. In just a little time, it will all become clear to you," Decara promised while mistreating Emma's hair, her deceptive smile breaking out the veins in her taut throat. "I shall see to it."

"Stop touching me!" Emma shouted.

"Enlighten me, won't you?" Decara asked, amusing herself by refusing to let go of her niece's curly blond hair. "What is it that the seals tell you, *hmmm?*"

Emma merely shook her head, not wanting to speak, but when she felt Decara's grasp on her hair tighten, she thought otherwise. "I don't know . . . dreadful, unspeakable things!"

"What kind of dreadful, unspeakable things?"

"I can hear them at night. At first I thought it to be a dream, but I know now that it was not. They cry out begging for help, but I don't know how to help them," she wept.

"How touching," Decara sneered, allowing for the subdued coldness to surface over her alabaster complexion, daring to tighten her twirling grip over the already seriously tangled clump of hair clustered around Emma's solemn and anguished face. "And what else do you hear, my precious wooden imp?"

"Nothing," Emma said, latching on to Decara's skeleton-like fingers, trying to untangle them from the clumps of hair she was pulling from her aching scalp. "You're hurting me! Stop it!"

"Yes, child, of course, of course," Decara nonchalantly said. "But first you must tell me what the seals are telling you," she suggested, tightening her pull.

"I told you! They merely cry out in pain for someone to help them. Now let go of me!" Emma screamed, digging her nails into her aunt's pale hand.

Decara smiled evilly, holding her cruel grip a time longer before abruptly releasing it. "Very well," she decreed, unweaving her long fingers in and out of the blond cobweb that she had created, quickly peeling off the matted strands of hair caught around her wicked grip. Emma's head sprang backward, at last free from Decara's monstrous hold. She bit her lip so as not to scream out in absolute abhorrence. She rubbed her head, easing the throbbing there and then looked at Decara with the foulest glare. In a flash, the dark woman bolted up and off the edge of the bed, her extraordinary cape outstretched like gargoyle wings, clawing outward, covering the floor she perpetually seemed to float upon. Then turning toward the small circular porthole situated near the bed's headboard, she uncoiled herself, just remaining silent, staring out through the frosted glass before her.

Still rubbing the throbbing place where Decara tore at her hair, Emma watched her wicked aunt. For a long time, the only sound abounding was the howling of the ever-whistling wind and the constant creaking of the ship, this and Decara's clicking fixation—a fingernail-tapping addiction she performed quite regularly, usually right before all hell broke loose. However, this time would allow for yet another exception. As Decara's long red painted nails tapped agonizingly against the wall, Emma continued in her study of the evil woman while Decara kept right on tap, tap, tapping, intently, staring out of the frosted obstruction before her.

"You're never going to let us go, are you?" Emma whispered.

Decara did not answer but kept right on tapping.

"What did you do to my brother? Where is he?"

Just more tapping followed.

"Answer me!" Emma shouted.

"Why should I when you will not consider telling me what I need to hear?"

"You mean about the seals?"

"Oh yesssss," Decara said, tap, tap, tapping, dragging out the *s*'s in her word, sounding like a snake.

Emma swallowed hard before answering. "Very well, but I can only tell you what my dreams have brought me."

"Go on." *Tap, tap, tap.*

"Last night, I dreamed of the white seal again. I'm not sure why, but he is someone you feel that you must destroy."

Decara surprisingly grinned, pleased to hear her niece confess such knowledge to her.

"He's not like the others, is he?"

"Never mind that, just tell me what else your dreams showed you."

"Why is that one particular seal so important to you?"

"The creature has what belongs to me, as well as what belongs to you." *Tap . . . tap . . . tap . . .*

"Me?"

"Yes." *Tap . . . tap . . . tap . . .*

Emma turned away from her aunt, trying to remember the entire dream. She pressed her fading thoughts, but only a vague image appeared. "I'm not sure, but I think it has to do with a stone of some kind, a rare and magic stone, but it isn't really a stone, is it?"

Decara did not answer directly. She just kept tapping as her dark eyes began to glow an eerie red color. "No, it is your deliverance . . . and mine," she offered in a low, hollowed groan, sending chills straight down Emma's back. Her knees began to tremble, and she quickly pushed down on them with her hands brazenly giving back her response.

"You mean *your* deliverance!"

Decara turned to give her a dastardly smile. "Until the white beast is apprehended and the stone he now carries around his wretched throat is returned to me, we both shall remain captives."

Suddenly, the room grew dark, as if a curtain of wind abruptly blew across a flame. Through the shadows, Decara made her way toward her niece, her eyes burning like two small balls of fiery coals. Emma wanted to run from her, but she knew she could not do so. All she could do was attempt to control her jumping nerves and try not to show just how frightened she had suddenly become. Decara hauntingly continued, her glowing eyes leading the way. "You are the doorway to a new existence. For you are my kin and through you we will both share a promised reward."

Emma waited for Decara to stop moving before looking up toward the wanton face of her aunt; she tried not to look into those shining eyes while addressing her. "I don't know what you are talking about."

"I think you do."

Emma stared at Decara for a long time, this time unable to keep from looking into those dreadful eyes. Then surprisingly, Emma smiled, her face exhibiting a peculiar new sense of awareness. "You can't destroy the white seal, can you?"

Decara just glared at her sadistically.

"That's why I am here, isn't it? You cannot kill it. If you do, the powers in the stone would die," Emma said, her gifted perceptions deepening. She rubbed at her temples, trying to make sense of it all. "But it isn't a stone, is it? It's something that is far more precious."

Decara's smile broadened, her eyes filling up with more glowing essence that clearly showed her wild anticipation over her niece's incredible perception.

Emma's head began to throb with a nauseating beat. "You actually intend for me to kill the white seal. That's what this is really all about. I must do it in order for you to keep the power alive. Wow, you really are insane, aren't you?" Emma exclaimed, almost laughing.

Decara evilly scowled at her.

Emma scowled back with a powerful share of added contempt and then spoke: *"Innocence destroying innocence?"*

All at once, there appeared a smile on the dark woman's lips. "That's my clever little witch. I knew you would see reason."

"Oh yes, you really are crazy! How could you ever think I would do such a thing? I would never harm it, never! I don't care what kind of powers his destruction would bring. I would never consider it, *never!*"

Decara's fake smile went on to become even more absolute, for her grimace now crawled mischievously across her face, eating it up with one enormous leer. "Oh, I think when the time comes, you will change your mind."

"No, I won't, never ever!"

"Hmm . . . ," Decara lightly hummed. "Really? Well, I think the reality of watching your dear precious sweet-boy brother die just might persuade you."

"You're a monster!"

"And not just suddenly, mind you, it will be long and excruciating. I can assure you."

"Stop it!" Emma shouted.

Decara maniacally laughed. "Just like the seals, my servant will peel him alive! Now that's got to hurt. *Ouch!* It will be a most impressive feat, one I just know you would not want to miss, but not to worry. I will see to it that you will be given a front-row seat to watch, knowing that for each time he screams, you and you alone will be held responsible!"

Terrified, Emma dropped her head inside the confines of her trembling lap, sobbing, shaking her head in disbelief, closing her eyes not wanting to look upon the evil dark woman ever again.

Weeping and covered in the surrounding darkness, she quickly recoiled further into her shadowed escape when she felt Decara's fingers begin to stroke the back of her head. "Hush, hush, my dear little prodigy," her aunt whispered, all the while her spiky fingers toying with Emma's blond hair again. "It will all work out in the end . . . you'll see," she said, her fingers leaving Emma's head while her voice trailed off with a wicked chuckle.

Emma did not stir or answer. She merely kept her face hidden inside the flowing folds of her nightdress, relieved that Decara's grip had pulled away from her. She remained this way for what seemed a frightfully long time, but when she heard the door open then quickly close and lock itself, she sprang up to find that Decara was no longer there. She had once again vanished.

Sitting at the end of the bed, Emma despairingly looked out into the flickering gloom before her. The shafts of sunlight had gone, and only slivers of opaque glare filled her existence. Turning from it all, she fell into the bed, her hands covering her face, weeping into the folds of the red-stained bedspread, her tiny form disappearing into its imposing boundlessness.

THE VAULT

Stealing tears from mother harps always made Decara giddy.

The removal of seal tears guaranteed in putting her in a good mood, for their exchange of teary suffering for diamonds always made her want to laugh out loud. Decara's love for the precious gems remained neurotic and obsessive. Just like the white seal furs she so often wore, her ostentatious want to flaunt her riches continued to consume her. She could never have enough and would always crave for more. She already had well over several thousand diamond chips made into fantastic and exquisite rings, bracelets, necklaces, as well as having had nearly eighteen hundred coats customized with hundreds of diamonds, again seal tears embellished throughout their snowy fur coats she alone kept exclusively for herself, valued well into the millions. Still, it was never enough.

Depending on the suffering the individual harp had experienced, the more heartbreaking and excruciating it was, the larger the tear, the bigger the diamond. It was always exciting for Decara for she never could be sure as what to expect. Fortunately for her, that is, the slimy varmints never disappointed; they always had plenty of tears left, always guaranteeing to produce a grandiose collection of the most glittering diamonds ever seen. Although she had not worn such fabulous furnishings since the death of her lover, Decara believed that it was now time for her to expand her wardrobe; she would add even more elaborate accessories to her already outrageous wares. Soon it would be the awaited Night of Screams, and she was expecting to look nothing less than absolutely fabulous! She knew her dark master would be watching her carefully, and she would pull out all the stops for that night; on that, all could be certain. However, until that time arrived, she would satisfy her lust for the sparkling seal extractions and further collections of dazzling heartaches.

It took a while for Oreguss to gather up all the remaining diamond chips. Falling asleep after one of his drunken binges, he had left two bulging sacks inside the laboratory from the night before. It was a good thing that Decara had not seen them still sitting there because he would be horsewhipped. Nevertheless, back to the laboratory he went to pick up the two bags full of crystallized tears and then off it was to the vault, the place where all the diamonds remained securely hidden and guarded.

The *Tiamat* had many secret passageways, and Oreguss knew and took advantage of every one of them. Down into the ship he crawled. He soon came to a tiny passageway where five small wooden steps disappeared into the dark vessel. Completing his descent, Oreguss squeezed through a tight opening leading into another corridor. His broad back entrapped him for a moment. He had recently put on another ten pounds and had to push and squeeze before he could be on his way again. Grumbling and moving through the scattered patches of darkness, he blindly went onward, cutting through the shadows until he reached a dimly lit area where a small shaft of pale green light slashed across his dark eyes. Throwing the sacks over his shoulders, he pushed his wide self through another scrubby hole. This opening was just as congested. However, determined in his efforts, Oreguss squeezed himself and the two sacks through, dropping over into another corridor awaiting him on the opposite side of the wall. Sprawling out onto the cold wooden floor, he crawled a few feet and then stood up, arching his aching back, hearing it snap back into place before he collected the sacks that he had temporarily lost hold of. He twisted his fingers around their drawstrings and began dragging the pair of treasured pouches down an incline back into the darkness, leading yet to another long corridor, not as narrow as its shadowy predecessor.

Snakelike, its twisted trail took Oreguss into a maze of intricate dimensions of more shadows. The obedient servant's fast pace showed his familiarity to this ambience of such a sightless path. As he left the darkness and entered a more illuminated area, he carelessly became too confident in his quick footing, tripping clumsily. He fell forward, pulling recklessly onto the two sacks, yanking and squashing them beneath his heavy frame. With a screaming, ripping sound, one of the sacks tore open, spilling out all over the floor. Outraged by his clumsiness, he began to curse and grumble, not caring about the fuss he was causing, spitting out all sorts of grunts and groans. Looking out at the endless spillage that he had just created, he furiously picked himself up; and while still grumbling and cursing, he began scooping up handfuls of the spilled treasure.

Angrily, he grasped at the dislodged glitter, throwing the treasures haphazardly back where they belonged. It took the agitated man all of fifteen minutes to refill the open sack. Just when he had finally picked up what he thought was the last remaining gem; one more stray would taunt him from across the way, defiantly twinkling at him from the semishadows. Wired with more frustration, he persisted in his grunting, knowing that when he tied up the sack, another lost straggler would peeve him all over again. Oreguss continued to curse under his dirty breath, stomping in exaggerated provocation, zeroing in on more shiny straggles, forcefully slapping down his giant hand, retrieving them and squashing them like miserable bugs.

When at last Oreguss finished chasing the bothersome seal tears, he once more came on yet another. Beyond furious, he wildly made his way over to it and grabbed it. Stomping like a mad man, he returned to the sack and tore it back open, throwing the insolent chip back inside. Then hoping it had better been the last time; he furiously took hold of the sack's dangling cloth string and tied it, making a hard knot. Grunting like a pig with clogged sinuses, he sluggishly turned; and slumping forward, he continued dragging the seal tears down to the end of the corridor, where a silvery colored door was waiting for him, appearing more like a mausoleum than a secret vault. Its imposing tombstone features stared at him through the shielded darkness. Fumbling and irritated, he threw down the sacks and aimlessly started searching through his breast pocket for the key that would unlock this cryptlike entity. After a flustering few minutes, Oreguss found what he needed. Then twisting his thick neck from side to side, he looked about suspiciously, making sure that no spying eyes were patrolling him, but there could be none. He was much too clever for anyone to see. Besides, he alone knew all the secret shortcuts; so secure in his deed, he choked the key between his large fingers, pushing it into a rectangular lock situated near the shining silver handle of the vault. A slight click sounded. Then with a burst of savage energy, he was flat up against the door of the vault pushing and shoving on it until it opened.

There, before the hairy brute, stood a rather large-sized room just crawling with more shadows. Although he could not see them all, he knew that the room was already more than half filled with hundreds upon hundreds of bulging sacks stuffed full of sparkling seal tears, enough diamonds for thousands of kings and then some. Pushing at the door with more of his bulging weight, some light spilled in from the corridor, slightly lighting up the inside. As the portal stood agape, Oreguss flung the two sacks into the massive safe. With an enormous grin slapped proudly across his whisker-laden face, the satisfied lackey took a firm hold of the vault door; and forcing himself against it one final time, he sent it thundering shut. As before, Oreguss gave a second look around, checking for intruders. Again, he found nothing. Quickly locking the door, he delighted at his successful and completed task, listening to the lock surrender itself with another hollow click, knowing just how pleased Decara would be. She might even reward him with an extra bottle of whiskey. He giggled to himself, slapping the key into his breast pocket, patting his apish fingers against his burly chest. Feeling particularly confident that both key and treasure remained tucked away, Oreguss began to chomp up and down on his yellow-stained teeth, expressing his smugness. Yes, Decara was not the only one to have cause to celebrate. After she gave him that bottle of whiskey, he too had plans for his own private celebration, alone in the confines of his own quarters, and why shouldn't he celebrate? He did everything she asked of him. As soon as he could tell her about his latest catch, his reward would be grand. For he just knew that the seal he most recently threw into the black cage had to be just packed full of tears. What's more, he knew he would be guaranteed plenty of alcoholic spoils, especially after one of Decara's seal-tear sessions. This made Oreguss a very happy man. He practically skipped down the corridors thinking about his expected share of firewater, pushing all the shadows away in his hasty departure. Yes, it was soon to be party time!

Oreguss continued to hurry back through the winding corridors, feeling his way through the darkness until he once again came to the small cubbyhole in the wall. He would have to repeat the process of squeezing his bulky frame through all over again to get to the other side. There, he would find the steps that would lead him back to his quarters. However, while, pushing himself through he abruptly, stopped, now halfway trapped inside the opening. With one leg poking straight out, he listened. He believed he could hear footsteps echoing off in the nearby corridor. Remaining just where he was, he listened some more; but this time, there were no footsteps, just the usual aching sounds of the *Tiamat*'s internal grumbling. Waiting just a few minutes longer, he decided he was mistaken and was now wasting his time. Besides, he was extremely uncomfortable, bent and crushed inside that hole that way, and was much too anxious to leave.

Pulling his leg inward and pushing against his thick midsection, Oreguss began cramming himself through the opening, gathering up his furry bulk, grunting aloud as the hairs that covered his chest and back pulled and stung, abrading against the angled sides of the puny aperture. After a bit of a fight, he finally sorted himself through, landing back onto the blackened floors of the corridors that would take him to his room. Impatient to return, he quickly found the stairs; and without the slightest difficulty, he swung his hulking body upward, grabbing firmly on to the railing, rapidly accelerating like a crazed insect. Wild with the need to guzzle the drink that he so desperately needed, Oreguss disappeared into the darkness.

Could he have waited just a brief time longer and had listened just a few seconds more, he would have not been in such an insatiable hurry to return to his quarters or to his mistress with such contented arrogance. For he would have learned that he had made a most serious blunder in thinking that he was alone down there. For directly after his quick departure from the secret vault, the sound of more shuffling footsteps had returned. The sound echoed down the forbidden halls as the shadows of two men scratched against the cold darkness.

SNOOPING SEALERS

Slowly, the two snooping men shifted through the shadows, both heading directly toward the cryptlike door housing Decara's incredible treasure, a supposedly well-guarded treasure accidentally exposed, its whereabouts made possible by the incompetence of their employer's peculiar manservant.

Excitedly, their warm breath frosted lightly over the silvery face of the vault's door. Surprisingly, a distinct crunching sound suddenly snapped beneath the boot of one of the intruders. With a tingling excitement sparking between them, both men turned to face each other. Quickly, a hand dropped down as its owner lifted his weather-beaten boot from where the crunching sound came. As the hand reached down further, it came upon a shining stone—another serious mistake left behind, proving to be yet another grave blunder left unseen by the hairy henchman. The shining stone caught a shaft of light coming from somewhere above. It glistened with brilliance, causing the two men to breathe in a gasp of excitement. Showing off the precious find to each other, both shadowy figures emerged from the darkness, coming directly under the shaft of light that was lighting up the stone.

There they stood—two sealers sailing upon the *Tiamat* under the command of Captain Thorne, gaining wealth for skinning the infant whitecoats of Sealssong. Like a couple of excited schoolboys, these two rebellious men appeared to be in their late thirties—one, tall, thin, and dark, sporting a most unkempt beard that poorly covered up his pockmarked complexion; the other, a round-shaped man, considerably overweight for such a difficult journey, with a red face and thinning, frizzy red hair to match. The two men sparked with feverish excitation, passing the sparkling chip back and forth while prospects of pirating their own treasure deliciously washed through their flashing thoughts.

Suspecting Oreguss and Decara of having been involved in matters other than mere seal hunting frequently occurred to most of the men aboard the *Tiamat*, but this discovery was unexpected and most enterprising. For it was with the unsavory boldness of these two men that the forbidden secrets would come to be first revealed, secrets that should have never been disturbed, for the repercussions would be fatal. However, now, such notions remained decidedly far away from the excited minds of both swilers. It was all too intoxicating. Their voracity would hold no boundaries. The diamond chip was right there, large and fantastic, shining brilliantly; and the best part of all, locked behind the vault door in front of them was a million more of its exorbitant relations!

"Just look at this beauty, Cyrus!" the pockmarked man uttered, rolling the large diamond around his callused fingers. "Ever see one this size before?"

"Don't reckon I ever did!" impetuously answered the plump red-haired man. "I knew that freaky flunky of hers was up to something, but I never thought that we'd find this!"

"Nor did I, my underhanded friend, nor did I."

"You said if we tailed the scurvy ape we'd come up with something. Guess it really paid off, huh, Yorick?"

"You bet it did, and just waiting for us behind this door are so many more of these delightful beauties!" rejoiced the pockmarked seal hunter, tapping his bony palm against the cold door of the silver vault.

"Joy! Joy! Rapture!" sang the red-faced man.

"Cyrus, do you realize what this means? We're rich, man—*rich!*"

The paunchy red-faced hunter nervously began to laugh before speaking with a hushed whisper. "I always wanted to pay back that wench for all the misery she's dumped on us."

"Yes," hissed Yorick. "But this time it's not a payback. This time it's a payoff, my friend, the biggest yet!"

Then surprisingly, Cyrus gave out a small unmanly gasp. "But tell me, Yorick, what if the spiteful hellcat suspects?"

"You mean the frigid dragon lady herself. Miss Butter-Wouldn't-Melt Decara?"

"Yeah, you know she's not to be fooled with, she'd have both our heads if she found out."

"Why? Are you planning to tell her?" Yorick laughed, struggling to keep his voice down.

"Of course not."

"Then shut up and help me so we could get better acquainted with more of those beauties just a-waitin' for me to caress them!"

"Okay, okay," Cyrus fumbled. "But, just say, she does find out?"

The bearded Yorick shook his head, still rolling the impressive stone between his dirty fingers, drooling hungrily over it. "By the time, that wench hears tell of her unfortunate loss, it will already be too late," he gloated. "Now come on! Snap out of it, or is little piggy Cyrus afraid of the big bad Decara?"

"No, of course, I'm not! Why should I be? Would I have come this far if I were?"

"Then stop your damn bellyaching, man, remember, my corpulent comrade—no guts, no glory!"

"I know that too! I'm only saying that we might wanna think this through first. You know, make a real plan and then come back."

"Oh, I was right. Little piggy Cyrus is scared!"

"It isn't that, I'm only saying—"

"Think, man, do you want to be a dirty swiler your whole life?" Yorick growled, grabbing the frizzy-haired chubby man just below the neck. "Do you think we're ever going to get a chance like this again?"

Cyrus timidly shook his head, trying to pry his greedy buddy off him, not succeeding very well.

"Then buck up, man!" Yorick growled, releasing his grip.

However, blindly determined, Cyrus opened his mouth, preparing to yet once more present his already agitated companion with another series of fretful doubts; but Yorick slapped his dirty palm over the chubby man's mouth, hitting the man's lips closed with a hard smack. *"Enough!"* he snarled. "I'm not going to let you screw this up for me. Am I making myself clear, fat boy?"

Hurriedly, Cyrus nodded inside the callused grade of Yorick's hold, waiting for his aggressive partner to release his filthy hand from his crimson face. "Now, you better get a grip!" Yorick warned, letting go with a forceful shove, nearly tumbling the round man backward. "Either help me or get lost! I don't want any sissy man, lily wimp spoiling things 'cause he's freakin' scared!"

The forever-blushing Cyrus turned an even deeper shade of red while his eyes blinked irregularly from his growing apprehension. "Don't say that, Yorick. You know that I'm good for it."

"Do I?" Yorick questioned, scratching into his scraggly beard. "Maybe I should reconsider this whole partnership."

"No, I only meant—"

"What?"

"Well," Cyrus said, pausing, taking a moment to swallow, his eyes restlessly scanning across the impending darkness closing in, the, sounds of the groaning *Tiamat* increasing. "It's just that there is something . . . well, something wrong about this place. Like, I don't know . . . like, if we take anything from it, we'll be punished."

"Talk sense, man!"

Cyrus did not answer directly. He neurotically glanced over his shoulder, asking, "Can't you feel it?"

"Feel what, man?"

Cyrus swallowed hard. "I don't know. I can't explain it."

"Are you bailing?"

"No!"

"Then help me with the freakin' door," Yorick groaned, partially kneeling down to take hold of a flat metal bar that he had propped up against the wall. Yorick had swiped the metal bar on his journey down to the vault. He never ventured anywhere without a weapon of some kind, but he never imagined that he would be using it for something entirely unexpected. Oreguss had obviously left the bar behind, using it for some kind of maintenance work. Yorick wasn't sure what the blasted thing was initially intended for, but he didn't care. Right now he had definite plains for this tool, and it was going to make him very rich.

"Wait," Cyrus warned. "Listen . . . What was that? Didn't you hear it? It's all around us!" Beyond annoyed, and ready to take a swing at the plump man, Yorick squeezed onto the metal bar, grasping even firmly around the sharp edge that ran across its bottom. He bit down on his taut and cracked lips, just glaring at his paranoid buddy.

"They say the ship is haunted, ya know?" Cyrus whispered with a nervous twitch tugging at the corner of his mouth.

"Do they now? And what else do they say?" Yorick teased, his voice sounding pretentious, his temper rising.

"That—that Decara is a witch of some kind and she can suck out people's souls. They also say that she steals little children from their beds at night and brings them here so she and that bear manservant of hers can drink their blood!"

"My, you sure know how to rouse my appetite."

"Well, it's true! I've seen things—I've heard things."

Yorick began to laugh, his dark eyes showing no signs of amusement. "You are bailing, aren't ya?"

"No, I can't explain it. It's just that, well . . . I think we need to leave this place for now. We'll come back later, okay?"

"All right, fat boy, I have had just about enough of your spook talk!" Yorick shouted, ready to grab for Cyrus's throat again, when suddenly the ship shifted sideways, rocking unsteadily back and forth, both sides of the vessel rattling like skeleton bones over a tombstone. It began to grow louder, sounding as if the entire ship was coming apart, this time nearly throwing both men to the floor. Again, the *Tiamat* ferociously shook, and Yorick and Cyrus found themselves to be clinging to the silver handle of the vault and each other. Clearly the ship was in trouble. However, as quickly as it erupted, in just a few moments, the vessel began to settle down. Both men remained silent, slowly rocking back and forth, holding on to each other and the silver handle of the vault, both frozen there in the semidarkness that continued to surround them.

The calmness did not last.

From out of the shadows, another disturbing sound shot across the blackened corridors. A loud banging sound surrounded them, allowing for even more goose bumps to pop and tingle beneath both men's skin. Then in a flash, the pounding disappeared down one of the dark corridors. Then silence.

"What the—" Yorick yelled, releasing his grip from the handle, as well as the shaking arm of his petrified crew mate.

Cyrus followed directly. "*S-s-s-s-*sounded like snapping bones and bouncing chains," he squealed, pathetically striving to situate his quivering feet onto the black floor beneath him.

"Good Lord, not only do you think we have ghosts, you have the damn things saddled with their own rattling chains!"

"But you had to hear it that time. You just had to!"

"Shut up, there were no bones or chains! It was just the ship moving and settling! That was all!" Yorick yelled while he kept right on listening to the new weird sounds that were currently echoing about. While they continued to listen, each man holding his breath, everything suddenly became unnaturally silent. Then out of nowhere, another violent-sounding CLINK-CLANKING frenzy returned. It banged and thumped uncontrollably for what seemed an eternity, and then it went away, rumbling and disappearing down the corridors, fading back into the previous unnatural silence.

Yorick was the first to break the muted quiet. "Maybe you're right. Maybe we'll come back another time. You know, before we're missed," he said, attempting to hide his uneasiness, holding tight to the giant diamond chip clenched deep inside his sweaty palm, having never let go despite the volatile shaking. "We'll come back better prepared, when things have settled down some. What do you say?"

"I'm right behind you!" the red-faced Cyrus hastily added.

Both men turned, heading once more down the corridors that would return them back to more stable and familiar places; and once more, the ship went berserk. It shook and vibrated, so much so that the floorboards began to break apart. Violently, the wooden floors clattered and jumped about, hitting the men hard across the legs, snapping mercilessly up at their ankles and shaking knees. It was as if some gigantic thing was attempting to come up from somewhere beneath the sea. Luckily, this disturbance, as did the other, did not last long and then like before, it simply vanished. A petrified Cyrus rubbed at his sore ankles and knees before scratching nervously at his big belly, his eyes bulging out of their sockets. "What's happening, Yorick?"

The pockmarked companion thought for a few seconds, rubbing and soothing his own feet and aching knee joints before he spoke, for he also needed time to swallow down the knot that had just squeezed around his throbbing tonsils. "We must have hit something!"

"Something big, huh, like a mother of an iceberg, do you think so, Yorick?"

"How in the hell should I know?"

"Well, whatever it is, Thorne will be checking it out. That's for sure!"

"Come on!" Yorick shouted with a disturbing edge to his voice, continuing to rub at his hurting ankles. "We best find Thorne." Cyrus gave a quick and nervous nod, ever anxious to leave as well. Then Yorick suddenly stopped, blocking the plump man's way with his arms, his scraggly beard only inches away from the, red-faced man's stubby little nose. "You got any more of that rum you keep hidden down in those dirty underdrawers of yours?"

"A little."

"Then let's have at it, man!" Yorick ordered, waving his hand fast, motioning to his companion to be quick about it.

"Well now, don't drink it all. There isn't much left, you know!"

"Come on, come on, give it up!"

Begrudgingly, Cyrus dug down inside his pants and pulled out a small shiny vial. Not waiting for the chubby man to give it to him, Yorick grabbed it, twisted off the mini lid, and took a gluttonous swig of the firewater he so desperately needed. Finishing his gulp, Yorick wiped his mouth with his dirty hand. Never returning the flask back to his friend, he claimed the vial for his own, pushing it into his back pocket, the huge diamond chip finding a place in his other pocket.

As both men left the vault, more shades of darkness fell around them while they walked through the twisting halls. They crowded each other, pushing, heading back down the long corridors, each man eager to join the other crew members above.

Not far from the vault, another sudden clanking sound came from a room that remained heavily cluttered in dreary, dark shadows. It was a room down the corridor located just opposite of the vault door, a room that neither of them had noticed. *Clink-clank* went the rattling sounds again, sounds of moving chains against a cold, drafty floor, but this was no speculated ghost. For this watcher was made of flesh and blood and had only recently been vanquished to this place by command of the vile Decara, taken by the cruel henchman who had broken his leg before gagging and dragging him there.

Here, in the blackness of this unfamiliar cell, Kenyan lay on his stomach, his hands bound, breathing heavily through a scratchy cloth gag tied tight around his mouth, his broken leg throbbing as he stared through a small crack under the door that incarcerated him; he could see everything that happened nearly two feet up from the stony flooring of his new and horrible prison cell. He had watched and listened to the words of the excited and greedy men discovering the diamond chip. Only one of his eyes could peer through the tiny break, but it was all that he needed to see Oreguss, the two nervous crew members, and best of all, the secret and strange silver door that protected an unimaginable and fantastic treasure! Quietly, the injured Kenyan remained prostrate against the incredibly cold, stony floor, holding to a penetrating stare aimed exclusively at the massive vault door guarding Decara's riches.

Oreguss would be back soon, bringing the usual slop. However, this time Kenyan actually was in definite anticipation for him to arrive, for the abrasive cloth cutting into his mouth had begun to hurt almost as much as his burned cheek and broken leg. As far as the dreadful slime Oreguss would bring for him to eat, something he would never welcome, he knew that as soon as he smelled it, his stomach would retch. He would puke up whatever was still stubborn enough to stick to his ribs, and yet he would do whatever it took to survive this nightmare.

Kenyan's mind sparked further with new hope. The two seal hunters would be back. They would not merely leave such a treasure without trying to take more of it, and that is what he would count on. It would be these two unsuspecting men who would free him from this hellish captivity.

The next time, Kenyan would make sure that the gag was not around his face no matter what. He would call out to them, and with a bit of luck, the sea would be calm and the men would hear him.

For this newfound prospect of optimism, he would endure anything. He would battle against all the odds and anything else Decara would send his way. Broken leg or not, he was going to beat this thing. For how else could he ever expect to execute the deed that had inspired salvation for both him and his sister? The moment that they could at last be free was all that kept him alive. It was the driving force that fed him daily, sustaining him, for he knew the moment would eventually come: the exact moment he would kill the witch!

This was all he could think of; it devoured and consumed his every waking moment.

However, for the time being, he would have to wait and plot in the darkness of his newly acquired cell, alone, peering out into the blackened halls that stretched toward a cryptlike vault door that coldly stared back with menacing defiance as if it were silently laughing at him, and . . . it was.

THE DROP-OFF

By the time the whale reached the main nursery, everyone aboard had been awake and most anxious, not one of them knowing what to expect. Another blanket of fog skimmed over the icy mountains, making it appear ghostly and uncertain, but this did not seem to faze the mad seal. In no time at all, Mum was screaming out commands that made no sense whatsoever; both walruses were already hanging over the edge, wanting a better look at the grounds below, while the penguin maintained his post near the very rear of the whale ship. Not wanting to venture near the others, especially the mad harpie, he constantly kept his distance.

The effects of the sleeping bubbles had long since worn off the white seal, and he had spent much of the remainder of the trip in quiet thought. He kept thinking about all the incredible things the whale had told him, and of course, his thoughts were never far from his mother. He knew that in just a little while, he would have to say goodbye to Mum and his new friends for the magnificent whale was about to set out to find his mama, but how long would he have to wait? What was this place called, *the Origin of Lights*? Above all, what or who was this *Kellis* they first had to find? Could she hold the answers? Was she an angelic creature, or an evil one, just like the kind of things that walked on two limbs called man? Should she be evil, would the whale and the others ever return, or would they, just like his mama, be lost to him forever? Miracle shivered with fear, feeling the whale surge forward, grating up against the island. The time had come. They had at last reached Sealssong.

Kishk melted into the surrounding floes, lining himself up directly in front of the island while Mum continued shouting out commands. "This way to the nurseries of Sealssong, single file, single file, if you please!" she barked with a deafening roar.

The feisty penguin did not waste any time in resuming his rightful commanding duty. Quickly, he scooted toward the others, his shrill voice cutting the air while zooming near the very top of the whale's reflected head. "Really, madam, that is quite enough! I give the orders here, not you!" Mum merely made a disgusted expression at the bird and then belched loudly in his face.

The bird, while trying to maintain his temper, closed his eyes, took in a deep breath, and stuck out one of his tiny penguin flippers. "This way if you please!" ushered the penguin, making room for

Crumpels while she came barreling forward, soon followed by her enormous son, Poo-Coo.

The excursion down was much easier than the one going up, for in no time, both walruses found that they were safe and sound and back on the island. They remained there silently staring up at Miracle, waiting for him to join them. Instead, they watched him turn and begin making his way back over toward Mum.

"Must I go?" asked the white seal, unable to stop the tears that were easily gathering in his huge shining black eyes.

Mum looked kindly at the pup and kissed him promptly on the head. "As much as I hate to surrender you over to those bumbling sacks of jellyfish poop, I know that you will be safe with the walruses. Besides, we don't know what we'll find out there, and such a journey is far too dangerous for the likes of you, *Love-ya,*" Mum said, then smiled tenderly. "It would be better if you remained with them, love."

"But, Mum, I promise I'll be good! Please take me with you! I won't be any trouble, honest!"

Mum gave a rather disapproving smirk, tilting her head sideways, showing that she was not about to give in to him. "*Love-ya . . . ,*" she scolded, holding to her smirk of disparagement. "Now go with the walruses. The whale has instructed them to find a secluded cave where you will be safe. They will know what to do," Mum said. "Now off with you, love."

It was then that the blue whale spoke his melodious voice, still kind, yet commanding. "Not to fret, little pup, it will do you good. Get you better acquainted with your own kind. See how they live, feed and interact with one another. You might find it to be something you did not expect," the whale said with a massive grin. "As soon as we learn of what happened to your mother, we will return, but we cannot do this unless we leave now, and the sooner we leave, the quicker we will find her, my brave new friend."

Complying, the seal nodded his head.

"We're as good as dead, kid!" screeched the penguin from way up top.

"Mulgrew!" scolded the whale.

"Well, I'm just saying!" the penguin chirped with a sighing groan stuffed neatly under his beak. His eyes suddenly came upon the Mad Mum now lying on her back, and he had to cringe while watching her engage in another round of her stupid and annoying Clap-Clap game. "Somebody kill me!" he lamented, his eyes rolling up into his head.

As the whale began to push away from the island, he spoke out toward the two walruses and the white seal. "Find a place with the others. Find solace here, but above all else, watch out for the man-beast! Never let your guard down for a moment! He is evil, and he will kill you! Never forget that!" Kishk warned.

Crumpels and Poo-Coo continued to wait for the white seal to join them before wishing all a farewell, impulsively waving their flippers at the whale, while Miracle whispered softly, the others hearing him plainly, "Please find her please, and come back to us. Come back to us."

"Good luck, my dear friends," the whale sang back. "Our thoughts and good wishes remain with you!"

Mum merely blew kisses covered in gooey snot bubbles while Mulgrew made disgusting and growling noises, glaring at the mad thing the entire time.

Miracle remained motionless, watching the blue chanter and his small crew set off for the Origin of Lights in search of answers that would somehow lead him to his beloved mother. Then as quick as a twinkle of a star, Kishk and his stupendous frame suddenly vanished under the shadow of a passing cloud. It was as if the giant creature had never even been there, for the rolling mist had completely covered him up.

*   *   *

Although it was morning, it would prove to be a day without the sun, dull and gray, but that would not hinder the residents of Sealssong. In whatever color, shape, or form it was to be, it was indeed early morning; and the entire nursery was about to wake up in all its usual celebration.

Nonetheless, the white seal and the two walruses hardly felt like celebrating, for they suddenly felt frightened and all alone. Without the protection of the wise chanter, the island no longer felt safe. Instead, it became abruptly strange and unfamiliar, turning into a scary place filled with weird and eerie sounds, each chilling them with a cold and rash apprehension. The rolling fog only helped to intensify the gloomy situation, but like it or not, they were there for the duration of whatever was about to be.

Quietly, they slowly turned from the slushy sea, and at that precise moment, something happened that frightened them all. The purple stone around Miracle's neck began to glow with a peculiar pulsating beat. It hummed too, sounding like distant wails of discarded voices, all of them singing a faraway and haunting melody. Without thinking, Miracle wished to break the seashell chain, casting it aside; but he quickly considered otherwise, remembering what Mum had warned him about. He shook his head and decided to forget the matter. Besides, by the time he looked down at it again, the voices were no more and the stone had gone out, but he did notice that he was not quite as afraid as he was moments before. It was as if the stone had magically taken away his fear—well, most of it.

The strange sounds of the island continued to unnerve him, but he remained determined to overcome whatever he might encounter. With a quick turn of his head, he looked at the walruses, which now sandwiched him, knowing that they must begin to make their way into the nursery. The sooner they found a cave of their own, the sooner they might shake the unsettling feelings grasping at them. In one common effort, the three voyagers began making their way into the secluded harp cradle. The rolling fog came pouring in around them, snatching them all away and leaving only the sounds of Sealssong to echo hauntingly after them.

Two Ships in the Fog

Once more, the *Tiamat* groaned, rattling its insides, making its way through the ice and snow, intent on reaching the islands of Sealssong. A thick and hanging shroud of fog infested itself perfectly over the ship, bringing visibility to absolute zero. Still, the vessel remained steadfast, cutting through the ghostly clinging mist. It jolted, tottering dangerously while Captain Thorne executed his skills, daring to navigate the ship, safely undeviating from the threatening obstructions, courageously breaking through the rebellious fog and the ice monstrosities hidden within its perilous surroundings.

Eventually, Thorne slowly brought the *Tiamat* to a near-nonexistent sail, completely unaware that through the murky nothingness, barely missing the, ship, one particular and massive blue whale had crossed dangerously before the foreboding vessel. He would have no possible clue that the fantastic creature was now only a few hundred yards away from the bow itself, its tail having missed it by just a few mere inches. The whale Kishk would continue swaying away from icebergs, missing each one due to his fortunate ability to produce sounds of sonic clicks and tones that he would send out and wait to return and, when they did, each recurrence would give him immediate forewarning to any unseen and dangerous formations of ice he might encounter.

The blue chanter would be far away from the ship, having long since disappeared within the fog, continuing to move onward, humming and clicking and chortling strange and various frequencies that would momentarily vibrate and reflect on zones that would hopefully spare them from danger, ultimately taking them into a remarkably different realm of reality—a secluded place, a forbidden place, an existence that few, if any, had ever seen before, a place known as the *Origin of Lights*.

WATERSPOUTS

A cold and penetrating blanket of mist hung mercilessly over the chanter's eyes, hindering any expectation of seeing mere inches beyond. Still, its obstruction appeared to make no difference to him whatsoever. However, it most definitely annoyed the short-tempered penguin. As for the Mad Mum of Sealssong, the dense fog most assuredly did not bother her. In fact, she was not aware of it. She merely remained indifferent to it, tending to her own private world of insanity, both seal and penguin sharing one thing in common: detesting each other and remaining far away from the other as possible. The intrepid whale, ignoring both of their peculiarities, glided effortlessly, completely focused on his innate progressions through the sea. Breaking through the silvery ice pathways, Kishk chortled out his high-pitched clicks and hums, making his way through the misty covering that concealed him from the rest of the world. As if recognizing the exact phrases the whale was making, Mum snorted and shook her head, heeding the sounds with diligence, seeming to understand the whale's projected frequencies. She continued listening, smiling, ridding herself of the constant dampness collecting on her snout. Mulgrew merely waddled back and forth, growling under his breath, glaring at the seal, neurotically pacing like some expectant father. Back and forth he went from the very tip to the very end of the whale that disappeared into the frigid silvery waters. Mum offered equally countless glances of disgust back toward the penguin. She irritatingly surveyed the fidgety seabird disappear and reappear in the cleaving fog, to and fro, in and out of the thickset mist. Having all she could take, she finally bellowed, "Will you stop that incessant promenading, birdbrain?"

The penguin merely growled. Holding his building abhorrence toward the impossible harpie, Mulgrew angrily attempted to steady his temper again, knowing that if he dared open his beak, he would undoubtedly pop off so badly it would prove disastrous. He was at the very breaking point as it was. Having already been subjected to traveling with the crazed thing and not having a say in the matter right from the start, he was already half mad himself. Enduring the babbling and the maddening slurping sounds that she made while sucking up her ever-dripping nose goop, he gnawed at his tiny flippers, not daring one single solitary syllable, unsure of what terrible things he might do to the demented hump-pig. Eventually, Mum tired of plaguing the seabird, deciding to settle herself into a comfortable slump, positioning herself right in front as she had since the very beginning, right on the very tip-top of Kishk's head, her trusty and tattered bonnet now placed ever so snug upon her saturated noggin. Staring out into the white nothingness, she hummed and sang pleasantly to herself, mumbling words of nonsense, each word sung with her usual robust enthusiasm: "*A lovely love-ya day to love and love . . . and just sail away!*"

Completely abandoning any self-control, the penguin gave out a rather disturbing squawk. With a stern and snappy slap to his waddle, he scooted up toward the mad singing seal. He glared at her while repeating his shrilling call before he spoke. "Is that really necessary? Is it, *is it!*" he kept asking, getting louder than ever with each demanding screech.

"Oh, do dry up and blow away, little bird," Mum scoffed, holding to a comfy-cozy smile, wiping her dampened flipper across her drenched muzzle, removing what she could of the sea mist and whatever else dripped there. "Just stop your fussing already!"

"*My fussing!*" squawked the bird.

"Yes, and if you do not stop your codswalloping, flap-doodling hubbub, you tedious ninny ass, I'm going to have to really smack you!"

"*Smack me?*" snapped Mulgrew, his tone soaring into a high falsetto shrill. "You'll never get the chance; you big bloat-back hump-pig!"

Mum only smirked, continuing with her humming.

"Besides, you're a fine one to talk!" Mulgrew ranted. "You've done nothing but fuss and boss everyone around ever since we found you! Not to mention vomit, belch, and stink while entertaining yourself with stupid songs that make no sense and play that ridiculous Clap-Clap game of yours, which I absolutely loathe, by the way. And let's not forget to mention that constant slurp-and-suck ritual of yours! Tell me, just how much of that revolting nose puke will we have to endure? Will you blow that slosh pit once and for all and be done with it for the sake of my sanity!"

Mum smiled again, this time contorting her cheeks, inflating them like a balloon, holding them that way until she let out a long drawn-out nasty belch.

"Disgusting hump-pig!" went the penguin, turning away with a most disturbing screech, quickly scampering up to the very bridge of the whale's head, making sure he was a safe distance from the vile belching creature. Looking down toward the blue chanter, he cried out in desperation. "You have got to do something about that horrible hump-pig! She is driving me crazy! CRAZY, I tell you! I'm about ready to snap!"

Kishk did not respond, nor had he spoken to the penguin in several days. As if in a trance, the mighty leviathan continued onward, his mysterious whale song prevailing. It was then that Mulgrew became concerned, for the whale's clicks and hums began to expand. They were more abrupt, sounding as if to forewarn that something dreadful was about to happen. Mulgrew listened with further nervousness, placing his tiny head directly upon the skin of the whale's head. "Oh, I don't like the sound of that, not one bit!"

Still, there came no reply, at least not the kind he would have hoped for. There was just more squeaks, hums, and more squeals, each one louder than the last, each one fluctuating harshly. "Sir," squeaked the nervous seabird, "what seems to be the problem? You know I could never make out that blue-chanter jibber-jabber of yours."

Louder chortling followed. That was all.

"No no no. I don't like this, not one bit, I tell you!" confessed the penguin. "With visibility at zero, this can't be good," he chirped, placing both ends of his tiny wings inside his shivering beak, listening with growing apprehension.

"Leave him be!" Mum commanded, moving her obese self closer to the already agitated seabird, adjusting her bonnet as a sudden wind played havoc with it. "He'll never find the passageway with all your yip-yapping! Now be still and let him concentrate!"

"Concentrate!" screamed the penguin. In absolute exasperation, he stomped his way over to the mad seal with unrestricted anger, wild, approaching with an exploding waddle. Reaching her, he suddenly hopped up, grabbed at a bunch of her whiskers and the saturated dangling bonnet ties, anchoring himself flush against her. Looking her directly in her drooling face, he squalled out, "First of all, let's get something straight! No one—and I mean *no one*—could possibly concentrate on anything with you around! You have not stopped babbling since we took off on this preposterous toot, you crackpot lunatic!"

Again, Mum merely grinned at the raving bird, delightfully entertained by his overblown tantrum. Mulgrew proceeded, still hanging on to her whiskers and a part of the bonnet, his webbed feet embedded securely into her bulging triple set of seal chins. "We have ourselves a serious situation here in case you hadn't noticed! And you had better get a grip, freak-O, or I won't be responsible for what happens!"

"So who's asking ya anyway, nitwit?"

At that very moment, the whale made a particularly quick and sudden turn, nearly throwing both the seal and penguin overboard while more of his boisterous clicks and hums sounded, his vast body abrading against the currents of the icy sea.

"Now, do you see that? What did I tell you!" screeched the bird, trying to hang on while Kishk continued with his sharp turn. "Something is seriously wrong here, the big guy's signals are getting louder . . . *stranger!* We're in a hullabaloo of trouble here! I just know it!"

"Oh, do hush up, Big Foot knows what he is doing," nonchalantly answered Mum, straightening out her bonnet, situating herself back in the same spot she was accustomed.

"And I guess you would know, wouldn't you?" sarcastically stung the bird. "After all, how can I even question but for a moment such accomplished reassurances from one so experienced in these matters as yourself?"

Mum suddenly opened wide her eyes and immediately broke into a fit of hysterics, grabbing on to the penguin and waving him in all sorts of unpleasant directions. Then with an added demented grin pasted to her drooling snout, she opened wide her eyes as if she intentionally wanted them to pop out from their sockets. Pushing the bird's face smack into hers, she crushed them both together with a disturbing squishing noise. In an exceedingly small voice that sounded crumbled up, she asked, *"Are you the Docta?"* While still ramming the bird into her wet snout, she belched. Not missing a beat, Mum quickly plopped the penguin on top of her bonnet, holding him there just like he was a mere extension of her ridiculous headdress. *"I'mmmm—hot! Sassy—hot!"* she blustered with vulgar conceit, all nasal-like, contentedly and unashamedly letting loose her overfilled bladder, hosing out a considerable puddle of urine that utterly surround them both.

"Aaaaeeeehhhh!" was all the appalled penguin could muster. Waiting for the shock to leave him or at least partially, the flabbergasted screeching seabird found the smarts to propel himself off the mad harpie's head, screaming, "Get it away! Get it . . . *aaa-way-eeee!"* He kept on screaming, jumping from the seal, frantic in his escape, unable to miss, naturally, the awaiting puddle below him. In utter revulsion, the bird slipped and fell facedown into the vile mess that the mad seal had so casually provided. Somehow finding his footing, he fled from the putrid waste, screaming out in further disgust.

Mum just sat there giggling, enjoying another fun round of Clap-Clap.

Making his way to the end of the whale, the half-crazed seabird quickly splashed about the freezing waters where the whale's tail remained submerged. In desperation, he began cleaning himself, hurling out penguin obscenities that of which would make a swiler blush, all the while commencing to rid himself of the acrid and soppy smells saturating his once pristine tuxedo-like attire. However, the moment after he had finally washed all the nasty mess from his coat, he froze, for it all suddenly stopped. Kishk's alarming clicking sounds and distressing hums had ceased, but with a most disturbing abruptness, making this silence even more unsettling than the whale's previous chatter. Mulgrew quickly shook the remaining water from himself, and twitching his small head out into the thickset mist, he listened carefully with a trembling heart. Mum had also stopped her Clap-Clap game, lending an exceedingly attentive ear to the complete silence that now prevailed over them. The hypnotic Kishk unexpectedly arched his enormous backside, forcing both the seal and the penguin toward the front of his head.

Momentarily dazed, the bird asked in a strained screech, "What is it? What's wrong, sir?"

Mum casually wriggled closer toward the whale's blowhole, wiggling her gooey mucus-filled nose about before she looked out into the hanging mist. "By Jove!" she barked with a robust voice. "He's found it! *Hal-a-roo!"*

"Hal-a-roo, my foot!" the penguin screeched. "We can't see a thing! What are you talking about?"

Mum only offered back another one of her bothersome smirks and then sucked up some more drool. The whale now remained intensely still, just barely swaying within the icy waters, still not uttering a sound. He just silently floated within the wisps of the clinging fog, all his clicks and hums altogether forgotten.

The penguin immediately waddled up to the blue giant's forehead and looked over it, holding on so as not to drop off. "Sir, please, what is it?"

Still no answer came.

"Oh, this is not good. I have never seen him like this before," lamented Mulgrew. "Perhaps he is sick. Maybe he's dead! What'll we do?"

Mum just rolled her eyes in a glassy saturation of disgust, irked by the never-ending melodramatics of the annoying penguin.

"Kishk, old buddy of mine, what is it? Are you all right?"

Still there came no reply. The frantic bird went on pacing back and forth again. "Talk to me, big guy, say something, anything! Just so I know that I'm not going to have to spend the last day of my life stuck with this nasty belching hump-pig!" he cried. "Come on, just let me know that you're okay!"

Again, no answer came.

Realizing that the whale was not about to speak, Mulgrew began to shake. Slowly, he knelt down onto the shining blue skin of his longtime companion. "You can't be dead. You just can't be!" he squeaked, fearing that his penguin tears were ready to overflow.

"Well, he's not dead," Mum said, brazenly wriggling her big self up to the bird. "He's not able to speak, stupid! He remains mesmerized by what he sees. He'll be fine."

"Mesmerized!"

"Yes, it's kind of like being in a state of hypnotic rapture! *Hal-a-roo!*"

"Stop that, he can't possibly see anything, you moron! The fog is as thick as jellyfish stew!"

"Well, he can!" she screamed. "And besides, it's all around us, tweedy-twit!"

"What's all around us?"

"The passageway, of course!"

"The what?"

"Hush up!" she barked, turning from the penguin, casting her glance upon the surface of the whale. "Isn't he the love?"

"What is your tête-à-tête babbling going off about this time, whack-O!"

"Don't you see, scare baby? He has found the pathway that will lead us directly to the Origin of Lights!"

"No, I don't see! In fact, I can't see anything but a sea packed full of matted mucked-up fog! And furthermore, I think—" The bird suddenly looked at the seal with disgust.

"What?" Mum chuckled, a demented lopsided grin running across her muzzle.

"You just stunk . . . didn't you?"

Mum only smirked, rolled her eyes, and then belched.

"Oh, this is like a nightmare!" screamed the bird.

"Yes, I may have silently relieved myself, and just what are you going to do about it, pinhead? Nothing! Because you're an idiot! Not to mention entirely mistrusting and suspicious! See with your heart, not with that incredulously raised brow and those doubting beady bird eyes of yours!" she bellowed, swatting down her saturated flipper, smacking the penguin's head, ridiculously bouncing it up and down.

"Stop that! I can't take you anymore!" Mulgrew screamed, waddling backward in utter contempt. "You're really crazy, do you know that? You're nothing but a fat, pompous, flatulating, deranged snot-spewing bully who has somehow tricked my buddy into believing there is something waiting for us out here. Something that both you and I know does not exist! It's just more of your insane ramblings and you know it!"

Mum only smacked her lips and rolled her eyes again.

"And now we are lost, left to smell your wretched seal gas, and it's all, your entire fault, *your fault, your fault!*"

"*Goosey loosey, love-ya!*" Mum teased while extending her grasping flipper, reaching for the bird, trying to tickle him beneath his beak. Then suddenly, she stopped. Raising her head, she sniffed at the fog vigorously. "He should be moving toward the lights at any moment now! You best hold on, tweedy-twit," she advised, scrunching herself next to the whale's blowhole, holding on to its concave bend. "It's going to be a bumpy ride, *Milly!*"

"Oh, is that supposed to scare me?" squawked the penguin. "It's just more of your mentally dysfunctional ramblings, that's all!"

Mulgrew would not have a chance to say another word, for suddenly the whale jerked forward, throwing the bird flat down on his back. He screamed all the way until he smashed up against the chanter's back end that had fortunately sprung up from out of the sea. Guided by sheer luck, the crazed penguin held on to a small slice of the whale's wavering tail, dramatically sputtering and swishing inside the rakish-moving currents while speeding through the blinding fog and icy sea. Suddenly, a thousand bursts of dancing lights shot out in every direction, each never relinquishing a single rumbling sound, igniting the mist, imitating trillions of glowing fireflies frantically swarming in some dark meadow. Then the situation intensified. The brilliant flickers changed from sparking lights into bolts of iridescent purple flashes—a thousand tongues of fiery purple spiderwebbed streaks bursting from the fog now set aflame in burning purple attire.

Unexpectedly, Kishk's tail crashed back into the sea, taking the panic-stricken penguin along for the ride. The bird screamed all the way, his cries muting pathetically inside the realms of the purple-stained ocean. Just when he thought he could no longer hold on to the whale's tail or his breath, up came the behemoth's backside, Kishk's astounding tail smashing upward once again. Mulgrew gagged, choked, and moaned in agony, about to pop from having filled to the brim with seawater. His lungs pounded like his racing heart. With his beak wide open, he desperately gasped, attempting to refill his tiny lungs. Shutting his eyes and holding on for dear life, the bird rattled and shook back and forth while Kishk sped through the water like a runaway torpedo. Mum sniffed the air about her, calm as could be, her bloated mass jiggling like a jellyfish while holding on securely. A strong wind blasted out, proving to be way too much for the tiny penguin. And the last thing that Mulgrew would recall before shooting off into the purple abyss was the way his eyes burned from the exploding lights even though his eyelids had remained shut the entire time. He would also never forget the terrible thunder of the rushing wind nor the crashing waves. It was as if the earth was crumbling apart, like one of his cracked barnacles. In a moment, he became covered in waves and exploding purple lights—and then vanished!

Suddenly, there came an earth-shattering vibration, so startling, so tremendous that the existing icebergs that stood nearby could not help but anchor down tight, hoping not to blow off into the same oblivion as did the penguin. However, just like the seabird, the situation proved to be too much for them as well. Instantly, they shattered and split apart, shattering into thousands of pieces of icy waste. Within seconds, the icebergs dissolved into the gushing waters, joining the enigmatic dance of the sea.

At last, the whale spoke. Unfortunately, his words would never be heard over the crashing sounds exploding from everywhere. "Hold on—we're almost through!"

As the sea whirled wildly about the blue chanter, Mum continued to sing out gloriously. She threw back her head, being careful not to lose her bonnet to the whipping winds, clutching one of her flippers about its tie strings, the other flipper continuing to snatch on to the whale's soggy spout. While the fantastic occurrence played on, even the whale became unnerved, preparing to brace himself inside the powerful pull of the sea, helpless inside its incredible grasp. Still, Mum went right on singing playfully, getting a jolly oceanic kick out of the whole experience.

Once again, things intensified. The happening aggrandized with added funnels of spiraling waterspouts, each coming up from places far below, merging, each ushering blasts of shooting spray over the whale and his mad traveling companion. One by one, the aqueous twisters became absorbed into what was rapidly becoming one dominant purple-stained vortex. Vibrantly winding its watery self in front of the whale, the thunderous funnel inverted. It bent before the blue chanter, having a monstrous mouth ingesting everything, exposing its whirling horizontal opening with a booming gasp! The whale closed his violet eyes as a child does when trying to block out images of the bogeyman. He began to shudder. Mum resumed her vocalizing; bringing her song up to a higher register, but none of it would be heard over the roar of the swirling suction slurping them up.

Then there was absolute silence.

LIQUID DOLPHINS

Kishk was the first to break the probing stillness.

"We're in! We made it! Is everyone all right?" he asked with a mighty voice, not sure of anything at this point. What he did notice was that after every word, every sound, there came a strange echo that added a million chiming tinkles to it. "Please answer me, are you all still with me?" he resounded.

Somewhere inside this void, Mum's response unmistakably reverberated. "A-OK, love ya!" she sang, her tinkling voice filling the vacant darkness. "You did it, fishy! You found the Origin of Lights!"

"Mulgrew!" called the whale. "Are you all right?"

No answer came from the penguin.

"Mulgrew!" insisted the whale.

Suddenly, a muffled grating sound echoed, followed by the same delicacy of tuneful ringing, indicating that somewhere out in the darkness Mulgrew had also survived, having been sucked into the vortex. Relieved, the whale prepared to speak; but before he managed a single sound, the extreme curtain of concealment began to slowly rise. It started with a single pinpoint of purple iridescence that gradually began to expand. Sparkling light beams shot down upon the whale, and a strange dimension of resplendent purple hues sharply came alive. It was everywhere! Impressed, but hardly overwhelmed, Mum proceeded in her unflinching nonchalance, slurping, the, lights of the fantastic dimension growing brighter and brighter, with each fleeting moment. Kishk blinked his lovely big violet eyes, trying to acclimate himself to the brightness surrounding him. More groans and half-formed giggles rang out in the distance. It was coming from Mulgrew. He was on his backside kicking his webbed feet like a playful newborn. Directly coming into view, the tiny seabird flipped and flopped comically in the water, splashing happily, laughing hysterically. It would seem that whatever was in the mysterious sea made him laugh uncontrollably. It was like nothing he had ever experienced before; for once in his life, he was ecstatically happy. In fact, he felt hysterically giddy and out of control, just like a delirious drunkard. He just could not keep from tittering even if he wanted to, for indeed, these waters remained utterly infected with a rare giggling contagion that rendered any creature who breathed in any part of its watery sparkle totally illogical with uncontrollable laughter.

It was not long before the penguin began to lose his breath; he was laughing so vigorously that he could hardly take in air. Poking himself further into the water, Mulgrew made one final attempt, zooming through the infectious sea until he was able to reunite with his companion. Up and out he emerged, landing smack on the whale's mouth, the extraneous laughter remaining with him. Flopping himself down onto the brim of Kishk's bulbous lips, Mulgrew continued chortling; slapping the whale's mouth with unbridled bliss the giggles rendered him helpless. Despite the frantic frivolity bubbling over him, the penguin knew that if he did not stop soon, he would run out of breath and die. Luckily, in just a little while, the effects began to subside; and in one heaping clump, he fell backward against the whale, nearly sliding back into the water. Thankfully, he was saved by the whale's open mouth. Carefully, Kishk held the semiconscious seabird on his tongue, raising him toward his sloping head where with a little bit of luck Mulgrew found his way back to safety.

The bird's laughter finally began to truly subside when he found himself next to the mad seal, his tuxedo-like attire still glowing from the strange ocean. He kept on trying to shake the wetness from himself, his eyes tainted purple from the fantastic sea he had ingested. Already Mum was becoming annoyed, for the penguin was getting her already wet coat even wetter with his bothersome wiggles and shakes.

"The spiteful act of a neurotic penguin!" Mum grunted, deciding to move away, disgusted, turning, her wide back on the agonizing bird that was still fighting to refill his lungs. When Mulgrew turned to look at the back end of the mad harpie, his laughter returned full-strength. He was not sure if the effects of the purple water made him this way or his own lameness from the whole exhausting experience. Whichever, the spent bird simply fell flat on his beak, laughing and chuckling, his voice cracking between snickers. "What's the matter, giggles?" Mum said dryly, tormenting the incoherent creature. "Your little swim proved to be too much for you, *MILLY*?"

The whale spoke instead. "How wondrous!" he chimed, enraptured in astonishment. "Such colors—such magic! Why, it is more beautiful than I could have ever imagined!"

The phosphorescent purple lights continued to sparkle around the three awestruck spectators, and the penguin began to regain his normal senses. It took a while for the watery effects of the sea to wear off, but eventually, Mulgrew lost his giggles, replenished his lungs, remaining as far away from the tormenting mad seal as possible. Lightheaded and feeling as if he had woken with an outrageous hangover, he tried to steady himself on the surface of the whale, his voice still shaking with uneasiness. "What's in that purple Jacuzzi, anyway?"

Although these remarkable waters flowed beneath the whale, shimmering with a life force all their own, there also appeared on both sides of this fantastic arena two distinctly curved panels made of the same spectacular fluid. What's more, these massive panels remained flowing—upward! It was unbelievable! The sparkling and intoxicating sea streamed not only on both sides of the whale but rushed up from every possible crevasse connecting to a shifting purple ocean way up in the watery sky above them.

Maintaining an unsteady stance, the penguin's beak opened, nearly falling off onto his tuxedo-painted breast. Immediately, he felt himself melting into sheer amazement, watching with bulging eyes while the moving waters frolicked wherever he might look. The sea stretched effortlessly in front of him, rising, completely unaffected by gravity or any similar restriction. Groaning, sounding sick, the bird sank further into his weary self. Ever since he came blasting out into the purple sea, he thought he was a goner. The reality, or rather the unreality of this bizarre predicament, rendered the penguin frightened and confused. He suddenly jumped when Mum abruptly broke the silence, her husky voice ringing out into thousands of tinkling vibrations. "A bit peaked, are we, twit?"

"Just stay away from me!" he snapped, finally able to speak out.

Mum laughed hardily, pushing herself closer toward the weary bird, saying, "Kind of like being swallowed up inside the belly of some squishy monster, isn't it, Milly?"

The whale was quick to reply. "Not quite," he answered, his words dancing about the walls of liquid space as the shimmering purple waters rippled upward, constantly accumulating into the immeasurable ocean above. "It's more like being swallowed up by the entire universe. It is truly amazing!"

Mum spoke, less affected by the spectacle than the others. "Yeah, yeah, yeah, so where is it?"

"You mean the Kellis? Shouldn't be far," Kishk suggested, slowly moving within the infectious waters. "From what I remember being told when I was a youth, we must first find a star of some kind."

"Oh bother!" Mum grumbled.

"Yes, I remember my grandfather telling me that the Kellis could only be seen when viewed beneath the light of a very rare and special star."

"Then let's have at it, shall we?" Mum barked, battening down her bonnet tightly over her head. Agreeing, the whale began to move faster within the purple waters; but after what seemed a terribly extraordinary long time, all had to agree it was just possible that this rare and noteworthy star, whatever and wherever it might be, did not exist. After all, how could a star fix itself inside a universe filled with flowing water? This rationality concerned and affected everyone—everyone but the mad seal. Once again, she began clapping excitedly. "One of us must go into the water. There are small passages that might be too small for Gargantuan to get through. Someone who is quick and cunning must try! That is how we will find the bloomin' star!"

"Well, don't look at me!" squawked the penguin, his purple-colored eyes filled with resentment.

"Don't worry, Milly, I wasn't about to!" she barked, sticking out her tongue in disgust. "Scare baby!" Then turning toward the head of the whale, she proclaimed, "I will swim out and find it!"

"But, madam," Kishk warned, "the waters are possessed with some kind of magically induced laughing serum! I myself have been most careful not to ingest the water. I think it best you stay on board."

"Oh bugger off, fish!" Mum growled. Turning from the whale's noggin before glaring off toward the penguin with exasperation, she rolled her eyes in revolt. "I'll find it long before any of you ever do, bloody wimps!" Tightening the strings of her drenched and tattered bonnet with both of her flippers, she simply had to add, "And after seeing the disgraceful performance our little daft Miss Milly gave, I shall strive to refrain from such disreputable behavior. A most unsuitable lack of self-control, I say," she ridiculed, looking viciously into the penguin's purple eyes.

"Did I mention I hate you?" Mulgrew spit.

Mum just stuck out her tongue and waited for a snot bubble to erupt, hoping it would pop smack on the bird's head, but she miscalculated and only managed to slime up her already wet and twisted snout. Wiping it away with one disgruntled sweep, she wriggled hastily toward the edge of the whale's head. Directly lifting her eyes to the ocean sky, her spellbound madness swarming about her, she intensely breathed in the air. Closing her eyes, she let her crazed but receptive mind waft inside whatever was now communing with her.

There she remained frozen, just standing near the edge of the whale, inhaling the unique mist and perfumed air inundating her. With eyes closed tight, she spoke in a queer voice, *"Follow the echo of the miraculous streams. In the heart of the star, is a well of dreams. As you ask, but seven times, beware . . . for only truth can be revealed there."* Mum suddenly stopped speaking and flipped open her eyes as if waking from a dream, a queer expression covering her muzzle. "What the heck kind of codswallop jibber-jabber just came out of me?" she bellowed.

Kishk immediately responded. "Don't you see? The Kellis is speaking through you!"

"Whatever! If you say so, fish, but it still doesn't help us find the star now, does it?" Mum questioned, slurping up a thick glob of nose drool. "Anyway, we are wasting precious time with our floundering presumptions. It is time I was on my way!"

Surprisingly, the penguin spoke, waddling toward the mad seal but being sure to keep a safe distance from her. "With a little bit of luck, maybe you won't come back, you stupid hump-pig!"

"That would be most unfortunate," explained Kishk, "for we might be forever trapped here without her psychic abilities."

"Enough flap doodling," Mum barked. "I'll be back, all right!" Preparing to dive into the purple sea, she turned her head long enough to stick out her tongue, directing it toward the annoying penguin. With this sassy gesture, the mad harpie dove off the whale's head. She immediately began to giggle as soon as she hit the water, making "weeing" noises flipping about just like a baby seal learning to swim for the first time, splashing and splashing farther and farther away from the whale, both her and her bonnet disappearing into the purple shimmers.

"Where'd she go?" Mulgrew squeaked.

"How curious, I'm not quite sure which way she went," the whale answered. "In any event, we must be very quiet until she returns."

"Why?"

"It is very important that I concentrate and send out as many positive thoughts to our brave friend."

"Brave! She's not brave, she's just crazy!"

"Quiet!"

"All right already!" piped the bird, folding his tiny flippers into his chest; and with an exasperated huff and puff, he slammed himself down on top of the whale's head, holding on to a most unattractive twist to his penguin beak.

It would prove to be an exceedingly long time before Mum would return. In fact, the whale was beginning to think that perhaps she had met up with a tragic end, but just as he was about to accept the worst, up crashed the mad harpie, laughing and giggling. She danced within the waters spinning and twirling effortlessly, chortling, her nose a sheer mass of erupting purple snot bubbles. Anxious to tell the others of her find, she quickly swam to the whale's mouth, still laughing, still cackling like the mad thing she was. Eventually making her way to the top of the whale, she found that she was entirely out of breath when she got there. It took her a while before she could speak, but she was raring to go. "I found it! I found it! The star! It is there, behind you!" she barked with only half a voice, her bonnet all askew. "You were going the wrong way, daft fool! Turn around!" she demanded, giggling while fixing her soggy hat, pointing in the opposite direction the whale was going.

"The Kellis, did you see her?" Kishk excitedly asked.

"No, just the star, but I know she was there just the same." Mum chuckled, shaking herself, splattering the purple water all over Mulgrew who had already dried off. A seething purple-stained penguin glared back at the seal, just wishing he could peck her to death, when suddenly he felt the massive whale turn his immense self around while Mum continued to point her flipper in the direction he need to go. What they found beyond was just more purple-painted sparkles. Kishk continued onward, sailing inside the twinkling arena, the sheer borders sweeping along upward into the flowing water-filled universe hanging above them.

On and on the whale swam. It would seem that he would go on swimming indefinitely. However, soon, minutes passed into hours and hours seemed to pass into days. The very essence of time remained altered in this far-off somewhere, so there was no real way of knowing just how long they had been there thus far. Their eyes had long since grown accustomed to the magnificent light, as did their initial excitement. After what seemed an eternity, it became apparent that there was an exceptionally strong chance that they were lost in this ongoing vacuum of purple shimmers and bubbling explosions that showed no signs of stopping or even running out of space. Having long since tired of the monotonous searching, Mulgrew, who preserved his distance from the mad seal, grumbled to himself, waddling toward the rear of the whale, plopping himself down, lying flat on his back looking up at the endless watery ceiling above. "I told him not to listen to that stupid hump-pig sea cow! There is no star! She just made it all up as usual! And now look where she got us, stuck in the middle of nowhere, stupid, stupid hump-pig!"

Suddenly Kishk stopped dead in the water and Mulgrew fell forward, his heart leaping to his throat. Something had happened. Something had changed. He was not sure, but something was indeed different; the penguin could smell it in the air. With a hurried waddle, Mulgrew scooted up toward Kishk's enormous head. "What is it, sir?" he asked with an out-of-breath voice, but Kishk did not answer. Mum merely continued with her clapping; only slowing down her pace just long enough to wait for a response from the whale. When there came no reply, she started up the clapping at her usual irritating, sporadic, and frantic pace. "Stop that stupid, ridiculous, insane clapping!" Mulgrew screamed.

Kishk then came to life. "It is near, I can feel it!"

Mulgrew did an about-face, corkscrewing his tiny head around several times. Seeing nothing but more purple bubbles and shimmers, the rattled seabird chirped, "What are you talking about, sir? There is nothing out there but tons of purple mishmash! That's all, nothing more!"

"You are mistaken, my friend. We have found what we have come looking for. It is here!" the blue chanter exclaimed with a dramatic voice.

In unison, and very slowly, they all raised their eyes to the ocean sky, each of them clearly seeing the incredible image shimmering brightly inside the waters it swam. "Praise be the powers above!" Kishk proclaimed, gazing up toward the magnificent find that remained wafting inside the watery circle surrounding it. Indeed, it was the star! A star surrounded by water, the star that would make it possible to see the strange creature known as the *Kellis.*

"Holy sea cow," piped Mulgrew. "Will ya take a lookie at that, will ya?"

"Told ya so, told ya so!" Mum tormented, shaking her rump playfully, taking a moment to smirk at the bird, sticking out her tongue before returning her eyes back to the water-filled skies. She smiled, looking upon the reflected image of the strange star, its silvery figure painted deep within the shimmer of the hanging sea, its silver light cascading down like a lit-up waterfall. Then something even stranger began to happen. The water everywhere began to bubble as if boiling, continuing to swell outward, creating vast ripples of blazing vibrations. Unscrewing her beefy neck, Mum chuckled, happily enjoying the water from the magnificent star showering down the liquid sun adorning her. It was ever so warm and ever so soft, a million sparkles captured in each and every drop. Then all at once, the purple sea below erupted.

A fantastic column of water transformed itself into a fantastic fountain, a spinning fountain painted with the same purple sparkles as the mysterious sea they floated upon. From the very core of the fountain, there emerged two silvery-colored misshapen forms. Evenly they oozed out from opposite sides. At first, these figures were globule, almost gluelike. Formless, they shot out of the waterspout in two different directions. Slowly, they began to take shape, continuing to move away from the fountain, their gluey features merging in and out of each other. Soon their shapes became long and tubelike, both resembling silver snails. Their undistinguished forms twisted inside and outside of their watery configurations with ecstatic speed, the entities becoming partially separated. Appearing like lucid bookends, their flaccid shapes stood erect, each form remaining linked to the amazing fountain.

Mum cocked her head back and forth, her eyes focused on the peculiar sight continuing with its metamorphosis. *"Jiminy Cricket!"* she howled, immediately hearing a heartfelt cry of a baby seal echoing somewhere way off in the distance. The cry lasted but for a short time. Then it was gone.

Little by little, the forms changed from the ambiguous to the familiar until at last, all could finally recognize the shapes the liquid-filled creatures had taken. They were dolphins—two beautiful silver water-filled dolphins. However, unlike their proverbial brothers and sisters, these strange fellows remained entirely made out of water, reflecting the pure essence of the magic glow that burned within the spinning column of purple sea. A wet gurgling sound moaned about the creatures, their translucent bodies becoming more distinct and three-dimensional. However, resembling the common dolphins of the sea, these see-through beings stood much taller than the others they had copied. They stationed themselves steadily around the spinning fountain, each fixed at opposite ends, no fluid spilling from their watery shapes. Only their eyes, which swam inside transparent skulls, held any kind of solid appearance. The eyes were abnormally large and perfectly circular and possessed a colorful pink brightness that hurt when looked upon. Mum, whose undivided attention had finally been won, gazed upon the fantastic creatures. She watched, her smile beaming contentment. The eyes of the creatures pulsated with an even more intense pink glow, perpetually dusting each dolphin's silhouette with a haunting veil of the incredible. It was at that moment both water-filled creations opened their mouths simultaneously. A loud piercing sound roared, choking the air, the eyes of the liquid creatures further igniting with brightness. Its light was so intense that it temporarily blinded all three spectators. However, in a short while, Kishk and the others' sight returned; and in the faraway distance, another small echo from the cries of a baby seal presented itself. Then a single voice of resilient purity radiated from the liquid dolphins, each summoning an understood language set in a low-pitched drone.

"We are the messengers of truth, one voice—one spirit. Within our Song we shall whisper what only your dreams can hear."

THE KELLIS

All at once, the dolphins flickered, their globlike bodies imitating the brilliant glow of their shining eyes. From the very center of the revolving pillar that continued to spin and stay connected to them, a strange figure appeared.

There, within the fantastic fountain encased inside its watery domain stood a most curious being. Quietly and supremely benevolently, it looked toward the whale. Consumed of a great light, the figure was difficult to see at first, but this impairment would not last. Kishk sighed aloud, for he immediately knew who it was. Floating before him was the legendary creature—the *Kellis!*

"Well, I'll be!" exclaimed the whale with a choked-up voice. "The mad harpie was right all the while. I just knew it had to be true!"

Plainly hearing the chanter, Mum boldly looked down toward the penguin, giving him another round of arrogant and cocky "I-told-ya-so's." However, Mulgrew would never know it, for he remained dazzled and spellbound by what he saw.

Enraptured inside its water boundaries, a creature possessing both human and mammal-like features serenely stared back through a limpid wall of weightlessness. She was the most fantastic being any of the three had ever seen or imagined. Immediately, they noticed the pronounced similarity of this creature to the land monster known as man and yet, at the same time, they had to acknowledge the definite characteristics of a strange aquatic race set within her features. Supreme purple-colored eyes having very little evidence of pupils five times as large as mortal man's graced her translucent oval face. She remained tinted in a purple glowing color that twinkled just like the sparkles of the purple sea. A fragile nose with what appeared to be a single nostril traced itself delicately below her magnificent eyes as an almost nonexistent mouth shadowed above her fragile chin. Her head was void of hair, and in its place, a resplendent crown of watery spines pierced through her shiny liquid skin. There, looking like some royal crown, sat a transparent wreath made up of seven pointed spikes, each not unusually long but adorning her nonetheless. Unlike the rest of her, this eternal headpiece remained dimly lit, allowing very little light to pass through its clear columns.

Her body was much more ambiguous than her face. For in one moment it appeared to retain arms and legs, but the wavering movement in which she seductively swam seemed to mutate her, erratically changing her into a semblance of something less human and more aquatic and, for a moment, almost seal-like. Legs became flippers and flippers became legs until one fused into the other. Still, two of the most striking features about this creature were its eyes and the sinless purification of its sweet voice. It was high to the pitch, sounding most unearthly and angelic. As it sang, it could communicate words, but not through its own accord; it would need the water-filled dolphins for that. Nonetheless, the voice stood alone in its wonder, a voice so utterly serene, so pure which upon hearing its song, the listener would be sympathetically rendered to unexpected vulnerability, even tears.

The being with the magnificent purple eyes nodded her head, acknowledging her audience, outstretching her translucent limbs, proceeding to sing to them, bidding them welcome, a low monotone hum underscoring her call, the dolphins translating her song into a mystical unison of voice: "I am Kellis. You will know this for I wear the seven stars of Patreeze, one for each of your longings. My eyes are the passageway of time, eyes that will cry tears from your pain so that you will not. Eyes fashioned from the first light that scattered through your emptiness. Through them, you shall experience the answers you now seek. Greetings," she gently sang, slowly signaling to the whale. "I know why you are here, for I have waited such a long time for your coming. In order to fulfill the prophecy, I must answer when only seven of your questions are asked, not one more, not one less. Here, you will find your truth. I pray that you ask wisely, for like Her Majesty, the Sea, you also hold fast to my destiny," she sang, her haunting and beautiful voice emanating from both dolphins. "Who will be the one to ask the first of seven?"

Without the slightest hesitation, Mum spoke out before anyone could stop her. "Are you the Docta?" she blurted out, flipping herself over on her backside, clapping all the while.

A loud trembling sound rumbled around the whale as the first spine upon the Kellis's head ignited like a newly lit Christmas tree.

"What's the matter with you!" shrieked the penguin. "Are you crazy! What are you doing, asking a stupid question like that?"

"It was asked, and so I must answer. No . . . I am not who you have asked that I am," the purple being disconcertingly replied, a sad look befalling over her haunting features.

Wanting to smack the seal as hard as he possibly could, Mulgrew angrily growled at Mum, then turned to look upon Kellis, waddling hurriedly up to the end of the whale's head. "I am so sorry, Your Eminence! You must forgive that asinine hump-pig! She is mad, and one big messy embarrassment. I thoroughly apologize for her absurdity. Please, couldn't we just forget she ever asked such a ridiculous and stupid question?" Slapping both his flippers over his beak, realizing he had just posed the second question, the penguin gasped. Once more, the waters rumbled, and the second spine upon the wavering creature's head ignited. "Oh no! *No! No! No! No!*" screeched Mulgrew. "I didn't mean it! I did not mean it! I take it back! I take it back! She made me do it! She made me do it!" beseeched the penguin, leaning over the whale, nearly falling overboard, his tiny flippers clasped in a begging position.

"Again, I must comply," answered the Kellis, her large purple eyes showing definite signs of disappointment, appearing as she was about to cry. "You have asked, and I must answer in the negative. You now have five more questions left."

Mum was not about to miss out on taunting the penguin. She flipped herself over and wriggled righteously up to the mortified seabird, carrying an antagonizing smirk along with her. "At least I have an excuse. I'm insane, you're just plain stupid. *Stupid!*"

Before the penguin could react or before either one dared utter another syllable, the whale quickly intervened. "Enough!" he shouted. "If there are to be any further questions asked, I shall ask them myself!" Quickly turning his violet eyes away from the top of his head and back over to the Kellis, he smiled apologetically. "Do forgive our ignorance. I'm afraid we are not well versed in such matters. I promise I will try to do better, Your Eminence," Kishk offered, bowing his head in humiliation, taking a moment to raise his eyes long enough to glare exasperatingly toward the two rivaling creatures.

Kellis smiled, also nodding, this time hoping for the best.

The whale cleared his voice, preparing to submit the third question. "Dearest lady, our quest is a simple one consisting of a few questions, the first and foremost being this: please tell us how we can help the white seal find his mother, providing she is still alive?"

The waters rumbled, and the creature that stood floating between the liquid-filled dolphins waited for the third spine from her aquatic crown to burst forth. It looked just like a freshly lit candle, its light bright and glowing with a fascinating shine almost too bright to look upon. "You seek to help the one called Miracle," she sang, her words pouring through the dolphins. She smiled approvingly. "You are wise, dear chanter; you have asked one question but have given it two parts." Looking pleased for the first time, the incredible creation with the magnificent purple eyes and purple translucent skin held to her incredible smile, a smile that could somehow be seen on lips that appeared to be almost invisible.

"Before I answer the first part of your question, I shall answer the second. When returning to the white seal that carries the sacred tear, you must tell him that his mother still lives. However, I must hasten to warn that the darkness has already claimed her for its own and will eagerly do the same to him should he not hold true to his heart, for the mother of the white seal is held prisoner upon a vessel that carries pure evil. Its name is *Tiamat*. Upon this vessel, a most sinister woman dwells. There she steals the tears of the innocent seals. She has used their sorrow for wealth, but now and foremost, she seeks the absolute power of the tear. She must first find the white seal, and during the approaching *Night of Screams,* there, before the bleeding moon, she will have him killed! Take warning once more: to prevent her from doing this will not be an easy task. She is pure evil and devilishly cunning and only pure goodness could possibly hope to defeat her. Again, be warned—nothing will stop the dark woman from destroying him so that she may consume the power of the omnipotent tear."

The whale closed his eyes, shivering with dread. However, realizing that Miracle's mother was still alive despite the gloomy possibility of woe, Mum released a sigh of relief; placing her head down, as if in prayer. She sighed once more before throwing back her head with a forceful thrust. "Hal-a-roo!" she barked, a big silly grin stamped on her face.

Kellis proceeded with her delicate song. "He wears the very essence of the sea over his heart. It is a most wondrous mystery and possesses a most powerful magic. It was stolen many years ago and has since changed many hands, all of them wicked. The white seal remains our final hope, for should the tear be returned by such an unselfish heart, the world will rejoice in a second chance. If not, she will suffer the final death of this most sacred gift of innocence. Even now, there is so little of it left," the purple-eyed wonder sorrowfully chanted.

The whale felt the mad seal wriggling toward the edge of his forehead, and fearing that she might blurt out another mad and irrelevant question, he quickly interjected. "Dear lady, if you please, what exactly is this power in the stone that the white seal now wears?"

The fourth spine readily exploded upon the Kellis' crown, and she once more sang out. "Captured in the stone is the preservation of the very first tear ever shed upon the earth; it came from the heart of Our Majesty, our mother, the Sea. It was shed when mankind first turned away from the light and became a part of the darkness and lost his innocence. And with this tear, a great force was born that was not like anything before or since, for there is unbelievable power in the birth of a single tear, especially a mother's tear. For this reason, it remains sought after these many years but always for evil's sake and never for good, for the righteous heart would have selflessly returned it," the purple creature grieved, her face filled with immense sadness.

Then once again, before Kishk or Mulgrew could stop her, Mum blurted out another one of her verbal curiosities. The penguin, try as he may, jumped up and slapped his webbed feet across her face, trying to stop her, but Mum only threw him aside like a flip of her ever-constant drool. "Tell me something, Lady Love," she belted out, slurping away at her nose goop. "Is it really true that the white seal will die if he removes the bloomin' stone?"

The fifth spine abruptly flared off and lit up the water-filled universe. "Yes," the Kellis told in her haunting song. "For no one is exempt. All who wear the stone, whether used for good or evil, and dare to remove it will forfeit their own life. That is the cost one must pay for possession of such a rare power."

"Hal-a-roo! You're keeping it real—*toots*, but tell me, honey—"

Again, the whale tried to stop Mum, even tried to toss her overboard with a sudden jerk of his head, but she quickly held on tight, finishing her words, asking, "Isn't there something you can do about it? After all, you are the gosh darn Kellis, for clapping out loud!"

The sixth spine immediately exploded and with it came an awful silence. Then a look so forlorn suddenly washed over the face of Kellis. "No . . . I am afraid there is nothing." That was all she would say—nothing more.

Mum became angry and was about to snap off again when suddenly the whale shook his head with a forceful shake, this time casting her back toward his tail, hoping she'd fall off, but she didn't.

"Stop," Kishk shouted most upset. "We now have but one last question left! Please, Mum, I beseech you to be still and allow me this last inquiry! *Please!*"

"Well, all right, all right!" Mum barked, all annoyed, wriggling back toward the center of the whale's head. "Bug off then! Codswalloping lip-lumps!" she ferociously growled, turning her back disdainfully away from the purple-colored creation, having heard all she needed to hear, disgusted, flopping herself down, holding to a most disgruntled expression.

"Once more, forgive us, dear lady," the whale implored in his suave way, the whole time feeling his heart leap into a faster beat, knowing that it was up to him to ask the final question.

The Kellis looked toward the whale with pleading eyes, hoping he would succeed.

Kishk slightly backed away from the creature, nervously swaying within the water, thinking his question over and over again. When finally he was ready, he cleared his massive throat and took in a difficult, long, and heavy breath, asking, "Dear lady, tell us, what have you to do with all of this?"

The seventh and final spine ignited, and the waters shook. The air sparked with electric discharges, and through it, the whale could see that the purple creature was pleased with his words. "I am Kellis . . . ," she sang, her words flowing through the watery forms of both dolphins attached to her wavering image. "The first seal to be slain, the first to be exalted, Guardian of the Purple Angels, the children of the snow, those who were slaughtered for the sake of man's greed. For we, among all beasts, the seals of Sealssong, are the most pure! We are the true cherubs of the ocean. Until the sacred tear is returned, we are unable to leave. Not because we cannot, but because we will not abandon Her Majesty. She is ill and suffers greatly because of man, but her affliction would no longer be once the sacred tear is returned. Then and only then will we take our leave, for both she and all of innocence will have been renewed and her waters made clean, but take warning. Should you allow the darkness to conquer this innocence, Her Majesty will dry up and vanish, and all who dwell in the sea shall be no more. We all will crumble, becoming dusty piles of nothingness that will be devoured by the arid winds of despair."

An absolute silence settled over the whale, the penguin, and the seal. Such tidings both confused and frightened them, for such a responsibility was far greater than they ever imagined. The whale again cleared his throat, feeling his heart race against his mammoth chest. He swallowed hard, gulping down his apprehension, trying to present a convincing smile for the purple creation swaying before them.

"Do not fear," the Kellis sang. "For above all who have tried to enter this place, you are all that have succeeded. The rest were crushed by the weight of selfishness, others remain lost in this void. You are not like them, for you have the pure and courageous heart to defeat the darkness," she sang with a smile. "I have waited for you a long time, blue chanter. I have never lost hope of your coming."

The whale felt the tears pile up against his violet eyes, his heart full yet filled with much apprehension. Still, graciously smiling back toward the purple creature, honor and sincerity beaming across his gallant face, his magnificent head lowered in gratitude. He remained bowing for several moments before he was able to speak again. "Benevolent Kellis, you have certainly given us a profound challenge, one I never expected, one I do not rightly know how to achieve, for there are so many more questions to ask. Please, is there anything more you can tell us that will help us in this most incredible of quests?"

Suddenly, the shining star above the Kellis exploded, becoming a part of the ever-flowing waters. These incredible tides suddenly began to crash down upon the blue chanter. "I must leave you now, for all seven questions have been asked," the Kellis sang, her song taking on a more serious tone. "Prevent the evil Decara from sacrificing the white seal, return the tear to Her Majesty, and forever rid the evil that has taken your innocence from your world. Fail and never look again to find me. We all shall be no more."

"Hal-a-roo!" Mum blurted, clapping insanely, looking at the penguin shrugging her shoulders. "Just say'in"

"Oh, that's just great!" Mulgrew squawked in a nervous wrecked voice. "How are a single whale, one small but valiant penguin, and a deranged messed-up, freaky hump-pig harpie supposed to stop the end of the world? Will you tell me please? Thank you very much!"

Mum immediately smacked the bird across the head, nearly tossing him overboard. "Oh, do hush up, scuttle-snot!"

The Kellis began to dissolve before the whale, her eyes looking out to him, imploringly, "My time is empty . . . I have remained far too long," she hummed in an almost unrecognized and powerless voice. "Be brave and fear not. My thoughts go with you . . . and may the sacred tear protect and guide thee."

The wind increased, and the waters began to race upward, this time with a wild and exhilarated speed. Fully encased with a complete headgear of fiery spines, Kellis cried out, her wail sounding like that of a baby seal, her words no longer understood, her unearthly operatic voice drowning in gurgles and gasps. And there before the three voyagers, the fantastic creature suddenly wrapped herself inside the embrace of her transparent limbs. Lowering her head, she closed her massive eyes. Within a flash, she thoroughly melted, rejoining her connected water-filled companions. All three creatures quickly merged into each other, becoming one mass of collapsing fluid. In a thunderous crash, every trace of the Kellis and the interpreting dolphins disappeared, the spinning fountain sinking deep into the purple sea.

Wrapped up in her own queer expression, Mum promptly wriggled toward the face of Kishk. Dropping her snout over the whale's forehead, she took in a cramped and blurred upside-down view of the whale's enormous face. "Well!" she huffed, slurping at her runny nose, plopping her roly-poly self down with a miserable grunt—"that was festive!"

"Festive?" screeched Mulgrew, frantically waddling toward the immense head of the whale, careful not to get too close to the mad thing that was adjusting her tattered and soggy bonnet. "Now what are we supposed to do?"

"What's the matter, scared, tweedy-twit?" Mum taunted.

"Enough!" shouted the whale. "Don't you realize the seriousness of what has happened here?"

Just then, Mum's lips unexpectedly broke into a large and silly grin. Rapidly rolling herself directly over to Mulgrew, she squashed her plump self down on top of him. There was a prominent shrill of panic, just before the penguin and his impish scream became sucked up between the blubbery folds of her foul-smelling girth. "You were saying, my dear Mr. Kishk," she nonchalantly prattled off, shimmying her backside in a thumping frenzy as if to relieve a most bothersome itch.

Kishk merely shook his head in disapproval, surrendering shamefully, too concerned over their present predicament to further comment on his crew's ongoing feud. They were indeed lost. If they were ever to help the white seal find his mother—that, and of course, save the rest of the world—they needed to find their way back to Sealssong. Surging further into his uncertainties, the whale felt a tingle spark down his entire body, making him feel uneasy as if someone, or something, was watching him. This feeling of dread, like his worries and concerns, began to intensify when looking around at the purple dimension of endless incertitude. Although he could not see anything but purple stars and upflowing waterspouts, he knew that somehow, some way, be it through the same passage way allowing him to enter, something had followed him or became sucked in with him and had intentionally, or perhaps unintentionally, come along for the ride. Still, more importantly, the blue whale remained involved with the urgency of returning back to Sealssong, but where was the exit? How could he find it? There was still so much he did not understand about this place or the quest he must undertake. Despite it all, leaving this topsy-turvy world of purple stars and water-domed skies remained his primary concern.

Remembering the Kellis's final words, Kishk quietly repeated them: "Fear not . . . ," he said, imitating her proclamation but not sounding convincing in the slightest degree. He followed up with a discouraging sigh, then simply rolled up his troubled violet eyes and sighed some more. *"Right,"* he lamented, probing anxiety flushing his broad cheeks, closing his eyes, not daring to imagine what terrible calamity could happen next.

CAPTAIN CHAOS

Captain Thorne first noticed that the *Tiamat* was in trouble the moment the ship's instruments malfunctioned.

With this, there came a sudden drop in temperature within the vessel itself. As accustomed to the cold as he was, and as was his crew, this chilling grip remained raw with a penetrating bitterness far surpassing the previous voyages. This cold seemed to burn with a venomous bite, not like anything he had ever experienced. All systems and functions had mysteriously shut down when a strange glowing purple mist covered the *Tiamat*. Several hours after this occurrence, the boards and the iron strips covering parts of the vessel began to snap—rattle, and buckle; resentfully reacting to the freakish turbulence it was enduring. The ship remained virtually paralyzed as Decara's piercing screams of frustration shot through the blackened corridors. Because of this mysterious setback, she was not in a good mood, not that she ever was. Convinced of Captain Thorne's inadequacies and blaming the entire delay on him, she stormed through the blackness, setting out in an uproar, furiously ascending to the shipmaster's quarters determined to find out just what the matter was. Her crazed and violent presence came as no surprise to Captain Thorne; he knew she would be expecting a full report just as soon as she became aware of the strange disturbance, a disturbance he would not be able to explain. He heard the rattling ravings long before she came crashing through the door, nearly jolting it off its frozen hinges. "How dare you deviate from the course of this ship! What kind of fool-hearted man could allow for such an asinine blunder?" she ranted.

"It appears to be some kind of intense fog bank," Thorne explained.

"A fog bank!"

Exhaling his sparking annoyance, Thorne turned away from Decara and looked out the giant porthole before him. "Madam, I assure you, it was quite unavoidable."

"Oh really?"

"I am not the keeper of the sea, dear lady. She can be quite the formidable matriarch, not unlike yourself if, I may be so bold to say."

"How dare you!" she lashed out, whipping her black cloak around her slender figure. "How long will this fog bank last, and will it detain us from reaching Sealssong as I had planned?"

Captain Thorne appeared unusually calm. "It's hard to say."

"Just answer my question, Captain Chaos!"

Bringing a taut grin to his rugged face, Thorne scratched at his chin, itching away at his thick blond stubble, remaining unmoved by her arrogance. "With all due respect, madam, in case you hadn't noticed, we have a little more than fog to contend with," he said, pointing to the porthole. "Something quite extraordinary is happening out there."

"The only thing extraordinary, my misguided captain, is your lack of skill and good sense! Exactly how far have you taken us into this extraordinary happening?"

"At the moment," Thorne replied in a nonchalant voice, "I haven't the foggiest inclination, if you'll forgive the pun."

"I will not forgive! Nor will I forgive your indifference or your blatant disregard for the responsibilities I pay you for, and very well, I might add!"

"My humblest apologies, madam, but I must confess I really don't know. As it stands right now, I can offer you no logical explanation for what we are experiencing."

Decara's face soured with exasperation pressing herself toward Thorne's face. "You're not only incompetent, you are an imbecile! Now tell me, what exactly is going on here?" she demanded.

"My dear woman," Thorne answered, holding back a nervous, but intolerant grin, "I am still collating the ship's malfunctions."

"Still collating!" she screamed. "Well, I suggest we collate a little faster here, shall we!"

"I'll simply need more time to evaluate our situation," he advised, now restraining a forming snarl. "I implore your patience, madam. Until I have proper access to the ship's instruments, I'm afraid we remain stalemated."

"The only thing stale is your wretched arrogance!" she sneered. "And just for the record, my dear Captain Thorne, I won't be forgetting this little blunder of yours either!"

Thorne turned his face away from her probing finger just in time to escape its slicing cut. Proceeding toward the ship's panel of nonfunctioning instruments, he merely stared on, his eye refusing to meet up once more with the dark and out-of-control woman fuming next to him.

Continued with his study of the paralyzed implements, Thorne felt Decara's eyes drilling holes in his skull. Conveniently, he quickly offered her side of his face where his eye patch eliminated her from sight. "My guess is that we somehow encountered some abnormal storm front. Still, I must admit, it's nothing I have ever seen before." Then with a devilish and deliberate smirk on his robust face, the blue-eyed man was filled with sudden brazenness. "Or perhaps we've all died and have gone straight to hell." This time he slowly turned to face the evil woman inside the black cloak. The one eye, the one that remained exposed, twinkled at her playfully. "See anyone you know?" he dangerously toyed, moving his blond thick eyebrows up and down, quivering his black eye patch.

Surprisingly, Decara did not explode all over him. Instead, she smiled cunningly. "Captain Thorne, I should be careful if I were you."

Sucking in his cheeks, Thorne resisted his forming grin, trying to replace it with a more serious expression. "Once again, my humblest apologies, dear lady," he said unable to get rid of his devilish smirk. "That was inexcusable and not worthy of such a fine woman as yourself."

"Spare me your pretentious babble."

As Thorne gazed upon Decara's evil sneer, he soon lost all traces of his smirk. Once again, carefully turning his gaze away, he immediately went back to the inoperable and crippled equipment, fully aware that he was unable to offer any rational explanation for the condition of the ship or the blurry purple fog incarcerating them. "I guarantee you, madam"—his voice began to strain—"I will do everything possible to assure our intended course." He became thoroughly involved in the useless gauges before him.

"Fool," Decara protested, slamming down her skeleton-like fist against the glass-covered instruments, keeping it there and preventing him from viewing them. "You better come up with a snappy solution for our little problem and be quick about it, or I assure you, Captain Thorne," she yelled in a condescending shriek, "this will prove to be your last voyage—*ever!* I'll see to it personally!"

Trying to control his flush of anger, Thorne bit down on his dry lips and began grinding his teeth, holding his tongue as well as his discarded stare. Quietly, he waited for the dark woman to remove her white bony fingers from the spiderwebbed cracks she had angrily brought to the ship's glass panel. When she finally did so, he watched Decara carefully. She remained looking down at the break she had made.

Furious, she exploded, this time drenching him with contempt. "Look what you made me do!" she screamed, pushing him aside, checking the damage she had caused. A strange, almost pathetic look of remorse strangled her face while she continued to mournfully look upon the broken glass, her eyes filling with bitter regret, appearing as if to cry. However, quickly discarding her sudden vulnerability, she snatched on to a most foul and evil expression, turning her face away from the broken panel, exposing her fury, lunging her demonic leer toward the startled man. She literally growled at him, baring her teeth like a savage animal, then hurled herself toward the door, leaving the captain to figure out their dilemma, slamming the door behind her, her black cape slipping beneath the door, barely escaping its wooden crunch.

Finding his devilish grin again, Thorne could not help but chuckle. "A most delicate creature," he mumbled out loud disbelievingly. Moving from the inept panel of spiderwebbed glass, he backed away and stood in front of the wooden wheel thought to command the *Tiamat*, still staring at the door. His grip was intense while he stood there squeezing its polished ligneous curves. Thinking of the dark woman, his knuckles began to turn almost as marble white as hers, this woman he had grown to despise and yet at the same time continued to be intrigued by.

Soon his expression fell into a mold of distress when faced once again with his uncertainty, digging into the truth of his own fears. Never had he experienced such a moment in all his years of exploration. It was just like the *Tiamat* had slipped into an unknown dimension all on its own, filled with purple sparkles and foggy mist that easily swallowed it up with just one quick gulp. It was a strange dimension, quite extraordinary, leaving the ship completely under a strange and compelling purple spell.

Quietly, in the stillness of that room, he stared on, wondering, unsure of what disturbed and unsettled him greater—the ambiguous purple void before him or the shadowy woman hidden deep beneath the dark shroud in which she floated.

*   *   *

Complying with whatever was asked of them, the men assisted the *Tiamat* with the best of their skills, but their skills remained considerably limited within the grasp of the mysterious purple phenomenon. However, it was not until they continued to penetrate further into the purple abyss that the men began to show signs of severe apprehension and confusion. Disturbed and fearful, the sealers began to abandon their posts in an unorganized pursuit to see the phenomenon develop, each man watching it from various regions of the ship.

A fear unequaled before struck the heart of every man as they looked up into the watery sky above. It was all too fantastic for the men to comprehend, each in his own way reacting as if some kind of unimaginable sea creature had swallowed them whole. The familiar skies they once knew were no longer. In their place, a ceiling of rushing purple water hung itself abnormally from where the sun once shone. Walls of the same flowing substance surrounded them as far as they could see, and soon, a sick feeling of claustrophobic hopelessness infested itself deep inside the men, inviting the beginning stages of desperation and hysteria.

All power had ceased. Nothing was operable. The *Tiamat* was defenseless, left dark and floating aimlessly in the interior of the strange and unexplained. The only visible light came from the outside regions of the purple glow that thoroughly washed itself over the darkened shadows of the ship, doing the same to the perplexed and nervous faces of the already spooked crew, many of the men already believing that they had died or that they had somehow reached the end of the world.

CROOKS

In another part of the ship, the only two men not watching the skies were Cyrus and Yorick.

Despite the fantastic goings-on all around them, these two shrewd pilferers were already on their way back to pay another visit to the dark bowels of the *Tiamat*, each man discovering newfound courage, allowing them to return. Having seized what they believed was the opportunity of a lifetime; they continued their descent, fueled with this new and sudden burst of bravery.

Armed with a long crowbar that he believed could pry open the door to the cryptlike vault housing the incredible treasure, Yorick unremittingly grasped the metal tool tight like a weapon. Expecting to leave the ship wealthier than they had ever imagined, the two avaricious thieves never envisioned that this would prove to be the last time they would ever walk together, for they soon would no longer possess legs or feet to do so. Should they ever be discovered, they would not be found dead and yet they would no longer be considered living, for their human flesh would no longer be recognized. It would have long since been mutilated into grotesque fibers of what would be regarded as definitive of living horrors, mere playthings to be later devoured by the evil of the living *Tiamat*.

TIME TO KILL THE WITCH

Waking from another nightmare, Kenyan's eyes flashed open, and he began to cough.

He was not sure how long he had been in this cell, but it seemed like forever. Despite the many coming and goings of the terrible Oreguss, time no longer seemed to exist. Although he was not sick, he felt quite warm—or was it the temperature in his cell? Where did all the cold suddenly go? His forehead remained drenched in sweat, and his throat burned and tingled while he drew in a long and needed breath. He held it for a moment and then slowly released it, allowing his senses to fall into place. He had apparently fallen asleep and had once again awakened to the usual filth and degradation of his horrid cell, as well as this unexpected heat wave.

Something was different, all right; he could actually taste it in the air.

Abruptly sitting up, he immediately realized that the chains that once constricted him had decayed into small piles of dust around his feet.

He was free!

Then something even far more fantastic occurred when he realized that the once excruciating pain in his leg, as well as the burn on his cheek, had altogether left him.

Still fearing that he was still asleep, Kenyan reached down and ran his hands against the shattered bone in his leg, only it did not seem shattered any longer. Shaking his head in disbelief, he cautiously began to bend it back and forth, slightly at first, then more vigorously. Experiencing absolutely no pain, he proceeded to sit on the floor, bending his knee clear up to his chin. He could do it with no strain at all! His leg was mended! It was incredible! He quickly felt his face, realizing that the burn was healed as well. Fantastically, his leg and his face were made whole again, but how?

Once more, he looked down where Oreguss had snapped the bone in his leg like a dried-up twig. Pinching the place in sheer disbelief, Kenyan stood up and jumped, landing on both of his feet. His head in a whirl, the ecstatic boy began jumping up and down in a crazed state. "Yes!" he roared, clenching his fist in triumph, feeling the adrenaline pump wildly inside of him. It no longer mattered how it happened. He was but outrageously happy to find himself in one piece again, but then, in a moment, his rejoicing came to a halt. He was aware that the door to his cell had made a distinctive clicking sound and was in the process of partially squeaking itself open. Kenyan jerked his head toward the door. He waited for someone to enter the cell. No one did. Dowsed with burning apprehension but doubly fired with compelling curiosity, he slowly made his way over to the heavy wooden door. Before he could reach it, the door opened itself the rest of the way with no apparent assistance from anyone.

Only dark purple shadows stared at him from beyond. Not understanding what was happening, but being a young man of impulse and having been gifted with the knack of getting out of jam when he had to, he fully intended on taking advantage of his chance, and what a chance! After all, should it be a dream, he would be no worse off than he already was. However, should it be real, such an occasion would never present itself again, especially if Decara had anything to do with it. Then again, how did he know that she did not? Perhaps it was all a trick. It did not matter; he did not care. He was going to take his chances. It was now or never! He had to act quickly, but not before he armed himself. He would not leave until he took with him the precise thing that would finally end the nightmare. It was what he obsessed over ever since the witch sentenced both him and his sister to this cold and bitter hell.

Cautiously he glanced around at the purple darkness invading his cell. Moving through the mysterious mist, he went to the farthest corner of the filthy cell. He crunched down, his knees meeting the floor. It was a small place where even more shadows gathered. Here was the exact spot that had incarcerated him for Lord knows how many days now. Squatting, he reached down and pulled up a small portion of the stony floor. He had hidden something there; the something was what he would use to destroy the witch. He relentlessly worked on it ever since he came to this horrible existence. It was all that kept him from giving up, knowing that one day he would use it on the obscene Decara. Kenyan smiled a most frightening smile while reaching down, grasping the something into his awaiting fingers.

There it was—his creation. He had made it with his own hands, his chained hands, during the many cold and lonely nights, forced to lie secluded in darkness against his will. Concealing it on his person was the hard part, but he had somehow managed it. It was not, however, until he came to this cruel cell that he would finally have the chance to finish it. Remembering the time lying there in the darkness, his leg throbbing in agony, his face burning as if it were on fire, when he desperately executed its final completion, creating the perfect weapon, his dry lips cracked, breaking into a smug grimace. He had found a long strip of broken stone originating from some part of the first decrepit cell way back where Decara had sentenced him to upon his wretched arrival. With such precision, he put his meticulous talents to work. He spent hours grinding its once blunt surface against the stony walls of his prisons, transforming it into the trenchant weapon it now was. It was the constant thought of Decara's evil that fueled his desire to create such a shaft, customized just for her.

The pointed dagger was approximately eight inches long, two inches wide, and razor sharp. Around the crafted handle he had twisted various fragments torn from his shredded pants, allowing for a better grip, one he believed necessary to penetrate Decara's accursed heart—that is, if she even had one. If she did, it was dark as sin, and he was going to scrape out that sin once and for all!

At last, the time had come to kill the witch.

He would indeed snap apart her ribs and take out her loathsome heart. Afterward, he would keep it in a jar, he thought. A souvenir of the evil dragon he alone had slain. Swiftly, he took the dagger and tucked it inside his deep and narrow pants pocket, securing it shut with the fashionable button that still remained there. Completely pulling out his bloodstained shirt or rather what remained of it, he once more concealed his weapon. The warm air surrounding him felt incredible; however, the entire circumstance made a chill run down his back. Despite the suddenly increased warmth, that of which he could not think of one single logical reason for, it was time for him to take his anxious leave. He surely did not have time to reflect upon such matters, not now.

It was time to go.

He glanced once more over his shoulders, back to the despicable cell, his thoughts returning to Decara and the dagger. He patted his hand against the place where the tattered shirt covered it and smiled. In seconds, the boy left the prison cell, disregarding the dark shadows that had remained with him during his stay. They were on their own now to do what they will, just as he was.

In a flash he disappeared!

PURPLE ANGELS

Emma was filled with a wondrous fascination.

Looking upon the purple world of twilight bursting outside the small window in her room, all fear seemed to dissipate. Her blue eyes danced back and forth, mesmerized by what she was watching. "How beautiful!" she said in a hushed voice, feeling the sudden warm air embrace her. It felt magical. She had been in a state of peculiar cheerfulness ever since the purple mist first surrounded the ship. Its presence had awakened her from sleep. It seemed to call to her and touch her with fingers that were much too small ever to recall, and yet somewhere in the deepest part of her mind, she knew it was not part of a dream but an incalculable reality.

Pressing her face against the small porthole, she could feel a warm vibration bearing down against her cheek. It was a steady, overwhelming presence, and it was everywhere! From whatever proposed such a cause, she was most grateful, for never in her life had she felt so alive, so full of hope, so rejuvenated. It was as if she had suddenly become reborn. However, she could not help but wonder what it all meant. What was causing such an incredible feeling, and where had the ship taken her? Had it been taken somewhere unknown to everyone, even Decara? Emma tried to press her face closer into the small window, her breath fogging the glass. Wiping the telltale signs of her breath away, she lowered her head, trying to see more of what was happening outside. However, the tiny porthole only allowed for such a small sliver of what was occurring. If only she could see more of what sparkled so purplishly beyond her tiny window. Continuing to contort her neck, she twisted and turned with frustration, unable to take in any more of the spectacle than she had already, unable to see the wonder playing on above somewhere among what was once the sky.

Suddenly, her door sprang open, creaking, sounding as if yawning after waking up from a nap. She jumped when she looked back at the door's handle. Watching it turn, she shuddered. Moving from the window, she allowed the room to fill with the strange purple glow, placing her hand to her mouth, trying to hold back a gasp. Instantly, her entire body became wrapped in the same purple color that utterly pervaded the room. Panicked, she waited for Decara to enter, but she never did. Slowly, Emma walked across the room, mixing with the purple shadows, her excessive pink nightdress now turning purple, trailing endlessly behind her. Blankly she stared at what she now believed to be her imagination playing tricks on her. It was surely just the movement of the ship enjoying its devilish trickery again. Compelled, however, to go to the open door, she could see that it was not the case. Whatever was happening was no illusion and certainly not caused by the ship; that much was for certain. The door was open wide, and there was no malicious Decara or terrible Oreguss to stop her from leaving. Still, it could have been one of Decara's horrible wiles, and yet the way the purple mist made her feel, she no longer cared. She felt released in a way that she never believed was possible. The feeling made her dizzy and almost giddy, and she loved every minute of it. Seizing this unthinkable moment, Emma decided to chance all her odds.

From outside her door, more shafts of purple glow spilled itself across her face, turning her blue eyes remarkably iridescent while she prepared to leave this room she so despised. Picking up the aftermath of her nightdress, she appeared to float across the room. Taking hold of the door's mighty handle, she confidently crossed over its diabolical threshold, momentarily hesitating. Not knowing what made her do it, she turned around and looked back at the strange room one last time, defying it from stopping her.

It did not.

Her glowing eyes flashed open wide, watching the door close all by itself. She smiled pleasantly and walked away, disappearing into the awaiting purple shadows. She was still smiling when the surrounding purple shades pressed themselves around her, lightly kissing her forehead.

MISFITS

A heavy blanket of freezing rain showered over the seal rookery. Icebergs of every shape and size went nosing up to its frozen borders. Morning had come once more, and once more, the nursery came alive with a hundred squeals, all inquisitively sounding off from the baby whitecoats recently born. Despite the inclement conditions, the seals seemed content, none appearing to mind the prickling sensation the freezing rain provided. In fact, most enjoyed the tickling flutter made upon their wet, furry heads.

The children of Sealssong, having been fed for the most part, remained happy and playful, many of the mothers settling back in an attempt to get some needed shut-eye before the next feeding took place. While they snoozed, some of the children made a game out of the freezing droplets that covered them unceasingly. Raising their black shining eyes, they stuck out their pink tongues, wiggling them about, giggling, while the icy rain danced inside their mouths. Other pups entertained themselves by lying flat on their backs. Having already learned the game Clap-Clap, they waved their tiny flippers, fanning the icy droplets, chasing them away from their furry faces. However, most children remained near their mothers, fascinated by the downpour, but just the same, not daring to venture away, at least not while the sky remained in such an unpredictable dither. Such was the life of a harp seal on this particular day, in this particular nursery in Sealssong.

As the exhausted mothers continued in their half-twilight snooze, one eye remaining on their pup, the other buried somewhere in dreamland, there were those who would not be so easily entertained by the rain; they would have more pressing things to consider. Almost forty times the great fireball in the sky had come and gone, and on this rainy afternoon, Miracle found himself pining for the return of his friends. The walrus Crumpels managed a fairly commendable job in watching over the white seal, finding shelter in a distant icy keep, far from the other seals. She fussed over him, doing everything she possibly could do for him, and yet for Miracle, something was missing. For in his heart, no one could ever take the place of his mother, nor could anyone ever compare to the outrageous, Mad Mum.

This day, they had temporarily left their home, having gone to the open floes. While looking out into a silver black sea that swarmed about dizzily inside the tosses of a most unruly storm, there upon this particular nursery on this particular afternoon, the young seal sighed. Not far from where he stood, directly behind him, a sea of roly-poly baby seals covered the floors of the buoyant cradle. Still, as fate would have it, Miracle remained set apart from them. Ever since his return, he made sure that he kept his distance, spending most of his time alone. He was not eating properly and was beginning to lose body fat, something not healthy for seals to do, but he just had lost his desire to eat. Poo-Coo, on the other flipper, was enormous and growing every day. He had long since tripled Miracle's size. In fact, at the rate he was expanding, in just a short time, he would soon surpass even his own mother. There was certainly nothing tiny about this baby walrus; he was growing in leaps and bounds, all bouncing into one spongy bundle of quivering blubber. Unfortunately, his awkward size, as well as his preposterous features, made him out to be a facetiously looking clown, especially to the other harps sharing the nursery. The moment Poo-Coo arrived; he suffered bursts of ridicule, as did both Miracle and Crumpels. It would seem that they all would be misfits here, and very little time would be devoted to social observance. This did not seem to bother Miracle as much as it did Poo-Coo. Being of an extreme curious and outgoing nature, the young walrus intended upon making new friends. However, he soon came to find that it would not be an easy task. Most of the younger harps merely laughed at him; others treated the walrus as a threat. Some simply chose to ignore him, others snapped cruelly, hoping to discourage any encounter with the queer-looking beast, while some called him names. There were adults that threatened to attack him, wanting nothing to do with the tusk-ridden, uninvited tooth walker. It was a problem, but it was about to change—on this most particular rainy afternoon.

Miracle continued his silent watch, overlooking the sea, its watery radius still alive, jumping with the pitter-patter of heavy rainfall, when Crumpels rumbled herself toward him. As she approached, the rest of her traipsing rolls unfolded like an accordion. Then with one quick and disturbing plop, Crumpels asked, "Whatcha thinking, White Puff?" Miracle chose not to answer her. He merely stared off, offering another faint sigh. Crumpels squeezed in for a tighter fit, turning her head toward the open sea. This time, she sighed too, imitating the same yearning moans as Miracle. "Wondering, where they be, boop-boop-dee-dee?" she pondered, shaking her enormous head.

Miracle turned to face the walrus. "It has been such a long time already. Do you suppose that something dreadful has happened to them?"

"Now there, there . . . Mr. Kishk would never allow for such a thing, would he?"

"Well no, but there are terrible things out there! Mum told me so!" he gasped, becoming terribly excited. "You don't suppose that one of those dreadful man-beasts got them, do you?"

"Oh gosh, no," Crumpels panicked, fear swathing her face while slapping one flipper hard across her open mouth. "No!" she exclaimed, this time realizing that her alarmed reaction was not helping the situation any. "I mean, no no no, of course not . . . no way, boop-boop-hey! *Hey!*" she quickly added in a desperate attempt to compose herself. "Whooo-whooo!" the disheveled walrus nervously piped. "Everything is A-OK, White Puff, boop-boop-dee-bluff! Not to worry, dear—not to worry."

Miracle just could not help but smile. He had come to adore the silly walrus. Besides, he knew what she was trying to do; still, he had to be true to the feelings now surging through him. Pretending them away just wasn't the answer. "You've been so wonderful to me, watching over me, both you and Poo-Coo. I just want you to know how grateful I am."

Crumpels blushed and then placed a flipper next to her mouth, rolling her eyes to the side of her large head. "*Whoody-whooo!* Why, there isn't anything I wouldn't do for you, White Puff. Besides, I am sure that whatever it was that Kishk and the others were meant to do, they will have finished doing it. And after having done it, they won't have to do it anymore, and they will be safe and sound and soon to be returning to us once more," she explained, batting her massive eyes in a wild frenzy.

Miracle only shook his head and giggled, rubbing his saturated head against her soused face. He remained that way until he felt the heavy weight of Poo-Coo's head resting on top of his own. "Chin up, little bro, it will turn out right, you'll see. Besides, we're family now," Poo-Coo announced, all his folds pressed against Miracle, nearly drowning him in squashy rolls of blubber. "Nothing, or nobody, will ever harm you while I'm around!"

Prying his tiny head from the rippled skin of both walruses, Miracle took in a deep breath. Looking at them, he smiled just before he began to playfully rub noses with both massive creatures that had shown him such loyalty and kindness. Then a tremendous black cloud suddenly snuck up from the east, aggravating the raindrops, as a mighty wind tore through the nursery with an impulsive fury. Miracle remained undaunted while Poo-Coo's maturing howl sounded off in the background. "We better take cover!" Crumpels shouted. "This storm is getting a little too rambunctious for me! Boop-boop-dee-flee! Hurry up," she bellowed. "We best get back to the ice keep. Come; let us be on our way!"

"Just a little longer please!" Miracle begged.

Crumpels shook her head, dusting the raindrops from her face. With understanding eyes, she tried to explain. "We have waited in this very spot for some time, dear heart. We are all tired," the walrus said, holding her drooping abdomen, looking as if she were about to upchuck. "So please, come along now. You need your rest. Besides, what would your mama think if she saw you sitting out here in the middle of this dreadful storm? Come, it's off to the keep! We can wait for Mr. Kishk and the others just as well there away from this *whooo-rendous* storm!"

Lifting his eyes and turning his glance once more to the dancing sea, Miracle gave the rippling waters one final sigh, turning, slowly wriggling back to the remoteness of the small secluded ice keep. With Poo-Coo leading the way, the white seal reluctantly followed. As the three misfits commenced onward, they passed the other seals. Several mothers and their pups watched with suspicious eyes, not wishing to associate themselves with the peculiar-looking trio.

Poo-Coo now triple the size of most of the inimical spectators surrounding him, could not help reacting to their indifference. *"Ppplltttwthhppwttthhp!"* he spat. "What are you looking at? Never seen a walrus before?"

"Walrus, indeed!" scoffed a nearby mother, tugging at her child, one who was trying her best to maneuver her way over to the young tooth walker who had clearly caught her attention. "Uninvited vagrants, if you ask me!" barked the mother harp.

"So who's asking?" Poo-Coo snapped.

"Tawdry trespassers!"

Crumpels became appalled. "Now see here, my good seal, we are not tawdry in the least! Boop-boop-you-beast! That is a most unsuitable way to conduct oneself, especially in front of the children, *whoody-whooo-whooo!*"

"Yeah!" spit Poo-Coo, making a grotesque face, sticking out his tongue as far as it would reach while the pup of the insulting mother broke away freely. Waddling fearlessly up to the young walrus before her mother could stop her, the inquisitive pup confronted Poo-Coo. "You sure are ugly! What are you supposed to be anyway, a smelly pig whale?"

Poo-Coo snorted in insult. "A—pig whale! *Noooo!* I already told you, stupid, that I am a walrus! Don't you know anything?" he said, shoving the pup aside.

"How dare you touch my child!" growled the mother of the pup. "Jillith, come back here at once! Stay away from such unnatural disease-ridden beasts!"

"Well!" exclaimed Crumpels, showing her utter exasperation.

Ignoring her mother's request, the shrewd intrusive Jillith pup persisted. She swatted one of Poo-Coo's tusks hard with her flipper. "Gross, what are those yucky pointy things sticking out of your mouth supposed to be anyway?"

"Don't you know?" spit Poo-Coo, opening wide his mouth, throwing his head back while showing off his premature set of shining tusks. He shot out a stream of spittle, forcefully hitting the sassy small fry right between her eyes. "It's what I use to chop up silly little snot-nosed busybodies like you! Now get lost you ignorant runt!"

The screaming pup immediately fled back to its mother, wailing at the top of her voice. "It tried to KILL me! It tried to KILL me! Mama, that fat pig whale tried to KILL me!" the spit-covered pup screamed crazily, scurrying into the folds of its mother, whimpering and shivering.

The infuriated mother harp, while nudging her pup out into the icy rain, began incessantly licking her child from top to bottom, helping the rain dissolve the remaining residue provided by the appalling tooth walker. "If you ever dare come near my child again, I swear I will—" Not furthering her threat, thinking it beneath her dignity, Jillith's mother snarled before finishing off her words, shielding her pup with her hindquarters. "Why don't you all go back to wherever it is you came from? This place was never meant for the likes of you! This is a sacred place, where decent seals come to give birth to the purest of pure. You have no right being here!"

"We most certainly do, boop-boop-boo-who!" Crumpels grumbled. "Who are you to tell us such things? There are no laws in Sealssong prohibiting us from remaining here!"

"There most certainly are! Why, your very presence here profanes all that is sacred to our law!"

"Sacred—schmacred!" Poo-Coo spit.

"Guttersnipe, all of you!" the infuriated mother harp thundered.

"My, aren't we the sassy snot nose," Crumpels grumbled

"Misfits, that's what you are, all of you! You're a pompous, belligerent beast just like your sloppy mouth degenerate!" Then quickly turning to Miracle who had remained silent and situated directly opposite her, the excited mother opened wide her eyes with a disturbing look that pierced his very soul. Lashing out with a chilling voice, she barked, "And you, how dare you leave your mother to worry while you disgracefully fraternize with these unwanted vagabonds? You should be ashamed of yourself!"

Miracle began to feel his heart race as the very tips of his saturated fur took on a faintly shining glow of purple. Even his eyes seemed to burn of the color. With his throat becoming dry, he managed to speak out. "I don't like how you talk, nor do I know why you act so angrily. These are my friends, and I don't think you should speak to them that way. Just because they are different from you, you call them names and try to hurt them. It is you who should be ashamed of yourself! Furthermore, as for my mama, well, she is none of your concern! Now leave us alone!"

Crumpels immediately went to Miracle's side, consoling the pup as best as possible.

Poo-Coo stood nearby while numerous seals began to pile in from everywhere. The scolding mother harp became silent, watching as Miracle turned his head from hers, his purple color intensifying more and more with each passing moment. Suddenly, the stone around his neck flared, startling the mother harp and the entire seal congregation.

"What sort of creature are you, anyway?" the alarmed and suspicious mother of Jillith demanded. Not waiting for a response, she quickly backed away, pulling her child along, completely disturbed by what she had just witnessed. Other seals began to grow apprehensive as well, intensifying the scene while the curious gathering continued to multiply.

"Look, Mama!" one pup called out, appearing more like a giant drowned white rat than a seal, his doused fur pasted heavily around his chubby frame. "Why does that seal have a funny color to it? Is it sick, mama?"

A disruptive murmur of extending alarm filled the maturing crowd while each mother gathered up her curious offspring. "Perhaps it is some kind of rare plague!" another oversized harpie suggested, scooping up her pup between her massive jaws, preparing to abscond away from the misfits.

"Yes, it may be contagious for all we know!" panicked another voice from somewhere in the crowd.

"My baby!" screamed several more misguided harpies, snatching their children in their mouths, pulling away from the crowd.

Much of the gathering seemed to agree, the panic infesting itself further with each fleeting moment. Then all at once, all the seals began barking and howling in a most unruly protest.

"Whoody! Schmoody!" sparked Crumpels her face a wad of irritated wrinkles, "the plague, indeed, boop-boo-dee-dweed! You're nothing but a bunch of blubbering buffoons, scuttle bum, every last one of you!"

"Yeah," Poo-Coo blurted, shooting out another unpleasant round of spittle, its stream blindly dousing the opposing crowd, cutting screams scattered everywhere, the spittle hosing over the barking seals, creating an even more unnerving situation. It did not look good. By now, all the seals were barking out alarming howls toward the three misfits. Some even tried to snap at them, wanting to harm them.

"Cut that out!" demanded Crumpels, shielding Miracle and Poo-Coo. "Cease your infernal hullabaloo, boop-boop-dee doo!" she nervously barked, a streak of panic stamped across her wrinkled face, her massive body a sea of quivers pressing tight around her child and Miracle.

The incessant barking and ridicule did not stop. In fact, it grew steadily worse. The growling seals closed in on them, their yips and yawls exhilarating in retaliation over the cold wash of spittle they received. The younger set seemed to concentrate on the freakish Poo-Coo. They all began to laugh at him, and it wasn't long before the constant barking became entwined by the young squeaky high-pitched voices of sheer mockery. *"Fat seal, fat seal, eats up everybody's meal!"* Some seals, even those old enough to know better, became caught up in the tease, scooping up flippers full of slushy snow and ice, flipping it devilishly into the faces of the three misfits.

Then without warning, a loud sound suddenly rumbled over the pitiless mob of yipping harpies. *"ENOUGH!"* Miracle shouted, a thunder roaring itself behind him, the sky momentarily lighting up with a strange greenish illumination. Another crack of thunder pealed off while Miracle pushed out his heaving chest, directing his words to the crowd, his purple stone glowing more brightly than ever before. "You who call yourself children of Sealssong, you dishonor this very place! You make the sea want to weep again!"

A peculiar stunning silence gripped the congregation as another tremor shook the icy grounds. Miracle looked out into the shocked gathering, staring at their perplexed faces while the island shook as if to come apart. Most of the frightened seals scurried for cover, nearly falling through the sudden gapes below them. Slumping forward, suddenly utterly exhausted, Miracle tried to keep from falling himself, waiting while the earth around him began to settle. Confused and frightened, not understanding what had just happened, becoming especially disturbed by what he had just blurted out to the crowd, he shivered. *How could such bravery come from me?* Closing his eyes, he shivered some more, trying to steady himself.

In a short while, Miracle began to feel like himself again; however, the feeling of having the wind knocked clear out of his lungs remained. He raised his head, slowly and carefully looking to the seals whose shining heads peeked out from behind scattered columns of icy sculptures. Seizing the moment and having each of their undivided attention, he shouted, "If you cannot be our friend, then just leave us alone! We wish nothing more from any of you!" he said as a final rumble shook behind him, its exploding light filling the sky with another surge of artificial green iridescence.

The sky was beginning to grow brighter about this time, sending with it the initial traces of a few strains of faint sunshine, gradually bringing each shaken harp back out into the open, its light unfolding across the nursery. A few fainter grumbles of thunder, bellyaching somewhere in the far distance, rolled themselves off submissively into oblivion, the remaining dark clouds disassembling themselves, leaving the sky a peculiar orange color, dotting it randomly with silver streaks of wispy, hanging vapor. More segregated areas of broken sunshine streamed down from the passing clouds with Miracle leading the way, this time back to the ice keep, not one single seal stirring. Even the wind and the rain had become less agitated, and with its demise, a gentlest breeze favored the island, one that seemed to invite a quieter moment upon this secluded nursery of Sealssong. It was not long when from high above through the abandoning clouds several expanding rays of sunshine showered down, moving swiftly over the hushed congregation, the conforming seals parting themselves, making way for the walruses and the queer white seal wearing the strange and fascinating purple stone.

THE KEEP

The great fireball in the sky had once again returned, bringing a measure of wonderment full of relaxation and sleep to most of the seal pups. It would seem that a sense of normalcy would embrace the land, at least for the time being.

Dozens and dozens of whitecoats glazed the shining cold grounds. It appeared that in just such a short time, every pup was cozily closing his eyes, reposing in the most preposterous positions, the majority managing to lie on their woolly backs, pleasantly warming their soft, tender bellies, their flippers askew as if dazed in some deplorable drunken state. Like furry sewn-together stuffed toys, the snowy children spotted the icy grounds in such a jumbled way, easily promoting the assumption that they had been randomly discarded from somewhere high above. However, despite their ill-fated poses, these adorable critters were most content, for after having been fed, the warmth and the tingle from the fireball's glow was all that was required to assure a well sought-after snooze. For the most part, the pups were no longer concerned about the misfits but only the delightful retreat to the happy place called dreamland. As for the mothers, just like the baby seals, the recent memory involving the three peculiar beasts temporarily seemed to vanish beneath the tingle of the warm sun as well. As long as the burning ball in the sky continued to shine and warm their soft bellies, caressing them with a somberly delight, each drowsy seal would forget about all else.

Indeed, it would seem that nothing could possibly matter, except the sheer delight of indulging oneself within the delicious charm of an afternoon seal siesta, complete with pleasant seal dreams for all. Painting every harp's lips with a humorous grin of complacent bliss, the shimmering rays brushed itself ever so delicately across every single muzzle. All, that is, except for the small and disheartened Miracle that remained secluded inside a remote icy keep some distance away from the snoozing whitecoats and their mothers.

*   *   *

There, somewhere off toward the very borders of the floating nursery, somewhere inside a jagged and rocky lair, an icy cave lay buried against a backdrop of endless valleys of snow. Treelike sculptures covered in billowy ruffles of snow and ice filled the grounds while an ominous yellow-colored haze hung lethargically from the sky. This keep stood secluded and shut off from all. It was an abandoned place accidentally discovered by Crumpels not long after they returned to the nursery. It was here that the young Miracle waited with a heavy heart for word of his mother.

The secluded keep was not a place easily found, for it remained surrounded by foreboding glaciers, broken and crumbled, offering difficulty for any intruding seal to investigate. However, what made this keep most discouraging from the prying eyes of others was its particular location—a dangerous place where numerous unpredictable ice floes shrouded much of its forsaken surroundings.

Only a few hundred yards from this cave, a dark circumfused sea stretched out as if endless. It bubbled with a strange and unusual steam. Blue graylike wisps of moisture twisted upward from this secluded sea, crystallizing in the rush of the cooling water, forming icy, thorny monstrosities, all skimming teasingly above the frosted swells that moved with sluggish oiliness. These forming crystals mutated and grew into and around the pancake ice forms, stippling the dark sea of Sealssong with a haunting uncertainty. The varying waves, which chanced near these parts, twisted and tugged at the icy pans, sometimes pulling them apart, breaking the surface as an oozing milky slush rimmed the floes over with a frosted mucuslike covering, the yellow haze intensifying its spectral bizarreness. If she had looked a hundred times over, Crumpels could not have found a more precarious or secluded retreat, but it was all that she could find, all that she believed was available. For the time being regardless of its hazardous qualities like it or not, the deserted cavern would prove to be home for the white seal and the two walruses.

WANNA GO SWIMMING?

Inside the keep, Crumpels and her son slumbered noisily while Miracle blankly stared over at them, both of their rowdy snores rattling the walls. Their enormous stomachs, which continuously rose up and down, made for a momentary distraction for the young seal. Before falling into their noisy heap of snores and grunts, Crumpels had gone out to the many surrounding floes, rendering dinner for everyone. Miracle never quite figured out what she had fished out of the slush holes, but whatever it was, it sure looked icky. Still, it seemed to please Crumpels and Poo-Coo quite satisfactorily. He believed that she called the crusty things shellfish. She did, however, tell him that it was essential that he learned how to swim to find food. For when he was old enough—that is, if he still hadn't found his mama—and he was ready to leave the nursery, she would teach him how to swim, but she would go on to talk about this another time, she explained. She simply was much too boop-boop-dee-pooped to consider such a notion, not right after finishing her lunch. "Yes, perhaps another time," she promised, shuffling her large self around in a circle trying to find a comfortable spot.

Reluctantly, Miracle studied some of the leftover shellfish that Crumpels had eaten partially. Unsure of exactly how to eat the crusty things, he tried to break through the hard covering with his teeth, only extracting some of its innards. After chewing a few times, he found that he actually liked the taste, but he still wasn't very hungry. He was much too preoccupied with his thoughts and continuously found himself mesmerized by the sleeping walruses' wobbly bellies bouncing and jiggling in a peculiar harmonious dance, up and down, over and over again. As he remained in this fixed trance, he suddenly began to feel queasy. Shaking this dizziness away, he wriggled himself out toward the opening of the disquieted keep, grunting to himself. The gentlest breeze passed over him, and he raised his head, pausing outside the opening, attempting to see beyond the broken chunks of icy debris piled heavily in the distance, the yellow alien sky emanating everywhere.

Breathing in the flowing air, he closed his eyes. Its sweetness filled him; and for a moment, if he tried terribly hard, it would seem that he could pretend the entire situation away by merely listening to the unremitting caresses given to the forming shore, imagining that his mother was out there calling to him, waiting for him. She would show him how to swim and catch the slimy crusty things called shellfish. She would sing to him once more, and this time, she would never go away, never ever!

The dreaming pup remained this way, his eyes closed, his nose wiggling, taking in the salty briskness of the blowing wind, when all at once a cold softness pressed itself against his vibrating nose, completely startling the unsuspecting seal. Nearly losing his balance, he abruptly pulled away, his shining black eyes shooting open, unprepared for what would happen next. Once again, the coldness came up against his nose. This time, a small mouth, furry and soft just as his was, quickly came up against his nose, repeating the same cold, wet sensation. Only this time, a tiny pink tongue peeked out from the velvety soft mouth just for a second, impetuously licking him with one fast scoop.

"I knew it was you!" a tiny but high-pitched voice rang. Backing away into the keep, Miracle blinked his eyes in disbelief. The voice grew louder with a higher shrill as a petite and fluffy female pup followed him daringly inside. "Hello!" she belted. "Remember me?"

Continuing to back away from her, Miracle only shook his head. "I'm Nikki!"

He remained confused.

"Don't you remember?" the intruding little pup said. "We've met before!"

Once again, Miracle only stared at her in disbelief.

"What a stupid look you have!" The young girlish pup laughed. "Come on, you just have to remember! It was the day you lost your mama. You looked so sad and lost. I couldn't help feeling sorry for you. Have you found her?"

Miracle tilted his head and gave the young seal a puzzling look, suddenly remembering. "Yes, I remember you. You were with your mama that day. She took you away from me."

The tiny female harp rolled up her eyes, proceeding to close in on Miracle. "Well," she said with a mocking grin about her snout, "you don't get points for ripping out nursing teats! I mean, really! I knew you were hungry, but what were you thinking? Mama forbade me from seeing you after your many attacks."

"Sorry," Miracle offered, lowering his head in embarrassment.

"Oh, not to bother, if she didn't have that to complain about, she would find something else! It's always something! She emotionally drains me!"

"How did you find me?" Miracle asked, backing away from Nikki.

"I followed you, silly!"

"But it's dangerous here. You could have gotten yourself lost or even killed!"

"Oh please! Hey! Why do you wear that stone around your neck? Can I see it?"

"No!" he barked, pulling away further. "What are you doing here anyway, haven't you heard? I'm some kind of freak!"

"So I've heard. At least that is what the word on the ice block is. They say you're kind of . . . what was it—*peculiar?* However, being a lady and not prone to the general assumptions of misguided mammals, I thought I would come here and find out for myself! Besides," she added with a bonus smile, "I think you're cute!" Then Nikki smiled some more and began sniffing about his snout. *"Hmmm,* seem pretty normal to me, except for that silly stone you wear, that and being just a tad colored purple, but nobody's perfect, *n'est pa?"* The inquisitive seal continued sniffing about, here and there, and then quickly wrinkled her mouth with a questionable frown. *"Hmmm?* Don't see what all the fuss is about."

"Fine, I'm glad!" Miracle snapped. "Well, you've come to see the freak and you've seen him, now if you don't mind—"

"Well, this is the thanks I get. I come all this way, almost kill myself on three separate occasions, just trying to get to this freaky place, and this is how you treat me, of all the nerve!" Nikki barked, quickly changing her tone to a burst of girlish excitement. "Come on, let me wear the stone! I'll give it back! I promise!"

Miracle swatted her snatching flippers away with one sharp swipe. "Leave me alone!" he warned.

"All right," Nikki retorted as a hurt expression fell over her snout. Retracting her neck and sitting up erect, she continued to stare at Miracle. "It's a stupid-looking stone, anyway! Who cares about it? Besides," she said, shaking her little behind in a defiant quiver, "I have a good mind not to take you to the Forbidden Place, after all!"

"You better leave if you know what's good for you! You'll get into such trouble if someone finds you here."

"Who cares?" she scoffed. "I'm not afraid of them. I'm not afraid of anybody! I'm not even afraid of you, so there!" she said, sticking out her wet pink tongue.

"What is it you want?"

Nikki quickly found her mischievous smile again. "Just being friendly, that's all."

"Why should you? No one else is."

"That's because they're all stuck-up bores."

"Well, that's all very interesting, now I think you should go home now."

"Besides, there is something very different about you."

"Yes, we have already settled on that. Now you better go before your mama finds out."

"I don't mean different in a bad way, I mean in a good way. I knew it from the moment I first laid eyes on you."

Miracle was about to ask her to leave again, but then for some strange reason he suddenly changed his mind. Looking at the daring young pup with a softer stare, still unsure as to her intentions, he realized that she was the first pup in the nursery that spoke kindly to him.

"*Sui generis,*" Nikki said with an adorable smile plastered over her puppy face.

"What?"

"*Sui generis* means you're in a class of your own, unique. I like that."

"You do?"

"Yes, in fact, I do."

Miracle felt his snout twitch. The young pup actually caused him to smile; it was a small smile, but a smile nonetheless.

"Now, you don't really want me to leave, do you?" she asked, batting her eyes in a foxy manner.

"Well, I guess you can stay for a short while, but that's all!"

Nikki smiled again and batted her eyes some more.

"Aren't you afraid that the seals of Sealssong might turn against you if they found out you came here?"

"I told you," she repeated with a growl to her soft voice. "I'm not afraid of anything, least of all any of those moronic blockheads!" Then tilting her head, she softened her voice, and continuing to press herself forward, she watched Miracle wriggle backward, trying to get away from her. "You mustn't let them worry you," she said, persistent in perusing him. "They really mean you no harm. It's just that, well, you're—"

"What?" Miracle growled, feeling his back fold up harshly against the frozen edges of the wall of the keep, completing any further chance of avoiding the advancing harp.

"Awfully cute," Nikki teased rubbing her tiny muzzle against his.

Miracle desperately searched to pursue another avenue of warding off her brazen persistence; however, he found that he was unable to move. Tensing up, not knowing how to react, he remained still.

"Besides," Nikki said, pulling slightly away, finally giving him a moment to breath, "who really gives a seal's behind what they think?" She tossed her furry white head to the opposite side and crunched up her charcoal-colored nose. "Don't really think it's so much you as it is those two silly-looking friends of yours."

"What do you mean by that?"

"Well, you know," Nikki admitted, adjusting her brow with a gentler bend. "You can't deny the fact that the two creepy seals you are bunking with, how shall I say, isn't helping your social seal status any."

"That's how much that you know! They are not seals!" Miracle protested in an outburst, pushing out from his cornered position, startling Nikki, and nearly toppling her backward as he continued in full voice. "They are walruses—*Walruses!* Don't you know anything?"

"I know more than you, I'm sure!"

"You do?" Miracle snapped. "Then you must also know that they are more than just walruses, they are family! This is more than I can say about you and any of the snooty seals on this island!"

"Calm down!" Nikki barked, shaking the powdered snow from her coat. "I didn't mean to upset you. It makes no difference to me if you like hanging out with creepy-looking seals."

"They are not seals!" he screamed in frustration, this time nearly waking the two sleeping walruses that were snoring just a few feet away, both momentarily pausing their snoring long enough to smack their wrinkled mouths together with their lumpy tongues, each making sucking noises with their bulbous lips before proceeding to snore off again. "Now see what you did, you nearly woke them!"

"Me? I'm not the one with the mouth!" Nikki answered, turning, her curiosity getting the best of her. Scurrying over toward the back of the keep, she drew closer to the two slumbering walruses. She cocked her head, just studying the fleshy creatures carry on with their exaggerated snoring. It made the young seal feel nauseous with disgust; still, she blatantly continued to watch close up as their enormous bellies expanded ridiculously in front of her. "Sure are the ugliest-looking seals I've ever seen," she groaned. Then suddenly spinning around, Nikki threw a crazed look back toward Miracle. "Hey, wanna go swimming?"

"Swimming?" Miracle reluctantly asked, shaking the film of ice from his backside.

"Yeah, swimming, you know, splash-splash, wiggle-wiggle!"

Miracle smirked. "I can't do that!" he confessed, panting, relieved that she was at last a comfortable distance away from him. "I don't know how."

Nikki began to giggle. "You can't be serious. You mean you're waiting for one of the grown-ups to show you how?"

"Well yes, that's how it's done, isn't it?"

"Yeah, if you're a real scare-baby, it is."

"Well, I'm not a *scare-baby!*"

"Prove it!"

Miracle frowned and twisted up his snout in annoyance. "What are you getting at?"

Nikki thought for a moment before she spoke and then grabbed at another mischievous grin. "I'll make a bet with you."

"What kind of bet?"

"It's okay, not to worry, silly! After one lesson with moi, you will be most proficient in this art I have perfected! I will teach you!"

"You? What could you possibly know about swimming?" Miracle argued, once again backing away from the advancing pup.

"Oh, I know lots and lots about it. You'll see!"

"I think not!" he ridiculed, edging himself blindly out through the rugged opening of the keep with Nikki in mad pursuit. As he crossed the threshold, he suddenly slipped on a long slab of broken ice, landing headfirst into a small and isolated pool of slush. Popping up and gasping for air, the white seal embarrassingly flipped about, fumbling awkwardly, trying to leave the water.

"Clearly, I see this is not going to be easy! Oh well." Nikki sighed, clearing her throat just before she took a flying leap into the tiny slush pool, mercilessly splashing them both, knocking Miracle back down just as he was about to pull himself out, pinning him precisely where she wanted him. Securely wedged inside the shallow pool's restricted confinements, Miracle jeeringly glared at the ostentatious female.

"Wanna smooch?" Nikki chirped.

"Cut that out!" Miracle yelled in a desperate attempt to get out of the water once more. It took him a few moments, but he finally managed to pry himself away, furiously shaking himself clean from the slushy mess covering him. Then once more, he glared at the immodest harpie who continued to smack her lips together in a mocking pretend kiss from the center of the pool.

"What ya wanna do that for!" he shouted in a not-so-friendly voice.

Nikki giggled. "Just trying to get you in the mood for swimming!"

"And I told you I don't know how!"

"But I will show you how!"

Miracle distorted his brow with growing annoyance. "Look, this is all very silly!"

"*Silly?* I'll have you know that I have already taught several others, and they didn't think it at all silly!"

"Why should I believe you? You're just trying to trick me. I know."

"Trick you? Look, would I have come all this way, struggled through all sorts of ghastly passageways just so I could trick you?"

Miracle scrunched up his nose and continued to shake out his wet coat. "You might."

"Oh, don't be absurd! I have much better things to do with my time. Now don't be such a gooey jellyfish! Besides, I only thought that since your mama isn't here to show you, I would help you out."

"Keep your crummy thoughts to yourself! I don't need your help or anyone else's!" barked the angry Miracle, shaking off the remainder of the saturated ice and water from his white coat.

"Now, don't get all testy!" Nikki said. "I only came here 'cause, well, I like you."

"More like feel sorry for me!"

"That simply isn't true," she told him, throwing both of her flippers over the side of the small slush hole, hoisting herself out with one push. She shook herself, ridding herself of the icy water, then turned and looked at Miracle with a disappointing stare. "I really thought you would like to see it."

"See what?"

"I already told you, goofy—*the Forbidden Place!*"

"The Forbidden Place, what's this 'Forbidden Place' you keep mentioning?"

Nikki's snout curved up considerably as she began to bat her eyes in a teasing manner. "Why, it is the only place to really experience the ultimate swimming in all of Sealssong! It's a place of challenge and excitement, a place where sissies dare not tread!"

"It sounds dangerous."

"Oh, it is, it is! Terribly! That's what makes it so great!" she barked with a snout full of wiggles. "So what do ya say? Wanna go swimming?"

"Oh, I don't know. It just doesn't feel right."

"Oh, you're gonna love it, promise!"

"You've been there before?"

"Of course, now come on, silly, let's go!"

"Does your mama know of this place?"

"Yes."

"And she knows that you are going there?"

"Of course not!"

"I thought not."

Nikki wriggled up toward Miracle and rubbed noses with him, giggling all the while. "Don't be such a sissy-seal scare baby!"

"Excuse me!" Miracle growled.

"We'll be back before the two weird-looking seals wake up."

"And what about your mama, won't she be worried about you?"

"Please, she doesn't even know I'm gone. Now—you coming or not?"

"And you really know how to swim?"

"I do."

"And it's okay to go to this . . . this—forbidden place?"

"It is."

"Then why do they call it forbidden?"

"Oh, how you do go on."

Miracle only stared at her apprehensively.

"There will be others there too. They're waiting for us now."

"Others?"

"Yes, a few more brave hearts I rounded up. Oh, just think of all the fun you're going to have!"

"I really don't know about this," Miracle confessed, shaking his head disapprovingly. "If it's such a great place, why won't you tell your mama that you're going there?"

"You are a SCARE-BABY, aren't ya?" Nikki banteringly teased.

"Am not, it's just that—"

"Then it's settled!" she concluded in a boisterous voice. "LET'S GO!"

Miracle could not believe that he was actually considering taking up the bold pup's invitation. However, with all things considered, he would have to learn how to swim sooner or later, and it might be nice to be with someone of his own kind, at least for a while—even if she happened to be the bossiest thing that he ever met. Hesitantly, he looked back at the keep and the sleeping walruses. Suddenly, he felt an urge to remain; but before he could renege, the aggressive Nikki was nudging him with her snout, pushing him away from the keep.

"Don't worry, silly, you'll be back before they even know you left!"

"How do I even know that you're experienced at this? After all, you're not that much older than I am. How could you be teaching swimming at your age?" Miracle grumbled.

"Oh, how you do go on!"

As Miracle felt himself to be forcefully escorted toward somewhere called the Forbidden Place, he clumsily lost his balance, falling into another small and unsuspecting slush hole. With whiskers dripping and one eye closed, the shivering seal relinquished a sour and soggy smirk. "Are you sure you know what you are doing?" he asked, angrily shaking the water from his fur again. "I can't believe I am actually thinking about going with you. Tell me now, no kidding; do you really and truly know how it is done?"

"How many times are you going to ask me that? I told you, I am most proficient at it!" Nikki exclaimed, and jumping into the tiny pool and cramming both of their bodies together in a most uncomfortable squeeze, she slurped out her tongue, perspicaciously licking the nose of the white seal before her. Then quickly sliding into another high-pitched giggle, Nikki excitedly thumped her hindquarters against the slushy bottom beneath her. "Come on, silly," she exclaimed—"Let's go swimming!"

THE FORBIDDEN PLACE

Miracle and the small sassy Nikki made their way through and over countless ice banks, home to snow-covered perennial plantlike sculptures minimizing the most intricate and magnificent manmade Christmas trees. The sky remained the same sour yellow color, giving the sparkling creations an unnatural glowing allure, taking on the semblance of some alien world. The many various ice floes they passed eagerly streamed along with them, the air itself having a shine of its own, glistening and churning with mounting breaths of effervescence. Occasionally, Miracle would stop and investigate the loud gurgles the icy waters made, fascinated by how the bubbles tickled his nose. His enticement, however, would not last long, for soon Nikki was nipping at him, pulling the fur on the back of his neck, aggravating him while snagging parts of the seashell chain he wore, catching it between her jaws.

"Cut that out!" Miracle warned. "You might break the stone!"

"My goodness," Nikki said, rolling up her pretty seal eyes. "The way you talk, you'd think something dreadful would happen if you took off the stupid thing. I mean, it's just a silly stone held together by a bunch of stupid seashells!"

Her words stopped him dead in his tracks. Remembering Mum's warning, he shivered in the snow. "You shouldn't talk about things you know absolutely nothing about."

"What's that supposed to mean?"

"Never mind, just forget it."

"Tell me."

"I said forget it."

"No please, I want to know, honest!"

"It's special. That's all."

"Did your mama give it to you?"

"No."

"Who did then?"

"None of your business, that's who!"

"Oh, I know," Nikki scoffed. "One of those fat, ugly seals gave it to you, didn't they?"

Miracle rolled his eyes in disgust, not even thinking of correcting her. "You don't know anything! I don't know why I'm even talking to you!"

"Oh hush; you are giving me a migraine!" Nikki muttered. "Look, if wearing that stupid stone means that much to you, then go right ahead, but surely you'll remove it when we commence with our proficient swimming lesson, won't you?"

"No."

"Why?"

"I told you, I'm not supposed to, Mum, told me not to. If I do, something awful is supposed to happen."

"Mum? Who's Mum?"

"She's . . . ," Miracle stumbled. "Well, she's someone who . . . Never mind!"

"Suit, yourself," Nikki callously said before scurrying off, "makes no difference to me!"

"Hey! Wait up!" he called out, wriggling after her, speeding up his pace.

Suddenly, Nikki vanished. She was nowhere to be found.

Miracle felt a sudden panic trickle down his spine. However, before it could develop further, Nikki surprisingly popped out from behind one of the ice trees scattered about, barking happily at the top of her lungs. Miracle barked back. Playfully, Nikki returned a jolly yelp. Back and forth it went until both finally collapsed in exhausted laughter. Soon, the two frolicsome seals rolled about, dusting themselves with the glistening particles of powered snow, laughing all the while. Down they tumbled over hills of snow and ice, constant in their laughter, blissful in their playfulness. It was the first time Miracle remembered actually laughing. It felt good.

Sliding onto a flat portion of glassy ice, the seals sprawled out unashamedly onto the slippery surface. Catching his breath, Miracle looked about questionably. "Is this it? Is this the *Forbidden Place?*"

"No, silly," Nikki laughed, "but we're almost there! Come on, let's hurry!" With one restless hop, the tiny pup delicately slid across the ice, shooting straight over to the other side where more ice and rugged chunks of snow awaited her. Miracle tried to emulate her symmetry but failed miserably. Slipping and sliding in a most deplorable manner, he ponderously made his way across the slick surface. When at last reaching the other side, he gave out a heavy sigh of relief.

"You're funny!" Nikki squealed. Miracle only managed a half-unimpressed smile, once again attempting to catch his breath. "Can't wait to get you in the water," she boasted with a laugh.

"Are you sure you know everything there is to know about swimming?"

"Are you going to start that again? Listen, I already told you that I know how! My mother has proven to be most proficient in her tutelage. Naturally, I improved upon her limited abilities considerably! Now stop being such a scare-baby!"

"I still don't know about all of this."

"How you do worry so," she huffed. "Come on, you're going to love it!" Springing into the air, the agile Nikki once more took the lead, wriggling off somewhere into the sparkling hills of snowy enchantment. All at once, the drooping yellow sky began to disappear, and the dazzle of the great fireball found its place above, burning off the flaxen clouds exploding all around Miracle while maintaining his pursuit of the spontaneous pup. Temporarily blinded by its light, he desperately tried to squint throughout the blazing rays bursting upon the reflecting snow, something that forever hindered the eyesight of the harp seal. It was beneath the depths of the icy waters that their true vision would be realized.

In a sudden flash, Nikki had once again vanished from sight.

"Nikki!" Miracle shouted. "Wait for me!"

No reply came from the out-of-sight pup.

A growing concern flooded his mind. He quickly veered to his right, somehow believing it was the path that Nikki had taken. Disappearing behind an immense hummock, the white seal continued to shout out Nikki's name, wriggling in a nervous fashion, squeezing his eyes together in another attempt to lessen the glare that assaulted him. Hurriedly, he searched for her, uncertain of his actions, fearing he had now taken a wrong turn. A twisting doubt began to burn at his stomach muscles, warning him that he had indeed chosen the incorrect path, reminding him that he should have never left the keep in the first place.

In sheer panic, Miracle realized that the strange and sassy seal had taken him through passages he was not familiar with, areas of wonder that had captured his fancy but had distracted him from ever retracing his journey. The panic intensified when Miracle realized the repercussions he would have to answer to if Nikki remained misplaced. It would mean that he was surely lost, and this frightened him more than he imagined. He began to pounce upon the ice, terrified of the possibilities, determined to find Nikki before it was too late. His bouncing form skid across the ice and snow in a sporadic flow while continuing to call after her. Finally, after reaching the end of a sizeable hummock only to find several more icy monuments awaiting him, Miracle skidded to a halt. Dwarfed pitiably between them, he turned the corner, tearing away from the frozen obstructions looming abruptly in his path. It was here that he fell to his side, opening his mouth, exhaling a sound of wonderment and relief. There before him was a most magnificent scene, that of which he could have never conceived. It was a remarkable place filled with ice structures towering over hundreds and hundreds of feet into the cold, frosty air, all painted a vibrant deep blue color.

As the great ball in the sky shed its dancing rays upon each grandiose composition of incredibility, Miracle felt as if he had been transported into a different dimension of light and illusion. He had never seen anything quite like it before. The world of ice to which he was accustomed had vividly been changed into the stunning abruptness of insurmountable color and shimmers. Beyond the incredible carvings that nature had so beautifully created, just a few hundred feet from where he stood, was the Forbidden Place—the exact spot Nikki had spoken of. Of this he was certain, for smiling back at him from an icy shore sculptured with far greater towers of glaze giving way to a spectacular sea of silvery endlessness stood Nikki. With absolute alleviation and without the slightest hesitation, Miracle promptly set out to discover this bright and shining new world.

It appeared that no gentle streams caressed these shores. However, on this particular day for some unknown reason, the slush-covered body of silvery water appeared to be content with the uncanny calmness of its own, and yet as Miracle neared the fascinating shore, he became apprehensive. Still, it did not prevent him from approaching such a place, and that included Nikki, who was surprisingly waiting for him and who was not alone. There she stood, unbelievably dominated by the towering mountains; and nestled on each side of her were four whitecoats, all gathered, each carefully watching as Miracle nervously, but excitedly, made his way over to them. He immediately noticed the expressions of sheer deviltry each seal exhibited toward him as if something quite unprincipled was about to occur.

Nikki could not wait for Miracle to make his debut. Hurriedly, she wriggled up so that she could greet him, shouting for all to hear. "What took you so long, pokey?"

"You shouldn't have done that!" Miracle scolded in a depleted voice. "I thought you left me to die!"

"Oh, how you do go on! Come, silly, I should like to introduce you to the rest of the class."

"The class?"

"Yes, now stop embarrassing yourself. Come and say hello to your fellow classmates," Nikki insisted, nudging and shoving him with the roundness of her furry head. When at last reaching the place where the four whitecoats waited, she unexpectedly burst into another flipper full of seal giggles. "Everyone, I would like you to meet—" Suddenly, she stopped laughing. "Goodness!" she gasped, grasping at a queer expression. "What exactly is your name?"

Miracle plainly rolled his eyes, and in a low voice, he lowered his head and meekly said his name.

"Yes, of course, Miracle." Nikki giggled. "And as you all know, I am your instructor—Nikki!" she said with an overzealous smile. "My recruit, Miracle, has come to prove the courage of his own brave heart. He too dares to learn the sacred seal ritual of swimming, that of which I have mastered and am most proficient at!" she boasted, brazenly maneuvering Miracle with the roundness of her head, forcibly directing him in front of each young seal, introducing them one by one. "This is Little Lukie," she explained, only allowing Miracle the chance to view the seal but for a split moment. "Nice enough, but a little ditzy," she added under her breath. "Has a bit of a problem in the potty department, if you know what I mean."

This pup looked even smaller than Nikki, but Miracle did not have enough time to size up the pup further for all too soon, Nikki was introducing him to the next young whitecoat. "This is Sneaky. Sneaky is just his nickname, he won't tell us his real name, but it doesn't matter. Sneaky fits him to a tee! Always trying to sneak up on somebody and scare them—never has, as I recall. At least he has never scared me!" she divulged with a snip. On to the next Miracle went, again, hardly having a chance to acknowledge the pup that was hastily shoved in front of him. "This is Big Petie!" Nikki announced. "He is a friendly sort of fellow," she said before including with a whisper, "but suffers from an obvious overweight problem. Poor thing eats everything that's not frozen down!"

Miracle watched an uncomfortable blush pass over the plump seal's face. "Salutations!" greeted the well-rounded harp, but Miracle regrettably was unable to return the gesture, for yet once again he was being ushered hastily toward the final seal awaiting her acknowledged prelude.

"And this," Nikki explained in a sarcastic tone, "is Jillith! Let it here be known that she was not invited. She threatened to tell my mama about this place if I didn't allow her to come. She is a snitch baby and is a most competitive brat that thinks she is better than everyone else, especially when it comes to the delicate art of proficient swimming. One only needs to look at her snooty face to see that she is obviously clueless to the entire endeavor!" Nikki divulged, breaking into an overexaggerated grimace, her eyes burning mercilessly into the seal she most clearly despised.

Returning the same searing glare, Jillith followed it up with her own bogus grin. "Jealousy is a terrible thing, Little Miss Persnickety Nikki!" she ridiculed. "You're just scared because you know I'm better than you are, that's all!" Jillith taunted, sticking out her tongue before looking the other way.

"Better? Ha! I'm sure!" Nikki jeered.

"Yes, better, and everyone will know it when they watch you drown yourself out there!"

Nikki scrunched up her brow, defiantly returning the insult by sticking out her tongue as well. "We'll see, won't we, jerkhead?"

"Yes, we will, pig meat!"

"And may I remind you, the only reason you are here in the first place is because you were going to snitch on us if I didn't let you come!"

"You don't own this place!" Jillith yelled. "And besides, I still may tell. I haven't made up my mind yet," she flaunted, looking directly at Miracle, who was staring strangely at her. Suspiciously, Jillith stared back and twisted her little snout with a cocky smirk. "Why, if it isn't the purple poop-faced palooka! What are you doing here?"

Nikki did not wait for Miracle to respond. "What's it to you?" she snapped.

"Come on now," Jillith said with a drawn-out fleer, keeping her eyes directly on Miracle. "He's that queer seal everyone is talking about. He's the one that came to Sealssong uninvited, along with those two gross and ugly fat seals. My mother says that you're some kind of freak and that after taking one look at you, your mama dumped you for shark meat."

Miracle was about to thrash into her, but Nikki once again beat him to the quick. "Shut your mouth, Jillith, your mama couldn't even give you to the sharks. They'd puke you back so fast they'd make your stupid head spin, and that is precisely what I'm going to do to you if you don't watch that scrappy mouth of yours!"

"Is that so?" dryly spit Jillith. "Got a little crush on the purple freak, do we?"

"You better be careful or I swear I'll deck you!"

"Oh, help, help!" the sarcastic seal squealed. "The big bad Nikki is going to attack!" Jillith barked before bursting out with a fit of laughter, her eyes inadvertently meeting Miracle's once again.

"What's that's supposed to be, anyway, huh, your good luck charm?" she degraded, reaching out with her flipper, slapping the stone around Miracle's neck, tossing it aside so that it faced directly behind him. "You'll need more than good luck if you're going to let that one teach you how to swim—she doesn't know a thing! She's nothing but a big liar!"

"You're such an ignoramus!" Nikki scoffed. "It just so happens that my mama was voted the best swimmer in all Sealssong, and she taught me everything she knows, so there!" she stung, spitting out her pink tongue again.

"Oh, you're just a liar, you always were!" Jillith barked.

"And you're a stupid seal-ass!"

Jillith made a disgruntled-looking face, glared at Nikki with more than her share of contempt, then looked back toward Miracle. "I don't even know if I want to go swimming any longer," she groaned in exasperation. "We may all get sick and die. After all, just look at him!" She clearly spoke about Miracle again. "He's got that queer, funny purplish color to him. Mother says that he is diseased, which he probably is if he's hanging out with you, Miss Persnickety Nikki, and besides, he'll most assuredly contaminate all the water in Sealssong once he dives in."

Miracle remained silent, simmering in a sensation of humiliation and anger.

"You be quiet, Jillith!" a tiny high-pitched voice erupted, belonging to the smallest seal already introduced as Little Lukie. "I like him. Anyway, I think whatever is around his head is very nice. I wish that I could wear such a pretty sparkly like that. You're just jealous because you don't have one!"

"*Jealous?*" Jillith barked. "Oh, you're hopeless. The entire lot of you is hopeless and stupid! I can't believe that I actually came here with the likes of all of you! I should turn right around and leave this juvenile fiasco and go straight to my mother and tell her precisely what all of you are up to!"

"Go right ahead," Nikki insisted. "Who cares, Miss Dastardly Jillith? However, when you do tell, make sure you don't leave out the part that it was *you* who told me about the Forbidden Place in the first place. And it was *you* who chose to disobey your mama for the third time by coming here today, even insisting you didn't care what she thought because you knew more than she could ever know when it came to the fine art of swimming. Isn't that right, Jillith dear?"

"Drop dead!" Jillith growled, following up with a most distasteful snarl. "I most certainly do know more about swimming than you'll ever know! And if it wasn't for the sheer satisfaction of watching you sink to the bottom of the sea, I would have never told you or any of your geeky friends about this place!"

"That's enough," the seal formally introduced as Sneaky barked. "We came here to learn how to swim and not listen to your stupid jibber-jabber, Jillith!"

"Like I really care what you think, *Sneaky!*" Jillith laughed. "Everybody knows that you're the biggest coward here! Why, I bet you never even get your nose wet!"

"*Kill-ith! Jillith!*" roared Sneaky, jumping crazily about her, teasing her, exaggerating his growl, determined to torment her. "Keep it up and I will show you just how much of a coward I am!" he retorted, growling and yipping louder than before in a particularly aggravated manner, causing the rest of the gathering to join in and do the same. Yips and yaps came from every direction, for it was obvious that the rowdy and opinionated Jillith had successfully unnerved every seal around her. It was not long before the plump Big Petie seal spoke out in a most robust voice. "Hush your big mouth, Jillith, why must you always be so mean and hateful?" he demanded, scrunching up his bloated cheeks, shaking his head.

Jillith only growled and glared at the corpulent pup as Miracle slowly moved closer toward the sarcastic seal, she whose dark eyes and snout contorted into a dreadful scowl. Somehow feeling pity for her instead of contempt, he continued cautiously approaching the angry harp, coating his tone, asking, "What makes you so unhappy?"

"Get lost, weirdo!" Jillith sneered.

"You shouldn't be so mean," Miracle told her. "You have a mama who loves you, who cares about you, and if given half the chance, I'm sure we could all be friends."

With the sudden recoil of a snake, Jillith hissed at him. "Stay away, *freak!* What makes you think I would ever want to be friends with the likes of you? A diseased mutant purple-stained thing! You probably have already contaminated half the island with your purple germs! Just stay away from me if you know what's good for you!"

Just then, the puny Little Lukie surprisingly spoke out. "Oh, don't waste your time on that one—she's most vicious! There is not another whitecoat in all of Sealssong like her. Never have I met any pup as mean and hateful as she is, and she is not as silly as she looks *neither!* She can be downright scary, as a matter of fact!" Little Lukie said, lowering his head inside his thick rolls of blubber, continuing in a nervous and hushed voice while turning his head in the opposite direction so that Jillith could not hear him. "If she doesn't like you," he cautiously whispered, looking back toward Jillith, making doubly sure his words could only be heard by Miracle, "she bites you *really hard!*" Maneuvering his hindquarters around, Little Lukie parted his fur with his tiny mouth, showing off a bruise sitting halfway down his shoulder. With his chin, he continued to part the delicate angel hairs there, further exposing his injury.

Miracle's eyes opened wide. "Gosh," he said, staring at the bite mark before slowly turning his stare back over to where he had last seen Jillith, finding that she was no longer there. Carefully, he asked the puny seal in a whispered voice so as not to be overheard. "Whatever did you do to her for that to happen?"

"Nothing!"

"You mean she just bit cha?"

"Yep, me, and Big Petie was playing when she and her mama happened to pass by. I stopped and looked at her just for a moment, that was all, and she bit me."

"Gee whiz!"

Little Lukie shrugged his little seal shoulders, saying, "She's simply dastardly, that's all. She actually told me that she didn't like the way I stared at her. Go figure!"

"Goodness. I'll try to remember not to stare at her, if I can help it."

"Best do that!" Little Lukie warned.

"Have you ever tried this before?"

"You mean this swimming thing?"

"Yes."

Little Lukie motioned with his head for Miracle to come closer as if to tell another secret. "Well, can't say that I have, but Nikki said it's a cinch to learn. Sure hope she knows what she's doing."

"I'm not certain, but isn't swimming something you should learn from your mama?"

"I'm not sure—*neither!*" Little Lukie confessed with a curious twist to his tiny mouth. "But I guess it's time we learned just the same. I suppose we're not getting any younger. Besides, soon we will begin to molt, and you know what that means?"

"No, I'm afraid I don't," Miracle answered.

"Quit foolin'."

"But I'm not."

"Hasn't your mama told you anything?"

Miracle's solemn face relinquished any further probing from the tiny pup. Sympathetically, Little Lukie prepared to make amends for his oversight. "I'm sorry, how perfectly rotten of me. Forget I ever opened my big trap," he said with a new smile. "I heard about your mama, you know, missing and all. But if we are ever to leave the nursery, it's time we learned how to swim, and now is as good a time as any, don't you agree?"

"Well, I guess," Miracle dubiously responded.

"Sure it is! How else do you suppose we will ever find the great feeding grounds?"

"Feeding grounds?"

"Yes, of course," Little Lukie excitedly divulged. "We will have to swim . . . let's see, if I can remember . . . Oh yes, we will have to swim thou-thousands of miles away. That is very, very far, you know. Mama said we must listen for the song that the northern winds sing—*our seal song!* Then we will know that it is time to leave."

Miracle brought down his head, remembering how he could never leave Sealssong until Mum, Mr. Kishk, and Mulgrew returned; but he wasn't about to discuss that now. "Where exactly will the song of the northern winds take us?"

"Told ya already—to the great feeding grounds. Mama said we would feast on delicious jumbo shrimp. Mama also says that they are . . . de-lick . . . de-lect-able." The little seal crumpled up his snout, asking, "What does, *de-lect-able* mean?"

Miracle did not answer right away; however, after mulling it over, he decided on an answer. "I don't know . . . *friendly,* maybe?"

"Friendly food?" The puny seal laughed. "I don't think so! No, Mama says that we can eat and eat until we burst! Not that I'll ever want to burst, mind you, but the great feeding grounds produce everything that is de-lick . . . de-lect . . . good to eat! Tasty things too, like capelin and herring, whatever that is," Little Lukie said with another giggle, rotating his enormous black eyes, retaining a playful smirk.

"Did someone mention herring? YUMMY!" the roly-poly Big Petie imposed, anxiously joining in on the conversation.

"Yes," answered Little Lukie. "Wait a minute, you never tasted herring before!"

"Nope," happily retorted Big Petie. "But I sure as flappin' can't wait until I do! *Yummy! Yum! Yum!*" Big Petie yapped, licking his lips and chomping his mouth up and down, dropping his plump self heartily in front of a convenient lump of ice. Without a pause, the roly-poly seal began to scratch his backside against the icy post. "My mama says that I will molt soon. I think I already am. She says that when I do, I will itch a lot and that I will stink."

Nikki was quick to join in rolling her eyes, souring her snout with an obnoxiously looking smirk. "I can hardly wait for that to happen!"

she barked, shooting over, eager to join in with the others. Wriggling up to Big Petie, she sniffed a few times at his lower extremities. "*Heeuf!* Seems like you also already stink!" she snorted in a disgusted groan. "Now how are any of you ever going to benefit from my proficient swimming lesson if you insist upon wasting your time and mine talking about gross things like stinking and molting, will you tell me, please? Thank you!"

"Mama says," Big Petie offered, "that after a while, the stink goes away."

"Yes," Nikki said in a sharp voice, "and did Mama also tell you that it gets worse before it gets better?"

Now Miracle's curiosity was quite aroused. "What will get worse?"

"The molting act, silly, what else?" gruffly explained Nikki.

"Yes, indeed!" agreed Sneaky. "My mama says we will lose the rest of our already fading white coats, and soon we will be on our way to becoming all grown up, just like my good old papa! We will be known as ice-lovers, with wishbone-shaped markings on our backs. That's when we'll be true harp seals!"

"Have you ever met your good old papa?" Nikki questioned, retaining a suspicious glare.

"Well, actually—"

"I didn't think so. How can you be sure papas even exist? None of us has ever seen one of them."

Sneaky became terribly upset and snorted out a disgruntled grunt. "That's what you think, Know-it-all Nikki! I'll have you know that I did see my papa once. Mama showed him to me."

"You're making it up."

"No, I'm not! Upon a cliff, we stood looking over, and beyond there I saw my papa and many others like him, all waiting for the time for us to leave the nursery. They wait there, protecting us, waiting to see us off, the day the northern winds sing to us our seal song."

"*Bunk!* And even if it were true," Nikki defended, "it doesn't seem fair that our mamas should do all the work!"

"That's because our papas are busy protecting us!" Sneaky barked as he too began to scratch at himself with his back flippers. "We've already lost much of our white coats, in case you hadn't noticed, Nikki! Well, all of us except for the new kid."

Jillith was quick to throw in her two cents, growling, "Because he's a diseased freak!"

"The only freak here is you, Jillith!" Nikki taunted, causing the seal she ridiculed to aggressively wriggle once again over to the gathering, appearing hostile and wanting to fight. Gripping on to a look that clearly exhibited her absolute revulsion toward Nikki, Jillith instead remained silent, just glaring at her.

"*Burp!* Excuse me, so sorry," Big Petie apologized, busting over with a surge of unexplained joy, enjoying the relief the ice block gave him as it temporarily relieved his itching tickles. "My mama says that when we get all growned up, we'll be called *'Ragged Jackets.'* That's when all our fur falls out."

"Goodness," Little Lukie lamented. "This is really depressing. Besides, how many names are we expected to be called, anyway? I'll never remember them all *neither!*"

"Just one," abruptly stated Jillith. "Stupid! Stupid and bald!" she growled.

"Oh, and I guess you think you are going to somehow dodge the molting act?" Nikki accused with a leer. "You're already looking pretty shabby there, sloppy face!"

Turning her back to the entire group, Jillith rudely snubbed them and began to make her way toward the ice ridges that bordered before the open sea. "I for one intend on remaining a recluse until the whole ghastly process is over."

Nikki dared to venture closer to Jillith, still clutching to her cutting leer. "Well, why don't you leave and get a head start?"

"Shut up, idiot!"

"Besides, the entire ghastly process takes a long time. For many days, the fireball will have to pass over us before we have our final coats. Tell us, just where will you hide that snooty face of yours for all that time? Not that any of us will mind in the least, I assure you!"

"Get away from me!" Jillith popped. "You don't know anything! None of what you said is true!"

Flipping over on her soft belly, Nikki shook the loose snow from her wiry whiskers, squeezing out another taunting smirk. "Yes, oh yes, it will take such a long time, a long—*longgg . . . time!* Oh, the agony of it all, the shedding, the itching, the rotting, the stinking! Yes, oh yes, the yuk-yuk-heeuf smells of it all!" Nikki squealed, throwing back her head in a final climax as if to faint. Jillith never turned her head. She seemed far removed from the entire situation, defiantly staring off somewhere into the silver glare of the frosty sea. Nikki appeared to be having too much fun to stop now. "Yes, after many days of excruciating pain, we will finally—should we live to see it—become true harp seals, just like Sneaky said, wishbone markings and all. Still, even if we do survive," she warned, finishing her sentence with a low and scary voice, "that doesn't mean we will escape the vile clutches of . . . THE MAN-BEAST!"

Instinctively, every seal's head, including Jillith's, turned to look at Nikki. "Oh no!" pleaded Little Lukie. "Please do not speak out loud of the man-beast! It is bad luck!"

"Yeah!" agreed Big Petie, bringing his scratching to a sudden halt. "And Mama says the man-beast is evil and wicked and always hungry." He briefly dipped his head in a nearby slush pool, hopeful, but finding nothing to eat there.

"And that's not all," Sneaky told in a quivering made-up voice. "If you say his name out loud and he hears you, he will cut out your tongue, rip out your guts, and pop out your eyes! And if he feels like it, he'll suck out the rest of your brains with one quick—*gulp!*" he blurted, dramatically making gross sucking noises, sneeringly stalking behind the head of the unsuspecting Jillith. "*Slurp!*" he devilishly teased, sharply startling the seal, making her jump several feet in midair. However, when she came back down, she didn't miss the opportunity to snap at the skulking harp, nearly clipping his cheek with her jaws. "You sneaky fool, you stay away from me, or I swear I'll—"

Nikki interrupted. "You better save your little threats for the terrible man-beast 'cause he's coming to suck out your rotten, smelly guts!"

Having had enough, Jillith lunged in Nikki's direction, all traces of composure vanishing, and there was a savage glare in her eyes. "You're nothing but shark slime, Nikki, and so is your stupid mother for telling such lies!"

Nikki appeared to be most confident, provocatively approaching the disturbed harpie. "Think so? Well," she sneered with defiant fire in her eyes, "we shall see who gets eaten, won't we?" With this, Nikki threw out her tongue in revolt and prepared to jump off in the opposite direction, but she never made it. For Jillith swung out her backside catching the seal in midjump, bringing her down with one hard thud. An uneasy disquiet immediately settled over the gathering as worried eyes and nervous hearts waited to see what Nikki would do next. She shook off the assaulting clumps of ice and snow, surprisingly showing no signs of hostile retaliation. Calmly wriggling up to the black-hooded bulging eyes of Jillith, she smiled, tilted her head, saying, "Real smooth, scamp!"

The gathering remained unusually still, not secure in Nikki's calmness. However, as Nikki continued to stare into the swelling eyes of Jillith, she dared to wriggle up a little closer. "Insidious move, I

must admit, but you know what? I have one that's even better!" With
a whisk of a snappy gesture, Nikki plowed both flippers into the snow
and ice and proceeded to wildly hurl a burst of snow directly into
the face of Jillith, making her look like an angrily faced snowman.
The snow seemed to glow red-hot from the seething shock of Jillith's
face, and as the cold wetness trickled down her mouth, staining the
sides of her lips and chin, with a bolt of fury, Jillith swung her neck
out with an alarming twist.

"LOOK OUT!" Little Lukie screamed. "It's attacking! *It's attacking!*
It's gonna bite! *It's gonna bite!*"

The crazed Jillith lowered her head in combat, savagely clipping
Nikki directly in the soft of her belly. Wincing aloud, Nikki felt
her breath leave her body. She fell backward, scraping her head
on the frozen world behind her. Out of breath, the determined
Nikki lunged forward, slamming her head against the head of her
out-of-control rival, only to infuriate Jillith further.

Once more, but this time with even more severity, Jillith dove
into the aching spot of her opponent's belly, catching her head
against the tender frame of Nikki's chin. An immediate blotch of
blood formed below Nikki's mouth as both raging pups rotated
within the confines of the snowy grounds, tumbling over and over
again, each growling as if they had both gone mad. In an attempt
to stop the two feuding seals, Miracle thought it was about time that
he did something. Frantically wriggling himself nearer to them, he
tried to stop them but only found himself lost inside the snowy cloud
twirling around the two fighting pups. He suddenly felt a sharp pain
spark and burn at the side of his nose, finding that he had placed
himself smack center in the crossfire. Unable to stop himself, Miracle
went hurdling backward into the bleary slopes of harsh and freezing
whiteness.

Momentarily breaking away, Nikki managed to raise her
stiffening rump, and in a split of a seal's breath, enlisting every last
bit of dauntless fury she could muster, she forcefully swatted the
weight of her backside against the unprotected snout of Jillith. A
cracking noise sounded, followed by a loud guttural moan as Jillith
defenselessly flopped backward, toppling dangerously toward the
ice floes that flimsily crested around the ridge leading down into the
slushy currents of the murky sea. Before Miracle or any of the others
had a chance to intervene, the panicking Jillith slipped helplessly
toward the frigid clutches of unfamiliar waters. In terror, she opened
her mouth wide, crying out, scratching wildly against the treacherous
incline of the ice ridge.

"Help me!" she begged through the corners of her distorted jaws, slipping further. A cold prickle of raw fear brutally tightened itself around her throat when her hindquarters touched upon the freezing waters.

Wriggling over and holding to a crazed smile, Nikki approached the dangling seal and looked down at her, still keeping that demented smirk smug about her lips. "From where I am, I can spit right in your dastardly mouth!"

"I'm going to get you, Nikki, if it's the last thing that I ever do, and when I do—" Jillith warned in a shrill voice, losing more of her grip and the rest of her threat while proceeding to fall toward the sea. "Get me out of here!" she screamed instead.

"What's the matter, big girl? I thought you knew everything there was to know about swimming!" Nikki tormented, lowering her head over the ridge, smiling at her, just staring down into her contorted face. A loud round of indecent threats and screams surfaced from the wedged jaws of Jillith. Infuriatingly, she clawed against the slick surface pressing next to her; she was rapidly losing the match, about to crash into the freezing sea. By this time, the rest of the seal gathering was already crowding around the icy ridge.

"This has gone far enough!" Miracle barked. "We have got to get her out of there!"

"Why?" Nikki asked nonchalantly.

"Why? Because she could drown, that's why!"

"And that's a problem because?" she asked, smiling contentedly. "After all, she claims to be most proficient, insisting that she knows everything there is to know about swimming. I'm only giving her a chance to prove it."

"Nikki! Please!" Miracle begged.

"Oh, how you do go on. Very well," she said in a disappointed sigh, holding out both her flippers while Big Petie sat on her rump, keeping her steady. "Come on, big girl, I don't have all day, ya know!" It was touch and go for a while, but Nikki managed to maneuver herself in just the right way so that Jillith could wrap herself around her woolly neck. Up she pulled Jillith over the icy ridge while Big Petie kept her backside pinned to the ground. When at last Jillith finally retained the handle over the situation, she threw herself upward, flopping disgracefully across the ridge there, panting excessively just staring at Nikki with a most contemptible look blazing in her black hooded eyes. "All right," Nikki instructed with a charge. "That's enough gaiety for one afternoon. Now, let's do what we came here to do! Let's put our fighting flippers in shallower waters where they really belong, and let's go swimming, shall we?"

Before any seal could respond, Jillith suddenly struck out with her open jaws, catching Nikki in the center of her throat. Using the quick twist of her neck, Jillith pulled Nikki down toward the icy waters, flipping Nikki over the edge with one vicious toss. However, to her surprise, and not counting on losing her own balance, Jillith also plunged over the edge, sending them both crashing backward into the open mouth of the freezing sea where the waters ran deep. There was a loud siren scream from the throat of Little Lukie as the other seals quickly bombarded the ice ridge. In panic, they looked down over the crest, terrified by what they saw. In the fall, young Nikki had struck her head against the slope, leaving her unconscious, her tiny body left merely to float lifelessly within the slow-moving currents of the freezing waters. Another piercing yelp shot out from Little Lukie, accompanied by a comparable shriek from Jillith. It was a most alarming scream that seemed to gut the entire lining of her throat, groping the unsteadiness of the bitter world washing over her. In the misery of fear, the panic-stricken seal blindly attacked the waters with her flippers, pathetically struggling against her own weight while the frozen currents pulled mercilessly at her. "Help me! Hel—" Jillith gurgled, her mouth and lungs rapidly filling with freezing water, her unbridled panic sinking her further into the blackness of the sea. "I'm drowning!" she cried in helpless terror, the remainder of her shiftless pleas swallowed whole by the murky bubbles contemptuously circling her.

"Go on and swim!" Miracle called. "Why don't you swim?" he imploringly repeated, nearly sliding over the crest in his frantic excitement.

One more time, the drowning seal managed to howl admittedly back, "Because I don't know how—you moron!" Feeling the waters pile up against her, they hauled Jillith down further still. In one final attempt to save her own life, she grippingly held on to the unconscious and floating Nikki, shamelessly kicking Nikki's lifeless body under the water, savagely scratching against the ice futilely, springing herself off Nikki's buoyant form. Failing horribly, and with one stifled gulp, Jillith brought herself and Nikki down further into the sucking gullet of the freezing sea. Quickly disappearing, they left behind only a few surfacing bubbles in their wake—nothing more.

The watching seals remained in a state of absolute shock while Miracle frantically paced the water's edge. "They are going to drown!

They will die if we don't help them! Nikki," Miracle barked in anguish. *"Nikki!"*

Little Lukie let out another scream, soiling the ice beneath him with unrestrained bursts of urine while all the while Big Petie cried out, "Mama! Help us! Help us!"

"It isn't going to help to scream. We got to do something now!" Sneaky howled, attempting to override the ear-piercing shrills of Little Lukie's lament. "I'm going to go for help! It's our only chance of saving them!"

"Yes! Hurry," Miracle shouted, fighting the tears burning in his eyes. "Hurry, before it's too late!" In a sudden blur, Sneaky took off, disappearing behind the brilliance of the light that seared within the statues of ice and snow. Just as Miracle turned his eyes over to the crest, he saw more forming bubbles ascend and rupture against one another. Not able to wait any longer, the terrified pup prepared to help the two drowning seals. Severely trembling, he edged himself onto the icy slope. Staring down at the grayish water, he spread out both flippers as far as he possibly could. Wedged himself against a small niche in the crest, he slowly inched himself downward, teeter-tottering dangerously above the place where the bubbles fizzed his heart, colliding with his chest. With his nails dug into the icy surface, he desperately tried to balance against the incline.

"Nikki!" he whimpered. "It's going to be all right, I'm coming to help you!" he muttered, unable to control the tears, nor his sudden fall toward the waters below. Instinctively throwing out one flipper in front of him, he braced himself while his other flipper gutted out some of the glossy wall of the slope. With his razor-sharp claws, he left a ragged trail screaming all the way down the slide until only the icy, watery impact below could silence him. With a tremendous splash, the frigid ocean was everywhere, its mighty weight holding him under, refusing to let him go. Manically splashing about, he struggled to stay afloat, piteously grasping to refill his throbbing lungs. More frantic splashing followed, and he began to choke. He suddenly felt himself sinking, despairingly fighting to refill his lungs once more before vanishing beneath the water's chilling exterior.

Down he sank, kicking all the way, aware even beneath the closure of the water that he could still hear Little Lukie and Big Petie's cries. For a split moment, just before his gradual decline clouded his sight, he thought he could see their barking muzzles staring down at him. Feeling as if his chest would break open at any minute, Miracle incurably paddled against the trapping waters, only to languish further into their shadowy squeeze. Darker and darker became his surroundings as he sank further and further. He opened his mouth in panic, depleting any oxygen remaining. Feeling the empty burning in his lungs, the crazed pup waved his flippers about, madly trying to resurface, but he was unable to do so. He was drowning, and in just a little while, it would all be over. Wearily, his exhausted flippers began to strain until he was no longer able to move them. His heart throbbed uncontrollably, his head collapsing to his chest, his eyes barely open. Feeling as if it were some kind of a bad dream, he thought, just for a moment, that he could see the floating bodies of Nikki and Jillith just a swim away from him. However, that was just it.

If only I could swim, he thought, his mind perceiving extraordinary dizziness, complete with purple explosions and sparking lights.

As the dark waters continued to swallow him up, he became still; and in his despondency, his fading thoughts suddenly went to his dear mother, knowing that he would never again see her. However, before he closed his eyes, his last thoughts were of Nikki. *Sorry . . . ,* he mourned, alone inside the murky darkness. *How I wish I could have saved us . . . So very sorry . . .*

Only fleetingly aware of the purple stone swimming hauntingly before him, his body convulsed and he closed his eyes, quietly relinquishing himself to the sea, sighing out the last of his breath: a single bubble to be remembered by. In agonizing silence his bubbled gasp climbed steadily up to the watery surface, only to sit there but a moment before erupting, once more giving itself back to the sea.

MOST PROFICIENTLY!

Another round of seal screams followed.

Little Lukie and Big Petie dangled over the icy ridge, barking out of control, each watching the bubble disappear. More spurting urine streamed from where the smaller pup stood, staining the snow and ice beneath him, the yellow excretion filtering downward while Big Petie sobbed between barks. Staring directly where the bubble had surfaced, he howled urgently. Then something quite unexpected happened: another bubble exploded above the skin of the sea.

In a purple blaze it erupted, abruptly changing the watery world of dark silvery gray to a wild iridescent purple. With it came the rocking and trembling of the nursery. Mammoth ice sculptures came to life, moving, contorting into weird shapes while rocking back and forth, all of them ablaze with the same fantastic purple glow. Without warning, the icy edge securing both Petie and Lukie suddenly split apart. With one final tremor, both seals dropped, joining the same watery fate as the others, each seal vanishing within the radiant waters below.

Absolute silence prevailed for a few moments until the clamorous sounds of the bubbling sea stirred the air. Louder and louder the noise grew, when, from its sheer depths, an implausible shaft of water erupted. A powerful icy geyser shot up hundreds of feet in the air. It shook the ice garden, once again gushing, rocking back and forth, imitating the same dance of the mammoth ice structures, its aesthetic movement wavering about magically, shimmering brilliantly in the sunlight. Following a definite beat, the flowing column abruptly split apart. In a flash, there were suddenly two whirling pillars. Immediately, both shafts began to slow dance. They merged and twirled delicately around one another, and from this spectacular minuet, a third and fourth and fifth pillar appeared! On and on it continued until the sea became adorned with numerous shooting fountainheads, all varying in shapes and sizes. Alive, dancing, bursting with the color purple almost too dazzling to look upon, one pillar remaining in the nucleus of this visionary gathering, allowing for the real showstopper to begin. Deep from within its watery confines, like a shot blast, up flew young Nikki all the way to the very top, giggling and singing every splash of the way.

From the adjacent pillar, a pudgy white missile shot upward; it was Big Petie, and he too was laughing all the way to the top. Hitting the watery summit, he burst over with additional happy hysterics. The third pillar promptly propelled Little Lukie. He shot out yelping and squirting. The fourth pillar soon exploded, blasting out Jillith, her bulging eyes a mass of insanity. Finally, from the center fountain that first extrapolated Nikki only moments before came Miracle in a rushing gush. There was a smile, brimming from ear to ear on his tiny snout, the purple stone around his neck burning with a magnificent light. And as the two giggling seals acknowledged each other, young Nikki kissed Miracle directly on his nose. Both seals, filling with a rebirth of life, turned from each other and looked down while Nikki joyfully sang out, "Let the proficient swimming lesson commence!"

Extending both flippers out as far as they would allow, both she and Miracle raised their happy muzzles to the flaming fireball watching from high above. Casting their flippers dramatically over their furry heads, they kicked off from the supporting pillar, diving effortlessly and flawlessly into the shining purple waters below. Down they went, most proficiently, perfect in their movements, impeccable in their decline. Splashing in the water at the precise moment, each very much under the magic of the tear, both Nikki and Miracle dove far beneath the bubbling surface.

Enraptured in the same enchantment, Big Petie and Little Lukie prepared to copy their diving friends, both fearlessly brimming with joy. Holding on to each other, they rode the spraying ridge of the extraordinary pillar, each showing off in the bluntest manner, circling its watery rim like a slow-moving carousel. Flippers over heads, backs bent forward, they aimed themselves at the water below. With one quick nod of their heads, they reared their back flippers, simultaneously shouting out, "One, two three!" before springing from the fountain. In the poetry of motion, both pups gracefully descended, still holding to each other's flippers, giggling heartily toward the shimmering waters, Little Lukie's bright yellow stream trailing loyally behind them.

Beneath the bubbling lid of the sea, all four dashing seals met. They swam near each other, moving and responding to each other's faultless rhythm, creating the most intricate and refined patterns within the iridescent waters blurring past them. Upside down and right side up they twirled, just as lithe with expeditious precision crisscrossing through a million sparkling shafts of filtrating sunshine from the world above. Aside from Miracle, not for a moment did they question their newfound abilities. Never did they give a thought to the burning stone around Miracle's neck or how he was glowing with an exceptional purple color, or that perhaps he had somehow made this wondrous experience possible. No, each seal was much too wrapped up in the magic. Now confident in their uncanny quickness, they exquisitely performed aquatic acrobatic feats never before dared by the adults, let alone the younger sect. Their fortitude held no bounds. The snow-white children of Sealssong were infallible among the splendor of the sunlit meadow in the sea.

Once more, the gliding pups met. From four different directions they came, whirling through the watery universe, directly coming together, creating a four-pointed star with their snouts, their black noses touching. Then in a surge of bubbling thrust, the whitecoats brought their starry configuration up through the shimmering bubble clouds. As if in a clinging pursuit, the bubbles followed closely behind, while together, in one body, the rocketing pups broke through the outer limits of the sea. Immediately, the brilliant rays of the fireball in the sky spied the surfacing harps. Like a blinding heliograph, their sudden flash bounced from one flowing gusher to the next, setting the stage for the marvels yet to come.

Big Petie could hardly take in the gushing air around him, for his foolhardy laughs and giggles were much too much out of control. "Look at me!" he whiffed. "I am swimming! *Ssss-aaahhhh-wimm-ing!*"

"Me too, me too, too, and most proficiently!" sang Little Lukie, zooming happily past his roly-poly buddy with the greatest of ease. *"Weeeee!"*—he squealed, hopping upon the rumbling waters, skipping like a stone across the glimmering sea's pavement.

Miracle made his second debut back into the water after twirling around from places high above. Never had he felt so alive! Never had he felt such a sense of belonging. It is too incredible to be true, he thought, splashing down, disappearing quickly inside the foaming bubbles that remained busy exploding everywhere, the stone glowing fantastically around him. Nikki, who remained occupied in showing off her own variations of somersaulting against the brilliant sky, now sang out in unceasing giggles while flipping about, most proficiently, in front of the gusher, still sustaining Jillith ever so high above. It was Miracle, however, who would spring up from below, reaching the place where the screaming Jillith was. He called out to her, "It's all right, the magic stone made the water magic!" Returning to the sea, he waited for the discomposed Jillith to join him. She refused, spitting out her tongue, too frightened to move. Sitting atop the gusher that terrified her, Jillith looked down, her eyes wild with fright.

Miracle called to her once again. "Something wonderful has happened! Don't be afraid! Everything is all right now! The stone, it makes magic!" he sang, springing up again to meet with her, his purple glowing fur and swaying medallion bursting with the same strange and fantastic light that was very much a part of all the enchantment. Still guided by her fear, Jillith shook her head in defiance, bulging out her hooded eyes, unable to answer, unable to join in with the others. She could only sit there upon the shooting fountain. Alone with her fear, imitating some kind of stony gargoyle jealously leering down at the world from distant shadows above, she shivered from the middle of the sky while the cold winds brushed past her. Then unexpectedly, the disgruntled Jillith became excited, filling up with a tingling bolt of hope. From where she stood, she could see the return of Sneaky. He had brought with him an entourage of approaching harps consisting of mothers and their clinging pups. They would know what to do! They would rescue her! Barking every wriggle of the way, the approaching creatures inundated the grounds with their alarming yips, the nervous mothers of the disobedient five following directly behind Sneaky. The others randomly crawled over each other, hoping to guarantee a better look at what all the fuss was about. Resembling a uniformed rescue team, each harp, both young and old, wildly continued with their barking, nearly drowning out Jillith's maniacal pleas. "What took you so long? Help me! Help me!" she yelped. "They're trying to kill me!"

Most of the watching seals seemed to dismiss the whining pup. For all too soon they became mesmerized by the incredible show of the four aquatic contortionists dancing about the shooting purple sea. In enthralled awe, the watchful seals began barking even louder, both confused and excited by what they were watching. "Someone, help my baby!" howled the mother of Jillith.

Again, no other seal seemed to care about the lone pup splashing high above them; they could all but take their eyes off the others and the dancing sea. Becoming enraged by the ignorant crowd and even more at her deceitful daughter, Jillith's mother angrily barked at her pup, "Jillith, you come down here this instant!" Nonetheless, her demands became muted in the confusion of the resounding barks from the others. Infuriated further, she began slamming her backside hard against the icy ridge beneath her, she herself barking at the height of her voice, insisting that her child come to her at once. However, Jillith remained paralyzed with fear, her mother's demands made silent by the crazy assembly jumping around her, the tips of the darting waters splashing forcefully against her ears.

Now even more unglued, the agitated mother repeated the pounding of her backside upon the ground. Furiously, she slammed her large buttocks against the ice, shouting at her daughter in the most unpleasant manner. Ironically, inspired by the estranged mother's gusto, the young whitecoats who shared the same icy ridge as she did also began to show unrestrained behavior, comically imitating her excitement upon the ice and snow. It was only a matter of time before the thumping craze caught on as wildfire, enticing every pup. Soon the entire assemblies of one hundred and three baby harp seals were thumping their bottoms against the ice with an electrifying beat, all blending together with the ongoing rhythm of the acrobatic seals, bursting gushers and slow-dancing ice, mountains, each one performing most splendidly. They vibrated the icy crest with their rippling thumps and shrilling yips and yaps, defiantly pushing themselves past their elders, determined to have the best seat in the house. Zealously, they continued to pile in along the sheer, glossy borders of the ice crest, creating a half-moon furry white circle.

As the baby whitecoats united in their barking cheers, their mothers became more and more unnerved, not at all sure what was taking place. Surely the pup nicknamed Sneaky had been mistaken. These pups were in no danger whatsoever. If anything, their prodigious behavior, along with the most peculiar backdrop they had ever seen, was certainly not of the norm; any red-blooded, shrimp-eating seal could see that! How could four whitecoats command such control over the waters? That which a lifetime would have taken any adult to perfect, if that was now simply executed brilliantly by four young pups who, whether they chose to admit it or not, shamed and far surpassed every experienced swimming adult in all of Sealssong.

Now, twice as many baby seals poured in and around the icy ridges, all wanting to see the fantastic water show still in progress, each managing to push their way through the solid white wall of additional baby harps. A very out-of-breath Sneaky squeezed his way to the front of the barking squad, nearly sliding over the edge as dozens of whitecoats bustled behind him, all of them hopping on the ice crest, yip-yapping and barking excitedly, all of them unable to swim, all quite unaware of the strain they were placing upon the ground beneath them, each one most unmindful of the snapping sound that the ice made while straining pitifully against their considerable weight. The ridge, grunting desperately trying to withstand the heaviness, groaning with the forewarning mere seconds before it collapsed, abruptly shattered apart with one thunderous sound, sending the humping whitecoats down into the palpitating waters below. In one prominent crashing gulp, they were all gone, all one hundred and three baby seals!

A PIECE OF MAGIC

A smothering gasp choked each mother's heart while she helplessly stared at the place that only moments before held her bouncing child, now unthinkably replaced by a purple sea bubbling and gushing, not like anything they had ever encountered before.

It was not long before a startling realization hit, bringing with it another round of urgent barks and howls, all springing forth from the open throats of the shocked mama seals left behind, horrified, as their children began to drown before their eyes. In wild pursuit, the mothers prepared to enter the strange waters in search of their dying pups, pups that were still too young to know how to swim. However, before they could do so, they stopped, frozen in their tracks. With the explosion of Old Faithful herself, the sea suddenly opened, showering off another multitude of screaming, giggling baby harps. In sets of sixty and more, they popped out of the water. Resembling tiny cannonballs made of clouds, they filled the air with their singing giggles, flurrying the skies with their milky forms, each one most defiantly throwing out their chests and flippers, preparing for their first dramatic dive into the gurgling waters rushing up to embrace them.

Lining straight across from one another in the semblance of a rehearsed, choreographed display of stunning theatrics, in one complete uniform splash, the high-diving whitecoats submerged into the waters, twenty-five of them at a time. Once more, the adults gasped in disbelief, some of them even fainting when the first set hit the waters. By the time the second line emerged, the mothers began to cheer and rejoice, proudly watching while they singled out their pup twirling effortlessly on the wings of the air. It was Nikki who would initiate what was to follow. Persuasive and brimming with confidence, she began to direct the new gathering of pups. Mirroring a shepherd in the sea, she commanded her flock while singing out to them. In her most proficient stratagem, she instructed the children of Sealssong, each obeying her every command. In perfect harmony of motion, half of the gathering extended to the outer regions of the water arena while the remaining half filled the center ring. They dove in and out of the water, somersaulting around each other, the first string going in one direction, the second going in the other.

Round and round they went, creating white blurry lines, accelerating in speed, waiting for Nikki to give the word; and when she did, they quickly began circling the gushers. Up they went, winding around the watery pillars, looking like woolly candy stripes, all the way up to the top of the many spouting fountains. Nikki, naturally, chose the highest gusher still sustaining the screaming Jillith, the others following close behind. Reaching the bug-eyed harp who remained too frightened to partake of the festivities, Nikki devilishly prepared to challenge the situation. Having but a second to make her move, she wrapped both her flippers around Jillith's furry neck, and pulling her over the edge, she boasted, "Come on, scare baby! We're going for a ride!"

Down they spattered together, Nikki and the stubborn Jillith, dropping through the collapsible see-through walls of the gusher. Jillith resisted in every way she possibly could, snapping and snarling at Nikki until at last they reached the bottom, splashing into a blur, momentarily stunning the obstinate seal. Not allowing Jillith a moment to react, swarming circles of parading baby harps quickly latched on to the screaming harp. With one bleary WHOOSH—they took hold of the shrieking pup, stealing her away, bouncing her ridiculously from seal nose to seal nose, whirling around the enchanted setting, each giggling and squealing with sheer excitement. They circled the watery pillars, twirling them into ivory purple blurs. Up and down they glided happily, dragging the opposing Jillith along, tossing her about like a plaything, blissfully indifferent toward her vile barks made silent by their own overriding cheers, squeaks, and squeals. Then in one climactic burst, the entire baby seal assemblage mushroomed high above the watching crowd. Holding steadily to one another, they closed their tiny jaws, clamping them tight about the rump of the pup in front of them. The acrobatic harps, creating a solid seal chain, swelled outward into one swirling mass, making sure that the screaming Jillith was at the throbbing pinnacle of their contagious eruption. Teeter-tottering high above, elbowing the clouds that jostled about the sky, the infuriated Jillith gave out a final bloodcurdling shriek as the floor of the living seal pups gave way to their awe-inspiring grand finale back to the gurgling waters below.

The speculating mama seals became covered with an unexpected wave that towered over them, nearly shadowing them for a full second, washing them clear back to safer grounds.

As this wave washed itself back to the sea, it left in its wake all one hundred and nine pups, everyone accounted for and left in the merriest of spirits, all except Jillith; she remained miserable. The others continued laughing and squealing, rolling about and hopping over one another, barking uncontrollably. It was not long before they sought out their mamas; in blissful reunion, each pup rejoiced; some of the mothers showing more excitation than their offspring. The entire marvel seemed to leave a lasting wonder over the seal congregation, mother and child finding a special moment between the laughter and play. Wrapped in an instant that was theirs to own, they secretly celebrated a unique love for one another, so content, so sacred, it would remain with each seal for always.

From a distance, still shaking the cold waters from his coat, a panting Miracle sat atop a broken panel of ice, watching the waters drain back into the sea. As the waters returned to their normalcy, so did the dancing surroundings, but one thing was most certain—he could not mimic their normalcy. How could he? He would never again be the seal he once was. It was as if he suddenly became rewritten from inside, and the pages of his being would be forever changed by the entire experience. Further still, and not knowing how he managed it, he knew that somehow he and the purple stone were responsible for the wonder of this day. How peculiar he felt. The magic stone, or whatever was inside, had saved him and the drowning pups. He would think of this while watching them all joyfully return to their waiting and excited mothers.

Big Petie, Little Lukie, Sneaky, and even the miserable Jillith soon found themselves reunited with their parental guardians. Aside from Jillith, who was greeted by a hard swat on her behind by her annoyed mother who then quickly dragged her away by the scruff of her neck, the baby harps would delight in the embrace of their togetherness. Each mother tenderly licking the head of her child left with a feeling of awe as she stared into the large black eyes of the small one looking up at her, she herself clueless to what exactly had taken place. However, for the time being, it would not matter. All that remained necessary was that each pup was safe and had once again been reunited with its mother, leaving them with memories of a wondrous moment, as well as curious visions of a strange orphaned pup that wore a peculiar stone about his neck, a stone that somehow saved all the pups in the nursery. Miracle knew this, as did every heart in Sealssong. Try as they may in dismissing this feeling, they could not, for the magic of the tear had also changed them that glorious day.

Soon, the inspired gathering began to settle, the head of every mother turning to look at the curious pup with the purple glow. Young Miracle noticed their stares, and shyly recoiling downward, he smiled, not knowing what else to do. In silence, the mothers remained motionless, gazing, their eyes, reflecting wonderment but showing no signs of friendly smiles, each trying to understand the peculiar emotions struggling inside them. Eventually, they began to turn away from him, scattering, and this significantly relieved Miracle. He continued to watch the seals returning to the center of the nursery, as one by one, the happy youngsters and their confused but prideful mamas slowly made their way back to familiar grounds.

It did not seem to hurt as much, his loneliness. He had already resigned himself that he would leave this place alone, hoping to find the keep on his own. Then quite unexpectedly, Miracle felt a tiny tap against his shoulder. It was Nikki. She was with her mother. "A most proficient swimming lesson if I say so, myself, don't you agree?" She giggled, rubbing her furry cheek affectionately against his. Turning her head and meeting with his eyes, she smiled. "Thank you," she purred before kissing him on the nose. "I'll never forget you, ever!"

Then something even more glorious happened. The mother of Nikki smiled too, and lowering her head, she affectionately rubbed noses with the orphaned pup. "I do not know what it is about you, little one, that makes me feel this way, but I believe today you have saved my child." Miracle's eyes widened, feeling Nikki, and her mother, tenderly brush up against him. "Come," the mother of Nikki said. "Remain with us. I will see that no harm comes to you."

"That is very kind of you," Miracle attempted to explain, "but you see, I have a mama out there somewhere, and I know she is very worried about me. I must find her." Clearing the burning disquiet away from his throat, he continued. "I'll be all right. I have friends on the nursery that will protect me."

The mother of Nikki nodded her head. "Very well," she agreed. "Come, I will return you safely to them."

Innocently Miracle looked up to the mother, doing as she asked.

As the great fireball in the sky progressed in shedding its dazzle upon the shimmering place blessed with a miracle of its own, three seals, the very last of the gathering, made their way back to where each belonged—each one taking with them a piece of magic that would forever change their hearts.

THE ITCHLINGS

T he days that followed were most difficult for the white seal.

Crumpels rejoiced in Miracle returning safely to the keep, bathing him with her unending shower of walrus kisses and hugs, nonetheless remaining upset with him for wandering off just the same. Having tried to explain the events of that particular afternoon at the Forbidden Place to both Crumpels and Poo-Coo made for a frustrating time, for Crumpels seemed to dismiss his unusual story, concentrating more on the fact that he had left home without her consent. Her motherly instincts had decidedly gotten in the way of her judgment, making her irritable, but it did not last. There were other things to be concerned with, for Poo-Coo was growing at extraordinary proportions and it would soon be time to find another ice keep. At the rate of his increasing spread, it would only be a matter of weeks before a change of address would be in order, so the next few weeks were spent in achieving just that. However, finding a new residence was not going to be as easy as they imagined. Miracle and Poo-Coo soon realized that most of the best spots had already been taken or destroyed by recent storms. It was a problem, but it was a problem that would soon become secondary to what was to follow.

Seventeen times the great fireball had come to the sky since the phenomenon at the Forbidden Place, and Miracle was kept busy searching for a new home for him and the walruses. It was in the heart of this quest that he chanced to come upon a welcomed reunion with his new friends, Big Petie and Little Lukie. Their immediate enthusiasm for the unexpected but welcomed social gathering was made quite obvious as they happily called out to Miracle. Still, something was different about his two young harp buddies. Miracle sensed it at once, but even before he understood the peculiar physical changes they were experiencing, he came directly up against an extremely pungent and offensive smell, making him crunch up his nose and snort aloud in disgust.

"Yeah, yeah!" Big Petie admitted, rolling over his huge black walnut-shaped eyes. "We know! We stink, and we got it bad!"

"What on earth?" Miracle questioned.

"The itchlings!" answered Little Lukie in a shriveled-up squeak.

"The itchlings?" young Miracle repeated. "What in the world are . . . *the itchlings?*"

"It's what we got!" grumbled Big Petie.

"And it ain't no fun—*neither!*" Little Lukie complained, looking as if he were about to cry.

"It's downright rotten!" Big Petie spit with a frown, nonchalant in his outward display of smelling himself beneath his buttocks. *"Pweft!"*

"Yes, oh yes!" Little Lukie exaggerated in a spit-spot. "You stink real bad!"

"Look who's talking!" Big Petie griped. "Whoever said this stupid molting thing was cool!"

"Well, I'm sure it wasn't me!" Little Lukie retaliated. "How can anything be cool when all you do is itch and itch, every part of yourself, including private things that should not be mentioned? And it isn't very pretty—*neither,* especially when every single part of your private things is chafed and irritated!" Unexpectedness happened as a whopping snot bubble broke across the little seal's face, only intensifying his disgrace even further. Little Lukie moaned, quickly wiping the grossness away with his scruffy little molting flipper, dragging it to the side of his snout, dispelling it somewhere into the lining of his disheveled fur. "I could just die," he pathetically grumbled.

Miracle's expression melted into a frown, suddenly feeling terribly sorry for his troubled friends. It would appear that both whitecoats had most certainly changed. In fact, what remained of their snowy fur was nearly nonexistent, for most of it had fallen out in tufts and in its place endured the outbreak of a black-spotted silver coat along with the distinct beginnings of the characteristic wishbone shaped-marking. Now nicknamed "ragged jackets" because of their shabby appearance, the seals savagely scratched at themselves as dogs infested with fleas.

"Gee whiz," Miracle gasped. "It seems just awful!"

"It is! It is!" speared the suffering martyrdom of Little Lukie.

"Yep, yep, yep!" wholeheartedly agreed Big Petie, wriggling his roly-poly self about while throwing himself next to an icicle, probing from a nearby ice slab. "It's a bummer," he confessed in a whisper, wiggling about discontentedly, scratching his rump against the icy protrusion.

"Is there anything I can do to help?" Miracle asked.

"Nope, not a thing," Little Lukie explained. "And that's not the worst—*neither!* We can't sleep or eat! Nothing! Not with all this nasty scratching stuff going on, nasty, nasty, nasty!" Suddenly, the shabby pup stopped scratching at himself. Looking wide-eyed and straight at Miracle, he slowly wriggled himself up close next to the curious white seal. Little Lukie pushed his snout down toward Miracle's lower extremities, sniffing hard several times. Raising his head, his eyes sloped off into a perplexed glaze, his face drenched with surprise. "Hey," the wide-eyed Little Lukie exclaimed, "you don't stink! How come?"

"Yeah," quickly added Big Petie, still too intent on his scratching frenzy to stop. "And besides that, he hasn't lost any of his white top, how come?"

Now it was Miracle's turn to widen his eyes with a question. Slowly, he looked down at himself, wondering. "I don't really know. Do you suppose something could be wrong with me?"

"Don't rightly know," Little Lukie confessed. "Maybe you're sick or something!"

Miracle thought for a moment, then shook his head. "Nope, don't think so."

"Well, whatever you did or didn't do I sure wish you'd let me in on it!" Big Petie spouted. "I don't think I could take one more day of the blasted itchlings! I'm plum itched out!"

"Me too!" coincided Little Lukie, very busy at studying Miracle's unaffected, pure, and fluffy purplish form, only to be shocked away from his concentration by another dreadful attack of the itchlings. "Mama says that the cold water can soothe the burning and itching," the little seal whimpered, his tiny flippers vibrating mechanically against himself with one solid whirling blur.

Big Petie remained in agreement. "Yeah, so what are we waiting for? Sorry, Miracle, we best be on our way back where we can sit in soothing waters. No offense, but my butt's a-burnin'! *Heewft!* Sure hope what we got isn't catchy," he said with a huff. Then with a smile for Miracle, he blurted out, "You're the lucky one, pal!" The shabby roly-poly seal dug at himself. "Come on, Lukie, we better go home now. I got to soak it and soak it good!"

"I hear that!" Lukie grumbled, rubbing his tiny behind up and over the rugged icy stones below. Preparing to leave, he suddenly stopped and turned to face Miracle. "Thank you."

"For what?"

"You saved us from drowning, didn't you?"

Not knowing how to answer, Miracle merely looked down at his chest and felt the purple stone glow and then warm against him. Lukie smiled and then wriggled up to the stone and touched his nose against it. "Sure is a pretty sparkly," he said, feeling it warm his cold nose before finishing off one more set of nearly tearing out the few patches of dry white fur. With one long and drawn-out scour across the ice, momentarily cooling off his twitching buttocks, he quickly added, "I have to go home now," turning away eager to catch up with his buddy.

A sudden quiet moved over Miracle while watching the two scraggly ragged jackets slump away from him, both complaining incessantly to the other while their swishing flippers propelled against their itching skin. Miracle watched some more while their beating flippers kicked at their sides and dug at the broken snow around them. His gaze followed them until they eventually became swallowed up by the dusty snow clouds they brought about, now explosively reflected in the last burning rays of the sinking fireball in the sky. Miracle did not stir. He only stared at the place where the burning orange sun maintained its removal from the heavens, leaving him alone with a luminous twilight and a hundred probing questions, each one more puzzling and disturbing than the next. He did not need the itchlings to be among the ragged jackets to go without sleep tonight. For once again, the seal would feel the bitter pain of loneliness, and the reality of his difference would be enough to keep him awake for some time.

Looking down at himself once again, he wearily surveyed his beautiful white coat, its purple glow fading in the swirling colors of the sunset, contemplating the curiousness of his situation. To be like the others was all he ever wanted, and yet as his eyes fell upon his glistening fur and the shining medallion swaying loosely below his chin, he somehow had the feeling this would never be the case. Sighing, he slowly turned and wriggled back to the keep.

CHANGING SHADOWS

The next few days continued to keep the walruses and Miracle busy with their search for a new home. They did not feel however, this time, like they were misfits as they had on previous accounts. In fact, it was just the opposite. The numerous harps they chanced to meet while in the midst of their house shopping treated them with a certain respect. Most acknowledged them with a smile and a slight nod of their head. Nonetheless, whenever their eyes met Miracle's, they could only stare and wonder. Meaning no disrespect, they remained this way, not knowing what they truly felt for the unusual pup wearing the strange stone unchanged in his appearance, unlike the other young seals that had continued on as normal, reshaping themselves for adulthood as it was meant to be. Just the same, despite his abnormal contrariness, the seals of Sealssong continued to acknowledge him respectfully.

However, for Miracle, their insisting inquisitiveness plagued him. He no longer resembled his peers, and his prolonged adolescence seemed to stand out wherever he was. It was beginning to wear thin on the small seal. He found himself shunning away from many of the younger harps, turning corners to avoid their peering eyes, ashamed to be seen. He even began to shrink away from Nikki and the others. The situation was becoming serious. Still, since the occurrence at the Forbidden Place, not one seal, young nor old, regarded him with anything less than delicate observance. Still, for Miracle, it was maddening. He began to hate his peculiar uniqueness. For each time he came upon his friends, he would be crudely reminded of his dissimilarity, and all the same ugly feelings would resurface, intimidating him into seclusion. How it hurt to watch them mature while he remained the same!

Why am I not changing? What is wrong with me? Miracle suddenly made a small gasping noise and then looked down at the stone around his neck, his fears and doubts crashing in around him. In desperate attempts of finding some kind of proof that he was changing and was not to be left a freak as the unkind Jillith suggested, Miracle examined himself regularly for any telltale signs of maturing, but it always ended the same way; he was most assuredly left hopelessly despairing when no shedding confirmation was evident. If anything, he had grown several inches, but not much more. The seal began to make himself ill, so much so that on one particular afternoon, he asked Crumpels if he could remain in the ice keep while she and Poo-Coo continued in their search for a home. Reluctantly, Crumpels agreed.

That night, a highly excited Crumpels and Poo-Coo returned to the keep. They immediately told Miracle that their troubles were over and that through the tremendous help of the friendly seals of Sealssong, they had found a perfect spot to move into. Crumpels quickly explained that it was conveniently located near the open sea where they could always keep a close lookout for Kishk and the others. "Isn't it marvey?" she exclaimed. "You're going to just love it, White Puff!"

"It's the biggest, bestest house I've ever seen!" Poo-Coo rejoiced, crippling the sides of the ice keep with his massiveness. "I don't know what you did to those silly seals, my bro, but they sure are acting awful polite."

"Yes indeed," Crumpels exclaimed. "Pleasant as a tickled-pink porpoise, they are. Why, they even told us that they would have the place ready for us by tomorrow."

"Yep," Poo-Coo said, smiling. "We could move in then, right into the king daddy of all ice castles! By tomorrow, all those seals will have cleared out, and it will be all ours!"

"I don't understand," Miracle said.

"Well, it is true, boop-boop-dee-doo!" popped Crumpels. "They won't be here tomorrow. They are leaving, you see!"

"What do you mean . . . they're leaving?"

Poo-Coo finished off the explanation with a wrinkled mass of smiles crisscrossing over his giant face. "It's something about the song of the northern winds or something like that and finding the great feeding grounds. Couldn't make heads or tails out of it, but the truth is, I suspect they'll all be gone by morning," he said, cleaning his tiny tusks on the wall of their soon-to-be deserted home.

"Are you sure you heard correctly?" Miracle asked in a restrained whisper. "They won't be here in Sealssong anymore, ever?"

"I don't think so, White Puff," Crumpels tenderly explained, putting her dangling fleshy flippers around the small seal, but he quickly pulled away from her.

"You're lying!" Miracle barked, fighting the tears.

"Now, dear," consoled Crumpels.

"I don't believe it!"

"But it's true, dear."

"Not Nikki, she won't leave. I know she won't!"

Crumpels's face began to melt until it looked as though it would drop to the icy floor and dissolve into the cracks beneath her. "She wants to say goodbye to you tomorrow, if you'll let her," Crumpels carefully said. "She told me so herself." Miracle let the tears flow, not caring to restrain them, knowing that if he tried he would only fail. He lowered his head for a moment and then flashed his stare across the threshold, out of the keep, and into the darkness beyond.

Crumpels's heart skipped a beat or two and then seemed to lodge itself in her throat. Cautiously, she approached the hurting pup. "Now, now, these things happen to us all the time. It is all in the sphere of the great chain of life. We are all connected to it—we are a part of it as it is a part of us, dear."

"With one exception," snapped Miracle. *"Me!"*

"Now, that's simply not true, White Puff."

"Stop calling me that stupid name, and stop telling me about how things are supposed to be and how we are all a part of some great plan! It's just a lot of stupid nonsense! I don't want to hear any more!" the white seal shouted, slamming both flippers abrasively against his skull.

"I know how you must feel," a hurt Crumpels said, proceeding to comfort the seal, drawing closer to him.

Again, Miracle recoiled. "No! Just leave me alone! How could you possibly know how I feel? You haven't even noticed that I have stopped growing or that I haven't really changed since I was born! Have you? Why should I expect you to know anything? You are stupid and silly!" he sobbed. "You're not my mama, she would know what to do; she would know how to help me!"

"Oh dear, oh dear," Crumpels fussed, drawing closer still to the seal. "Please don't upset yourself, dear."

"Just stay away from me! I hate you and this stupid place and everybody in it!" Miracle cried, accidentally swatting the stone, swinging it across the front of his snout. "And I hate this stupid, ridiculous stone most of all! I don't want it anymore!" he shouted in sobbing hysterics. "I don't care what Mum said, I don't want it!" Deliberately trying to tear it from around his throat, he wedged his flipper between the stone and himself. Still, try as he might, he could not break the chain of seashells. Eventually giving up in an exhausted collapse, he fell to the floor, crying in a pathetic way that broke Crumpels's heart.

Poo-Coo proceeded to go to him, but his mother quickly stopped him. "Leave him be," she whimpered, her eyes swollen shut with tears. "He is very sad now. We must leave him alone," she bewailed through her broken feelings, turning her enormous self from the keep, finishing off with a bruised "Boop-boop-dee-dee," said in the saddest, choked-up voice she had ever muttered. In a moment, she managed to get her gargantuan self out of the keep and left. Poo-Coo followed her out, but before doing so, he glanced back at the sobbing Miracle for a moment before casting his stare toward the exaggerated wailing of his mother's cries echoing somewhere in the night. Shaking his head in annoyance, he bloated out his bulbous cheeks and spit. "It's going to be a long night!" Sighing, he quickly left the keep in search of his mother.

The following morning, the great fireball leisurely appeared but did so to a most reluctant sky filled with sullen clouds and dropping mist. A shrilling wind whipped itself around the seal rockery, aggravating the sea between the floes, sending fistful of slapping spurts of foam against the icy shores. In the distance, the lonely call of a lost gull echoed throughout the overhanging breath of the sea while the dying rays of the sun warned of its retreat from such a dismal place.

Changing shadows that came from some unseen cloud crawled menacingly over the keep, bringing spurious life to the icy structure. As it fluctuated in movements of grays and blacks, a tiny face peered out from its veiled entry. A particularly solemn Miracle gazed into the drizzle, the shadows splashing and covering his face, making him appear like the keep itself, ghostlike and unreal. Neither Crumpels nor Poo-Coo had returned that night, of this he was certain for he had remained awake most of the night, left to contend with the haunts of his wrongful behavior. Although he remained deeply affected by the disconcerted emotions that had governed such an outburst, he knew he had indeed acted poorly. He had spoken badly to Crumpels, and now she too had left him. He had only himself to blame. He did not mean what he said to her, but now he would have to pay for his unkindness. Somehow, he just had to find her and make her understand, but what would he say? He suddenly felt dreadful and highly ashamed again.

Out he came from the shadows, feeling the immediate sting of the chilly soaking wind. The creepy shadows followed the seal along as he made his way through their transparent clusters, with no sight of Crumpels or her son anywhere. A sudden spark of coldness shot up his spine, and Miracle thought that he heard a muffled movement somewhere behind him. Miracle turned his head, stopped, and listened. Only aware of the persistent groans that the wind made, he decidedly suggested that he continue on his way until once again the sound returned. This time, it was even more distinct than before. Slowly, he turned his head once again to confront the disturbance, desperately hoping it to be Crumpels. However, once again, only the whistling wind answered him. Then all at once, he was suddenly met by a startling attack. Flipping backward, the stunned seal went crashing into a snowy embankment. As his eyes fought to focus, he saw a shadowy figure swiftly bounce toward him.

"*Surprise!*" the figure squealed. "It's me, Sneaky! Did I scare ya?" proudly asked the tricky harp. He was a whole lot bigger now. With his white fur nearly gone, his new coat sporting black-spotted silver attire, he looked like an entirely new seal. "Sure glad I found you!" exclaimed the spotty prankster, "been looking for you for some time now!"

"What is it you want?" snorted Miracle, pushing Sneaky off and away from him, not particularly pleased with the seal's unexpected greeting.

"Well, for one thing, it is *you* that I am wanting! I've come to say goodbye!"

Miracle began shaking off the dusty clumps of snow before he spoke, disappointment melting his annoyance. "Then it's true. You are leaving Sealssong."

"Yep, off to the great feeding grounds where the food is plentiful and the adventures bountiful, at least that's what Mama says." Then suddenly, Sneaky appeared sad, his bright eyes slanting into uncertainty. "Sure wish you would come with us."

Wistfully, Miracle shook his head.

"We all have missed you," Sneaky confessed.

Miracle did not answer; he merely looked at the seal, not knowing what to say.

"It's okay. I understand. It's because you haven't changed from white to spots yet, isn't it?"

"I don't want to talk about it!"

"Gosh! I'm sorry, didn't mean to upset you. In fact, I've been meaning to tell you just how great I think you look! Honest! All snowy white with purple tips! Cool!"

This time, he avoided his eyes. "You came to say goodbye, and you did. Is there anything else you wish to tell me?"

"Yes, two things, actually. First, you don't have to call me Sneaky anymore. Mama says everyone should call me by my true name, now that I am becoming a bull and all. I am named after my papa."

"All right," Miracle asked with an uncaring voice. "What is it?"

"Bellgar."

"Interesting . . . and the other?"

"Well, it's just that . . ." The new Bellgar paused, just for a moment. "Won't you reconsider coming with us, won't you?" he asked, his eyes sparkling with hope.

Miracle blankly stared at the spotted seal whose name had just changed from Sneaky to Bellgar, not truly knowing how to respond again. His heart becoming heavy, he shook his head, looking downcast. "I can't, I have to stay. I promised," he finished off, holding to his stare to the shifting shadows beneath him.

"I know. I know." The spotted seal sighed. "The two fat seals already told us that you wouldn't be coming with us. Things just won't be the same without you."

"I'm sorry."

"So am I," Bellgar offered.

"You have seen Crumpels and Poo-Coo then?"

"Well yes, of course."

"Are they all right?"

"They are fine, I imagine. It's hard to tell. They're so weird looking. They're waiting down at the shore of the nursery. They came to say goodbye to all of us. They are sad you are not there with them, especially Nikki. She is the saddest of all, and very upset that you won't speak with her."

"She is waiting for me?"

"We all are, Miracle."

Miracle slowly raised his head. "Please take me to them."

"Well, come on!" Bellgar sang, another smile filling his snout, its warmth momentarily chasing the pestering shadows away that happened to pass over him. "Follow me!" he called.

And with no further words, both seals headed toward the very borders of the nursery, the siren calls of the wind leading the way to the place where the soon-to-be departing seals had gathered.

SEAL SONG

The great fireball had utterly abandoned its post, leaving the sky dark and foreboding.

More black clouds were draping themselves over the frigid waters that roughly kissed the shores, seemingly caught up in their restless attempts of bidding farewell to both mother and child of Sealssong.

It was not long before the white seal and Bellgar arrived. In a hushed wave, the entire seal gathering stilled and calmed as Miracle approached them, most of the mothers remaining quiet while the young seals suddenly bombarded him in droves. Joyfully, they danced about him, singing their farewells, not one of them commenting on his spotless appearance. It did not seem to matter to the children of the ice. Forgetting his ever-conscious uniqueness at least for a moment, Miracle freely embraced them. Affectionately, they rubbed heads and noses, all one hundred and three of them, each one saying goodbye to the small seal who had magically taught them to swim and who saved their lives that memorable day not so long ago. Then from within the heart of the blowing winds, a powerful sound emerged. As a brilliant flute made up entirely of swirling air and fluttering wind, a haunting intonation pierced the nursery. Instinctively, every seal responded to its unexampled call. Knowing that the children would soon fall under its hypnotic spell, the mothers were saddened as the northern winds blew about them. The winds had come, and they would continue to play their haunting seal song, calling each of the children to the sea while each mother gazed upon their child with sympathetic eyes. And yet still for a brief moment, unable to resist, every mother's head turned to look upon Miracle who remained a way in the distance. One by one, the mama harps lowered their heads to the seal wearing the purple stone, each harp offering him their respect, gratitude, and soundless farewells.

After a short time, they began to disperse, their maturing pups at their side. The dreaded time had come for Miracle, the pups, and the mother harps. The sad time of saying goodbye was upon them all. It was time to leave Sealssong, time to begin the separation from one another. Although each pup would eventually accept this crude detachment only under serious protest, this day, the children of the ice would have to begin their lives away from the nursery and from their mothers.

Once again, the haunting sound came, flooding the seal nursery with its driven refrain. Reluctantly, the mothers acknowledged the urgent summons. Disheartened, they began to guide their children toward the open passages of the sea where just beyond, the male harps, the guarding bulls, waited and watched in breathless anticipation. For they at last celebrated the long awaited moment. They would once again be reunited with the mate they had waited for these many long and frigid days and nights; and should fortune smile upon them, if they were exceptionally lucky, the bulls might even get a glimpse of their son or daughter. However, like all seal moments, these encounters were brief and short-lived. It was harsh, but it was the way of their existence.

Tenderly, each mother directed her child to the sea, encouraging him to listen carefully to the seal song chanting all about them, telling them that every sound they ever heard was at that very moment singing to them. It would be so much easier for their children if they would not fight its commands. Instinctively, every spotted seal recognized its voice and knew its reason for coming. It was time to go.

Many mothers began to weep as the piercing cries of their precious ones stabbed into their breaking hearts, each torn between the children they had brought into the world and the distinctive barks of their mates calling them from an icy sea. This would always remain the most difficult moment in every mother seal and child's life. Suddenly, the entire gathering of spotted children began to scream out in pathetic cries and desperate pleas of yearning to remain, never dreaming that they would have to make the trip to the great feeding grounds all on their own. Again, the cries of the children sliced excruciatingly through every mother's soul, nearly crushing it.

"Listen to the song!" they called out to each spotted child. "It will guide you and will remain with you for always. It will help you find your way. Do not resist!" the heartbroken mothers wailed. Then in their final voice, they lowered their tear-swollen eyes to the icy floor beneath them, trembling, whispering in torment, "It will help you forget me . . ."

From a distance, as Miracle watched and listened, the seal song did not summon him, but its effect on the others disturbed him immensely. Why, even the dreaded Jillith seemed to have difficulty with its intoxicating tune. He watched her wincing, curling into a ball, resisting its call, cushioning her ears against her spotted blubber. Still, even in her torment, she managed to raise her head and stare off in the direction where Miracle followed her every move. Somehow sensing his presence, she turned to him and spit out her tongue. This would be her final goodbye to the strange white seal, but her actions hardly surprised him.

The cries of the children of Sealssong continued in agony until Miracle had all he could endure. Depressed and careworn, he turned from the pitiable sight, unable to watch any further.

Once again, the haunting sound whistled itself through the misty breeze, sounding more pressing than before. Beyond the nursery, the male population was getting even more anxious. They barked impatiently, bobbing up and down, howling out for their mates and conducting themselves in a rowdy and extremely boisterous manner. The bedlam of excited grunts, yelps, and squeals echoed against the swelling of the invoking seal song.

As Miracle began to leave, concluding that he had seen more than his share, he turned to ascend a snowy embankment. Instead, when he did, he found himself staring into the eyes of a maturing and spotted Nikki. Miracle's lips reached for a small gasp as both seals stared at each other. Nikki's black-spotted silver coat seemed to sparkle in the shadows, but her eyes, as well as Miracle's, were sad and lightless.

"It doesn't call to you, does it?" Nikki gently asked.

Miracle painfully shook his head.

Nikki hesitated before speaking again. "You never said goodbye." She appeared as if she had been crying.

"I wanted to. I came to look for you," he said with a quiver. "But with all of this, I—"

"It isn't pretty, I know. But Mama says we shouldn't fear the seal song. She says it is what will heal our broken hearts."

"How can you say that? It is calling you away from Sealssong."

Nikki tried to smile an impossible smile. "Mama says if we listen to it sing to us, we won't feel the hurt inside our hearts anymore. She says it will give us the courage to become a part of it and the sea."

"I don't understand," Miracle confessed. "Why must you leave?"

"To find my life, I imagine," Nikki answered in a helpless voice. "At least that is what Mama says, but Mama is not always proficient in her way of thinking. You know Mama." Both she and Miracle smiled through their tears, both becoming unusually quiet, fighting to control the breaking pain they shared. "Come with us," she finally pleaded.

"I can't," Miracle told her, unable to say anymore. Instead, he lowered his head and touched it lightly against Nikki's. Despite the seal cries echoing endlessly or the restless seal song exploding all around them, this was where they would remain for all time. Nothing could separate them now, but with a steal of a seal's breath, it was over. The voice of Nikki's mother had come to confirm such demise. "Nikki," she said in a choked-up voice. "It's time to go."

Nikki tried to grab for another impossible smile. "Goodbye," she said sadly, partially turning away. "I hope you find your mama and all that your heart searches for."

"Come, Nikki," her mother wept, trying to remain strong, agonizing, pushing her daughter toward the calling sea. Still resisting, Nikki turned her head back to face Miracle, wanting to go to him just as she had the very first time they met. She began wriggling toward him and then stopped. All at once, the young Nikki seemed to hear the seal song for the first time as it began to escalate to near-deafening proportions. Proving to be even too powerful for the determined Nikki, her eyes suddenly went blank, filling with an opaque color, changing her black eyes into an unnatural haze. Now under its hypnotic spell, young Nikki, as did the rest of the pale-eyed children, began to prepare to leave the nursery, each submitting to its final call. With every beat of its refrain, the spellbound seals began to enter the sea, their cries becoming silent to the haunting enchantment cast over them.

The white seal watched with a heavy heart as the young seals splashed into the sea and began to swim away from the island. Never did they turn to face him again, for they now belonged to the sea and she belonged to them. The haunting seal song called to each harp in its own unique way, mothers veering to the left, their children veering to the right, neither side reflecting upon the other.

Nikki and her mother were the last to leave the nursery, and although Nikki's mother looked back at Miracle one final time, Nikki did not. With one quick flip of her backside, she entered the sea, swimming out into the freezing waters, her trancelike stare leading her onward, the singing wind in full voice.

Miracle remained in the place where he had said goodbye to Nikki, watching blurry-eyed while his spotted friend disappeared into the clouded horizon, her mother cutting through frigid waters, heartsick, watchful of her only daughter one last time before returning herself to her awaiting mate somewhere in the distance. In a matter of moments, it was all over. The chortling of the males, the hypnotic seal song, the, mother harps, as well as every last pup that had once filled the secluded nursery, all of them gone.

Once more, Miracle remained alone, or so he thought. Suddenly, and quite unexpectedly from out of the shadows, he felt the reassurance of Crumpels's flipper curl itself around him, Poo-Coo near her side. The drizzle had returned to freezing rain when Miracle looked up into the enormous but sympathetic eyes of Crumpels. Hardly even aware of the stings the icy droplets brought to his eyes, he remained steadfast at the ridiculous but beloved mustached and long-tusked tooth walker's side, thinking to himself how truly grateful he was that she was there with him now. Closing his eyes, he lowered his head and buried it into the many folds of Crumpels. They would remain that way until the freezing rain would change from its lucid dress of ice into a billowy gown of snow. Then they would go to their new home. There they would await the return of Kishk and the others, there in the deserted ice castle at the top of the hill just above the water's edge.

NASTY LITTLE BOYS

He could not have planned it better. Even if he had executed such a scheme a hundred times over, it could never be more faultless. "It's perfect!" Yorick said while both him and Cyrus, his corpulent partner in crime, made their way down through the ship's corridors back to the vault where the incredible diamond treasure awaited them. Whatever freakish strangeness had consumed the *Tiamat* would now prove to be most favorable, making their dark deed all that much easier. Most, if not all, of the crew was too busy hiding from or in awe of the peculiar purple fog to ever notice their absence. If they were going to make their move, now was the time; there would be no other.

Once more, they found themselves squeezing through narrow passageways and black tunnels. Cyrus clumsily fell about the darkness, barely able to hold the long iron crowbar he carried while the bearded Yorick held tight to a heavy mallet, squeezing its handle, turning his knuckles a ghostly white. After having dealt with added grief from his partner's stumbling mishaps, Yorick was more than ready to begin the pursuit the second his beady eyes looked upon the morbid face of the vault door, delighting in the knowledge of what lay just beyond.

"Are you sure that they'll never suspect it was us?" lamely questioned Cyrus.

"Damn it, man, don't start that up again!" Yorick bit sweat dripping down from his pockmarked brow. "I told you, they won't even know we are missing! They're all too busy wondering if we've been swallowed up by some kind of sea serpent, the lily-livered sissies, every last one of them!" Yorick spit his saliva, disappearing into the shadows. "We'll take as much of the booty as we can, stash it good and safe, where no one on this godforsaken ship will ever find it. Then when it's safe, we'll sneak it off the ship and take the shiny wad to those gentlemen of persuasion willing to give us our just rewards!" he said with a mouthful of foul grin.

"I just hope Ms. Decara doesn't give us our just rewards first!" Cyrus mumbled, nibbling on his chubby fingers, nervously looking about the purple shadows that stretched everywhere.

"You know, I don't know why I have anything to do with you! Come on, let's do what we came here to do!" snapped the sweaty bearded man.

Cyrus agreed with a slight nod, first swallowing down a lump of isolated nerves. Hurrying, both men clenched their sweaty fingers around the tools intended to break the vault's seal. Bringing the edge of the iron crowbar to the lip, Cyrus nervously held it in place while Yorick raised the mallet, but before the mallet could ever strike, the unforeseen happened.

Suddenly, there was a queer clicking sound somewhere inside the vault, both men distinctively hearing the noise, the door proceeding to open slowly, all, by itself. Taken aback, both men jumped, clutching to the heavy objects in their hands, not knowing what to expect. The vault's door continued to open, squeaking in agony as it groaned contemptuously. Neither one spoke until the door came to a complete stop, the lurking gloom spilling across its threshold, only illuminating the entrance, but a little. "What's going on?" Cyrus asked in a panic.

"Shut up, fool!" Yorick growled, more sweat oozing down his rippled forehead and into his unkempt beard. Only the whistling wind responded along with a few creaking floorboards that was all that seemed to sound a manageable alarm.

"What is it?" insisted Cyrus, all jittery, his voice already in a hard, whispered knot.

Yorick growled some more. "Will you shut that fat lip of yours!" he snapped, the whites of his eyes flashing inside the shadows. Then, from just beyond the open door, came another sound. Both men listened, the tension tightening inside them. It was a noise resembling the vibration of thousands of crawling insects scurrying across the floorboards. It rattled the room for a moment, moving from side to side, and then stopped. With his knuckles nearly breaking through the taut skin, Yorick raised his mallet and began to enter the room, ready to strike out at the first encounter.

Cyrus followed close behind, not wanting to remain alone with the purple water thin shafts of light peering down at him from unexplained places above. However, as they entered the vault, only the welcomed display of bulging sacks stretched out before them, several bundles made visible by the outside flickering gloom. Hastily filling up with a spark of encouraged greediness, the plump Cyrus waddled himself over to the sack closest to him. Preparing to grab its tie string, he abruptly froze when more sounds came from somewhere in the room. Thinking he had heard something crawling up the side of the wall just beyond where the darkness was thickest, Cyrus began to shiver.

"Rats! There must be rats in here! Hope the filthy things don't think we're sharing any of this!" the plump man nervously teased in passing, his quivering voice revealing the building heebie-jeebies caught in his throat; all the while, he continued to munch on his chubby fingers.

"Damn it, man, do you ever shut up!" Yorick snarled, still suspicious of the circumstances of their effortless entry. Holding tight to his mallet, his bulging eyes darted about the room. Numerous sacks occupied the room as far as he could see, at least that was all the existing light would dare to reveal. It could have very well been rats. There was no way of telling, but no pesky rodents could open a steel door, that was for sure. Still, it didn't matter; he wasn't about to be scared away now. Not hearing any further sounds, the overzealous Cyrus once again reached for the tie strings of the sack he had already been eyeing up. Pulling on the string, the sack opened. Immediately, the sparkling glimpse of a thousand diamonds set his heart a-thumping. "You crazy ass fool, what are you doing?" the bearded hunter howled.

Cyrus jumped back while he feasted on his soggy fingers some more. "I just wanted to make sure it was really there," he deliberately misled, trying to smile through the plump wad of soggy fingers crammed halfway inside his mouth.

"Come on!" Yorick angrily groaned. "Take what you can and let's get out of here!"

Agreeing wholeheartedly and with another feeble nod, Cyrus complied, taking two large sacks into his grip while reaching for yet another; but in his rapacious eagerness, unable to support such a load, one of the sacks fell to the floor, spilling its contents everywhere.

"Clumsy oaf!" was all Yorick could utter before the rest of his blood turned to ice. From the darkness, the room began to crawl again, and this time Yorick could feel it move beneath his heels. The crunching noise intensified until it faded, suddenly filling with torturous moans and groans so utterly forlorn. This in itself was enough to scare them silly, but when the vault door suddenly slammed shut, locking them inside, this set them over the edge. Cyrus let out a shrilling womanly scream as the light got sucked out, while Yorick stood frozen, trapped within the terror of the lightless vault.

Suddenly, Decara's evil laughter pervaded the musky air, her red eyes shining a harsh glare against their flabbergasted expressions. "Well, well, well, what do we have here?" she uttered. "Two more bad boys caught with their dirty hands in the treasure jar. Naughty, naughty, naughty!" she crudely teased, clucking her tongue, slithering through the shadows, her nails tapping against what sounded like the walls. Not allowing either man to react further to her sudden presence, she mechanically threw out her arms, squeezing her bony fingers around each man's throat, sending them crashing into the awaiting wall behind them. With aggressive anticipation, the wall sprang to life, folding itself over both men, covering their bodies, leaving their heads exposed for Decara to play with, like flies in a wooden spiderweb, their broken limbs becoming useless as their screams became mute. Unable to breathe, the eyes of the men bulged, nearly tearing from their sockets, each one watching in maddening terror as Decara drew closer to them.

"Did you come to see the pretty diamonds, boys?" Is that what you came for?" she hissed, holding up a large diamond chip between her bony fingers. With another hellish shudder, the walls of the room folded in on the doomed men further, crushing their insides, churning their flesh, dissolving and transforming their bones into the very fibers of itself. Decara grinned happily, looking nonchalantly into their puffed-out terror-filled eyes, their constrained heads and small pieces of their elongated necks remaining horrifically exposed, telling of all that remotely remained human, the remainder of what was once arms, legs, and fingers now smeared grotesquely down into the buckling panels of the wall like molding putty. Holding up her bony hand, she clutched to the huge gem now burning with a weird glow of its own.

"Look at it!" she hissed, waving its blaze in front of their twisted faces. "Remember it well, my nasty little boys, for it will be the last thing you see before I send you straight to hell!" Reaching out, she touched the eyes of each man with the glowing seal tear, its shine suddenly turning a morbid green color. In one final burst of screams, the men became blind. For where there were once eyes, now in their place, through charred and empty sockets, were two mangled diamond chips crystallized inside their heads just before the rest of the wall swallowed them up, peeling off the outside of their faces until all human traces vanished, leaving behind the malformed skulls of the damned. Up the vile wall the hideous skeleton heads were sucked, snapping and crunching like scurrying insects over the wooden boards, their diamond eyes forever fixed inside their ghastly skulls.

Decara waited for the room to settle down before turning to leave. The cryptlike door opened once again on its own accord, grumbling with a steady moan. Some purple light snuck into the room, giving it an even more diabolical glow. "Guard well my riches, my nasty, greedy boys," Decara sang, looking up toward the creeping ceiling of the vault. "You who wanted my treasure, you who would do anything to get it, well, alas, you have it for all eternity!" Breaking into a whirlwind of wicked laughter, she tightly clutched the glowing diamond. With her arm protruding from her blackened cape, she reached into the darkness above her. The gem demonically burned in her hand as the entire room glistened with hundreds of twisted skulls, their diamond eyes glowing in the semidark like devil bats, each contorted mouth left agape, their deformed faces decorating the walls and ceiling high above.

A hundred different hellish moans were howling through the vault when Decara finally decided to leave. Standing partially inside the half-closed door, she smiled wickedly, gazing upon her ghoulish gathering. More ugly laughter followed. She closed the door gently, shutting out the light, leaving whatever remained of Cyrus and Yorick's moans to transfuse with the other ghoulish sentinels hanging from the darkened places where no human eyes should ever dare look.

In a little while, the room became still, except for the steady breathing of the tortured ones who would forever live inside the walls.

WHO'S THERE?

From a darkened corner Kenyan watched, silently staring at the invading shadows that clawed over the face of the crypt vault. He had been watching long enough to witness Decara's admission into the strange, dark place.

Inside his murkiness and waiting for her to exit the secret treasure room, he held tightly to the stony dagger. Drawing in a sudden breath, his heart jumped when the vault door suddenly screamed open, revealing Decara's shrouded figure heavily covered inside the flickering purple gloom. Kenyan pressed back into the darkness, hiding, all traces of himself, as Decara shut the vault door, a wicked smile pulling tediously at her scarlet lips. There she stood, carved inside the deep shadows still holding to the diamond chip. Clasping it in her hand, she held it up high again, and the crystallized seal tear exploded, scattering the defiant shadows aside. Startled, Kenyan pressed further into the blackness of his guarded nook when unexpectedly, he heard the wooden floor beneath him let out an excruciating moan. Instantly, Decara's eyes flashed in the direction of the sound. Remaining deathly still, he squeezed off every muscle of his body, not daring to breathe.

In search of the curious sound, Decara began to stalk the corridor. Slowly, she floated, slinking through the crevasses of the shadows, moving directly toward the exact corner where Kenyan's breathless self and aching limbs arched, straining above the boards that had betrayed him. His heart felt as if it was about to explode. It beat with such outrageousness, drumming mercilessly in his ears, and even more violently against the walls of his chest until he was certain that the out-of-control hammering had given him away for sure. The witch had heard it! How could she not? Its throbbing sound had to be rattling the ship itself! Still, he dared not move. Not able to stand the torment, he rebelliously prepared to come face-to-face with the witch, determined to send his stony blade through her black heart. Like a tightened spring, he came undone, shooting out of the shadows, thrusting down his blade, stabbing hard with every ounce of strength left inside him. However, it only took a second to realize that the stony blade was now striking effortlessly through the emptiness of the taunting blackness; the witch had suddenly vanished and was nowhere to be seen. Cautiously, the boy edged out from the darkness, unsure of his next move, uncertain if he was truly alone. As his eyes scanned across the long vague corridor ahead, he could see the clawlike shadows infesting themselves around the vault's contemptible face. Initiating small steps, he sparingly made his way toward the mysterious door, his curiously mended leg enigmatically leading him onward.

Only the talon-shaped shadows seemed to stir when he at last came to Decara's morbid treasure box. Forcefully, he pulled down on the handle, and sparking tingles of adrenaline shot through his spine. To his surprise, the door opened without the slightest hesitation. Clutching to the dagger, he entered, waiting for the screeching hinges to stop their infernal shrieks. Only a small sliver of purple gloom dared to sneak in with him while furthering himself inside the room. Suddenly, he felt someone, or something, breathe heavily down the back of his neck. Frightened, the boy quickly raised his dagger. Preparing to bring it down hard into the guts of Decara, he pierced the air; however, the room held even more surprises for him. It was not only void of Decara, but there also appeared to be no one else inside its dark confines. All he could manage to see were the many bulging sacks filled with what he believed constituted the secret of this most sinister of places.

Kenyan's feet remained badly bruised and barely covered by what was left of his shoes. Now frayed and torn, their withering frame hardly gave his aching feet any real protection from the cold and abrasive world he had been sadistically thrown into. Making his way toward one of the bloated sacks, his exposed toes scratched on something sharp and hard. At first, he thought he had stepped on broken glass, but when he bent down, to inspect the floor, his eyes quickly flashed with excitement. He had found some of the witch's treasure! A pool of diamonds flooded beneath him.

"Yes!" he soared, not caring who would hear him. Placing the dagger safely inside the lining of his shabby breast pocket, he immediately began to fill up his remaining pockets with handfuls of the shining wonders surrounding him. He would fill up every nook and cranny of himself.

Again, the room had other plans.

He nervously shuddered, startled by what he thought sounded like millions of insects crawling across the wooden floorboards. Kenyan flinched and accidentally let some of the diamonds fall from his busy fingers. "Who's there?" he demanded in a hoarse whisper. No one answered. Only more of the same disturbing insect sounds repeated as the hinges of the vault's door unexpectedly began to finish off the rest of its squeaking resentment. In a blur, Kenyan spun around, turning to the sound while the clicking of the insect-spawned crunching noises closed in on him.

In a moment, the sound of a familiar voice flooded the room. "Take my hand," the voice called out. Kenyan froze, just staring in the direction of the voice. In less than the quick take of a breath, Kenyan knew who it was. "Quickly, come away from the room before it's too late!" Emma warned, her tiny silhouette soaked within the existing deep purple shadows. Instinctively, Kenyan threw out his hand and felt his sister snatch it away. In a flash, she pulled him out of the vault just as the crawling walls fell forward, concluding to devour him. Emma released her brother's hand and slammed the heavy door closed, pressing against it with all her weight, making sure nothing dared to follow. In a relieved sigh, she opened wide her iridescent blue eyes, tenderly looking at her brother. Together in their longing, they both embraced. Kenyan squeezed Emma so firmly, bringing her close to his chest. Emma squeezed back just as tightly, clinging to a hold that promised never to let go.

"Are you all right, did the witch hurt you?" Kenyan asked against his sister's tight embrace.

Emma did not answer; she merely held on to her brother with no intentions of freeing him. However, with the necessity of stealing a needed breath, he pulled his sister away from his beating heart. "Emma, you must tell me," he begged, wiping the tears away with one quick sweep, "did that dirty witch hurt you?"

"No, not really," his sister answered, once again consumed in adorning her brother with another round of padlocked hugs. "Oh, my poor brother," she cried, pulling slightly away just enough so that her eyes could meet comfortably with his. "What did she do to you?" She wept, embracing him even tighter than before.

Once again, Kenyan held his sister in his arms, burrowing his face in her hair, dampening her curls of gold with his own obstinate tears. "How did you come to be here?" he asked, breathing through the locks of hair pressing against his nose.

"It was the purple angels. They led me to you."

"What do you mean purple angels?"

"It's true!" Emma said, still not wanting to let go.

Realizing that their prolonged sentiments were a luxury neither one could afford, Kenyan once again pulled his sister away and looked deeply into her eyes. "I don't understand, Emma. What is it?"

"They came to tell me about the seals," she told with a surprising smile. "It seemed like a dream at first, but it wasn't. You do believe me, don't you?"

"All right, all right, just calm down and try to tell me exactly what happened."

Emma took a deep breath, smiled, and began. "It happened shortly after the strange mist came over us. Like angels made of tiny clouds, they came to me silently, peacefully releasing me from that dreadful place," she said, looking down toward her brother's mended leg before touching it gently. "They came to help you too, it seems," she added, placing her dainty fingers against his cheek where he had been burned, his skin now smooth and untouched.

Kenyan twitched his leg and sucked in the air around him, holding to a perplexed expression. "But how can such things be? Please, Emma, we haven't much time!"

"I'm not sure, but as the purple angels released me from Decara's room, they began taking me through many different tunnels of light, tunnels that made me see and feel things."

"What kind of things?"

"It was there that the seals spoke to me, hundreds of baby seals, all of them snow white and so very sad, all of them crying out to me, pleading for me to help them! I saw and heard things I never imagined. Then the purple angels told me things of Decara and of you, and that I would find you here alive and that I must save you from the evil in that room!"

"Did you know about the treasure?"

"Yes."

"How?"

"But I have just told you."

"Right, I know—purple angels."

"Yes, I wasn't sure if I could reach you in time, I was so scared. There are horrible tortured souls locked in there, souls that are damned for all time. They were about to destroy you only moments before I came for you. They are the monstrous guardians of Decara's treasure," she explained, finishing off with a sudden shiver.

Kenyan slowly turned to look at the menacing face of the vaulted room, his own personal shiver playing havoc with his nerves. "Emma, you are really starting to freak me out," he said through a swelling lump in his throat.

"What scares me, dear brother, is that for reasons still unknown to me, I somehow knew much of what they told me," she confessed, holding to a dreamy gaze. "They only confirmed what I already knew."

"Confirmed what?"

"About the seals, of course."

"What about the seals?"

"The poor mother harp seals whose tears she steals."

"Tears?"

"Yes, after she steals their tears, she changes them into diamonds."

"The seals?"

"No," Emma said, shaking her head with frustration. "She changes their tears! Decara has captured many sad and destroyed mother seals, mothers who have lost their children to the savagery of man. She has some of them hidden away right now on this dreadful ship. She torments them with her evil magic, just as she torments us. We must save them. We must save them all!"

Kenyan could not find words to continue; his head hurt and his mind throbbed with a chaotic confusion that made him nauseous.

"And above all else," Emma explained as a peaceful look abruptly came upon her delicate features, all traces of distress leaving her angelic face, "the most beautiful vision of all was the image of the same beautiful seal I have dreamed about so many times before."

"Emma, please, I know you have abilities that I still don't understand, but you've got to stop this talk about talking seals and purple angels!" the boy pleaded, looking as if he were about to lose his sanity.

"Oh, but they can speak. I heard them. I've seen them." She closed her eyes, recalling it all as a dreamy smile lingered across her moist pink lips. "And inside the purple clouds that came for me, I could see the white seal. He was all around me and so beautiful, but so sad," Emma said, her blue eyes growing larger with wonder, the tears welling up, blurring the iridescent color of her extraordinary eyes. "I know he is the one Decara wants me to destroy."

"What are you talking about now?" Kenyan insisted, his patience dwindling, frustration taking hold of him.

"She needs my power to destroy all of innocence. That is why she has brought us here."

"I don't understand."

"I don't either, not really, but if she can get me to kill the white seal who wears the purple tear, she will reign over the earth and all will be lost."

"Emma, do you realize how impossible this all sounds?"

"I do, and yet I know it is all true and I know that I must somehow find the seal and protect him from Decara's monstrous madness. We must help all the seals! They are in grave danger!"

"We are the ones who need help, don't you understand?"

Emma did not offer any further explanations; she could only stare at him with solemn eyes that were impossible to dismiss.

"Okay, okay, tell me then, how do we help the seals?"

"We have to stop her from taking any more tears from the grieving mothers."

"And how do we do that?"

"I'm not sure," she lamented, rubbing neurotically at her forehead.

"Well, I am."

"How?"

"Simple. The witch must die."

Emma merely looked at her brother with burning eyes that grew apprehensive.

"I'm going to take out her heart," he said while reaching back inside his breast pocket—"with this!" Showing his sister the stone dagger that he fashioned himself, he watched as the full understanding of what he intended to do menacingly, surfaced over her fragile features. Emma continued to look at the dagger, her eyes filling with dread, but her look did not last long. Quickly, she nodded her head, knowing it was the only way to free themselves and the seals no matter what the cost.

As Kenyan looked upon his sister, he became suddenly struck with awe, as if spellbound. Never had she looked more beautiful than she did just then. It was quite remarkable. He did not understand how he could not have noticed this before. She was exceptionally radiant, looking like an angel herself. He could not explain it any other way for the shafts of thin light that filtered down from places high above gently settled upon her, illuminating her with a glow of purple magic. Her hair was vibrant and alive with a shimmering twist of soft golden curls that flowed luxuriously down from her crown, touching lightly upon her shoulders, bathed with a fragrance of flowers, sweet and gentle. Her iridescent blue eyes looked unreal, large and filled with sparkle. Her skin was pink and soft, flawless in its lustrous warmth. Her once cracked and irritated lips were made smooth with a rosy pink color, imitating the same wondrous hue gleaming from her satiny cheeks. The only thing about her that did not compliment her was the way she was dressed. It was that large brazen nightgown that Decara had dressed her in—how he hated it! Aside from the gown being obviously too large, it made her appear more elflike than usual. Its irreverent color and style was clearly made for an older woman, certainly not for a young girl of Emma's age. "I don't have to ask where that freaky dress came from, do I?"

Emma lowered her eyes, retaining an uncomfortable expression. "I hate it too! It's awful!"

"Why are you taking things from her?"

"I didn't, it just happened. She dressed me while I slept. A gift, she said, but it wasn't. It was another bribe, an awful bribe so I could do dreadful things for her."

Kenyan moved toward his sister, and the diamonds bulging from his pockets crushed up against them both. Feeling inside his pocket, he took out a few of the shimmering stones and looked at them, then looked at Emma with a million questions pervading in his eyes.

Emma queerly smiled, frightening her brother again, sending more shivers down his spine. "They are not real."

"What?"

"The diamonds, they're not real."

"What do you mean?" Kenyan asked, almost afraid to listen to her response.

"I already told you that what you have are seal tears and one day they will return to what they were. Every diamond on earth is a seal's tear, actually. Decara's treasure is one big lie of torment," Emma sadly announced.

"Are you sure?" Kenyan asked, not wanting to believe her.

Emma reluctantly nodded. "I'm sure."

Angrily, Kenyan began tearing the stones from his pockets, casting pieces of the treasure that he had taken down to the cold floor. "Then I don't want any crappy voodoo sorcery that belongs to her!" he shouted. "Freaking witch!"

Emma quickly went to the floor, her dress overflowing all around her. Embracing a handful of the shining diamond chips, she brought the stones close to her heart. She closed her eyes and sighed. "They don't belong to her either. They never did. She took them. They belong to the seals, no one else."

"We've got to find the witch and destroy her before it's too late!" Kenyan instructed with a loud voice, not wanting to hear anymore. "Come on," he said, leading the way. "We haven't much time! We've got to get out of here now!" However, as Kenyan prepared to leave, he slipped on something wet. Looking down, he saw that the piles of diamonds had been changed back to what he could only believe were, in fact, precisely what Emma said they were—*seal tears.* "Then it's true," he said with his heart pounding profusely against his tight chest.

"Yes," Emma answered slowly, rising from the floor, her dress now saturated and dripping from the abundance of harp tears. Then something else happened. Some of the diamonds that secretly remained stashed inside Kenyan's pockets also turned back into their original form. Completely appalled by the dripping wetness that soaked his tattered clothing, he let out an unexpected gasp. He shuddered for a few moments, trying to steady his shaking hands. "Did you do that?" he nervously asked his sister.

Emma offered a slight nod. "Guess you still had some tucked away, sorry about that, but I tried to warn you," Emma said, watching the seal tears leak all over him back down to the floor, joining the tiny puddles below. Kenyan stared at his sister for a long time. He should have believed her. He would only listen now; he did not dare to begin to rationalize any of what was taking place or what she was telling him. Emma continued with a more detailed approach, perplexity coloring her expression. "Decara is going to order me to do a most dreadful thing to the white seal that carries the purple stone."

"Purple stone?"

"Yes, and hidden inside it, there is a tear."

"More seal tears?"

"No," Emma tried to explain. "This tear belongs to the sea. It is a tear that holds an incredible power. That is why Decara will stop at nothing to get it, and she needs me to kill the seal and take the tear!"

"This is insane!" the boy ranted, swatting at himself. With neurotic spasms, he slapped at his soggy threads until all at once he began to laugh aloud. He had suddenly found the entire bizarre situation oddly amusing. "Why not, why not purple angels, witches, crying seals and ocean tears and vanishing treasures? It happens every day!"

"We must find them," Emma implored. "We must find them and stop her, once and for all!"

"Oh, we are going to stop her, all right, don't you worry about that!" Kenyan vowed, his eyes still filled with a queer madness of his own.

"And don't you worry either," Emma promised. "I will be very careful this time, not like before, and I won't be afraid, I'll be strong. I promise." She reached out, holding on to her brother's hand. A sudden breeze came out from the shadows as she did this, ruffling their dampened clothing about as it sent a handful of purple sparkles to dance over them. In a moment, their wet clothing became dry, the seal tears having evaporated inside their hanging garments, their skin left warm by its newly found warmth. "They are protecting us," she softly answered. Then Emma hugged her brother, whispering in his ear, "Thank you for believing in them because now they can believe in you."

"I'm not sure what I believe anymore." He sighed in defeat.

Emma paused, hoping that he would understand. "Whatever has come to this ship has set me free and has left its powerful message in my heart," she said, touching her chest gently with delicate fingers.

Kenyan found himself fixed within her mystic smile. She had once more deluged him with her glowing innocence. "Very well, Emma, you win. Who am I to reason against crying seals and purple angels?" he said, his fingers joining the place where hers remained. "But first, you must take me to the witch. Can you do that? Can you take me to her now?"

"I think so."

"You must be sure. We can't afford to make any more mistakes."

Emma thought for a moment, lowering her eyes to the dark shadows beneath her. "I'll find her," she vowed. Raising her glance toward the purple filtering light, she took in a deep breath and then closed her eyes. "I feel that Decara is with the seals now. I will listen for their cries, and they will lead us to her."

"Good. And you will do whatever I ask of you?"

"I will. I promise," Emma said with an almost unnoticeable quiver.

Taking Emma's fragile hand, Kenyan held on securely. "Then lead on, little sister. Lead on!"

They vanished into the blackness of the ship, crawling as mice through the mazelike corridors, leaving behind the clawing shadows who readily decided to stay behind in order that they might continue their bleak vigil about the vaulted face of the secret room.

As both siblings walked through the dark corridors of the *Tiamat*, Kenyan held on to his sister's guiding hand, secretly clasping to the stony blade with his other, intending to rip open the heart of Decara just as soon as they would once again meet.

DECARA'S LABORATORY

Emma's eyes remained closed walking through the twisted hallways of the creaking ship, the gloom scattering as she and Kenyan headed upward to a hidden and remote section of the ship. She would listen to the sounds inside her mind's ear, sounds, that would inevitably lead her to the most dangerous and forbidden place on this most accursed vessel.

Emma seemed to float along the blackened floorboards, holding ever so tightly to her brother's hand, leading the way through endless passageways of shadows. With the stony blade embedded firmly in his grip, Kenyan quietly followed. Without the least of warnings, Emma suddenly stopped. Profoundly, she listened as an invisible vibration abraded her senses.

"*Shhh!* I can hear them!" she quietly said, opening her eyes right before discovering a long and foreboding set of stairs that disappeared straight up into the awaiting blackness above. As she listened, she could hear the seals' pitiful cries. It was mournful and most delicate. Kenyan listened, but hearing nothing, he waited for his sister to propose their next move. Slowly, Emma scanned her eyes up toward the imposing staircase. Kenyan did the same while she whispered in a hushed voice, "Above us . . . inside a dark room . . . I can hear them," she uttered before taking a deep swallow. "The seals are there with her now!"

"All right, so what are we waiting for? Let's go!" Kenyan commanded.

"Wait!" Emma warned, her hand stopping him from passing. "There is a great danger in this room, worse than I suspected. It is a room filled with much evil."

"Is the witch there?" Kenyan quickly asked, dismissing her warning.

Emma cautiously nodded, her eyes filling with growing fearfulness.

"Then that's all I need to know. Let's go!"

"But, Kenyan—"

"I thought you weren't going to be afraid, Emma."

"It isn't that."

"Then what is it?"

"I'm not sure."

"Come on," Kenyan insisted, growing impatient, his hands sweating from the tight grip he placed around the dagger's handle.

"We're wasting time!" Pushing past his sister, he began to creep up the long and narrow staircase, this time, Emma following closely behind. Trying to keep up with his steady pace, she remained silent, concentrating on her movements so as not to slip on the uneven wooden stairs beneath her bare feet. Higher and higher they climbed, neither one saying a word, their hearts pounding in their eardrums, their breath becoming short, the gloom swallowing them up while proceeding upward.

In a little while, Kenyan could see a dim light at the end of the staircase. Onward he climbed with a little more kick to his stride, straddling the wooden stairs, adrenaline pumping wildly throughout his body. Feeling faint, Emma tried to catch her breath, stopping but a moment so as not to topple backward. Still, she did not call out to her brother. Finally, Kenyan came to the end of the winding stairs leading up into a vast hallway filled with even more shadows and more stairs. Speedily, the boy climbed, turning around, looking down toward his sister as she began to make her ascension. Stretching out his hand, he held it out for her. With one grasp, she held on and was pulled into another long corridor.

"What is this place?" Kenyan asked in a whisper full of huffs and puffs.

Catching her breath, Emma remained silent, closing her eyes, listening carefully to the sounds she alone could understand. A soft breeze passed above her, ruffling a few strands of her golden hair. "Down this hall, toward its very end, we can enter the room through a broken wall panel," she explained with startling reassurance.

"Have you been here before?" her brother asked with a hesitant and uncertain tone. Emma only shook her head, leading the way down the dark and frightening hallway. As the *Tiamat* shifted to and fro, back and forth, it began to sound as if every floorboard was alive beneath their feet. The walls seemed to bend and crumble into bizarre and grotesque shapes. All at once, the entire hallway filled with a strange moaning murmur. It seemed to be coming from somewhere within the dreadful walls that remained endlessly moving right along with them.

Reaching the end of the corridor, Emma stopped. "Come on, I believe there is an opening somewhere around the panels here," she said, crouching down, feeling the dark walls with her palms. Believing she had found the precise spot, she pushed forward. The wooden panel cringed, buckled outward, touching her naked ankles. "Gotcha!" she said with an almost happy voice. "This will take us high above the room, up into the ceiling. We will be able to see everything from there." She took the protruding panel in both of her hands, sliding it upward.

Crunched into a tiny ball, she began squeezing into the hole, her small frame slipping in effortlessly. Now, it was Kenyan's turn. Finding courage in the blade he held, he moved on. Using his free hand to aid him, he pushed through the panel in the wall. Entering, he imitated his sister's crouching gestures. Through more tunnels, they crawled, this time on their bellies. Like snakes, they moved along a very narrow and pitch-black passageway, Emma in the lead, never once faltering, but for a moment. Amazed at her courage, Kenyan strived to maintain his own pace, trying to keep up with her.

"We are almost there," Emma whispered out. In obedient compliance, the boy continued on his undiscovered pursuit when his head abruptly pushed into the bony back end of his sister's rump. She had stopped again. They had at last reached their awaited destination. "We will have to crawl across a few of the ceiling boards."

"Then let's do it!" Kenyan said, ready for anything.

Scurrying off, Emma crawled along the stretching of several two-by-four wooden planks located high above the mysterious compartment. Sallow shades of gloom vaporized against her nervous features while she carefully made her way across the woody tightrope. Concentrating, she slowly pulled herself along, focusing only upon the small secluded scaffold directly ahead. Fewer shadows had settled there, making it easy for her to make her way over to its landing. Halfway over, she suddenly lost her balance, nearly falling. Choking on a muffled scream, she quickly pulled herself up onto the wooden beams with a startling wrench. Panicked, she began to steady herself, dangling high above the shadows of the mysterious room below, her hanging nightdress spilling ridiculously all around her.

"Emma, are you all right?"

"Yes," she called back in a raspy voice, still trying to catch her breath. "It's okay! I'm nearly there!" she whispered excitedly, once again focusing on the scaffolding in front of her before snaking across its narrow path. Kenyan held his breath, watching his sister with a flogging heart as she inched toward the scaffolding. Nearing it, she outstretched her trembling arm and pulled herself over with some help from a protruding wooden shaft. Onto its unsecured platform she slid herself, holding on for dear life. She made it!

The scaffolding swayed, moving slowly back and forth but not showing any signs of plunging downward. Kenyan immediately sighed out a long breath of relief, preparing to follow her. Carefully, he felt the wooden beam with his free hand, making sure that it would support his weight. He would have to put the dagger away for the time being. Returning it skillfully into his breast pocket, he slowly began to edge himself across the boarded plank. Unable to help himself, Kenyan glanced down. Only a green vapor of mist looked up at him. He felt his stomach turn. He would not look down again, at least not until his crossover was complete. After a few close calls, nearly falling himself, he at last joined his sister on the already swaying scaffolding. Emma quickly outstretched her arms, aiding her brother while the unstable landing dangerously shifted back and forth, making ghastly squeaking sounds. Kenyan clutched tightly to his sister, not saying a word, holding to her as if he intended to never let her go.

Suddenly, from below, both siblings heard a strange sound, and then the entire room seemed to explode with a brilliant light of iridescent green. A wild wind stirred the air as the scaffolding moved about, jerking as if in torment. They clung to each other, each trying not to fall into the blinding pit. A smoldering streak of electricity shot up from below, burning the air, charring it, turning it into a heavy, sallow condensation that sizzled. Emma blocked her mouth, stifling a scream while the scaffolding banged mercilessly against the black walls surrounding it, its jolt nearly hurling both her and her brother to the pit below. More shocks of green bolts of lightning crazily seared through the room. The entire place flashed green, once again followed by stillness so quiet it would have evaded death itself. Emma tightly grasped on to her brother, trying to steady herself while the scaffolding rocked back and forth, painfully squeaking. Eventually, it came to rest, and they prepared to look down, not knowing what possibly to expect.

A large glowing crystal ball floated ghostly inside the middle of this room. It pulsated with a green glow, splattering its devilish light over everything. At first, the shine was too intense to look upon. However, as Kenyan's and Emma's eyes adjusted to its strange light, more shapes began to take form. The suspended glowing ball seemed to be made from some kind of transparent watery substance, and within its confines, more sporadic shocks of green fire bolts wavered and lashed out in every direction. And standing before its magnetic glare stood the dark figure of Decara. Cloaked within her raven cape, she looked upon the three-headed serpent floating inside.

"Salutations, oh illustrious-*sss* and dark miss-tress-*sss*," hissed the serpent named Sin, she who always so devilishly coiled herself upon the pinnacle of the glowing green spheroid. "We have been waiting . . . Speak and ask what you wish to know."

Decara was quick to reply. "Where is he?"

"Where is who?"

"Oh, don't already rile me, snake! You know very well *who!* The master has allowed me but a short time to find the white beast, reclaim the tear, and have him destroyed. The beast's presence has not yet been revealed to me, serpent! You must show me where in all the damned realms of Sealssong I may find the despicable slug!" Decara shrieked.

"Patience-*sss*, oh paranoid miss-tress-*sss*, there is still time before the Night of Screams!" slurped the sinister snake.

"Listen, you blundering fools, I've got to find the beastly thing, and I mean now!" she wailed, losing her patience. "Besides, I don't know just how much longer I can keep those two galling brats alive!"

"Well, it would be to your advantage to *sss*-see that they remain alive and unharmed, especially the girl," warned Sin.

"I know that, you irritating thing, you!"

"Have you decided how you will get the child to destroy it?"

"Of course, as long as I have 'sweet-brother boy,' she'll give me no trouble, and as soon as the deed is complete, like the imprudent seal itself, I shall take great pleasure in peeling off both their hides, one inch at a time, rotten little pish-freaks!" Decara screamed, slamming down both of her feet, appearing as if she were about to fly off into a childish tantrum. "I've been patient long enough! I want that tear, and I want that snowy-white piece of seal scum destroyed, once and for all!"

"Yes, of course, of course, and yet only the child, your dear *sss*-sweet niece," Sin tormented with a devilish grin, "can perform such a deed!"

"Oh, you really are begging for obliteration, you moldy snake!" Decara raved. "I am well aware of that, you stretch of twisted filth! Just tell me where to find the damn slug!"

"He is closer than you sus-*sss*-pect."

"What do you mean?"

"However, before you can find him, the *Tiamat* must first be set free from the shroud of purple mist, for the mist is now your main concern."

"What?"

"Do you not recognize the ones who hide inside the purple clouds?"

Decara's face became distorted with outrage, her black hair wildly framing her slender face. "I'm far ahead of you, snake. I have come to know this recently with no help from you, I might add. It is the wretched, goody-goody purple diehards of the sea, the martyred children of Sealssong, who else! Those benevolent bunglers have come to prevent the girl from killing the white seal, but they will not succeed."

"Did you know that they have helped her escape?"

"That's impossible, she remains locked in her room."

Sin began to giggle in a demonic fashion. "I don't think *sss*-so!"

"Go on—revolting reptile!"

"They have come to prepare her for *the Night of Screams*," Sin revealed with another contemptuous grin. Then suddenly, Sin's yellow glowing eyes flashed upward. "She is not far away, can you not smell her presence?"

"You mean she is just wandering free on this ship?"

"Yes-*sss*."

"Lies*! Lies!*"

"It is true. The purple mist is most clever and very powerful. It plays havoc with time, shifting it, making it unstable as it aids the child."

"Are you telling me that we are in some kind of time warp?"

"Yes, but to what extent is not yet known."

"Tell me this then, has it affected our course?"

"We remain in favor of Sealssong, but the time shifting has prolonged our stay upon the waters."

Decara's face twisted into a horrible mask of raw hatred. "Then I have been robbed of time!"

"Yes-sss. That was their intention."

"A curse upon those purple pathetic do-gooders!"

"Cursing this innocence of the sea will not help. The Night of Screams will be very close at hand when you do finally arrive on the shores of Sealssong," the evil serpent head told with a wicked grin, her sisters following up with the same evil mockery.

"Spare me your addle-headed pandemonium and just tell me if I will have enough time to find the beast!" Decara shrieked.

"You will," answered all three serpent heads. "Time will have been cheated, but our master will see to it that we reach the nursery before that final hour."

"And the slug—" Decara furiously ranted, "where shall I find him?" When no further reply came, she exploded. "All right then, enough! Tell me before I tear your rotten tongues out! Where will I find the wretched white seal?"

Sin coiled around again and again, stringing both of her sisters clumsily along. "It shall be revealed soon, dear miss-tre*sss*. Not to fear, in the end, evil shall prosper, and all the powers of darkness shall be yours!" Sin delighted, giggling through her many hisses.

Decara glared at the snake. "How kind of you to offer me your divine assurance," she angrily spit, grabbing on to a most inhuman scowl, pushing her face up against the floating ball. "Listen, you demonic flouter, if I go down, you go down with me! Don't forget that! So I would not be so smug, serpent! You have just as much to lose as I do!"

"Not to worry, miss-tre*sss*, we have *sss*-sufficient reliance in your proficiency."

"Oh, do you now?"

"Oh, most assuredly, most dastardly one!" the three-headed serpent answered, slithering about, flicking all its tongues out at her. "It has been yours, as well as man's incessant evil that has continued to fuel our existence. The slaughtering of the seals of Sealssong has continued our survival upon this cold planet for one thing. Even now, as man persists in destroying what is sacred upon his world, we are made invincible! He consistently replenishes our powers, making our strength far greater than even we ever hoped for!"

Decara smirked. "Well, you better hope we find that wretched seal, and soon! I want him, and I want the mad slug that robbed me of the tear in the first place," she snarled, gnashing her teeth. "I want their remains, rotting and drenched about my bare hands before the next full moon, do you understand!" she screamed, stretching out her bony fingers, crushing them together, making a gnarly fist.

"We can do nothing until the purple mist leaves," explained the three heads. "May we suggest, meanwhile, you *sss*-satisfy yourself with the seal tears you so skillfully *sss*-swindle. That always seems to calm you, oh horrendous one."

Decara surprisingly laughed. "Yes, my precious diamonds, how they truly adorn me," she dementedly purred, reaching into the lining of her pocket, pulling out a long string of shimmering seal tears. Lavishly she wrapped them around her neck, stroking the stones sensually.

"How rapacious we've become!" teased the serpent through a twisted grimace. "How it does become you! When will you dispose of the men upon this vessel?"

"Well, it wouldn't be bloody advisable to do it before we reach the nursery!" Decara shouted. "After the men have skinned the despicable beasts, I shall fashion a most extravagant coat out of the lily white hides of every newborn in Sealssong! The scalpers shall destroy the entire nursery, young and old alike! I'll have them destroy all of Sealssong! After they return to the ship, the same fate shall await them!" she said, breaking out into her usual insane laughter.

Sin hissed and gurgled humorously along with Decara until the evil woman abrasively stopped, shouting in a bloodcurdling voice, "Silence! Are both of your sisters ready to begin?"

"Yes-*sss*, mistress-*sss*," Sin hissed, springing open its mouth, revealing its yellow fangs as did the other two reptilian sisters. With eyes bulging as if to burst, the serpent heads hissed a demonic shrill, directly bringing down their sharpened fangs, each snake biting viciously into each other's scaly skin, a wash of green blood spattering over them, splashing everywhere, momentarily covering the top of the glowing water sphere. As the verdant excretion filtered back down, it quickly evaporated, turning itself into the same green vapor both Emma and Kenyan saw when they first came to this most unholy of places. Once again, Emma choked off a forming scream, stopping it just before it tore out from her pounding throat.

Down dripped the sallow green vapor, moving like a cloud of death, dark and villainous, contaminated with the breath of the very devil. Slowly, it descended upon the room, Emma's and Kenyan's eyes wild with fear, both trembling as the vile cloud began to shift over to the opposite side of the mysterious room. From where they stood looking down, most of what they viewed remained foreign to them. Much of the room consisted of strange contraptions, all of which seemed to glow and move just as their eyes left them. Glass tubing curved around and circled one another, collecting on top of golden stands that stood several feet off the floor. Inside the slender transparent funnels crawling about this dismal setting appeared a strange luminously flowing liquid. Magically, it continuously changed from blue to green to red to yellow, so on and so forth until it surpassed every color of the rainbow. Round phosphorescent crystal cylinders also filled up the room, placed about strategically on elongated black tables covered in dark satin coverings.

The room was alive with the flicker of candlelight now. Where it came from Emma and Kenyan knew not, but the dancing glow shimmered upon millions of diamond chips heavily coating the floor. Standing across the room, precisely where the green vapor was oozing stood Decara's manservant. A large silver chain remained buried deep inside both of his hands. Pulling forcefully upon it, he raised something bulky and ponderous. Emma strained through her forming tears, trying desperately to see what the peculiar manservant could possibly be doing now. Up came a massive cage made of a black and shiny heavy mesh. As it rose, water drained profusely from its tiny openings, its oblong massiveness swaying directly over the place it was retrieved. On and on it continued with its noisy exuding while brother and sister tried to see what was inside the mesh contraption, but the small woven steel-like openings did not allow for them to peer inside. They were just too far away to see what might be entrapped; still, Emma had a strong notion about what was suffering there.

Oreguss proceeded pulling down with all his strength, almost lifting himself off the floor preparing to wrap the chain around a steel stake impaled inside the blackened skin of the adjacent wall. Once in place, the nearly drained cage squeaked with a rebellious squeal, moving back and forth, away from the glass water tank from which it had been snatched. Oreguss began to chomp on his limited yellow teeth in a most disgusting frenzy, watching the green mist finish its descent, its final destination, heading directly into the thousands of tiny openings of the rocking cage. Down it floated, saturating itself within the boundaries of the unexplained meshed contrivance. It was then Emma and Kenyan saw the cage jolt. A horrible howling flooded over the room, and the cage began to buck violently, protesting to the green vapors drenching over it. Clearly, whatever was inside remained terrified and was wild to get away from the dreadful green fog.

More howls of absolute torment sounded. Oreguss danced up and down, shamefully aroused by the pathetic cries coming from inside the mesh cage. Decara continued to stare at the glowing water ball, all three serpent heads slithering toward its midsection. This time, the sister snake Suffering spoke. "Yes, find comfort in the taking of their tears-sss, oh wicked mistress-sss, and while you do, we shall reveal what you so most desire . . . BEHOLD!"

All three serpent heads hissed, each one coiling wildly over each other's scaly union. There was a flash, and then the mysterious water ball began to glow brightly. As the images of the three serpent heads began to fade, a flickering impression of something most familiar to Emma began to appear inside the watery domains of the floating globe. There he was, as plain as day, the white seal looking exactly as she had seen him in her dreams, just as she had seen him when sketched on the hems of clouds by the purple angels themselves. Emma cupped her tiny mouth unsure as to what would escape from her trembling lips. She continued to look at him in awe, viewing him through the glowing water ball. He appeared to be sitting on a snowy slope, situated before an icy hole, just staring off into the sea as if he were waiting for someone. The small piece of sky that dropped behind him was cold and cruel. It looked like a storm might be brewing, but its importance paled in comparison to the sad and forlorn eyes of the creature who wore the treasured tear, his beautiful image glowing vibrantly inside the floating water ball before her.

Abruptly, Decara growled, "Now for the last time, for the sake of hell itself—where is the damned thing hiding!"

"He waits for us, mistress-*sss*, on the main nursery of Sealssong. The white seal that wears the tear will have remained there for one year by the time we finally arrive. He now waits for the whale to bring him news of his mother."

"*Whale?* Mother? What in blazes are you talking about?"

"Yes-*sss*, she is still alive!"

"What are you blabbering about, fool? Its mother's welfare means nothing to me!"

"It should," the snakes foretold. "She can further help with your quest to reclaim the tear."

"How?" Decara snapped.

"Your servant has captured her. She is here now and sits before you in this very room!"

A large wiry smile cut across Decara's face. "Interesting," she said, her eyes bulging while her long red-painted fingernails tapped neurotically against her chin. "Tell me this," she asked, her eyes slanting into a vicious squint, "is she not the same seal who destroyed my companion and stole the tear that now hangs around the neck of the wretched beast that I see before me?"

"No. She is not!"

"Then what do I care! Let her die then! I only want to find the mad seal that took away all that I desired, for my revenge shall be unmerciful!"

"The white seal waits for her now, this mad beast. She is his protector and will arrive on the icy shores of Sealssong by the aid of the blue whale. They too remain trapped inside the realms of the purple mist," the snakes explained. "As we remain trapped . . . so are they."

"Go on!"

"Not to worry, you still have the upper hand, most vile one. Just like the boy, you can use the seal's mother to assure your destiny," hissed the three-headed snake, each head winking an eye, unmasking its ghastly amusement. "Just think of it as additional collateral," they slurped.

"Yes . . . I see what you mean," Decara said with a wicked grimace. "Oh . . . you are good! Devilishly good, irritating as hell, but wickedly good! There may still be hope for you yet, snake!"

Suddenly, the three heads began to twirl around each other in a frenzy of excitement. "The Night of Screams is at hand!" they monstrously decreed.

STEALING SEAL TEARS

Leaving the radiance of the glowing ball, Decara carefully turned away and headed to where Oreguss obnoxiously fluttered. Knowing what he had to do, Oreguss lowered his head subserviently and walked across the room. There, he would collect the mysterious chalice and bring it to his volatile mistress.

Taking the dark shining cup in both hands, Decara wrapped her long fingers around it, walking sinisterly toward the mesh cage, clinging to the black chalice, looking mercilessly at the swaying cage before her, a ghastly grimace cut deeply into her face. Obediently once more, Oreguss was at her side, still chomping devilishly on his yellowish brown-stained teeth. He began to grunt excitedly. Grasping on to a long and twisted bolt from the cage's door, he pushed it aside with one vehement hit, ushering open this unholy jail. Instantly, the cage feebly fell to its side, wiggling with dangerous severity against the heavy chains that constrained it. Uncontrollable howls and barks escaped into the room, sending chills down the spines of the watching siblings.

Emma immediately recognized the cries. *"The seals!"* she gasped. Quickly cupping her hand over her quivering lips, she shot her brother a frightened look. With tear-stained eyes, she swallowed, trying to muffle the pounding sound in her throat. Kenyan sharply threw a glance down toward Decara, making sure that she had not heard the emotional murmurs of his sister. He held his breath, looking upon the witch, but she did not stir in the slightest, nor show any signs of provocation. Exhaling, he closed his eyes, relieved that they were safe, at least for the moment.

As the mesh cage jerked and shook, Decara held out the mysterious cup, waving it tauntingly before the creatures imprisoned inside. Terrified, seven emaciated mother harp seals went cowering toward the back of the mesh entrapment. Once again, in unison, the seals all cried out with an unbounded lament, a wail so pitiful that severed Emma's heart. She could hear and understand everything that they were crying out. She tried verbally to explain the torment to her brother; however, Kenyan quickly shook his head and placed his trembling fingers over her lips. Now was not the time. Bathed in sorrow, Emma listened to the seals while they continued to cry.

"Have mercy," the seals begged. "Not again! For the love of all that is sacred, leave us in peace, we have no more tears to give!"

Decara let out a most ghastly laugh and then struck her bony hand against the sides of the cage, rattling it as if to snap it free. "Shut up, snail-scum!" she hissed, her mouth tightening with a horrific twist, all traces of laughter gone. All at once, the green vapor that had remained over the mesh cage began to move toward her. It twirled and rushed around the evil woman, swirling like grotesque green-skinned demons before melting into the chalice. Bringing the shining cup to her lips, she drank. Decara threw back her head and opened wide her mouth. Then like a fiery breathing dragon, the vapor spewed from her, exploding over the mesh cage. However, this time, when it hit, it crackled and hissed out as burning acid. The seals began screaming, and the entire room was filled with unimagined terror!

As the diabolical mist dripped from the cage, Decara daintily wiped her mouth with her fingers, removing any of its obscene residues. She was smiling hideously when she did this, her free hand flipping shut the lid of the chalice before handing it over to her servant. She waited for him to return the black cup back to its proper place before she shrieked out his name.

"*Oreguss!*" she screamed, summoning her manservant with a quick twist of her head. There, in a flash, Oreguss stood, grunting, still chomping on his twisted teeth while reaching into the cage.

All seven seals were barking and howling with untold suffering, unable to control the anguish exploding from their tormented eyes. Pushing themselves hard against the rear of the mesh cage, unable to free themselves, three of the seals began to slice up their skin, but their bloody injuries did not stop them from trying to penetrate their brutish jail. Nothing could be worse than the pain they had been made to endure once again.

Scrounging his hairy fingers into the flapping pack, Oreguss randomly grabbed at the first seal. This seal was seriously ill, undernourished, and burning with a fever. She could not possibly fight the squeeze that Oreguss had placed around her throat. With a cruel tug, he pulled the harp forward further into the green mist that heavily infested the cage. Instantly, the harp wailed out. Decara lowered her hand and wiped it across the seal's ailing eyes; the seal screamed, shutting its eyes as if acid had been thrown into them. In a sickened faint, the harp fell forward as if dead, its limp tongue protruding through its foaming mouth, its flowing tears immediately turning into diamonds. The seal's tears spilled into the mesh cage then onto the cold black floor. Oreguss waited until the beast had no more tears to give, looking as if it were dead. Taking hold of the drained creature, he quickly discarded her like some dirty rag, casting her to the side, preparing to seize the next unfortunate harpie. Decara's smile, now filled with venomous gaiety, quickly changed when she looked upon the small quantity of diamond tears the first seal had produced. It just was not enough. It never was enough. Smirking disappointingly, she raised her eyes in disgust while Oreguss gruffly grabbed the next creature.

This second seal was not a stranger to pain and sorrow. She too had lost her child, but not to the cruelty of man as did the others. Her grief was that of shame and guilt. She had left her child alone on a floating slab of ice one morning, alone with a strange walrus. Alone so that she might feed, only never to see him again. She had abandoned her son and had lived to regret it. Oreguss grabbed hold of Arayna, shaking her repeatedly, trying to stifle her spastic movements.

"Please end this!" Arayna pleaded in a weak and whispered voice. "We cannot go through this again! We will surely die!"

Decara laughed. "Die then, what do I care! There are plenty where you came from, but first, surrender your tears to me, pathetic slug!" she screeched, slapping Arayna across the snout while Oreguss yanked her out into the green mist.

From across the way, the wicked head of the serpent Sin hissed out to Decara. "*Ah, ah, ahhh,* best be careful with that one," the snake cautioned. "She is the mother of the white *sss*-seal we have told you about."

Decara abruptly froze and then smiled wickedly. "Ahhh," she murmured. "Then I will enjoy doing this all that much more!"

Arayna tried to pull back her head, fighting Oreguss's grasp, nearly snapping her neck in the process. In a demented craze,

Decara abrasively swiped her skeleton fingers across Arayna's eyes. At once, Arayna crushed her eyes together and opened her mouth as far as it would go, and taking in a long and rattled breath, she let out a cry that neither, Decara, Oreguss, nor the young ones watching from above had ever experienced. It was so pitiful and full of heartache that it rumbled the ghastly room. Directly, Arayna fell lifelessly to the floor of the mesh cage. Oreguss began to laugh aloud as Decara watched the multitudes of diamond tears pour down over Arayna's saturated snout. "Now that's more like it!" the wicked woman sang.

Emma watched, or at least tried to watch through her teary eyes, as Oreguss went sadistically about his foul duties, shaking and pounding each seal right down to the last of the seven while Decara brushed their grieving faces with her unholy skeleton fingers. Emma wanted to jump down from the scaffolding she clung to, no longer caring about her well-being, her only concern now of somehow helping each one of the poor, unfortunate creatures locked in the horrible mesh cage below. Still, not knowing how she could, in fact, ever stop the terror taking place before her and her brother, Emma painfully sighed out in anguish. With her own tears drenching her delicate cheeks, she was not sure just how much more she could endure. In misery, she continued to watch the green mist swirl around the hands of Decara, knowing somehow that within its eerie green glow, it had the power to rekindle the vivid heart-shattering memories of lost children.

"Kenyan," Emma whispered out, unable to help the shaking in her throat. "We've got to stop her! She will surely kill them if we don't!"

Kenyan began to motion to his sister to remain quiet, when all at once, the entire framework beneath them jolted with a tremendous bang! Flopping sideways, the scaffold sent the siblings hurling to the opposite side, nearly sending each one crashing to the floor below. Panic stricken, Kenyan threw out his arms, one arm holding tightly to his sister, the other twisting around the sides of the swinging platform. Emma would have screamed regardless, but her scream quickly became inflamed with even more terror when her eyes suddenly came face-to-face with the evil grimace of Decara!

Unable to move, Emma and her brother hung helplessly in front of the dark woman who, only moments before, walked upon the diamond-filled floor. Like the swoop of a bat, she had winged her way up from the floorboards beneath; and in the swipe of a tear, she had fastened herself against the scaffolding, becoming suspended high above like some repulsive insect. With her black cape hanging over the sides of her slender body, which remarkably resembled shiny black wings, she stared at them both, her face only inches away, her red eyes burning hideously before them. With both bony hands wrapped horrifically around the front of the lopsided platform, Decara opened wide her eyes, expanding her satanic grimace until it swallowed up her entire face.

"PEEKABOO!" she hissed. "I SMELL YOU!" In a fit of maniacal laughter, the evil woman began to shake the scaffolding in such a wild way that the sections of the ceiling began to snap and crumble. Back and forth, Decara savagely wrestled with the unstable platform as more chunks of ceiling showered down. Emma shrieked out in terror, tumbling near the edge while Kenyan desperately tried to steady both himself and his sister. He could not hold on much longer. "Precious child," Decara hissed. "Come, let me KISS you!"

Emma began screaming bloodcurdling screams, swinging and clawing at the deranged woman dangling in front of her. Her tiny fist hit Decara's nose straight on, but this would not stop the crazed woman. Using both of her naked feet, Emma kicked out toward her monstrous aunt, striking another hit directly against the woman's blood-colored lips, but Decara was quick. In a flash, she seized both of Emma's ankles, pushing them aside with a feral thrust. Casting out her arm, Decara embedded her forceful grip into the bulk of Emma's blond hair, dragging the girl toward her.

"Rotten little pismire!" she sputtered, teasing her with another wave of maniacal laughter, rolling it off her tongue, making it rattle the walls like thunder. Then all at once, the loathsome Decara let go of the platform, only holding on to Emma's hair as a sole means of support. Throwing himself on top of Emma's legs before she was hurled off, Kenyan held his sister down. Emma's shrieks of torment shattered the room while she tried to fight the vile woman's powerful hold. In sheer agony, the frantic girl scratched deep into the hands of her aunt, the diabolical woman's fingers remaining wrapped around her niece's hair.

"Let go of me!" Emma screamed. "Let go of my hair, you maniac!"

The bouncing platform suddenly made a dangerous cracking noise, and Kenyan felt both himself and the unstable landing begin to slip away from the ceiling. Insanely, the boy reached for the blade inside his pocket. He would not go down without first driving its blade right between the witch's eyes, but he would never get the chance. For as Decara hung there, twisting mercilessly off the ends of Emma's hair, bouncing sadistically about as a wiggling worm impaled on a hook, the entire platform went hurling down to the awaiting floor below.

The crashing sound that echoed throughout the room vibrated the walls, splintering their wooden veins as if threatening to split them apart. The collapsed scaffold all but missed the serpent's floating lair by a few inches, sending the three snake heads into an unhinged alarm as the room filled with a cloud of milky dust. Round and around the unholy trio squirmed, all crazylike, inside their transparent glowing ball, hissing with shrills of hysterics. And as the swirling dirt began to settle, Decara emerged from its opaque cloud, unharmed. Her face was covered in a mask of mummylike dust, revealing absolute madness while still clinging viciously onto Emma's hair, pulling her out into the open over to the mesh cage that housed the seven unconscious seals. As lifeless as the seals themselves, a dust-covered Emma was dragged pathetically across the cold diamond-covered floor and handed over to Oreguss who was eagerly waiting to snatch her up.

"Interested in seals, is she? No problem! Take the ungrateful brat and lock the little princess up with the rest of the slimy slugs!" Decara growled her hair a wild mass of twisted disorder, its once-black sheen now powered with the decaying dust of the room.

Just as Oreguss seized the girl, Decara gave out an earsplitting scream and then fell to the floor. Hitting the crystallized piles of tears, she felt her spine crack against its hardness. Her clawing hands reached out toward her bony ankle; it was covered in blood. Then she felt another pain shoot up her leg. The dust had dissolved enough, and she could see the boy swiftly approaching. Kenyan had survived the crash, and he was ready to plunge his knife in her for the third time, only this time he had crawled directly on top of the insane woman. He was now sitting on her chest, ready to scoop out her black heart. Raising his arm, Kenyan brought down his dagger hard, shattering open Decara's bony chest, pushing the stony blade through her heart, impaling her instantly into the black floor that hid itself under the discarded seal tears beneath her.

SEWER RAT

It took a few seconds before Kenyan could comprehend what he had just done. Out of breath, his heaving chest exploding beneath him, he wiped the tears from his dust-covered eyes.

Still positioned directly on top of the lifeless woman, he looked down at her contemptuously, trying to regain his fleeting gasps of breath. At last, the witch was dead, and not even Oreguss had enough time to stop him from doing the deadly deed. However, what would happen next would far surpass any dreadful feat he could possible conceive. From below, a white bony hand shot up, grabbing the boy by his throat! Decara opened her black eyes and pulled Kenyan down toward her cold, stale breath.

"Sweet boy, we have really got to stop meeting like this!" she hissed with a psychotic giggle. A burning scream flew out of the boy, paralyzing him. He was not certain if it was he who was still screaming when Decara sat up from the floor, rising like a grotesque corpse from its coffin. With one hand fastened around his throat, she used the other to painfully tear the dagger from the gaping wound in her chest. "I hate it when that happens, it's always so messy!" she growled, crumbling the blade in her hand as if it were mere paper, the broken chips falling to the floor like pieces of confetti. With her eyes wild and having both arms stretched out as far as she could, Decara opened wide her mouth; and from its foulness came a howling blast of wind, hurling the dazed boy clear across the room.

Suddenly, the air was alive with strange sounds. Decara's black eyes abruptly turned a fiery red, and as her burning sockets blazed, she exploded into thousands of crawling spiders. Kenyan fell to the floor, crashing into the diamond seal tears while the hideous insects charged around him, covering him up in mere seconds. The wailing wind helped rattle up the room as the grotesque things encased the boy, turning him into a horrific unshaped glob of vibrating appendages, swallowing up his screams before monstrously picking him up off the floor. In a flash, the crawling infestation whisked him out and away from the room.

Once again, there was deathly silence.

This would last only for a short while, for all too soon the menacing grunts of Oreguss pierced the dusty air; he would be making sure that the lock of the cage remained secure after having thrown Emma inside.

That'll teach ya! Won't make any trouble now, sewer rat! Oreguss thought. He had handled her without consequence, throwing her into the cage with a heavy hand. Pushing an eye near the tiny holes of the mesh enclosure, he peered inside for another peek. From the way her pint-sized body lay twisted and bent, wet and lifeless on top of two of the slimy unconscious seals; she could have jolly well been dead. He would have to continue to remind himself over and over again to be gentler when handling the scrawny sewer rat, at least until the time came for him to peel her apart. Shaking the cage, he waited for the girl to stir. When she did not, he slammed his heavy fists against its massive sides. Again, nothing happened. Frustrated, he began to rock the cage violently, scattering all the seals and Emma about, nearly crushing Emma with the massive weight of the seals. Watching the scraggly sewer rat flop about aimlessly, he was able to detect that she was still breathing. Relieved, he chuckled sinisterly and turned away from the cage. He knew that he would have to be seeing after the boy again, for Decara would have most likely had him already chained inside yet another cell, one even worse than the last. Knowing that she would be impatiently waiting, Oreguss left the room.

MESH PRISON

The serpent had witnessed everything.

Upon each grotesque mouth, each head held fast to a most sinister grin. They would settle back inside the glowing guts of their liquid ball and wait. For in a little while, the young girl would awaken, and then the fun would really begin. They could not help hiss with evil laughter one final time, silently listening, watching with devilish delight.

*   *   *

Emma awoke with a slight stir and the most painful headache. Her eyes fluttered and then opened, staring directly up into the black universe of the mesh cage. She could feel that she was wet, and she felt slimy and cold, her bare skin touching against something already clammy and slippery.

When she sat up, her skull felt as if it were about to split. Slowly, she positioned herself upright, balancing on something quite extraordinary. With a small gasp, she retreated when she saw that her shaky palms had pressed against the whiskered face of an unconscious mother harp seal. Again, she took in an unexpected gasp and looked around.

The seals were everywhere—all seven of them!

Furthermore, she was, lying right smack in the middle of the entire lot of them! Her eyes nervously surveyed their motionless forms, and all of them appeared to be dead. Frightened, she reached out her trembling hand, touching the harp closest to her. As she did this, her entire body unexpectedly fell into the center crease of the slippery heap. Inside their silky folds, she fought to breathe, casting out her arms, grabbing on to the back of another harp. Unable to latch on, she kept turning the seal over and over like a hallowed barrel floating in unstable waters. Disconcerted, she stuck out both of her bare feet and swung them over the sides of the creatures, sandwiching herself into one crumpled heap. Determined to free herself, she pushed with all that she had against their slippery hides. Lifting herself, she began crawling partially over them, managing to find her way to the front of the meshed cage. Taking hold of the gate that locked her inside, Emma pulled herself away from the lifeless creatures and began to cry. It was then she heard a voice. Turning, she stared and listened carefully.

It came once again. "You will not harm us, will you?"

Emma blinked her weary eyes and pulled the wet and disheveled hair away that stuck to the sides and front of her face. "I knew it! I knew you could talk to me!" Emma cried, feeling as if she would begin to weep again.

"You are not like the others, are you?" asked the seal.

Emma tried to kneel before the incredible creature talking to her. "No, and you mustn't be afraid, I am here to help you."

"How is this possible? Aside from that horrible devil woman, we have never been able to communicate with man. We would not dare. I thought that all mankind was made up of wickedness and evil."

"Not all of mankind, I think that there is still some good in us left," Emma said, pushing up even closer toward the seal, her expression drenched in awe and wonder.

"Tell me," asked the harp, "has the horrible she-devil stolen your tears?"

"No, she wants to steal something entirely different from me," Emma answered, attempting to touch the seal's face.

Immediately, the seal recoiled, crouching into the unconscious pile of harps behind her. Sadness shadowed Emma's eyes while gazing upon the solemn face of the starving and bewildered mother harp. "I am so sorry, I didn't mean to frighten you. Please forgive me."

"It isn't that," said the seal. "It's just that you are . . . well, you are—"

"Man?" answered Emma.

The seal slowly nodded. "I'm afraid I never met one that did not wish me harm."

Again, Emma's eyes filled with sheer sadness. "And for that, I am truly sorry, but I promise that I am nothing like them, and I will do everything I can to help you."

The seal looked at Emma strangely. "I don't know why it is that I believe you, but I do." Then the harp suddenly smiled and looked back at Emma through teary eyes filled with both compassion and wonderment. "My name is Arayna," spoke the seal. "She tried to kill you, didn't she?"

Emma did not answer, but only looked in awe at the articulating mammal that was now wriggling closer toward her. Daring to come up as close as she possibly could, Arayna placed her wet snout near the bridge of Emma's nose and eyes and sniffed. "Can it be true? Are you truly our salvation?"

"Yes, at least I hope to be."

"Can you save us from this dreadful prison?"

Emma swallowed hard and waited for the lump in her throat to subside. "I think so," she said while trying to speak through the throbbing pain in her head that showed her not the slightest mercy. "I mean, yes, at least I must believe that I can," she explained, unable to hold back her doubts or the flood of tears just waiting to escape. "But now she's gone and locked me up inside this horrible cage, and I must concentrate hard on getting us all out of here." Her fingers immediately went up toward her pounding temples. Pulling away her hand, she noticed that there was a trace of blood on her fingertips. "I'll be okay. I just need for the throbbing in my head to stop so that I can concentrate."

"Concentrate?"

"Yes, if I concentrate hard enough, I can do things."

Arayna pulled herself even closer to the young girl and looked deep into Emma's eyes, her own enormous and swollen eyes glistening as she gazed at her. "I am not sure why any of this is happening, but I know that we have been brought together for a reason. I believe in you, young man-beast—you who are of man, yet possess not his deceitful heart," whispered the mother of the white seal.

Emma placed both of her hands around her mouth, cupping them as if in prayer. She suddenly knew who Arayna was.

Directly, there came another voice. This voice was deeper, older, and filled with great wisdom. "I have known of your coming for a long time now. You are the child of innocence."

Emma turned her head to find another seal talking to her. This one was twice the size of Arayna and appeared to be extremely ill. "I am old, yet I have been able to withstand the likes of the demon-woman, and so shall you!"

"Who are you?" Emma asked.

"My name is Lakannia. I have lived many years. Each child that I have given life to was taken from me, either by the storms or the evil of man. I have despised and hated man ever since that moment as does my race, until now . . . *until you!*"

"I don't understand."

"Your story is very old, 'tis an ancient story of a human girl who would be called the child of Innocence. She would come to render us from the unspeakable evil of man. Since the beginning of time, this has been written in the hearts of all that were born of the sea. She would create a world where man could never inflict his murderous and evil ways upon us ever again. Many of us had given up feeling that it was just that, a story to give us false hopes, for surely, nothing good could ever come from man. He has done nothing but help eradicate each other and us! However, you are proof that this prophecy has always been true," the seal named Lakannia uttered, coughing and wheezing, sounding as if she were about to collapse. In a little while, she began to speak again in a mucus-filled throat. "Use your power, your gift, for you can speak with us and are set above the rest, for you possess the ability to conquer the evil one!"

Before Emma could answer, she noticed that the other five seals were beginning to stir and were slowly awakening. At first, each one retreated to the sides of the cage, each terribly frightened by the strange likes of Emma, but soon the eldest seal once again spoke out. "Do not fear the child. She has come to save us!"

"SAVE US!" scorned the others. "She is one of them! A man-beast! She is the demon-woman's servant!"

"No!" Arayna protested. "Listen to Lakannia, what she says is true!"

"Search your hearts!" pleaded the older seal. "For it is written within you! Find it! For it is there!"

A brief moment of silence passed over each harpie until one finally said, "How can she help us when she remains locked inside with us? If she is not of the evil one, how can she release us!"

Arayna was quick to speak. "Lakannia was washed away by the terrible storm that hit Sealssong. I thought that she was dead. It is fate and this man-beast that brings us together once more. You must listen to what she has to say."

Lakannia swung her massive neck around, nearly knocking Emma over in the process. Like a great dinosaur, she wriggled up to Emma, saying in a low and whispered voice, "You will be asked to do the impossible, but if you have faith in the impossible, it shall be your strength."

Emma nodded, wiping the tears away from her eyes, wanting to focus on the mammoth beast in front of her. "Find the white seal and take him to your heart. Protect him, let no harm come to him, for through him, you shall find your destiny."

Arayna began to weep when she heard Lakannia's words. Having only recently learned that her son was still alive, unable to hold back, Arayna jolted forward, rocking the cage, nearly toppling over Emma again. "Find him! *Find him!*" Arayna wept, still shaking the mesh prison back and forth in her emotional outburst.

Emma held on to both sides of the cage, trying not to topple over. It took some time for both the cage and Arayna to come to steady themselves. Emma patiently waited while her head throbbed and stung from where Decara had clawed at her hair. Gently, she rubbed her aching scalp. "I know who you are. You are his mother," Emma gently said.

Arayna nodded, her tears freely washing over her beautiful seal face.

"I will find him. I don't know how, but I will find him. Besides, I have the purple angels to help me. They are still here with me. I can feel them all around us," Emma disclosed, looking above the mesh as if expecting to see them there.

"The purple angels?" Arayna sniffled.

"Yes, they are the lost children of the sea, the slaughtered pups of Sealssong, and they have somehow enchanted this wretched ship. They are the ones that led me to you," she tried to explain, not sure if she understood any of it herself.

"And you will find my son?" pleaded the broken-hearted Arayna.

"I will find him. I promise."

Lakannia cleared her parched and irritated throat. "Leave your doubts and fears behind. Have faith in her words and these purple angels she speaks of. We must believe in the child now or all will be lost!"

"Decara is pure evil!" Emma told the seals. "She has stolen your tears to corrupt and deceive man, and worst of all, she is my kin. I am ashamed that she could be so wicked," she confessed sorrowfully, clutching her wet bosom, protesting. "She has somehow been given a wonderful gift as I have but has chosen to misuse its powers. She has taken your tears and has turned them into diamonds."

"Diamonds?" Arayna questioned.

"Yes, shining rare stones that adorn her and continue to fool man," Emma grieved. "How sorry I am that she does this to you. I know it hurts you terribly."

"More than we can tell you," Lakannia woefully murmured. "She makes us relive the moments of our children's death repeatedly."

Each seal suddenly became still, bowing its head, shaking it as if not to remember.

"It's monstrous!" Emma cried, watching a single tear fall from the older seal's weathered face.

Lakannia quickly spoke out again. "The demon-woman is planning something diabolical that may change all that we have come to know."

Emma nodded. "Yes, it is just as you said, it involves me and the white seal."

Arayna wept some more. Striving to speak through a trembling voice, she asked, "But why, what could she possibly want with my son?"

"She wants the tear, a most powerful treasure, a treasure he now possesses," Emma tenderly said, stroking Arayna's soft head, the seal allowing her now to do so.

Again, the older seal spoke, her eyes now on Arayna. "How you can still weep continues to amaze me," Lakannia offered, a queer smile glistening on her dry lips. "Even after the demon-woman has stolen your tears time and time again, you still defy her by having yet more to give."

Arayna looked back at Lakannia with eyes glistening with crimson. "There is no end to my grief," she said, clearing her burning throat.

Emma lowered her head in absolute sadness. "She will have him killed in order to claim the sacred tear that he wears. Then she will become all-powerful, and from that moment on, our world will cease to be."

Arayna suddenly pulled away from Emma and stared at her with a horrified look. "And it is *you* who she intends to corrupt so that you may murder my child!"

"I would die first before I would ever harm him!" Emma shouted. "You must believe me!"

"Promise me, promise you will never let any harm come to him! Promise me!" wailed the exhausted and grieving Arayna.

"I promise! I promise!" Emma cried, grabbing on to the seal, hugging her close to her heart.

In a little while, Arayna carefully pulled away from Emma, staring at her with those same intense, heartfelt eyes. "But how? How can you stop her?"

Compassionately, Emma looked at the distressed seal, continuing to stroke her face softly, attempting to wipe the discolored stains the tears made under her magnificent eyes. All at once, Emma turned to look at the floating liquid ball just beyond her meshed imprisonment. "Don't you worry, I'll find him," Emma defiantly said. "And they are going to help me!"

"The serpent?" Arayna gasped.

"Yes!"

"No, you mustn't!" Arayna protested. "They will not help you! They will destroy you!"

"No, they won't!" Emma retorted, looking and sounding remarkably confident. "But first I've got to get out of here."

"But how will you ever manage to—"

"Dear heart," Lakannia interrupted, "leave the child be and watch the wonders of her gift."

Emma closed her eyes tightly and tried desperately to go beyond the drumming sounds of her terrible headache. For a moment, each one of the seals felt a cold electric tingle rattle against its bones. A soft wind stirred up out of nowhere as Emma touched the icy, harsh skin of the meshed entrapment, and right before each harp, a small purple cloud began to settle gently over them.

Emma watched the purple mist while it floated down around her. The seals began to stir nervously when all at once they could see that Emma's tiny hand had suddenly become transparent, as did the rest of her body. With eyes closed, she neared the locked gate. Placing her hand against it, she could feel her palm penetrate the mesh, her translucent fingers reaching out. More wind billowed, rocking the cage back and forth while the purple mist swirled around her. Out of thin air, a hand made of purple stardust and vaporous purple clouds began pulling Emma through the cage as if she was as thin as a ghost. Falling to the floor, she crashed against the many diamonds there. Picking herself up, she looked back to the seals, a wide smile of triumph pasted brazenly across her delicate lips. Standing before them, Emma watched the wearied harps attempt to join her. Their crunched-up snouts scraped against the harsh mesh covering, and try as they may, they could not penetrate the cage. Regretfully, they would have to remain. Somberly, each looked upon the girl who promised to save them, their eyes filling with more tears, tears that would undoubtedly be swiped from them yet once again.

Looking back at the seals, touching her hand against the cold, abrasive skin of the mesh, Emma softly spoke to them. "Maybe the angels want you to remain. Perhaps you will be safer here, at least for the time being. I will return as soon as I can, I will be back to set you free, I promise."

Each harp pathetically stared back at the girl, not knowing if they would survive the next few hours, as it was. Keeping alive until her possible return did not seem likely. Even Arayna did not speak. As did the others, she only stared at the young girl, wondering what the peculiar man-beast would do next. It would not be long before she would find out.

DOORWAY OF DIMENSIONS

Gathering up her nerve, Emma slowly approached the serpent lair. She could see the three connected heads suspiciously watching her, their glowing yellow eyes studying her every bit of the way. "Okay, here's the deal. Tell me what I wish to know, or I will find a way to dry up that stupid ball you hide in!" she warned with a most insolent snarl across her mouth. "If you don't, I'm afraid I will be forced to step on all three of your heads and squish them like blueberries!"

"*Sss*-sassy little thing, isn't she?" hissed the snake heads.

"I mean it!"

"Why should we?" Sin asked, wiggling about, pulling its sisters along, pushing its vile head against the watery boundary sustaining it.

Emma bravely pushed her face toward the floating ball, just barely touching the tip of Sin's nose. "Because I said so, that's why!"

"And should we refuse?" the snake head named Suffering asked, clinging to an obnoxiously looking grin.

Emma partly closed her eyes and stretched out her finger, preparing to puncture the watery ball. A snapping spark exploded as the tip of her finger pushed against the lymphatic globe. A million bubbles began to surface from the bottom, instantly bringing the strange gooey fluid inside to an excruciating boil. Snapping its head back, Sin gave out a cutting cry, recoiling back inside its watery lair, feeling the bubbling fluid eat away at its scaly skin. The other two serpent heads convulsed in pain while Emma's finger mercilessly wiggled around inside their translucent encasements. Stirring its water-filled innards, tormenting the heads, she asked, "Now tell me, where I will find the white seal?"

"*Sss*-stop this insidious boiling pot, you odious, repulsive thing, you!" begged the beast, its heads flopping around wildly, imitating a gasping fish lying on a searing cement pavement. "Give us-*sss* relief!" they demanded, their scales glowing red-hot as they squirmed in anguish.

"Not until you tell me where and how I can find the white seal!"

"Very well, but first release us from this torment!"

Emma looked questionably at the three flip-flopping reptilian heads before her. Biting down gently on her pink lips, she contemplated their plea. However, still keeping her finger right where it was, she suspiciously glared back at them. "You will tell me all I wish to know?"

"Yes-*ssss!*" the three tortured things wailed out in three different high-pitched squeals.

"All right then," Emma said, retracting her finger from the floating globe. She waited but a moment for the bubbling fluid to settle down before she laid into the creatures once more. "I'm waiting! Where will I find the white seal who wears the sacred tear?"

Infuriated from defeat, the head named Sadness spoke out. "You will find him at the main nursery of Sealssong. It is the island that sits between the mountains of ice that reflect the images of two kissing seals-*sss*," it hissed, seething now from within for having to confess to the likes of her. "There you will find each other."

Emma thought for a moment before speaking. "I want to go to him now."

The snake heads started to laugh.

"I said, I want to go to him *now!*"

"That is impossible!"

"Don't play with me, serpent! I know you can make it possible for me to go directly to Sealssong."

"Yes-*sss*, we have the power," the serpent explained. "But we won't—and you can't make us. Think we're afraid of you?"

"Very well, I'm done fooling with you," Emma said, preparing to rip her finger into their watery lair again.

"*Sssssss*-stop!" they cried. "All right, all right, we will help you find the whitecoat, only stop doing that despicable, insidious thing to us, you mean beastly beast, you!"

"Okay, but I have just about run out of patience! Now tell me—and be quick about it!" Emma snapped.

The three evil serpent heads began to squirm around each other, each still trying to soothe the burning sting that crawled across their scaly flesh. It was Sin who spoke out again. "We will send you through the Doorway of Dimensions. You just might be small enough to squeeze through. Upon doing so, you will find one of the nurseries of Sealssong—you will find him there."

"Good!" Emma was delighted. "I had a feeling you might see it my way!" she boasted, staring at them with contempt. "Well, come on, what must I do first?"

"After you squeeze through the doorway, the rest will be up to you!" they hissed as if ready to strike out at her.

"How will I survive the bitter cold?" Emma asked, catching them off guard.

The heads did not respond.

"Well, answer me!" Emma demanded. "You must give me something to protect me from the cold!"

Dumbfounded, the snake heads looked toward each other, slithering clumsily and nervously while Emma continued to order them about shamefully. "Come on, don't play stupid! I know some way; somehow, you have the power to do whatever I ask of you, so stop wasting my time! Now," she added in a strained tone, "you will concoct for me a magic amulet of some kind, something that will protect me from the bitter cold and whatever else I will encounter, and no tricks or else!"

The three fused serpent heads flared their pulsating nostrils and threw a most vicious stare at the girl. "I'm *ssss*-so sure!" Suffering snapped out sarcastically. "I have had just about enough of your sassy insolence! Be gone from here before—"

"Before what?" Emma asked, pointing her finger directly toward the suspended body of liquid encasing them, preparing to plague them all over again.

"ENOUGH! Do as she asks!" vehemently hissed Sin, a wretched shroud of defeat melting over her scaly face as she lowered her head.

"But the mistress-*sss*!" the two-joint sisters asked in a panic. "She will not be pleased!"

"No, she will not be!" hissed Sin. "But the child is far more powerful than even she suspects!"

"It is her innocence that defiles us!" both scaly sisters argued.

"Yes-*sss*, now do as she asks-*sss!*"

In compliance, but with absolute indignation, Sin's infuriated sisters nodded their heads. "Hold out your hand!" Sin hatefully decreed, motioning to Emma with a quick turn of her serpent neck. "Place it below the sphere, and do not move it!"

Emma did as she was told, watching each snake head as they drew closer to one another, each mouth hissing out its red demonic tongue, each crimson and vile forked projection wrapping around themselves, tightening as if to snap. Then from the knotted flap of their straining tongues, three tiny drops of blood appeared. Slowly, each spot oozed from the snake head's foul mouths, trickling down to the bottom of the globe precisely where Emma's hand remained extended and waiting. For a moment, the three drops of blood gathered there, penetrating the sphere, dangling just inches above Emma's hand. Suddenly, the drops fell, splashing onto the center of her opened palm. She gave out a cry when they burned her flesh. Wanting to wipe the filthy excretion away but not doing so, she watched again as the blood cooled quickly, congealing taking on another form. Within moments, the scarlet trickles had changed into something else. Eventually, the burning stopped and Emma gazed at the altered configuration in her hand. It was an ugly thing. An oblong diamond chip about two inches was fixed between two gnarled gold bands, both bands having been twisted into a queer shape. As she flipped it over in her hand, she could see that from its underside, there were three pointed snake fangs about two and a half inches long, each tooth also made of diamonds, each fang curving around, pinching down into her delicate flesh. "What is this horrible thing?" she questioned, not knowing what to make of it.

"You must wear it in your hair," the heads echoed forth. "You must wear it always. It will protect you," they hissed.

Emma looked at the scaly creatures with contemptible suspicion. "How do I know what you tell me is true?"

"You don't. Accept it or refuse it, makes no difference to us-*sss!*" the snake heads decreed in unison.

Emma thought for a moment and then nodded her head. "All right!" she said, studying the disturbing barrette in her hand. Taking it toward her head, she quickly combed the grotesque thing into her golden hair, the snake fangs immediately grabbing on, holding steadily in place. "Okay!" she said. "I'm ready!"

All three serpent heads suddenly smiled wickedly.

"Release me before Decara returns! Send me to the white seal!" Emma confidently demanded, never allowing the serpent to see how her hands were trembling.

Each head turned to look at one another. Their eyes flared brightly with a blinding blaze of yellow sparks while stretching the taut muscles of their mouths, continuing to grin at each other, each saying to the young girl, "*Ssss*-so be it!"

Emma jumped back a few feet, nearly falling to the floor when the floating globe began to erupt with a blinding burst of light. At first, the ball altogether disappeared and then reappeared, this time returning in the semblance of a horizontal line. Within its small dimensional space, it exploded with a brilliant glow. Emma covered her face, protecting her eyes from the severe glare that it made. Then the blinding aperture opened like a mammoth eyeball nearly consuming the entire room. A flashing dark space opened before her, and she could feel the sudden presence of sparking electricity fill the room, making it hard for her to breathe. She would have to leave now, but not before returning to the seals one last time. Making her way back to them, Emma touched the mesh with both palms. The cage shifted as the seven seals helplessly wriggled over to her. She gently rested her cheek against the mesh.

"You must be strong and believe that we will meet again when the *Tiamat* comes to Sealssong," Emma said and looking toward Arayna, she smiled. "Have faith, I will find him and you will be together again. I promise," she vowed, barely seeing the face of Arayna through the veil of black meshwork, but feeling her soft whiskers poke through as her heavy seal breath warmed against her cheek. A loud snapping noise echoed behind. Feeling faint and light-headed, Emma listened as the three voices of the serpent heads pervaded the room.

"Man-child, prepare to leave this place and enter the world of *sss*-Sealssong. The porthole is very small; you may not be able to get through should you detain yourself further. Even as we speak, it becomes smaller. Go now before the porthole seals itself shut—for once it has closed, it cannot be reopened."

"Gotta go," Emma said, feeling more of the depleting oxygen dwindle about her. She bravely smiled one final goodbye, knowing that the seals were watching from within the dark cage, their black eyes filled with worry, despair, and yet somehow with hope. Turning, she prepared to enter the shadowy Doorway of Dimensions. Reaching up to feel the peculiar hair comb the serpent had given her, she pressed it further into her golden curls, driving its diamond fangs nearer to her scalp. She then looked back into the darkness of the room, remembering her brother. Tears quickly filled Emma's eyes the moment Kenyan's image came flooding into her mind, but she could not afford to languish over it now. She hadn't much time left. She would see him again. She had to believe this and would not have it any other way. Throwing out her chest and taking a deep swallow, she courageously walked toward the sparking cavity. Without the slightest hesitation, Emma squeezed through the bizarre opening. It felt as if she had jumped from an incredibly high mountain. She could feel the rush of warm air press against her, tossing her about like a crazily twirling leaf.

At first, Emma felt as if she was falling. It was feet first then it was as if she were plunging downward head first. Back and forth this went, the warm air trampling all over her as she twirled around the innards of the black void, twisting about, believing that she would surely be torn apart. Instead, a rush of millions of burning pricks bombarded her. It was as if she was on fire, but she soon came to realize that the experience ravishing her was that not of heat but of intense and bitter cold. Blasts of savage icy winds crashed around her while she continued to fall through the black hole, whirling and spiraling out of control, deeper and deeper into the dark abyss that the serpent had created for her. She was freezing and shaking uncontrollably. Never had she felt such absolute cold. She fought to keep consciousness, continuing to fall, suddenly aware that somewhere inside this black hole, a tiny light was shining. Initially, it appeared as a pinpoint of light and then it began to grow and spin around her, sending out different colors from its core, resembling a fantastic kaleidoscope. As the rainbow hues continued to rotate, expanding and becoming brighter and brighter with more intensity, so did the gusts of the cold and chilling winds.

What followed next happened remarkably fast, almost as if time had suddenly run out for her, jumping and speeding abruptly as if, to catch up with itself right before it exploded, finishing itself off with a thrust and then a tremendous clashing bang.

THE CHILD IS CUNNING

Seven seals stood fearfully silent, not budging, not even breathing. They watched the black hole that Emma squeezed through secure itself shut before disappearing into a burst of light. When their flashing eyes once again adjusted to the room, each seal could see the suspended globe plainly; back where the three vile serpent heads were. However, this time, each one speared itself through the watery sides of their globe, stretching their reptilian necks out in such a grotesque fashion that they no longer looked real. Further still exaggerating the pull of their necks, the moving snake heads stretched monstrously over to the place where the seals remained trapped. Slowly, the heads began to squirm around the cage, crawling over it, only using their growing necks as a means of tying themselves around the mesh entrapment. In circles, they covered the cage, hissing and laughing in a maniacal way, "Foolish man-child!"

"What have you done to the child!" howled the ailing Lakannia.

"*Sssssssss!*" The serpent laughed. "We *sss*-simply did as she asked. She is there now in Sealssong."

Arayna shuddered as she listened to the serpent continue.

"The stupid overzealous-*sss* girl has failed to realize that we are suspended in a time barrier and that she has arrived in Sealssong at this moment in time, nearly seven months before the *Tiamat* will actually crash upon its very grounds!" hissed the three smiling serpent heads.

"You tricked her!" Arayna snapped.

"Yes-*ssss*, . . . of course!"

"You mean she must learn to survive until then?"

"Such a bright harpie! Right again," taunted the serpent. "Once the porthole closes, it cannot be reopened!"

One of the other harps nervously spoke out. "Will the mystic object protect her, or is that another of your wicked tricks?"

"The talisman will protect her from the cold. However, should she discard it, she will be at the mercy of the elements."

"But why would she remove it?" asked the suspicious seals. "Surely, she knows how dangerous that would be!"

The snake heads smiled the most sinister of all congregated smiles. "Yes, of course-*sss*," they hissed. "Can't imagine what would ever possess her to remove it!" they hissed again, holding to their pretentious grin.

Arayna strained to see the heads up close. She pushed her snout into the mesh holes, looking up toward the crawling things. "Monsters, I don't know how we could have ever trusted you!"

"Your mistrust wounds us deeply," spewed the serpent failing to hold back its grin.

"I bet it does!" Arayna sarcastically barked.

Lakannia quickly followed Arayna's snap. "Aren't you forgetting something, foul beast? If something happens to that child, your mistress will have each one of your heads. You know that, don't you? She needs the man-child to remain alive."

"But it would seem that fate has suddenly made an unsuspecting turn for Decara, making the odds all that more interesting, I should think!" Sin gloated.

"You evil thing, you!" Arayna snarled.

The serpent heads only answered with a morbid chuckle.

Arayna spoke through her pounding throat, looking up at the snakes staring down at her from three different places. "Decara will be wild when she finds out what you did. She will destroy you if any harm comes to the young man-beast!"

"She cannot destroy us," said the snake heads. "It is Decara who will be destroyed if the man-beast dies and does not complete the dark prophecy. We have but merely to watch and wait . . . wait and watch. It should be most interesting."

"The child is cunning! She is brave!" Lakannia defended, coughing aloud, trying to settle the rattle in her chest.

"Ssss-sure she is-sss," hissed the heads. "Sss-so there is nothing for you to worry about, surely she will ssss-survive the storms, the cold, the sss-starvation, and the most dangerous of all—man himself!"

"Man!" cried the seals.

"Yes-sss, man—he is there now!"

"At Sealssong?"

"Oh yes-sss, it is the time man has come to slaughter the baby seals, and she has placed herself plumb smack down in its delightful blood bath!"

"Oh no!" Arayna cried.

"Oh yes, at this very moment, your little solider girl has arrived just in time to witness an actual seal slaughter, how delicious-sss!"

"You vile things!" Lakannia stung.

"You horrible monsters!" Arayna protested.

"Don't sss-snap at us-sss!" hissed the serpent. "After all, it was she who insisted that she find the white seal. We only gave her what she asked. Now let's see if she is as brave as she pretends to be. Let's see just how supreme the man-child really is, shall we?"

"Whatever ever shall we do?" Arayna cried, directing her tearful eyes toward the solemn Lakannia.

The elderly and sickly seal just slumped down, rocking the mesh cage with a disturbing, creaking grate. Releasing a harsh and harrowed breath, Lakannia spoke her final words before she surrendered over her life. "Whatever she finds she will find through the eyes of an innocent heart, and therefore, just as she must, we too must dare hold on to this innocence while we wait for our salvation." With this, the seal closed her eyes and expired.

AND THE ANGELS CRIED

Once again, all the colored lights dispersed from Emma's sight, and there was darkness. She had fallen and had landed with a great crash. Was she dead? She had to be. She could never have survived such an impact. However, the cold that bit into her flesh confirmed that she was still alive.

Slowly, she opened her eyes. A brilliant glare assaulted her, blinding her, forcing her to close her hurting eyes until she could adjust to its harsh blaze. Rubbing her eyes, Emma squinted, filtering out the highest rays of glare. It took longer than she had expected; however, eventually she was able to see the stunning surroundings before her. She had made it! She was certain; the snowy grounds made this clear. Picking herself up, she stood erect, dusting off the clumps of snow from her nightgown. As the bitter cold assaulted her, Emma's thoughts immediately went to the curious object that the serpent gave her; its enchanted powers would warm her from the intense cold. Placing her hand to her head, she felt the bewitched barrette give off distinct warmth that quickly swept over her, warming her from head to toe. Unbelievably, the serpent had kept its word. Deeper, she reached into her golden locks, her fingers wrapping around the mystic safeguard. All at once, she felt a sting upon her index finger. Retracting it, Emma examined her fingertip. Forming at the tip was a small circle of blood. She had apparently pricked her finger on its sharp fangs. She must be more careful; she had not realized just how sharp the diamond snake fangs were. Nonetheless, when reaching for it a second time, the same startling thing happened, only this time its bite was much more severe.

Pulling her hand away, she felt the grotesque comb inside her hair begin to move!

She screamed. The thing had come to life and was slithering at the bottom of her scalp. Wild with panic, Emma began raking through her hair in desperate pursuit of removing the crawling monstrosity from her head. Once more, she felt another bite. Inexorably, Emma's fingers scrambled through her scalp, scratching for the evil that squirmed through her golden locks, viciously attacking her every time she tried to grab at it. Finally, with one lucky move, she took hold of it and pulled it from her hair, casting it hard to the snowy ground below. Falling backward, she caught her balance before tumbling over onto the ice, shaken and trembling, her bulging eyes fearfully scanning the whiteness in front of her. Instantly, she saw the horribly crawling thing. It had turned into a small replica of the three-headed serpent, its foul mouth open, exposing its long diamond fangs, now bloodied and glistening. The thing had come alive, just as the three evil serpent heads intended, just as the deceitful things knew that Emma would cast it away, leaving her helpless, cold, and defenseless within the icy world of Sealssong.

Emma shivered violently, watching the mocking snake glare at her. Its eyes were made of diamonds; one actually winked at her right before opening its mouth. It began convulsing, knowing that away from her person, it could no longer survive or attack. With a quick jerk, the hideous amulet melted into the snow, leaving only a light green slimy steam, dissipating and proceeding to dissolve into the interim of the snow beneath it. Clutching to her breast, Emma looked down at the green slime still misting in the bitter cold. Realizing she had ended the evil spell, she shivered when a gust of freezing air swirled around her. She knelt down creaking above the snow, shivering and pulling on her nightgown, the incredibly cold now penetrating every morsel of her being. Then suddenly, without warning, the entire earth beneath her began to tremble.

Quickly standing, Emma soon discovered its source. Pouring down from the snowy embankments about several hundred yards from where she stood, seventy or more screaming mother harp seals and white-coated children flooded the snowy grounds in absolute terror. The rumbling sound they made as they approached her was that of nothing she had experienced before. It was what she had imagined an earthquake sounded and felt like. Watching in absolute amazement, she stood frozen while the roaring stampede of wriggling enormous mother harps and their pups fell like a tidal wave directly in her path, each one giving off a piercing cry even more disturbing than the severe reverberation that rolled along with them. Not knowing what to do but realizing that she had mere seconds to somehow move away from their path before being trampled to death, Emma began to run, bolting faster than she could have ever imagined. Her tiny legs were spinning diagonally, cutting across mounds of snow and ice, her red nightgown pasted to her like a wet shroud. She desperately raced against the impending mountain of mammoth seals, never daring to look back, yet able to see their dark shapes pressing in close around her. A few terrifying moments later, she ran out of snowy floor, unable to go any further but down. Not knowing if she would be jumping to her death, she gasped, looking into the dark blue pit below her. If the seals reached her now, their velocity and weight would crush her in seconds. Gasping again, Emma closed her eyes—and jumped.

Finding herself still alive, she realized she had only fallen a few feet. However, it was enough to protect her from the rampage of the seals. Covered in snow, crouched and protected inside the hole of a splintered glacier, Emma stared straight up into the brilliance of the blue sky, listening as the thunderous quake of seals fell in all around her. In seconds, the sky turned black as the jumping and pouncing seals leaped over the icy ridge above her. Crashing over onto the other side, they continued in their inconceivable charge. Most of the rushing seals made it across. However, there were a few who hastily slipped, falling into the icy pit, nearly crashing on top of her. Some of their weight pressed against her, pinning her down further into the snow, covering her up, concealing her from their panicked states. In utter alarm, the fallen harps scurried off into the open channels of the glacier, completely unaware of the girl while frantically disappearing into the glaring ice and snow, their children buried deep between their jaws.

Emma lay frozen, turning numb in the cold snow, the stampede of seals, unbroken, rushing over her. It seemed like an eternity before the earth finally stopped rumbling and the sky turned blue again. Her skin was beginning to turn a purplish blue color, and the intense pain that she felt from the snow against her naked feet was more than she could bear. Wiping the litter of powdered snow away from her face, pulling herself up, knowing she had to get out of the pit before it was too late, Emma somehow found the strength to crawl from the freezing cavity, clawing her way up to the top. Slumping over the ridge of its icy lip, she pulled herself up. She sat there weeping, her head buried against her knees, pulling her long wet nightgown over her frostbitten feet. Rubbing her toes, she gently covered them with her nightdress. She would be able to rest there only a moment, for once again, another disturbing sound split the air. It was the sound of gunshots. Emma's head swiftly turned around, her tear-stained eyes searching through the frosty world in front of her. What she would see next would terrify her even more than the surging seals. It was man! He was there! He had come to hunt the seals! She could see the men coming from over the same hill where the racing seals had come from moments before.

The hunters were the reason the seals were crazed and fleeing!

Emma struggled to stand erect, watching the approaching men dot themselves over the snowy embankments. She could see that they carried guns and clubs, and the thrown-together seal skins that they used to cover their bodies made them look like abominable snow monsters she had once read about. Suddenly, she heard a shotgun explode and then felt something brush past her cheek, making it burn. Not far from where she stood, Emma saw a mother harp slump down against the snow. She knew the seal was dead and the bullet that killed her had just brushed past her cheek, nearly striking her first. Quickly, she took cover, hiding behind an underpass covered in scattered slabs and chunks of broken icebergs. From where she hid, she could see the trail of seal hunters descend upon their kill. The horrific image of the mother harp seal now left dead in the snow, leaving her defenseless pup behind as the men gathered there as hideous vultures, turned Emma's blood colder than her freezing flesh. She cringed in unspeakable horror when the fur-covered men reached the baby seal. Its shining, dark innocent eyes filled with wonderment as it looked up at the strange invaders. Shivering, the pup began to wriggle toward the men as if to find sanctuary, never expecting the hunters to bring down their heavy club, striking it several times in the head before it perished. Emma covered her mouth and blocked her scream, the tears freezing against her paralyzed flesh.

She had to stop this, but how?

Once again, she heard another gunshot blast off in the opposite direction. More of the seal killers were there. Swiftly spinning her glance in its direction, her wild eyes scanned to see what horrors now lay before her. More of the same hell was in store for her. This time, she could see that there were five or six men gathered there. They had shot and killed two mother harps simultaneously, enabling them to move toward their white-coated children, each mother leaving behind their doomed pups to the unmerciful fate that they themselves had succumbed.

The men on the floe separated as if previously rehearsed a hundred times over, leaving three seal hunters to remain. The tallest of the three men held out his gaff, clutching it tightly in both hands, thrusting it sharply into the head of a snow-white baby seal, instantly killing it. The tall hunter did not stop there. Without the slightest hesitation, he looked down at another abandoned pup not far off. He could see that the tiny creature was confused. The baby seal looked up at him with angelic eyes of wonder, shivering in the cold. The seal killer watched the pup but for a split moment. Then aiming his gaff, he brought it down hard, cracking the skull of the infant. One profound blow was usually enough to do the job.

However, this execution was not so precise; the dazed baby slumped forward, stunned, trying to cry but unable to, partially paralyzed, making a pathetic wheezing noise while it tried feebly to move about, dying there before the watchful seal hunter. Its shaking little flipper reached out, trying to pull itself away, its one eye buried in the snow, the other focused directly on the man and his gaff already raised. The baby harp tried to cry out again, but never got the chance. In a moment, it was over, the execution this time a success.

Immediately a second harp killer, not as tall as the other, moved in, exposing a large knife. With dexterous mastery, the killer brought down the weapon, cutting open the first dead baby seal. It easily tore into the whitecoat, and with one bestial jerk, its pelt peeled off like an old sock. Reaching over, he did the same thing to the other dead infant.

The third man, he being the smallest of the three, effortlessly began to thread the infant seal fur on a black and shiny wire of some kind. It did not take him long to finish this task. In fact, within minutes, he had slung the wire and the pelt over his back and was already heading across the snow and ice with the other three hunters, each man staining the once-virgin snow beneath him with the dripping blood of the innocent children of Sealssong.

Emma watched with added revolt when the snow below the men began to change from white to red, the spilled blood marking their trail while proceeding over the ice in search of more seals. Emma felt as if she were about to go mad. Could this possibly be happening, and if so, what in heaven's name could she do to stop it? Another gunshot sounded. This one was closer than the others were. Hurling around half frozen and burning with pain, Emma saw another mother go down; this seal was only several feet from where she stood.

"My god," she cried, flopping through the snow, falling directly in front of it. The dying mother looked at Emma through blood-filled eyes, terrified but able to pull away, but very little. "Please," Emma cried through her half-frozen eyelids. "I want to stop this, but I don't know how! Forgive me!" She wept. *"Forgive me!"*

The mother harp never heard her final words. She was already gone. Emma slumped on top of the dead seal and began wailing, wishing herself dead for not being able to stop the unthinkable bloodshed. It was then that something caught her attention. She heard the whimpering cry of the orphaned baby seal next to her. She looked at it, fighting the tears ripping through her eyes.

"Oh dear god . . . ," she whispered, pressing her tiny numbed fingers across her mouth. "I am so sorry, little one . . . so sorry." She mournfully wept, holding her trembling lips between her shaking fingers, reaching out toward the crying infant. It looked at her solemnly for a moment and then began to wriggle itself closer to her. "Mama!" it cried, nearly reaching her, but not quite. Suddenly Emma realized that a strong pair of hands were grabbing at her and hurling her backward.

"What in the devil's name?" the voice yelled, its words coming from a stupefied seal hunter.

Emma could feel his hands break into her delicate skin. She gave out a bloodcurdling scream, bringing down her heels against the man's boot-covered shin, wiggling savagely in his grip, determined to get away from him, kicking and screaming all the way. Not believing his eyes, the seal hunter continued to struggle with Emma. Striking her frozen heels against his protected rubbery shins, Emma shrieked, "Let go of me!" She kept screaming, flapping inside the man's sturdy grip. The bewildered seal killer tried to restrain her as best as possible, but when his arm curled around her shoulders, a small piece of his naked wrist bared itself. Emma swiftly bit down hard, breaking the man's skin. Cursing out, he dropped Emma into the snow below. Landing next to the crying pup, she took the orphaned seal into her trembling arms. Clutching the shivering infant to her bosom, Emma's blue face and tearing eyes bitterly looked up into the shocked expressions of the three men covered in seal fur. Speechless, they gawked down at her as Emma cried out, "No more!"

The earth seemed to jump as if startled from Emma's words; however, it stilled, leaving behind an unbalanced and tormenting silence. It prevailed over the men momentarily before the ground began to shake again. All together, each man's fur-covered head swung around, their mouths dropping open once more, watching the snowy mountains surrounding them begin to break apart. Somehow scooping up the baby seal, Emma began to run from the men as an incredible wall of tumbling ice and snow headed directly to where she and the hunters gathered. The panic-stricken men scattered, dropping their guns, clubs, gaffs, and peeled-off seal pelts, each one running off in opposite directions but having no chance of ever escaping the swiftness of the thundering avalanche closing in around them. Wildly, Emma ran through the snow, her frozen, numb feet somehow carrying her and the small seal inside her trembling arms. Despite the thunderous shaking, she could still hear gunshots going off all around her. Horrifically, more baby seals and their mothers were still dying while she tried to evade the approaching calamity of gushing white snow. An entourage of twenty ivory gulls exploded into the skies the moment she broke through their morbid gathering, their black beaks covered in the blood of the slain seal carcasses they had already been feeding upon. Rushing past them, her heart nearly exploding in her throat, she realized that her feet no longer were able to feel the warm blood from the mutilated seals beneath her or the splitting ground.

The speeding avalanche had just about reached her before she comprehended that she could not possibly go another step. She had run out of breath and time, and there was nothing she could do about it. She could go no further. It was all over. With the pup still tucked inside her frozen arms, she turned and looked straight up into the towering wave of surging glare and pounding ice and snow approaching. Closing her eyes and repeating a silent prayer, she waited as the earth suddenly fell apart from under her. Once again, Emma felt as if she were falling, only this time she truly was. The ice beneath her had given way, and with the cushioning of the rushing snow, she washed over the side of the mountain. Down she spun repeatedly, the snow cascading heavily all around her, blinding her, covering her up, pushing her, shoving her with such strength that she believed she would certainly come apart at the seams. Then the feeling of absolute weightlessness overcame her. She could feel the freezing air brush past her with such vengeance. She could see blazes of light pass over her closed eyelids, unable to open them, until at last she hit something that snapped them open.

It would be several minutes, or more, before she could move again, only after she had a chance to clear the caked-on snow away that had embedded itself over her face and eyes and had packed her nostrils shut. Unable to breathe, she blew out the snow from her frozen nose and then tried to open her burning red eyes. The exploding glare took away her breath. She tried to swallow, but even the lining of her throat felt frozen. Everything remained paralyzed. She felt as if she were dying. In fact, she was certain that she was.

Very slowly, she got up and out of the snow, stumbling. As she pried herself back out of the snow, she found herself looking up into the sky directly at two fantastic mountains. They stared down at her, mountains that resembled two seals caught in a moment of a kiss. She had incredibly somehow found the place she needed to be. However, she first had to find the pup. Deliriously she lowered her gaze and stared into the snowy blur before her, her only thoughts now remaining on the small seal that she saved, praying that it was still alive. As if trapped within a slow-motion dream sequence, she turned her head back and forth, still half blind from the onslaught of fiercely shining light, almost deaf from the contorting high-pitched whistles going off inside her throbbing head, determined to find the infant seal before her life ran out.

A sudden swarm of billowing wind stirred up around her, covering her further with snowy white stars from the cold grounds below. Her vision was failing rapidly, and she could feel her heart race as if to explode. Blindly, she began to trudge through the alien world of frost and bitter cold, its icy path stretching out perilously in front of her. Stumbling, once more, she collapsed to the frozen floor. Barely able to raise her head, the dying girl suddenly turned, straining the taut muscles of her neck, listening to what she thought was a faint cry. With the last gasps of her faltering breath, Emma tried to focus her stare on what appeared to be a snowy cave. Believing that the pup may have wandered inside and deciding that she would free herself from the blowing winds determined to cover her up, she began pathetically crawling toward the cave, wanting to see the infant harp before she died. Painstakingly, she pulled herself through the snow, not sure where she got her strength but knowing that it would soon give itself out, forever, in only moments. Her body began to thump inadvertently against the snow, shaking in a most unseen manner. Every part of her now had turned a pale blue, and it would be only minutes before she would perish. Still, somehow she found herself in the cave—a cold and remote place, a secluded spot, nonetheless a place that she never dreamed would serve as her final resting place. For a moment the wind stilled, and she believed that she could hold on for yet a short time longer for inside this small sanctuary of ice and snow, she felt the world about her turn a softer shade of bitter cold.

She had failed the seals and her brother miserably, and for this, perhaps she deserved to die. How could she ever consider trusting the evil serpent? What was she thinking? Nonetheless, it did not matter anymore; she would die a foolish, useless girl who disappointed everyone she loved, and that included the orphaned baby harp that she tried to protect. Even if the baby seal did survive, she would never live long enough to hold the pup in her arms again. No, she would die a failure; and the sooner she succumbed to death, the better off everyone would be. However, just as she was about to give up her life, something happened, something she had not been prepared for. Until that very moment, she did not know that her determined heart still had every intention of preparing her for yet even more wonders.

At first, it appeared as a dream or the last stages of a dying girl's hallucinatory dementia, but whatever was happening, she would embrace it with every part of her being. Still prostrate in the snow, Emma wearily raised her head. A multitude of blurry visions swirled about her as she fought to remain conscious, the wet snow clumping to her face and hair. While desperately trying to focus her debilitated sight, she quickly found herself drawing in a startled breath. It was he! She recognized him at once! In awe, she found herself looking straight into the eyes of the remarkably beautiful white seal that she had dreamed of—the very one she had come to find! He appeared just as she remembered him in her dreams; the same white seal that the purple angels manifested. It was the same creature that the three serpent heads spoke of—the very seal that Decara wished for her to destroy, and she was not dreaming, not this time! He was real and he was right there, right before her, and he was even more wondrous than even she could have imagined!

Somewhere inside this remarkable vision, Emma found newborn rejuvenation, enabling her to raise herself out of the snow long enough so that she could go to him. In a strange hypnotic daze, she rose, moving toward him ever so slowly, her head swimming in intoxicating dizziness never felt before, her eyes swimming in pools of wetness, her vision, both blurring and refocusing with crystal clarity.

There, in a niche of the snow cave, stood the white seal, Miracle.

Emma could not help but smile at the sight before her. He was so radiant, so beautiful!

Miracle backed up further into the nook of the cave, complete shock filling his shining black eyes. He shook violently, staring at the girl, burying his presence as far as he possibly could against the back walls of the cave. It was a man-beast, and it had come for him! Miracle closed his eyes tight, wishing the man-beast away, but she remained when he reopened them. When he looked upon her the second time, he could not help but notice that the creature before him gazed at him in a most unusual but benevolent way. Outstretching her pale blue hand, Emma smiled gently. Kneeling in the snowy carpet beneath her, the frozen nightdress spilling around her as her trembling fingers touched through the icy breath of the cave, she reached out to him. Miracle pulled back, frightened, and yet he could not help feeling some strange fascination toward the curious visitor. With his eyes wide, brimming with wonderment, he cautiously followed Emma's fingers as she held them in front of him, wanting to touch him. He stared at her, fear draining from him while he gazed into her incredible blue eyes. Never had he seen such a being.

Cautiously, Miracle moved away from the nook of the cave, surprising himself as he slightly wriggled toward the strange invader, no longer afraid but filled with intrigue while contemplating the definite possibility of allowing her to touch upon his head. Emma swayed in her kneel, her hand still outstretched to him. "It's all right. I promise," she murmured, her hand lighting upon his wintry white head of fur. "I have seen you in my dreams so many times before," she told the seal, her face full of a wondrous awe in seeing that the white beast was actually allowing her to touch him. Then suddenly, Emma collapsed, slumping into the many folds of her frozen nightdress.

Miracle remained motionless, not knowing what to do. Quietly, he watched and waited for the girl to stir, but she only lay there, struggling through irregular breaths that seemed to rattle through her throat. Miracle raised his head, sniffing the cold air around him. Moving toward her, he wriggled himself nearer, still sniffing the air, still holding wide his saucer eyes of black wonder. He could see that the strange creature had closed her eyes and was now gasping. A spark of panic stung inside his chest when he believed that she might die right there before him.

Who was this strange creature, and why had she come to him? Why wasn't he afraid of her? He had to find out why this being, a man-beast of all things, had such an extraordinary effect on him. Silently, he studied her, looking for any signs of life. Cautiously, he dropped his tiny snout even further, sniffing about her, never suspecting at that moment the dying girl's eyes would open. Instinctively, Miracle pulled away again, startled by her sudden awareness. Again, surprisingly, he did not turn away from her. Once more, he felt himself drawn to her; and with the stirring of his fluttering heart, he lowered himself, her weak and frail fingers reaching out to him, wanting to touch him again. This time, the white seal would allow her to feel upon the depths of his soft and plush crown. Barely able to raise her frozen blue-tinted hand, Emma tried to smile against the frozen skin pulling around her mouth, her eyes longing to look into the beautiful seal's eyes one last time, but regrettably she had finally run out of time. Emma's hand fell down lifelessly, brushing upon the purple stone resting against Miracle's chest. She felt a slight tingle when her hand whisked across the stone before falling down to the cold snowy floor of the ice castle. She lay still and quiet, her eyes closed, her breath finished.

Fearing this time that the strange man-beast had ceased to be, he poked his black nose gently about her face, hoping to wake her, but the curious stranger did not stir. She was dead. Still, once more, Miracle would be amazed by the power of the tear. Suddenly, Emma's eyes fluttered and then opened widely. She smiled again, the pink hue of her delicate skin shading over as all traces of the deathly pallor vanished. Taking in a deep breath, Emma sat up.

Miracle immediately retreated, his fear returning. Once again, staring at the girl in awe, the white seal felt the stone about him warm against his soft fur. It was glowing when he looked down upon it, and so was the stranger. Her eyes were aglow with the same purple color of the magical tear resting near his heart. As Emma sat there, she continued to smile at the seal, watching the glowing tear around him light up the ice cave. Then in a small moment, the stone began to dim. Emma began to crawl toward the seal, her hand outstretched, wanting to touch upon the tear once again. Miracle felt a sudden apprehension wash over him, but he did not pull away this time. He knew that she meant him no harm and that the tear had somehow saved her life. Emma gazed at the stone, also knowing it had rendered her from death. Reaching out to Miracle, she touched his incredible seal face. Petting him ever so softly, ever so tenderly, she sighed. *"Ahhh . . . ,"* she sighed, holding dearly to her delicate smile, looking at the white seal as if she had wandered into a dream.

Miracle closed his eyes and drew in toward her, allowing her soft and tiny fingers to caress him. What was happening? He thought while his sparkling dark eyes rolled up into his head. How could he feel so at peace with such a strange and foreign creature? She surely was but a dream of sorts. He must be deep in sleep, and when he woke, she would be gone. However, when he opened his eyes, he could see that the fascinating and strange man-beast remained, her hands still softly running themselves over his snow-white cheeks.

"How beautiful you are," Emma spoke, never noticing that her skin was once more warm and pink, her hair dry and flowing, her eyes filled with the same blue sparkles as before, or that she was once again restored with an even greater vibrancy.

Slanting his head, Miracle stared back at the girl with the same exciting wonder. "You can speak to me, and I am able to speak back and understand. Now I know I must be dreaming."

Emma merely smiled, tickling the white fur beneath his chin.

"Who are you?" he asked in an ever-so-small voice.

Emma took in a soft breath, her hands remaining about the seal's radiant features. *"Hmmm?"* she purred as if in a faraway trance.

"Why are you here?"

"Oh," Emma answered as if waking from a dream. "I am Emma. I have come to save you,"

Miracle continued basking in the warmth of her caress, dreamily repeating, "Save me?"

"Yes," she whispered back, reaching down toward the purple stone that had spared her life, holding it gently in her hand, the seal surprisingly not pulling away from her.

"Why?" he asked, sounding as if he was in a misty fairy-tale daydream of his own.

"I have come to bring you news of your mother," she softly told.

With a sudden jolt, Miracle's eyes flashed open, the sacred tear sliding out of Emma's hand. "My mother?" he dared repeat.

Emma never gave up her smile. "Yes," she said. "She is alive."

An appearance of shock and sudden panic fell across Miracle's face. He stared at the girl and tried to speak and found that he could not. Emma reached out again to him. This time Miracle did pull away, staring at her with black staggering eyes of unyielding perplexity and piercing uncertainty. "It's all right," she promised, drawing closer to him. Placing her arms around him, she embraced the white seal. To his unbelievable dismay, Miracle stood motionless inside the warmth of the strange creature's caress. Incredibly finding himself lost within the fold of her arms, he placed his head upon her delicate shoulders and softly began to weep.

FAMILIAR HEARTS

A dream, only a dream it had to be.

It was quiet when she awoke.

Emma opened her eyes, taking in the ultimate whiteness surrounding her. It was almost instantaneous that both she and the white seal awakened. Miracle initiated a slight yawn, and Emma quickly finished it. Miracle smacked his sticky jaws together once or twice and yawned a second time quite contentedly, then smiled, preparing to close his eyes again when he suddenly jolted upward. Emma watched the beautiful white seal become afraid; alarmed, he twitched his head, looking dazed. He was not hallucinating, and it wasn't a dream—she was real! Reassuringly, Emma reached out to him, but Miracle pulled away from her. None of what was happening made any sense, especially if it was not a dream. The man-beast had comforted him as he cried himself to sleep. That in itself was unthinkable! More importantly, she had brought him unbelievable news, words he could scarcely believe, words he believed he had dreamed until now.

He could not dismiss her away she and her unparalleled smile, with eyes that glistened like marvelous sapphires. However, fully awake, all traces of the dreamlike experience having left him he certainly could not overlook the fact that she was still *a man-beast!*

"Good morning," Emma said, stretching her arms, careful not to brush against the white seal so as not to frighten him further. "Sleep well?"

"This can't be happening! You're just an illusion; I'm not really awake yet. I must still be sleeping!"

"If you are, then which one of us is awake and which one of us is still dreaming?" Emma asked in a tiny sweet voice.

Miracle corked his head into his shoulders, looking at her as though she was a ghost. "No no no! This cannot be happening! I was sure you were just a dream! A dream, I tell you! What's happening? I know if I close my eyes really hard, you'll vanish! You are just another nightmare, nothing more!" Smacking his snout several times with his front flippers, he tried to wake from his apparent delusion. Despite his attempt, when the seal reopened his eyes, Emma was still there, merely smiling at him. "Gosh . . . you *are* real, aren't you?" he whispered.

Emma gracefully nodded.

Miracle gulped down more apprehensive thoughts and then looked at Emma with eyes that spoke of fear and yet wonder. "It all seems so strange now, as if last night was a fantasy. Perhaps it was. Is! Oh gosh, why is it that when I speak you can understand me? This is not the way of things, it just doesn't happen! It cannot happen! And above all, the fact still remains that you are a man-beast! Man is evil—a killer! He destroys all he comes upon. He has murdered my own kind. I have seen his evil ways repeatedly!"

Emma became sad. "Yes, I know, but I do not share his evil. I would not be here if I did. Surely, your heart must tell you that."

Miracle looked deeply into the human girl's eyes. His stare softened as if he was trying to recall something whimsical. "It seems I can almost remember some far-off memory that—" He stopped and looked even deeper into her sparkling blue eyes, daring to wriggle closer, hoping to fuel his recollection. "We have never met before, and yet you are somehow familiar to me. How is this even possible?"

"I know," she said, straightening herself in the snow, pulling at her nightdress, trying not to disturb the air that caressed her. "I have seen you many times before, you know."

"You have, but where?"

"In my dreams," Emma recalled happily, reaching out toward the white seal yet once again, gently touching the sparkling purple stone. Surprisingly, the white seal did not pull himself away this time. He could only stare at her, wondering while she looked into his extraordinary eyes, watching her own reflection in his gaze, still smiling, holding on to the sacred tear. "This has brought you happiness and has brought you sadness, and it has brought us together," she said in a dreamy whisper.

Miracle's eyes sparkled, then suddenly closed, experiencing the same tingles that remained whirling inside the warmest parts of Emma's heart. It made him shudder. "You make me dizzy," the seal confessed, his eyes still closed. "How can I begin to understand what is happening to me?"

"You are no longer afraid of me, are you?" Emma asked.

"I'm not sure," the white seal admitted, opening his eyes, settling them quietly before the young human.

"She waits for you inside a ship, your mother. Her heart breaks, fearing she may never again see you."

Miracle stiffened and looked at the girl with a concentrated stare of an unyielding suspect.

"Arayna endures the evil of Decara and remains captured within the darkness of the *Tiamat*."

"You know my mother's name?

"It's a beautiful name, isn't it? It's as beautiful as she."

A single tear slid underneath the bridge of Miracle's snout, dropping off, splashing against the stone. "Then it is true. She is alive!"

Emma nodded.

"How do you know such things? Please, you must tell me, man-beast!"

A sad and lonely look crossed over Emma's face. Outstretching her thin arm, she wiped the tears away that brimmed just above his snout. "I too was held captive upon that wretched ship because like your mama, my brother is also a prisoner there, along with other seals. They all so desperately need our help."

"Other seals?"

"Yes, and I believe the sacred tear that you wear will guide us so that we may help them," she said, snatching the purple stone in her hand. "It has already saved my life and it has protected you, and it is what Decara wants more than anything!"

"I don't understand. If it will help my mother, then I will give it up!" Miracle hurriedly decided.

"No!" Emma said with a heavy hand pressing the stone deep into the seal's white fur. "You must never remove it, or you will die!"

"I already know this, man-beast, but if it will help my mother and the others—"

"You will only help them by wearing the tear next to your heart, for that is where the true powers lie."

"Then Mum was right, all along!"

"Who?"

Miracle shook his head. "Never mind. Please tell me, won't you—who or what is this . . . Decara creature?"

"She is pure evil all wrapped up into one big ugly nightmare, far worse than any man-beast you can ever imagine," she answered, not quite sure which way her words would take her next. "She has great powers of darkness, and she uses them to destroy and corrupt. Still, her powers pale greatly to the tear you wear. That's why she wants it so badly."

Miracle shivered when he looked down at the purple stone. "*The tear . . .*," he uttered, sounding afraid again.

"Yes, and she will stop at nothing to get it! The only way that the tear can be removed and keep its power is for her to destroy you while you still wear it. She means to kill you."

The white seal's eyes sprang open. "Kill me, whatever for?"

Emma took a deep breath and drew closer to the pondering creature. "If she destroys you while you wear the tear, whatever little innocence remains in this world will also be destroyed . . . forever!"

"You best start at the beginning," the white seal implored, shaking his head with another shudder.

"It's the gift of innocence. We both have it, and from what I understand, it is most powerful. It is almost as powerful as love itself," Emma explained, directly arranging her legs comfortably beneath the oversized nightdress gushing around her, pinching on her toes as she began to tell the seal all she knew.

The next hour in the ice castle was filled with much, for Emma told him all about Decara and how the evil woman had snatched both her and her brother away and had kept them prisoners on the dark vessel. She reminded him about the other seals trapped there now and how Decara stole their tears, turning them into diamonds. She spoke of the treasure and the ghouls that protected it. She spoke of the horrid Oreguss and how he had hurt her brother, and how the purple angels came to help by showing her Miracle's vision. She told him all about the evil three-headed serpent and all she had witnessed inside Decara's chamber room and how she had seen incredible things inside the floating ball that the serpent swam in, allowing her to come to Sealssong. She reiterated about the special gift that she was born with and that Decara was regretfully her kin. The white seal sat there, spellbound by the entire duration of Emma's discourse, not knowing what to make out of it, but not daring to move or utter a sound. Finally, Emma stopped talking long enough to catch her breath. "I'm making myself all queasylike," she said, still pinching her toes, adjusting her legs that had fallen asleep meanwhile.

Miracle thought a long time before speaking. "How did you know how to find me?"

"I didn't. It just happened."

"It just happened?"

"Yes, it was right after the men had killed the seals."

"You brought man here?"

"No, of course not, I told you, I am nothing like him! The serpent permitted me to come through some kind of portal. I suddenly found myself in the middle of a seal slaughter. It was so horrible!" Emma fought the tears. "I somehow managed to crawl through the snow so that I could protect a small pup that the evil men were about to skin."

Miracle could not help but to shudder again.

Emma continued. "Then something strange happened. Suddenly, there were mountains of snow crashing down around me from everywhere. It was as if the entire planet was crumbling apart. I remember falling and then suddenly hitting the ice. I remember being in so much pain, the snow burning me as if I was on fire. It was then I heard a cry. I knew that I was dying, but I somehow found the strength to crawl into this cave, hoping to find the baby seal here but found you instead."

Miracle crunched up his snout with more confusion. "But how could you dare come to Sealssong with no protection? You must admit that you do not possess any fur, and what you have in its place is hardly suitable. How could you think to survive here? It's just too cold!"

"Oh that," grumbled Emma, rolling up her eyes in disgust. "The three-headed serpent gave me a bogus trinket that was supposed to protect me from the cold, something I will share with you at a different time. Of course, it was a trick, and soon I was at the mercy of the elements. In just a short while, I knew that I did not have long to live." Suddenly, she stopped once more, taking hold of the tear around Miracle's neck. "Thank goodness for this." She sighed.

"I think I'm going to be sick," the white seal moaned.

"Oh, you mustn't . . . You must be strong, you are a very special seal, you know."

"No, I'm not. It's the tear that is special. I am just a misfit, nothing more."

"But that's simply isn't true."

"Your words continue to alarm me. I am still not sure what you are about, man-beast. Perhaps you can tell me how to find my mother and then you should leave Sealssong. Man cannot, and should not, speak with understanding words to my kind. It does not happen. It cannot happen!"

"But it is happening!" Emma bluntly reminded.

"No! I would be a fool ever to believe that man possibly could be trusted. Your kind knows nothing of truth!"

"But I keep telling you, I am not like them!"

"No!"

Emma's face flushed with sudden defeat and worry. "Please, you must listen!"

"You frightened me, man-creature," the white seal barked. "There has been too much blood that has passed between our worlds. I must not forget! *I cannot forget!* I would not know how!"

"I'm not asking you to forget. I am asking you to trust me!" Emma unintentionally shouted.

The white seal wriggled away from her, startled. "Trust you? Perhaps it is time you left, man-beast."

"But you just have to listen to me!"

Suddenly, both Emma and Miracle froze, both listening to a peculiar scratching noise spark around the entire frame of the ice castle. From somewhere out beyond the doorway, a strange shadow began to splatter its creeping silhouette against the icy walls of the deep blue structure casting its elongated shape over both of their cemented faces. They watched with pounding hearts, unable to move or utter a sound as the shadow grew larger and larger, looking as if it had crawled out from the blackest regions of the sea, only to devour them with one swift gulp. A sudden whimper sounded, then a small squeal surfaced right before the owner of the mysterious shadow revealed itself in the doorway. It was the dwarfed pup that Emma had saved, his shadow exaggerated further by the reflected light of the rays of the sun.

"It's you!" Emma exclaimed, getting up from her crouched position, hurrying over toward the snowy white infant with both arms outstretched. Not allowing the pup even to consider a retreat, she had already secured both hands firmly beneath its front flippers and proceeded to pull it up toward her chest, curtly sinking back to the frozen floor. Incessantly petting the pup, she kissed its head repeatedly. "I thought I'd lost you, but you are alive! I'm so glad!" she cried, allowing her tears to wash against the newborn's soft fur. "Where have you been hiding, you beautiful snowball of fur?"

Miracle stood silently watching the man-creature while she continued to squeeze and love up the baby harp. He studied her for a long time before he even considered drawing closer. Then as if he had suddenly recognized something so familiar, he gave her an interminable gaze before turning himself and wriggling toward the tiny pup wrapped securely in her arms. Emma was not even aware of Miracle's approach, for her eyes remained closed while she held the baby seal's head next to her heart, softly stroking it. "I was so afraid, little one, but just to see your dear little face . . . Oh, my precious one, how happy I am to see you again!" she said, finishing up her kisses. Miracle tipped his head back and forth, lowering his muzzle, finding his nose nestling near the top of the baby seal. He sniffed a few times and then sniffed again. Instinctively, the pup raised its head and licked Miracle directly on the nose. Miracle pulled away with a queer look on his snout.

"Don't be afraid," Emma teased. "He won't bite."

Surprisingly, a curious smile found its way over to Miracle. "He is awful small, isn't he?" he said in a light voice.

"Yes, thank goodness, I could have never carried him otherwise," Emma told, grabbing for a better grip, holding the pup up higher, kissing it on the head again.

"You have saved him from the savagery of man?"

Emma stopped kissing the pup's head and looked directly into the eyes of the majestic seal before her, gently nodding. "As I have come to do the same for you," she said with all the sweetness of sincerity imagined.

Miracle listened to the pup whimper a few moments before saying, "You hold him as if you love him, just like his mama would love him."

Emma happily nodded.

"What you said before . . . is it really true?"

"All I have said is true."

"Have you really seen her?"

Emma nodded once more. "I have."

"And you can take me to her?"

"Yes, soon the *Tiamat* will come to the shores of Sealssong. Then I will see that you and your mother shall be together again."

"You will do that for me?"

"Of course," she answered without the slightest hesitation.

"And it is not a trick?"

Emma kept right on smiling and shook her head.

Miracle closed his eyes and solemnly said, "The whale told me that I must listen to my heart, not my mind, and that is what I will do." Opening his eyes, he solemnly gazed upon Emma. "There was something very different about you from the moment that I first saw you . . . something my heart found difficult to dismiss. You continue to confuse me, man-creature, and yet I believe you. I believe you."

Reaching out to the tear-collared mammal, Emma embraced both him and the infant pup simultaneously. There was a moment of silence that seemed to go on forever, then, Miracle spoke. "How long will it be until I can see her again?"

Emma released her grip and looked at the seal while still cuddling the pup within her arms. "I'm not sure. I overheard the serpent mentioning something about a time warp, so there is no real way of knowing."

"What does this mean . . . time warp?"

Emma moistened her pink lips with her tongue and then sighed and shrugged her shoulders. "I think it has to do with changing time itself."

"Strange man-creature, you make it so very hard for me to understand."

"I'm sorry," she sympathized. "It confuses me as well, but know this—in the deepest part of my heart, I know that you will see her again, I promise."

The baby seal began to whimper then cry as Emma stroked his soft head. "Poor wee little one, he is hungry."

"Well, I'm afraid I won't be able to help in that department," Miracle retorted.

Dismissing his statement with a shrug and a smirk, Emma lifted the pup nearer to her heart, continuing to pat his backside with a gently reassuring beat. "We'll have to think about that one, won't we?"

"Well, it might be a problem," Miracle added.

Emma scrunched up her face and thought some more. "It doesn't have to be, especially since the answer is right under your nose, or if you'll pardon, your snout," she explained while reaching

out toward Miracle, taking the wondrous tear from around his neck
in her hand. Pulling Miracle's head down toward the baby seal, she
began to rub the stone in a circular motion across the pup's furry
belly. Instantly, the stone began to glow with a most spectacular
purple blaze and then went out. Immediately, the pup's cries turned
to a contented purr. He licked Emma's face and softly nestled into
her further and then quickly fell fast asleep.

"There," Emma said with a full smile across her delicate lips. "All
better."

Miracle lowered his head and looked at the stone, his dark eyes
filling with more wonder. "How is it that you know so much?"

"I wish I knew more, but I believe the tear will see us through
many hardships for its magic is most powerful."

"But you make it do things I cannot."

"You have already done amazing things with the tear and will
continue to do so. I know because it has changed you, colored you
with the same beautiful glow of the purple angels."

Miracle carefully inspected the purple tips coloring his fur before
returning his gaze back to Emma's tender features, his large seal
eyes scanning her over and over again until she blurred into a soft
and filmy image, her sapphire eyes never losing their sharp intrinsic
gleam. "You are most fascinating, man-creature, most fascinating,
indeed."

"Emma."

"What?"

"My name is Emma."

"Oh," said the white seal. "—Miracle."

"Hmm?"

"Miracle, that's me."

Emma became enchanted. *"Miracle,* what a perfectly lovely name!
How it does fit you!" With the baby seal fast asleep in her arms,
Emma amiably bowed to the white seal wearing the purple stone. "It
is an honor, Miracle."

"Do you have a mother?"

A sad, yet contented misty look seemed to swirl around Emma's
face. "Yes, but she is in heaven," she said, raising her eyes up toward
the crest of the ice castle.

"Will she ever come back from this place called heaven?"

"No, but someday I will join her there."

Miracle shook his head and snorted. "Oh yes yes, you are most
strange, man-creature." Cocking his head sideways, he thought and

then thought some more. "Perhaps that is where Crumpels and Poo-Coo have wandered off to, do you suppose?"

"Brumpels and Who-Koo?"

"The walrus and her son, they must have smelled the flesh of man upon the ice of Sealssong. They are able to do that, you know. They must have gone to warn the others! They have been gone for such a long time now. Do you suppose they have gotten lost in this . . . heaven?"

Emma shook her head slowly, retaining her dainty smile. "I sure hope not. You can only get to heaven after you die."

"DIE! You don't suppose that they—"

"Now don't panic. I will help you look for them if you wish."

Miracle was moved by her direct unselfish nature. "I guess that will be all right."

"Okay then," she said, placing the tiny harp against the snowy floor of the ice castle. "He'll sleep most of the day, I'm sure."

"May I ask you something first before we go?"

Emma nodded, getting up, pulling on her long dress, adjusting herself as she listened.

"Have you always been able to speak to nonhumans?"

She raised her head slightly and drifted off into a calm and dreamy contemplation. "Yes, as far back as I can remember." Then quickly bringing herself back to the moment she said, "Well, we best be on our way. I am sure you are anxious to find Dumply and Moo-Coo."

"It's Crumpels and Poo-Coo," the seal corrected.

"Sorry," Emma offered in a small voice. "Are you ready?"

"Yes."

"Then let's go!" she said, heading for the opening of the ice castle.

"Wait!" Miracle called after her.

Turning, Emma waited for the seal to approach her. "Hadn't you best touch the tear again before going outside? I'd feel a lot better if you did."

"Of course, how silly of me," Emma answered, touching the stone once more. She felt it warm in her hand. Soon her entire body began to tingle with a delightfully cozy warm feeling as she took her first step out into the blazing sunlight and into the wintry wonderland of uncertainty. A blast of wind immediately assaulted her, but its biting grip passed right through her for her body remained renewed from the warmth of the stone. Even her naked feet remained wrapped inside a secure and snugly blanket of invisible warmth. The freezing breeze actually felt good against her delicate pink skin, as did the sun. In seconds, Miracle was at her side. Taking the initiative, he jerked his head to the left, indicating for Emma to follow him. Without question, she did.

The incredible avalanche had rearranged and had changed much of Sealssong's landscaping, turning its once familiar surface into a strange and indecisive place. Every common signpost that the white seal previously knew had been erased; yet instinctively, he wriggled onward, barking out the names of Crumpels and Poo-Coo, Emma following close behind him, unable to find the breathtaking surroundings resistible. Within their unequaled perpetuity of shining wonders, she surrendered herself. Never could she have imagined such a snow-white fantasy of billowing boundlessness. The sun seemed to dance over them, sending down thousands of exalted streamers of reflected wisps of dazzling lights as they made their way through the snow. Miracle maintained his position as the leader, calling out to the walruses while Emma followed closely behind him, still entranced by all the bedazzling glitter before her, enraptured by the gentle touch of the soft breeze against her warm skin. She could not help but smile to herself while experiencing the snow squish through her bare toes. It tickled so.

As the two pursuers flashed toward scaled cliffs of frost and chiseled mountains of glass, Emma watched the white creature before her. Not once did he turn to see if she had managed to keep up with him or if she had somehow lost her way. His quest was great, and she knew then just how important these two other creatures were to him. "I know that there is a floe nearby, a very large and vast floe," Miracle explained. "It may be difficult to find, but I know it is here, somewhere. It is a place Crumpels has visited many times before. We may find the walruses there."

Emma nodded in compliance, jumping over an impromptu block of jagged ice so that she might imitate the scurrying seal's swift maneuvers. Down they glided, over slippery curvatures of sloping pockets of silver blue glaciers, combing off their vibrant layers of wintry snow-white locks, swirling effortlessly down toward the deepest part of its origin. Emma blocked her mouth, feeling as if she were about to squeal in delight, remembering how different this sensation was from the one she encountered upon first entering this strange new world. Miracle hit the bottom first. Emma was right behind him. Instantly, they both shot out into the very center of an enormous ice pond. At first, the glare was almost too much for Emma. However, in a short while, she could adjust to its blinding sparkle. The cliffs that towered high above had already painted themselves over the icy pallet that both seal and man-creature now lay sprawled upon, the mountainous transparent reflections of royal blue covering them both. They shook the snow from themselves, looking straight ahead—straight out toward another magnificent sight of breathtaking illumination. A sparking jolt filled Emma's soul. They had indeed found the ice floe that the seal spoke of—she was certain of it!

Without hesitation, Miracle was off. Swiftly, he cut through the ultramarine transparency of the looming shadows of fantastic blues and grays designed upon the icy floor. Quickly, he wiggled over to the very edge of the floe, hopefully looking out into its seeming endlessness. A soft and delicate drizzle mistily filtered down with a feathery settle of light snow, its twinkles glistening over the two spectators who continued to cast their stare upon the silvery waters before them. "I'll have to search for them," Miracle said while studying the shining waters. "It's all right if you wait here."

"No," Emma answered directly. "I want to come with you." She waited through the lapsing silence.

The white seal looked at her with eyes of sheer wonder. Tilting his furry head, he again looked at her queerly. "How strange you truly are, man-creature."

"Emma, if you please," she reminded.

He smiled at her. It was a sincere smile if he had ever offered one. "All right, Emma, then come you shall." Miracle stuck out his furry white chest, inviting her to touch upon the miraculous tear yet once again. "Don't want to take any chances." Another fascinating and delicious tingle zipped through Emma's hand, spiraling like an out-of-control corkscrew, burrowing itself directly into her heart. Gasping aloud, feeling as if her breath had been momentarily taken from her, she felt the strange sensation to laugh. In fact, she did laugh because the entire experience had suddenly become all too much for her—it was all so wondrous!

Emma watched with careful eyes as the white seal slowly entered the icy waters. With the insatiable inquisitiveness that perpetuated her growing enthrallment over the creature, she felt the water splash warm against her face when Miracle dove into his familiar and graceful element. Another splash hit her as the wriggling bump of a seal forced to pull himself clumsily along the snow and ice, suddenly transformed into a flying shadow, there within the quivers of the silvery liquid space. A few die-hard droplets of water kissed Emma's cheeks, then her lips, turning them warm and moist while the seal's behind occasionally broke the watery surface before her. Sliding her tongue over her mouth, she could taste the tepid sea upon her lips. It was warm, all right, just as warm and delightful as was every transfigured morsel of her entire self. Then looking directly up into the blinding blue firmament, she smiled, closed her eyes, and dove into the ice-ridden waters.

HIS SECRET WORLD

Emma at first felt a little afraid, but she was also feeling exceedingly warm. With both eyes closed, she fumbled blindly within the currents of the water; however, something stronger than fear relentlessly tugged at her, commanding her to open her eyes. Obeying, she instantly saw a most spectacular world crest over her. A scintillating sun sparked high above the dark blue silver sea, painting Emma's skin with the same stunning hue. The sun deliberately invigorated the shimmering water with its majestic potency. Every column of ice found growing before her, surrounding her, adorning her, suddenly burst into multitudes of shining lights like the colors of multicolored stained-glass windows, splashing over the walls of a beautiful and grand cathedral. Great shafts of brilliant sunlight broke through the water from every angle, illuminating the magnificent glaciers, flashing their brilliance throughout the translucence of the sea, furthering the semblance of the floating arena into a churchlike setting of glittering ambiance, humbling Emma to fold her hands together in prayer.

Keeping herself near the white seal, she delighted in watching him cut through the dazzle of the prismatic reflections in glorious motion, stirring up the sea dust around and round. As they frolicked in the flashes of the glimmering waters, she no longer contemplated how warm she was or how she did not require oxygen to remain within this heavenly existence. She was much too preoccupied with the sheer wonder and awesomeness of this incredible universe. In the sun-stream dreaminess of the sea, the motley reflectors of ice deliriously painted rainbows over the two swimmers. Within its brimming colors, they effortlessly flew, both inordinately aware of each other's presence. Reaching out her hand, Emma took hold of Miracle's hindquarters, allowing him to pull her along at his own pace. With a slight turn of his head, he looked back at Emma smilingly. In silent observance, he could see those incredible eyes of hers. It seemed that all the flashing colors radiating from everywhere within the sea had suddenly merged, creating a soft and misty sun bow inside those eyes—eyes that continued to fascinate him. Suddenly, and without reservation, he decided that he would show her his world—a world he alone had come to know.

Making sure that Emma had a firm grip, he began to pull her downward, most confident that she would make the escorted journey. More spectacular flashes of stained-glass imagery cascaded lusciously over them as Miracle slid past the smooth edges of a gigantic glacier, its shooting trunk towering upward, bending into the realm of another rising glacier, both structures arching into the semblance of a magnificent church steeple. Passing through, they merged before sinking deeper and deeper. As they descended, a continual daring ritual followed them, each performing movements that flawlessly complimented each other while diving further into the flashing sea. Down they went, in and out of icy grottos, the rushing cathedral lights slowly relinquishing themselves to the abyss until the light had gone out of the sea. Their enchanting pursuit commenced onward exclusively by perception of touch alone.

At first, this obscure cosmos offered no signposts of any kind, nothing that could be viewed. At best, whatever happened to pass before Emma's eyes merely looked as dark blue shadows made heavy by the oppressing dimness that continued to weigh upon her. Still guided by and holding on to the white seal, Emma did not fear this uncertain universe. It was as if, like the seal, she too was at home in her element and was rejoicing in its wonder. Her heart did not lash with surprise, at least not until the entire sea decided to turn on its reserved string of backup lights. Emma gasped, swallowing in some of the water now showcasing a most magnificent exposition of swirling and twirling lights. She imagined that she had been transported to a magical Christmas world, a place made up of spectacular stars and flashing glimmers. She shook her head against the pressures of the slow-motion universe, amazed at the glory before her. There was a sudden burst of glow, temporarily shorting out Emma's eyes, leaving her blind to its direct glare. Furthermore, it was not until her sight once again returned that this Christmas-like existence really came alive, the phosphorescent lights of the strange inhabitants of the sea graciously receiving her.

These creatures were not like anything she had ever seen. Mysteriously looking jellyfish appeared, some like vibrant stars and others like private galaxies preciously hoarding within its domain all the colors of the universe. Others blinked on and off like fireflies. Many were iridescent, transposing from dark blue to the brightest of reds. Some consisted of starry strips of spiderwebs held together by a glowing transparent substance its quivering insides squirting out and about itself like a radioactive water fountain. Then there were those made up of gooey flowery-shaped things, their colors ranging from metallic green to iridescent yellow, their translucent shoots planted invisibly inside the confines of a floating brain that favored the better part of a giant cauliflower. Cordially they switched on and off their lights, properly submitting their silent hellos, submerged deep within this revealing and the most impressive twilight world.

There were even spiny-shaped things that floated directly up to Emma's eyes, flashing their salutations from somewhere inside their fluctuant foreheads. Some zoomed by, stopping but for a moment, their glowing skins wrapped tightly inside saucerlike creations, looking like alien spacecrafts. They hovered there only long enough to investigate the peculiar visitor's presence. Then as quickly as they appeared, these swift-moving flying creatures once again zoomed off, disappearing into the darkness of the sea, leaving behind a multitude of rainbow bubble trails. Just as the bubbles tickled Emma's nose, so did the shimmying whiskers of additionally weird and foreign spectators, they too looking like bubbles themselves. Some swam while others bowed to her in eternal dance. Others rolled and even split apart, dragging their gooey inserts along until they reglued themselves back together again, each one bursting into a resplendent explosion made up of more spectacular colors bidding their exclusive greetings unto the two curious visitors.

As Emma and Miracle dove deeper, still watching their very own private underwater show, they suddenly became aware of the distinct choral voices of the flashing sea creatures, the streams of starry fallout descending upon them. The voices seemed to honor them, voices who sang to them as if in joyous prayer. These strange sequester's of the sea no longer extended mere greetings; they were acknowledging something far more endearing. Neither one understanding why such regards should come from the seldom, if ever, seen residents of Sealssong, Miracle and Emma, nonetheless, embraced this veneration as sudden wonders filled their hearts. Though they did not know it at the time, the sea, on this most wondrous of moments, had given to the seal and the young girl her anointed blessing.

SILLY SONGS OF LOVE-YA

"Are we almost there!" asked an exasperated Mum while holding the screaming Mulgrew penguin tightly between the smelly folds of her backside. The penguin's high-pitched shrieks muffled themselves against the girth of the mad harpie while she pondered over the heavy fog pouring in and around the whale they sailed upon. How long it had been since they had seen anything solid. The incredible topsy-turvy world they had chanced upon had vanished, and in its place, an endless passage of fog prevailed. However, the memories of their experience inside the strange purple upside-down world kept right on playing steadily inside their heads.

"I'm afraid I still cannot say," answered the intrepid whale. "I regret once again to tell you that we are still most definitely lost within the grip of this dreadful fog."

Mum snorted. "Well, at least we are no longer in that stupid purple mishmash! If I ever see one more bloody drop of purple water, I think I'll puke! We must be going in the right direction though. I mean, seeing that entire codswalloping purple jumble is behind us, we should be on course, don't you agree, love?"

"It's hard to say," Kishk answered. "In as much as I have not been able to hear myself, think with all, that racket coming from Mulgrew! Please!" the whale begged in an exhausted breath. "Before I completely become unhinged, release him!"

"Why should I?" Mum quarreled. "I warned him to stop teasing me, and he chose to ignore me, so this is what he gets, stupid bird!"

"But he will suffocate if you continue this way."

"And once again, your point is?"

"Please, Mum, just like the many other times before, think of it as a personal favor to me, won't you?"

"But he's such an obnoxious, silly-ass lip-lump!"

"Madame, I must tell you that his screeches are prohibiting me from concentrating and if I cannot concentrate I will not be able to maintain our course back to Sealssong."

"Oh, very well," Mum grumbled, rolling up her eyes, scrunching down even harder, breaking wind on the screaming bird beneath her, all the while it pecking viciously at her rump. Becoming bored with the situation, she raised her buttocks and aimed her backhanded flipper bluntly at the bird's scrawny head. Hauling off, she gave the shrieking Mulgrew a whopping big smack, flipping him indignantly up into the foggy air.

"Bug off!" Mum growled, watching the twirling penguin sail upward then quickly drop directly into Kishk's blowhole. Instantly, the whale sneezed and out popped the penguin, screeching and screaming as if it was as mad as Mum. With a wild vengeance, it scurried up toward the deranged seal, intent on doing some serious damage to her—well, as serious as a penguin could possibly inflict on a several-hundred-pound seal. However, as he did this, he suddenly halted straight in his tracks, for his determined strut was intercepted by the great call of the mighty whale.

"Look!" the blue chanter exclaimed. "The fog is retreating! We must be beyond the borders of the Origin of Lights! Sealssong is not far away! I know it! We have found our way back!" Nonetheless, before the seal and the penguin could rejoice in the matter, a sudden and most massive and sinister shape crossed before them, nearly striking them. Having no time to reflect the situation, Kishk dove into the water, only praying that his two passengers would survive the unexpected plunge. In a flash, the whale and his two companions disappeared into the giant spray, collapsing into the swash of the sea.

What happened next truly startled the great blue whale. For as the abrasive spray of the sea spat at him from every side, he could still see that what he had nearly collided with had missed him within only a few short feet. It was nothing he could have ever predicted, for it was not of the sea, but of man! Slicing the waves, the whale's massive structure cut through the water, engaging every morsel of his muscular brawn to aid him away and beyond from this sudden monstrosity.

The thing at first seemed black and foreboding and remained that way. If it was not for its numerous beacons of ghostly yellow lights peering out from crevasses sketched like eyes inside its massive and dark structure, Kishk would have surely hit it. Knowing of man and his floating machines, he recognized the near-fatal obstruction referred to as a ship, only this ship had a name, and he now knew it—this tyrant was called the *Tiamat*.

The vessel bounced against the waves like a toy, looking as though it would flip over onto its side, only to fill up with the pounding flow of the disapproving sea. However, instead, it somehow maintained its unstable symmetry, nose-diving directly into the gushing waters, pivoting aimlessly against the surging waves, somehow managing to sustain its counterbalance with the help of some dark, unseen advantage.

The whale swerved sideways, crashing savagely against the swell of the tenacious hurdles of building waves, barely dodging the ship as it continued to slide directly into his path. With all the skill instilled in him since birth, Kishk fought to stay out of the dark thing's way. Incessantly, he pushed against the obstructing current of the waves and the *Tiamat*'s powerful pull, only to find himself once more on a collision course with the stern of the malevolent vessel. How he managed it he knew not, but somehow, the mighty whale missed the corner of the speeding thing by only a mere few inches. Down he came with a tremendous crash, instantly blinded by the insurmountable wash of the turbulent waters pulling back his massive head, preparing to maintain his balance inside the rocking waters beneath him. As the sea prepared to settle down, Kishk waited for the spray to clear while swinging his magnificent head about, tormented by the notion of having another confrontation with the treacherous *Tiamat*.

Nevertheless, as the mist began to compose itself, the whale could see that the dreaded thing was several hundred feet in front of him, already making its way slowly toward a multitude of vapors hanging low on the distant horizon. The gloomy mist seemed to come out of nowhere, just sitting there upon the open waters just waiting for the evil vessel as if to swallow it up, shielding it against further scrutiny. In just a few short moments, the despicable thing vanished, and the whale was finally able to expel a well-deserved sigh of relief. Closing his eyes, the mighty Kishk drifted aimlessly inside the watery arms of the sea, bobbing choppily against the current, thinking to himself that he was safe and that he had indeed defeated man and his distasteful floating annoyance. However, in doing so, had he also defeated the purpose of safeguarding the two that sat upon him? Kishk's violet eyes flashed open, and he quickly began calling out to them. "Mulgrew, Mum, are you all right?" He waited and listened, but there came no answer.

Once again, the whale's eyes frantically twisted and turned while he moved his head back and forth. Again, he called out to them, and this time he heard a reply, a most distinctive but skimble-skamble reply. *"Love to love my love when my love—love's my love!"* the Mad Mum seal sang from the center of the whale's head. There she sat contentedly, holding on to the side of the mammal's blowhole, her bonnet sliding halfway down the side of her head, the terrified penguin stuck tight next to her, once more wedged against her girth.

Pushing away from the mad beast, Mulgrew growled incessantly. Inasmuch as the penguin wished to peck the mad seal's eyes out or begin gnawing on her provoking and meddlesome tongue, she did prevent him from being hurled overboard, not that it was ever her intention. Still, for this, he would make concessions, but he would not enjoy himself while doing it—not one bit! He still despised her, and nothing would ever change that! Nothing!

Kishk felt Mum flop away from his whale nostril while Mulgrew chose to remain silent, not knowing how he would ever be able to control his abhorrence toward the crazy seal's insane gibberish, clapping her flippers together, singing silly songs of Love-ya! Along with other chitter-chatter the bird could not make heads or tails of. Not being able to listen any longer, he scooted madly from her, shrieking every inch of the way.

Comically, Mum decided it would be fun to roll herself toward the edge of the whale. When finally reaching a satisfactory spot, she popped up and looked out into the partially clearing sky that kissed the open sea before her. "Shouldn't be too much longer now," she said.

This time, Mulgrew spoke up. "What was that nasty thing we almost hit?"

"I believe it to be that evil ship that the Kellis warned us about," the whale answered with a worried underscore carrying his words.

Mum rolled her eyes in disgust. "Of course, it was of man—it stunk of his corruption!"

The penguin who was still shaking himself clean added, "Well, good riddance to rotten rubbish, wouldn't want to see that thing again!"

"But we will see it again most definitely," Kishk explained, a strange realization flooding over him tenfold stronger than the waves that had just washed over him. "And if I'm not mistaken . . . very soon."

"Well," Mum added. "Just get us to Sealssong first, and in one piece if you please."

"Yes, my rambunctious harpie, that I will do," promised the exhausted whale. "We must return and tell the white seal all that we have learned."

"Yes, oh yes!" Mum giggled, clapping her flippers together in feverish excitement. "A little bit of sunshine that one will surely be a-needing, I'm sure."

Mulgrew, who was steadily listening but still expelling the wetness from his person, suddenly spoke up once more. "How are we ever to find the blasted nursery? We don't even know where we are!"

"Oh, do bug off, birdie!" Mum spit. "The whale will find the way!"

All at once, as before, the mighty blue chanter began to sing out his chant, casting its reverberation into the sea, listening for a returned signal that would in some way confirm his course. On and on his whale song continued while cutting through the moving waters, no longer certain if his intonation was an SOS or just a way one whistles to oneself, rendering fear away in a feeble attempt when one is anything but valiant. Still, the courageous and steadfast whale sailed forth with both Mum and the penguin sitting at the bow of his enormous head pushing onward, determined to find the icy shores of Sealssong and once again reunite with the extraordinary white seal waiting for him.

WE MUSTN'T FORGET
ABOUT THE WALRUSES

An arctic tern sailed closely above the white seal and Emma just as they broke through the surface of the shimmering water. The unsuspecting gull continued to glide effortlessly, mere inches away from them, the frigid spray of the sea breaching around its slender body, thoroughly washing over its narrow wings, bill, and black cap. Nevertheless, it did not seem to mind the impulsive washing. In fact, the gliding gull seemed to be fascinated by the two swimming creations, continuing to follow them closely, finding itself captivated by their aquatic ballet, unsure if it were made up of one or two creatures. It was the way both seal and human merged into each other, nearly becoming part of the watery background that they shadowed against that seemed to fill the gull with a heavier dose of curiosity. Trying to keep up with the seal and its strange counterpart, the gull found itself moving to the same haunting dance as they. In a delirious trance, the bird continued sailing next to them, disappearing into the exhilarating rushes of air and sporadic douses of icy sprays now consuming it. Gliding effortlessly, it listened to both seal and girl who remained engaged in the most delightful bursts of giggles, not like anything it had ever encountered before.

With another whoosh into the sea, both seal and girl disappeared, and when the gull watched them resurface, it lowered its place in the sky, enthusiastically rejoining them in a flying rush. Experiencing the vibrations of both creatures swimming next to him, the gull felt their rushing bodies touch upon the soft tips of its wingspread. Holding to its flight, it continued to watch Miracle and Emma swirl around inside the waves. Over and over they turned, entwining with each other until they melted and became one. It sounded as if they were singing to each other in such a way that even the gull could understand. Suddenly, more gulls came down from the heavens, the brilliant sun bathing everyone in endless streaks of sparkle, turning them and the sea into a silvery luminous misty marvel.

Temporarily breaking away from her, Miracle circled Emma in playful flight, swooping beneath her several times before he jumped high into the sky, bringing with him all the watery stars of the sea, momentarily blinding off the sun as his body kissed the air. Then in one sudden plunge, he dove into the water, descending far beneath Emma, covering her with more of the liquid stars. Up he swam directly beneath Emma, and pushing up his seal snout, he quickly touched upon the bottoms of Emma's delicate feet. Supporting her as she stood fully upright, her tiny feet flush against his whiskered snout, the white seal rushed upward once again, breaking through the sparkling surface of the sea, balancing Emma on his nose all the way up into the sky so that she too could kiss the sun.

The gulls made way for the two soaring creatures sailing upon the flowing winds that carried them along, each bird trilling out to the strange duo in their native tongues. Enthralled, Emma smiled. Happily, she delighted again being able to understand the birds, their song clear as the sapphire sky that she brushed against. They were singing out such beautiful greetings as she swam in their warbling chorus. However, it was not long before she and Miracle sank back into the foaming waters, disappearing, the definitive sea bubbles following them. Emma laughed and grabbed onto the velvety seal touching against her, laughing again in sheer wonder, holding on, feeling like she had never felt before such happiness, such bliss. It was as if she had magically stepped into one of her favorite fairy tales and she was bewitched for all time. She had not a care in the world. There was only the silvery sea, the glittering bursts of the sea stars surrounding her, the harmonious choir of gulls, the ever-sweet smell of the rushing breeze, the brilliant sapphire sky, the wizardry of the sun, but most of all, and best of all, the white seal that now danced next to her inside the floating ballroom in the sea.

Every move the seal made appeared to be spectacular. Why, even Miracle felt invincible! He, like the human, never felt so alive and liberated, so much so that it was all he could do but to hold back the building squeal of seal laughter oozing from every pore of his being. With his glowing purple stone radiating just like the fireball in the sky, he pulled Emma along in playful bliss, the freezing waters turning lukewarm each time it touched upon her skin. And as the bubbling bedazzle exploded around them, from the very heart of the sea, there appeared dozens of blue-colored dolphins. They quickly broke through the water, crisscrossing over the two frolicking companions, splashing about them, wanting to get in on the fun. It only took a moment. Instantaneously, the multitude of leaping and spattering dolphins, like the gulls, fixed themselves to the happy scene, becoming a part of all the wonder. The dolphins danced about them, swimming right along with them. Once more, Emma could clearly hear them. They, too, sang to her! How incredible it all was. She felt like laughing again, and she would have done just that if it were not for the way Miracle suddenly looked at her while cutting through the eurhythmic waters. His eyes, although still filled with the song of the performing sea, now held an underscore of something more serious, something that would take them back to matters at hand. Emma knew what he would say before he did, but she listened politely, almost repeating the words back to him in silent duplication.

"The walruses—" the seal, said, still retaining a sliver of laughter in his voice, "—we mustn't forget about the walruses."

The dolphins, offering their unison display of aquatic theatrics, dove in and around the seal and human, vibrating their heads in jovial friendliness, yet acknowledging the urgency emanating from the curious white seal. For like all creatures of the sea, they too were capable of a guarded sensitivity for one another—unlike the beast called man, who could not see beyond his own involvement—the dolphins, having perfected this sacred faculty long before most readily decided to help the seal and human across the waters over toward the floes. The porpoises began to squeak and click to one another, shaking their heads, motioning at the two strange and fascinating creatures to follow them. In single file, they began to formulate a choreographed arrowhead of each other. In a perpetual porpoise pyramid, the escorting dolphins splashed across the water in a stellar fugue that sang its way across the sea, ushering both seal and human back to where the floes grew vastly. To where the floes, if perhaps allowing, would lead them to the place where wandering lost walruses grew tired just waiting to be found again.

FADING GLOW

Many days passed by for the seal and girl, and still there was no sign of Crumpels or Poo-Coo. Through countless passages of floes, they searched with unceasing persistence. Still, no hopeful evidence presented itself that they might come upon the missing walruses.

Miracle led the way, wriggling on top of many stable as well as unstable stockades of ice losing himself to the uncertain waters, his weight breaking through the crust, plunging downward as the frigid waters pillaged the names of his lost friends from his lips. Emma was always close by, keeping one eye on her new companion and the other on what she hoped she would recognize as what the seal referred to as Crumpels and Poo-Coo. Although the miraculous tear still glowed about the seal's neck, upholding its protection over the two seeking explorers, a distinct and overwhelming desire to seek shelter, food, and sleep had most certainly come over the seal and the girl. A steady wind that had followed them suddenly turned malevolently. Its southerly blow was abruptly thrust back by a most obstinate and powerful northern blast, knocking Emma off her feet with one quick sweep. Miracle watched her collapse into the surrounding icy waters, sinking rapidly, unable to stop her as the wind pounded against him. It was then the white seal noticed the stone that lay near his heart was beginning to dim, and with it, more urgency of exhaustion and weariness overcame them.

Diving into the water, Miracle swiftly swam to Emma, nudging her with his head, allowing her to take hold of him. In a moment, the seal and the girl broke the water's surface and were once more at the mercy of the whipping winds. Immediately, Miracle watched the blush in Emma's cheeks dim, imitating the stone he carried. She tried to smile but only halfway made the effort, suddenly too tired to complete her feeble attempt. Emma tried to speak, but the now deafening winds overpowered her words, but words were not needed. Miracle knew what had to be done. They were going back to the ice castle. They would rest, eat what he brought them from the sea, and in the morning, they would once again resume their search. The white seal made a motion indicating that Emma take hold of him once more. Without hesitation, she scooped her arms around the seal's neck and rested her head against his furry back, the fading glow of the tear still managing to keep her from freezing, but not able to spare her from the incredible weakness possessing her. She would have to fight not to fall asleep while the white seal made his way back toward the place where he had first discovered her.

Dusk had come, and the wind had momentarily let up when Miracle reached the halfway mark that would soon bring them to familiar grounds. Still contentedly resting her head against the seal, Emma looked up into the darkening skies. Noticing the wisps of purple clouds painted ever so slightly below the deep royal blue heavens that had just begun to turn on their twinkling night lights, she felt safe and profoundly protected pressed near the wondrous white seal, the passing waters holding them together in silent flight. They would reach the island soon, and what they would find would not have tusks and have been once lost. No, for what was waiting for them was something neither one could have ever expected.

Man was back. More hunters had returned to Sealssong.

WATCHERS

The oil and fur of seals were many sought-after articles, and this in human terms meant money—and considerable amounts if enough seals were killed. It was for this purpose that two particular sealing ships had invaded dangerously near the sacred ice gardens of Sealssong. For first and foremost, the hunters would have to locate the seals' lair. This particular rookery in its entire icy splendor offered just such an undertaking. Whether by mere chance or carefully calculated strategy, the seal hunters were about to port near its icy shore, each sealer filled with a throbbing excitement inspired by his much anticipated find. Perhaps a part of the former expedition of seal hunters who recently came ironically meeting their own death instead due to mysterious and unexpected avalanches, these obstinate sealing ships slipped through the crunchy waters with uncanny and unsettling quietness like a stalking thief in the night; only this peculator was far more menacing. To every harp seal, he was the messenger of death.

Coincidental or mere deviltry of fate, one hundred and seven pregnant harp seals had recently come to the ice garden. The untiring mothers, summoned to its icy borders, came to the dazzling nursery, as if in a unified trance, the unyielding arctic winds following closely behind, always pushing them onward. Traveling across hundreds upon hundreds of aqueous miles, each significant mother relentlessly swam toward the nursery as if it were a remote candle in the darkness, its light calling out from the storm, promising shelter and rest. Placidly it called to the many that ventured near it, opening its portals to its chosen and gallant gathering. Upon reaching its glassy stairway, when once finding a sturdy hold upon the ice, the sizable and expectant mothers hoisted themselves out of the sea, one by one exhaustively sliding onto what they believed to be a haven for themselves and the unborn precious ones they carried inside. Shaking the sea from their saturated coat, the mothers in silent procession wriggled up laboriously through countless passages of ice floes, dropping in and out of sight, crossing over segregated pools of slush. With one thought probing their burning minds, the expecting harps sought out their own niche within the shining grounds of Sealssong. With one desire, they rumbled upon the ice garden like lethargic dinosaurs most eager to rest their weary ponderousness down upon the fantastic crystal cradle that would soon rock to sleep the tiny miracles living inside each of them.

Within the moments that took the easterly wind to sweep up and merge with the westerly wind in such an embrace that would remain for some time, the one hundred and seven mother seals had finally settled down. Each one, although somewhat crowded near the next, found comfort in each other's similar circumstance, blissfully finding that one special spot of ice that would bear witness to a truly sacred birth.

In almost immediate slumber, the exhausted seals closed their weighty eyelids, temporarily removed from their exclusive reality. They no longer were aware of their calling mates somewhere out in the already fog-enshrouded regions of the endless sea, also remaining clueless to the two sealing ships hiding in the packed shrouds of ghostly fog. Its gravelike veil more than adequately concealed the hunter's ominous presence, even from the unsuspecting nursery. However, as the sealing vessels moved through fog-infested waters, a sudden stern wind came from the southwest, coldly dismissing their once ghostly bodyguard.

As the iridescent fog began to lift, the sealing ships, both led by their own designated watcher, a master watch and a veteran sealer began to signal to each other from their vessels. The buckling floes retaliated against their presence; still, the determined vessels approached in silent procession, each watcher ever mindful of what was at hand, each smelling the sheer essence of harp hides mixed in the air itself. A stirring shot of adrenaline lined each man's veins as they stood frozen inside the dark shadows, each man looking out toward the gathering of pregnant harpies. How lucky they were,

the men believed, for they would be able to set across the floes on
foot without the ships splintering against the solid ice. These floes,
unlike so many others, seemed to offer no real danger to their vessel,
enabling them to go ashore without too much difficulty.

This burly bundle of he-men was the toughest of the tough. Half
starved and freezing, having already managed to survive the bitter
and nearly impossible of elements, these brutes relinquished any
previous anxiousness about this hunt, relieved in knowing that this
particular slaughter was fortunately not going to be as rough as they
first believed. The crucial task was always maintaining the ship from
becoming caught up in uncertain and dangerous ice floes so often
responsible for destroying the sealing ships, leaving the men to starve
or freeze to death; not even the staunchest of swilers could defeat
this fate. Nevertheless, this would not be the case, for the winds of
fortune were indeed blowing upon their backs.

The watchers continued to watch; their narrowly slit eyes
fixed directly upon the dark blue stretch of the nursery. Although
the visibility was now thick with semihalf nightfall, the, watchers
continued to survey the pack of seals only several hundred yards
ahead. The harps seemed to form a perfect circle all wrapped up
together, holding to an element of make-believe; but they were real,
this the men was certain—they could still smell them.

*   *   *

In the crow's nest on top of one of the sealing vessels, one of the
men, a tall man, large and packed full of muscle, glared out quietly
into the night. He could see that some of the mothers were in the
process of giving birth while others already had their newborn pups
by their side. He would wait until the time was right before entering
upon the nursery. From the number of seals that he could count,
this brood would guarantee some decent coin, at least enough to
compensate somewhat for the hardships they had to endure thus far.

Inhaling and then sighing out a breath half muffled by the
rawness of his throat, the brawny hunter anxiously held his tongue.
He would have to wait before verbally roaring the awaited signal, but
from what he suspected, this reckoning would be coming forthright.
Hidden in the darkness, he let out a slight chuckle and lit up a
smoke. The burning eye of the butt looked out menacingly through
the darkness like a one-eyed demon eating up the shadows, growing
more ravenous, more aroused with each wretched swallow.

Then it began to snow.

BACK TO THE NURSERY

Emma felt the falling snowflakes dance against her eyelids, the sky remaining twisted in wisps of sickly yellows and dark pink colors. She hugged and floated with the white seal, her eyelids continuing to feel terribly heavy. Still, her want for sleep would not last long. Suddenly, she jolted forward, nearly pushing both her and Miracle under the sheet of the rippling sea. "Miracle!" she gasped.

"What is it, Emma? I thought you were asleep."

"No!" she snapped. "Can you smell it?"

The seal flared his nostrils for a long time then answered, "I'm not sure. What is it I should smell?"

The scent was unmistakable in origin. Emma would have recognized it anywhere. She remembered every morsel of its dreaded familiarity. She closed her eyes and shuddered.

"What is it?" Miracle repeated, stretching around his furry wet head as far as he possibly could, but not too much as to topple her over.

Emma's eyes remained closed, fused together, while the nightmare flooded over her. There, in the darkness of herself . . . alone . . . she remembered.

"Emma," Miracle called. "Please tell me what is wrong!"

Finally, her eyes opened then widened. "Hardtack!" she cried.

"Hardtack?"

"It was what they sometimes fed me while I was held captive upon that horrible ship!" Emma retorted while more images and dreaded remembering occurred. "It was what she gave me when I tried to escape. It was how Decara punished me. It was all I could smell—it consumed me, even in my dreams!" she explained, the painful memory of her brother's horrible incarceration searing her brain. She cupped a hand up to her mouth, closed her eyes, and shuddered again. "Man!" she gasped. "He is here!"

Miracle suddenly found himself frozen. It was as if someone had just pulled out an inner plug that powered his reasoning. Cautiously, he began to submerge into the water, taking Emma with him, but before the water's currents flooded over his eyes, he caught a glimpse of something that sent another jolt of fear through him. Once again, his eyesight was not as keen above the water as it was below, and that made things difficult. Still, near the darkening horizon, he managed to detect what he believed was the gathering of the male population—the bulls. They remained a considerable distance away, but his gut feeling regrettably told him that they were nervous bulls, anxious fathers of baby whitecoats; and if that were true, another unsuspecting pack of the expectant mothers had gathered on the island and had already given birth to their children. With a whirling twist of his head, Miracle looked out toward the floating nursery directly beyond, now in sight, and about a quarter of a mile away from where they stood.

"The seals!" Emma shouted. "More have come to the nursery, haven't they?"

"Yes! We've got to get back to the nursery as quickly as possible! We have to warn them!" the white seal shouted in a trembling voice. "Hold on tight!" he howled, waiting for Emma to squeeze her grip around him. "There's no time to lose!" With this said, Miracle and the girl took off like a speeding torpedo, all signs of fatigue having long since vanished. Whitecaps collided with one another in the seal's aftermath, infesting the waters with foamy waves of chaos while they soared toward the nursery of Sealssong.

How could so many thoughts haunt me now? Emma thought, the slapping waves washing over her. Her mind should have only centered upon the threatened seals and their newborns, but images of her brother were mixed in with it all. Had the evil Decara destroyed him? Was there even a "him" to return to, and what of Miracle's mother, Arayna, and the helpless seals she had left behind? Had she ultimately failed them, as well, just as she might fail the ones that she and Miracle was racing toward now?

It seemed that the wind's current was on their side. It had to be. For Emma felt as if she were flying there upon Miracle's back. It was as if the white seal had suddenly sprung wings. And just as she felt as if the seal would take to the skies, both hit the icy nursery with a powerhouse punch! There was a disturbing crunching sound in Emma's side. Jolting from Miracle, she fell to the newly formed winter-ice feeling that she might faint, her vision blurring. She immediately shook her head, trying to regain her sight. In a clouded smear of light and dazzle, she could see the shape of the white seal next to her.

"Are you all right?" he asked in a puff of shortened breath. Emma nodded, not really knowing if she was, but it did not matter. They had to get to the nucleus of the nursery before it was too late. Miracle wriggled up to her further and spoke in a hushed voice. "It will be dangerous there. Perhaps you should wait for me here," he said with troubled eyes, still puffing heavily.

She but had to look at the shining stone about his neck beginning to glow again. With a quick scoop of her hand, she held on to it, feeling it warm in her palm. In a moment, she let it fall free and waited for her vision to return; and as it did, she stood up with a renewed strength, calling, "Come on, it may already be too late!" With these disturbing words, both quickly set off toward the nursery.

The recent winds that had invaded the ice garden had rearranged the icy furniture again, reforming the ice in large clusters in the bays with a wicked vengeance. It made for a most difficult journey with both companions losing each other several times while falling into unsuspecting slush holes. As the frigid water froze over her skin, Emma could only detect a tiny burning sensation from its bite, the effects of the white seal's stone sustaining her miraculously. Both slid down countless mountains of glassy slopes, colliding and sticking to each other in the fall, creating a peculiar cigar shape with their bodies as they rolled down hill after icy hill. Still, they wasted no time in enumerating over their toilsome mishaps. After hitting the solid bottom of each hummock from which they toppled, without even dusting themselves off, they were once again rushing to the newborn whitecoats and their mothers with the perilous warning.

"Look!" Emma choked her eyes, falling upon the footprints in the snow, the teeth of the boots worn by the seal hunters freshly gnawed into the white surface below. "They're already here!" she cried out.

One final hummock rose before them, not nearly as large as the others they had already conquered. Emma tried to lick this one in half the time. With the same instinct as the seal beside her, she began to climb the rocky hill. Slipping twice, she caught her chin on an elongated slab of hard ice. The warm taste of blood only lasted a few moments and then vanished just as the white seal did, disappearing over the frosted slope that finally led to the seal nursery. Emma came sliding down the embankment, slamming into Miracle's backside. The seal gave a slight grunt when she hit him, pushing him further into the ice.

Never could she have imagined such beauty and serenity set against the presence of darkness she knew was out there somewhere—watching, waiting to devour such a placid and sacred gathering. Be that as it may, for some unknown reason, the sealers had not yet struck, for the newborn seals and their mothers were still safe. Relieved, she and Miracle had indeed reached them before the hunters had. They would be able to warn and save them all! Like two preposterous snow creatures, they clumsily trekked toward the seals.

Instantly, every mother's head turned each sensing alarm as Miracle and Emma approached with a hurried rush. A distinct buzzing sound infiltrated the harps, every mother radically and anxiously feeling that something was seriously wrong, everyone pulling closer to her child, stiffening into dispositions of listening. A grunting sound coupled with a high-pitched squealing noise washed itself over the gathering, the adults stirring in a nervous and extremely apprehensive restlessness. The children awoke from their slumber, hungry, wanting to feed while their mothers wrestled with their tiny mouths, unable to lie still any longer. As the shrillness of the pup's cries filled the wind, Emma suddenly stopped.

"Wait! How foolish!" she realized. "They won't know about me until you tell them, the poor things. In wanting to help them, I've frightened them so. You best go ahead, Miracle. I'll follow after you tell me to."

Miracle nodded in agreement, inadvertently throwing off clumps of snow and ice from his brow. However, while proceeding, he too suddenly stopped, only this time he did not stop altogether. He was shaking, and not from the cold. At first, it was slight, but nonetheless, he felt it just the same. He could feel through the ice an indistinct vibration, something not belonging to the jeweled nursery of Sealssong or to the wind, nor the not-so-distant waves of the sea. A murky stain in the sky came down and settled upon him, temporarily blocking the seals from his sight. When it lifted, a bright full moon filled the heavens, splattering uncanny brightness upon the jeweled nursery. It was as if the great fireball in the sky had decided to come out for the night but was too afraid to be completely seen, forced to simulate a strange shade over itself, still illuminating the grounds in the abundance of glowing light despite its cowering.

Miracle quivered, experiencing the intermittent resounding bounce beneath him. Quickly jerking his head, he looked at Emma. Judging from her expression most vividly addressed in the moonlight, he could see that she felt it too. She looked back at him with alarming awareness. The darkness was coming! They were too late! It had already been there waiting for them!

The din of the crying whitecoats abruptly stilled as each wire-drawn mouth of every mother pulled painstakingly across her face in silent terror. Miracle felt his front flippers weaken, dropping him nearer to the icy ground, shaking him. Bravely, he continued to approach the defenseless seals that he was determined to save. Arching his back, he hauled his hindquarters and opened wide his mouth, preparing to howl out a cry of forewarning, but again, it was too late. A fierce rumbling suddenly overtook the moonlit nursery and the innocent ones who, but only this night, found sanctuary there. Nearly fifty clamoring footsteps slammed hard against the ice, creating long jagged cracks, each shooting through the glass-laden floor, splintering off in every conceivable direction. The nursery shook and then shook once more with an even more inconceivable and terrifying blast. A thunderous sound rolled itself across the ice as the army of seal hunters invaded Sealssong. Zealously disciplined and fiercely loyal to their captains, the sealers piled into the sacred rookery, obeying their commander's every word, the words to slaughter and skin the seals they had sought out, working through the night if need be to store the peeled-off pelts they came to take.

Another monstrous blast suddenly exploded.

Emma immediately recognized the sound of its fiery tongue. The men had brought firearms. It was the two watchers who had given the authority to initiate this slaughter, a slaughter that would once again cause heaven to cry and the angels to weep.

Death had returned to Sealssong.

HACK IT! CRACK IT! SMACK IT!

The firearms banged and then kept on banging.

Emma watched the seals go wild. The shots rocked the defiled cradle, and in the discordance of screams, the mothers and their children dispersed with panicked and uncontrolled madness. Pathetically crashing into one another, the terrorized harps fled from the abomination that invaded their home.

More shots split the air, exploding into a most ghastly thud, hitting one of the mothers, one of the few to reach the nursery first before the others. She who had traveled so far to give birth to her child, happy and blessed to be among the first to settle on the ice, now lay sprawled and crippled beside her pup. Her innocent child, still not understanding what the presence of man meant or the destruction he personified, wriggled up to his dying mother. Whimpering and sounding like a human baby himself, he began to cry out to her. Blood poured freely from the mother's wound, staining the pup's face. The baby seal suddenly stopped his crying before licking at the open gash in his mama's chest, violently shaking his head in distaste. Cautiously, the pup pulled closer, smelling the

wound haphazardly before looking up into her clouded eyes waiting
for her to nuzzle him, but she did not. She merely lay still upon the
crimson-colored snow, the warmth of her blood leaving her, steaming
in the cold as she gave out her final breath. The baby lowered his
head and began to wail despondently. Nuzzling his head into her
side, he continued to cry, his hindquarters shaking, there within her
bloodstained folds his heartfelt bawls muffled, pathetically weeping,
"*Ma-ma-a-a-a-a!*"

Mercifully, he would never know what hit him. As swift as an
unexpected gasp, four towering hunters surrounded him, one of
them bringing down his crude instrument, instantly killing the
unsuspecting orphan, bringing sheer wildness throughout the
nursery. In droves, the savage sealers came, their guns signaling
their forthcoming upon the ice, the wailing sounds of the baby seals
further filling the bloody wet smells that the air now upheld. Added
gunshots kept piercing the wind, and the chorus of high shrills tore
from every baby seal's throat.

While the men inundated the ice garden, their intention of
shooting the mothers and clubbing and skinning their children
consuming their every move, a shocked Miracle witnessed the
ascending horror. Having not had time enough to consider what he
could do to prevent such a horrific casualty, the tormented seal now
found himself directly in the path of four fast-moving hunters. These
individuals having already skinned two whitecoats quickly made their
way toward him. The blood-spattered remains of dead baby seals
flapped wantonly against the backs of some of the men, the seals'
wet, limp fur strewn aimlessly over their broad shoulders. They
trekked through the snow with new stimulation in their stride, and as
they neared, Miracle watched the man-beasts motion to one another.
Placing down the bloodstained pelts of the recently murdered
infants, Miracle looked on in mounting terror as the hunters went
for him, their monstrous clubs plowing out before them. For a
moment, it appeared as another dreamed nightmare. This could not
be happening. Surely not; however, while the guns banged and the
seals screamed, he knew it all to be as real as the terror churning
in his gut. He turned his head around, slicing the cold air. *Emma?*
Where is Emma? Once more, the guns banged and the seals screamed
and the nursery rattled mercilessly. All he could see were the fleeing
harps stampeding in front and behind him.

Some of the mothers carried their children in their mouth,
some accidentally dropping their pups in broken floes, diving in
after them before they drowned. Others tried to dodge the blasting

explosions in the air, having to leave their torn-away children behind. Devastation soured his being when Miracle helplessly viewed a fleeing mother pounce through the ice and snow, wild in her attempt to save her child from the approaching hands of the murdering hunters. She herself having already been hit twice suddenly collapsed to the ground when the third shot ripped through her chest. This final hit exploded mercilessly against Miracle's eardrums. He had to stop this, but how, and where was Emma? "Emma!" he howled, the screams around him intensifying. That was when the four men pounced on him. There was nowhere to go! There was no place to hide! Still, he could not allow for such anarchy to continue. He had to do something! Surely the power about his neck would not fail him, not now, not after all it had done already!

Slam! The first of the four men hit Miracle on the back of his head with something flat and hard. The second and the third man forced something around his neck, pinning him to the frozen floor, holding him there tight. The snow caked in Miracle's nostrils, making it hard to breathe. The ice burrowed into his eyes. He tried to move, but he was not able. He tried to breathe again, but could not. Then he felt the power of the fourth man-beast. Something hit him across the backside, skewing him further into the ice and snow. Hovering over him, the men's foul-smelling boots crunched about the snow while one gripped a massive club, aiming it directly at his head, and that was enough to send a million different chills through Miracle. He felt the stone around his throat pressing up harshly against him, and he could feel its sudden warmth. He waited and waited for something to happen. Anything!

However, only more of the muted vibrating and crunching noise of the men's boots and the sound of their monstrous voices fiendishly played on and on insanely about him. Miracle felt the boot of one of the men push down on top of his left flipper.

Why doesn't he just kill me and get it over with? He thought. More warmth from inside the stone penetrated his fur, but still no magic happened. Nothing! Had he lost faith in the tear? He could not have. He would not let that happen. Perhaps the power in the tear had lost faith in him. Odd, the things that go througha seal's mind before he is going to die. Fighting the layers of snow caked against his snout, he coughed and spit out the obstruction chocking him. He had to be brave now no matter what. He would think of Emma and his mother. He would be strong for them. Not even the deviltry of man could take their final memory from his heart. He would die remembering them, praying for their delivery from all this darkness.

Another blast from a rifle exploded. Miracle cringed, thinking it would be the final sound he would ever hear before he took his last breath. Surely, the gunshot was meant for him, but if this were so, why could he still hear sounds, resonance that sounded like Emma screaming, "Leave that seal alone!" More gunshots flared; however, the sound that followed next made the blasts of the guns sound like autumn leaves brushing upon the barren ground.

CRUNCH! SPLIT! WHOOSH! CRASH!

The entire ice garden lifted upward, shooting apart directly beneath Miracle. Like a massive and unparalleled explosion set off from somewhere at the bottom of the sea, the white seal was cast up toward the sky. With a hurling gust, the seal hunters also became tossed about ridiculously like matchsticks in the great booms' aftermath.

Kishk, the mighty blue chanter, was back!

Breaking the icy floor of the defiled seal nursery with booming vengeance all his own, the whale sliced through the ice like a torpedo, causing just as much fuss in his wake, if not more. Ice and snow spattered everywhere, and for a moment, it was as if the whole world evaporated in one blinding flash of brilliance. The gulls were the first to make a quick exit, some not escaping the flying debris, scratching them across the crowded firmament with a wicked blast, throwing them off somewhere into swirling oblivion. Sheets of ripped ice slashed upward and sideways, colliding violently with one another, shattering open the nursery with a shocking roar.

As the sensational 103-foot, 100-ton creature ripped the ice, he continued on a rapid incline, shooting upward toward the heavens. He seemed to float in the brisk moonlit sky, weightless, his massive form abruptly snatching the light, casting a dark, bluish shadow over the split-up grounds below. Kishk's passing shadow covered every nook and cranny of Sealssong, leaving nothing untouched in its shady path, not even the whites of the eyes belonging to the doomed men who were about to be smashed beyond recognition. If it was not for the sound that the wind made while rushing beneath the massive belly of the sailing whale high in the sky, blocking out the rays of the moon, there would have been only unnerving silence. This silence would last until Kishk's hulking form began to descend back down toward the ice garden. With the wind now screaming behind him, the chanter made his final descent. All the hunters who remained on the ice were instantly and most readily squished out of existence with one enormous *PLOP!*

Another blinding flash exploded over the torn-up nursery. A million shooting pieces of ice filtered down from the once again moonlit sky, replenishing each pulverized speck of shimmer with a spooky, luminous glow. Looking more like a meteor shower, the icy particles showered downward, accompanied with more chunks and slabs of heavy sheets of ragged floorboards of the seal nursery, making for several nasty sounds of repetitive and unsettling thunder blasts. The island rocked steadily back and forth, much of it already broken, continued to be bombarded with massive sheets of falling ice raining down from the moonlit heavens. Kishk had slid several hundred feet in his outrageous landing, ripping up even more of the nursery floor, eventually coming to a loud and crunching halt somewhere, smack-dab in the center of an already split-apart hummock. His head would sting and then burn and ache, but for the most part, the whale would have escaped injury. Nonetheless, his senses would be dazed for a bit and he would wait for them to return, decidedly lingering there half conscious while the rest of the glowing sky fell down all around him.

From out of a pile of snow and choppy ice, Miracle's head suddenly emerged. Foolhardy, he looked up into the sky before shaking the crunchy debris from his head and snout. He looked around, stunned in his motions, waiting, listening for the sound of man; but there came none.

Slowly pulling himself out from the shattered spillage of ice, the white seal wriggled out into the clearing, shaking more of the broken ice from his immaculate coat. The familiar sights of the nursery had vanished again. The extraneous split-apart grounds grew heavy around the seal while he tried to grasp what had just happened. More icy specks fell from the sky, exaggerating, themselves in the moonlight, looking as if it had somehow begun to snow amidst a most vivid, cloudless, crystal-clear, and star-filled winter's sky. Again, the dazed seal shook the snow from his coat and proceeded to wriggle further into the clearing, making sure he would avoid the rips in the nursery floor so as not to fall into the gaping shafts of slush-ridden floes. Suddenly, he gasped. What he saw defied all reason, and yet he dared to believe that what lay sprawled before him, all 103 feet, 100 tons of man-obliterating muscle, belonged to someone he had waited for, prayed for, all these many, many endless days. With a soundless tread, the white seal moved toward the giant monstrosity stretching out immeasurably before him. A soft wind cascaded freely over the seal's form; all the while he continued to stare at the only direction possible—*everywhere!* For no matter where his eyes fell, he could exclusively see the massive and the encompassing creature now set aglow by the moon's iridescent beams.

As the shattered slabs of nursery squeaked and gurgled, Miracle never relinquished his stare, not at any time looking down upon the shattered ice beneath him. His eyes fixed on the giant before him, the white seal trekked onward until he finally reached the sprawled out man-crusher.

Placing his black wet nose next to the creature's side, he sniffed in Kishk's scent. Hurling his head back, Miracle tried to look upon the face of the blue giant but was unable. He would have to scurry around to the front of this behemoth if he were to do so. The broken sheets of the seal nursery grumbled and hissed as he bounced from each of these floating stepping-stones until at last he made it to the very mouth of the dazed creature. Without a moment's pause, the blue whale, who had also sensed the seal's presence, immediately opened wide his huge and shining violet eyes.

"Kishk, it's really you!" Miracle shouted, tears filming over his shiny eyes. "I knew you would come back! I just knew that you would return, and you saved me once again! You saved so many of us!" Miracle sang, rubbing his tiny head against the blue whale's everlasting face.

The mighty Kishk's mouth suddenly broke into a wide and endless grin as he too gently rubbed his massive lips across the tiny creature before him. "I must say," exclaimed the whale, "leaving that topsy-turvy world sure gives off a powerful punch!"

Miracle continued to rub his cheek against the massive chanter. "I'm so glad you are here, oh, how I have waited for your return!"

Without a word, the whale invited the seal to come aboard. Lowering his head, Kishk waited while Miracle wriggled toward him. However, Miracle suddenly stopped, not wanting to go another wriggle before seeing that Emma was safe. Turning, he could not find her. Then from above him, Miracle heard a most familiar voice, outrageous and robust, getting louder and louder while making its way down the snout of the whale. What was rapidly coming down the slide of the blue chanter's nose was about to smash into him most abruptly. CRASH—went the white seal, nearly falling into a nearby slush pool, the loud voice and its many rolls of bulging blubber barreling down over him.

"LOVE-YA!" shouted Mum in a most excited and unconfined voice. Miracle tried to catch his breath but lost it again when the crazed seal wrapped both of her flippers about his furry and ice-drenched neck. Holding on to him, maybe just a tad bit longer than she should have, Miracle felt his breath heave from his chest, the mad beast squeezing him with all her might. However, just in the nick of time, Mum relinquished her powerful bear hug long enough for him to catch a sudden gasp. Still, it was not long before she was back to wrapping her bulbous self around him.

"Oh, my little lovely *Love-ya*, let me look at the love!" the blubbery mad creature exclaimed swiftly, holding the seal between her flippers in a sloppy attempt while smothering him with endless kisses of wet and slimy salutations. "Still a little wee thing, aren't we, love?" Mum giggled. Most determined to shower him further with more saturated adorations, she clinched her grip around the seal's head and began to pull him toward her large and ridiculous face, smacking her lips loud with an almost frightening and exaggerated noise. Satisfied with her overzealous kissing frenzy, the mad seal startled Miracle when she suddenly screamed, *"Love-ya!"* Smacking the seal on the back of his rump, she sent him sailing straight up onto the whale directly on top of the small penguin that was just beginning to find consciousness. With a helpless and an embarrassing plop, Miracle rolled over Mulgrew, squishing him. It seemed to take a while before the penguin calmed down, huffing and puffing scooting away, allowing Miracle to once again catch his breath.

The wide violet eyes of Kishk crossed themselves in double vision so that he could witness the reuniting of the young seal on top of his vast head while Mum hurriedly wriggled back up his nose, eager to join them again. Miracle's next thought was of Emma, but he would not be able to act upon this for Mum was not quite through with him. "How I have missed you, my little *Love-ya*," she added with a soft snuggle of her head. Helpless, he could only press himself closer to the outrageous creature that he had come to love. Besides his own mother, he would always cherish the crazy seal who wore the ridiculous bonnet now blessed with a moment of a peaceful mind. Relishing in the joy of this union, not knowing how long it would last, Miracle snuggled noses with Mum.

However, as quick as a good-night kiss upon a baby's head, Mum abruptly pulled out her bonnet, slapped it on top of her head, and blurted out, *"I-m-mmm—sassy hot!"* Then throwing herself on her back, nearly crushing the penguin for the second time, she commenced madly with another round of Clap-Clap.

"What happened to us?" Mulgrew squeaked, scurrying over to the tip of Kishk's massive mouth, looking down, sounding and feeling dazed.

Kishk tried to clear his voice as well as his swirling mind and spoke. "We have returned to Sealssong."

"I got that, sir, but how?"

"We broke through the barriers that had suspended us."

"Whatever! Just glad that's over with!"

Kishk immediately remembered the Kellis and all that she had told them. Somehow her words would replay themselves over and over to him. "We have returned safely to help the white seal find his mother and to destroy the evil that will soon return to Sealssong."

"You call that returning safely?" Mulgrew squawked, remaining shaken up from the whale's explosive departure from the sky. "And speaking of the white seal," the bird said with a snap, "did you get a good look at him? He's hardly changed. He's grown some, I guess, but he still hasn't traded in his birthday suit. What's up with that?"

"Don't let his white coat fool you. He has indeed matured, just as time has."

"What?"

"Yes, Mulgrew, somehow time has passed over the nursery in our absence, but for us who were among the Kellis, time has stood still."

It was then Miracle's voice prevailed, and what the white seal said suddenly and emphatically confused and silenced even the theatrical clamor of the insane seal next to him. "I know about my mother," Miracle said in a small but excited voice, moving away from Mum and over to the declining tip of the whale's mouth. "Much has happened since you left Sealssong. Word has reached me that she is still alive."

Kishk's violet eyes sprang wide open. "But how? Who has brought such news to you?"

Suddenly, Miracle looked out toward the broken-up nursery. There in the shattered world beneath him, Miracle could see the human girl who had brought him such tidings. Sitting alone upon a broken slab of ice, Emma stared in awe at the magnificent sight before her. Relieved, Miracle smiled. "Emma," he called out happily. "Come and meet the family I told you about, they have returned!"

Kishk remained silent, carefully watching Emma continue to make her way toward his massive self. With her iridescent eyes glowing, she proceeded to gaze up in awe toward the enormous creature before her. There were numerous ice floes rising and bumping into each other so it was difficult for her feet to find a place between their clouded obscurities. Eventually, skimming the icy shores for support, she found a temporary spot. A soft breeze, almost as delicate as Emma's feet, brushed past her, tossing her golden locks across her forehead, her toes holding on to a sturdy beam of ice. Rising, she steadied herself, nearly falling. Then with her shining eyes still fixated on the blue whale, she blindly felt her way over to the place where Miracle and the mammoth Kishk awaited her. Slowly, she approached, her heart racing, her eyes never leaving the whale, even when Miracle spoke out to her. "Come, Emma, meet my dear friend Kishk."

Emma's smiled and curtsied prettily. "It is an honor, sir," she recited, her half-shredded nightdress clinging to her like wet seaweed.

Miracle wriggled toward the snout of the whale and slid down, heading directly toward Emma. When reaching her, he looked at her and smiled a strange and endearing smile, almost as if he had just realized something most significant. Rubbing his head gently against her knee, the seal said with an unrehearsed exaltation, "And this, my dear family, is Emma. She too has come to help us."

The mighty Kishk tilted his massive head, pulling back slightly, crushing dozens of smaller ice floes stubbornly boxing around him. "You can speak to us!" exclaimed the blue whale. "How can this be?"

Emma smiled, this time feeling an unexpected chill race up her spine as another breeze came upon her. She would have to touch the white seal's stone if she were to continue to remain on such frigid grounds. Miracle, sensing her need, wriggled into her further. Placing his soft head against her side, he snuggled even closer, his shining purple stone touching an open strip of her flesh. Immediately, a flood of warmth caressed her, and her cheeks blossomed with the color of vibrant red roses. Despite the vehemence of splendor given to her by the magic tear's power, Emma knew that it would be she herself that would have to replace her dress. If she waited any longer, she would be rendered almost naked, with only wet and ratty strings barely to cover her. However, as to achieving such means, she hadn't a clue. "Yes, kind sir, I can understand you. All of you," she said in a quiet voice.

Kishk looked most confused. "Man-child, you present to me the impossible."

"Impossible?" Emma chuckled. "Sir, with all due respect, I have long since finished with expecting the possible. It is only the *impossible* that is now possible."

Suddenly, Mum's voice bellowed, way atop the whale's head, her head peeking out just enough to be heard. "KILL IT! It is MAN! Crush the foul thing!" she screamed in a bloodcurdling voice. "Hack it! Crack it! Smack it!"

Emma's eyes flashed up toward the angry seal's voice. Savagely, Mum snarled at Emma, showing off her fangs, preparing to tear the girl a part. "Back off, man-beast, we will have no more of your kind here! You have spilled enough blood! Get out before I spill yours!"

"Wait!" Miracle quickly interjected. "Mum, you don't understand!"

"Understand?" abruptly spit the voice of Mulgrew. The nervous and fidgety penguin had also dared to show himself, however, reaming as far away from the despicable mad creature. "It is you who don't understand, you boneheaded seal!" the penguin chirped. "You must be crazy as that mental-hospital-lunatic Mum you're saddled with if you think this man-beast can do anything but destroy you! Kill it! Kill it before it kills us all!"

"Nonsense," Emma explained. "I could never do such a thing. You must believe me."

"Crap-crock!" howled the incensed Mum from high above. "Lash it! Crash it! Smash it!"

Emma exhaled and shook her head, frustrated in not being able to explain her intentions toward the magnificent creatures before her. Reclining herself over as far as she could go while attempting to look into the violet eyes of the blue whale, Emma pleaded. "Please, you must listen. I can only imagine what you must think, but I assure you—" Emma did not have the chance of finishing her words. Quite unexpectedly, the Mad Mum jumped from the head of the whale; and with a thunderous rumble, she came barreling down faster than Emma could ever prepare for. With an appalling thud, Emma fell backward, half landing in a pool of broken ice, the snarling Mum seal tacking her to the sharp ridges of the ice pool. The massive seal's weighty blubber piled against the startled girl, crushing her, Mum's sharp teeth exposed, ready to tear Emma to shreds.

SNOWBIRDS

"Stop," Miracle frantically shouted, wriggling himself up to the mad seal. "You'll kill her!"

"Crack the head off first!" the unnerved penguin screamed, still surveying the scene from atop the whale, skittishly pacing back and forth at a blurring speed. "Crack the head off first, crack the head off first!" he kept squealing.

Once again, Miracle interceded. "Stop, stop I say!"

However, Mum ignored the white seal's pleas and lowered herself further over the man-beast, growling, white foam building up at the corners of her misshapen jaws. Emma felt the breath crushed out of her, unable to speak, unable to move. She could only lay there, half encompassed by drooping seal skin and broken icicles.

Thrusting his head into the side of the mad seal, Miracle once again begged for the seal to stop, but the determined Mum would not relinquish her prey, not even for the white seal. With a furious howl, she lowered her oversized head and pressed herself directly over Emma's face. Hot breath splashed over Emma's lips. She heard the mad seal speak to her in a voice that chilled her blood, far more than the ice ever could. "You and your kind have plagued and murdered my world long enough! It stops now here . . . with you!"

"Mum! Stop," Miracle begged. "You don't know what you are saying!"

"You are of the female gender, therefore," Mum growled, foaming, her eyes burning, red, "you must die before you can spread life to your filthy species, and for this and for the murder of my Sasha, I shall kill you—now!"

Miracle screamed out, trying to stop what was about to take place. However, Mum only had to swish her back flipper, sending him crashing into a pile of icy rubble amidst a broken background. With her fangs exposed against her twisted and upbraided lips, the mad creature went down for the kill.

It was not the muffled scream coming from the throat of Emma that made the Mum seal stop; it was something else—something most curious. It was something Mum had not planned for. In short, it was simply that she forgot what she was so inflamed about. Mum, without notice, suddenly did not have a clue; and in a flash, her dangling and discomposed mouth of dripping foam was swinging upward, forming the grandest and silliest smile she had ever engaged upon.

As if all that built-up rage inside her had abruptly turned to jelly, the unbalanced harpie lifted her head and belched. Looking directly into the terrified face of Emma, she asked simply, *"Are you the Docta?"* Then she fell over to her side with one stupendous crash, clapping madly all the way.

"Dysfunctional CRACKPOT!" screeched the disappointed penguin. "Huh, knew she couldn't do it, daft-loon!"

In seconds, Miracle was at Emma's side, helping her up out of the ice pool. Emma's hands were shaking, and she was out of breath when she put her arms around Miracle. Closing her eyes, she took in the air about her, hoping not to faint. With Miracle's help, she stood erect and looked over toward the icy floor where her near-assassin remained sprawled out, still clapping her flippers in frantic play. *"Love ya, love, LOVE!"* Mum sang, rolling about the cracked ice nursery, smacking her flippers together, all traces of vengeance, gone the bewitching madness flooding itself through her tortured mind.

"Poor thing," Emma lamented, still trying to catch her breath.

Suddenly, the mighty voice of Kishk prevailed. "Come here, man-child," he said in a strict command. Turning her gaze from the mad seal, Emma once more looked at the majestic blue whale summoning her. As she began to walk toward him, she nearly lost her balance. "I'm afraid I'm still a little dizzy," she confessed in a playful voice. Still, she showed no signs of faltering. Continuing, she once more tried to steady her walk, arching her head, trying to look into its violet and probing eyes.

"I cannot tell you how sorry I am," Miracle said regrettably, wriggling along with her. "It's just that Mum goes . . . well . . . a bit mad sometimes. It's not her fault, you see. It happened when she swiped the magic tear from Decara. She really isn't as dreadful as she seems," he offered, shaking his head, feeling as light-headed as Emma.

"I know," Emma replied. "My heart breaks for her. She has endured so much suffering."

"And what has your heart suffered?" the mighty Kishk asked.

Emma looked up, still unable to see the full spectrum of his eyes. She could only see the very bottom of the violet orbs swimming above her. "Me?" she answered with a small, but fading smile. "I can only imagine a mere drop of what the seals have had to endure. I am ashamed of my race and for all the pain that they have caused you." Lowering, her eyes away from the blue giant just for a moment, they returned with an added sparkle. "My name is Emma. I come to you in peace and wish only to help," she said quickly, straining to look up into the base of those violet eyes.

Kishk had to smile. "A man-child that can understand and that can communicate her words to us, hmmm . . . ," he murmured waggishly. "Can it be that you are she?"

"What are you talking about?" screeched Mulgrew. "Quick, squash it!"

"Silence, we will do nothing of the sort!"

Mulgrew became outraged. "What? Have you joined that half-witted Mum seal's way of thinking? The girl is of man! She comes from the same apes that have caused a permanent migraine in the skull of every living organism on this planet! You know, MAN, the ones that have butchered and destroyed all that we hold sacred, the same creature that walks around on two limbs, selfishly and willfully ending all of life as we have known since the beginning of time!"

"I am aware of man and his neanderthal intelligence," Kishk said. "But she is not like them. She is different. She has been spared his malignancy. Don't you see? She is the one the Kellis told us about!" the whale excitedly explained with greater revelation. "She is the one who still holds the last traces of innocence. It is she who will save the white seal and will be our redemption!"

Suddenly, Mum rolled over onto her stomach and screamed out, "Redeem my love!" Then she wriggled up to Emma, sniffing about her, probing her in the most unfashionable of places.

Nervously, Emma tried to pull the tattered nightdress about her but to no avail. There just wasn't enough dress to go around anymore. *"Hewef!"* Mum revolted, still sniffing at places Emma preferred the mad creature had never ventured.

"Mum, you must try to understand," Miracle pleaded. "She is not like the man-beast! She means us no harm. She has come to save us from—"

Kishk quickly finished the seal's sentence. "From the evil of the dark woman and to free us from man's wickedness, reuniting you at last with your dear mother."

"You're not listening," insisted Miracle. "She has come to—" He abruptly stopped and glanced at Emma, then back toward the mighty giant, doubting his own ears. "What did you say?"

Kishk smiled down at him endearingly. "You have heard me correctly, dear friend," the whale said, trying to lower his head nearer to the white seal. As more ice crushed and snapped, the mighty Kishk began to tell the story of the journey both he and his comrades had encountered. He told him of the Kellis and what she had told them, how the evil woman would destroy all of innocence by corrupting the man-child into destroying the white seal. Having already heard much of these words from Emma, Miracle graciously continued to listen, digesting the remarkable events that the blue chanter and the others had encountered. On and on he listened despite Mum's incessant sniffing about Emma's private parts. "But,why me? That's what I can't understand."

"There are no answers, not now, I'm afraid," gently explained the whale.

Bowing his head, Miracle closed his eyes. He did not open them until he felt Emma's gentle touch upon his head. Nestling closer to her, he placed his head within her tiny hands and felt her rub his forehead. Now this demonstration of affection was much too much for the penguin. "You got to be kidding! You let it touch you? What's wrong with you!" screeched the bird.

"Mulgrew," Kishk demanded. "Come down here at once! We have much to discuss, and I can no longer allow for your outrageous and bigoted assumptions!"

"Assumptions? But she's—"

"Not another word!"

"Yeah, but—"

"Mulgrew!"

Disgusted and throwing up his tiny flippers, the exasperated penguin rolled his eyes, growling viciously under his breath, stomping his webbed feet up and down in a tantrum. He obeyed the giant's command. "Idiots, every last one of them!" he squawked, jumping into the air before diving head first, down and then over the whale's face.

"The purple tear you have about your neck must allow for the man-child to survive in our world, does it not?" Kishk asked.

"Yes," Miracle replied. "It's magical. That's why Decara wants it so badly."

"From what I gather, there are three important elements involved here in order to bring about the end of innocence: Yourself, the man-child, and the tear."

"That is correct," Emma embellished. "But please, won't you call me Emma?"

Kishk looked strangely at the human before him, dwarfed pitifully amidst the backdrop of the icy shambles that his timely arrival had caused, and then smiled. "But of course, as you wish, Emma," agreed the blue whale. "Tell me, Emma," the whale asked, clearing his voice before speaking, "how is it that you escaped from the vessel that imprisoned you?"

Answering for Emma, Miracle boastfully spoke out. "She tricked the three-headed serpent!"

"Serpent?" Kishk uttered. "Good heavens, serpents and tears and humans who can speak our language, what next?" he said, chuckling playfully. "Have you always been able to communicate with the creatures on this planet?"

"Yes, as long as I can remember."

Mulgrew heard enough. "Oh, you're too much, kid!" he spat, shaking about, splashing the ice and watery droplets all over Emma and Miracle, chirping incessantly. "I don't care what you say! I still don't trust you! No matter what, you're still one of them!"

With a small part of her madness fading, Mum gruffly huffed. "As much as I hate to agree with the annoying and rotten little imp, he may have a point. After all," Mum said, sniffing suspiciously about

Emma once more before pushing her wet snout directly into Emma's face, "man's blood still runs through her veins."

"Where is your faith?" the whale asked in a wrathful tone. "Did you not see the images or hear the words that the Kellis gave to us? Why, the very reason she is here, alive, sustaining the elements, speaking to us is proof enough!"

Mulgrew looked even more unconvinced, daring to waddle up to Emma, only coming halfway up to her exposed knees, looking as if he thought about pecking off a few chunks of skin. "How do we know it's not some witch's trick? After all, she did come from that evil floating machine. Besides, just look at her. She has no fur, no feathers—no hide—just those—knees and that thin layer of pink waddle covering her spiny skeleton! What's that about?"

"Oh, enough of this," Kishk sternly announced turning his kind gaze to Emma. "I believe in you, and we will do whatever it is you ask, Emma."

Once again, the whale caused Emma to smile. "Thank you," she said. "But if you please, some of what the small bird said is true. Not having fur or feathers are somewhat of a problem. I will need something more substantial to wear while I am here."

"Yes, of course," Kishk agreed. "However, to find such coverings may not be a simple task."

"Wait!" Miracle called out. "Let's see if the tear can help. Come, Emma, touch it. Make a wish." The seal gave a very extensive, happy smile.

Emma agreed. "Yes, it just might work."

"Well, we won't know until we try."

Crouching down near the seal, she took the stone in her hand, closed her eyes; and as the seal suggested, she made a wish. A gentle breeze came upon her, its softness painted the most magical shade of purple. As if in a trance, Emma slowly stood upright and began to move away from the seal, holding on to a few broken slabs of ice pillars while moving to a higher level of broken ground strong enough to sustain her. The glow of the cracked island began to dim as newly formed clouds arrived, each one, little by little, snuffing out the light of the moon.

It began to snow.

Miracle followed close behind, wondering what she would do next, as did the rest. He did not utter a word, but only stared at her in awe as the delicately trailing snow fell all around her. There, in the midst of the falling snow, Emma looked up and began to outstretch her arms toward the heavens, turning slowly in a circle, the twinkling of the shimmering snow and the purple mist showering over her. In a quiet voice, she began to sing, her song more like a chant, its melodious refrain most pleasing and quite magical. The snowflakes seemed to dance to the musical wonder. They fluttered about her like ice-covered butterflies, swirling up and down and all around as powdery gusts of snow began to blow off the icy peaks high up in the sky. It cascaded over her, majestically covering her up in a billowy mist of dazzle. Then from the very heart of the clouds that gently tucked away the moon came the sounds of many birds, their warbling song preceding them. In a moment, the sky filled with large snow-white dove-looking creatures, all of them singing the same voice of chant that she sang. One by one, the magnificent white birds descended upon Emma adoringly. They, like the dancing snowflakes, twirled about her, rotating and swarming in circles until they became lost in a blur, becoming one with her.

As Emma became thoroughly covered up inside the feathery and snowy twister, Miracle could see that her tiny feet had left the icy ground and that she was floating there among the wintry wonderland, captured in the whirling splendor. Her suspended feet seemed to dance within the snowflakes and the flutter of the bird's wings, each one tickling her, spinning around and around her before vanishing inside their rhythmic ambulation.

Emma's song was the first to end. As graceful as it all began, she slowly sank from the swirling sky and fluttering snowflakes. Her tiny pink feet, now covered in a strange and misty cloud, touched ever so gently upon the slope of ice she had been taken from, her hands clutched as if in prayer. Although the sparkling snowflakes remained at that moment, reflecting brilliantly as the moon came alive, once more shafting down its own personal spotlight upon the girl was the astonishing garment that now embellished her. The snow birds had vanished, leaving their selfless and precious gift. They had shed their feathers so that she may have warmth and protection from the cold night air. Now covered in an immaculate wisp of snowy-white gatherings of plumage, Emma stood glistening in the snow of Sealssong. Intricately, the presented wings of the birds overspread themselves about her, each feather woven into the next, creating a dress of embroidered wings, every part, every seam a sheer work of art. For even her delicate pink feet were covered in white feathers, every section interlaced in such a fashion, resembling the most dainty of slippers. Emma looked adoringly at her incredible dress and slippers. Smiling happily, she brought her hands to her lips and blew a kiss up toward the snowy heavens. "Thank you," she said. "It's lovely."

Miracle was again immediately at her side. A far-reaching smile broke out all over the white seal's face, marveling at his remarkable companion and her fabulous new wings. The mighty blue whale that had witnessed the magnificent makings of the feather dress could only look on in wonder, nodding his head in reassurance. The penguin remained unimpressed. "So watcha gonna do now, fly?" snapped the flabbergasted bird.

"*Love-ya, love love!*" Mum bellowed, looking at Emma, drool running down her cheek. "Pretty, little swan—pretty little swan!" She tilted her head back and forth, not knowing what to make out of the whole ordeal. Suddenly, Mum grunted and blew a snot bubble from her nose, once again sniffing the ground where Emma was standing. "Hmmm?" she pondered, then snorted and spat.

With this final confirmation that the tear had provided, Kishk would forever be convinced. "Come forward, child."

Emma quickly turned to face the whale, temporarily leaving the awestruck Miracle to remain, his eyes not leaving her for a moment. Her feather dress danced whimsically in the night breeze, each feather painted with the glow of the full moon. Carefully, she walked across the snow and ice, her feather-covered feet breaking through the crust. Upon reaching Kishk, she curtsied.

"Let there be no doubt," Kishk declared, "that this man-child will be akin to each of us from this night forward. Unlike her species, she is of a pure heart and will forever be set apart from the evil one called man. She has come to us in peace with a promise of our salvation," he announced, looking at her, spellbound, his violet eyes shining. "Let it be known throughout the land," the blue leviathan proclaimed, "Emma has come to save Sealssong!"

THE MONSTERS CLAIMED MANY

It was all too much for the penguin to swallow. He just could not understand how it was possible that the whale could be fooled by the vileness of man. "So let me get this straight," the penguin squeaked. "We're really going to trust this tricky man-beast, bird impersonator, or whatever she is? She gives me the creeps! Look at her, parading around like some spooky goose! Why, it's just downright embarrassing!" The penguin squawked, waddling further off the whale's head so he could get a better look at Emma. "Feathers just don't work for some of us, honey!" Mulgrew chirped.

Mum was quick to chime in. "Oh hush, I think the pretty bird lady just might save the seals of Sealssong," she contentedly exclaimed, yawning through her words as if she had just awakened from a snooze. "There's a good love," Mum said with a nod of unexpected acknowledgment.

Mulgrew was far from convinced. "And what about the predicted killing of the white seal and your dirty little part in it, are we simply to forget that, man-beast?" the penguin lashed while hanging off from the whale's head.

"I assure you," Emma said with more sincerity than she had ever managed. "I would die first before I let any harm ever come to him."

Kishk, who remained thoroughly convinced, spoke. "I believe her, and so must all of Sealssong if we ever hope to defeat the evil Decara."

Once again, Mum stopped her yawning and began sniffing about Emma again. She was about to sniff the feathers covering her toes when a large explosion of snow and ice suddenly interrupted her. Its blast covered not only her but also the human girl and the white seal next to her.

"I saw the whale's return! And I finally found you! I found you! Whoody-whoody-whooo!" howled the voice of the returned walrus Crumpels. "I've been searching everywhere for you! I have been to the ice castle, and you were not there! What has happened? Are you all right?" Crumpels begged, still holding to a near-deafening howl, pushing her massive face directly into the snout of Miracle who remained covered up in the snow blast that she had only moments before covered him with most thoroughly.

"The monsters were here with their loud killing sticks!" Crumpels shrieked. "They came upon the nursery, out of the darkness, out of nowhere! They tried to kill me! They tried to kill Poo-Coo, but we managed to escape and hide from them! But oh dear me, boop-boop-dee-dee, I'm afraid that—" The walrus slowly lost the highly pitched screaming voice of hers. This happened when her eyes came upon the human girl now in the process of dusting herself from the blast of snow as well. "—Many of the others—" Crumpels stopped again, her voice becoming squeaky and lost while she eyed up the human creature before her, holding to a look that indicated that she might start screaming all over again. Instead, she nervously swallowed her growing fear, continuing with her story, her mouth and long whiskers wobbling about with apprehension and nervousness. "Well . . . ," she uttered, swallowing another gulp of dread. "Many of the others didn't make it." She then started to tremble with added fear, her eyes flooding open, looking upon the strangely feathered-up creature before her.

"Salutations!" the silver-tongued blue chanter offered. "It is good to see you again, Ms. Crumpels."

Overcome with fear and uncertainty, Crumpels merely looked up toward Kishk with a befuddled expression splashed all over her face, slowly waving a tiny portion of her flipper to him.

Mulgrew remained indifferent. "What's so good about it?" he popped off again, shaking himself clean from the walrus's annoying entrance.

"Crumpels," Miracle exclaimed, "you're all right!" He wriggled excitedly up to her, rubbing his furry face against hers. "We were so worried!"

The stupefied walrus did not reply or even show signs that she was aware of the white seal's presence. She could only stare at the peculiar birdlike thing staring at her.

"It's okay," Miracle tried to explain. "She's come to help us!"

Crumpels shook her head and grunted confoundedly. "Wha-wha-what is it?" she mumbled, her voice cracking before backing away, getting ready to run off again.

"You mustn't be afraid," assured Kishk's calming deep voice. "We have returned with good news of the seal's mother. She lives, and this human creature is going to help us find her."

"Oh, that's nice," Crumpels choked in an almost emotionless voice. "Does the birdie bite . . . boop-boop-dee-fright?"

"No, I'm afraid you don't understand," Emma tried to tell the walrus. "I'm not a bird, I am a girl."

"Oh, I see—boop-boop-dee-dee!" Crumpels nervously chuckled. "Then it would be safe to assume that you are a human girl, would it not, dear?"

"That's right," answered Emma.

"HUMAN!" roared the panicking walrus, cringing, commencing on backing away, this time nearly flipping backward into the open floes.

"Now if you will allow me to explain—" begged Emma, desperately attempting to go to the terrified creature.

"Stay away!" Crumpels howled. "Human creatures, be they, dressed up like crazy birds, are still monsters! Killers! *Murderers!*"

"No!" Emma pleaded.

"They carry loud killing sticks!" Crumpels insisted. "They come only to destroy us!"

"No, not all of them," Emma pleaded. "I am only here to help, I promise." She offered her hand to the walrus, but Crumpels would not allow it.

"It's okay!" Miracle pledged. "This man-beast is good and kind. She is not like the others. She is going to find my mother and save all of Sealssong! Honest!"

"The white seal speaks the truth, silly walrus," Mum told the disheveled creature. "The blasted thing seems harmless enough. However, it does freaky things with birds—go figure."

Backing up against a solid wall of ice, the frightened walrus looked at Emma with a terrified and suspicious stare. Realizing that they had spent enough precious time already, the blue whale spoke. "Crumpels, you have said that many others have not survived. What about the ones that have survived?"

It took a moment for the walrus to respond. Ungluing her eyes from the peculiar human was not easy, but eventually she was able to do so. Once more returning her awkward stare toward the whale, Crumpels spoke out through her wiggling mustache. "Yes," she answered in a chopped-up voice. "My boy Poo-Coo is with some of them now."

"Are the casualties great?"

Crumpels sadly nodded. "I'm afraid so. The monsters claimed so many this time."

"Is the man-beast still upon the island?" Kishk asked outright, fear tugging at his words.

"No, thanks to you, they're all dead, boop-boop-dee-dread, I hope. Still, there is trouble, bad trouble!"

"Get to the point, my good walrus!" the whale demanded.

"She's mad. I think she will really kill it if they try to stop her!"

"Who will?"

"Jillith!"

"*Jillith!*" Miracle repeated, cutting his eyes at Crumpels. "What has Jillith to do with any of this?"

"They have all come, even some of the familiar seals. For some reason, they all followed the winds to Sealssong, many coming to give birth to their young ones, the poor dears. It was a sad fate that brought them here this time—believe you, me! Boop-boop-dee-flee!"

Not wasting any time, Miracle asked, "Where is Jillith now, and what has she done?"

Crumpels looked at the strange human creature one more time and then turned away quickly with a shudder, directing her words back to the white seal. "Jillith was with child. She too came as did the others to the island before man arrived. Her child was not fortunate to be missed by their loud and noisy killing sticks! It is dead," she said with a sad and dismal stare.

"And what of Jillith?"

"She has gone mad! She has already tried to take several whitecoats from their mothers in an insane rage to replace her murdered pup!"

"Oh no!" Miracle uttered.

"But she failed. Poo-Coo was able to get the stolen children away from her unharmed, returning them to their rightful mothers!" Crumpels wept. "My son had already suffered many a near-death fight with that terrible Jillith, that is, until this last time when she . . . she—"

Once again, the penguin exploded. "Jumpin' jittery nerves get on with it already!"

Crumpels nodded her head in flustered compliance. "She has taken another infant and has it trapped inside a cave with her. She says that she will kill it if any of us tries to stop her from keeping it! Please," Crumpels implored. "We must stop her! Nikki tried as best as she possibly could, but the poor dear just wasn't a strong enough match for such a horrible creature! I'm afraid she never even—"

"*Nikki!*" Miracle cried, not believing what the walrus had just said. Wriggling quickly up to Crumpels, he thumped his hindquarters against the snow, impatiently waiting for her to continue.

"Yes," Crumpels told him. "She too has come to Sealssong to deliver her child. Time has aged us all, White Puff, and after all, she is of age now and has grown into such a lovely young dear, bless her heart."

"Is she all right? You must tell me!"

Lowering her head, the sad walrus slowly shook it. "She tried to stop Jillith, and now she lies dying at the bottom of the hill not far from where her child was stolen. You see, it is Nikki's child whom Jillith has taken this time. She means to kill it if we stop her!"

"Take me to her at once!" Miracle demanded.

"Yes, whooody-whooo, follow me!" Crumpels wailed.

"Wait!" halted the voice of the blue chanter. "You will need all our help. We too shall come. Lead on, walrus, lead on!"

LOST LOVE

Emma tried to keep up with the others as best as possible, the moonlight shedding light upon her uncertain path, Miracle remaining at her side. In the many days that the seal and girl shared, Miracle told her of his friends, Nikki, and the wicked Jillith, but never did he expect that Emma would eventually meet them, and meet them she did.

Suddenly, Miracle stopped dead in his tracks.

It was they! They were there right before him! Miracle shook his head, trying to take in the incredible happening; it was Big Petie and Little Lukie!

"It is you!" Big Petie shouted, now a fully grown bull, all traces of his white fur gone, completely covered in smooth silver covering of fur, the wishbone marking most evident. He hurried in a frantic wriggle to meet his longtime friend. "Miracle, I knew that you'd come! I just knew it, the walrus told us that you were here!"

It was not long before Little Lukie came up to greet the perpetual white seal in a gush of wriggling excitement. Lukie, still smaller than an average adult bull, had also grown all traces of his former snow-white youth long since forgotten.

"Big Petie, Little Lukie!" Miracle exclaimed as the wind billowed about him, the silver streams of the moonlight blanketing both him and his newly found friends. "I never thought I'd see you again!"

"Yes, yes, it is we!" Lukie squealed his voice slightly of a lower register, however still retaining its excitable highly pitched singsong tone.

"What are you doing here?" Miracle asked them in excited breath.

Big Petie spoke up his eyes as full as the moon that shone upon him. "Wow, you haven't changed a bit, Miracle, how come?"

Annoyed, Lukie spoke out. "Never mind about that *neither*. Tell him about Bellgar and Nikki! It is their child whom Jillith has taken!"

It was as if a shard of ice had cut its way into Miracle's heart. "Bellgar is Nikki's mate?"

"Yep," Big Petie yelped. "And we have to help save their child, that is, if it's not too late already!"

Miracle shivered in the wind, then spoke out softly. "I see," he whispered, a deluge of surging emotions slapping mercilessly all about him.

"It was not long after our mates arrived upon Sealssong," Petie explained, "that we saw their ships. We then knew that the evil man-beasts were planning to kill the whitecoats! We came here to warn them, but we were too late."

"Yes, so many have died," Lukie hurriedly disclosed, "so many were destroyed by the claws of the horrible man-beast! So many were—" Unable to finish, Lukie just shook his head and closed his eyes, failing to block out the tears.

"Come," Big Petie barked. "We must hurry! We must go to the cave at the top of the slop, which is where Bellgar is. That is where the crazed Jillith and the child are!"

Turning, Miracle and Lukie followed the robust bull. It wasn't long before Miracle could see the tiny form of Nikki at the bottom of a hill. In an instant, he was sliding down an icy incline toward her. As he made his descent, the snow under his flippers kicked out from beneath him, the snow and ice slapping the prostrate Nikki across the chest. Seeing her just lying there as if dead took his breath from him. Somehow finding the strength, Miracle called out to Crumpels who was already at Nikki's side.

"Listen to me, you must take Nikki back to the ice castle and watch over her. I must help Bellgar and the child!"

"Oh, whoody-whooo," Crumpels wept. "The poor dear, she doesn't seem to be—"

It was Emma's voice that sounded next. "Yes, and I will help you, Crumpels," she said while sliding down the remainder of the snowy hill, startling the walrus, her feathers caked with snow.

"*You?* Whooo!" Crumpels resisted, pulling away from the girl that remained decorated in the queer feathery dress.

"Do as she asks!" Miracle sternly instructed.

Seeing the human girl, Big Petie immediately went in for the kill. With one gigantic thrust, the enormous bull pounced in Emma's direction, bearing his fangs, ready to rip her to pieces.

"Stop!" Miracle shouted, but Big Petie ignored his pleas. Emma tried to speak to the wild creature, but in seconds, Petie prepared to lacerate her into a million slivers. Miracle immediately rushed up to defend Emma. Blocking Petie from reaching her, the white seal again shouted, "Stop! She means you no harm!"

"Are you crazy?" Big Petie howled. "She is one of them!"

"No, she is not!" Miracle roared, the hairs on his back standing straight up, preparing to fight if necessary. "She is my friend. She has come to help us. She knows where my mother is, and if we are ever to save Nikki and her child, you had better trust and believe me or it will be too late!"

The raging Petie stared at Miracle for a moment, studying the white seal's purple-tipped fur blow back and forth in the moonlight. Instinctively, Petie closed his mouth and covered his teeth. Lowering his head in submission, he began to back away from the human girl, Lukie following his retreat. In a circle, they gathered near Nikki, each one bending his head to look down at her. She was still alive when Miracle touched her nose with his. Quietly, and almost immediately, the injured Nikki looked up into the white seal's face, her black eyes sparkling as she looked at him as if none of what had happened ever did. It was as if they were still young, looking at each other in the same way that they did before all of this sadness came to them. Nikki's eyes began to fill with tears, catching the blurry reflections from the fleeting stars and moon above. As the clouds began to stretch away from one another, a shooting star mirrored itself in Nikki's eyes; and for a moment, every other star seemed to watch as the shooting blaze shot across the newly lit twinkling night sky.

"What has she done to you?" Miracle begged, tears filling his own eyes.

Nikki spoke. "That stupid seal, neither she nor the man-beasts could kill me. I wouldn't let them!" Nikki said, coughing up blood. Swallowing, she found the strength to raise her head. "Save my child, Miracle, please save my son!" was all Nikki said before her head slumped down and her eyes closed off the twinkling night sky.

Suddenly, from out of the shadows, a large form emerged, then a mighty roar refuted as if the ice garden was breaking apart, convulsing the hearts of everyone listening. Miracle twisted his gaze toward the icy mountains, watching the massive walrus Poo-Coo crash down the slippery slopes that now seemed to sustain him barely. He flipped and turned over several times before hitting the solid ice. Emma gasped, as did the rest, when she saw the blood covering his face and chest. The walrus was hurt, and from the looks of his matted and bloodstained hide, the wounds were deep. The dazed walrus tried to wriggle forth once more, but he quickly fell back to the cold ground. A hysterical scream left the throat of his mother. Miracle and the others went to him, Emma remaining behind with the lifeless seal who had asked that her child be saved before closing her eyes.

"Poo-Coo—" Crumpels shrieked, blatantly falling pitifully against her son's weighty bulk. Poo-Coo shook his head, again trying to sit up, but the injuries he had sustained would not allow it. In agony, he yet once more fell to the icy floor of the ice garden. "My poor Poo-Coo, what has happened?" she blasted out while her tears hosed over him.

The other seals gathered in close, circling the cut-up walrus, and Poo-Coo spoke to them in a tortured voice. "Jillith has killed Nikki's child."

What followed seemed to shatter into the surreal. It was as if his words did not belong against his lips. The walrus had to be mistaken. However, once more, Poo-Coo made the monstrous statement a cruel and intolerable reality. "She took Nikki's child. I tried to stop her!" he coughed, a burning grip in his throat devouring him. "I even had the little guy in my grasp. Everything was going to be all right. Everything should have been all right!" The suffering walrus choked; there was additional coughing before he continued. "I had saved Nikki's child! We were on our way to where we are now"—Poo-Coo looked at his mother—"when out of nowhere she cut me off, that damned Jillith! There was no way I could have known! I thought that she was dead! I thought I had killed her!"

Not waiting to hear any more, Miracle quickly threw his stare up toward the caves, both rage and pity reflecting in his burning eyes. Turning his gaze, he looked back to the walrus. "You did everything you possibly could. We all know this, Poo-Coo," Miracle said, returning his stare toward the sad gathering. "Go back to the ice castle, all of you. Do all you can for Nikki and Poo-Coo. I will join you when I am able." With these words, Miracle began his ascent toward the cave and Jillith, only the penguin daring to follow not far behind.

EVIL HARP

Just as Miracle reached the top of the icy slope, from out of a dark, bluish snow cave, the now massive and lethal Jillith emerged the dead pup between her crimson jaws.

"I warned them not to stop me! I told them if they dared to interfere the child would die!" Jillith viscously growled, moving the dead body of the baby seal monstrously between her distorted lips. "And if you dare come near me, you will die as well!" she ranted through a ghastly snarl.

Unscathed by her threats, Miracle wriggled forward, but then stopped when he came directly upon the body of Bellgar. The father of the deceased infant was lying snout down in the snow. Lowering his head, Miracle tried to turn the bull over. "Bellgar!" the white seal begged. "You must get up . . . Bellgar!"

"I warned him to stay away, but he would not listen," Jillith insisted coldheartedly. "He tried to stop me. He failed."

Turning his face away from Bellgar, Miracle looked at Jillith with sheer contempt burning in his eyes. "How could you do this? You are worse than all of the man-beasts!"

"So it is you, freak! Is it the child you have come for?"

Suddenly, Bellgar stirred, regaining his consciousness. Slowly turning himself around, the distraught father wearily raised himself out of the snow, his glaring eyes shooting directly at Jillith. Miracle tried to help Bellgar, but the incensed bull pushed him away, looking at Miracle for a moment, acknowledging him in silence. Then crunching his snout into a mad snarl, Bellgar began to wriggle unsteadily toward Jillith, a demented look burning in his eyes.

"Look who's back from the dead!" Jillith crudely teased. "Does Papa want some more?" Dropping the dead pup from her mouth, the crazed seal once again exposed her sharp fangs. "Come on, this time I'll make sure I finish the job!"

"Give me my son!" Bellgar growled, madness foaming from the sides of his mouth.

"But it's dead," she nonchalantly answered.

"Give me my son!" Bellgar repeated, his eyes growing wilder by the moment as he continued his way toward the evil Jillith.

"It is of no use to me now," she said, once again taking the lifeless creature between her jaws. "Here, take it and be gone with you!" Casting the lifeless form of the dead pup before its father, Jillith spat the last traces of its blood from her savage jaws. With a wild and crazed howl, Bellgar lunged at Jillith, but he remained dazed and desperate for consciousness and in no shape to fight the savage beast. Nevertheless, he went in for the kill, missing his mark, only grazing her cheek. With insane retaliation, Jillith swung open her mouth, catching the disjointed bull between her sharpened jaws. Biting down hard, she tore into his flesh, shaking his neck about savagely. Miracle screamed out for them to stop but to no avail. Jillith quickly flipped her backside around, hitting the dazed father in the head, knocking him senseless against a large ice bolder.

Miracle surged across the snow, wildlike, barking out in a frantic voice. "If you do not stop, I will destroy you, Jillith, I swear I will!"

As the full moon strained and slipped through the moving clouds of the midnight sky, it caught Jillith's scarlet lips in its light, making her look more like a monster than a seal. "Oh, and what are you going to do?" She laughed. "Look at you, still dressed up in your little white dress, I see. What's the matter, too much of a coward to become a real bull, freak?"

"You hurt Nikki and killed her child!" roared the white seal, the tips of his purple fur boiling over with the same emotional fire that now erupted in his veins. "How could you? How could you do such a thing and feel no remorse?"

"Get lost, pansy!"

"This is your last chance, Jillith! Leave Sealssong now and never return, or you will live to regret it!" Miracle shouted, the stone around his neck flaring a brighter shade of purple with each word he commanded.

She laughed wickedly, the blood glistening over her snout. "You're still as ridiculous as you were when you were a wimpy, sissy pup!"

"Don't force me to do something we'll both regret!"

"Oh, stop it! Everyone knows you're afraid to take on a baby seahorse, freak! Be gone!" she cursed. "Or I'll kill you right here and now!"

"Jillith, I realize that you too have suffered a loss this night, but acting like this is not going to bring back your pup."

"I'm warning you," she growled. "I already killed this night. One more death won't make any difference to me, especially yours!"

"You no longer belong to Sealssong! Get out!" Miracle shouted.

With one bolting leap, Jillith cut through the chilling night air, slamming into Miracle, her incisive fangs sparking from the moonlight as they sliced into his side. Miracle pulled away, leaving a chunk of fur and flesh in her mouth. Somehow managing to plow an uppercut against her jaws, he swatted shut Jillith's mouth tight, catching her tongue, nearly severing it. Wild with insanity, the wicked seal spat more blood from her mouth, exposing her crimson fangs, preparing to tear open his throat. Miracle jolted away just as her snapping teeth brushed against his neck, only instead of biting down into his furry hide she inadvertently caught the purple stone, cracking it, splintering it while ferociously biting down. Jillith screamed out, and the stone flashed a brilliant purple color. Hurling backward, she fell hard against the ice, its harsh impact crushing the breath from her while more sparks from the splintered stone shot out like a newly lit flare.

Dazed, the vicious seal flipped over numerous times trying to get her bearings. Her lips felt as if they had been literally torn to shreds and then set on fire. Collapsing from the pain, she struggled to get her bearings. Gripping the ground tightly, Jillith began to rampage through the snow with her burning mouth exploding before her. Unhinged, she buried her muzzle deep in the cold snow, shaking her singed, raw lips against its coolness. She kept rolling about, digging through the crushed ice while blindly edging her way across the mountain, rapidly nearing its end. Coming dangerously close to a rocky cliff, one that without warning seemed to drop down into the darkness of nothingness, Jillith dangerously tottered back and forth. Never had any seal ventured to this part of Sealssong before—until now! Just as the murderous seal was about to plummet into the darkness below, she suddenly jolted from the snow, sensing the fatal drop only inches from where she stood. She watched as a chunk of snow fell from her severely burned lips down into the endless pit before her that was believed to lead somewhere into the cold and forbidden parts of the earth. Slowly, she began to edge away from the radical drop, making sure that her flippers remained steady upon the ice; however, steady or not, she was not about to escape, not this time.

SMACK! was the sound she would hear besides the sound of her own screams. A sharp blow to the back of her head sent her toppling over the edge; the smack and the screams would be in the company of yet one more pronounced blare. For as Jillith toppled over the cliff, she could plainly hear the robust voice of the mad seal snapping, "BUG OFF, bozo! Ya lip-flappin', codswalloping donkey-ass fool!" Mum barked, finishing off with one long stretched-out belch blasting off from behind before turning away from what she had just done.

Down the dark shaft of nothingness Jillith fell, tumbling further and further, her tortured screams fading while she disappeared into the blackness. In a short while, Mum wriggled her way over to Miracle, who remained bent over in a small heap near the unconscious Bellgar. Upon reaching the white seal, Mum sniffed a few times at his furry head. "*Love-ya*," she said in a quiet voice, "it's all right now. She's gone. She won't hurt you or anyone else ever again."

"Mum," Miracle answered in a voice that held imposing anguish. "She has damaged the tear. Something is wrong. Something is very wrong!"

Bellgar was slowly coming around just as the feisty penguin waddled up to his side. "Is he dead?" Mulgrew asked in a high shrill.

"Oh, back off, birdie!" Mum snapped. "Of course, he isn't dead, pinhead!"

Miracle tried to sit up but quickly fell to the ice-cold ground. Bellgar, however, was sitting upright. Shaking his head, the father of the deceased pup tried to regain his senses, pathetically crawling back toward his dead son. Taking the pup gently into his shaking jaws Bellgar brought his child away toward the water's edge. He would return his infant to the sea, burying his remains among the freezing waters surrounding the icy cradle that his boy would no longer need. Again, Miracle tried to sit up, this time succeeding. Mum helped him the rest of the way, supporting him with her weight, both descending the hill, the small penguin nervously dancing behind them.

It began to snow heavily. Sadly, Bellgar looked down into the slushy ice floe where he had relinquished his pup. A single tear fell as he bade the dead infant goodbye. Suddenly, a loud cracking sound shook the ice. Kishk had returned. Pushing onward, the colossal leviathan waited for a small portion of the icy floor to crumple and bend. It broke off from its frosty host while the whale watched silently. A piece of the nursery floated toward the distressed creatures looking back at him.

Suddenly, the voice of Lukie sounded. "Miracle, you must come at once!" he cried.

Miracle quickly spoke out. "Lukie, I thought I told you all to go back to the ice castle."

"We did! We were even fortunate to catch a ride on a nearby ice raft, but I had to come back and find you after the strange bird lady began to turn blue!"

"Blue?"

"Something has happened to the man-beast!"

"Emma?"

"One minute she was fine and then suddenly she fainted and has not moved a muscle since *neither!*"

Miracle's eyes widened with fear. He lowered them to look upon the stone. "The tear, Jillith has damaged the tear! I knew something bad would come of it."

Realizing that the enormous whale was only a few feet away, the nervous Lukie looked at him. "My, you are a big one, aren't cha? You sure go a long way up!"

"Oh, love us," Mum exclaimed, happy to see the whale. However, maintaining a bit of exasperation, she said, "'Tis about time you showed up, fishy!"

There, upon the moving waters filled with its crushed and icy driftage, the blue chanter gave the assemblage a doleful look of sympathy for the tragic misfortunes they were enduring.

Eventually, the broken floor of ice reached the gathering. Bobbing back and forth against the nursery, the giant raft tapped incessantly against the icy shores of Sealssong.

"I must get back to Emma!" Miracle barked before wriggling away from the others.

"Wait," Kishk called after him. "I will return you all safely to the ice castle. Come." He waited for them to gather on the ice raft he provided.

BACK TO THE ICE CASTLE

Moving in a sea of total sound, the blue whale listened to the perpetual orchestra of life moving about him, its sweet voice calming him, telling him that everything would turn out all right for the unfortunate creatures sailing before him. Allowing for the piece of the floating nursery to embark upon its journey, Kishk listened further as Miracle gave the commands from the center of the raft, instructing the whale in the direction of the ice castle, the others cushioning around him as he licked at his wounds unceasingly.

The penguin upheld his nervous flutter, circling the edge of the raft. Lukie sat next to the grieving Bellgar, both remaining silent staring out toward the soon-to-be distant portion of the shattered nursery still glistening from the spilled blood of the innocence that knew life but for a moment. Not once mentioning this heart-wrenching loss aloud, Lukie would also remember how he, as well as his faithful companion, lost their pups this night, each having lost his mate to, the evil of man as well. Reflecting upon this, the weary Lukie lowered himself to the icy floor; and for the first time since this heartrending occurrence took place, he began to weep, not only for himself and his lost family, but for his cherished friend Petie too. Then Lukie sat up and looked out into the ocean, just as Petie, who was already back at the ice castle, looked out into the same open sea, both simultaneously lowering their heads in reverent memory of all that remained lost, each forever to be honored and regarded as the unsung but eternally true and brave warriors of Sealssong. As the tears fell, Lukie imagined he was no longer floating on an ice raft, just as Petie believed he was no longer waiting at the entrance of a distance cave. They were together again in spirit, just as if they were sitting side by side, their silver-colored heads resting upon one another, their silver coats with piebald markings shining in the frosty night air, each silently and simply staring off—remembering, forever remembering.

Now Miracle's thoughts were of Emma, the strange human girl who had somehow not only captivated him, but had also managed to capture his heart, knowing that when he returned to her, she might already be dead. Once more, he looked down at the dimly lit stone. All he could do was to shudder while gazing upon it, his heart growing heavier, hundreds of possibilities overwhelming him. Mum would stay awake for most of the ride, seating herself next to the white seal, keeping her fleshy flippers tight around him, singing to him her nonsensical jibber-jabber, her shabby bonnet partially sailing in the breeze.

As the moon finally left the dark sky that remained swarmed over by the falling snow, the drifting creatures continued onward. With the snow twinkling upon each one of them, Kishk remaining ever constantly alert, the music of the sea pressed itself tenderly against the mighty blue giant's frame, an even and abiding sounding board that would endlessly and faithfully remain next to him as a newlywed bride.

It would stop snowing when they would arrive at the ice castle; however, what was impending in the blackest waters of the sea could not be stopped.

The *Tiamat* was almost there.

VILE THINGS

For Kenyan, the darkness was never far from him. Oddly, it was becoming a part of him, so complete and unrestricted. Once more, he was pulling at chains that bit into his wrists. Feeling them weigh against the cold stone wall, he fell forward with a pathetic groan of utter hopelessness. However, his resilience would not permit him to remain this way. All too soon, he was again pulling and clanging the bracelets of steel, not daring to give into their squeeze, shaking them as if to keep from slipping into madness. Kenyan was not sure how long he had been in this darkness, nor was he certain of just how long he had been awake in this shadowed universe of squeaking boards and dripping water. Lately, he was no longer certain of anything.

More squeaks and creaks sounded. Was it the boards within this blackness that continued to squeak, or was it more rats? The furry creatures were plentiful and most curious about him, crisscrossing over his bare feet, brushing past his arms and face as they scurried up the wet and slimy wall that bent around him. One brazen foul-smelling rat with red shining eyes, just like the witch's, was even bold enough to take a nip at his chin. As if that were not sufficient, the wretched thing went on investigating by clawing up his face, steadying its dirty little rat feet against the folded and clinched skin of his squeezed-shut eyelids, taking a bite out of his forehead with one quick nip. Guessing that the filthy thing did not like the taste, Kenyan felt the beastly creature dropping off abruptly before scurrying into the obscurity, pressing ever so tightly from every corner of this dismal place.

Once again, he tolled his heavy chains, rattling them wildly against the evil nighttime surrounding him. He pulled on them savagely, but the wet and dripping wall had no intention of releasing its cold, vicious bite. More thoughts of the vile witch clogged his already crazed and exhausted mind, recalling over and over again his sister and how that sadistic, evil woman who resembled the filthy rats with the red eyes had attacked her.

"Emma!" he screamed. "Emma, can you hear me?" All that answered were more sounds of dribbling water, that and more sounds of squeaks and pitter-patter of more little filthy rat feet. Indeed, the rodents came preparing to taste more of his toes or suck on some old nibbles previously sampled. Again, he rattled and banged his chains, screaming out his sister's name. Not sure if Emma was even still alive, he suddenly pictured the witch's face right there in the black heart of this blind and unbearable midnight, clinching his fists, shrieking the dreaded name. "Decara!" he howled. "I know you can hear me so listen up, you worm-eaten piece of rat scum! I swear I'm going to get you! I'm not going to stop until I rip out that dirty heart of yours, do you hear me—witch!"

There were no verbal responses to be heard, not at first. However, a response, one that he was not ready for, made its presence known to him. He heard it plainly. Someone, or something, was there with him in the darkness. He could hear it breathing, and this time it was no rat. Her tried to still himself while he strained to listen, consumed by the wild drumming inside his head.

"Who's there? Is that you—*witch?*" he hoarsely whispered. Again, no answer came. Then suddenly, he heard a slight stir. Something moved, something sounding much like the clinking of chains. Again, he called out, "Decara, is that you, or is it your hairy flunky? Answer me!" he shouted.

Kenyan jumped back, hitting the wet wall with his shoulder when he heard the voice answer him. It was deep and masculine, belonging neither to the witch nor the hairy stooge. "Tell me who you are, boy," the mysterious voice asked, clearing itself as if it had been asleep. "How is it that you are here? What in god's name could she want with you?" Kenyan did not answer. At first, he was not sure if it was the witch's trick. Again, the deep voice called out from the pit of blackness. "Answer me, boy, who are you?"

"I'm a prisoner just like you," Kenyan answered.

"My god, you are real. For a moment, I thought—"

"I was a ghost or something the witch conjured up? No, I'm no ghost. My name is Kenyan, and you are?"

The voice cleared itself again. "I'm not sure anymore," the deep inflection replied. "Ask me who I was instead."

"All right then, who were you?"

"I was once the captain of this accursed ship, or so I thought. My name is Thorne."

"Are you hurt?"

"Never mind that. Tell me, how long has she held you captive here?"

Kenyan shook his invisible head and scoffed out a half-breath of humorous disgust. "I'm not sure anymore myself. Both my sister and I have been prisoners on this filthy ship what seems forever now."

"You mean there is another youth upon this vessel? How was she able to conceal you so completely, and why? For the love of God, boy, tell me what is happening here?" the exhausted Captain Thorne implored, something he had not remembered doing ever.

"I don't know where my sister is," Kenyan said, restraining his burning tears. "I don't know if she's alive or dead."

"What is it Decara wants?"

"She is a witch; surely you must know that by now."

Silence scratched through the black nothingness surrounding them for what seemed a long time, and then Thorne broke the quiet with his deep and irritated voice. "This must be a nightmare of sorts. I am ill, I must have the fever or something even worse."

"I assure you that you are not imagining this. She is a witch, and she intends to kill us both!"

"Why?"

"That's just it. I don't rightly know myself, but it has something to do with my sister and the seals."

"The seals?"

"Yes," Kenyan explained. "My sister has abilities—powers. She can do things, see things we cannot."

"That's all fine and well, son, but what has this to do with me and my ship and the men aboard the *Tiamat?*"

"I just told you that I don't know, but the witch has something rotten planned for all of us!"

Both sets of chains rattled at the same time, sounding as if they were playing to each other in stereo. Captain Thorne once again spoke out, his raw voice penetrating the darkness. "She has taken over the ship and the men," Thorne said, slumping against his own set of chains. "She has somehow bewitched them, taken their minds and souls," he said, shaking his invisible head wrapped deeply inside the darkness. "But for reasons I cannot explain."

"How did you end up here?"

"When I was unable to find the way out of the devil's fog, she came to me like the black of night, threatening me, accusing me of recklessness, being a fool, an incapable commander. She . . . she—" He suddenly stopped. Swallowing hard before speaking again, Thorne felt a menacing shiver crawl up his back. "She . . . she did things to me."

"What kind of things?"

"Vile things not of the flesh—*but the soul!*"

"Go on."

"She was able to weaken me, tear at my spirit, almost as if she were sucking it dry." Suddenly, he became outraged and yelled, "Who, or what is this hellish wench? How can she mandate such influence over me, strip me of my will until . . . until . . ." he started to cough, his words diminishing into the black lining of the world covering him. "Until I was weak, debilitated, and easy prey for that neanderthal pig that brought me here and chained me up in this stench hole!" Once more, he became enraged. "For the love of God, what has she done to me?"

"She has done what she has done because as I have already told you," Kenyan explained nonchalantly, "she is a witch, and she must die."

"But witches cannot be. There are no such things!"

"Keep telling yourself that, you might begin to believe it, but not for long, not for long."

Like the rats, more silence crawled over both prisoners. "What could she want?" Thorne moaned, his deep voice made tired and raspy.

Kenyan did not answer straight away; instead, he kicked at the worming rodents covering his feet and nipping at his toes, swinging them off before he spoke. "To destroy innocence and the seals, at least that is what my sister believes."

"The seals, what have they to do with anything?" Thorne snapped, his voice breaking up again.

"I'm not sure. Perhaps nothing," Kenyan told him, pushing more of the determined hairy creatures away from his bleeding toes. "Then again," he continued, smiling wickedly at the blackness,—perhaps everything!" Closing his eyes and momentarily giving himself up to the darkness, Kenyan sighed, Thorne doing the same. In silence, both dropped their heads, resting them against the heaving movements of their chests, both breathing heavily, not knowing what to say or feel, or what to do. This would last for but a moment, before Kenyan raised his invisible head, defiantly staring back into the obscurity. Pushing his feet back and forth, he aimlessly threw off more of the furry creatures piling up on top of his toes, knowing what had to be done. He had to break free to kill the witch. Somehow, some way, the witch was going to die, and this time failure was not an option. Before he could contemplate his plans further, he heard the captain start to yell. The rats had finally come for Thorne, and the way that he howled, they must have thoroughly enjoyed the sampling of his hide.

Once more, the darkness rejoiced.

WAITING

Arayna tried to support the weight of the harp next to her, attempting to hold the seal's head with her own, pushing her body against her, keeping the seal from falling. Sadly, it was too late. She was already gone.

Arayna watched when at that same moment, yet another tormented mother seal closed her eyes for the last time, just as Lakannia had done days before. This last death would make five; there was just one other left besides herself. Slowly, and with all the strength she could invoke, the weary Arayna gently and reverently relinquished the body to the cold floor of the mesh cage. She lowered her snout and softly kissed the dead harp's forehead. "Sleep well, my dear sister," Arayna whispered. Eventually, she raised her head, looking to the other surviving seal, each mourning the loss of the harps that were unable to survive the cruel and torturous ways of the wicked devil woman. The stealing of tears had this time been fatal, for this time, the monstrous act extracted more than their precious fluids; this last session was the worst of the worst, finally taking with it the core of their life force.

Not sure how she withstood the horrible process that Decara inflicted, Arayna shuddered, glancing down at the pile of dead seals she had come to know and love. It was all too much for her. Surely, she felt her mind could not withstand another session of the monster woman's hellish power. Slumping forward, she began to weep. Aware of the remaining seal, she made her way over to its side. As the two suffering mothers finally met, they immediately fell into one another, weeping pathetically, each collapsing to the black floor. No words would be spoken here. What they felt and what they had been forced into experiencing went far beyond the possibilities of mere words, for these emotions burned deep through what remained of their broken hearts.

Starving, and at death's doorstep herself, Arayna realized that the seal next to her was becoming despondent. Collapsing further, the unconscious harp sank across the swaying bottom of the cage. Arayna, however, did not stir. She merely looked at the heaving motion of the seal's chest. For now, this harpie remained alive. She would not disturb her. It was better this way. For the time being, this woeful mother would find peace. She would no longer be made to feel the memory of her dead child, nor remember the deplorable feeling of having her tears sucked from her spirit just so they could be changed to what the man-child called diamonds.

Arayna continued to weep. Now afraid and dying, she fought the sensation to slip into the unconscious or death itself. If the human child did not return soon, Decara would. And this time, she too would join her dead sisters of the sea. She was sure of this. There was no possible way she could endure one more encounter with the devil woman. Turning, she arched her neck and looked toward the place where Emma had vanished. She could hear the serpent hissing and fizzing across the dark and gloomy room. It sounded as if it was laughing, and it was. She closed her eyes, capturing the last image she remembered of the human girl just before she disappeared. Her eyes blurred when returning her stare back to the unconscious harp next to her, as well as the deceased seals covering the floor. They remained mercifully released from Decara's hideous horrors—horrors she would still have to face.

More thoughts of the human creature piled in around her.

Had the human girl forgotten her promise? Had the serpent sent her to a death too frightening to consider? Was she still alive? Furthermore, if she were, where was she? Would she still be able to return to save both her and the unconscious seal resting next to her? If she did return, would she return with her lost son? The mesh cage swayed back and forth from Arayna's movements, causing the gathering of the unconscious mother and the dead seals to shift along with her. She blinked the tears away and let her gaze fall solely upon the unconscious harp beneath her, wanting to see the rhythm of her breath once more. However, when she did this, Arayna drew in a sudden gasp. No movement came from the chest of the collapsed seal. When it stopped she knew not, but the poor creature had succumbed, joining the others that would for always sleep.

Arayna resisted utterly collapsing herself, though she was well on the verge of joining her dead companions. Fighting to maintain consciousness, she clenched her jaw tightly and shook her head in defiance; she would not surrender to death. She would not give up her spirit. She would wait, somehow believing in the human girl's promise to her and the covenant etched somewhere within the deepest part of her heart, one that promised the return of her lost Miracle. With the saddest of eyes, Arayna looked down upon the recently deceased seal. She stared at her for a long time and then moved her sorrowful gaze, meeting the other harps that were drained dry by such unspeakable evil. She closed her eyes and said a silent prayer, and when she reopened them, she would return to waiting, believing, somehow trusting that she would not fall victim to the nightmare. She would wait, only this time she would wait—alone. There was no one left who could comfort her. Only the memory of her lost child would remain and offer her solace now. For here, inside the darkness of this prison, she would continue to believe; she would not dare do otherwise. For if she did, she would truly be exiled, and there, within this dreaded seclusion she would most assuredly meet death itself.

No. She would wait, and she would believe; she simply had to believe. She had no choice.

UNIQUE MADNESS

Emma was still alive when Miracle returned to the ice castle.

The tear, however damaged, had not entirely gone out; there was still enough light left inside the magical wonder to help Emma, Nikki, and Poo-Coo. Miracle did not waste any time in having them each touch the stone, and in a little while, they seemed to respond, Nikki taking somewhat longer to recuperate.

The ice castle proved to be more than adequate to accommodate the entire gathering, aside from Kishk, of course. He remained stationary in some nearby body of water next to the shore that washed itself faithfully up to the entrance of the castle. The tides had become most anxious. In the distance, a storm was approaching. The dark menacing clouds that were assembling there foretold quite the tempest. Miracle, Big Petie, Bellgar, Little Lukie, and even Mulgrew had worked through the day and most of the night gathering the bodies of the baby seals, returning their sacred forms back to the sea in a silent vigil of somber veneration. In silent procession, the heavyhearted seals brought the tiny infants to the watery fingers of the waves, watching, stirring near the very edges of the frosty floes. In humble reverence, the downtrodden harps came bearing their sad offerings, each holding the remains of lifeless pups within the soft crevasse of their mouths. As each came near the wavering shoreline, they lowered their heads and closed their eyes, saying a prayer before relinquishing the tiny infants back into the sea. Once more, their precious souls would unite with the absolute mother of their kind, the omnipotent sea herself. She would reclaim her lost children, perpetually gathering them within the rushing waters of her heart. Whenever she swelled and washed against some forgotten shore, they would be there embracing distant lands, each tiny harp reformed into frothy circles of foam that would kiss the hands of many strangers millions of miles away over and over again. She would, for always, keep their memory alive this way; they would never be forgotten.

The seals did not utter a single sound, nor did they acknowledge one another during the burial of the children. Not even the birds of the air sang this day; the very air itself mourned. The storm was rapidly approaching, and the groaning rattles in the throat of the disarranged wind cutting through the jeweled world came with a disturbing hollowed roar. Miracle would be the one to release the final infant back to the sea. He stared at the pup, watching it settle into the watery arms of the sea, gradually turning into a soft blur before vanishing. The raging wind tore at Miracle, but he did not stir.

As the approaching storm continued to rumble, growing more enraged by the minute, as if alive with fuming wrath over the unspeakable slaying of innocence, Mum went about her business. In a calm and determined manner, the mad harpie sang to herself while doing a deed that brought her a peculiar satisfaction; she was on a most definite mission. Trekking through the snow, Mum eagerly sought after the remains of the monsters that had stained her world with the color of blood and tears. One by one, she sniffed out the bodies of the dead men, the ones that she could find; and one by one she tore off the hunter's clothing, snipping the edges of the furry raiment that had once protected them. With her teeth clenched tightly, Mum pulled and tugged at their garments, ripping them off harshly, never stopping until she had left behind numerous naked man-beasts. After the dead men had been completely stripped, she returned back and forth repeatedly to the chosen site where all the torn-away clothing had been gathered. Casting each article gaily into an already spilling pile, the mad seal clapped her flippers together excitedly. Proudly surveying her stolen collection, she clapped some more. However, before preparing to take her poached souvenirs back to the ice castle, Mum would have to return to the dead, naked man-beasts one last time. Coming upon one of the deceased hunters, she looked down at it and belched loudly, so loud that it caused her nose to shoot out more of its familiar gooey discharge all over her bosom. Having already turned a most unpleasant and ghastly shade of blue, the corpse of the man lay partially covered in the snow beneath her. Gazing at it, Mum just could not resist taking one final thing from the murdering vile beast—its so-called dignity. To do so, she must first leave something, but not just any something. For upon his dead carcass, she intended to leave the foulest and most displeasing excrement she knew of; and so plopping directly on top of the frozen cadaver, the mad seal forcibly pushed on her filled abdomen, opened—and squirted! She would do this to every dead, naked seal hunter whom she should chance by. When she was at last satisfied, with a wicked smile, she turned away from the last of the defiled men and wriggled happily back to the heap of stolen man-beast coverings. It would require some time to bring the pilfered belongings to the ice castle, but she would endure. No storm would stop her. In her unique madness, she knew exactly what she was doing.

Another violent crash of thunder filled the heavens. Miracle felt the rumble upon the icy ground while Big Petie approached him from behind. "We must return to the ice castle before the storm gets worse," Big Petie barked, the storm roaring about him.

"But the others, I am sure there are more," Miracle pleaded.

"Miracle, we must get back to the ice castle. We've done all we can."

"It's not enough!"

Big Petie stared at Miracle and offered a tired smile. "I know, dear friend, I know, but it won't do any of us any good if you go and get yourself taken away by this nasty typhoon. Please come back with me now. The others need you. I need you. Come on, chum, it's time we were on our way."

Hanging his head, Miracle lamented over the murdered baby seals. Realizing that Big Petie was right, he complied. With one more look at the icy waters before him, he made one last prayer over the mellifluous place of interment granted to the innocent baby harp seals of Sealssong now returned to the sea. Meanwhile, the Mad Mum made several trips back to the ice castle, adding to her growing mass of collected assortments of man-beast coverings while Mulgrew neurotically paced back and forth in front of the guarded entrance, shaking his tiny penguin head in aggravated amazement over the question of her deranged endeavors.

Big Petie, Bellgar, and Little Lukie finally made their return to the temporary sanctuary. Crumpels, who had remained to watch over both Poo-Coo and Nikki, suddenly rumbled her massive self about the ice castle. Flaking off parts of the walls with her big old self in a definite attempt to greet the others as they returned, the entire place reverberated as if to fall apart while she wriggled up to its icy doorframe. Slamming against a large icy boulder propped against the entrance, Crumpels pushed and pulled at it with her extensive tusks. Rolling the heavy blockade away, she waited for all to enter and then forced it shut with one exaggerated and emphatic slam. A peculiar quiet encased the ice castle as a flock of eerie sirens of howling winds, although muffled, moaned about the structure, haunting it with its disturbing groans sounding like angry and restless ghosts. A soft and diminished blue glow burned within the glassy walls, making visible only the silhouettes of the creatures within. Bellgar was immediately at Nikki's side, looking down at her, caressing her with his frosty and saturated cheek. Crumpels returned to her sleeping son, Big Petie and Little Lukie remaining near the entrance of the doorway, defying the storm or anyone else to enter.

Mulgrew continued with his neurotic pace circling the entire place. He occasionally threw Mum dirty looks of disgust when he saw her shifting through the pile of man-beast coverings, acting just like a human sorting through the laundry after the wash and dry.

Emma lay prostrate. Most of the beautiful bird feathers remained lost and strewed, crushed about her, rendering her almost naked, her thin arms wrapped around the tiny pup that she had saved. When Miracle came upon her, he could not help think how curious she looked. Unlike anything that he had ever seen, she continued to hold such awe and wonder for him. She remained beautiful although why, he was not sure. Looking down at her, his heart stirred. So many feelings were passing through him. Drawing closer, he heard from across the ice castle the sigh of the one he would for always cherish. It was Nikki. She was awakening.

Without hesitation, the white seal wriggled himself over to her. Slowly, Miracle approached the semiconscious Nikki as hundreds of sensations flooded over him. Her mate, Bellgar, continued his affectionate rubbing of his cheek against hers as Miracle tenderly looked down at Nikki and smiled. Lowering his head, ready to speak to her, he plainly heard her first words; they were not for him. "Bellgar," she whispered in a low and weakened voice. "I want Bellgar," she called with such a voice of longing.

The feelings that arose inside the white seal hurt with a biting sting; it was something he did not anticipate. Unremitting, he continued to look down at his dear Nikki; his vision blurring, the tears filling his dark shining eyes. "Nikki," Miracle softly implored, but she did not answer. Once more, she called out for her mate, and once more, Miracle felt the shooting stinger pierce his heart. Sadly, he bowed his head, allowing Bellgar to comfort her. Watching the two in their joyous reunion, he wept silently, slowly removing himself from their sight, not for a moment believing that they were ever aware that he was there.

"It's as it should be, boop-boop dee-dee," the kind Crumpels said, rubbing her rubbery head of wrinkles against Miracle's snowy-white cheek. "They are one now, dear."

Miracle looked at the walrus for a moment, brushing the last of his tears away with his shoulder, bravely giving Crumpels's a faint smile. Then with one final pause, he once again looked at his dear Nikki. Her eyes were wide open now as she and Bellgar remained tenderly nestled into each other. Abruptly, Mum belched. "She's going to be just fine, *Love-ya!*" the mad seal chimed, nearly falling over the walrus, almost crashing straight through the side of the ice castle, just about bringing down the whole place in order to get the last word in, as usual.

The penguin was quick to snap. "Hey, watch where you're going, you clumsy thing, you!"

"Why don't you go bye-bye, birdie, and bugger off!" Mum bellowed, snubbing the bird with disgust—"Popinjay barbarian fool!" Then suddenly, the mad seal let loose a wicked sound from her rump.

"I don't believe it! Did you just stink? She just stunk! The disgusting hump-pig! With all of us stuck in here, she went ahead and stunk! Somebody—kill me!" the nauseated bird shrilled.

The walrus rolled its eyes in further disgust over the sudden offensive smell, just as annoyed over the mad seal's and the penguin's nonstop abhorrence for each other. Crumpels became even offended, further, by the second enormous gaseous explosion Mum gave out while attempting to get up off the icy floor, looking like an enormously drunken dinosaur fighting to maintain her stance. Mulgrew held his flipper over his beak and quickly scampered away while Crumpels endured.

"Boop-boop-disgrace, she sure can stink up the place," she groaned, fanning her face with her flipper. Waiting for the air to clear, the tooth walker attempted to comfort the white seal further. "Not to worry, White Puff, Nikki will be okay now," she told Miracle, inflating her cheeks, returning a gentler stare toward him. "One never knows where the heart will find its true home, my precious White Puff. Have faith, dear," the spongy walrus said, intending to return to her son, who was still very much asleep with heavy exhaustion. Then all at once, she stopped and looked toward the man-beast who was beginning to stir within the broken universe of the immolated bird feathers scattered and crushed about her. "It would seem someone else needs you now," Crumpels offered before quickly turning away, scratching the ice castle with her great big self, sending down a flipper full of shavings of ice upon the head of the white seal.

Shaking the icy debris off, Miracle snorted and then wriggled himself up to the awakening Emma. She sat up almost immediately, grasping on to Miracle, hugging him close, touching the damaged stone, covering her nakedness with his fur. The tiny pup who was also waking, rambunctious and as hungry as could be, suddenly wriggled away from her. As quickly as a seal's wink, the pup scurried toward the rear of the ice castle, sniffing the air like a curious hound dog. The pup made funny faces, scrunching up his lower lip, bouncing his teeny black nose with a comical wiggle-waggle. Happy tiny growls chirped from his mouth, his furry tummy filling with even louder growling noises driving him onward in the search for food. Miracle rubbed his soft cheek endearingly against Emma's for a brief moment before speaking. "We tried to bring as many of the lost children back to the sea, but time was against us. A dreadful storm now approaches."

"Yes, I know. I can feel it all about us," Emma said, hearing the wind shriek like maniacal banshees around the walls of the ice castle. Miracle's stone suddenly brushed across Emma's face. Taking it into her hands again, she squeezed it.

"I think it's broken," Miracle nervously divulged.

Emma closed her eyes, breathing in the sensation. She smiled at the seal while her eyes remained closed. Miracle's brow furrowed then softened. He waited for the human girl's eyes to open, and when they did, he gazed deep into those still intriguing eyes of hers. He noticed that they were glowing like strange lights he had once seen shining in the twilight skies of Sealssong. "It is trying to rebuild itself," Emma explained. "The tear grows weak now each time we use its power. It will, however, grow strong again, but from what I feel, it may take some time. I'm afraid we will just have to face the world without its complete help for the time being." She began to cough, shivering; clutching herself around the seal, not quite sure what to do about her apparent nakedness when out of the flickering gloom of the ice castle, something fell upon her bare shoulders.

"Cover that ungainly butt of yours, will ya!" the Mad Mum seal snapped. "The mere sight of your denuded rump gives me the bloody willies!" She sniffed the air, belching louder than she had ever done, smiling most proudlike.

Both Emma and Miracle stared at each other for a moment as the something about her shoulders suddenly dropped, spilling out in front of her. Emma recognized it instantly. It was clothing, or what remained of it, somehow retrieved from the likes of the recent, but dead seal hunters. It appeared to be the better part of a partially torn tan-colored parka, its lining sewn and stuffed together with several strips of seal skins. Emma embraced it, certainly not because of its once-upon-a-time previous owner, but because it meant protection and warmth, regardless of its depraved origin. Slipping into it effortlessly, Emma wrapped it tightly around her waist, fastening it shut with a crisscross of her arms.

Through the twisted corners of her jaws, Mum drooled and slurped while filling her mouth with another gulp of stolen strips of man-beast coverings, the furry linings an ever-remindful memorial of the seals who had died so that the man-beasts could sustain their vile existence a time longer. "Filthy vermin," Mum spit, continuing to toss more of the human clothes, about this time striking Emma smack in the face. "Here, cover up the rest of your scrawny hide! Disgraceful, I say!"

Emma took the hit with a gracious smile, stunned as she was. Looking down at this fresh toss, she scrambled through the pile like a child tearing open a Christmas present, discovering it to be a pair of hunter's pants entirely intact. How the mad seal had ever managed this feat, Emma could not be sure, nor did she care. All that mattered was that the deranged beast had indeed managed it, and she was only too happy to crawl inside them, cold and damp as they were. The material was of a heavy make, the insides lined with baby seal remains. "Oh, thank you, Mum!" Emma exclaimed, continuing to climb into the extremely large pair of hunting pants, pants far exceeding past her tiny feet and toes. The next installment consisted of gloves and socks, each one a different size, each one belonging to a different seal hunter. Still, again, it didn't matter. Emma soon came upon another strip of seal fur. She looked at it sadly, knowing, realizing that the fur had come from a murdered whitecoat. Slowly, she put the strip of fur down, humiliation covering her face.

"Take it," Mum ordered. "At least the poor love would not have died in vain."

With a remorseful nod, Emma did as the crazed seal asked while the mad harp assaulted her with more strips of coverings. Mum even hurled over a floppy, rubberlike hunter's boot, slapping it down abruptly on top of Emma's unsuspecting head. "That's more than sufficient," Emma said, taking the boot away from her head.

Miracle tried to help Emma as best as possible. "Mum, how in the world did you manage to get these things?" he asked, sifting through the menagerie of items that the determined harpie was heaving.

"Easy!" Mum boasted with a formulated belch. "It was dead, and the only good man-beast is a dead man-beast!" She belched again, this time long and sloppylike. "I simply snatched the man-beast skin from its dirty, smelly dead self, that's all!"

Emma crawled along the icy floor, reaching out in every direction, collecting more of the strewn cuts and pieces of clothing. Finding several more strips, she tied them together then hastily wrapped it around her waist like a belt, doing the same for the jacket, holding them both in place. Some stray mashed and broken feathers dropped from her enormous dangling sleeves. All that remained from her previous illustrious feather dress now lay crushed beneath her feet. With the cunning and swiftness of a seal herself, Emma searched for the boot she had discarded from her head. Finding it, she quickly began to search for another.

Mulgrew, who was still pacing the ice castle and was now engaged in a disgruntled discourse with himself, accidentally came upon the intended man-beast's strange, yet impressive footwear. Finally, here was just such a place where he could find solitude away from the others.

Slowly, the bird placed his tiny penguin head inside the boot and sniffed about a few times. Deciding that it was safe for entry, Mulgrew squatted down and turned himself around, waddling unsteadily backward. Squishing his pudgy backside against the opening of the boot, a boot lined with warm seal skin strips, the feisty penguin believed that he had indeed found a place that would finally hide him from the rest. It was a beautiful thing. He was ecstatic. Twitching his rump in all sorts of approaches, he found that he only half fit inside the mouth of the boot, convinced that if he pushed and probed, he would force himself inside, at last finding the cozy and warm retreat away from everyone, especially from the tormenting Mum seal; but as usual, he was wrong. Aside from only half fitting inside and not very well at that, with one quick and swiping flash, the tormenting Mad Mum grasped both boot and bird in her mouth, flinging them unwieldy toward Emma. The penguin-stuffed boot missed Emma by a seal's hair, slapping itself hard against the icy wall like a dead fish. Pathetically, it hung there; just sticking against the side of the castle momentarily before dumping the remains of Mulgrew out and onto the floor, plopping him down only seconds before it came unglued, slapping itself on top of the screaming bird's head. In a wild furor, the smashed-up Mulgrew shook about, ranting and raving, ruffling himself up into an even crazier state before absconding off somewhere toward the rear of the ice castle.

Disregarding the entire penguin drama, Emma politely thanked Mum with a queer smile, went over and picked up the flopped-over footwear, and sat down, attempting to straddle both hunting boots over her frozen feet. Because of their enormous size, Emma's delicate feet sailed straight through, but this would not be the only problem. When she finally sank into the boots, she discovered that each was intended to be worn on the left foot—once again, belonging to two separate hunters.

"Oh well," she sighed in a disappointing breath. "I guess it will just have to do." It was not going to be easy walking with two left feet, but she was grateful for their wobbly and furry protection. Reaching up toward her head, Emma shuffled about, her golden hair drawing in a sudden breath. "I'm going to need something for the top," she said, proceeding to sort through more scraps of clothing.

"Take it!" Mum grumbled in disgust, casting something else at her. "I'm tired of carrying the bloody thing around already. Besides, it's not sassy hot anymore. I need something much more ostentatious!"

Carefully, Emma reached down, unfolding the object. It was Mum's bonnet. Although extremely tattered, torn, and washed out, Emma was most grateful for it.

"But, Mum," Miracle interjected, a surprised expression wrapped around his small mouth, "It's your bonnet!"

"I know that, and I don't give a tinker's damn either!" Mum snapped, sticking out her tongue before turning away abruptly. "I'm-mmm hot, and I don't need no gosh-darn bonnet to prove it!"

Miracle could not hold back his smile. "Thank you, Mum."

"Well, she needs something to cover that head of hers, doesn't she?" Mum barked, her snout still facing the opposite direction.

"I imagine she does," Miracle said playfully.

"And I will cherish it always!" Emma sang, fastening the scraggly bonnet ties about her neck.

"See to it that you do!" Mum barked.

After fussing with it, still not sure if she had situated it properly, Emma turned and looked at Mum, her entire preposterous-looking ensemble flooding ridiculously over her as she stood upright. "There!" Emma exclaimed. "How'd I look?"

Mum started laughing, rolling her eyes, losing them somewhere half inside her gigantic head. Rumbling her massive self backward, she nearly crushed Nikki as well as the side of the ice castle, shaking the structure with her sudden movements. "You look just like—" Mum stopped in midsentence before suddenly flopping herself backward on the ice, just missing the sleeping Poo-Coo by a mere breath. Exposing her large belly, she finished off her sentence clapping away at her flippers, whispering, *The Docta.* Abruptly freezing in motion, Mum lethargically dropped her head off to one side, staring at Emma, holding to a drunken gape.

"Poor thing," Emma lamented, dripping inside her enormous clothes, "poor—poor thing."

However, Mum did not seem affected by her sudden surge of madness. She kept right on smacking her flippers together, the drool pouring down the side of her demented seal face. "Docta, love-ya!" she exploded again, bursting into an uncontrollable roll of giggles, her snout covered in mucus and gooey extract.

Emma and Miracle, as well as most of the occupants in the ice castle, suddenly looked at the mad creature and became very sad. "Poor, poor Mum," a terribly upset Little Lukie offered, wriggling near the flip-flopping, flipper-flagging mad creature.

"Horrible, evil woman," Emma cried. "Decara is responsible for this and so much more!" Striking her fist against the dead seal hunter's pants, losing her hands within its many folds, she squeezed the excess material between her fingers, feeling her blood boil.

"Decara has just got to be stopped!" Miracle barked.

"But who's gonna stop her?" Lukie squeaked. "She seems most dastardly and powerful, a real bully! I don't think I'd like her one bit—*neither!*"

"We're going to stop her!" Emma commanded.

Crumpels suddenly filled with dread. "What do you mean? Surely you're not suggesting that Miracle should go anywhere near that-that . . . devil woman, are you? I mean—whooo-whooo!" the mother walrus cried, leaving her son for a moment, shifting the ice castle, approaching the girl. "I may not know all of your strange talk, child, but isn't White Puff the one that this monster woman is after?"

"Well yes, but—"

"But nothing, he won't go anywhere near her, I tell you!"

Suddenly, Miracle nuzzled his head against Emma and then tenderly pulled away from her, wriggling over to the walrus. Looking deeply into the glistening windows of Crumpels's eyes, Miracle said, "I have to go, don't you see? It's what I must do."

"Oh no, you simply mustn't! You're going to stay right here with us, we who need you, boop-boop-dee-doo!"

An amicable smile sparkled on the seal's lips for a mere second and then disappeared. "Listen to your heart now, not your fear."

"It's that man-beast!" screeched the penguin, fluttering near the walrus. "She's bewitched you! She's the one who put these gaa-gaa ideas into your head!"

"No!" Miracle told the bird, looking toward Emma. "They have been there from the start. She only opened my heart, and now that it is open, I won't close it. I know what I must do."

"Nonsense!" squeaked the bird again. "You're both going to die! That shrewd chippie witch has powers that you possibly could not understand. You don't have a clue or a remote chance to defeat her, you'll see! She'll squish you like shark snot!"

"But we have this!" Emma said, holding on to the tear.

"Big deal!" scoffed the bird. "It doesn't even work right anymore! You said so yourself."

"We have something else," Miracle added, drawing closer to Emma. "*Innocence.* I am not exactly sure what that is, but I know we both share it and somehow I know it will protect us."

Rolling his eyes, the bird crept contemptuously toward them, scrutinizing them with his slit-covered eyeballs. "*Innocence! Spitocence!* Sounds like something pretty dirty to me!" Mulgrew spat.

"Be still!" Crumpels snapped, ready to discard the annoying bird with a swipe of her hind flippers but not having the chance for Mum suddenly rolled on top of him, snuffing both him and his comments out like a light. Miracle wriggled closer to the walruses, trying his best to ignore the penguin's constant muffled screams. Realizing that she was indeed weakening, he knew that it would not be long before Crumpels granted her blessings.

"Mama Walrus," Miracle implored, "I have been desperate to find out what happened to me as well as finding out where my mother is. I must find out if she is still alive. Besides Mum, you, above all others, know how important this is to me, do you not?"

Crumpels lowered her enormous head. "Yes, I do—boop-boop-it's true."

"Mama Crumpels, don't you see, she may be sick and dying. This may be the only chance that I may have to find her. Surely, you can understand."

Crumpels wiped the tears away from her dancing whiskers, looking surprised when Poo-Coo, now stronger and well on the way to becoming whole again, suddenly joined her side. Both of their immense girths cracked a piece of the ice castle when Poo-Coo placed his shaky flipper about his mother, resting his head tenderly on her ample rolls of thickset blubber. "Tell me, White Puff," Poo-Coo asked through a mucus-filled throat, "about this man-beast friend of yours. Are you really sure she knows what she is doing? She looks kind of weird to me, bro."

Miracle smiled and looked at Emma. There she was, all bundled up, all lopsided and furry, looking more like a refugee from outer space than any living thing on the planet. The crazy and tattered headpiece on her head chewed and sucked on a many a night by the Mad Mum seal was a sight enough to disturbed anyone. However, her entire body wrapped in different strips of seal fur, killer man-beast leg coverings, draped about her three times her size, totally masking any shape or form of her legs or herself as far as that went, was just too much. In truth, she remotely looked human. If anything, she looked more like some strange furry animal, and then there were the boots: one pair half the size of her legs, made for the same foot, as if it truly mattered at this point.

Suddenly, having the need to walk over to the walruses, Emma began dragging herself toward them, but when she did, one of her oversized wobbly boots flopped out from beneath her, causing her to fall hard against the icy floor.

"Oh good heavens," Crumpels said, shaking her head.

"I just have to get the hang of these stupid boots!" Emma grunted.

Miracle looked at her with more smiles and even giggled himself when Emma tried to get up only to fall again, this time altogether losing the boot. It shot off her foot, sailing straight across the room, hitting the opposite wall of the ice castle. "You're no help," Emma scolded, attempting to fix herself up again.

"Oh codswallop, I'll get the blasted thing!" Mum abruptly offered, rolling to her side, at last freeing the suffocating penguin. Mulgrew screamed and jumped up and down, even popped himself onto the mad seal's head and started pecking at her, all crazylike, but alas, as always, one simple smack sent the bird sailing. "Here," Mum said, returning the boot. "Make sure you keep it stuck tight this time!"

Emma nodded, quickly taking the boot, placing it on her foot, securing it with an extra strip of seal fur. After finishing, Emma thought it best to keep seated. Later, when there was not such a gawking audience, she would try for another walk. Crumpels then wriggled closer toward Emma, her face a wrinkled smorgasbord of worry. Miracle slowly backed away, allowing the walrus to place her enormous face in front of the human girl.

"I do not understand you, man-child, or your strange ways, but you have enchanted my little White Puff. Therefore, despite your appearance and the fact that you are a human creature, I have decided that there is something most different about you," she said. "I don't know what it is, but nonetheless," she added with a sturdy nod, "it is quite different, indeed." She then paused, looking more serious than ever. "Please, let no bad come to him. Promise me, boop-boop-I plea!" she begged through teary walrus eyes.

Emma smiled. "With all my heart, I promise."

The walrus looked at the human girl with strange eyes, tilted her head back and forth, and then suddenly drew very close to Emma.

"Then go with him and watch over him every minute. No bad must happen, please," she said, pulling away slightly.

Suddenly, the sound of the hungry pup filled the ice castle. It was not long before the entire congregation circled near the baby seal and Nikki. Having welcomed the pup to her side, Nikki looked up toward the curious inhabitants of the castle. "He seems to like it here," she said, happily feeding the hungry pup nestled ever so close to her for some time now. As Miracle watched, both Nikki's eyes and his met. "Thank you," she said smilingly, allowing a tear to slowly trail its way down her beautiful face. "Because of you, today I have been blessed with a son." Miracle smiled back, watching the tiny baby seal suckle her seal milk, then begin to grow tired and finally fall asleep, all tucked in next to her. "My heart was broken . . . and now it feels joy." Nikki sighed wholeheartedly.

Miracle looked at Emma and then returned his misty stare to Nikki. "It was Emma," he said, "who found the pup. She saved him from the killer man-beasts all on her own."

Nikki slowly raised her head and widened her smile. "Most proficient man-child, bless you both," she said, striving to stretch her neck, wanting to speak further with Miracle. "Go with her, my dear and faithful friend. I believe in her for she is filled with a magic wonder, just as you are." Then looking at the stone about the white seal's neck, Nikki noticed that it was slightly aglow. "Perhaps the real magic," Nikki surmised, "is that the stone has somehow brought you both together." Made dizzy with her efforts, the recuperating harp sank down with exhaustion, sighing. "Always knew you were different . . . wonderfully . . . beautifully . . . different . . . ," Nikki whispered, sounding as if she would fall back into unconsciousness.

"Rest now," Bellgar told her. "You can talk later. Sleep is what you need."

Miracle looked at Nikki one last time, seeing her eyes close while Bellgar cuddled up next to both her and his unexpected and welcomed newly adopted son. These moments would remain sacred and would not linger. It was late, and Bellgar, as did the rest, were beginning to feel the spell of sleep press itself heavily upon them. Wriggling near Emma, Miracle curled up next to her; no further words would be spoken this night. The only sound that would prevail would be the lashing of the storm against the ice castle.

The storm was far from finished, and in the morning, both Emma and the white seal would discover that there were many things worse than storms. The black of night was moving inside the tempest, and soon it would be as real and as deadly and heinous than any nightmare they could ever imagine. The most important, and perhaps final, journey that they would venture upon was only hours away now. The ice castle would rattle and moan until the first rays of light would come for them.

NEXT STOP: THE *TIAMAT*

Kishk hardly slept a wink that night. Thoughts of his loved ones filled his mind every moment. He realized that if sleep came, it would visit but for a short while, or not at all. Someone had to watch over the others while they slept, and it would be no one other than himself.

The whale had remained near the cramped and coupled floes near the ice castle, half submerged in the frozen waters, determined to wait out the storm, a storm that had no intention of sparing whoever crossed its path. Tossing and turning in his unmerciful restraints of freezing bits of ocean, the mighty blue whale could not help but feel the unnerving suspicion that something far sinister than a storm was on its way. He could feel the evil approaching, and it was approaching swiftly.

Slowly, almost painfully, he tried to resurface in the water, breaking a substantial icy floorboard as he did this. Probably having taken months to form across the independent floes he now invaded, he half lay upon it, crumbling it down into the uncertain floes beneath him. Pulling himself up as far as would allow before taking another chunk of the island with him, Kishk steadied himself, listening through the constant pops the icy rain made against his thick skin. Although the dark clouds and annoying raindrops made it, most difficult, he could see something small and dark begin to surface near the horizon. With an upsetting grunt, he blew an endless gust of bubbles into the crystallized universe. With another grunt, he blasted the skies, scolding the rain for striking him while striving to get a better look at whatever was appearing in the sky's unending vista beyond.

Suddenly, the rains increased. Their sheeting downpour covered the whale and island with one unbelievable cloudburst. Visibility was zero. Then without any warning, an incredible piece of glacier hanging directly above Kishk's head, twice his size, began to crack before sliding down icy walls. Not nearly moving as fast as he should have, Kishk felt the hit. He shot out of the water, scraping against the colossal wall of plummeting matter. Temporarily finding leverage, he pushed off from the diving glacier, hurling himself entirely out of the sea. Aimlessly falling onto the island, another incredible crash followed both glacier and whale, hitting the ice precisely the same time. With an explosion that rocked and split the ground, Kishk rolled over several times, smashing and crashing into other nearby glaciers, forming floes and twisting pillars of ice and snow before skidding, with no way of stopping himself, directly into the path of the ice castle!

Miracle, who was half asleep, first heard the explosive sound. Jolting up, the white seal directly woke Emma. She immediately jumped to her feet and headed toward the doorway, her ridiculous boots nearly causing her to fall again. Taking hold of the ice boulder, she attempted to push it away from the cave's entrance. Slowly, it budged; but it was not until Mum flip-flopped her rotund self against the boulder's edge, hitting it headfirst, grousing wicked seal curse words at it as the icy stone finally rolled away, crashing into the side of the wall. A cruel and overpowering gust of howling wind blasted the castle, rattling the walls, as well as everyone inside. Crumpels screamed. Nikki quickly held on to her new pup as Bellgar buckled down, attempting to protect them from the savagery of the winds. Big Petie, Lukie, and Poo-Coo merely sat there in shock while Mulgrew, who was also screaming, remained suspended in midair. The fanatic twirls of the wind would keep him stationary, offering him a rather perfect view to the outside world. In shrieking glory, the bird could plainly see everything, including Miracle and Emma, both awestruck, their bodies shaking from the shake of the winds. Both frozen in their stare, the sight of the rolling and sliding whale that was heading right toward them, shaking the island like a rattle sliding in their direction, frightfully crammed their vision. From the hurried way that the whale was approaching, it would not be long before he reached them. Mulgrew would remember screaming one more time before he fainted.

With all the screeching restraints of a barge that tries to swerve away from hitting something it has no business ever hitting, the great blue whale gushed toward the helpless gathering with uncontrolled and increasing speed. Another scream pierced the air, this one coming from Emma, just before the whale hit the icy castle.

CRASH! It was all over!

Miracle felt the blast then the hurling impact and the sound of everything falling down around him. The shrieks of the exploding castle preceded any other screams that may have shrilled out. As the whole place fell apart, so did the floor. More crashes and exploding sounds added their voice to the already saturated stormy cacophony. Immediately, Emma felt the freezing waters. She could not breathe, having been carried down into the sea by the blast. Knowing she had to surface, she tried to swim, but the weight of the hunting gear pulled down at her brutally; she was drowning. She tried to scream, but only more bluish black slushy water filled her, already exploding lungs. Chunks of ice brushed against her, and she felt herself sinking further. Just when she believed all was lost, she felt him there; it was Miracle. His touch was indescribably unique. He had come to save her. Quickly slipping beneath her, the white seal began to push her up toward the surface. More chunks of ice, some from the once-standing ice castle itself, hit against her. Still, Miracle swam bravely, motioning to Emma to take hold of him around his neck. As weak as she was, she did as he asked and felt herself rushing through the waters. Then something else happened quite unexpectedly. They hit something solid, and it was not an iceberg or a part of another glacier. Practically unconscious, Emma could feel the strong pull in the water as millions of pieces of broken ice whizzed past her as if she were somewhere in space in the middle of a meteor storm.

Another incredible surge in the water detonated within the icy veins of the sea, nearly shaking Emma free from the white seal. With a power neither one had ever felt before, the thing that had stopped them from resurfacing now began to pull them out of the water at an extraordinary speed. In a matter of seconds, they broke through the watery floor of the sea. Coughing out, Emma continued to gasp for air, the rain assaulting her, the wind once more taking away her breath. It was not until she could breathe properly and could look about that she realized she was on top of the whale. Kishk had somehow found them just as he had found the others; for as she and Miracle coughed and sneezed and hacked and spit, there, on the very top of the head of the amazing Kishk, all remained accounted for—wet, frightened, semiconscious, but all alive and once again together.

In a small saturated circle stood Nikki, still clinging to her newly acquired pup, Bellgar beside her. Big Petie, Little Lukie, Crumpels, and Poo-Coo remained crammed together, Mulgrew remaining unconscious and sprawled out, lying near the whale's blowhole like a drunken sailor. Stunned, yet unharmed, most moved about lethargically in a dazed concern, but not Mum. She was at the head of the whale-ship sitting at the fleshy bow, playing Clap-Clap with the raindrops. "Clumsy galumph!" she grumbled at the whale. "Don't you ever get tired of smashing into things, for goodness love!" Scoffing and belching, she clapped some more. Then she abruptly stopped, sniffed the air, and pointed a flipper toward the horizon. "There it is!" she spouted—*"The devil's ship!"*

There would be no mourning for idleness. As the rushes of water poured from the whale, Emma and Miracle fought their way toward the bow of the blue chanter, dodging chunks and slabs of splintered icy floorboards and slush, all in a hurried race to drain from the dazed mammoth. "That's it!" Emma cried, still coughing out the water in her lungs—"The *Tiamat*!" She also pointed toward the horizon.

The mighty whale furrowed his brow in sadness and spoke. "How deplorable, in trying to warn you, I nearly killed us all!"

"No!" Emma exclaimed with another choked offset of gasps. "We would have never seen it had it not been for you. Look, the witch is coming!" She still pointed her finger toward the horizon, the rain and wind shaking her arm raucously. A faint roll of thunder murmured in the way off distance, somewhere around the *Tiamat*. From what it looked like, the vessel seemed to be stationary as if biding its time before some devious attack. "She's planning something extra evil!" Emma said, sitting down on the whale to empty her water-filled two left-footed boots before taking off her bonnet to wring out as much water as possible.

"She's coming for me, isn't she?" Miracle asked.

"For us both, she will wait for the Night of Screams before she does anything really horrible."

"The Night of Screams, when will that be?"

"When the moon turns red in the sky."

"How will the moon turn red?"

"Not sure, but you can bet it won't be good."

"It is then that she will try and destroy me?"

Sadly, Emma nodded, shivering in her wet seal hunting clothes while putting back the bonnet before straddling back into her soggy boots.

"But before this dreaded time, we will be able to rescue my mother, won't we?"

"Yes! We must!"

"Then I must go to her now!"

"Shhh," Emma commanded. "Listen!"

An alarming quiet overtook the gathering, the rain subsiding, the wind, for no apparent reason, doing the same. "What is it?" Miracle asked in a hushed voice.

"It's not good," Emma told him with a regrettable quiver.

"My mother, she is dead?" he trembled, afraid of hearing the words that might come from the human girl. For a second, he would have settled for never hearing Emma speak again.

"No, she is still alive, but I'm afraid the others—" Unable to go on, Emma lowered her head, closed her eyes, and felt the tears push against her lids. "There are only so many tears shed before, they—"

"Then my mother could be next!"

"Yes, we have no time to lose!" Emma warned, standing up ready to leave—"Hurry!"

Not waiting, the white seal dived off the head of the whale and into the sea, Emma following. They headed toward the blackened horizon, Emma hugging on tightly while Miracle made his way through the icy waters. Suddenly, they heard the whale calling out to them. "Wait; do not let your heart preclude strategy. The heart needs to be protected as well. Please come back!" By the time they swam up to Kishk's enormous mouth, Emma was shivering uncontrollably. "Now you see, how far do you think you would get before you turned into an icicle?" Kishk asked.

"B-b-b-b-but the tear . . . ," she tried to offer, shaking from the cold.

"Its powers are still uncertain. No, I have a better plan. Come," said the whale, "return to me."

Mulgrew was now conscious and quick to squawk. "How in blazes are they supposed to get onto that blasted ship with that creepy witch just waiting to eat them up like a spider?" he spouted, adjusting to his comeback from the world of the discombobulated. "They haven't a chance! Drop me back! Drop me back! Drop me back at the nursery! I'll have no part of this farce!"

"We will only be dropping off two passengers," Kishk retorted, "and I'm afraid you're not one of them."

"What? Aw, come on now, I'm not going anywhere near that-that . . . floating devil thingamajig or whatever it is! I'll have no part of it, I tell you!"

"You certainly will, Mulgrew, and so will the rest of us, all except for Nikki and the child. I'm afraid it would prove too dangerous for them."

"And what about me?" popped the penguin. "In case you hadn't noticed, I'm approximately the size of one of the barnacles on your rump. I have little stumpy winglike flippers that I don't even know what they're there for!" he said, flipping his flippers about absurdly. "What good would I be fighting off witches and mean old monsters?"

Kishk offered the ranting penguin a wide smile. "Even the sea crab and the octopus with their nonconforming limbs can create sanctuaries that we cannot. We are each given our own unique gift, and you, my friend, are no exception."

"Whatever! I still don't want to go, and you can't make me!" Mulgrew squeaked, preparing to jump ship.

"Oh, let the little goon ass go!" Mum belched. "He'd only get in the way anyways. Stupid coward!" she said, sticking out her tongue.

"Who are you calling a coward? You, fat, demented stinking thing, you!"

Mum merely sneered at him and then belched directly into his red and irritated face.

Mulgrew became outraged. "I'll have you know that I've been sailing these seas longer than you, tubby! And I'll also have you know that I have been involved in some pretty heavy combat, miss know-it-all! Here, look at this!" shouted the bird, daringly drawing closer, leaning in toward her and showing Mum a nonexistent battle wound just below his tiny wing. "That beauty came from wrestling with a great white, so there! *Pppllith!*" he spat.

Miracle suddenly barked. "Can you two discuss this later?"

Mum then blew up her face and smashed it directly into the penguin's, just daring him to chicken out. He did, shrieking and fluttering away toward the other seals, Lukie being the first he reached. "Well, Mr. Great White Shark Slayer, what's it gonna be, are you in or not? Betcha don't come—*neither!*" Lukie said, all wide-eyed, smacking his jaws, enjoying his plaguing of the seabird.

"All right, I'll go! I'll go! But you'll see we're all going to die, I tell you! We're all going to die!"

Also, having heard enough, Nikki spoke. "Whatever, bird!" she plainly discarded. "Do you have a plan?" she asked the whale, still weak from the dreadful experience.

"Yes," Kishk responded. "After taking you back to the nursery, we will sail out to the *Tiamat.*"

Crumpels then spoke up with a hardy voice. "But they'll see you coming! I mean, you're no tiny tuna, for goodness sake. No offense, I'm sure, dear, boop-boop-I fear!"

"I shall only surface several inches from the surface of the water, however, keeping you safely aboard all the while. They will not suspect our advance."

This time it was Emma's turn to speak. She was shaking from the cold, so her words were somewhat distorted. "W-w-w-we need to s-s-s-s-sail to the extreme stern of the ship, I know of a spot, a small b-b-b-b-broken porthole we can enter. Arayna and the three-headed serpent won't b-b-b-be far from this point."

"Three-headed serpent? Good Lord!" Mulgrew cried. "We're doomed!"

"Whooo-wee! We best get Nikki and the pup back to the nursery, boop-boop dee-dee!" Crumpels exclaimed. "I'm sure the poor little dears are exhausted."

"I don't want to leave you," Bellgar said to his mate. "Surely they will understand."

"Perhaps it would be best if you did remain with her on the island," Kishk offered. "You, as well as your mate, have not fully recovered from your ordeal. I really do think it best you return to Sealssong."

Nikki's mate nodded, grateful that he could remain with his family.

The sky was beginning to turn a violet color as dark blue clouds scratched themselves about from every direction in the firmament; if they were about to embark upon their journey, it had to be then. With a great sweep of his tail, Kishk splashed tremendous surges of water beneath his massive bulk. Turning, the whale flowed like the tides shimmering in the spirals of the breathing light. It was not long before the blue chanter reached the chopped-up and splintered nursery of Sealssong. There were plenty of the nurseries left to allow Nikki, her mate, and the pup to settle there upon, plenty of room for others should they come preparing to give birth. The adopted now chubby little pup that Nikki named *Promise* squealed on a wee bit, the whale bending his head, causing the congregation to move forward in a sudden heap. As quickly as possible, Bellgar escorted his family away from the whale and onto the ice.

"Go now," said the whale. "Go and find a safe place. With any luck, we will all meet when this is all over." Nikki and her pup turned to look back toward the whale, and Nikki appeared as if she were about to say something but instead turned slowly into the niche of her mate and her adopted child. Kishk smiled his gigantic smile toward her. "May Godspeed go with you!" the leviathan said, his voice filling the wind.

Bellgar turned and looked back toward Miracle. He stared hard at his longtime friend, his eyes expressing his own torn feelings. Looking down at the icy covering of the sea, he turned away from the white seal, once more cutting through the waters, once again en route to help his delivered family away from the floes. Miracle watched them wriggle off, the brilliant glaring of the sea temperately washing their forms from sight.

The blue chanter that would forever keep the face of youth would exhibit susceptibilities of wonder across that permanent smile endowed to him at birth. It was time to leave the nursery, time to find the white seal's mother, time to unite the human girl with her brother, time to confront the evil upon the sailing vessel. Time to meet the witch!

Miracle, Emma, Crumpels, and Poo-Coo stood nestled at the mast of the whale while Mulgrew remained his distance away from the mad beast. Mum proudly stood at the bow, an enormous dazzling smile pasted rigorously to her crazed muzzle, clapping her flippers like a spoiled child who had just won her way, belting out, "Getty up, love-ya!"

Lukie and Petie stayed together, both surrounded in silence, their eyes remaining on the nursery, still forever remembering. Like a moving land mass, the colossal whale exploded out of a private sea of his own. From the center of his spouting head, he tooted off, sounding like a whistle drawing his strength from the majestic waters of the sea. As the crunching and frothing ocean danced before him in a symphony of light and sound, Kishk turned from Sealssong.

SILENT WONDERING

The sky was yielding to scattering patches of deep blue with occasional bursts of sunlight while the heavenly fireball snuck occasional glimpses at the journeyers below. Kishk looked out into the distance directly at the pulsating horizon, its ardent flicker beating to the counts of the waves like a telltale heart; he could still see the *Tiamat*, faded as it was. He estimated it would take less than an hour to reach it, but in doing so, he would have to be extremely careful so as not to be sighted. It could mean success or failure to such a valiant enterprise.

Another blast of ocean water emerged from Kishk drenchinghis entire crew. Most did not mind. Well, except for Mulgrew. He shook and danced up and down in a disgusted ritual, not unlike to his character. Crumpels and Poo-Coo circled then flopped lethargically against the wet surface of the blue giant while Little Lukie and Big

Petie remained inseparable, both continuing to watch the nursery grow smaller and smaller, the whale moving farther away from it.

Miracle and Emma stood close to each other, looking out toward the vibrating horizon. The clouds continued to gather in dark unison, draping the glimmer of the icy domain into a shadowed and unpredictable region. Even the waters began to turn hostile, the wind scratching over its spurring surface. A sudden and foreboding darkness furthered itself across the sky, bringing with it a veil of mist, blocking out the horizon from view and thoroughly taking the *Tiamat* from sight. Kishk shook his large head slightly and narrowed his violet eyes. It did not matter; fog or no fog, his senses would not fail him. He had seen the dreaded vessel; he had marked its image against the sky. He would find it.

"Not to worry, the sudden fog will shield us from the probing eyes of those who sail upon the evil ship," Kishk assured, not sure if anyone heard him.

A distinct quiet crossed over the whale and his crew while the drizzle performed a chaotic dance over their heads. It all seemed so unreal. The sea stilled, hushed within her apprehensions, and yet Kishk would not ponder this occurrence deeply, for there was no time for mere contemplation. Besides, it would only come to represent smooth sailing for him, and he was not about to question such fortune. The fog would be enough to contend with; nonetheless, the blue chanter began to accelerate his speed. He and the faithful ones nestled there on top of him would buckle down and endure. The newfound quiet would dictate finding solace in its boundlessness, the walruses finding the moment to close their eyes and wink off for a short time while it was still possible. Kishk, of course, would remain watchful, guiding his course toward the invisible mark somewhere out in the ghostly mist. The Mad Mum, who persistently propped herself at the bow of the whale, continuously clapped to her heart's content. The white seal and the human girl would remain ever so close to each other. Together they would look out into the obscurity before them, their saturated faces emotionless, staring into a silent wondering that would all but consume them.

Merging thoughts crammed with mothers and brothers, witches and demons, serpents, purple angels and tears, diamonds and seals filled their heads; but foremost, the fearsome premonition as to the end of the world, or at best the end of their world, chilled their blood, as did the image of the ship that now waited for them in the not-so-faraway horizon.

COCKY MOUTH

Kenyan remembered opening his eyes after he heard the door scream, or was it the screams of the captain who startled him? He just could not be certain. It was still dark in the room when he saw the glowing of fire-red eyes flicker for a moment inside the damp and disgusting rat-infested cell. "Thorne," Kenyan called out, desperately needing a witness to the validation of the flashing red-eyes sighting. "Are you awake?"

Only sickening silence echoed endlessly before him. "Thorne!" he shouted when once more he saw a fleeting line of red blur before him. That time, he felt hot breath burn against his damp skin, but there was no sign of the glowing red eyes. All at once, he felt something move across his forehead. With a string of groans, Kenyan began to tug wildly at the chains confining him in a crazed and feeble attempt of chasing the rats away from his face; but in midswing of his swaying arms, something grabbed him, squeezing his forearm with a tight and electrifying grip.

"We will have no shouting here," the voice commanded with a trace of condescension. "What would our distinguished Captain Thorne think of such behavior?"

Recognizing the voice at once, Kenyan's eyes flashed as a candle ignited before his eyes, splashing its greenish glow over the skeleton countenance of the witch. Her eyes, although surrounded in blackness, seemed to squirm out of a red bloody glow of gooey discharge. Her face was exceptionally white, her lips exceptionally red from what Kenyan could manage through the blackness. Her mouth was drawn tight, revealing a grotesque sneer as if all the muscles in her face had been paralyzed.

The witch raised the candelabra that held only one black candle, shining it about his face, glaring at him in utter fascination. "You are a feisty one, aren't you, sweet boy?" she hissed, attempting to stroke his cheek.

Kenyan pulled back, hitting the wall behind him with the back of his head. It hurt, but he did not flinch. He only turned his head as far as possible, discouraging any further contact with the witch, but Decara was far from through with him. Suddenly, from the other side of the room, a distinctive moan echoed through the dismal place. Decara quickly swept through the shadows, appearing before the awakening but ailing Captain Thorne.

"Enjoying our little nap, are we?" she taunted, flashing the candlelight against his sensitive eye. Captain Thorne only coughed groggily, slowly raising his head while she flashed more of the candle's eerie glow about him. Visible scratch and bite marks marred his handsome face, left there by the roaming rats. Blood covered parts of his unkempt beard, some having already been chewed away by the same grisly pests.

"Why are you doing this? *Why!*" the captain screamed through a raspy throat barely audible.

Decara smiled a wicked smile as greater darkness invaded her twisted reasoning. "I don't know what you're talking about, you really must be sick."

"You're the one who is sick, you crazed demented wench!"

"Now now," Decara taunted again, "name-calling is such a callow attempt when trying to express oneself, don't you agree? Besides, I thought you might want to know, dear Captain, that we are very close to our destination."

"What are you talking about?"

"Awe, poor nibbled-up Captain Thorne," she mocked, poking at the different torn-away places on his face, stinging the wounds with her skeleton fingers. Twisting his head away, Thorne coughed again, almost throwing up his insides as she continued. "You never had a clue, none of you! Like all the others, you thought you were dealing with just an ordinary woman. Eccentric? Perhaps. Mad? Possibly, nonetheless a mere mortal woman driven by greed for money that came from the slaughtered pelts of pathetic slug like creatures that roamed the ice. After all, you and your men did it a hundred times before. Such valiant hunters, assertive, fearless, and bold, lacking nothing but fortitude as they marched across the ice, clubbing and skinning to their heart's delight, hearts magnificently void of any remorse, barren of any sympathy for the poor, defenseless seals of Sealssong!" Decara clucked her tongue and shook her head, no longer able to contain her laughter.

"But who could blame you for knocking off the little piss-worms?" she sneered, blurting out a vile and blasting scream of laughter directly in the captain's face. "How marvelous—sinfully, reprehensibly marvelous!" she bellowed, breaking out into more maniacal hysterics. "And what made it even more charming was the avarice notion that this mere woman, this crazy man-hating woman, was offering the highest of remuneration for such services. Services you alone could command! Services only your experienced professionalism could propose!" She began to laugh even wilder.

"You fool!" she chortled trying to restrain herself, but failing pitifully. "All I ever needed was the craving greediness and heartless arrogance fueled by you and your foul-smelling, dirty-trash, seal-skinning crew! It was you, all of you, who continued giving life to this vessel!"

"You're insane!" Thorne protested.

"Hmm?" Decara teased, drawing even closer to him. "Insane? Think so?"

Suddenly, Thorne felt the wall behind him jump forward, and with it came a most horrifying thumping sensation. There came a disturbing wail, followed by the sensation of thousands of insects crawling up and down his back, each one repulsively pressing through the lining of the walls. "Good God!" he shouted as the pulsating backdrop came alive. Decara stepped back a few feet and raised her candelabra, illuminating the room so Kenyan could also see the same horror. As the crunching insect noises grew louder and stronger, the walls began to crawl over the captain. Two stony but pliable limbs vaulted forward, stretching, twisting their grasp around the chained man's face. Before he could even attempt another scream, three raveled fossilized fingers growing from the extended armlike stumps of the walls wrapped themselves about his bearded bloodstained mouth. Horrifically, the black ceiling began to breathe, dropping and sloping downward, rippling and crawling with the same monstrous parade of moving insect noises, each monstrosity hidden somewhere within the blackened pores of its stony skin.

In a moment, the excruciating sounds stopped, and the room froze dead. All that could be heard were the desperate breathing sounds made by the captain's bloodstained lips. Thorne's crazed and bloodshot eye peered through a small gap in the twisted stony structure of the heavy grapple smothering him. As he gasped for air, Decara slowly approached him, careful not to hit her head on the downgrade of the slouching ceiling. Thereupon reaching him, she slightly held up her candle. The decline of the ceiling made the shadows flicker and burst even greater about his one bulging and bloodshot eye, the tight-fitting surroundings aiding and amplifying the strangled breaths for which he fought.

"You see, you clueless fool," Decara said in a trifle and matter-of-fact tone, "the ship is alive!" Thorne tried to continue breathing, attempting to scratch off the vile thing from his face, but all these endeavors would prove useless. Decara drew even closer, whispering in the eye that now blinked in terror as her warm breath hit upon it. "Alive, Captain Thorne, alive, with the memory of my dead lover! He who was destroyed by the slugs of the ice, conjured

up by my summons! Yes, kept alive by the essence of ignorance and
the selfishness of man! Your men! A murderous mercenary collection
of men filled with greed, and most importantly, men having already
been damned with the blood of the slaughtered innocence that
came from the hundreds and hundreds of precious baby seals
they butchered by your command alone, over and over again!" she
shrieked and then kept on laughing until she finally ran out of
breath. Eventually returning to his crazed and twitching bloodshot
eye, she pressed her dry lips against it.

"Oh, and incidentally," she huffed, still trying to catch her breath
as a more repressed and unsettling voice pressed out from her,
"just wait until you see the magnificent coat that I made from the
last lot of skins you and your cryptic crew provided! It is an absolute
masterpiece, if I say so myself! Oh, please do forgive my arrogance,
but I seem to have a distinctive flair for sewing dead things together,
but it is all in the illustrious name of fashion, isn't it, my dear
Captain? You will want to see it, won't you? Why, I could have never
made it if it hadn't been for you." She pressed her mouth right into
his eye, close enough to swallow it up if she wanted. Whispering her
hot breath into it, she continued. "Why, it's to die for!" she hissed.
Quickly flying into another peal of mad laughter, she disdainfully
blew a kiss into his screaming red eye.

"Leave him alone!" Kenyan shouted from across the room, barely
escaping the drop of the ceiling now only inches away from crushing
him.

Decara directly aimed the glimmering glow of the candle's
light toward Kenyan. Moving hauntingly through the shadows, she
growled, "Darling sweet boy, you're already on thin ice . . . Don't
push it."

"Shut your dirty mouth, witch!"

"Such disrespect," Decara complained. "Well, no matter." Her
face suddenly turned ghoulish in the shadows. "Your cocky mouth
won't be snapping about much longer. Soon, your world will end,
and it shall be as it was in the beginning—a dark, powerful place,
where the light of innocence shall be snuffed out forever!" She
abruptly turned and crashed the candelabra into the stony mask
around Thorne's face, shattering the pieces of stone and candle
into his popping eyeball. She again laughed fiendishly, raising what
remained of the candelabra hitting the sloping ceiling, startling it.
The hideous fingers recoiled, yielding their hold over the captain's
face, melting back into the rigid wall from which they came. The
crunching noises lasted for a few short moments before fading off

into the shadows as did Decara. Once again, the darkness swallowed up both prisoners.

Kenyan's flashing eyes darted around the room while Thorne's heart exploded with his undertaking of refilling his hammering lungs. Decara's evil laughter promenaded about the damp foul-smelling air as she sang from somewhere in the shadows, "Oh, and sweet boy . . . ," her red eyes now visible like two tiny pinpoints of ghostly light. "I would think twice about escaping again if I were you. The walls have ears! Literally!" she jeered with a restless laugh. "But then again, you don't have your little sister to help you out, do you? Not to worry, I'll keep you alive, so you won't miss the grand arrival of your precious, precious Emma."

Kenyan suddenly froze in the darkness at the mention of his sister's name.

"Oh, didn't I tell you? How careless of me. You see, she took a little vacation from our happy abode, just for a little while, but not to fret. She's coming home. In fact, she's on her way as we speak, the little darling, oh, how I have missed her. It's going to be like old times again. Isn't it, sweet boy? It will be one whopping family reunion! How thrilling! I can hardly wait! Won't it be grand to see the happy expressions of joy smudged all over your adorable little faces? Why, I can almost cry," she said sweetly, stalking forward with eyes shining red, her voice sinking into wickedness. *"Almost . . ."*

Another disturbing series of hollow and sinister cackles filled the room, and just before Decara evaporated in a flash of crimson light, she offered her final words: "Remember, it is alive! It is watching you, and soon it will gobble you up like candy!" Her laughs exploding into the crack of thunder.

Kenyan stood fearfully still within the blackness surrounding him while the choking captain continued to pump air through his dying body. The fighting gasps were the only sound Kenyan heard, that and the squeaking of the rats coming to eat them again.

LULLABY

Arayna was wide awake. She had been that way ever since the evil woman and her manservant had left her; it would not be long before they would return. Arayna could not help but remember the words the horrible woman said this last time. With insufferable torment, Decara blatantly proclaimed how she would yet once more perform the stealing of seal tears, her tears, the mother of the white worm, before she returned to Sealssong.

Arayna remembered how the witch ranted and raved, furious that the serpent had allowed the young girl to leave the ship, but she would deal with the slimy trio later, she vowed. They would pay for such a blunder; still, Decara remained unworried. She would find the conniving brat, and this time, there would be no further escape. For in just a short while, she would once again be reunited with her ungrateful niece for the very last time. This brought Decara much pleasure, almost as much pleasure as knowing that she would be draining the concluding bit of tears from the very slug whose child dared to carry the stone that rightfully belonged to her. Yes, she would certainly enjoy this last extraction of diamonds, for they were the final lots to be stolen before all hell broke loose!

Arayna closed her eyes and shuddered as more of the devil woman's words came back to haunt her. "Yes, I'll particularly enjoy sucking out the last drop from the white seal's precious mama!" the devil woman promised. The seal also vividly recalled how the witch said that afterward, she was going to have her remains stuffed and sewn together, turning her into a throw pillow. She went on to promise her manservant her stretched-out flesh so that he could plop his giant head into her twisted seal skin every night. Decara would make sure that Emma and the white slug looked upon her rotting, mutilated leftover's moments before she ordered her niece to plunge the devil's blade deep into Miracle's heart.

Arayna shuddered again, rocking the black mesh cage back and forth. The remains of the dead seals that had been locked in the cage with her, as well as Lakannia, had been shamefully discarded by the hairy manservant. One by one, Arayna watched in horror as Oreguss grappled with them, pulling and tugging at their lifeless bodies like old sacks, dismantling their remains from one another in such a cruel and tortured way, turning her blood to ice.

After he had removed each of their bodies, throwing them carelessly to the side of the room in a massive heap, he waited for the devil woman to give him further instructions, and the wicked woman did just that. She told Oreguss to get rid of them at once. "Dump their slimy carcasses overboard!" she screamed. "Their rotting skin is beginning to make me gag! Get rid of those things!"

Arayna remembered with a chill how the bearish man delighted in his horrid task, dragging them to a darkened part of the room where he opened some kind of portal, jamming their remains through it, his teeth chomping away in horrific bliss. He must have forced their remains through the small opening because she could hear the shadowed portal snapping and splintering as he crazily attacked it, the devil woman in the background shrieking not to break the glass. "Wretched seal scum!" was the only eulogy that the evil Decara used over these precious creatures, creatures that would for always remain in Arayna's heart. However, the cruel and vile woman who did these terrible things had no heart, this the seal was certain!

Arayna thought about her dream again, that same dream that had somehow kept her alive during this entire nightmare. She closed her eyes, the memory etched against the fine borders of her remembering, the delicate blueprints of recall that would forever paint the image of both her and her son upon the morning when they sailed on that memorable ice raft only hours after his birth. His dear little face looking up to her, his beautiful shining black eyes dazzling far greater than the fireball that danced in the sky, this and the lullaby she sang to him. She could still hear the music playing, all around her, and she began to hum along while it played on in her heart, giving her the reason to believe, to remember to find the courage to sustain a dream that would not be silenced. For there in the essence of her being, that heavenly lullaby of her maternal seal song had timelessly perpetuated its voice within her. Nothing could take it from her. Nothing! No one! It was her gift to treasure, to shield, to shelter, and no devil woman, no creature, no man-beast could take it from her this time. It was an absolute part of her, and not even death could separate them.

Once more, Arayna looked toward the place where Emma had vanished, remembering her promise of returning. She could hear the malicious three-headed trickster snickering, all three of its heads slurping out words she wanted no part of. No, she would close her eyes and block out their nasty sounds and wait for Emma's return. Slumping against the cage, she found herself half smiling, for within that smile, she found serenity rocking back and forth, protected by the music, music that came from her tired and parched throat, the same lovely and haunting refrain of the lullaby she sang once upon a time, only yesterday, and yet forever ago. She would keep singing her seal lullaby repeatedly until its music somehow brought him back. Soon Arayna felt no pain, no sorrow, but only the music—the music of her sacred seal lullaby.

ALMOST THERE

A slight breeze was blowing, making but a slight sound above the water.

The magnificent Kishk sailed onward, rearing upon the topmost crest of the jellylike currents, blowing off water from his spout toward the misty gray skies, blasting obstinacy into their shrouded presence. Through fog or rain, snow or sleet, he would soon make his way to the *Tiamat*.

The sky had somehow turned an even meaner shade of black by the time the whale made what he believed was the halfway mark from where the vessel met the evading horizon. Only Her Majesty, the Sea, consistent, washed and splashed against his moving body, daring to make any sounds while he traveled through his watery quest. Even the repetitious singing of the Mad Mum seemed to cease.

Emma and Miracle made their way to the bow of the whale, joining Mum, who, believe it or not, had fallen into a dead sleep. Her enormous body remained buckled over several times, transforming itself into a whopping pile of snoring blubber. Mulgrew retained his distance somewhere in the stern of the whale, watching the moving current dissolve into a grayish blur as Crumpels and her son continued their refuge in a half-dozing walrus nap. Big Petie and Lukie remained stationary since their departure from Sealssong, each still looking in the direction of where the nursery once stood, its icy borders long since eaten up by the surrounding fog.

"It's funny," Emma suddenly spoke out with a definite shiver to her words. "I know that we are headed for something that quite possibly may end all our lives, and yet I can't help feeling so fortunate."

Miracle turned his head and stared strangely at the girl. His fur was damp, left dangling in front of his snout, saturated from the swirling mist, and yet through it, he could plainly see her iridescent blue eyes. He looked into them deeply and smiled. "You confuse me, Emma."

Emma connected with the white seal's enchanting smile. She crouched down in a shivering shudder, her ridiculous seal hunting clothing buckling all about her, her loose-fitting boots folding over as she tried to sit comfortably next to the seal. "Except for Kenyan, I guess I never actually had a friend before. I've been much of a loner, I'm afraid," she confessed, her eyes leaving the seal, losing her sight inside the ghostly vapors surrounding them. "I'm glad I found you, Miracle. I don't know what I would do if you were not here with me now." Quickly, she wiped a tear beginning to form. "And yet I somehow always knew you existed and that one day I would find you," she said, shivering through her words again.

"It's strange, but I feel the same way," Miracle confessed, drawing closer to her. "I never felt like I belonged . . . not until . . . well, not until you."

Emma's smile was enchanting. "No matter what happens from this moment on, you'll always be a part of my heart, Miracle. Always," she vowed, reaching over to pet his face right before she bent over and kissed him on top of his head, just as she had done so many times before. "Thank you," she said.

Miracle smiled his cutest seal smile ever.

"Your muzzle cracks rather easily," Emma playfully teased.

"You're thanking me?"

"Yes, for giving me something I thought I had long lost."

Miracle cocked his head and once again looked strangely into those incredibly blue eyes of hers. "And what is that?" he asked in a soft whisper.

"Home," Emma replied, turning, looking at the hanging gray vapors, her eyes searching through the growing fog encasing her.

Miracle nodded affectionately then rested his head upon her knee. "*Home . . . ,*" he acknowledged with a heartfelt sigh, gazing out toward the mist-covered world before them, his purple stone curling inside the folds of Emma's unsettling attire.

As the seal and young girl merged deeper into the ghost world of wispy shapes and blurring nothingness, their thoughts were far from obscure. With the memory of home came the deep reflection of Kenyan and Arayna, both now just beyond the swirling vapors that clung ever so close to them. "We're almost there," Emma cautioned with another jolting shiver, reaching toward Miracle, pulling him close to her, her own share of probing fears pressing down mercilessly upon her. "I can feel it."

Mum continued to grunt and snore, and Crumpels and Poo-Coo continued with their own share of noisy slumber. Big Petie and Lukie remained somewhere in the back trails of the whale, the agitated penguin maintaining his vigil of staring off into the blur of the wake created by the blue chanter, and chanting he was, at least for a brief moment. Kishk's whale sounds continued quietly going off into the abyss with hopes of resounding off the evil vessel in question. Unable to see anything, the whale carefully submitted his song with the hopes of hearing a difference in its returning vibration. He was not exactly certain; however, he knew deep in his gut that the vile *Tiamat* was not far away now. In just a short while, he knew that he and the dear ones he carried were about to face their final journey together.

In the distance, a roll of thunder sounded, and then everything turned deathly still.

The time had come.

The blue chanter had found what he had been looking for.

INSIDE!

This time, the sea darkened and the air grew heavy, weighing closely about the blue whale.

Kishk could taste the raw smell of evil with every breath he took. It sickened him to draw in the foul scent, here in this unfamiliar breeding ground of spoiled malignancy. Still, it did not matter. There would be no retreating, no sudden panic attacks of any kind. Nothing would stop him from doing what he must do, even if the ponderous fog made him almost blind; he knew he must see this through to the very end—whatever that might turn out to be.

Not even the *Tiamat* and the witch herself, who was but a chilling breath away, could stop him now. After all, he was a renowned blue chanter born of a proud race, one that existed in a world older than most that lived in the sea, blessed with lengthening senses, both man as well as beast, having long since lost, or perhaps never procured. He was gifted by eternal voices that would remain with him for always. Voices that would guide him and protect him, voices he alone could hear and create—voices that sang the ultimate Song of Songs—his melodious whale song. It was his heritage from birth, and there inside this infinite haze of uncertainty, one thing was certain, the pure voice of the sea now whispered to him a dreaded alarm—the devil ship was but a gasp away now. He could literally feel the floating thing's filthy eyes upon him, watching him, laughing at him. Nonetheless, its deliberate foreboding would be in vain; he would not surrender to its wicked leer. With every part of his eternal heritage, the violet-eyed leviathan cleared his enormous throat, preparing to begin the inevitable confrontation with the darkest enemy he could have ever dared imagine. Suddenly, Kishk heard Emma's voice warning him. With an impulsive jump, the mighty whale fought to gather his bearings, nearly toppling everyone overboard.

"Don't move a muscle!" Emma shouted through her chattering teeth. "Look!" she announced in a choked-off whisper, slowly raising her hand, outstretching it, carefully piercing the thick and fleshy skin of the fog, her fingers shaking from the bitter cold as she clenched her gloved hand, making a small fist, trying to pump some blood into herself. She kept her arm outstretched and then pointed a single finger into the ghostly vagueness. With a certainty that scared her more than she had expected, she proceeded to knock out a sound that would send millions of shivers through both her and the whale.

As her frozen knuckles came upon the *Tiamat*, she shook violently as if death was passing over her. With her eyes fixed shut, she defiantly tapped again, its depraved echo sounding off. A haunting groan from within sent another set of icy creeps through her blood. Emma closed her eyes even tighter, the stunning realization finally slamming hard against her—she was back!

"Oh, Love us! We're here!" the Mad Mum abruptly shouted, clapping her flippers together exceptionally loud in a freakish state of bliss.

Mulgrew jumped three feet in the air. "Okay, here's the deal, slappy, keep that stupid mouth of yours closed tight before I slap it shut!" he snapped. "You're going to get us all killed!"

"Twitter off, stupid lip-lump," Mum spat, sticking out her tongue, wagging it spitefully toward the annoying bird, continuing in smacking her flippers together, this time directly in front of his tiny head.

Before the bird could retaliate, Miracle intercepted. "Mum," he pleaded, trying not to upset her, "I know how you love to play Clap-Clap, but now is the one time that playing Clap-Clap is not such a good idea!"

Big Petie quickly spoke out. "*Wow-eee!* That's one butt-ugly floating thingamajig!"

Little Lukie agreed. "Oh yes!" he added with a shiver. "Don't like this not one bit *neither!* What if that dreadful witch knows that we are here? Oh, I shouldn't like to think that."

"It already knows," Emma said with an unsettling certainty.

"Big deal," Mum snapped. "I'll smack the—" Abruptly, Mum's belligerent yell was suddenly cut short. For all too quickly, Miracle slapped a flipper over her dangling mouth, restraining the remainder of her obstinate insanity. "Please, Mum, you've got to be very quiet! We could be in serious trouble if the witch finds us here."

Mum gave the white seal a disgruntled once-over before rolling her big and heavy head back toward the pesky Mulgrew, once again sticking out her tongue at the bird before turning around addressing Miracle. "Very well, *Love-ya*, mum's the word!" she sang. "But just for you!" Then once more, she flipped around her head, jabbing out her tongue toward the penguin, who this time was nowhere in sight. He was clear across the other side of the whale, far from her as space would allow, rolling his eyes in revulsion, watching her begin to play that plaguing Clap-Clap rubbish he so desperately despised.

Again, Miracle interceded with more of a disciplined flipper. "Mum! *Please!*"

Crumpels suddenly spoke out to her, nerves now raw and rattled, gasping, "Whatever shall we do, boop-boop-dee do!"

Kishk's voice was clear so all could hear. "Well, the first proposal is that each of us remains calm and remembers not to panic."

"I left the panic pulpit long ago!" Mulgrew uttered. "I'm well into the screaming Nelly-sissy soapbox now! Damn you all for roping me into this crazy hullabaloo!"

Suddenly, Emma thought she saw something move across the shadows of the tiny porthole fixed directly in front of her. Carefully, she crawled toward it, balancing herself on top of the whale's head while the mighty leviathan remained plunged almost level with the sea so as not to be seen.

"What is it?" Miracle asked in a hushed panic.

"Someone is watching us."

"Boop-boop-dee-bay—we best swim away!" Crumpels pleaded, hurrying her roly-poly self toward her son, who remained looking onward toward the mysterious devil ship. All remained hushed, studying the porthole, each questioning the two glowing eyes looking back at them. Then in a moment, they were gone!

"Who could it have been, child, the witch?" the blue whale asked.

Emma shook her head. "I'm not sure."

Miracle looked at Emma, then back to the vile *Tiamat* and pushed the fear down his throat. "I don't care! We go on as planned."

"That's my little *Love-ya!*" Mum happily screamed out.

"Oh, we are *so-ooo* dead!" Mulgrew moaned from where he stood. "That fat, crazy mouth of hers has finally done us all in!"

In a mad rush, Mum rumbled up to the penguin, her wobbly tongue dancing all about, smacking her flipper against him, pinning him down, thoroughly covering up the bird's puny head with her tongue, swiping it twice.

"*Get it aaa-wwway!*"

"Please!" Kishk commanded. "I beg of you both to stop this at once!"

"It no longer matters," Emma said with another stabbing shiver. "I told you, it already knows we're here." She turned to look at the porthole once more. Only darkness stared back. There was nothing there but the moving shadows. "Go around to the back of the ship," she instructed. "I believe that is where we will find Arayna." She began to cough, shaking and shivering violently.

Miracle rushed to her side. "You are growing weak," he said.

Emma shook her head, adjusting the silly torn-up bonnet. "I'm just cold, that's all."

The white seal looked at her with a painful stare. "Emma, please hold the magic tear, it will warm you. I know it will." Emma smiled and did as the white seal asked. Clutching it, she held the mystical stone and closed her eyes. "It has helped, hasn't it?"

Emma fought against the intense shivers and the burning fever ravishing her insides and then smiled. "Yes," she pretended. "I feel better now."

Miracle was not convinced. Something was terribly wrong. He never felt the stone warm around him. He did not see it glow, so he knew Emma never felt its power. Yes, something was seriously wrong.

Unexpectedly, all the passengers felt an abrupt turn as Kishk sliced through the indomitable fog, desperately trying not to bang into the ship. "We must hurry," Emma explained. "It could get really ugly fast now!" She then reached out toward the seal, her hands shaking so, feeling as if she were about to come apart. Taking hold of Miracle's face, she inadvertently bounced it around her numb fingertips, her gaze centering upon those magnificent seal eyes of his. "I'm with you to the very end," she promised. "Understand?"

Miracle smiled and nodded bravely, and then Kishk's voice predominated over all. "Are we anywhere near the porthole you speak of?"

Emma strained through the intense fog with squinting eyes when suddenly, something caught her attention. It looked and felt eerily familiar. "Wait!" she cried. "I feel this is it!" Cautiously, the mighty leviathan drifted closer to the *Tiamat*, careful not to strike it as the rest of the squad came forward upon his tremendous brow. "Come," Emma instructed. "I'll go ahead first. When I give you the signal, you follow." She turned from the white seal, crawling along the shape of the whale's mouth, holding one hand onto the porthole and the other upon his slippery head, trying not to fall into the sea.

"Oh, do be care-fee!" Crumpels chimed.

Emma leaned forward against the small windowed porthole, pushing hard, listening to its frozen hinges scream back in retaliation. It did not budge. Again, she pushed this time with more fury in her thrust. Frustrated, Emma made a fist and slammed it hard against the willful opening. After three more slams, the porthole finally gave in, but only halfway. It would be a tight fit, but she believed that both her and the seal would pass through.

Grabbing on to the inner ledge of the opening, she lifted herself, preparing to enter when suddenly, Crumpels screamed, "Whooo! There is someone inside! I saw them! *I saw them!*" While still holding on with both hands, Emma found herself dangling from the porthole unsupported. Realizing this, Kishk quickly went to her aid, maintaining her feet, preventing her from falling into the icy waters.

"I didn't see anything!" Mulgrew squawked, wanting desperately to wish away the entire experience.

"No! I saw it too!" Big Petie barked.

"Me too, too!" agreed Lukie.

Mum suddenly came to life with a loud and boisterous bellow. "Is it the Docta?"

"Mum," Crumpels hushed. "Be quiet, they'll hear you, goodness me, boop-boop-dee-dee!"

Poo-Coo, finally speaking, added, "Dude, you really have to stop that!"

"Well then, are you the Docta?" the mad harpie asked, looking to the confused walrus.

Poo-Coo just rolled his eyes, but the penguin was quick to jump in, sounding mad himself daring to come closer. "Oh, somebody kill her and feed her to the polar bears! I beg of you!"

A troubled Miracle bit down on his quivering lips. "It's true! There was something there."

"I believe you're right," Kishk added.

"Hellooo!" Emma called to the whale with an exaggerated voice. "I'm about to fall into the sea here!"

"Oh, do forgive me," Kishk humbly apologized, not realizing that he had temporarily drifted away again, leaving the girl to dangle outside the porthole. Nervously, Emma briefly touched down on the whale, trying not to fall.

"I have an idea!" Miracle announced, snatching on to an accomplished smile. "Use the sleeping bubbles!"

"The sleeping bubbles!" the whale exclaimed. "Of course, the sleeping bubbles!"

"Yes," Miracle fluttered. "It could work on the man-beasts inside, could it not?"

Kishk smiled. "I don't see why not. We'll have nothing to lose!"

"You're losing something right now!" Emma uttered, dangling again with no whale skin to support her.

Aggravated by the situation, Mum huffed out a loud grumble. "Oh, good Lordie, fish, do pay attention!"

"So sorry," Kishk lamented, moving to meet the girl's swinging legs. "So very—very sorry, it shan't happen again."

"Can we talk about this after I'm inside, do you suppose?" Emma begged, twisting in frustration, her legs spreading every which way while trying to hold on to the ledge of the porthole.

With a swift wriggle, Miracle dashed up to Emma's feet, supporting her with his back. "It's some kind of whale thing. Don't rightly know how it works, but somehow the big guy can create bubbles that can put whoever, happen to find, themselves near him fast asleep!"

"Terrific!" Emma said in a careless voice, still swinging deplorably from the ledge.

"Yes!" Kishk figured in excitedly. "And with a little manipulative mammal maneuvering, multiplied by what I hope to be a devious dash of whale ingenuity, I think I can send the little floaters directly inside the ship!"

"Great!" Emma agreed with failing patience. "But do you think you could get me directly inside the ship first?"

"Oh, but of course, such fatuous folly," apologized the whale, once again coming to her aid, just as she was about to fall into the freezing sea. He pushed his immense self up to the very edge of the *Tiamat*, remaining there long enough until Emma managed to grasp the porthole properly. Making sure she was able to pull herself through its narrow passage, she began squeezing herself through the opening.

"Give 'em hell, *LOVE-YA*!" Mum's loud voice followed.

"Knock it off, cracked-nuts!" Mulgrew spit.

"Bug off, tweedy-twit!" Mum snarled, smacking the bird across the head, slamming him into the exposed backside of Emma, giving her just the right push to get inside. With a loud thud, Emma found herself lying on the cold and icy floor. There was now a bump on her head and her hands remained raw with frostbite, the gloves only adding to her torment, but she was inside and that was all that mattered. "Thanks a bunch," she moaned, pulling off the hard and frozen gloves, casting them to the floor before rubbing the sting out of her head, her pathetic bonnet upside down hanging around her chin.

"Are you all right?" Miracle barked.

"Peachy!" Emma snapped, forcefully pulling up the weathered bonnet.

A frightened Lukie quickly spoke out. "Are there any witches in there?"

It was terribly dark in the place where Emma entered, dark and creepy, just like the entire ship. Although there was no sign of Decara, there was no sign of the familiar surroundings either. She had indeed made the wrong choice. This was not where she departed from; she was lost, or so it would seem. Enclosed in the shadows, Emma would wait until the white seal would join her there before she decided what to do next.

"Man-child," Lukie nervously called out again in a squeaky voice, sounding more like a newborn pup than a grown harp seal. "I say, are there any witches in there?"

Big Petie immediately corrected his companion. "Don't be silly, if there was a witch in there just waiting to devour her, we would have heard the man-child's bloodcurdling screams and possibly bone-crunching dismemberment snaps by now, don't you suppose?"

Lukie nodded his uneasy head. "Yes, I suppose."

Suddenly, a sigh of relief rang out when Emma's tiny face appeared at the half-opened porthole. "Everything is all right, but we had better hurry, don't know how much time we have before we are discovered."

"The child is right!" Kishk announced. "Go on, Miracle,—I'll give you some time before I grind up the bubbles. Now, remember, try not to let the bubbles touch you, do not inhale them, and whatever you do, do not swallow them! In addition, it would also be advised not to—"

Miracle looked down at the whale with a crossed expression that plainly stated that he got the point. Kishk quickly retreated from his words, clearing his throat. "Right," He groveled. "Now, we'll be waiting here all the time," Kishk advised. "At the slightest sign of provocation, you are to come and make your presence known to me immediately! If you are unable to, I will not tarry long. I will only allow for a certain amount of time. If you have not returned within the hour," the whale said, his violet eyes growing enormously, "I'm coming in!"

Miracle agreed with a nod. Then gazing down at his now half-glowing stone, he rubbed his furry chin next to it. It felt somewhat warm, but he could not be certain. Nevertheless, he would make sure that Emma held it just as soon as he was inside. INSIDE! He was finally going inside! There was no turning back now! "Come," Kishk said. "Let me help you aboard, my most brave and honored comrade."

"Whoooo!" wailed Crumpels, the gigantic walrus tears running down her pliable and wrinkled face. "Hurry back to us, dear!"

"I'll be back. I promise," said the white seal, trying to catch his breath, casting his eyes toward Mum. She did not come to him. She merely smiled at him then winked and blew him a kiss with her flipper and waved. She kept right on waving, her flipper moving up and down unceasingly.

Turning to face the ship, Miracle neared the porthole, waiting for the whale to help him up.

"Hold on!" Kishk commanded, arching himself as far as he possibly could so that the seal could wriggle flush against the opening. With a heavy swallow and one final glance at his medallion, Miracle stuck his head through the opening. His chubby seal body pondered there for a moment as he pushed and forced himself about, twitching deplorably. He was going in, one way or another! After a few moments of real pushing and shoving, he finally plopped forward, flipping inside the ship head first, landing in almost the same fashion as Emma had; only he had her to catch him when he fell down toward the blackened floor of the vile *Tiamat*.

From outside the ship, Kishk and the others remained silent, worriment filling their eyes, uneasiness filling their hearts. Reverently, the blue whale cast his violet eyes up into the enshrouded heavens, closing them tight, praying quietly, his colossal form framed inside the gathering fog.

CHATTERING LIPS

Miracle never ever remembered seeing so much darkness. He never thought such blackness was possible. His eyes could not adjust fast enough. Frantically, he fought the eternal nighttime of this most ghastly of places. While the dismal essence of the ship drenched over him, he felt Emma's hand touch his head. "Are you all right?" she asked in a bundled buzz of shivers.

"Yes—and you?"

"I'm okay."

Wide-eyed and ready for almost anything, Miracle experienced his own set of shivers come over him, Emma remaining clueless as to their whereabouts. Although the interior of the ship offered her more warmth than the frigid outside world did, she could feel its unearthly clamminess crawling over her. Then almost as if the vile ship had waited precisely for this moment, she could smell the putrid reek of dead fish and hardtack, the mere nasal recollection causing her to become violently nauseous. Expecting her insides to come propelling out her mouth, she held the vomit back, desperately attempting to concentrate solely on her mission.

"What's that smell?" the white seal asked.

"It's what they serve around here. It's the entrée, the à la carte, and the à la mode, exclusively served upon this swank floating bistro consisting of fish guts and some kind of stale bread and Lord knows what else."

Miracle made a disgusted face before perceiving that Emma had left his side; he could barely see her walk away into the immediate shadows. Wrapping her arms around herself, she tried to ease the trembling taking place inside her. She walked a few more feet before stopping. She had come to the end of a passageway connected to yet another dark corridor, this one leading far beyond, disappearing entirely into further darkness more cruel and forbidding than where they now stood. "I don't know why, but I feel that we should go this way," she instructed.

Miracle quickly wriggled next to her, doing as she asked, saying, "Emma, hold the stone before we go another step." Complying, she knelt down and grasped the lightless stone. Feeling nothing, she stood up before furthering herself into the darkness, waiting for the white seal to join her. As he did, the seal felt a stir of panic rise within himself. "Emma," he whispered in a taut voice, "I'm blind. My eyes cannot adjust to this darkness."

"It's not just your eyes," she said through trembling and chattering lips. "I can't see anything either. I think we are in the pit of this monster's belly."

Suddenly the mysterious tear within the stone began to glow. It was slight, but a distinct glow just the same. "Emma! Look!" exclaimed the seal.

Emma quickly turned to see the faint, soft light of the purple stone emanating in the sea of perfectly surrounding blackness. "Touch it again!" Miracle pleaded. "Touch it before we go another inch! I know it will make you well this time. It must!"

Emma bent down, guided by its light, and grasping it tightly, she remained there holding the glowing stone. In just a short while, she felt something tingle inside her. Then like hundreds of butterflies fluttering against her insides, she felt a slight relief from the bitter cold struggling to defeat her. Although it was not near as lavish in its easement as in previous times, she did begin to grow warmer, especially her hands. However, still experiencing shivers and what she believed to be a burning fever, for whatever reason, the stone had once again aided her, at least partially. She could breathe easier now as a slight, soft wash of warm essence embraced her, the very thing that she needed to continue.

"Did it help? Please say it did!" beseeched Miracle.

The stone remained disarranged, of this she was certain; but it was fighting to return whole, she could feel it plainly. Exaggerating her claim, she answered, saying, "Yes, I almost feel like my old self again. Are you ready?"

The seal paused for a moment, closed his eyes, fought off the shivers, gulped hard and fast, and then nodded his head firmly. "Yes! Let's go!" he said, waiting for Emma to lead the way.

Standing upright, Emma turned and faced the charcoal shadows. Turning around, she gave Miracle one final glance before entering the pitch-black opening. Miracle was directly behind her every wriggle of the way and found himself continuously bombarding against her boot-clad feet, not daring to be more than a half-inch away from her. Unexpectedly, he suddenly gasped.

"What is it?" Emma asked, startled, staggering in the unbelievable blackness.

"Don't know, something touched my nose, I felt it plainly!"

"Your nose?"

"Yes!" cried the white seal. "Ahh! There it goes again; it's something wet and slimy!"

"It's all right! It's all right!" Emma explained, reaching down to pat her jittery companion. "The bubbles, remember? Kishk said that he would send in the bubbles after us. Surely, it must be what you feel."

"Of course," he agreed just as another of the transparent balls exploded across his snout. "The bubbles!" he cried, suddenly panic stricken. "We mustn't inhale or swallow the bubbles!"

"I may have just swallowed one," Emma yawned, feeling the effects of the whale's mystic spray swarm about her.

"Hurry! They work fast! Very fast!" he barked, his eyelids growing heavy. "We best get away from them, and quickly!"

Finishing another yawn, Emma agreed lethargically. "Come on, Miracle, one more dose of Kishk's slumbering sea snooze, I'm afraid I'll be a goner!"

"Me too!" the white seal groaned, battling against another yawn. Blindly, they tumbled into the one-way path of the corridor; its passageway suddenly making an abrupt and sharp turn just in time to counter off what remained of the invading army of bubbles, both evaporating into its nothingness as if being sucked up into the mouth of a gigantic black hole.

BUMBLING BUBBLES

The bubbles kept pouring out of Kishk, and getting them all to follow direct route into the vile ship had proven not to be an easy maneuver. However, the blue chanter did not let the difficulty interfere with his plan. Before he even began the whole bubbling enterprise, he had asked his crew to dislodge themselves from the center of his head, asking them to veer to the rear as he slanted and adjusted his incredible head, aiming his blowhole directly into the half-open mouth of the ship's porthole. With his face now half covered up inside the freezing waters, the whale began puffing out his floating menagerie of sleepiness, and everything would have gone precisely to the acute calculations of the intrepid whale's design if it had not been for the mad seal. Compelled to stick her enormous head forcefully into the porthole, Mum began offering more deranged seal kisses to the white harp. Becoming half stuck inside its obviously too small opening, Mum's bloated backside abruptly prevented any more of the wafting legion of bubbles from entering the ship, instantly commanding them to come to a complete halt!

"Oh no!" moaned the whale, incapable of doing anything before the massive army of bubbles, made strong by the strengthening winds, now unable to enter the ship because of Mum's widespread rump, suddenly switched gears, returning, bursting down around everyone! They were most potent in their pursuit, completely covering the whale as he tried to warn the others, but in a matter of moments, it was all over. The tranquilizing whale spray immediately went to work; and one by one, Mulgrew, Crumpels, Poo-Coo, Big Petie, Lukie, and the chanter himself suddenly flopped down in every direction, each succumbing to the whale's magic sleeping spell.

Slumped on his side, Kishk nearly tossed the unconscious gathering overboard. With his violet eyes beginning to close, he yawned out a resistant whale yelp. Scrunching up his face with the most unpleasant exasperation, his last view of his surroundings caught a glimpse of the enormous dangling rump of the mad and blundering Mum seal before he too fell prey to his own sleeping enchantment.

STUCK TIGHT

Mum bounced around inside the tight-fitting porthole, grunting and blasting off from both ends, trying to free herself; but like it or not, she was stuck tight! She continued to try to slide her enormous self through the opening, but of course, she could not. Soon tiring of her incompetent attempts, the mad harpie merely went limp, looking out into the darkness of the *Tiamat.*

"Are you the Docta?" she asked the shadows. Then she called out for Miracle several times, but no answer came to her. Exhausted, she continued to study the stirring shadows of the evil ship that she had idiotically entrapped herself within. "Oh, bother love!" Mum lamented, smacking her lips together before ending with a most pitiful belch that echoed off into the bleak shadows. She sighed then suddenly started up a fast game of Clap-Clap but quickly lost interest in the frolic of her favorite pastime.

She was in trouble, and even she in her clueless madness knew that she had really botched things up this time. Feeling a sudden itch spread across her backside, Mum attempted to scratch the annoying sensation away and found that she was not able to relieve the annoying tickle. This was because her other half was outside the dreadful ship, and judging from the way her girth remained corked in there, try as she may repeatedly, she was incapable of meeting up with herself no matter what. Nor would she be able to join the sleeping ones only a short distance from her unplugged rump, not that she even had the remotest idea of what she had just done. She sighed again and let the drool slowly run down her nose. She deserved it. After all, she had been a bad, bad seal. Another sigh came, another belch and then another sigh and a few more smacks of her saturated lips. She would just have to wait this one out alone, stuck somewhere in a place that was not a place anyone would ever want to be trapped.

After a while, Mum was not sure if her nose was still leaking or if she had begun to cry. It did not matter; after all, no one could see her there. Still, after looking out into the disturbing shadows of the *Tiamat*, she was no longer sure.

More Tears

Arayna's seal song had gotten weaker, almost faint now, and this terrified the seal.

Furthermore, she had not slept since the vile henchmen had come to her prison. Except for the slithering and disgusting noises that the three-headed serpent made, she was utterly alone. Occasionally, strange creaking sounds came from somewhere above. Every time the floors or the walls made a sound, the frightened harp would jump, preparing to meet the evil woman again. Every time she was certain that it was Decara, only more of the loathing sounds of the ship would call back to her.

Arayna's stomach had been long since finished with making its hunger noise. She was starving and not sure just how long she could hold out. The hairy servant had not come to bring her food in such a long time; although why she remained alive when the others had died plagued her endlessly. She knew it somehow had to do with her son and the evils of the devil woman, but in her confused and exhausted state, nothing made sense anymore. She felt so small inside the massive mesh cage. With the others gone, she perceived the darkness with greater dread. She closed her eyes and tried to listen for her seal song, imagining the face of her child when suddenly the snake heads began to stir louder than usual. She shuddered, unable to block out their dissonant sounds. They were growing restless as if they sensed someone approaching the dark-infested room.

All at once, a door hidden inside the blackness swung open. It slammed hard against the wall, shaking the whole room. Arayna cringed, buckling down, cowering toward the back of the mesh prison. She sniffed the air and at once recognized the foul smell. The devil woman had indeed returned! Suddenly, there, before the mesh cage stood Decara, clothed in an all-consuming and extensively long and dragging-across-the-floor, red-tinted furry robe. Despite the diluted scarlet color, Arayna identified the crimson-stained garment immediately. It was baby seal fur having been sewn together, its once white array now drenched in the color of dread. The devil woman had debased the harp fur in seal's blood—its own!

The witch stood quietly in the shadows, blending into the flickering gloom perfectly as if she were a part of it. Aside from the vulgar display of murdered seal skin that made for an enormous and lengthy vestment, an overbearing mantle veiled her head. A wide and brimming hood made of the same desecrated seal fur cloaked the devil woman's head, covering it up entirely, making her look like the grim reaper its tiny seal hairs fluttering scarlet in the dark air, the room suddenly surging with a diabolical static charge. Arayna stared at the vile woman, scrutinizing her through the gloom, but Decara's face remained eaten away by the squirming shadows. All she could see was those shining red eyes of hers; that was all.

Decara dramatically raised her arm, extending a single unlit candlestick, black. Suddenly, the wick ignited, dismissing hundreds of creepy phantoms. Retreating into the gathering darkness, the shadows allowed the flickering glow to remain, at least for the time being. As her arm continued with its ascent, Decara threw more candlelight upon the seal. Arayna could see the black candle firmly fixed tight inside a silver holder shaped like a skeleton claw, its bony grasp resembling the devil woman's own fingers, each finger clenched tightly around its waxy stem. A flash flared, and Decara exposed the underside of her bloodstained seal robe. Lined with a rigid red and satiny material, it appeared not like anything Arayna had ever seen. A disturbing sound sparked and rasped, intimidating the seal further.

"*Aw . . . ,*" Decara lamented in a fake and condescending tone, licking her lips in the privacy of her own secluded darkness. "Such a sour face, we'll have no gloomy puss around here," she said in a long drawn-out breath. "'Tis a happy day for me, that is, my soon-to-be mammal leftovers, for your tears will be the final tears that will adorn me as I complete the task the darkness has chosen me for. The death of innocence has finally descended upon us, my darling slug, so let us begin, shall we?" The vile Decara chuckled. "Oreguss!" she abruptly commanded in a suddenly piercing scream. "Prepare our honored guest for her final 'boohooing' chastisement!" She began to cackle maniacally. Arayna did not move a muscle. She only stared at the devil woman with a new and sudden defiance.

Deciding to show her face, Decara allowed the hood of her cloak to fall around her shoulders. Her face was exceptionally white, fixed, and bloodless, her red eyes glaring maliciously at the mother harp. Surprisingly, Arayna was no longer afraid; she would not die having the evil man-beast think her a coward. With her eyes fastened to the woman, she watched Decara's statuette appearance disappear and reappear within the streaking splashes of candlelight. Arayna pressed herself up close to the steel webbed prison, her snout slightly touching the cold mesh. Stunned silence progressed over her as Oreguss appeared, unlocking the cage, leaving her vulnerable to their villainous savagery. As the door screamed back and forth, Decara spoke.

"One last time," she vowed, evilly standing before the cage. "Prepare, wretched mother of the white worm, for the end of your world is upon you! And by all that is truly evil, I shall take your precious child—and swallow his soul!"

Arayna's eyes stung while keeping her stare upon the beastly woman. It hurt to keep them open. She remained exhausted, starving; and the distress flaming in her eyes disabled her sight considerably, causing her nausea, but she maintained her decided trance. Decara grinned inside the defending shadows that crept across her ghostly face, just surveying the defiant mother harp as she sinisterly approached her. "OREGUSS!" she screamed again. "Bring me the chalice!"

Nodding his head, Oreguss turned away into the awaiting shadows, reappearing in only a matter of moments. In his hand, he held the black and shining sealed-up chalice, its coal-black smooth surface like newly polished ebony, glossy and glistening. With its sculptured dragon head wrapped around its lid its dreadful mouth, open, and pointing toward the ceiling as the rest of its body embedded itself in a wild spin, Decara monstrously smiled. Then with a theatrical swoop of her arms, she swept herself before the terrified harp the bloodstained, long and dripping seal cape, pouring out everywhere from around her. In the shadows of herself, Decara upheld her head, speaking out to the blackness of the room and the black chalice before her:

"Breath of Hades, awaken! Come forth! Take the suffering of this beast and defile it for the last time that I may complete your will—Breath of Heaven—at last—be—still!"

The irreverent chalice began to glow brightly, expelling a dark green mist. It seeped through the tiny opening, reflecting itself against the reptilian-sculpted covering just as it had the many times before. Arayna drew herself up to her full height, defying the witch. Intently staring at Decara, she waited for her to raise the chalice, and she did. Opening its lid, the wicked woman released a small part of hell from within. Arayna cringed when the green vapor hissed, leaving the cup sizzling in the air heading directly toward her. Powerless and heartsick, knowing fully what to expect next, she closed her eyes in horror, listening to the cracking and fizzing. Slowly, the hellish fog floated out on wisps of demon claws that crawled across the shadows, filling the air with its foul smell ominously descending upon the helpless seal.

Swiftly, the devil's breath crippled Arayna, drenching her face with wetness. She tried to recoil inside herself further, pushing her head down into the girth of herself, wanting desperately to block out the heart-wrenching wails exploding inside her, but she was not strong enough. With continued fixed shut eyes and buried head, her screams expelled with such fervor she thought her heart would explode; for no matter how many times she became exposed to this monstrous torture, the stealing of tears remained unbelievably excruciating.

The hell-spawned mist swirled devilishly around the mesh cage, wavering and sizzling in ghostly pursuit, reaching out in all directions, permeating itself around Arayna, forcing her to relive such brutal memories. Again, she screamed out in sheer agony, her burning tears turning into diamond chips. Oreguss started to chuckle, preparing to crawl into the cage, ever so eager to collect the shining wonders now turned to gemstones. The cage was overflowing with dazzling seal tears when he spitefully stepped on Arayna's collapsed body. While pilfering the shimmering anguish, Oreguss forcefully scooped up the diamond chips, stuffing them inside a large burlap sack.

A morbid and unsettling quiet seeped across the room.

Arayna remained lifeless inside the confines of the cruel mesh cage, countless shining diamonds scattered beneath her. They covered up her face, almost appearing as ice like the frosty homeland she had once lived upon . . . once upon a time . . . not so long ago.

Decara's loud voice jarred Arayna from her delirium, forcing the seal to look upon her yet once again. Incredibly weak and unable to hold her head steady, Arayna pathetically tried to focus on Decara, her eyesight almost reduced to blindness, feeling as if death was just waiting to claim her any minute now.

"Let the nightmare begin!" Decara shrieked with a gurgling sound, madly committed to her hysterical laughter, disappearing into the blackness of the room, her cackling roar echoing after her. Turning his eyes back to the cage, Oreguss smashed his fist against the mesh, forcing the tortured Arayna to a slow and piteous retreat. Falling ashamedly into the multitudes of her own tears, she once again collapsed. Bordering consciousness, she still found the strength to glare and snarl at Oreguss while he clumsily went about with his dastardly business. Squalling on its hinges, the door abruptly flew back and forth as he filled up his abrasive sack, taking every last trace of the treasure before he slapped shut the cage, once more locking Arayna inside. After a few moments, she took a deep breath, trying to somehow remain conscious. In a quiet turn, she lamely wriggled over toward the locked door. Slumping forward, her weary head struck against the cold bite of the prison. If she could have cried again, she would have, and yet she was unable for Decara had taken every last tear from her. There was nothing left inside her—no tears, no hope. She was dying, and the heartache that filled her now was unbearable. She managed to pull her heavy head away from the mesh screen, feeling all traces of belief drain from her. She felt numb. Perhaps she was dead. She could not be sure of anything. Certainly, by the way she felt, she should be dead. Despite the promises of the man-child, everything seemed hopeless now. After all, what made her ever think that the human girl spoke the truth? Everything she had ever known of man remained defiled with the blood of the tortured and the murdered. Man was a savage liar, spreading nothing but heartache and tears wherever it went; and now, the evil Decara had even taken that from her—every last tear. Pathetically ironic, she thought.

Shaking her weary head, she now fought for consciousness.

Exhausted and near death herself, the brokenhearted, tear-barren Arayna opened her burning eyes and turned to face the mesh wall mere inches before her blurring vision. Falling forward, she once more lethargically bumped her aching head against its cold surface only to close her eyes again and sigh—utterly sigh. And that was all. For she knew in a little while, if heaven still employed its mercy, she would soon join the other dead seals of Sealssong.

RATTLING CHAINS

Miracle thought that he had lost Emma for one terrifying moment for the darkness was thick. Then suddenly, Emma gasped.

"THE VAULT!" she cried, stopping abruptly, the shadows settling down around her.

Miracle came crashing from behind, striking his head on the lopsided wrong-foot hunting boot. Stunned, he shook his head, trying to catch his bearings. *"The vault?"*

"Yes, that is where the diamonds are! I've definitely been here before!" Emma said, trying to hold back another cough, waiting for the darkness to settle, again barely able to see the light directly ahead. "Shhh—" she hushed. "Listen!"

Miracle quickly stopped in his wriggle, listening to a low moaning sound. "What's that?"

"It's THEM!"

"Them?"

"The sentinels, the watchers of the diamond vault, the cursed creatures that guard her treasure. Anyone who enters and steals the seal tears is doomed forever!"

Miracle moved closer toward Emma, needing to feel her body next to him. More haunting groaning moans echoed through the black corridors, each sound mixed in with more spooky sounds of the moving *Tiamat*. Emma started walking again, her floppy irregular boots making their abrasive squeaking sounds, stopping directly in front of the crypt vault. A softly filtrating light from above cascaded down, creating dark shadows over the face of the vault, making it look even more sinister than she remembered. More ghastly sounds seemed to come from inside, making Emma shiver with fright.

Miracle's heart began to beat alarmingly. "I can hear them! Let's go away from here!"

"They won't hurt us unless we go inside. I nearly lost Kenyan to them. They are cursed to recruit anyone who dares swindle the stolen treasure," she reiterated, wiping her dripping nose with her bulky seal hunting sleeve three times too large. "But you are right. We need to keep moving. Time is running out. I can feel it. Come on, let's go." But in her attempt to stand, her legs buckled and she suddenly collapsed, returning to the white seal, slumping hard against the vault.

"Emma!" Miracle cried. "What is it?"

It took a moment for the room to stop spinning before she could speak again. She cleared her parched throat, shivering, resting her back against the grotesque face of the vault. Bending her knees, she placed her head between them. "Just a little dizzy, I'm afraid. I'll be all right."

Miracle pushed closer still, extending his head to meet up against her cheek. "You're sick. You're burning up inside. Emma, you need to rest."

"No," she answered, raising her head, looking back to the seal. "We must keep moving. We've got to save them! We've got to save them all, and we are running out of time!"

Another ghastly moan came from behind the face of the vaulted room. Strange crackling noises crawled across the surface of the door, sounding like millions of insects. Its horrific motion suddenly pressed against both their spines, chilling them to the bone. Instantaneously, they pulled away from the ghastly vault. A loud unbearable banging sound thundered throughout the dark corridors. Emma jolted up, her wild eyes darting down the blackened halls before her.

CRASH! Another explosion rumbled through the corridors as a large diamond-packed sack hit the walls and floor, sliding several feet before striking another portion of the corridor. "It's Oreguss!" Emma gasped. "He's coming to the vault with more seal tears! Quick, let's get out of here!" With a rushing gush, they disappeared into the sullen shadows, turning down another endless hallway, this one semilit with an eerie glow slightly tinged with green. Miracle tried to keep up once more, smacking hard into Emma's boot when suddenly he came to another unexpected halt.

"Who's there?" asked another voice. "Is that you, witch?"

Miracle stretched his neck way beyond what a seal should ever be required to stretch while looking over his shoulder. His head jerked to and fro, listening intently, his dark shining eyes made wide with fear. He could hear some kind of rattling sound, and it was coming from somewhere close—frightfully close! Then the voice returned, this time even louder. "I said, is that you, witch?"

The voice was hoarse and raspy, but Emma recognized it immediately.

She looked up only a few feet in front of her. Seeing a large wooden door, she quickly approached it. A small open window bearing four stony bars securely embedded deep inside its wooden gums, resembling sinister-looking chipped teeth, grinned out at her menacingly. If she stood on her tiptoes, she would be able to see inside. If only Oreguss hadn't come, if only! Miracle wriggled close beside her, listening to her call out her brother's name. "Kenyan!" she cried, grabbing on to the stony teeth of the prison door temporarily suspending herself off the floor.

"Emma . . . ," the shocked and raspy voice called back. *"Emma?"* Although much of the cell remained covered in darkness, she could see her brother's face, compliments of some unknown faltering light. Her mouth fell open and her eyes immediately filled with tears, for she could scarcely recognize him. He had gotten so thin and pale and had appeared to have suffered numerous cuts and abrasions, which covered most of his once handsome and youthful face, his eyes dark and sickly. "Emma!" Kenyan once again called out through a clot of mucus. "Is that really you?"

"Yes!" Emma cried. "It's me, but you must be very quiet Oreguss isn't far away!"

"Are you all right? How did you ever—"

"My poor brother, what has she done to you?" Emma wept, quickly grasping tighter to the cell and its split-apart rotting door handle. Twisting it back and forth, pulling on it, nearly snapping its decaying remains off in her hands, she tried to enter but was unable. Once more, she grabbed the cell's stony teeth, pulling herself up off the floor, her ridiculous boots dangling in midair, the even more ridiculous bonnet still somehow remaining askew on top of her head. "It's going to be all right. I promise!" she said through teary eyes. "We've come to save you and the seals!"

Suddenly, another strange voice, much deeper and raspier than Kenyan's, broke through the dismal blackness of the cell. "Who is it, boy?"

"It's my sister!" Kenyan answered in an excited jolt.

Emma gasped. "Who is that? Is someone else in there with you?"

"It's the captain of this filthy, rotten ship!"

"Captain?"

"Yes, the witch put him here after she had no more use for him, nearly killed him, poor guy. I'm still not sure how he's managed to stay alive. He's real sick, thought he was dead—well, until now."

"The poor man," Emma lamented with choking discomfort. "I've got to get you both out of there!" She dropped to the floor, taking the crumbling door handle in her hand, once again shaking it, spitting pieces of itself all over her hands. Still, the door never opened. Exhausting herself in the feeble attempt, Emma stopped, reverting to her suspension in the air while holding on to the teeth, but not before wiping away her tears, smearing a dirty streak across her creamy pink face. "Let me try it my way," she blurted, her frustration and fever driving her to outrageousness.

"Do you think you can?" Kenyan called out.

"I think so," she said, jumping away from the door, concentrating as hard as she possibly could. However, she suddenly lost her balance and fell crashing to the floor, her head spinning, her vision blurring.

"Emma!" Miracle barked. "Are you all right?"

"I don't know. I don't think I'm strong enough," she moaned, attempting to stand up again. Eventually finding the strength to hold on to the bars of the prison door, she called to her brother. "I'm not able . . . Too weak, I guess, to fight the evil here."

Suddenly Captain Thorne spoke out. "There is another way," said the dying blond man, unable to finish off his sentence before he cleared the blood from his throat. "The key . . ." He coughed, fighting for consciousness. "I stole it"—*cough*—"the key . . . skeleton key . . . opens everything." That was all Thorne could muster before the blood filled back up in his throat.

"Where is it?" asked an excited Emma, slanting her tiny face, pressing it hard against the stony teeth, straining to send her words over to him.

Thorne tried to swallow down the rising sickness, his one blue eye oozing fluid it should have never known, his face fully bearded except for some bald patches torn away from nips and bites of pesky rats. His dirty blond hair hung limp, sticking to the dried blood on his forehead from many nibbles before. "In the bridge—not far from the wheel, a black wooden desk—Look inside—," he wheezed, then coughed some more. "Get the key," he begged through parched and hollow lips. He exhaled, sending his breath into a whizzing gurgle right before his head fell limp into his bony chest. He did not speak again.

Emma released her grip. "Oh dear God, help me," she whispered. "Please help me." Miracle wriggled up close to the door partially resting half of himself against the wood, his flippers up against the door's rough base, looking like a dog wanting to come in from the cold. Emma then quickly wiped more dirty streaks of tears across her face. "She's nearly killed them," she said as Miracle lowered his head in sadness. Once again, she rose to her feet, squeezing the stony teeth. "I'll get the key! I'll get whatever it takes! I'm going to get you both out of there! I promise you," she called out, unable to control the trembling in her voice.

Hurried, Kenyan spoke back. "Emma, how did you survive the witch?"

"The seals!"

"The seals?"

"Yes, Kenyan, you must believe me!"

It was then Emma heard Miracle's nails scrape the prison door. Once more, she released herself from the stony teeth, dropping down to the seal, an intense, yet hopeful expression probing across her red face. Swiftly, she took hold of Miracle's half-glowing medallion. "I need whatever strength you could spare," she said to the tear. "I believe . . . I believe," she repeated with her eyes closed, holding tight to the stone.

"What are you going to do?" Miracle whispered.

"Kenyan needs to believe now. He is still filled with doubts. He needs to believe. He needs to see and hear you!"

"Me?"

"Yes, and I need the power of the tear to help me lift you to the window."

"Oh . . . ," Miracle said readily before quickly changing his tone when realizing what she had just suggested. "*Oh, Emma,* I don't know if that's such a good idea."

"Hush, it will be okay. Just trust me." She took hold of the half-glowing medallion. "Come on," she said out loud, squeezing the tear again. "Give me all you got!" She closed her eyes tightly, saying in a long drawn-out voice, "I believe . . . I believe!"

"Emma, you're not well, maybe we should—"

"It's okay," she interjected, opening her eyes, still feeling the warmth of the stone against her skin. "It still glows. Weak as it is, its power remains with us." Suddenly, her face lit up with a flushed glow, a broadening smile breaking out across her pink lips. "Are you ready?" she asked with newfound endurance.

Miracle remained still, blinking his eyes nervously, not knowing what to expect next. Emma groped him from underneath, nearly falling on top of him, striving to lift up his floppy, soft, and furry body, dropping him down between her legs with one lumbering hoist. Miracle's head bumped the floor several times as she tried to flip him over. Trying to hold him just below his front flippers, she nearly dropped him again before finally lifting the seal upward. With the help of the wondrous tear, she was lifting Miracle up to the window with the stony chipped teeth. Up he went, his furry round tummy brushing up against the door, his white seal head propped to one side as he continued rising up directly in front of the prison casement. A stunned and freakish gaze exaggerated over the seal's face while his eyes popped open. Feeling as if he were about to flip backward, Miracle braced himself for the crash, his wild stare fixating on the darkness of the cell before him; the whole time, Emma continued to push with all her newly acquired strength, maintaining her stand.

"Talk to him!" she called out in a constipated muffle, bouncing the seal humorously in front of the stony teeth of the prison window.

At first Kenyan could not make out what the bobbing image was or what it possibly was doing there. His eyes squinted through the gloominess of the cell, watching the strange thing dance ridiculously, the existing light from beyond overstating its silly movements. It only took a few more moments before the boy's jaw dropped openly, his staggering stare a mass of disorderly disbelief. He shook his head and then shook it once again, trying to chase the image away, but it remained. Once again, he merely stared off with a queer "you've got to be kidding" expression stamped across his face.

Miracle looked down to Emma for needed reassurance, far from knowing what his next move would be. Emma kept on pushing up the seal, grunting from his weight. "Say something!" she repeated—"*anything!*" With a jittery and excited nod, Miracle kept looking back down at her and then turned his head to face the opening to the cell, just barely able to make out the outline of the man-beast who was Emma's brother. Miracle cleared his throat and smiled an awkward seal smile before he simply offered a shy, but sturdy "Hello there."

Kenyan's mouth, although thought to have already dropped as far as it possibly could, somehow managed to drop out even further, and from the way it hung there, it felt as if it had dropped right off his face. In an absolute stupor, he shook his buzzing head again, believing he was either dreaming or hallucinating or ill from some kind of fatal seasickness. Several more times Kenyan and his swinging unattached jaw shook with defiance over the bizarre image. He blinked and squeezed shut then opened his eyes repeatedly, but the outlandish thing continued to stare at him. There it was, a smiling face of a white seal—a seal somehow upheld by his frail sister and not only a seal but a TALKING seal who easily offered articulate salutations. It was just too much!

"You must be Emma's brother, Kenyan," Miracle said. "Very nice to meet you finally, so sorry about all of this, but not to worry, if anyone can save you, I know Emma will," the seal said, all bumblinglike. "She's magnificent!" he nervously added, proceeding to smile a great big cartoon grin, exposing all of his seal teeth, only making himself appear even more freakish than ever. Just then, Emma's strength gave out and Miracle came toppling down on top of her with a crashing slam. Fearful of being caught, both darted off into the nearest nook of shadows adjacent to the prison door, certain that the prowling Oreguss had heard them for sure, and in fact, he did! They could hear his lumbering footsteps echoing across the nearby corridor; they hugged each other, their eyes shutting tight, straining to block out the likes of the vicious henchman, both of their heads buried deep into each other's shoulders.

In a matter of seconds, Oreguss was at the end of the corridor. His beady brown eyes peered down into the darkness before he suddenly tore down the hall, smelling the dank air like a wild animal. Miracle pushed up even closer to Emma, crunching up tight against her, but somehow he lost his hold. Incredibly, he felt himself fall away from her. It had somehow felt like the wall they had huddled next to had suddenly sprung to life, becoming resentful of their hidden refuge, pushing him straight out into the open corridor. Emma tried to grab on to him, but she was not fast enough. With one quick *whoosh*, his furry white body slid out past the guarding shadows as Oreguss made his way toward him. Determined, Emma reached out for Miracle once more, this time grabbing the tip of his quivering hind flipper, pulling him back toward her with one swift tug. Throwing her arms around him, she covered the seal with her body. Oreguss suspiciously came to a halting stop right there in the middle of the gloomy corridor. He continued to sniff the air like a demented hound dog. Although Emma had been able to retrieve the white seal back into the murky obscurity, was it too late? Had Oreguss seen them?

A demonic crazed grimace wiggled wickedly across the burly man's scruffy face as he once more headed down the hall, laughing to himself, sniffing the shadows, punching the air, hopping along with a deranged gait. He was close enough to reach them just a few fingers away when from out of the blackness a shrilling voice rocked the very corridors. Oreguss surprisingly jumped several feet, not expecting such a rattling ruckus. Instinctively, he most assuredly knew the shrieking voice that filled the black hallways. It was, of course, his dark mistress. Her earsplitting unquestionable scream bombarded the man with an unnerving and vicious assault, demanding that he finish his task of taking the diamonds to the vault before reporting immediately back to her; she had more for him to do—much more! He winced in disgust, kicking the wall in fury, knowing that if he did not respond at once, there would undoubtedly be hell to pay—literally! He did not want to go through that again. He had enough of Decara's wicked dramatics. He would respond immediately just as she commanded so as to avoid any severe punishment. Grunting aloud, he kicked the wall again and turned, heading back down the corridor, shrewdly turning his head around periodically, hoping to find whatever, or whomever, aroused his suspicions. Nevertheless, it didn't matter. He would return, and when he did, he would find whoever was hiding there. You could bet your life on it. He would find them, and this time they would not escape! Not this time, he would find them and take care of them, all right!

Emma and Miracle remained holding each other and their breath when Oreguss disappeared into the shadows. They could still hear him dragging the sack to the vault, hurling it into its haunted domain before returning to his awaiting mistress. Emma exhaled a deep breath before patting the seal on the head, preparing to return to the toothy cell window.

Suspended once again, Emma looked upon her brother, calling to him in a choked whisper. "Kenyan, it's all right. Oreguss has gone!"

Her brother did not utter a sound. He was just as the white seal had left him, still holding to the same dumbfounded "you've got to be kidding" expression stuck all over his face, his mouth remaining agape, his eyes wide and glazed, looking as if he had been hit in the head a couple of times. Again, Emma called out to her brother, "I'm going to find the key, I promise! We have friends to help us now! Big friends and they will help us escape and destroy Decara before her awful Night of Screams begins!"

Kenyan remained silent, still terribly stunned, with drool dribbling from his open mouth.

"She wants me to kill the white seal during the Night of Screams, but with the help of Kishk, he's the blue whale who's responsible for us being here, the two walruses, the penguin, the two bulls, the Mum, she's mad, you see, and of course, the white seal—"

"That's me!" Miracle called out from some unknown place below.

"We're going to finally, once and for all, beat the stink out of that miserable woman!"

A stunned stupor expression remained on Kenyan's shocked face, his thin, pale features made limp and jellylike.

"You just keep the faith until I return, and return I shall just as soon as I can!"

Kenyan tried to speak, but only a high-pitched squeal tweeted out.

"Don't worry," Emma offered softly, hanging from the stony teeth. "The purple angels won't let any bad happen. I promise." She smiled at him, watching his still shocked face. Then somehow managing it, the boy struggled out a few words. "It . . . it spoke to me."

Emma continued smilingly, nodding her head. "Yes, I know."

"But . . . but you don't understand! A seal . . . a seal wearing a necklace with a white head and funny lips spoke to me!"

Emma nodded again—"Of course."

"But you're not listening. Its lips moved. It talked to me!"

"I know, he talks to me all the time. I always knew if you listened hard enough, you'd hear what I can hear. After all, you are my brother."

"Hurry," Miracle called to Emma. "I think someone is coming!"

Emma glanced down to the white seal, nodding her head, raising it, turning to look at Kenyan one final time. With her heart breaking all over again, she knew that she had to leave him yet once again. Courageously, she let go of the stony teeth for the last time. Then she turned away from the prison door, leaving Kenyan alone with the unconscious Captain Thorne and the hungry rats with the red eyes that were just waiting for her to leave so they could continue with their nibbling.

Kenyan would not realize his sister's absence for some time. He would remain in the twilight of disbelief for yet a time longer, left to contemplate his own sanity, or even more, the incredible possibility that all this time, his sister spoke the absolute truth. Suddenly, a rather funny and curious thought spun itself into his already twisted mind.

If there were such things as witches, why couldn't there be talking seals? After all, anything was possible with Emma. He, above all else, should have realized this from the beginning. Laughing to himself for being such an ignoramus, he exhaled slowly, his bony chest caving in as he sank back against the cold stone wall, the shackles tight around his wrists just barely rattling. His eyes were wild now with a deranged glare, his mouth still slack-jawed as he murmured, "Seals with lips that talk, man, oh man!" His mind swimming in sheer amazement, not even aware that one of his hungry roommates had just begun to nibble on his toes again. The rat was only able to maintain his snacking but for a short time before Kenyan's automatic reflex kicked in, sending the pesky vermin across the room with one swift kick, smashing it somewhere off into the filthy corners of the cell. Nonchalantly, and yet ever so precisely, Kenyan settled his stinging foot down, resting it back into the damp and murky floor, his dazed expression merely staring off toward the cell window with the stony teeth. A consuming, crazed smile ponderously broke out across the boy's face, continuing with his ingrained stare, marveling in awe, his wild eyes forever remembering the talking white seal with the funny moving lips and his magnificent, small, and frail sister who had once again left him absolutely dumbfounded.

I Can Still Feel Her

Emma blindly felt the walls, careful not to bump into their sudden turns and abrasive bends. It was pitch-black, and neither one could see anything. They had long since passed the vault, and as to their whereabouts, Emma had not a clue.

As her tiny fingers touched the walls, she found that she could only keep them stationary for a brief moment. The peculiar surface suddenly felt disturbing, feeling comprised of nasty lizard scales and decaying snake skin. It revolted her thoroughly, and yet she valorously pushed onward, relying on her blind touch until at last some stray light found its way over to them.

"Look," Miracle called from behind. "There is something up ahead!"

Emma could see a strange emanating glow splashing across the black floor, its splattering light freeing her from touching the disgusting reptilian wallpaper. "That's it!" she said, feeling her heart skip a beat. Her heart would skip several more beats as the walls surrounding her abruptly began to breathe! In and out they stretched cracking and splintering, with ear-shattering sounds pulsating grotesquely. A chilling draft suddenly swirled up, howling like a mad ghost, twisting itself down the corridor, its powerful blast hurling off the withered bonnet she had somehow managed to keep on her head thus far. Into the endless corridor it flew, disappearing into the darkness. Her blond hair whipped mercilessly around her head, violently lashing at her eyes.

Miracle felt the pressure of the powerful wind turning him over, rolling him about like a play thing, flipping him over on his back. He scratched at the floor as the vicious blast carried him away down the black halls of the *Tiamat*. He quickly blew past Emma; however, she was quick enough to snatch him. Grabbing on to one of his flippers, she held on, both dragged mercilessly through the filthy corridors of the devil ship. They scraped along the splintering floors, the boards beneath them snapping and shaking with a horrible and ungodly banging sound, flapping at them ferociously.

Then suddenly, it stopped.

Both remained still, trembling, Emma facedown and Miracle face up, his head twisted around his furry tummy, all scrunched up into a round furry ball. Emma sprang up abruptly as if waking from a nightmare, looking back toward the white seal, his dark eyes staring upward, swimming in a sea of mossy green light. "Good heavens!"

Emma cried, reaching over to flip Miracle right side up. "Poor thing!" she said, hugging him, once again feeling her burning fever return with a most distasteful vengeance. The temporary effects of the tear were slowly fading from her. Once more, she grasped the stone, closed her eyes, mouthing a silent prayer. Then slowly she opened her eyes and took in a heavy gasp.

"I see it!" she cried, standing up, nearly falling over in her ridiculous boots, pointing into the semigloom. "Decara's laboratory!" she announced.

The white seal, still somewhat dazed, tried to swallow down the mounting fear, his heart beating faster than before. "My mother?" he inadvertently uttered in a pathetically questioning voice. "She is in there?"

Emma knelt next to the seal, her ridiculous boots spreading out everywhere. Taking his trembling snow-white face into both of her hands, she simply smiled. Before collecting the skeleton key from the bridge, they would first rescue his mother. "Yes, she is there, I know she is waiting for you, right where I last left her when I promised I would return. I can still feel her."

The white seal looked at the girl in a strange way, wanting so much to believe in her words.

Emma hugged Miracle, bringing her face next to his. "Come," she said, standing up inside her silly boots, trying not to touch the wall, looking exceedingly brave and decided. Her eyes quickly fixed upon the door leading into the room where she had last seen Arayna, the precise chamber that kept within its darkness the three-headed serpent and all of Decara's evil spells. Clearing her parched throat, fighting the burning cough and fever raging within, Emma shook her head, trying to ward off the incessant ringing in her ears as she stood erect and surefooted.

This time she did not look back to the white seal so as not to break her concentration, speaking out one final time before entering the vile room. "Let's go get your mama!" she announced, pushing the shadows aside.

POP! GOES THE WEASEL

Defiant, Emma approached the double doors that lead to Decara's ghoulish chamber.

The doors shone bloodred, almost glowing as if they had just recently been stained with the most vibrant of red paint. Emma believed it was blood. No matter. She outstretched one of her tiny hands and prepared to test her impeccable perception. The door immediately burned her skin like a hot skillet. Quickly, she snatched back her hand; no traces of blood, but blisters were already forming on her fingertips. Unscathed, in her reasoning, she reached down and touched one of the peculiar half-moon door handles. Surprisingly, it was cool to the touch. By this time, Miracle was directly behind her, his seal heart pounding so deafeningly he thought for a moment that the terrible banging sound had returned to the dismal corridors once again. Emma's golden locks, which remained mashed down against her forehead from the previous pull of the soggy torn-up bonnet, now lay scattered wildly on top of her head, the seal-chewed bonnet nowhere to be seen, its tattered memory lost somewhere inside the *Tiamat*'s insides. A gathering of yellow hair hung in front of her iridescent blue eyes, blurring her vision long enough to aggravate her. Impatiently pushing her disarrayed locks abruptly aside, ignoring the blister stings on her fingertips, she reached for one of the half-moon doorknobs resting close to the surface of the bloodstained doors. Taking it firmly in her hand, she slowly turned it, hearing its latch immediately spring free.

The door, having suddenly sprung open only a few inches, creaked back and forth for a moment before coming to a stop. She was in! It was that simple—perhaps too simple. She listened attentively, remaining remarkably still near the small crack in the door's opening, the white seal directly behind her. Both anticipated another violent spasm of thunder to roll down the halls as she pushed the door open a few more inches, but only dead silence crept out through the crack of its narrow opening. With full force, she pushed the divided doorway with a quick shove from her hanging sleeve protecting her blistered fingertips. A scurrying shiver ran up and down her spine as the door only halfway opened. A disturbing heavy silence poured around her. Not even the three-headed serpent made a sound. Taking in a deep breath, Emma again shoved the door, swinging it forward, its creaking resistance screaming off as it slowly opened wide.

She stepped quietly into the room. A multitude of gray shadows swiftly infested themselves around her. She continued onward, almost tripping over her oversized, mismatched hunting boots, nearly falling facedown into the blackness below. Miracle rushed to her assistance, slamming the door up against the shadows of the wall in his hurried pursuit. Emma managed to maintain her wobbly gait while Miracle followed. A distinct chill began to curdle the seal's blood. Emma, whose continuance of boldness seemed to disturb the assaulting shadows as she defiantly pushed past them, remained undaunted in her quest.

All at once, the seal halted in his tracks. His heart lunged to his throat, a tiny gasp escaping from his lips while looking upward. He had to close and reopen his eyes, attempting to dislodge the horror he would not easily forget the sight of, causing him to scream outright. From high above, suspended from cruel-looking steel prongs, dangled suspended horrors, each an atrocity unto themselves, their once beautiful, innocent forms reconstructed into mutilated nightmares. One after another they hung there in rows, mostly what remained of butchered harp pups, their insides gone, their suspended white coats separated from one another by the steel hooks holding them. Some still retained their heads, their pathetic dead eyes forever suspended in an upward death glance, their tiny mouths partially open as if still screaming. As the horror expanded, Miracle's uncontrolled yelps grew louder and louder, immediately setting off the three-headed serpent that was already giggling from the shadows.

Yes, Suffering, Sin, and Sorrow could not help but hiss and fizz in devious delight, each head fully aware of the seal and the human's presence from the very beginning. As the scaly snake heads slithered over each other, laughing sinisterly, swarming inside their floating sphere, their evil eyes ignited into a flaming yellow blaze.

In an accelerated backward crawl, Miracle continued yelping, shaking his head in revolt, not yet seeing the second terror awaiting him from behind. It happened so fast that he could scarcely catch his breath when he felt himself slam into a stretched-out seal canvas. It was unusually large, undoubtedly the leftovers of a mother harp, her removed skin stretched tight around four wooden strips shaping her into a perfect square frame. Wincing out in horror, Miracle became crazed, his pitiable screams expanding, as he wriggled away from the unthinkable sacrilege before him. He was not aware that Emma was already there embracing him, holding him tight, trying to ease his shrilling yelps of grief and terror.

"It's okay! It's okay!" Emma cried, holding his jerking head under her chin. "It's okay. I'm here! I'm here!" she said, fighting to control his twisting head.

"They killed her! They killed her! They tore her apart and killed her!" the crazed seal winced out despondently.

"No! It's not her! I promise!" Emma cried back, desperate to control his convulsing body within her trembling arms. "Please listen to me! It isn't her! It's some poor, unfortunate seal, but it isn't your mother! It is not Arayna!" Somehow, the sound of his mother's name suddenly stunned the terrified seal, rendering him into a disabled silence, unable to speak, his heart bursting in his ears, his mouth wheezing for air. Emma held tight to the seal, pressing herself next to him, both of their raging hearts engaged in an outrageous rhythm of disbelief and shock. "It's okay," she consoled, wholeheartedly holding the seal's head close to her, her eyes brimming with tears.

Miracle's head remained rigid. "What kind of monsters are these . . . these . . . things called man?" the seal wept, recoiling into his own shoulders with a snapping jolt, his snout tight as a fist.

Emma sighed, sounding disheartened. "I am ashamed to be a part of them," she confessed.

"You're not a part of them! Don't ever say that again!" Miracle snapped. "You will never be anything like them—*never!*"

"Shhh . . ." Emma continued sustaining the seal, rubbing his head and bringing him close to her heart. "Still," she said, "none of them could ever compare to Decara. She's worse than all of them put together."

"She did this?"

"Well, not entirely, it is what the men on this ship do, but most of this is Decara's sick mania!"

"She killed them and put them like this?"

Emma regretfully nodded. "We must be strong, Miracle. We've come too far to let her twisted insanity stop us now!"

"She will pay for this sin! I swear! By everything holy, she will pay!" vowed the enraged white seal. Suddenly, the stone around his neck flared a bright purple color, his already glowing tips mimicking the glimmer.

"Look," Emma cried. "It's glowing again!" Reaching for it, she grasped it tight in her hand, the warmth of its glow heating up her tiny palm. However, it was to be short-lived. For as before, it began to dim, nearly going out altogether this time. Emma was about to stand up when she heard the loud ruthless snickering of the three-headed serpent. Squeezing her mouth together in revolted distaste, she looked toward their hissing frenzy then returned her eyes to Miracle.

"I'll be right back," she said, standing erect as best as she possibly could in the ridiculous boots, walking straight through the shadows again, her wobbly, ridiculous footwear squeaking rebelliously all the way as she headed directly for the serpents' floating crystal-like ball. Approaching it noisily, she puckered her brow, making slits out of her eyes, staring brazenly at the three devilish things. She stood in front of the floating water sphere, just glaring at them with mean, calculating eyes. "And isn't it funny?" she sneered. "Just a whole heap of rip-roaring, snake belly laughs, isn't it?"

"Well, ain't we sassy and *sss*-swank!" hissed Suffering. "All dolled up in our little miss-*sss*-soldier costume!"

Sin immediately interjected. "You've never looked better, it *sss*-simply *sss*-screams you all over!"

Sorrow stuck out her vile serpent, tongue hissing with vile laughter, coiling around her scaly sisters. "What's this-*sss*, not wearing the *sss*-splendid hair comb we gave you? Insolent youth! *Sss*-such an ungrateful and *sss*-spoiled adolescent! Why, the very thing cost us an arm and a leg! Get it, *arm and leg?*" Sorrow hissed blasting out another crazy giggle while holding out her own limbless scaly snake trunk.

Her reptilian sister Sin quickly took center stage. "No legs or arms-*sss*, what's that about?" she hissed dementedly, her snake mouth wide and open, running her slimy lips up and down, over and over her own limbless torso with a rapid exaggerated biting fit.

Pulling away in disgust, Emma spit at the globe. "*Monsters!* You seem to find everything that is cruel and wicked most humorous. Everything is a joke to you, isn't it?"

"Of course!" the unholy trio hissed simultaneously, snickering through their darting tongues, flashing them up against their stretched-out floating lair, each licking at Emma's dripping saliva.

"I guess you really got a big chuckle sending me out into the freezing 500 million degrees below zero icebox with a demonic barrette stuck to my head, didn't you?"

"Oh yes-*sss!* Yes-*sss!*" They laughed uncontrollably in a frenzy of hysterics. "That was-*sss* good, wasn't it?"

Emma stood there with tongue in cheek while the snake heads carried on before her.

"*Sssss!* You bought that gag quick enough." Sin laughed. "You're just too easy, kid! A bit of a bungler, aren't we?"

"My," Emma said casually, "we must think me quite the fool, mustn't we?" She stared at them straight-faced. "And yet I can't help thinking who the bigger fool is. That little prank of yours nearly got me killed, and if that happened as it very well may have, that just might have really ticked off Decara, especially since she so desperately needs me around to fulfill her twisted fantasy," she taunted, drawing closer to the floating ball. "Did you ever think about that?"

"Yeah, we thought about that," the hissing serpent sneered.

"And you think that's funny?"

"Oh, do lighten up, soldier girl." The serpent giggled, covering up each one of its snake lips with parts of its swarming trunk, shamelessly snickering, "Nothing really happened to you, so what's all the fuss-*sss* about?"

"Is that what you think? Nothing really happened?"

"Oh, enough of your squawking, irritating human," Suffering snarled.

"Besides-*sss*," Sorrow offered with her snake mouth wide, her sharpened fangs exposed, her yellow eyes glowing sinisterly, "it was well worth the risk just to see you dodging gunfire and running from those sliding avalanches! You should have seen your silly man-beast face, we just about wet ourselves-*sss!*"

Then Sin sinisterly slipped in with her own set of burning yellow eyes and vicious innuendoes. "How hysterically outrageous!, You! The destined redeemer of Sealssong! Going to save the whole sloppy preposterous race—what a nimble-witted fool!" they roared with hysterical hissing. "You really are *too* much, *sss*-soldier girl!"

Emma remained motionless, her head slightly tilted, her eyes slits, her lips drawn her cheeks sucked in tight. "Evidently," she said, "the slaughtering of these animals amuses you?"

"Intensely amuses, us-*sss!*" they fizzed through tongues full of titters.

Emma smiled surprisingly. "Hmmm . . . ," she hummed, her delicate finger suddenly exposed. "You know what intensely amuses me?" she asked while making a partial fist, extending her index finger toward them. *"THIS!"* Emma yelled, punching straight through the membrane of the floating sphere, pulling hard on it and tearing it wide open.

Despite the wicked blast of watery gush that threw her backward, Emma could see the thwarted, shocked expression on each of the snake head's faces as their wet world exploded around them. For only a few short-lived moments, Suffering, Sin, and Sorrow floated in midair without the aid of their floating ball, for their supporting sphere was suddenly gone and splattered endlessly over Emma and the *Tiamat*'s walls and floors. Their tangled-up necks were now one big messy scaly knot, each head staring at Emma with gigantic eyes of staggering dumbfounded shock, each calling out, "Oh no, she didn't!"

Emma heard them start to scream right before their heads popped like water balloons. The watery spew was noisy, and what remained of the three-headed serpent had already begun to shrivel up and disintegrate, slapping what remained of itself against the wet black floor.

She looked down through the gooey strings of fluid dribbling from around her eyes. Blinking and wiping her face, she watched their fading forms flip and fizz, melting into one another, mixing with the already massive pool of tacky muck that had heavily washed over her hunting boots. "Oh yes, she did!" she boasted, snapping her slimy fingers together with a wet and muffled click. "Now, how's that for wetting yourselves?" she said, wiping away more of the muck from her face, flipping the gathered goop from her fingers back to the gooey pool below. "Stupid serpent," she said, sloshing away from their remains.

Miracle was already at her side; half saturated himself from the powerful watery blast, his soggy behind sitting in the sticky pool, his eyes wide and questioning. He looked down at the slime-covered floor once before reestablishing his gaze to Emma. "Where'd they go?" he asked simply, a peculiar quiet settling over him.

"Back to the pit they crawled out of, I'm sure," Emma answered.

"Gosh! How'd you do it?"

"Not really sure, they just made me so mad!"

Miracle returned his snout to the wet floor, sniffing a few times before he grunted in distaste. "Well," he grunted again, "whatever it was that you did, I'm sure glad you did it—horrible creatures!"

"I've managed to deal with some heavy issues here, but those three mean and hateful things just had to go!"

Miracle smiled, giving her a look of awe. "You are truly magnificent indeed! A rare wonder, you are!"

"No!" Emma said. "I'm angry! Decara and her unholy stooges have gone too far! She has caused enough pain and grief. It's time they all paid for their wickedness!"

He nodded, snorting out his agreement while looking down at the shallow pool beneath him. Lifting his gummy behind off the sticky floor, he lowered his snout and sniffed at the wetness, still no traces of the three-headed serpent to be found anywhere. There was only slimy wetness. Some of it touched his nose, and he pulled away quickly. However, inside the shallow pool, he could see the wondrous reflection of Emma's face and her sparkling iridescent blue eyes. Suddenly, her placid reflection blurred as she came forward, gently touching the nape of his furry white neck.

"Now," she said, swinging her drenched golden hair around to the back of her head where it remained as if glued. "Let's do what we came here to do." She then stood up, breaking through the lingering shadows again. Unhesitating, Miracle broke free from the gooey wetness. He wriggled forward, swallowed deeply, and began to follow her, trying to chase the cutting chill away jostling against his spine, the horrific images that he had recently seen still burning in his mind.

As Emma forged through the stubborn shadows, her peculiar hunting boots squealed and squeaked their watery sounds, trumpeting her approach. Directly behind, the uneasy seal followed with eyes full of wonder. From not so far away, a familiar grinding noise echoed through Decara's morbid chamber of spells and ghastliness. Emma recognized the sound immediately. It was the grating of the black mesh cage swaying back and forth. Arayna was now only a few footsteps beyond. Her footsteps suddenly came to an abrupt halt when her eyes came upon the mesh prison. It remained suspended from thick chains wrapped around the large wooden beams fastened to the dark ceiling way above. Although the massive cage was creaking back and forth, Emma soon realized it was due to the movement of the ship. A sick nauseating sensation suddenly inundated her insides, making her feel as if she would be drastically ill. Her heart began to pound, and small beads of sweat began to break out across her brow. She tried to refocus her stare while proceeding toward the cage, all the time watching with no sign of Arayna anywhere—at least not alive. In fact, it appeared as if the cage was empty.

Another severe pang of nausea flipped over Emma's stomach as she maintained her look over the inert remains of shadows, remembering the tortured mother harp seals, fearing that she had indeed come too late. There was no movement. There was no Arayna. Was her initial intuition wrong, was the mother of the white seal truly dead? She had to be, for it was becoming evident that Arayna was no longer there. Oreguss must have had long since dispensed of her remains. Emma's eyes began to hurt with a stinging, burning sensation, forcing her to close them. She began to weep softly. It was all over. She had failed miserably in her plight. Arayna was dead. She had betrayed the mother of Miracle, leaving her to suffer at the murderous hands of her own bloodline.

Shamelessly, she lowered her head, continuing to squeeze shut her eyes, unable to shut out the disgrace she felt or the feverish tears that found their way down her cheeks. Falling forward, she fell into the mesh cage, hitting the front gate with her shoulder, clutching onto its rough surface with her blistering fingertips, wavering back and forth, mimicking its pendulous motion, her tiny face pressed close to its cold mesh exterior. She kept her eyes closed, feeling incredibly sick as a gripping knot grew in her stomach, tightening as it restricted her breathing. Unable to speak with the white seal who was calling out to her, Emma remained silent, misplaced in the desolate slow dance of the swinging mesh prison. She heard the seal calling out something to her, but his words were incomprehensible. How could she ever look into his eyes again? How could she ever tell him how sorry she was for failing him, for giving him false hope, and for promising him something that would never be? What words could she find that would ever pardon such a betrayal? There were none. And she knew it.

UNITED HEARTS

Miracle had stopped his outcries long enough to hear noises coming from within the black mesh contraption. He moved closer, his eyes wide, staring upon the dark and seemingly abandoned cage now almost totally unaware of Emma still clinging there.

The mesh prison began to rumble. It rocked back and forth with a steady beat, swaying to and fro as more rumbling sounds shook from within. Miracle felt his blood flush with both excitement and fear, its potency nearly crippling him, yet he bravely wriggled forward, the cage uninterrupted in its sway and rumble, his black shining eyes barely level to its rocking base.

Suddenly, Emma flashed open her eyes. Slowly, she stepped away from the cage and its swinging rhythm. She plainly could hear and feel the strange rumbling too. She listened to its distinctive sound, continuing with her backward retreat, staring intensely at the sea of shadows before her.

From this noisy obscurity, there suddenly appeared a single seal's head, its eyes unsure and apprehensive. Emma cupped her mouth, blocking out a startled gasp, her eyes becoming extremely large, filling with more tears. She froze in her tracks, gazing at the one she recognized. It was Arayna! She was alive and had somehow survived the evils of Decara!

Arayna sniffed the air desperately. Her eyes flashed boundless with conjecture, yet a marvelous excitement saturated her nostrils while she breathed in the vision before her. At first, she could not make out the strange shapes that had come to her, and yet her heart leapt, praying, hoping, but not daring to be certain until her eyes focused and came directly upon the white seal that had filled her heart since the very beginning. And then it happened. She could see him. It was he, the exact image that had haunted her dreams and had sanctioned such a sacred lullaby to survive, permitting her mere existence to continue when she surely believed she could not.

Still, was this a dream, a mere hallucination of a dying mother's last recall before death? No, there could be no doubt; it had to be him, for she could once again hear the music playing in her soul. She heard it unquestionably—the wondrous seal lullaby that belonged to both her and her beloved child was back, playing louder and sweeter than ever before. Dispelling the chronic exhaustion and hunger away, Arayna found the strength to thrust forward. Weak and trembling, she managed to drag herself toward the white seal, only slipping partially. Breathing heavily, she did not stop to rest, praying all the while for her inner strength to carry her.

Emma looked down toward Miracle whose own entranced stare remained attached permanently onto the mother harp that remained locked inside the peculiar mesh prison whose approach was near frantic now, her image blurring and streaking as if part of some strange symbolic dream. Backing up further, Emma's boots continued to squish and squash, fading back into the shadows, her hand still cupped over her mouth, concealing her unfolding smile, her eyes dazed in pools of glistening wonderment. She raised her head, closed her eyes for a moment, thanking the powers that be, remembering the purple angels. Resisting the uncontrollable desire to run to the mother harp that she had made such promises to, Emma remained in the shadows. This time was not for her. This revered moment of moments was to be shared by another—he who had suffered, yearned, and waited for this union for so long now.

At first, Miracle did not quite know how to react to the exceptional situation stirring inside him. His eyes blurred as the large black cage before him kept on swaying, holding the obscure image of the living seal trapped inside, her face merging into one distorted vision of confusion. However, as the cage began to slow in its declining swing, through his teary sight, he was able to look directly into the unforgettable eyes of *HOME*. Instantly, the vision immersed him like the swelling of the magnificent tides.

Despite her severely depleted condition, Arayna pushed forward until one of her flippers suddenly gave in and she fell to the floor, her eyes never leaving the white seal, not for a single moment. Fumbling and sliding helplessly, and caught up in an excited lunge, Arayna once again wriggled ahead with a driving instinct that forced her breath away. Once more, her weakened flippers gave way, causing her to tumble, her head crashing to the front of the cage as the rest of herself followed down with a harsh slam. A detached moan lodged itself in Miracle's throat while looking at the cage. It rumbled as it rocked back and forth from his mother's disturbing fall. Dazed, Arayna tried to pull herself up. Her body trembled from the strained nerves ravaging her front flippers. Struggling to pull her taut face away from the tiny openings spread across the sharp-cutting floor, she gave out a pathetic groan.

Miracle jumped forward, sitting up directly in front of her, maintaining half of himself up against the cage, both flippers outstretched, resembling a dog begging for food. However, the only begging now came from the pleading in his eyes. Raising himself slightly off the floor, the white seal firmly pressed his front flippers against the cage, stretching out his nails, securely holding on between the tiny mesh openings. His small frame swayed back and forth with its rocking rhythm. With his face pressed next to the mesh, his weeping eyes began to melt into hers. It was then Miracle yelped out to his mother as if in pain. *"Maa-maaa!"* he cried with his black glistening gaze full of teary wonder, his sharp nails scraping nervously against the moving thing that heartlessly separated him from his mother.

As the cage swayed, Miracle could plainly breathe in her never-forgotten, one-of-a-kind scent—a scent that was hers and hers alone. The bulking mesh cage began to settle itself when Arayna's throat opened with a heartbreaking cry, one that punctured the sheer air, shaming it back into the cringing shadows. Here at last, at last, was her son returned to her, half sitting before her, his precious face exactly as she left him, his fur the same immaculate snow white, except for the purple glow on the very tips. If it were not that he had grown some and not a considerable stretch at that for she knew he was not nearly the size a seal of his age should be, it could have almost seemed as if no time had passed between them. Nothing had changed in those beautiful eyes. They were the same—unchanged, untouched, and filled with the remarkable innocence that pierced her heart with awe.

Arayna's disabled body suddenly collapsed to the mesh floor for the third time, yet she continued to pull herself up with determined perseverance. Extending her worn-out flipper, she scratched her nails against the mesh screen, her flipper touching against Miracle's. She held on with a shaking tremble. With her burning eyes slanting into a sentimental embrace, she pressed her worn face against the cage, crying out her heartfelt seal moan as her child's unique scent poured over her. Miracle whimpered with another sudden emotional ache of his own. Here was his mother, the one he had lost, the one he had searched for, longed for. The face he had looked for in every face but never found, leaving him to wander alone in a strange world that would not understand or recognize him, but now, his weary journey was at an end. He had at last found Home.

Pushing his snout against the cage, crushing his snow-white fur against hers, Miracle wept, purring out a low seal moan. "*Mama . . . ,*" he whimpered again, his eyes overflowed with tears, both flippers stretched up against the cage, pressing as close as he possibly could, fervently scratching at it as if able to dig through, rubbing his head up and down its harsh grid, trying to feel his mother's face.

It was during this extended moment of tactile yearning that a wondrous thing happened. Arayna's eyes began to burn with a strange sensation unlike before. As she pressed her face toward the mesh in a desperate attempt to caress her child, she suddenly felt something warm and wet run down her cheeks and trickle across her snout. Arayna immediately knew what it was. She could cry again! Her tears had come back, returning like a newfound spring breaking through barren ground. The miracle of her son's return had made her full again. Her tears poured freely from her eyes as she continued rubbing her head against the mesh screen. "My baby, my baby," she wept, both her and her son straining to pass their heads up and down over the mesh. Their muzzles grated over the dividing screen, the endearing seal song lullaby playing strong and emphatically within each seal's heart, as all the while she continued rubbing her head against the grid, feeling Miracle's dampened fur brush close to her tear-stained cheek.

Emma had remained within the shadows, compassionately watching both mother and child embrace each other, stroking heads, both ignoring the deplorable mesh barrier dividing them. Then slowly emerging from the hiding darkness, Emma's boots sprang to life, squeaking and squishing as she walked toward the two returned seals. Feeling the need to go to them, she once again fought the temptation. However, she knew that time was of the essence. She still had to release Arayna, and the only way would be through her powers, but were they strong enough? Wiping the tears from her iridescent eyes, unseen within the shadowed background, she approached the cage slowly, desperate to work her magic, however unnoticed by both seals.

As her delicate fingers touched the locked door of Arayna's prison, she could not help watch as both seals commenced in their rubbing embrace. Emma smiled joyously, observing the white seal propped in front of the cage, his head sliding over the grate, his eyes closed, feeling his mother's nearness, listening contentedly to the beautiful song that she sang to him.

Continuing with her concentration, as difficult as it ever was, Emma knew that whatever happened now, no matter what the outcome, the white seal had finally found what he was searching for, and no one could take this moment away from him. Still, she could not help but think how lonely her life would be without him. There would be no place for her now, not like before. Still, she quickly dismissed the thought, once more filling up with the wonders of the incredible creatures before her. She had actually done something extraordinary and powerful and would forever be grateful in remembering this most blessed and rare homecoming of lost hearts once more found. She smiled a most tender and loving smile while looking upon them both, her tiny hands pressing softly against her full heart. However, despite such a joyous reunion, she knew that time was running out and she had to work the lock with her unique ability. As difficult as it was, considering the fantastic circumstances, she simply had to concentrate.

Softly, Miracle hummed along with his mother, the splendor and familiar lullaby easing their yearning, soothing their tears, their flippers pressed to each other, their heads nestled ever so close, and the wondrous seal song they shared forever cradling their hearts.

Emma, engaged in her telekinesis knowhow, was once again startled by the resisting evil power of the ship. No matter how hard she tried, just like her brother's prison door, she simply could not budge the lock.

"*Hmm . . . mmmm . . . ,*" purled the seals, pure voices in faultless union, each murmuring on with closed eyes fluttering, affectionately purring, still rubbing their heads against the obstructing mesh, wanting to remain with each other, pretending all the hurt and anguish away that they were made to suffer, and they would have done so if the unthinkable did not happen.

Crash! Crack!

Without warning, the *Tiamat* hit something tremendous! The shocking impact was strong enough to rip several tears in the walls of Decara's chamber. Water began to bleed into the split-apart room when the ship took a second hit! This one rocked the room violently, snapping the chains of the mesh prison, sending the cage crashing to the floor, breaking its door open, throwing Emma and both seals forcefully across the room right before the *Tiamat* tipped over sideways.

FLYING DEVIL

The way the ship fell to its side felt as though some fiendish explosive knocked it over, the sudden impact plunging it off into the wash of the sea. The diabolical ship contemptuously fought back, prevailing, allowing for yet another violent rupture. The vessel had momentarily fallen asleep, just as the others had. Even the *Tiamat* was not immune to the sleeping magic of the blue whale's sleepy bubbles. In its brief repose, it consequently struck a sizable iceberg, clipping its bow, sending it down with a skittish nosedive before listing, brutally scraping against the ice.

Arayna felt herself falling before hitting the floor with a tremendous crash. The door of the cage instantly tore off, crumbling and bending. Her vision went black, but she remained conscious, skidding harshly over the ship's black floor. She felt the tip of her nose tear as she pathetically rolled across the wood, only stopping when colliding with what was once part of the chamber walls. Most of the ceiling had fallen down. Many of the numerous glass tubes, crystal balls, shining mirrors, and various apparatuses, along with shelves after shelves of glowing glass jars of potions and forbidden books, suddenly began to spark. They all hissed with an eerie explosive resentment, each sinking into the already flooded room. Back and forth rocked the *Tiamat* in forensic dismay, boards, walls, halls, glassy portholes, doors, every aspect, and every inch of it alive and livid! With one piercing and horrific scream of fury, the ship shook, having a deranged temper tantrum. Despite its hellish origin, it was still able to experience pain. It screamed and howled, frightfully alive as it had been for some time now.

Arayna's front flipper suddenly became wedged between a broken chair and part of what appeared to be something that could have been a table. Using it and pulling herself up over the strong pull of the gushing waters, she broke free, seeing her son and the young girl that had indeed kept her promise.

"Mama!" screamed Miracle. "Stay there! I'm coming for you!"

Arayna tried to call back to him, but her wheezing throat only filled with more gushing water. The ship desperately tried to even itself out from the critical hit, but try as it might, the evil *Tiamat* could not straighten up. It continued to shriek and rumble with unbridled rage like an injured animal, provoked and about to strike. Dodging the floating debris, Emma grasped tight to Miracle's backside, holding on with everything she had as the white seal swam toward his mother, the interior of the vessel crashing down from high off places above.

Once more, Miracle shouted, "We're almost there, Mother! We're almost—" *Crunch!* A heavy slab of furniture hit the seal, sending him back, nearly causing Emma to lose her grip. Sinking down into the rushing waters, Emma fought the current, her lungs filling with seawater. Arayna's sight remained severely impeded from the watery explosions; nonetheless, she could still see the girl and her son once more swimming toward her. Her aching flipper was torn and bleeding, and she could feel the cold saltwater sting against her wound. Gasping, she fought to refill her lungs, the convulsing waters washing over her.

Regaining his place in the unsteady rapids, Miracle waited for Emma to tighten her grip before diving back into the stringent current. Through the gushing stomach of the vessel, he swam, wiggling like a tadpole, trying to escape the pieces of the falling ceiling still crashing all about him. Bravely, he pressed forward until at last he reached his mother. In a mad panic, Arayna waited for her son to surround her. Emma quickly put her arm around the harp while holding on to Miracle. Releasing her weary grip, Arayna felt the gushing current push her toward her son. For a moment, they were facing each other. She looked into Miracle's eyes with teary wonder, the panic somehow dwindling from her sight when looking upon him once again. She felt the hand of the young girl close to her, all of them shivering like newborn pups in the freezing snow. That was when the entire floor suddenly gave in, shattering and ripping apart, sending them down further into the bowels of the ship.

CRASH!

As the chamber floor fell, there came a horrendous and foul scream of agony shrieking forth from the core of the vessel. Parts of the ship, as well as the rest of Decara's torture chamber, broke apart like an old seashell under a strong and sturdy boot. All three continued plunging downward, along with the rest of the *Tiamat's* broken insides. Before she shut her eyes, Emma thought she had seen the helm of the ship pass before her, flinging off beneath somewhere. Another CRASH exploded, and more water shot down from above, covering them with a powerful and blinding blast. Additional parts of the heinous chamber fell with a section of the upper deck. The sound it made was deafening and ferocious. Miracle continued to scream out to Emma and his mother, both lost to him within the bursting stomach of the ship.

"Emma, Mother!" shrieked the white seal, his eyes blinded by the blast, his eardrums deadened by the thunderous screams the gushing waters made; or was it the screams belonging to the *Tiamat?* He would never be sure. Over and over again, he called out their names in relentless anguish. He continued barking until he felt his mother near his side, her wounded nose touching up against his cheek. She embraced him with her shaking flippers, pulling him close to her. Not wanting to, but knowing that she must, she released her hold.

"Hurry, my son," Arayna called out in a choked-up undertone. "We must save the man-child. She is hurt!" Miracle's eyes shot open with a wild terror seeing his mother turn from him, beckoning him to follow her. Instantly, both seals took off into the rushing flood like salmon fighting the currents.

Emma was lying facedown in the moving flux of the water when they reached her. Not wasting a single moment, Miracle dove beneath Emma, pushing hard on her stomach, turning her over. Arayna arched herself under Emma's shoulder while her son aided her. Both treaded the water, keeping the unconscious girl afloat for what seemed an eternity. As the ocean continued to fill the ship, a passing smoothness came over the waters, allowing both seals to swim with more assurance and direction. Both headed toward a floating part of the room already half swallowed up. Another chunk of the helm drifted by when they approached the partially exposed deck and what might have been part of a winding corridor.

"It's going to be okay, Emma," Miracle barked through pounding lungs. "I won't let anything happen to you." He was desperate to believe his own words.

Arayna reached the half-submerged deck first. Slowly, she bowed out, allowing Miracle to take over, pushing the girl onto the solid piece of wood. Emma flopped forward, striking her chest against the wet deck. A sudden gasp came from her throat while fighting to refill her lungs. Regurgitating seawater, she began to cough, panting and feeling as if she were about to faint. Turning, she saw the white seal and his mother. Throwing her arms around them, she half fell into the water. Arayna paddled tirelessly with her foreflippers, helping Miracle keep Emma's head upright, trying not to let any water near the girl's mouth and nose. Emma readily kept on coughing, pulling the seals down into the water, her body convulsing from her choking. Back to the half-submerged deck the harp seals went. Emma tried to speak but only started to cough again. Carefully, she pulled herself onto the broken-up deck, shivering and pulling on her saturated seal hunting coat. She had lost both irregular boots in the fall and some of her protective clothing. She pulled her arms around herself and squeezed hard at her chest, trying to stop the uncontrollable shivers consuming her. Trickling pinched-out puddles of water ran down around her, the seizing grasp of cold never surrendering.

Leaving the water, Miracle pulled himself onto the deck. "Here," he said. "Take hold of the stone!" Emma quickly obeyed, and for a moment, the stone began to flicker, its usual purple glow filling her with a temporary relief of inner warmth. She at last stopped coughing, finally able to catch her breath. Nodding her head, she smiled a reaffirming sign of success. Arayna remained nearby, moving about nervously in the waters that still poured around the ship's vile insides. Miracle cuddled closer to Emma, his heart beating wildly, hoping to warm her further. Emma clutched onto him, pushing her face into his wet fur. She could smell him plainly. It was a sweet smell, so pure and clean. She remained that way for a while, breathing in his delicate seal scent, embracing every moment. Soon, she felt the horrible and bitter cold lessen and she could breathe without coughing.

All at once, and with a vicious squirm of outrage over the successful rescue, the *Tiamat* jerked itself sideways, bucking, its internal mishmash snapping whatever remained dangling from its insides, hurling it downward with a nasty punch. More boards and parts of darkened corridors and pieces of the mast came crashing down. There was a violent explosion as they heard the men upon the ship scream out in unison, many still alive, unable to abandon ship, each held captive by Decara's unthinkable evil. Some of the seal hunters hung pitiably to the starboard, all clinging to the broken boards and fallen debris that came down upon them heavily. Some of the men had already died, having been crushed by the falling parts of the ship. The men who had survived now wished they had not, as their broken bodies and torn-up flesh remained paralyzed by forces wicked and unknown to them upon the most evil vessel that ever sailed the seas, a vessel that was alive with the very breath of hell. Several men dangled from the stern, their twisted bodies clinging to each other like a stretched-out row of knitted yarn, while the remaining seal hunters stayed scattered about the ship, hurled in the most obscene conditions, all of them screaming, all of them unable to move, all of them only able to watch as the *Tiamat* once more rebelled in an unholy and fiendish retaliation.

Arayna screamed first and then Emma when the ship made its savage attempt of flipping itself over. With one crazed gesture of propulsion, it jumped forward. Shrieking from the icy waters, the *Tiamat* left the sea for a split moment, howling and screeching out with contemptible infuriation in its lifeless throat of broken boards and splintered ruin, gagging on itself with a sick, yet renewed spawn of horrific fury. Arayna and Miracle upheld Emma, both trying to protect her from the return of the swarming waters, each tossed about, each listening to the snapping sounds of the ship and the unnerving and deplorable screams of the seal hunters—these the same men who had come to slaughter the children of Sealssong, now broken and rendered helpless under the indomitable bewitchment of the depraved and malevolent *Tiamat*.

SHAKEN UP

Kishk had been the first to awaken; he was able to see the entire spectacle. In fact, he almost hit the iceberg himself only moments before he awoke, dodging fragments of the giant ice monster along with shattered and ripped-away pieces of the ship. "Wake up!" he commanded. One by one, the creatures on top of his head began to stir, but he knew that they had no time to acclimate themselves for drowsy stretching and yawning. "Get up!" he shouted, this time even louder, his blowhole exploding cold, icy water all over his crew.

Mulgrew was the first to protest in anger, shaking himself silly from the blast of seawater when he, as did the others, saw what was taking place. Crumpels screamed and rumbled toward her son, whooo-whooing in such disarray, falling into an embarrassing skid before she even reached him. Both Big Petie and Little Lukie wriggled close to each other, shaking their coats like wet dogs, rewetting themselves repeatedly.

The *Tiamat* suddenly became enraged again and made another sudden thrust sideways straight toward Kishk, aiming its damaged (what was left of it) bow directly at the blue whale. With remarkably little time to prepare for such an encounter, Kishk jerked backward, feeling the occupants above scatter about in every direction. Then the mighty chanter partially dived beneath the water, bending his enormous body, becoming circular in his twist. With a powerful flip of his tail, he prepared for the upheaval of the vicious vessel. *CRASH*—went the *Tiamat* as it lifted from the sea, falling to its side again, slashing against the cold and wild tides, momentarily disappearing in an explosion of the frothy downpour, every seal hunter screaming out again like frightened boys. Kishk had knocked the ship off its murderous course, saving himself from a near-fatal collision by just a few feet; but as to the whereabouts of his own crew, he was no longer certain. They had all been washed overboard.

TALKING HEADS

Emma screamed along with Arayna as they were helplessly hurled down the ship's innards, washing down half-broken hallways, scraping along the sides of the loathsome half-flooded corridors until they came to a place barely maintaining a broken staircase. Only two wooden steps remained covered by the tons of pouring water draining through its black opening. Emma and Miracle continued to be pulled along mercilessly, Arayna following some distance behind them. In only moments, they would be emptied into the dark sewer roaring before them. Unable to grab onto the walls, they scraped the sides until their nails broke, grating harshly against the surface of the *Tiamat*'s insides. Emma reached out for Miracle, both spinning helplessly inside their, own private whirlpool. Grabbing on to the white seal, she held on tightly. Just, then, Arayna came flying around the corner on a wave of gushing sea, unable to stop. Striking them, Arayna forcefully shoved all three of them down into the opening of the ghastly black sewer that continued to swallow up the once spiral staircase, the gushing ocean spilling uproariously into its gaping mouth.

Down they fell like Alice through the rabbit hole, only there was not a Wonderland below. When they hit, they once again felt the sting of the cold, icy water, but it was much shallower this time. In fact, it hardly broke their fall. Emma tried to block the screams from her mouth, searching for Miracle and his mother. Finding them, she rushed to them, falling before she reached them. Miraculously, all had survived. They remained in a circular embrace for a moment, then Emma gasped. She knew exactly where they were!

"The vault," Emma cried through soggy lungs. "We're right back where we started from!" Both seals quickly flipped their heads about and began to wriggle toward the cryptlike door of the vault, following close behind Emma. The running water now only came up just past her ankles, the room displaced on a teeter-tottering incline. Emma slipped against its slippery grate, coming upon the closed door of the vault. In an excited voice, Miracle barked out, "It's the place where she keeps all the tears!"

Arayna looked at her son with a solemn expression, its sadness darkening across her face, her breath short and irregular. "So it is here that she has hidden them."

"Yes, this is the terrible place," Miracle gulped. "Here, Mama, touch the stone. It will help you."

Without question, Arayna did as her son asked.

Emma cleared her throat while keeping her eyes steadily on the vault, its cruel face now lined with veins of surging water. "She's running out of time," Emma announced in an unnerving, yet still calm voice. "Decara has made a bargain with the devil, and the time has come when she must pay the ultimate price. All the stolen seal tears in the world won't help her now."

"Mother," Miracle barked. "This terrible devil woman wants me killed. She cannot do it herself. It has something to do with our innocence. It drives her to do awful things so she will have all the power ever imagined!"

"When will this nightmare ever end?" Arayna cried, abruptly pulling away from Emma, wriggling up to her son, wrapping herself around him, never wanting to let go.

"Arayna," Emma said, kneeling down in the rising waters. "As I promised before, I would die before I let anything happen to your son. You must always believe this." She let out a sigh. "It is what Decara has planned for tonight that frightens me." Her frosted breath made weird-shaped clouds around the two seals, her aching head fit for cracking.

"Tonight?" the mother harp feared.

"Yes," Emma answered, looking back toward the haunted vault. "I think the time is at hand for her to make her final move."

Arayna straightened her head and looked at Emma, pushing down the terror lodged in her throat, asking, "And should this horrible devil woman somehow succeed in destroying this—this very powerful thing of which you speak, this—this—innocence, what will happen then?"

Emma never looked at Arayna; she merely kept her gaze upon the vault, whispering in a low and hesitant voice, the creepy foggy mist still dancing around her lips. "It will be the end of our world."

Arayna wriggled closer to Emma as did Miracle, his own gaze now also fixed at the vault as was hers. Not sure why she too had turned and was staring at the cruel-faced door with its watery veins bleeding all over its face, Arayna spoke out in the same hushed and frightened voice, asking, "This force of innocence, is it greater than the wealth and power that man seems to consistently kill for?"

"Oh yes," Emma answered, nodding her head reassuringly. "The treasured gifts I speak of are the greatest gifts ever bestowed to our world, innocence, and the most powerful of all—love."

Arayna thought carefully before addressing the girl. "Then how could it ever be destroyed?"

Sadly, Emma looked down at the seal, feeling as if she might faint, "because man will have stopped believing in it." Suddenly, Emma reached out her hand, feeling the slick surface of the drenched vault door. As her frozen fingers touched upon its wicked features, a most horrible and hideous shriek filled the watery corridors. The very fibers of the vault began to shake and vibrate in such a way that it became three-dimensional, quivering with a double-blurred vision of disarrangement. From somewhere inside the steel-like fabrics of itself, the horrid door began to stretch as if someone, or something, was trapped inside its minuscule face. Like melting copper the thing from inside continued to crawl out like a probing worm from the dirt. It made an awful noise moving about, sounding like millions of insects scratching and crawling from inside. All watched in horror as the face of the treasure room shivered in revolting spasms. The thing pushed itself out further, still consumed by the fibers of the steel-like skin it erupted from, reaching outward until at last it had the semblance of someone, or rather something, remotely familiar.

Emma gasped, and Arayna quickly wriggled behind her water-covered ankles, Miracle at her side. There, before them, was a human skull, or what resembled a skull. Only this monstrosity consisted of molding steel-like fibers that seemed to melt continuously. From the empty eye socket of the thing, another form squeezed out. It grew rapidly, revealing itself to be yet another skull, both permanently connected, both distorted and grotesque. Each horror had mouths that remained torn open in constant torment, both skulls tugging and pulling in such a horrid way as if to tear themselves free from each other, but unable to no matter how fiendishly they tried. Suddenly, the skeleton faces spoke from the center of the vibrating door.

"Beware, for this night holds your doom!" the voices shrieked.

"Who are you?" Emma asked through a raspy voice.

"We have become no one—*No one!*"

"What is it that you want with us? Who are you?"

"It is rather who we were," spoke the things.

"Tell us!" Emma demanded.

"We were once men who sailed upon this ship—seal killers—thieves—swindlers—men who dared defy the evil one!"

"Decara did this to you?"

"Both she and our greed are responsible." Suddenly, both monstrosities began to scream out and cry, each still attempting to tear altogether away from the other in unchanging misery.

"Your names," Emma pleaded. "What were your names?"

"It no longer matters—for we no longer exist—we are no one . . . We are nothing . . ."

"Who were you before you became nothing?"

"Why?"

"Perhaps if I can reach what remains human inside you, I can help you!"

A long, uneven silence sliced itself over the split-up head while their pulled-apart faces moaned and contorted. Both skulls turned only once to look at each other in utter anguish. By recalling their names, they suddenly became forced into remembering their former selves. However, they fully knew that it would be the final time they could remember or ever look upon each other's monstrous deformity again.

"Cyrus—!" called out one head.

"Yorick—!" called out the other.

Then both split-apart skulls started to scream.

Arayna pushed herself close to her son while Emma pushed her hands over her ears, trying to block out their horrendous torment.

"Beware, innocent one. THE NIGHT OF SCREAMS is upon you all!"

Miracle growled. "We already know this! Tell us; is there a way to defeat Decara?"

"You must NOT remove the stone you possess for any reason or you will die! You will be nothing—no one, just as we . . . for we are nothing—we are no one!"

Again, the white seal shouted out his words in a forensic bark. "Answer me, is there a way we can defeat the witch?"

"Yes," answered the split-apart head.

"How?"

"She must fail before the first ray of the morning sun awakens the heavens, ending THE NIGHT OF SCREAMS while the bleeding moon is still in the sky."

Emma pulled down her hands from her ears and looked at the frightening torn-up thing sticking out of the vault, having heard everything it had revealed. "What do you mean 'and the bleeding moon is still in the sky?'"

The split-apart horrors continued to rip away from each other, answering in a torturous voice. "This night belongs to the bowels of hell—the moon and the earth itself will begin to weep. Take heed, when the moon has vanished, that is the beginning of your end. Decara and her NIGHT OF SCREAMS will attempt to crush you if you dare to stop her before the moon is taken from the sky. Destroy her and your world will be reborn. Fail and both Decara and hell itself shall take residence here, forever, upon this wretched planet."

"Why should we believe you?" Arayna bravely barked. "Why should you want to help us?"

"We are no one and shall remain so long after this night is over. We have nothing to lose for we are already lost. We cry out one last time in shame for ourselves and for whom we once were," the thing with the split-open skeleton head said. "Let this be our final cry before we become absolute darkness."

"Please," Emma begged, trying to appeal to the once-human monsters. "Cyrus, Yorick, I beg of you, please help us now! Help me find my brother! Surely, you must know where he is! Won't you show me how to find him?"

Once again, the thing began to scream. "WE ARE NO ONE! *No one!* We are nothing!"

Emma tried to plead with the dual-faced abomination yet once more, but it was impossible for its horrible screams just increased and grew wilder and more maniacal. It continued to tear away from itself, melting, snapping, and stretching in opposite directions until all at once, it popped like a water balloon, bursting abruptly all over the face of the vault. The sudden explosion acted like a gunshot provoking an avalanche. Instantly, from above, a deluge of trapped water broke through the remainder of the already half-opened ceiling. As the water hit the vault with its tremendous punch, the door to the vault sprang open. Quickly, the water level began to rise, and Emma and the seals found themselves amidst a multitude of diamond-filled sacks. In tangled clusters, the encased diamonds poured out like spittle from the gaping mouth of the vault. Once again, the *Tiamat* rumbled in infuriated hostility, thrusting the door of the vault shut, keeping what little remained of the treasure inside. All at once, a strong wind began to shriek, sounding like the screams of a hundred banshees howling at an October moon.

Emma and the harps could only look onward in complete horror as the newly arrived shrills manifested into ghostly vapors of deep red, all swirling out in different directions, their elongated forms slashing the cold breath of the ship. Morphing further, the forms became transparent with grotesque faces, devil-like; their mouths torturously left wide open. Suddenly, the entire room seemed to experience another internal blast of cold and bitter air, taking with it all the swarming red glowing goblins. In absolute ferociousness, they blared through the broken boards and shattered portholes, squeezing out through any such crevasse nearby, no matter how small or seemingly impenetrable. Once outside the evil vessel, the screaming fiends circled the *Tiamat*. Faster and faster they twirled until they turned into a crimson devilish blur. Linked together in hellish union, the scarlet phantoms twisted themselves around the broken ship. Insanely, they ensnared the front of the vessel, shrieking out in horrific howls. Then something unthinkable happened. The *Tiamat* jerked forward with a gigantic thrust. As parts of the demonic devil chain choked itself into a knot, tying itself around what remained of the jagged bow, the remnants of its fiendish connection blasted up into the open sky. On the claws of the howling wind, the demon link shot across the black sky and headed toward the jeweled seal nursery that now was clearly visible in the not-so-faraway distance. An eerie red eruption flared off somewhere on Sealssong as the goblins took to anchor there, securely embedding their hellish fangs into the icy ground. Then with another round of shrieks and screams, the goblins with their ripped open mouths began to pull the *Tiamat* across the sea—directly toward Sealssong!

From inside the ship, Emma screamed, toppling over Arayna. Miracle quickly came to her aid while more boards snapped and the ship leveled itself within the wild currents. "It's moving again!" Miracle shouted, the boards from the leftover realms falling and crashing. The water was rising significantly, and Emma could see that all that remained of the haunted vault was just the top portion of its nasty self. In a moment, the awful cryptlike treasure box would vanish, but the diamond-filled sacks that escaped would remain floating about her momentarily, sinking to the bottom of the ship.

"I have to find my brother! I'm not leaving without Kenyan!" Emma called out to the seals.

"But this terrible place is sinking," Arayna shouted back with a terror-filled bark. "You will drown, child!"

More ceiling boards came crashing down, and the *Tiamat* thrust forward with a vengeful and powerful tug. It was beginning to move faster, unstoppable, and with no intentions of plunging into the bowels of the sea. "We have to get out of here now!" Miracle cried just as the rest of the room began to fall all around them. Instinctively, Emma jumped onto Miracle's back, Arayna following closely beside them. In a unison of fear, both seals dove into the water with exact precision, slashing through the water with a wild torpedo-like speed, barely missing the remainder of the dropping room when it came crashing down in a thunderous outcry. Both seals' front flippers continued to beat the water at racing speed, shooting across the crumbling place. The watery insides of the *Tiamat* bubbled past and under their slick chest, each skidding under and over the water's surface like tossed pebbles. Infected by the seal's uncompromising excitement, Emma held on tightly, beating her feet through the swishing current, closing her eyes as she heard the room fall apart. Another violent yank struck, and the *Tiamat* went soaring across the sea straight toward the nursery!

"Quick," Arayna called out to her son. "Bring the child here or she will perish!"

Pushing forward, Miracle rushed up to a substantial chunk of floating ice, waiting for the shivering and coughing Emma to hoist herself onto its slick surface. Miracle followed. In just a little while, all three were floating there upon the buoyant iceberg. Arayna looked at her son, once again overwhelmed by the memory of that moment of moments of his birth. When once upon a time, they both sailed upon a piece of icy carpet much like the one they now occupied. However then, there was not a young girl that had saved their lives. There was not a human being that looked upon her son with eyes of compassion that of which she never believed imaginable for any man-beast.

As Miracle's mother floated there watching them, the heads of her son and the young girl rested against each other, both fitting precisely like a closed locket. Arayna could not help but notice that when their faces turned to face each other, their eyes fell into place with such perfect belonging. They were utterly and entirely different creatures, coming from two altogether different worlds sharing feelings they should have never experienced, and yet their eyes remained upon each other in such a way that made her uneasy and confused. Still, somehow, it filled her heart with a familiar understanding that she never thought was possible.

"Mama," called Miracle. "Are you all right?"

Arayna just stared at her son, still wondering. "Yes," she finally answered in a surprisingly quiet voice, steadily examining his precious face.

Once again, the floating icy carpet they sailed on began to descend to the lower level, picking up speed, swirling ridiculously inside the water until it struck the side of a corridor. Instantly, it shattered into several large pieces, most of itself dispersing as quickly as it appeared, down into the throat of the water-filled corridor. Emma stood up, the water now covering her knees, the drenched pants and coat pasted heavily against her as if it was a permanent outer layer of shriveled skin. The ship shifted again while the red goblins persisted with their ghastly towing, as part of the wall connected to the corridor collapsed, almost falling in on Emma.

"We must leave this place at once!" Arayna begged. Miracle nervously wriggled up to Emma's side, making sure that she was all right. Emma stood up, directly holding on to another side of a wall that had not yet caved in. With a flash of instinctive perception, Arayna turned her head around. Just a few hundred feet away, she saw the chance to escape. Through the long and torn-up corridors, the seal could see a large hole in the vessel leading directly out into the sea. In fact, she could not help but gasp in excitement when she saw the blue whale directly beyond the gaping hole. She would only be able to view the chanter for a moment, for as the ship continued to be pulled along by the red monstrosities, the mammoth figure of the whale became hidden and impossible to see.

"If we leave now," Arayna pleaded, "we could find our way to the sea, but we must leave now, I tell you! Now before it's too late!"

Emma felt the ship shake, this time feeling it accelerate inside the freezing waters it skipped upon. Kneeling down to meet the face of Arayna, Emma looked into the imploring mother's large lucid black eyes. "Could you truly ask me to leave my brother here?" she asked, just staring at the seal, swaying back and forth while the *Tiamat* speared through the sea toward the nursery. Shamefully, Arayna put her head down and closed her eyes, regretting, understanding—remembering. Another brutal tug threw Emma off her feet and sent the seals colliding against the smashed corridor of the ship. Emma hurled her glance to the crumbling passageway bouncing before them. "Miracle, take your mother through the opening to Kishk, he'll know what to do!"

"No," Arayna plainly barked. "We will remain with you! We're not leaving you, Emma!"

Emma would not hear of it. "You'll be killed! Nothing must happen to you!"

Quickly and without hesitation, the white seal spoke up, shaking his head as he slid from wall to wall on a glaze of slippery floor. "Remember, we are in this together. I am not leaving either one of you! Now come, we have no time to discuss this further. We must hurry! We're almost out of time!"

Just then, the wall next to them caved in and down they all fell once more. Emma felt the frozen palms of her hands sting when she fell against something sharp and grainy. Both seals wriggled about, sliding in a shallow stream of flowing water that now circled and trickled over a clump of wood and slippery, wet strips of what looked like stony bars. Emma gasped. It was the teeth that held her brother and the Captain Thorne prisoner! Only this time it lay broken and twisted, imprisoned beneath the streaming water below.

"He's here!" Emma shouted. "I know it!"

"How can you be sure?" Arayna asked with an out of breath bark.

"This is the cell that Decara had locked him in, I can feel him! I know that he is here!" Emma cried, stepping on the decaying stony teeth, kicking them, scattering them aimlessly inside their watery grave. "Kenyan!" she shouted in a high-pitched and shaking voice. "Where are you? Answer me please! Tell me where you are! Dear God, please, *please* make him be all right! Please be all right," she begged, splashing and stumbling over what remained of the broken-up prison.

More water began to fill up the crumbling cell, and although she could see remains of dead rats floating by, some in multiple pairs, there was no sign of her brother or the captain who once dared command this diseased ship. The water was up past her waist when she began to panic. Soon the room would be filled, and if she remained, she would drown. It was simply a matter of fact and a mere matter of time before it happened, and time had just about run out.

"Kenyan," Emma cried—"*Kenyan!*" The *Tiamat* rocked again, flopping both seals and Emma hard into the gushing waters steadily pumping into the room. "*Kenyan—*" Emma despairingly called out once more in a hoarse and raw voice splashing pathetically about the swelling water, pushing aside floating dead rats and broken up debris. "Please, answer me!" she implored, unable to continue for she had begun to cry sorrowfully.

"Look," the white seal suddenly yelped out in a wild bark—"There he is!"

Emma swung herself around, nearly hurling herself back into the water. She twisted about in every direction until at last her frantic eyes suddenly fell upon her brother! She watched Miracle jump from under the water while holding Kenyan, his seal jaws pulling him, holding to the shredded piece of shirt still wrapped around him.

""*Kenyan,*" Emma screamed her voice rising louder, splashing her way to be next to him. "We have found you!" As Miracle flipped the boy from side to side in the water, trying to keep him from turning over, Emma reached him and pulled him toward her. "Dear God in heaven, please open your eyes, Kenyan!" she cried out in a strangulated hoarse sob. "Please be alive! God, God, Kenyan, answer me!"

No response came from the boy.

NIGHT OF SCREAMS

Emma continued to pull her brother toward her, desperately trying not to sink further into the rising water. She noticed that he still wore the horrid shackles around his feet and one iron bracelet around his white swollen wrist. She could feel the cold swipe of what remained of the shackles' abrasive tentacles brush up against her legs while retrieving him from the water. Just then, the boy's eyes began to quiver. He started to cough with a raspy and bubbling sound. Miracle continued to support his weight, allowing Kenyan to expel the cold water from his throbbing lungs. In a whispered prayer, Emma thanked the heavens as her own body convulsed from the bitter bite of the frigid waters. She rocked her brother back and forth, weeping, until she heard him softly say her name.

"*Emma . . . ,*" he moaned, his voice fading off into a gurgled mutter. "I knew you'd come." He offered her a slight smile. Their tearful eyes remained locked the whole time, Kenyan coughed with uncontrolled spasms. He had lost so much weight that removing the shackles from his wrist and feet did not take very long. As the restraints slipped off somewhere beneath, Emma held on to her brother with all of her strength, feeling her tears freeze against her cheeks. Kenyan tried to speak to her, but loud barking sounds suddenly blasted through the open corridors and half-standing hallways.

"This way!" the barking voices channeled, echoing against the constant sounds of the moving ship and the quickened gushing sounds the water made, determined to fill up the shattered prison.

Miracle barked back in a quick tireless voice. "Poo-Coo, Petie, Lukie, you're here! You're really here!"

Emma took in a sudden breath, her eyes gazing upon the very welcomed sight. There was the gigantic rhyming walrus, her son, and the two bulls, Big Petie and Lukie, all en route to save her and her brother. Poo-Coo skirted the edge of the water-filled corridor, his half-human face with his ridiculous mustache and three-foot tusks contorting into a mask of panic. The walrus, now howling out in a loud voice, proceeded to create large bubbles around his preposterous whiskered muzzle. "The blue whale awaits us, but we must hurry! This evil scrap of trash is headed for the seal nursery, and from the way it is shedding its skin, I don't know if it's going to make it in one piece!"

"Yes," Miracle agreed. "But first, we must help the boy!"

"Very well, but hurry, bro," Poo-Coo roared.

Emma quickly looked at her brother, promising, "Everything will be all right. You must go with the walrus!"

Kenyan slowly turned his head and blinked his eyes, amazed at the ridiculous face of the walrus only inches away from his lips. Feeling as if he had just awakened from a drunken stupor, Kenyan could not help but laugh aimlessly. He smiled and surrendered to the entire madness, wantonly moaning, *"Crazy . . ."* while Emma took hold of his hands, placing them both on Poo-Coo's tusks. She kissed Kenyan on the forehead, and just as the walrus began to hurriedly escort her brother out toward the sea where the blue whale was waiting impatiently, Kenyan pulled his hand away from the walrus and grabbed onto his sister's wrist. "Thorne, you have to save him too!"

"You mean this soggy-looking man-beast?" Big Petie smugly barked. He and Lukie were dashing across the surface of the waters, pulling the unconscious remains of the once-esteemed Captain Thorne.

"Saw the dribbling man-beast floating along down the black passageway. Had a feeling he might belong to you. Where shall we put it?" Lukie squeaked, mumbling from the corner of his mouth, his teeth hooked to the captain's tattered shirt, enabling him to carry him along inside the rushing waters. "Not sure if it's still alive *neither!*" Lukie solemnly shook of his head. Hurriedly, Emma splashed herself over to the unconscious man. She was not sure if he was indeed breathing either. There was no way of telling until they were free from the *Tiamat.*

"Big Petie," Emma called out. "Quick, you and Lukie must take him directly to Kishk!" She was unsure if the seals heard her over the roaring sounds exploding inside the *Tiamat.* However, when both bulls quickly tossed the seemingly dead man onto their backs, she knew they had understood.

Another violent spasm shook the expeditious *Tiamat,* and more shocking sounds began to vibrate over the broken insides of the ship. "Hurry," Poo-Coo roared. "We have to get out of here, and I mean right now!"

Just then, the fleeting ship began to wobble and quiver just like a spinning top, losing its momentum, but still heading straight toward the seal nursery, now only moments away from crashing upon its shores. Arayna again spotted the blue whale. Kishk was directly in front of them, the evil *Tiamat* once more aimed straightway at the giant creature. Trembling, Arayna remained near her son. She waited for Emma to take hold of Miracle while the walrus swept the boy onward. Both bulls tried to maintain possession of the flip-flopping captain bouncing back and forth upon their backsides, Lukie holding on to his arm with his quivering jaws striving desperately to make it out the opening before the ship exploded into the whale's head.

Poo-Coo and Kenyan made it out first, then Miracle and Emma. Arayna quickly followed, but it did not look as though the two bulls would be able to get out before the fatal impact shattered the skull of the mighty chanter. However, Kishk, in his consummate wisdom, waited for just the precise moment to jolt sideways, causing the *Tiamat* to miss its mark, allowing both bulls and the captain to make it out just in the nick of time! Kishk heard the penguin, who had found his way back, scream out from the top of his head as the *Tiamat* sped toward Sealssong. Within seconds, the maniacal ship burst onto its icy shores, sounding as if the great fire ball in the sky had fallen and landed smack down on earth itself! The sea went wild with a commotion never before seen. The waves grew and collided with a great roar, scattering the seals and the humans about in every direction. For a moment, all that remained afloat in the raging sea was the blue whale. In a little while, the provoked sea began to calm, and Kishk could see his friends pop out from the water one by one.

Lukie came out of the sea gasping and snorting, blowing the salty ocean out of his clogged-up nostrils, connected to Big Petie, still holding on to the soggy and lifeless creature called a captain. Not wasting a moment, Poo-Coo took Kenyan right up to the huge face of the whale. Kishk looked at the boy the walrus was escorting.

"Hmmm," hummed the chanter in amazement, "must be Emma's brother. Praise the powers that be!" Kenyan's eyes opened. He tried to blink away the sea, gasping at the air filling up his lungs. He blinked some more, then looked directly into the wide and mammoth face of the blue giant. Kishk's enormous violet eyes looked back at the boy still blinking out their own private ocean of dripping seawater and wonder. "Welcome, man-beast," the whale said. Kenyan's eyes turned white, rolling back, and that was when all the lights went out in his head.

The excited Crumpels feverishly rumbled over, trying to help her son. "Whooo-whooo!" she sang out in a frenzied panic, not sure whom to assist first, her son or the strange-looking man-beast he had brought her.

"Mother," Poo-Coo called out. "Please take him to the center of the whale, and watch out for him!"

"It won't bite, will it?"

"Don't think so, it might even be dead."

"Oh goodness me, boop-boop dee-dee!" she hooted, not wanting to leave her son, but doing exactly what he told her.

The penguin suddenly popped out from the whale's blowhole. He shivered and shook himself as if to wake himself up from a bad dream. Disgusting sounds came from his throat. He quickly waddled over to the dead-looking human boy, making his way down and around Kenyan's limp legs that dangled as if broken. "This one is a goner!" Mulgrew squeaked, shaking the spray from his head.

"Hey, birdie," ordered the walrus. "Help my mother look after the young man-beast!" Mulgrew rattled, his head flinging off more beads of seawater. Surprisingly, the spell of the sleeping bubbles was not yet entirely out of his system, and a silly droopy expression remained on his penguin face. He nodded in compliance. Poo-Coo continued. "I must help the two bulls carry the other human beast," he said, quickly turning away from the bird, not concerned in the slightest as to what the penguin possibly could utter next.

"There's another one? Lord!" Mulgrew fussed, raising his little flipper wings up into the air, rolling his eyes, grumbling to himself.

"What next?" He wiggled briskly up toward Crumpels and the unconscious boy.

Poo-Coo passed Miracle on his way over to the two bulls carrying the lifeless Captain Thorne while Emma straddled the white seal and his mother, trying to steady herself climbing up the whale's enormous face. She was coughing and shivering so violently that for a moment, Miracle thought she would lose her footing and fall. Bravely, she preceded, cautiously, Miracle and Arayna wriggling right behind her. Soon Poo-Coo and the two bulls swam under the gigantic lip of the blue whale. Poo-Coo looked back at the lifeless human who wore a patch over one eye now and again, making sure that he remained attached to both seals. Having all been accounted for upon the whale's head, the seals, the walruses, the penguin, and the humans, be they conscious or unconscious, all eventually ended near the whale's blowhole—all except the Mum. Miracle was the first to bring her absence to everyone's attention. "Where is she? Where is Mum?"

Emma looked at the white seal questioningly and then turned her eyes toward her unconscious brother, stroking his pale forehead, trying not to touch the places where the rats had nipped at him. She began to cry softly, turning slowly toward the seal nursery. Miracle asked another time, wiggling about the top of the whale's head, his eyes flashing, hoping to see the mad seal. At first, a peculiar silence wavered over the congregation, all of them not sure how to answer. Each creature looked out toward the seal nursery that stared back at them with its perpetual luminous shoreline now alive with a unique, eerie glowing light of its own. The red goblins succeeded in pulling the *Tiamat* toward Sealssong, crashing it alongside its shore while somehow sinisterly holding it together, protecting it from the incredible impact. From where they stood, the entire congregation could see that the once pearly island had suddenly darkened in hue, changing from a vibrant snowy white to a dull and murky pink color, eventually changing into a deep red color, taking on the same shade as the freakish goblins themselves. Each creature on the whale's head could see the silhouette of the vile *Tiamat* and all the crimson flying demons that hauled it there, all of them swarming around the ship like angry hornets protecting their nest.

"She is there, trapped inside that horrible ship," the mighty blue Kishk softly said in a sorrowful voice.

"What do you mean?" Miracle cried.

The whale furrowed his giant brow and sighed. "After, I had begun to send in the bubbles, for some reason known only to her, that mad creature decided to join you and Emma."

"Oh no," Emma cried, no longer stroking her brother's head.

"Yes," the whale continued. "She was too large to get through the porthole, naturally, and she . . . well, she became trapped there, unable to move. That is where I lastly saw her."

"Stuck tight!" added the penguin with an almost devilish chirp in his bird throat.

Kishk continued ashamedly. "Yes, it was all that I saw before . . . well, before we all fell asleep."

Mulgrew interrupted again, adding, "Yes, that crazy hump-pig got her big fat butt stuck in the opening, blocking out all the bubbles. They bounced back at us, putting us all to sleep, stupid sea cow!"

Emma slowly shook her head, allowing her iridescent blue eyes to overflow with sadness, "Poor mad thing."

Miracle prudently stared toward Sealssong where the *Tiamat* had come to crash, taking with it all its red-colored hobgoblins. He continued to watch them circle the evil ship, saying in a low, almost whispered voice of dread, "I must go to her."

Kishk slowly nodded, unintentionally scattering about everyone. "Yes, we must do all we can for the poor creature."

Unable to contain himself, Mulgrew chirped out with an inappropriate smirk on his bird face, "Why bother? She's probably dead."

Crumpels quickly came to the mad seal's defense. "Mulgrew, that's a terrible thing to say, boop-boop-hey-hey!"

"I won't believe that!" Miracle barked.

"Nor I," Emma said as a strange look came over her while she kept her eyes fixed on the wicked and evil ship. "She's still there. I can feel it."

"But-but-but . . . ," stammered the penguin, "if we go there, we'll be dead just like her, that much is for certain! Did you forget that the witch is there? I say we leave this terrible place while we still can!"

Crumpels, having heard enough and all she could take from the bird, rumbled up toward the penguin, giving him a most discontented glare. "Of course, you do, you ridiculous bird, you! Now be still! We didn't come this far to hear what you have to say! *Hey—hey—hey!*"

"Well," snapped the bird. "Neither did we come this far to hear what you have to say! Ney, ney, ney!"

"Stop it!" Miracle barked. "Don't you see what is happening here? If we turn on one another now, we will surely lose this battle. We must be as one. Mum needs our help and so do the seals of Sealssong!"

Mulgrew wasn't giving in. "But if we go there, that awful witch thing will kill us! She'll kill you! Isn't that what's this is all about?"

Miracle turned to look at the bird. "No, it is not just about me anymore. Mum, Nikki and her family, as well as the seals need our help."

Again, the penguin was quick to respond. "If Nikki and the other seals are out there, who knows where they are. From the looks of things, I wouldn't' think anyone was still alive . . . And that includes that ridiculous mad seal!"

Wanting so much to rip into the penguin, angry at the bird's continued indifference, Miracle drew closer, anger burning in his eyes, appearing as if he was unquestionably contemplating taking a bite out of the penguin. Emma, however, was quick to intercede before anything terrible happened. Quickly, reaching out her shivering hand, she stopped the seal in his tracks, placing her trembling arm around him. Looking up into the sky, she put her hand directly under his snout, directing his gaze so that he too could watch as the moon that was now unusually large and full in the twilight of the sky suddenly began to bleed. It was happening very slowly, but she could see a small part of the moon change in color.

"Look and understand all of you, we are witnessing the end of the world, the end of what remains of purity, love, and kindness," she said. "Unless we can stop the terrible evil that has washed up against Sealssong, everything we believe in will be wiped away forever." She quickly took the stone around Miracle's neck in her hand, feeling it relinquish its last bit of power over to her as the moon continued to bleed, turning crimson bit by bit.

"Isn't there anything we can do to stop this terrible thing?" Crumpels asked quickly, darting her eyes back toward the seal nursery.

"I'm not sure, but arguing amongst ourselves certainly is not the answer," Emma said simply, releasing the cold stone from her hand, allowing it to fall around the seal's neck.

Miracle was quick to bark. "We must go to the island now!" Suddenly, he felt the stone tremble. He immediately looked down, watching the purple color altogether go out of the tear. It slowly began turning dark until it gradually went pitch-black. "It's gone out!" Miracle cried, trying to hold back his increasing fears.

"Yes, I know," Emma said.

Looking deep into her eyes, he calmly said to her, "Guess this is it."

Emma nodded, stroking the white seal's precious face. "Guess so," she agreed. Another set of shivers filled her as her gaze fell upon the island.

The whale cleared his throat with the intent of gaining everyone's attention. "Look!" he exclaimed, his eyes staring up into the peculiar half-lit heavens. "Something terrible is happening!"

"What's happening?" cried Lukie.

"The moon is weeping tears of blood," Emma told in a soft and ghostlike whisper, "and soon the whole world will begin to do the same."

"Shhh," Arayna warned, feeling a sudden shiver crawl over her. "Listen!"

Slowly, and with a complete mimic of each other, each head turned and looked toward the crippled *Tiamat* sprawled across the threshold of Sealssong. An incomprehensible assortment of added creeps gripped each listener, the sounds from the *Tiamat* growing louder and more desperate. It started out as a low moan, exceptionally deep and sullen, and then began to mature, sounding more human.

Emma gasped. "It's the men! The seal hunters! Some of them are still alive!" With not a moment to linger, she turned her head from the ship and raised her fragile finger. Pointing toward the sky, her finger came across the moon again, now full with gore, a single stream of light, bloodlike in its glow, shooting down from its crimson surface. Its eerie red-stained shine washed a haunted shadow over her savory features, the blood-drenched smolder streaming down on the once snow-white nursery. The crimson shafts beamed from the moon like a beacon cutting through clouds, spilling a gory hue not only over the seal nursery, but also the entire world.

Emma cupped her delicate hands over her mouth, whispering, "Yes, my faithful friends, this is it—*The Night of Screams.*"

DEAR PURPLE ANGELS . . .

Suddenly, the cries from the men who remained trapped began to grow maniacal.

The red goblins circled the crippled structure, and the sounds the hunters made were intolerable and excruciating in torment. As the villainous hobgoblins revolved madly around the ship, the men's cries became even more uncontrolled and more unbearable. Around, and around the red-colored demons screeched, sending the men into absolute realms of insanity. Then in a matter of moments, the goblins began to descend back into the destroyed vessel, each one nose-diving, disappearing into a ghostly blur. An unexpected boom sounded as the last of the bloody goblins vanished with a supernatural eruption.

A hot flash of air charred the wind. The scorching blast blew about Emma, tossing her hair wildly against the red glow of the bleeding heavens, pushing her to her knees with the force of a hurricane. Poo-Coo and Crumpels lowered their heads, feeling the explosion pull at them, moving them backward several feet. It was sheer luck that Poo-Coo saw the blowing penguin suspended in midair. Catching the bird, the walrus slapped the bird down onto the whale, pinning him down with his flipper, the deafening winds howling about them. Big Petie and Little Lukie crouched down, shivering and shaking near Emma, Arayna, and Miracle, all of them waiting for the awful gusting sound to stop.

Then as suddenly as it began, it ended.

Emma gradually raised her head. She could feel the air about her. It had turned warm, at least for the moment. It was as if a bizarre kind of summer had suddenly come over Sealssong. The air burned the skin like saltwater to an open wound. She coughed trying to maintain the dizziness and nausea eating its way inside her. Carefully, she stood up, her hand resting on the white seal supporting her. Only the wisps of the sporadic trail of air made its presence known, for beside the whistling winds, the earth itself remained hushed in the aftermath.

"Is everyone all right?" the white seal asked.

Everyone nodded, no one answering except the flustered penguin. "Was that headlock really necessary?" Mulgrew screeched, pulling himself out from the hold of Poo-Coo's flipper.

Emma stood looking toward the island, watching the silent *Tiamat* glare at her as the now semiwarm wind played havoc with her golden locks; however, little by little, she could feel the chill in the air return. She shivered and coughed, feeling light-headed; continuing to survey what was just beyond.

"Young human," began the blue whale. "I realize that under the circumstances, we have not had time truly to speak to each other as I would have hoped. There is so much about you that I wish to learn, and yet I know that time is of the essence. On behalf of the penguin, the two seals, the walruses, and me, and Sealssong, we thank you for saving Miracle and his mother. You have done a great and wondrous thing. You bring honor to your species, a consideration I never thought would be granted to your kind."

Emma smiled. Getting down on her knees, she began to crawl to the very tip of the whale's face. Looking at the gigantic mouth that stretched on forever beneath her, she said, "Thank you, but your words may be a bit premature. Perhaps it was our destiny to have found each other. I only hope I don't let destiny and everyone else down." She told him, swallowing deep, her eyes rolling up into her head. "I hope I can do this right," she confessed with another shiver. Slowly, she turned away, looking back to her unconscious brother and the lifeless Captain Thorne.

The whale spoke again. "They will be all right, this I promise. When we get to the island, I will make sure that they are well taken care of."

Again, Emma looked toward the island that now bled like the moon itself. She felt the white seal put his head under her arm, cuddling there for a moment. "The time has come, my dearest friend," Miracle said with a heavy voice. "No matter what happens from this moment on, I want you to know that it has been an honor and a privilege in meeting someone like you. I will never forget you, Emma, never."

Emma quickly wiped the tears away from her eyes before she embraced the seal. She did not speak. She only remained wrapped inside his snow-white coat, never wanting to leave there. She watched the purple tips of his fur grow dim while more of the sky dissolved into chunks of blood. Feeling lightheaded, she nearly lost her balance, fatigue ravishing her body. Both Miracle and his mother were at her side directly, both trying to steady her gait while she looked intently at the bloodstained nursery.

"Are we ready?" the whale asked.

"No-ooo!" spit the penguin, the only one still resisting.

Everyone else nodded, slowly looking to one another. Then a strange yet powerful thing occurred. In an unspoken understanding, the congregation formed a small circle, each one putting out a flipper, or a hand, each touching on one another filled with a silent moment of prayer, all but the penguin. He stood in the background, just glaring at them. "Fools, all of you, risking your lives for a stupid, mad thing which probably is already dead!" he said under his breath, sure that his words went unheard, but not actually caring if they weren't.

The wind began to change its direction, growing bitterer with deeper coldness than before. More strips of red moon glow descended from the boiling heavens. The scarlet rays shot down everywhere, coloring the whale red and the crew. The gathering continued in their silent prayer, each one in their own way, asking the heavens for help and protection from the evil that awaited them. However, before the circle dispersed, Emma added something else, the only one daring to speak aloud.

"Dear purple angels, if you can hear me, be with us this night, and protect us while—" Stopping, she slowly relinquished herself from the circle, looking once again at the nursery, finishing with, "Just please give me the courage I need now more than ever!"

The penguin waited for the circle to disperse before waddling up to Emma. His questioning eyes scrutinized her up and down, all the time wondering how it all would end. That of which, for the first time, was in parallel to everyone else's pondering. The whale looked up once again, up into the scarlet heavens now in utter chaos. Closing his violet eyes that remained stained red, he said his last prayer as well. He would not speak again, not until they would reach the nursery. The wind began to whip around him, sending an unmerciful chill over him and his crew. Springing open his eyes, the chanter cleared his throat as if to speak, but he spoke not a word. He waited for the crew to gather at the center of his massive head before taking off toward Sealssong.

Emma rolled from side to side, guarded by Miracle and his mother, the rest of the crew, even Mulgrew, remaining connected, once again forming another circle. Emma felt Arayna's rigid body beside her. The seal's constant support kept her from falling outside the circle as the whale took to the flight of the sea. She looked tenderly at the mother of the white seal. Squeezing her tiny hand around the seal's flipper, she held on to Arayna and smiled reassuringly. The seal stared at her for a moment and then suddenly returned the same warm smile. Arayna's eyes told of the struggle of fear conflicting inside her, her eyes telling of nothing but gratitude and admiration for the man-child going to do battle for the sake of her son, the seals, and the entire world. Arayna smiled again, affectionately rubbing her head against the human girl's arm.

It was not long before Emma found herself to be looking at the white seal again. She embraced him one more time, feeling that it would be the last time she would remember peace or happiness. For soon they would reach the bloodstained seal nursery, and Emma knew that somewhere deep inside her being, nothing would ever be the same again.

THE HAPPENING AT SEALSSONG

Nikki had been the first of the fresh, new seal mothers to grace the island with her recently acquired pup that she aptly named Promise. In fact, she, her pup, and Bellgar arrived just moments before the other journeying seals reached Sealssong.

Exhausted and most anxious to deliver their young ones, the others came, one by one, each coming upon the island as if somehow delivered by some unknown calling. There were nearly one hundred of them when Nikki awoke that morning before the *Tiamat*'s arrival, all of them ready to give birth, all of them unaware of what was about to take place on their private sanctuary away from man and his unthinkable cruelty.

The miraculous moment came when each mother harp relinquished unto the world her precious gift, her miracle of miracles, her very own child. The island was alive with sounds of excitement as the distant sky darkened with twirling seagulls, each calling out, proclaiming the births of the newly born whitecoats of Sealssong. The birds sped in a tremendous curve around the shining island, disappearing into the sky, their trumpeting songs echoing after them, disappearing in a few moments just as they had, their calls suddenly changing into a disturbing forewarned cry.

In just a short while, the nursery had doubled its magnificent assembly. One hundred and ninety-nine seals, half adults, the remainder newborn pups, spread out endlessly over the jeweled nursery. Nikki excitedly looked about at the new generation of young pups. She smiled happily, but then something uneasy overtook her. It was as if the smell of evil had crawled between the spaces of the carrying wind, bringing its foul warning to all her senses. She slowly raised her head and sniffed heavily at the rushing air. She looked up into the dimly lit heavens, just as they had gradually begun to take on the color of scarlet. Quickly, she pulled down her neck, looking at the multitudes of whitecoats scattered endlessly about her. She could plainly hear the pups moaning, some crying, others grunting, and some even making their first bark upon the island. From as far off as she could see, the island was alive with a squirm and a shiver, all once again rejuvenating the glittering world of the nursery as it had done so many times before.

However, this time would be different, most different. Even Nikki had no clue as to what was about to happen, and yet some unknown probing uneasiness taunted her. Perhaps it was the concern for Miracle, as well as the others, which made her feel this way. It had to be. For now, she was safe, completely safe at the seal nursery, wasn't she? Away from man and his murderous nature, they all would be safe. She remained graced with a newborn that she would love and protect for always. She had been given a second chance, and there could be no room for such apprehensive concerns. She knew she must have faith in the white seal; she knew that no matter what frightened her, she must take refuge and comfort in the belief that Miracle would set things right. This belief is where she would place her faith and so it would be, there before the moon would bleed and the sky would turn scarlet in color, and the monster ship called the *Tiamat* would come crashing into her world, changing it forever. Nikki would continue to hold to this faithful contentedness while gazing down at her adopted child. "Nothing must happen to us now," she whispered.

The tiny pup looked up to his new mother, his eyes teary and sleepy, reflecting such wondrous gentleness, innocence, which would forever captivate her. Happily, Nikki lowered her head and rubbed the tiny pup's nose. She, for always, would remember and mourn the death of her first child, nothing would ever change that, but the comfort that this newly acquired baby brought to her was certainly heaven sent and for this she would be eternally grateful.

Hearing her child's pocket-sized giggle, Nikki rejoiced in her motherhood. Her mate Bellgar was by her side, now curling around her and his newly arranged son. As the only male on the island, Bellgar looked toward the other females and their pups pleased that his presence on the sacred ice had not upset them. The mother seals hardly noticed him for they remained mesmerized by the unique wonder that they had just given life to, much too occupied to care about his presence, too occupied to smell the evil danger blowing heavily in the air. They remained far too involved not seeing the sky change to blood, too engaged in the wonderment of motherhood ever to see the monstrous speeding *Tiamat* heading straight for them.

The last thing Nikki would remember before the *Tiamat* exploded on their once sacred world was the contented giggling face of her precious newborn looking up at her, the red devilish reflection of the sky mirrored exquisitely in his teary and sleepy black shining eyes.

BLEEDING HEAVENS

Kishk approached the island as quietly as he possibly could, or at least as quiet as a giant blue whale possibly could. The wind continued to whip around him and his crew, the sky persistent on growing even sinister, changing into more ghoulish shades of bloodlike hues, tinting the gathering on his head the same shade of unearthly red as if dyed that color permanently.

Gingerly, Kishk crested near the shore of the nursery, a large sweeping wing of broken glacier stretching out from the sea, its icy resilience maintained for many years by all indications, its monumental arm pointing upward. It branched out, shooting into the burning heavens, disappearing into the seething skies. It would prove to be a perfectly resting place for the whale and his crew. Although the glacier supplied ample protection from prying eyes, each member of the whale's crew could clearly see the *Tiamat* from where they stood.

"I'm not going, so don't even ask me!" Mulgrew spit. "I'm not risking my life for that stupid sea cow!"

Finally, the whale retaliated, "Very well, since you have decided not to go, you will remain here with the walrus to watch over the two humans!" he commanded.

"She's such a know-it-all! Let her do it herself!" screeched the penguin.

"Silence!" the whale shouted, ashamed he had to raise his voice at such a moment. "Please do not add shame and disgrace to your already weak-minded conduct. It has already grieved me more than I can tell you."

The whale paused for a moment, raising his red-stained, once-vibrant colored violet eyes, addressing the eldest walrus. "Crumpels," he said aloud, trying to compose himself, waiting as she rumbled toward the tremendous edge of his head. "Please remain with Mulgrew and see that no harm shall come to the humans. I am not sure if I can trust the penguin any longer. His lack of stoutheartedness has left me uncertain, but I must ask him, nonetheless, to join you. We are not sure what we will find out there, our time away may be considerable. You may very well need his help, regardless of its gutless impotence."

Mulgrew grew outraged. "Gutless impotence, what's that's supposed to mean? Huh? Gutless impotence! With all due respect, sir, are you calling me a coward?"

Crumpels could not help but plague the bird further. "If the beak fits . . . *wear it!* 'Cause it is true! Yes, that's you—boop-boop-dee-doo!"

"Prattling fool," the penguin spat. "Shut up!"

"Lily-livered mollycoddle-boop-boop-dee-fiddle-foddle!" retorted the walrus.

"Enough!" roared the whale. "You both will remain to guard the humans now, not another word!"

Mulgrew remained highly scorned. Feeling belittled and filled with contempt, he too waddled quickly up to the vast mouth of the chanter. "I won't have that half-witted, rhyming moronic twit speak to me that way! It's bad enough that I have had to listen to that demented fat seal this whole time, plaguing me . . . *Plaguing me!* If you ask me, I hope she—"

"Well, I am not asking you," smugly replied the whale. "You have not introduced one suggestion or have once offered a trace of compassion, patience, or any kind of reminiscence of bravery. Your only concern has been for yourself and yourself alone!"

"But, Kishk sir!" pleaded the bird with a sudden voice of humility. "I only meant—"

"It was clear what you meant. Now before you leave this planet, as well as we all very well may do in just a short while, please leave yourself some kind of dignity, and for the sake of my sanity, please keep that beak of yours shut and aid the walrus to watch over the two humans! They will need all the help they can get."

Mulgrew's heart filled with a great hurt. The whale had never spoken to him like that before. They had sailed the many seas together for so long now, and not once had the great leviathan ever addressed him in such a manner, nor had he ever publicly renounced him as the coward he might very well be. The whale had had many the opportunities; the bird knew this exceptionally well. However, the chanter had somehow always had the ultimate forbearance for all of his numerous shortcomings. Shortcomings Mulgrew knew existed, yet never could face up to, until this moment. Not even his own obstinate resilience could aid him now. He felt stripped naked, betrayed, and ashamed; and for the first time in a long time, he felt terribly alone, without a friend in the world. The penguin also felt something happen that had not occurred in a long, long time. He began to cry. He hated himself for it, but he could not help it. His best friend in the entire world had just rejected him, and his heart, cowardly or not, was breaking. Mulgrew slowly lowered his head, offering not another word, hiding his tears.

"Now," continued the whale. "If there are no further objections, please find your place with the walrus and the humans."

Mulgrew wiped at his eyes with his small flippers, nodding, keeping his head lowered, not daring to let the whale see him cry, his tiny body covered up thick in the red glow from the bleeding heavens. Nevertheless, Crumpels saw his tears. Suddenly feeling sorry for the little bird, she tried to go to Mulgrew, outstretching her flipper; but the penguin quickly recoiled away from her, scampering over toward the unconscious humans. He would wait for her there.

Carefully walking past her brother and the unconscious Captain Thorne, Emma surprisingly knelt next to the penguin. She grabbed at a smile; the horrible shivers making her bluish lips tremble. "You okay?" she asked, outstretching her quivering hand.

The penguin pulled away, turning his eyes from the girl. "Aren't you going to be late?" he growled. "I mean, don't you have to go and save the world, man-beast?"

Emma looked at the upset penguin, still offering her smile. "You don't fool me for one second. Your words may be sharp, but your heart is kind. You're not such a tough guy. Maybe just a little misunderstood like most of us, I imagine."

Flinching, Mulgrew recoiled again from Emma, but not before she managed to touch the very tip of his tiny penguin head. "Don't touch me, just leave me alone!" he snapped.

Emma nodded. "All right," she agreed before looking toward her brother, his eyes still fixed shut. "Watch over him, and when he wakes, tell him . . . tell him . . ." She paused, sad, closing her eyes, shutting out the tears, engaging the bird to turn to face her. "Just tell him that I love him."

Mulgrew stared at Emma as if seeing her for the first time. Slowly, he waddled up next to her and leaned backward, trying to look into her iridescent eyes that were somehow not affected by the red glare from the tremulous skies above. The bird offered no words, but as he stood there, he looked again at Emma in a strange way, sucking his beak into his cheeks, his eyes filled with puzzlement.

Crumpels was soon at Emma's side, her massive head against the girl's frail body, embracing her just for a moment with one of her flippers. "Not to worry, dear heart, we'll watch over him. I promise."

Emma nodded, offering the walrus a grateful thank-you, then walked away, allowing Crumpels to tell her goodbyes to her son. She listened as the walrus's outrageous whimpers and cries surrounded her. Although the walrus did not say it aloud, Emma knew that Crumpels's tears came from not knowing if she would ever again see Poo-Coo. Despite the intense sense of alarm, both walruses gallantly prevail in the awareness of honor and valor. Where it came from they knew not, each wholeheartedly accepting it without reservation. Then suddenly, Emma felt a wetness strike against the back of her cold hand. As she looked to see what it was, she shivered seeing it stream down, merging into her fingers like a distorted lightning bolt. Whatever hit her was warm, almost hot to the touch, and that frightened her. Still, what frightened her even more was its color. It was red—deep red! Emma looked up into the sky and watched as more droplets fall. The sky had begun to bleed. "Quick!" she shouted in an already out-of-breath voice. "It's begun! We must hurry!"

The bleeding rain came down like a slow mist. In moments, the gathering turned a deep muddy scarlet color, wet from the teardrops of the bleeding heavens. However, frightening and alarming, the droplets did manage to warm Emma's skin momentarily, and for this she was grateful. The blue whale gave no further warning. He immediately began to swim toward the icy island. He moved slowly like a stalking beast, moving his immense body closer toward the red-stained, once-jeweled Sealssong. Finally, the whale felt his massiveness touch upon the incline of the island. The incredible sheathed icy structure grated against him with a sudden bump. He stopped when he noticed a secluded inverted landscape of ice. Its surroundings remained crippled with heavy ice floes, and much of the broken ice already frozen over made it look like a gigantically opened seashell with dozens of pearly stones scattered about its entrance. Here would be just the place to hide the two humans. Its icy canopy would protect them from the weeping sky.

Carefully, Kishk pushed himself up next to the island. Crumpels and Poo-Coo did not waste a moment assisting each other in rolling the humans over the whale's head down onto his mouth, then onto the cold and red-stained ground, Emma and Miracle, as well as Arayna, also descending. Looking back at the blue whale that remained covered in vibrant shades of red, Emma patted the incredible face of the mammoth beast.

"Thank you," she said with another violent shiver, " . . . for everything."

Kishk smiled majestically. "May the purple angels go with you," he replied solemnly, gazing at Emma, seeing in her face the grim mask of extreme sickness. The whale's heart broke as he floated there, covered not only in a sea of redness, but in a wake of helplessness.

The girl was dying, and he could not do a single thing for her. Where she found the strength to continue onward amazed him.

Emma did not answer the whale. She merely exchanged a weak smile and turned. Miracle and Arayna were there to help her walk toward the place resembling the giant seashell, the place that would momentarily offer shelter to her brother and the unconscious, and perhaps dead, captain from the end of time. Soon, Big Petie and Lukie helped the walruses by pulling the lifeless bodies of the two humans over to the slushy ice floes leading to the vast dome. The concave slopes inside and the tight-fitting space would keep them warm as Crumpels and the penguin stood vigil over them. Mulgrew was the last to slide off the whale's nose.

As he prepared to scamper away, Kishk called after him. "Mulgrew, I am sorry for my words. You must understand. It's just that—"

"That's okay, Captain. Don't worry about it, no big deal," quickly answered the bird, his head never turning around to face the gigantic beast. "Like you said, I best go help the others." He scampered off most abruptly.

Kishk watched his little friend scramble over the floes, heading toward the seashell-like opening of the icy cave before him. Sighing, the whale closed his eyes, feeling the tiny droplets of blood that were falling from the heavens pitter-patter all over his body.

At the giant seashell, Emma, Miracle, and Arayna made sure that both humans were properly and securely situated inside. "Mother, please, I ask that you remain with the walrus and penguin," Miracle said in a low voice. "There is no telling what we will find out there. You'll be safer here."

Without hesitation, Arayna shook her head. "No!" she answered, sucking in her breath. "I already told you, I lost you once, I'm not ever going to lose you again. I'm coming with you!"

Miracle looked at his mother with a discontented glance that paled in comparison to her steadfast determination.

"You better get going," Mulgrew surprisingly warned. "The sky seems to be getting darker—redder! We must be running out of time for sure!"

Arayna quickly looked up into the sky. It seemed that the heavens had indeed grown darker, redder, and with it, the moon had grown gruesome, fully drenched with the color of blood. However, something even more incredible began to happen. The moon began to break apart! Tiny flakes began to fall toward the earth, mingling with the droplets of blood, sending it down on them like a strawberry hailstorm. Emma, the seals, and Poo-Coo flinched with painful discomfort as the rocky particles stung unpleasantly against their aching, cold skin all the while they trekked through the slushy red-stained ice floes. Kishk maintained his station in the waters, watching them intentionally trespass toward the foreboding *Tiamat* now only silhouetted black against a red-glowing background fueled by demon fire, looking more like an insect than a vessel. Its splintered spiny remains of broken boards and building beams had fallen free and unfolded outside its damaged structure like insect legs, making it resemble a gigantic black widow spider wakeful in its lair, ready to suck out the guts of anything foolish enough to come near it.

"Mother," Miracle barked. "Listen to me, you mustn't come any further, it's too dangerous."

"Son, I don't want to leave you!"

"As you wish, Mother, however, I only say this because we don't have much time left," he begged with pleading eyes. "I need you to do something then, something most important! Will you do this for me?

"Yes, of course, what is it?"

"Warn the others."

"The others?"

"Yes, go to the nursery and warn the seals. Tell everyone what has happened, take them to Kishk!"

Once again, Arayna shook her head in disagreement. "No! Please! I want to remain with you!"

"Mama, I need you to do this for me! The seals will understand and trust you far better than they will trust any of us. I know you can do this!" Miracle implored, the heavy rains of the rocky moon debris stinging him. "Try to find Nikki, gather the seals, and bring them to Kishk. He'll know what to do," he said, feeling Emma's hand suddenly sink inside his saturated shoulder, hurriedly placed there to prevent her from falling over.

"But, son—" Arayna begged.

"Mother," Miracle begged. "Please trust me."

Arayna felt the stony rain sting at her eyes, but she did not close them. She looked at her child with a compelling dedication that seemed to command her faltering will. Holding back the tears, she quietly answered with a pathetic sigh, "All right." The moon's remains danced harshly about her while she surrendered to him. Then closing her dark and vibrant eyes, she pressed her face close to her child's snout. "My heart and my song go with you, my precious son. Please return to me . . . *Please* . . ." She began to weep, her heart breaking.

Miracle bravely smiled. "I will, Mother, I promise." He gently rubbed his cheek against hers, feeling the stubble of the gritty moon rocks scrape against their seal skin. "Now go, quickly!"

The blood from the weeping heavens had turned the white seal's fur just as red as the bleeding sky by this time, but his wondrous eyes shone brightly through the darkness, offering his mother one final promise of his return. Arayna forced a smile before turning to see the human girl. Slowly, Arayna wriggled up to Emma, rubbing her saturated fur against the girl's shivering legs. What remained of Emma's clothing hung tattered and torn away, leaving little protection against the unbelievable elements battling against her. Arayna gently looked up into Emma's eyes, wanting so much to speak, but unable to. What she felt far surpassed anything she could have ever articulated. Understanding, Emma smiled and reached down and gently rubbed the side of Arayna's drenched head as if to say that everything would be all right. From the way the human girl looked, and knowing what she still had to combat, everything certainly did not seem all right. Arayna did not think she would ever see the girl alive again. She so wanted to beg her not to go, to run away from all this madness and evil, but she knew better. It was too late to turn back now. No, both her son and this human girl, no matter how ill, were about to undertake something far greater than she could ever hope to prevent. Once more, Arayna pressed her face against Emma's side. A sudden rumbling in the earth surfaced, jolting Arayna's heart. Her glance quickly darted toward her son, the panic in her seal eyes growing as the sound of the awakening earth grew more intense.

"Hurry, Mother," Miracle begged—"Quickly!"

Arayna's eyes flared, opening even wider, as more crushing terror consumed her. Not waiting for it to devour her further, the mother of the white seal turned and wriggled off into the blur of the demonic glow emanating from everywhere. The earth continued to groan in agony, the skies raining down its red tears and pieces of the moon. A powerful wind came from out of the west, howling in such a monstrous way it took away Emma's breath. "Quick," she managed to call out—"This way!"

Miracle, the bulls, and the walrus instinctively turned and followed her heedfully, wriggling close behind, all the while the savage wind screaming and wailing, the earth shaking and the sky falling apart. Emma fell many times, and each time Miracle was there to help her back up. His heart broke watching the human he had come to love deteriorating before his eyes, helpless to stop the sickness inside her. Once more, Emma fell to the cold and slushy ground colored bloodred. Once again, Miracle was at her side. She reached up and held tight, holding him close to her, his precious face next to hers. "The stone, hold on to the stone!" the white seal cried over the incredible screams of the prevailing winds.

She shook her head. "The stone has no power now, not on this night. This night belongs to the powers of darkness," she told him, able to finish off her sentence before she ran out of breath, her brutal cough taking what little breath remained.

"I'm afraid!" the seal barked out. "I'm afraid for you! You are so ill!"

Emma fought to regain her fading breath. "I will be all right," she bravely answered, putting her arms around him again. "It's almost finished now."

Miracle felt the tears freeze up in his eyes. "I don't want to lose you. I could not bear to lose you! Please let me take you back to the cave where Crumpels and Mulgrew could watch over you. I will go and destroy the witch, I promise! Please!" cried the seal. "Do as I ask, you will surely die if you try to go any further!"

Again, Emma shook her head. "No," she cried back. "I am going with you. We are in this together, remember, and I won't leave you now. Together we are going to kill the witch! Come!" She pushed herself up from the red-spoiled snow and slush, her body numb from the cold. "The *Tiamat* is not far. It's only a few moments away!"

Unable to stop her, Miracle watched in disbelief while Emma began to trek toward the vessel with an unwavering stride that not even the gusting winds, nor the quaking earth, nor the bleeding skies, nor the decomposing moon could hold back.

Miracle and the pack wriggled onward, and soon they neared the threshold of the damaged *Tiamat*. Suddenly, and quite unexpectedly, Poo-Coo fell through a thin layer of ice. An enormous and loud splash echoed out like an explosion. "Dudes, it's okay! It's *Ooo-Kay!*" shouted the stunned and embarrassed walrus, his voice twice as loud as the splash. His booming shrill bounced all over the place while spattering inside the slush-filled opening. "Everything is . . . status quo, bro! No prob-o-la!" he howled, desperately clawing his way up and out of the mucky hole, temporarily washed clean from the bloodstained debris. Miracle only closed his eyes, trying to maintain his composure, certain their presence was a secret no longer.

"I can't breathe," Lukie squealed.

"What is it now?" Big Petie bellowed.

"My nose is filled with moon snot!"

"Well, blow it out!"

"I can't."

"What?"

"It's stuck tight!"

"Stuck tight?"

"Yes," Little Lukie said in a nasal tone, "and I can't breathe—*neither!*"

"Oh, for the love of—" Big Petie complained, smacking the smaller seal on the back of the head with his flipper, causing the impacted nose to come free with the sticky red-colored moon rubble.

Lukie wiggled his nose about and blew from it just to make sure the passage was clear. "Thanks!" he barked, overriding the wind with bellowing gratefulness.

"QUIET," Miracle begged, his eyes never leaving Emma for a moment. "We mustn't let them hear us!"

Emma cocked her head in a curious pose, looking at the ship with a silent understanding. "I already told you, it knows we are here. It has been expecting us all along," she said when she suddenly gasped. "Quick! Someone is coming! We must hide!" she cried, looking as if to be covered in strawberry syrup, turning from the vessel toward a clump of thrown-together slabs of ice and snow. The others followed in a flash, each dodging behind the bloody blockade that was wide enough to hide each one of them, all of them watching with pounding hearts as the *Tiamat* began to creak, crack, and rumble.

It was footsteps, an entourage of footsteps! *Crunch! Crunch! Crunch!* The marching footsteps grew louder as they approached a small cabin door, dented and bent in sideways from the crash the vessel had sustained. Its opening would still allow for admission or departure, for whomever or whatever wished to pass through its distorted threshold. Emma and the others crouched down low, the loud and echoing footsteps exploding all around them, the moon and the bleeding rains constant in their assault. They all gasped as the footsteps came smashing through the misshapen cabin door in a burst of fury, breaking through the threshold.

The footsteps had a form! They had a name! They belonged to the menace that had plagued these parts many times before! They belonged to the beast called MAN—the seal killers!

"*The hunters!*" Emma announced, quickly taking in a sudden breath, cupping her mouth, holding back another gasp.

"I thought they would have all died! Where are they going?" Big Petie asked. "And what's with their faces?"

Emma also noticed the change in the men's faces. However, it was their eyes that frightened her the most. "They are possessed!" she cried.

"Possessed?" Lukie screamed.

"Yes," Emma explained, staring into the lifeless eyes of the zombielike seal hunters. They ghoulishly continued to barge through the small opening of the wreckage, unaffected by their wounds and tattered skin, their eyes vacant of life and yet filled with a living death; a death hungry to destroy all that was pure of heart.

"They are possessed by the witch," Emma cried never taking her gaze off the hollow eyes of the seal hunters continuing in their zombielike procession, each man heading away from the broken vessel, out into the glowing red island. Over a dozen surviving hunters pushed through the deformed opening of the ship, spilling onto the platform, all of them having the same vacant dead eyes, each one carrying firearms or weapons that looked like clubs or sticks, all of them consumed by the witch's power. The bleeding sky and moon rubble turned the men's hair into stringy red globs of gummy molasses. The heads of the men who were bald quickly became drenched by the crimson rains, turning them into bloody grotesque monster heads. However, no matter how much the heavens bled upon them, nothing could change the empty holes in their faces that once were human eyes.

"What are they going to do?" Big Petie asked with a quiver.

Emma continued to watch the possessed men walk across the ship's broken deck, their vacant eyes leading the way as they headed out onto the tormented island. "She's sending them out to the seal nursery!"

"Oh no," Lukie cried. "But if they go there, the seals will surely—"

"Be killed!" Emma finished.

"My mother, the seals," Miracle cried. "We've got to warn them!"

Big Petie volunteered immediately. "I will go!"

Miracle turned to Petie with eyes that remained infused with both fear and admiration. "You must get there before the hunters do! Before my mother does! You must warn the seals! Nikki! Warn them all! Can you do it?"

Big Petie nodded his big head with a rumbling assurance. "I may be large, but I'm fast! I'll get there before the humans do. Not to worry, Miracle!"

Miracle nodded and gave the seal a reputable glance. "Then hurry, *hurry!*"

The white seal watched the bull quickly evaporate into the crimson-colored ice floes. Soon the ghoulish parade of seal hunters became swallowed whole by the glowing island, and yet their recent images remained steadfast within his mind's eye, for Miracle could still see their harsh and grotesque faces stamped with the witch's vile insignia. He could still feel the thud of their feet thunder against the cold, icy floor of the island, battering and thumping, their unholy drumming invading his heartbeat, possessing it.

"Come on!" Poo-Coo howled, feeling a sizeable chunk of the moon slam down on top of his rubbery head. "Ouch! If we're going to do this, I think now would be a good time, don't ya think!"

Emma was already at the deformed pushed-in doorway. Hunching under a broken canopy that had undoubtedly belonged to another part of the ship from someplace else, perhaps the bridge, Emma waited. The moon continued to crumble, making the wooden floor of the *Tiamat* come alive with a million tapping sounds. She looked around, surveying the splintered remains of the vessel, shuddering. Miracle, Poo-Coo, and Lukie soon wriggled near the pitter-pattering canopy.

The walrus, unable to fit under its protection, continued to be bombarded with the collapsing ceiling of the sky. "Could we move this along, do ya suppose? Please? I'm dying here!" growled the aching tooth walker.

Miracle took the lead, looking back to Emma one final time before entering, closing his eyes, swallowing hard before penetrating the deformed door. Emma followed close behind him, Lukie next, and after a few agonizing moments of pushing, shoving, wrestling, holding in his bulging gut long enough to squeeze through its tight opening, the walrus joined the others inside the darkness of the vessel.

They were only inside the *Tiamat* but for a moment before the door collapsed with a thunderous explosion, sealing them all inside, the absolute darkness pouncing mercilessly around them. Lukie was about to squeal when the high shrill of the witch's maniacal laughter pierced the blackness and a cold hand squeezed itself around his neck, choking off his terror-filled scream. The witch's laughter further assaulted each of them with a horrific blast, nearly deafening them. That was when the ship jolted and shook like never before. Emma fell to the cold, splintery floor, knowing without a doubt that the vile ship was no longer anchored to the icy shores. No, this time, the vile vessel was not sailing. This time the defiled ship was flying! Hoisted to the very seams of the bleeding heavens, the broken *Tiamat* wavered in the crimson sky, hovering high above the once sacred nursery of Sealssong.

EVIL LAUGHTER

The *Tiamat* swam in the sky like a giant barracuda. It twitched and it snapped as the wind fled from it, making deafening whistling sounds while rushing past it. The ship roared rumbling in the clouds, this time sounding as if somewhere in its hollowed-out throat it had at last found the ability to laugh, and this time, it was! It was laughing with a haunting, devilish howl.

Little Lukie tried to scream again when the massive hand tightened its grip around his throat. Oreguss had almost drained the seal of all his breath, nearly killing him. Poo-Coo, however, would not allow it. The walrus pushed off from the floor, his head dangling, his spongy bottom flip-flopping upward, smashing the hairy brute in the jaw. Oreguss fell backward in a surprised daze. A few of his already scarce teeth broke loose and washed around in his mouth, bloody and splintered from the sudden impact. Spitting them out, Oreguss swung around, staggering, and then fell into the black walls of the ship, his head still in a spin. He growled out in anger, reaching for the beast he meant to strangle, intent on finishing the job. However, when he turned to grab at the seal, it was gone!

Lukie and Poo-Coo managed to escape down the broken and twisted corridors of the flying devil ship. Unfortunately, Miracle and Emma were not that lucky. Regrettably, they too would have escaped from the brutish Oreguss, but Emma fell when rushing down the ship's mazelike pathways. Exhausted and burning with fever, she collapsed right before Oreguss grabbed onto her frail shoulders. Not leaving her side, Miracle remained and felt the wicked Oreguss's brutal retaliation come down upon him with a most vile and cruel vengeance.

The evil man did not grab at Miracle as he had with Emma. Instead, he smashed down his heavy boot, crushing the seal's left flipper. Miracle screamed out in agony, nearly losing consciousness from the pain that shot through him. Unable to move, he felt Oreguss's hands stretch around his neck before he was hurled across the room. The seal's head hit against the wall, and then he fell limp to the floor. Miracle watched, partially conscious, as Oreguss stomped his way over to him once again, his heavy boots thundering his approach. Once more, the seal felt the man's fingers squeeze around his throat, and before everything turned to black, all that he could think of was Emma and whether she was still alive . . . that was all. Then all too quickly, Decara's evil laughter linked itself with the unrestrained hysterics of the haunted *Tiamat*. Again, there was blackness.

CRYING PUPS

Arayna hurriedly wriggled along. In the meantime, the sky steadily fell from the bleeding heavens, bringing more than its share of the broken moon down upon Sealssong. She could hear her own thumping heartbeat strike against her chest, growing louder and more furious than the crashing chunks of lunar droppings. She would soon reach the place where the mother seals and their newborn whitecoats gathered.

Minutes seemed to lengthen into hours; however, finally, Arayna's, breath faded into a stunned rhythm, and she began to wind down while approaching a thirty-foot hummock nearing the floe leading directly to the place she had come to find. While in the great shadow of the icy hummock, she tried to steady her breath, knowing she would need all the strength that she could possibly conjure. She was able to see all the seals, all frightened and anxious because of the bleeding sky, but all were still alive. Relieved that she had reached the seals before the horrible man-beasts, Arayna's mind sparked as she wriggled up toward the gathered fields of apprehensive creatures. Instantly, the crowd was alive with a hundred different sounds. Each one filled with a reverberation of alarm and confusion. The bleeding sky had caused a terrific deal of uncertainty and dread among the harps. Even the whitecoats seemed to sense the menace at hand. Most of the pups began to cry out vehemently, their mothers surrounding them, pushing them closer into themselves, trying to protect them from the falling parts of the red glowing heavens.

Nikki continued to protect Promise from the falling debris. In a perfectly formed circle, she placed her adopted pup in the center of her curved body. Her head wavered over the small seal, the back of her neck getting most of the sky droppings while continuing to look at her baby, trying not to show the panic building in her eyes. Promise was a healthy pup, well nourished by now, smart too; but the sick feeling in his tiny stomach told him that bad things were happening and would continue happening despite his mother's attempts of proving otherwise.

"It's all right," Nikki soothed. "Everything is going to be all right." Promise began to squirm within the circle Nikki had made for him to protect him all the while. Bellgar had momentarily moved toward the crowds of mother harps and their children and was making his way back to Nikki, when a cruel and biting wind suddenly filled the air. "What is it?" Nikki nervously called out to her mate her eyes never leaving her child.

"Don't really know," Bellgar answered, closing in on his family, his eyes filled with a sea of dismay. "But whatever it is, it certainly has every seal frightened out of their minds."

"Are we going to die?" Nikki asked, surprising herself for asking such a question, her heart racing as if to explode.

Bellgar quickly snatched his eyes from the sky and looked down at Nikki with a jolted unsettling feeling. "No!" he quickly told her, not daring to probe into her disturbing uncertainty. It was an issue that was suddenly filled with horrendous, unbelievable possibilities. He would not ever admit to it, but he never remembered having been so frightened in his entire life. Once again, his refusal to accept the obvious mocked his words. "Whatever it is, it will pass," he said, looking back up into the sky, his eyes burning from the debris, barely able to see anymore.

Nikki knew otherwise and knew he did as well. "No," she softly said while taking away her face from her child. Looking deeply at her mate, she felt her eyes well up with tears. "Something is wrong. Something is very wrong. You can feel it just as I can."

Bellgar tried to blink out the bleeding rubble from his burning eyes, and with a heavy thrust downward, he dropped, covering up both Nikki and Promise. He remained quiet and still, feeling Nikki's heart beat frantically against his own. He went on listening, hearing the other whitecoats begin to grow more alarmed and restless, as were their mothers, all beginning to cry and moan unceasingly against the furor of the fitful wind, the dropping heavens, and the snapping and gnashing of the screwing ice floes.

"I'm afraid," Nikki quietly confessed, shivering, pushing even closer to her mate. Promise, as did his father, continued to remain silent despite the sounds of the falling sky and the increasing cries of the whitecoats and their mothers. To each one, Bellgar lifted his head, wanting to ease their fear, wishing to calm the torment that sent them wandering around in circles as they held their pups tightly between their nervous jaws as if for the last time. He wished he could smooth away all their foreboding, but just as they, he was filled with the same fear; and no matter what, he would not be able to explain away what now appeared to be the end of their world. He would remain quiet, pressing close to his mate and the baby Promise, trying to protect them from the rest of the broken sky that continued to break down over them.

THE WARNING

For a moment, the uproar of the wind settled, allowing Arayna's voice to be heard, but its strength did not last. Where Nikki and her family had settled, the ice was nearest to the opening of the largest floes, the same floes that Arayna had followed, leading her straight to them. "Listen to me," she shouted in an out-of-breath bark. "You are all in danger! All of you, please, you must leave here at once!" However, the sounds the sky made, as well as the nervous reverberations that the seals produced, made it extremely difficult for Arayna to be heard. Suddenly, Bellgar jolted upward and quickly wriggled himself toward the strange seal that had somehow come to save them. "You need to leave this place now!" she warned as all the while the bleeding heavens assaulted her with its scarlet tears. "Man is on the island! He is coming here to kill you!"

Bellgar wriggled closer to Arayna, asking in a loud bark filled with alarm: "What is happening, who are you?"

"I am called Arayna. I am the mother of the white seal, Miracle, who carries the tear. I have come to warn you all!"

"Miracle?"

"Yes, he has sent me here to warn you about man! Man is on the island! He will be here soon! You must help me take the others to the great whale! This is your only salvation! He waits near the shore to take the pups away from here! Please, you must help me! This night belongs to the powers of darkness, and unless we leave here now, we all will die!" she cried, out of breath, fully covered red from the weeping heavens.

Bellgar looked deep into the eyes of Miracle's mother. What he saw there frightened him even more than the falling skies, but told him that she spoke the truth. Turning around to face the nervous and nearly out-of-control crowd, he shouted in a loud and clear bark, "Listen, all of you! Man is on the island! He has come to destroy us! We must seek refuge near the great shorelines—there we will find the whale Kishk. He will take our children away from here!"

Arayna watched as the seals and the whitecoats squealed and wriggled to and fro, none of them sure as what to make out of the horrors surrounding them. "Please!" Arayna added in a yelping bark. "We haven't much time! Man will be here any moment!"

Nikki, having listened to every word, quickly took Promise into her jaws and wriggled up toward Arayna and her mate. "I will help," she said, gently placing her pup near her mate's side. Then taking off like a shot, she ran into the frenzied seal gathering. "Did you not hear? We are in terrible danger! Man is on the island! If we have any chance of surviving, we must leave now! Take your children to the great shorelines, bring them to the whale, he will protect them. Now hurry! We must leave here at once!" she screamed. With one panic-filled thrust, the entire seal herd began to disperse into a wild burst of hysteria. That was when the first gunshot was heard. It was already too late. Man had come for them once again, bringing more bloodshed to Sealssong.

The first shot took the life of a mother harp that just happened to be directly in the line of fire. The gunshot had exploded her heart away, and she fell down into the scarlet-colored snow with a loud and powerful slosh. As her pup began to scream out, the entire seal congregation became utterly insane! In total pandemonium, the seals scattered, screeching and barking, sliding into one another, their babies falling from their jaws, disappearing beneath the chaotic stampede of absolute madness.

More gunshots pierced the bloody air as the hunters, with their empty eyes, surrounded the place where only hours before was a solace of joy and rebirth of hearts. Nikki scooped up Promise securely between her jaws, allowing Arayna to lead the way, everyone wriggling wildly from the trampling seals and the invading army of man-beasts. "This way," Arayna howled to Bellgar who had been temporarily swept away by the entourage of maniacal seals and their pups, all trying to escape the wrath of man.

Bang! Another shot went out, this time exploding right in front of Nikki. The ice shattered over Nikki's snout like broken glass, cutting into her eyes, causing her to drop her pup. She screamed out in wild disbelief, fumbling blindly for Promise in the red snow while the multitudes of panicked seals fled past her. As she blinked the ice away from her eyes, she found that she could no longer see. The gunshot and the razor-sharp splinters of ice had blinded her. "Promise," Nikki screamed in sobbing torment. "Promise, *Promise!*"

Another blast broke the ice before her. Nikki screamed again, her sight gone, the cold stings of the icy blast still fresh on her face. Bellgar tried to go to her, but another exploding gunshot stopped him. Arayna also tried to intercede, but the same bursting spray of ice stopped her directly in her tracks.

Once more, a hysterical Nikki screamed out for her child. Frantically, she tried to feel for Promise. In blind panic, Nikki raked her bleeding snout wildly over the surface of the ice, trying to find her pup, but she could not find him. "Baby!" she cried madly. "Where are you?" She began rubbing at her burning eyes with her flippers, trying to bring back her sight, but only gray blackness glared back at her.

"Mama, Mama," cried Promise, trying to wriggle up to his mother.

Arayna could see several of the zombie hunters approaching swiftly. From the corners of the floes, they came with their loud and monstrous weapons. Once more, Arayna and Bellgar barreled toward the injured Nikki. Suddenly, another round of gunshots exploded about them, and Nikki could feel the ice break over her face just as it had right before it took away her sight. "Quick!" Bellgar barked, pulling her, guiding her in the opposite direction. "The humans have surrounded the mountain!"

"This way," Arayna cried, taking hold of the pup, allowing Bellgar to steer Nikki in the right direction.

"My baby," Nikki screamed out. "Where did you take my baby?"

"It's all right!" Bellgar shouted as the gunshots flew past them. "Miracle's mother, Arayna, has him! He's all right!"

"Promise!" the blind Nikki howled, feeling her mate pull her along, pushing her with his massive head, Arayna and the pup following hurriedly at their side, all of them wriggling back to the dangerous floes, all of them disappearing inside the slushy waters as the gunshots pulverized the wet, bloodied ice directly behind them.

UP IN THE SKY

When Miracle first opened his eyes, he did not quite know where he was. However, when the incredible pain dug into him with fiery eruption, he quickly remembered. His eyes opened with a jolt when he felt something touch him. He abruptly pulled away, wheezing out with a dreaded squeal, but he suddenly stopped when he realized that it was Emma. She was awake and right next to him.

"Emma," cried the white seal, "are you okay!"

Emma nodded and put her arms tightly around the seal's face positioned directly in her tiny lap. "Try not to move," she warned in an exhausted voice. "That horrible brute hurt you. I'm not sure how much damage he has caused."

Miracle felt the pain explode in his torn-up flipper while attempting to pull himself up and move his head. "Where are we?"

Emma smirked before sighing. She looked around, rolled her eyes, and with an exasperated voice, said, "Back in another cage . . . again!"

"He's locked us in, just like Mama!" Miracle retorted. "Oh, Emma, did he hurt you?"

"He tried to," she said with a tight stretch pulling at her lips. "But I kicked him. In fact, I kicked him right in the privates! I had enough of that nasty-looking ape man!"

"Good for you!" Miracle said, smiling happily.

Without the slightest warning, the *Tiamat* suddenly shifted in the sky.

Slanting sideways, the cage that now imprisoned them, a cage much smaller than the one Emma and Arayna previously occupied, began to swing from the rafters of the ship. Suddenly, one of the cables holding it snapped. The small mesh enclosure went crashing into the ribs of the ship, hitting it hard, breaking into its side, taking off a chunk of the *Tiamat*'s innards while snapping off the latch and the entire door of the cage. Miracle and Emma hung there, merely dangling by one swinging and unstable cable. Back and forth they swayed, the cold air gushing all around them. For directly below, they could see another missing chunk of the ship, a portion large enough that they could see to the very bottom, straight down to the sacred seal nursery that they continued to soar far, far above! Emma tried to reach for Miracle when the cage shifted and shook as if to break apart. "Move away from the opening!" she screamed.

"You got it!" the white seal barked back, terrified. With a surge of fright, he was able to pull himself from the edge of the cage's aperture. Emma tried not to scream, pulling Miracle along the mesh surface, trying not to fall backward. As the cage began to settle down both found each other and quickly locked into a tight impenetrable hold. "We're flying!" Miracle cried.

"Yes."

"In the sky!"

"I know!" Emma bellowed over the roar of the wind.

"But how is it possible?"

"Don't ask!" she shouted back.

"Decara?"

"Who else? Just don't look down, it will make you dizzy!" she warned, straining to position both of her feet up against the cage so as not to drop out. The burning in her throat began again, and she started to cough. The wind increased, and with it came a more intense wailing, a most disturbing sound of high-pitched moans and groans, all wrapped up inside one long and icy breath, chilling her and the seal down to their bones.

"Emma . . . ," Miracle said in a hushed, constricted groan, holding on tight, his head resting against her tiny shoulders. "I'm afraid."

Emma closed her eyes, feeling the wind snap around her, tightening her hug about the seal's body. "I know, I am too," she revealed, keeping her eyes closed. Having no door to keep them from falling to their death, the ship spitefully continued to vibrate, shaking them mercilessly.

With the wind whistling, the moon falling down all around them, they remained silent, just rocking back and forth, squeaking inside the swinging mesh contraption, just dangling there thousands of feet above the once sacred seal nursery.

A WHALE OF A GUY

Kishk could see the flying ship plainly. A serious worry broke over the blue whale's face as he looked up into the red collapsing sky. He continued to shake the falling moon rubble from himself, jerking its remains into the slushy waters. Along with the flying ship, he had witnessed the moon grow smaller and smaller as it disintegrated before his very eyes.

In absolute frustration and helplessness, the chanter moved to and fro in the dark waters. He continued to watch the infamous sealing ship crumble, as did most everything else in the sky. Pieces of the *Tiamat* kept falling down around him like sheeting rain ruffling the sea even further. This made the blue whale all the more frightened because he knew that Miracle, Emma, as well as the others, remained inside that ship when it suddenly took to its unholy flight. Kishk knew that the terrible Decara had everything to do with it. He also knew deep down in his whale gut that if he did not do something soon, they all would die up there! The way that the already dismantled ship was falling apart, it wouldn't be long before something awful occurred, but what could he possibly do?

Just then, a group of frightened gulls flew over him. He watched them fly off into the distance, trying as best as they could to duck from the falling sky, but one of the birds did not fare that well. With a sharp blow, it was bluntly hit by a piece of the moon, or was it a part of the sealing ship that sailed in the sky? The whale could not be sure. Whatever hit the bird sent the creature plunging down into the frosty sea.

WHALE SONG

At first, Kishk thought that the bird was dead; however, it suddenly came bursting out from under the icy waters with a piercing shriek. The whale watched the bird continue to shriek, flying madly in a frantic attempt to meet up with the other gulls. Thinking for a moment, Kishk smiled before abruptly shouting out in a firm voice, *"That's it!"*

Casting his eyes down into the icy waters, he grinned some more. "The help will come from the sea!" he said, his violet eyes lighting up like the stars that once shone down upon the once pearly garden of Sealssong. Staring up into the falling red sky, the blue chanter called out toward the flying *Tiamat*, "Not to worry, my friends, help is on its way!" Sufficiently clearing out his illustrious throat, he closed his eyes, saying in a soft whisper, "This song is for you, Miracle." And taking in as much air as his massive lungs would allow, the blue whale began to do what he was born to do—*Sing!*

The sound that the chanter made came out slowly at first it was almost unrecognizable. Just like an orchestra prepping up for the great concert, the many melodic sounds that only a blessed creature as himself could produce suddenly filled the sheer borders along the icy stadium. It surrounded the magnificent beast as well as the heart of the watery arena beneath him. His wondrous whale song saturated the breath through the winds that circled him, taking his powerful and yet delicate melody within itself, scattering its enchanting heartfelt composition everywhere. However, the singing whale did not stop here; he had every intention of singing on and on forever if he had to, until every last creature in the sea heard his imploring whale vocalization. Then all at once, the blue chanter dove into the icy sea and vanished.

CLINGING VINE

In the greenly drenched darkness of the ocean nearly forty feet below, Kishk continued to sing out his song. The whale's score exploded into the water, making millions of bubbles, a million tiny notes of music all singing out in one magnificent voice of splendor!

As the chanting beast dove deeper and deeper, he could see past the massive walls of the ice floes growing far below. A gathering collection of sea creatures, all of them drawn together by his glorious voice, suddenly emerged. They convened not only around the stages of the floes that stretched endlessly beneath him, but his magnificent song also brought in creatures from far-off places not normally found in these parts. From everywhere they came to hear the whale's song, its powerful supplication drawing them onward, unable to resist even if they wanted to.

In just a matter of moments, the entire sea filled with hundreds of fish, mammals, and thousands of creatures, each animal knowing what must be done for every command was there in the chanter's exalted song. Kishk resurfaced, and in great unison of exploding amazement, the sea opened with a stunning shower of music, the chanter shooting up into the sky, bringing with him an assortment of underwater performers, all following him like the hypnotic Pied Piper that he truly was!

Crashing upon the surface, Kishk immediately realized that he was a smashing success. He watched as his entreating melody called to everyone everywhere! From every part of the ocean they came! Multitudes of the sea's inhabitants appeared, all of them swimming toward the sacred nursery. Dolphins of every shape and size filled the waters, as did the many other seals that lived in the ocean, many from parts far, far away. Eels, jellyfish, tortoises, starfish, octopuses, fish of every kind came! All one in voice! All one in spirit, all of them guided under the great direction of the greatest singing conductor himself, Kishk, the magnificent! However, it was not until the whale saw that his song had invoked the added voices of three other chanters, blue whales—just like himself, that he actually became overwhelmed. From way out in the distance, out near the red-glowing, cloud-infested horizon, he could see three of them, side by side, coming toward the island. Their tremendous forms, while filling the realm of the scarlet vista, shimmered in the intervening space before him. He could see the whales approaching, massive, gigantic, their voices full and vibrant. The three leviathans appeared to be sailing through the red-tinted clouds, each singing out its own whale chant, blending in perfect operatic harmony, bringing with them the rare and treasured music of the sea never before presented in such a prayerful marriage of song.

Kishk excitedly studied the whales singing back to them. They drew closer and closer, their song growing stronger, abounding with an unforgettable serenade, that of which even the heavens hastened to listen to—and they did listen, as did every creature on earth. Every stir of the wind, every wave of the sea, every flutter of the wings of the birds that wavered there, every sound that echoed in the earth listened. Even the ice and snow listened, for all were one, each knowing the importance of the song and what they must do.

Suddenly, the gulls who flew overhead, who only moments before were frightened by the falling sky, suddenly reformed; they were now filled with a new sense of hope and redirection. Without hesitation, the gulls suddenly dove into the frosty waters, forty, fifty, or more at a time, one after another they splashed into the slushy sea with tremendous swiftness. As the ocean exploded from their multitude of dives and splashes, the sea held her breath, waiting for the birds to resurface; and they did! One by one, hundreds at a time broke through the frosty lid of the ocean, each one carrying enormously long and lush vines of seaweed. The hundreds upon hundreds of gulls retrieved the flowing sea plants from the freezing waters, the whales singing out their song while the sea creatures prepared to save the ones who remained in the sky locked inside a monstrous vessel.

Starfish began to jump out of the sea, attaching themselves to the lush vines of sea growth, forming links between each section of the extracted marine plants. The shadowy forms of nearby dolphins and seals helped collect the prize assortment. Two at a time, side by side, the dolphins and seals held separated lines in their mouths, each waiting until another round of starfish, eels, and even squishy octopuses jumped up and attached themselves, pulling both ends together, making the glistening strings fuller and longer. In no time at all, the sea animals had created a slew of thick and sturdy ropes of connected sea plants. Then once more, the gulls flew back down to gather up more stringy cords, half the flock taking the ends of the collected ropes back down, meeting up with the three singing whales who were just making their way toward the massive Kishk. Instinctively, two selected leviathans opened their mouths, biting firmly on the ends of the plants, each making sure they had a secure hold, careful not to crunch down on the starfish and other clinging creatures. The remaining half of gulls quickly picked up the ends of the ropes before taking to flight. Up they flew toward the flying *Tiamat*, dodging the falling sky carrying the long and endless trails of seaweed and sea life. Reaching the vile ship, the swarming gulls began to encircle the *Tiamat*. Around and around they spun, covering up the broken vessel, twirling the pliable plant growth around it, making it look more like a ball of leafy yarn than a crumbling sealing ship.

When the gulls believed that they had tangled enough of the plants around the ship, still maintaining enough length to take back down to the island, they quickly took a nosedive, returning to Kishk and the other whale. Dropping the connected ends of the rope into their readily opened jaws, the gulls watched the giants snap down with a hearty bite. Then all together, all four whales, with one mighty pull, sank into the freezing waters, each pair facing one another, each pair pulling with all his might upon the twisted vines ensnaring the vicious vessel. The chanters watched the flying *Tiamat* jerk from their initial tug as if startled, never anticipating such a shrewd ambush. Down the whales went, pulling with all their strength, each one still remaining at opposite sides of the island, sinking further and further into the greenish sea.

Again, the *Tiamat* wrenched in the heavens, but upon the second pull, the sealing ship lost its grip in the sky, taking a noticeable plunge toward the sea that was growing closer as the four mammoth giants submerged deeper and deeper into the water, holding the leafy ropes firmly between their massive jaws. A considerable amount of the twisted lines snapped and broke from the extreme strain the chanters placed upon them, but enough plants and sea life remained fastened while the sinking whales continued to pull the bucking *Tiamat* out of the sky back down into the awaiting sea.

COLD HANDS

Inside the *Tiamat*, they heard the sudden shriek of Decara. Emma felt her already chilled blood freeze when the ensnared *Tiamat* felt the startling yank from the whales beneath them. The mighty tug was enough to snap the remaining cable holding the cage. Striking the side of the ship with another mighty punch, Miracle and Emma began to fall. Fortunately, the mesh contraption slammed into a part of the vessel that still maintained a portion of floorboards. They screamed, both shutting their eyes, holding on to each other, trying not to fall again, still screaming when the mesh enclosure flipped over sideways, lodging them between a narrow gap in such a way that the cage became temporarily immobile. Sadly, that was not about to last for long. Emma flipped backward, and Miracle flipped forward, just missing each other in midair. They went crashing to the opposite sides of the mesh prison, Emma landing next to the place once possessing a door. Her face was pressed against the side of the mesh, her hands gripping it, her feet dangling outside the cage. She could not help but look straight down onto the island that was swiftly growing closer, right before her eyes as the ship was pulled back down into the sea. Miracle, unable to hold on, toppled over; hitting Emma hard in the chest; and that was enough to send the cage, the ship, and everything inside the *Tiamat* out of the sky.

More seaweed and sea life snapped away, but there was still enough line left to give it one final needed pull. One last time, the diving whales yanked hard, and the *Tiamat* crashed into the sea with an astonishing splash of unimagined foam and flying ice. The shooting icy splinters ripped through the scarlet sky like a shower of daggers. The foaming sea continued to erupt, causing the disheveled *Tiamat* to rock back and forth inside its trembling arms. The sound the crash made when the ship exploded upon the water was deafening, leaving a terrible ringing in Emma's and Miracle's ears. Despite the impact, the evil *Tiamat* did not sink, nor did the

seal and Emma. They had somehow remained inside the ship, as well
as the confounded mesh prison. Immediately, both looked at each
other, making sure that the other was all right. Upon seeing that
they miraculously survived the ordeal, without a word and with only
the officious ringing inside their heads to guide them, they crawled
out of the dented mesh contraption. Emma came out first and then
quickly assisted the white seal. Turning toward the openness of the
smashed-up ship, unable to hear the groaning the vessel made or
the rapidly approaching footsteps coming their way, these sounds
hindered by the still strong ringing in their ears, Emma and the seal
spotted another long partially collapsed corridor. Emma pointed
toward it, suggesting it might be the way out. Miracle nodded and
quickly began to follow her, but the footsteps were now directly
behind them!

The last thing Emma remembered before giving out one final
scream before she fainted was cringing from how cold the touch
upon the back of her neck was. It was colder than the rushing waters
flooding around her—frigid, clammy, yet familiar, a touch belonging
to but one person and one person alone—*Decara!*

BEHOLD . . . YOUR DESTINY

When Emma finally opened her eyes, she could sense
hundreds of vibrations buzzing over her, and she could smell dozens
of different fragrances too. It was as if she had somehow been placed
within an endless field of the most sweetly perfumed flowers ever
known to grow.

Slowly, she rubbed at her eyes, breathing in the delicious aroma
that washed itself plentifully over her. She was lying down on a small
bed that was utterly made up of tiny pink blossoms, extraordinary
blossoms, able to make tiny little breathy crooning sounds every
time her body pressed against them. She placed one hand to her
side; and feeling the tiny flowers beneath her hand, she listened to
them make *ahhhaaaa* sounds, each note most delicate and sounding
as if they came from mystical gnome-like choruses of reverberating
sopranos, each note following her every move. She pushed herself
up from the flower bed and became immediately aware of something
else—her clothing. The torn and tattered hunter's rags had been
transformed into queenly raiment. She looked down at herself in

awe, touching the floor-length royal blue robe that was covered in tiny shimmering diamonds fit for a princess. Its long sleeves were daintily and intricately cuffed with the finest silk, which sparkled and shone with an alluring silver color whenever movement caressed it or the light came upon it a certain way. Emma felt her neck tingle and quickly placed her tiny hands just below her throat, feeling the smooth, velvety collar that was bordered with the most precise and involved pattern of woven branches bearing the smallest flowers ever reproduced. They too shone of the same vibrant silver that danced like the stars themselves. As if in a foggy dream, she tried to straighten herself up, the tiny petals of flowers beneath her feet continuing in their choral song, her beautiful garment shining like a million sparkles. As she tried to step forward, an invisible wall suddenly stopped her. She fell backward a few inches, crushing the flowers below, realizing she was barefoot and feeling the blossoms squishing through her toes, tickling her feet as she stood there.

Then there came a voice.

It was softly calling her name.

Emma immediately recognized the voice and strained to view its owner through the swirling mist that suddenly appeared there. Slowly, she reached out her hand, feeling the invisible barrier directly in front of her. It felt soft and pliable to the touch but was impenetrable. She tried to push her hand through its surface, but was unable.

Once more the voice spoke her name.

Once more she listened, fully knowing who it was.

"Decara," Emma shouted, her voice strong and healthy, the burning sensation completely gone from her. "I know it's you! Stop these sick games of yours, and just do what you have to do!"

"Such impatience," the voice politely sang back, clucking its tongue in false surprise.

"Oh, just stop it already!" Emma shouted. "Where am I now?"

"Where you belong . . . ," answered the voice. *"With me."*

"What have you done to Miracle?"

The voice did not answer.

"Where is he, Decara?"

"The seal is safe . . . for now . . . ," the voice told her.

"Let me see him!"

"In time!"

"Now!"

"Soon . . ."

"Where is he?" Emma shouted in panic, feeling the veins in her neck expand and press up against the velvety embroidered collar of her royal blue robe.

"Never mind about the seal, I want you to see something," insisted the voice.

Emma remained exceptionally still, watching the spinning mist dance chaotically about her before condensing into a fine rainy mist, a mist that did not saturate her skin or the regal garment of shining diamond chips. Carefully, she approached the strange barrier that would not release her, observing the figure before her solidify into the dark shape of Decara.

Emma immediately was aware that the dark woman was dressed in the same majestic robe as she, only Decara's was solid black and had an extensive hood attached to it, the same diamond chips garnishing its every movement. Her hair was braided in a stylish fashion, and for the first time ever, Emma actually thought her aunt looked breathtaking. Still, as always, Decara's eyes were as dark and cold as ever, calculating and ill-starred, her high cobra cheekbones catching the light sinisterly. Her aunt seemed to be pushing something that reflected blinding flashes of light toward her. Emma squinted from the harsh glare, listening as Decara spoke to her. "Look," Decara said in a still calm and almost pleasant fashion. "Look how truly beautiful you are!"

It took a while for Emma's eyes to adjust to the suddenly appearing full-length gold-framed mirror before her. She watched Decara's skeleton hands adjust its position so that the light would reflect her image just perfectly. Emma stared at her reflection in the sparkling mirror, compliments of the witch, with all its devilish designs integrated into and around its elaborate and immense gold frame. She looked at herself in the uniquely looking glass as if she was staring at someone else entirely. She could hardly believe her eyes. She was beautiful as she was sensual. Her iridescent eyes glistened with more radiance than ever before, glowing in the dark. Her skin was soft and milky, tinted with a blush of red roses at each corner, and her lips were moist and pink with a lustrous shine kissed across them. Her hair was not only fashioned, as was Decara's, twisted up against the back of her head as it snaked up around into a tight bun on top of her head, but it also appeared to have been mysteriously painted with a golden glow that sparkled like the flashes inside the mirror. She closed her eyes tightly and shook her head, unable to comprehend herself.

Decara was smiling from the shadows, whispering, "Behold your destiny, for it is what and who you are."

Once again, Emma continued to stare at herself in a confused manner. "What have you done to me?"

"I have allowed your true identity to show itself at last, are you not insatiable?" the witch taunted. "You are from my blood, from my kin. You are a part of me, and the dark god has shown favor upon you and will deliver you from destruction. You will reign at my side for all eternity, forever beautiful—forever young! You will have powers beyond anything you could ever imagine, and you will live in a world very different from the one you know now," Decara told her.

Emma turned her eyes away from the mirror, focusing solely on her aunt. "I see," she said in a plaintive, unimpressed voice.

"Yes," Decara went on to say. "You will no longer be an outcast, but a god! And you will never know sickness, my child. There will no longer be the frail, pathetic little Emma everyone has come to know. Instead, you will become a ravishing beauty that will evoke even the most powerful forces of darkness to find envy in you!"

"Ah-haa," Emma said, trying to suppress the anger rising in her. "And let's see, all I have to do is—what was it again?—kill the white seal, is that right?"

"'Tis a meaningless life-form—nothing more. A slug that has no purpose, a pestilence upon the earth whose only reason for living is that you should destroy its—"

"Innocence?" Emma finished.

Decara smiled sinisterly again from within the shadows. "Let's just say, it's pathetic existence. It is a freak, a morbid mistake of nature. Destroying it would actually be a mercy killing, and you would be putting it out of its misery. Don't you see, all you have to do is surrender to—" Decara paused for a moment then quickly started up again. "Look at it this way. If you don't kill the damn thing, sooner or later some self-appointed seal skinner will," she said with a hardy chuckle. "It's always the same story, and just think of all that you will be getting in return."

"No, never!" Emma shouted from inside the invisible bubble dome imprisoning her. "This innocence must be one very powerful force, Decara. It's made even you grovel."

"Careful," Decara warned. "It would not be wise to upset me, not now, not on such a moment as the day you came home to claim what is rightfully yours." She suddenly took away the shining gold-framed mirror, replacing her dark form before her niece. "You belong to the night, you have since birth, and it has at last come to claim you."

"Get away from me!" Emma shouted, punching her fist into the elastic bubble of swirling mist.

"Give in to it. It is what you were created for, precious child," Decara purred.

"I said get away from me! And don't call me precious child!"

Decara's purring suddenly turned into a snarl. "Another warning and I promise you this one will be your last. Give in to the darkness and take your rightful place with me and surrender your innocence. Kill the white seal and join me in eternal life!"

"Never," Emma screamed back.

"Oh, Emma, surrender this meaningless chastity!" commanded Decara in the full range of her thunderous voice. "It has always been a hindrance to you! Come share the powers of darkness with me! You can have it all! Beauty! Eternal life! More power than you ever dreamed of! All this can be yours for the mere sacrifice of one pathetic beast, a worthless slug that slinks through slimy seas and has no rhyme or reason for its existence!"

"I am not listening to you!" Emma shouted, firmly covering both of her ears with her hands.

"Kill the seal! Take the stone he wears! Share its power! BECOME THE POWER! The two of us together! For always! Come, be one with me!"

"Stop it! Stop it!" Emma screamed.

Decara's words just kept growing louder and more maniacal, raging. "Take my hand!" she shrieked, tearing into the flexible membrane of the floating dome imprisoning her niece. "This is your chance for immortality! You know I'm right! You know you want it! Beauty! Wealth! Power! Take my hand!" she commanded viciously. "Take it, I say!"

Suddenly, Emma stopped shouting. Releasing her hands from her ears, she quietly stared at the hand of the witch now probing through the transparent wall before her. In a slow approach, Emma extended her hand, the beautiful blue sleeve of the robe spilling all around her, the affixed diamonds glaring in her eyes. With this trembling hand, Emma continued to outstretch it; and just as she was about to touch the taut skin that wrapped itself around the fingers of Decara, she forcefully pulled back before striking the hand of her evil aunt with one stinging slap!

"Now, will you go away from me, *witch?*" Emma said indignantly. "I will never join you! *Never!* I am ashamed that you are a part of my family!" She was filled up with emotion, her eyes rimmed with red, choking on her words. "I am ashamed that I carry your blood."

Emma quickly turned away from Decara just in time not to see the way the corners of Decara's mouth twitched, barely noticeable at first, but soon becoming more marked and twisted. "Yes-*sss* . . . ," Decara hissed. "Your bloodline lies within me, there is no denying this! We are a part of each other, whippersnapper, we are of the same true blood, and there is nothing you can do about it. *Nothing!"*

Emma's eyes flashed wide, open. She looked upon her aunt, her eyes burning. Allowing the saliva to well up in her mouth, with disgust and contempt, she neared the elastic and misty bubble. Pulling up the wetness, she spit against the clear wall of her floating prison, just glaring at Decara before eventually drawing back into the blurred mist. "I will never be like you! I will die first!"

"That can be easily arranged, ungrateful, cocky brat!"

"Then do it!" Emma recoiled. "I've had enough of this! I've had enough of you! I've had all I could take of your threats and all your lies! Enough of all your cages and tricks! Enough of you calling me precious child! Enough of you touching me and pulling my hair! Enough of your madness! Just do it and get it over with!"

"It won't be that easy!" Decara's harsh, rasping voice spewed. "Besides, I still have other ways of persuading you."

Suddenly the room seemed to explode with a hundred different flashes of light, and Emma felt the floating bubble entrapping her begin to spin. And as she spun, she was aware that also floating before her were two more suspended bubble jails, both of which held prisoner her beloved friends.

There was Miracle, prisoner in his own personal bubble cell. Little Lukie and Poo-Coo were sadistically crammed into another of the wafting domes. Emma looked at their faces, each one filled with terror and sadness, tears shining from all of their tortured eyes. "You monster, you horrible monster," Emma cried.

In a horrific rage, Decara flew from Emma's side like a huge bat, and hurling her long black diamond-sequin-filled robe, she plunged her hand into the clear wall that imprisoned the white seal. The devil woman grabbed Miracle by the throat, squeezing the air out of him, hurling her words to Emma. "Are we still so cocksure of ourselves? Shall I rip his eyes from his face? Shall I have Oreguss cut out his tongue and feed it to the sharks, or maybe I'll have him eat it right before your eyes? What shall it be, precious child?"

"Stop, you're hurting him, you maniac!"

Decara laughed. "Oh, I'll do more than hurt him by the time this is finished," she promised grimly. "You can bet on that!" Releasing her tight grip from Miracle's throat, she pushed him forcefully back into the mist of the suspended bubble. "It's true," she continued to jeer. "I cannot kill him now as I would have it, but I can play with him . . . a little." She cleared her throat, coming back with a more intense voice, chuckling. "I can play with all of them!" Then once again, Decara attacked Miracle's floating cell, hurling herself against it with all her might. The bubble cage abruptly swung back, striking the other suspended jail incarcerating Lukie and Poo-Coo. The shocking impact sent them crashing into Emma, causing all three buoyant domes to slam into one another repeatedly.

Oreguss suddenly entered the room. With an inhuman groan and a queer and deranged grin smeared across his brutish unshaven face, he threw himself on the floor, his back hitting the wood hard. With his massive legs, he began kicking at the floating prisons, making them further hurl against each other in a more deranged manner. He kept laughing and kicking like a mad man until Decara suddenly grabbed hold of both his feet, pinning them crudely to the floor. Turning sharply from him, she began to writhe away toward the floating bubble jails. Oreguss slowly sat up from the cold floor. He grinned, carefully watchful of Decara crawling across the black floor, resembling a stalking panther. Stopping just in front and directly below the bubble that held Lukie and the walrus, the evil woman smiled a most sinister grimace before abruptly springing upward, ripping into the bottom portion of the dome, using only her head, her torso dividing both the seal and the walrus from one another while continuing to tear upward.

With a ghastly twist of her neck, her mouth opened wide. She viciously struck out at Little Lukie like a viper, biting into his flipper. Lukie screamed out in sheer panic. "She bit me! She bit me!" he squealed in horror, crying aloud in pain. "That crazy man-beast bit me!"

Then even before he could pull away, Decara's arms shot up, breaking through the invisible membrane of the bubble. Seizing tightly one of Poo-Coo's long tusks, with one mighty demonic snap, she broke half of it off his wobbly face. The walrus yelped out in sheer agony, falling to the transparent floor of the cramped jail. In a splurge of laughs and morbid-sounding giggles, Decara pulled herself from the dome, wickedly holding on to the half-broken tusk. She looked smug, slithering over to Emma, holding out the sharp pointed end of the walrus's tooth, glaring at her niece, the cutting edge of the tusk barely touching the thin wall where Emma stood. Inching the piercing tip through the elastic skin of the dome, Decara rested Poo-Coo's severed tooth against Emma's throat.

"Now you see, precious child, you done gone and made me cranky. Now that wasn't very nice, was it?"

Emma did not budge. She remained still with the tip of the broken tusk pressed against her delicate throat. She swallowed hard, and finding her voice, she said, "You're running out of time, Decara. Soon it will be daylight, and everything you hoped for will be gone, everything including you!"

Decara merely laughed, just holding the severed tusk at her niece's exposed throat. "Think so?" she said, smiling sinisterly the whole time. "We shall see. We shall see."

"I will never kill the white seal. Never! No matter what you do, I will never harm him."

Again, Decara merely laughed. "It's funny, just now I had to stop myself from shredding apart that stupid walrus and prissy whining seal. They mean nothing to me and can be disposed of at any time, and yet I wonder what stopped me. Can it be that I am actually acquiring a woman's heart, precious child?" Decara taunted, stroking her niece's neck with the blunt tooth, laughing to herself in a low, guttural tone. Emma just glared defiantly at her, not answering, not moving. Decara sighed, admitting in a mocking voice, *"Nhaah . . ."* Her black eyes opened wide. "I don't think so!" she added with an irritating cackle. "They will be disposed of soon enough, I should think. Besides, I have bigger fish to fry, don't I?" She rubbed the splintered tusk carefully up and down the tender part of Emma's throat.

"What do you mean?"

"Come now, precious child, you know fully what I mean. Let's not start playing games, not with, your auntie Decara, not now."

"I don't know what you are talking about, and I told you, stop calling me precious child!" she said, still not pulling away from the sharp point of the tusk.

"But you are my precious child," Decara teased. "And to show you just how precious you are, I'm going to give you one last chance to join me. Stop all of this unnecessary resistance and live as the gods have from the very beginning of time, and spare that idolized brother of yours a considerable amount of torture!"

Emma looked straight into Decara's face, and without blinking an eye or attempting to move away from the piece of the walrus's tooth that remained closely pressed against her neck, she said, "You just don't get it, do you?" Decara remained motionless, smiling grimly, batting her eyes in a ridiculing fashion. "Do you?" she mocked dryly. "I hate everything about you. Everything you represent. You are a pathetic, lonely woman who feeds off the pain and grief of everyone around her. You're right, Decara, you have no heart, nor do you have any allies in your dark kingdom! Just you wait, you'll see! When they are finished with you, your precious darkness will turn on you and throw you away like a used and broken thing!"

"Oh—really?" Decara sang in a casual voice, pressing the severed tooth deeper against Emma's throat, this time pushing it just a little further into her niece's skin, a spot of blood beginning to show itself. "Well," she further sneered, her dark features holding to a cunning grin. "There are some truths you better face, *missy!*"

In the next instant, Decara's bony fingers smashed through the wall of Emma's bubble. Grabbing hold of her niece's neck, Decara forcibly pulled Emma forward. Emma screamed as the bony fingers tightened about her throat. "Listen to me, you thankless, empty-headed little brat! I have had my fill of your cockiness! Do you understand, girl?" Decara's grip intensified even further as she continued to rant and rave. "I tried to make this easy for you. I offered you gifts of unimagined glory, and you have scoffed and refused every one of them, but no more, missy, no more!"

From across the room, Miracle shouted from his bubble cell, "Leave her alone! It's me that you want, not her!"

Within seconds, Oreguss was beside Miracle's floating prison, hitting it, making it sweep back and forth like an out-of-control swing. The other cage holding Lukie and the injured walrus also sparked with life as they hurled their own share of resentment toward the witch. "Dude, if I ever get out of here alive," Poo-Coo growled, the incredible pain of his attack remaining fresh and excruciating, "I'll crush you! I swear I'll crush you, you rotten sack of garbage!" His words became entangled with the boisterous and excited Lukie who was screaming, "Kick it, Emma! Kick it!" However, Emma could not move for Decara's vile grip remained all too powerful.

"You will kill the white beast!" Decara shrieked.

"Never!" Emma shrieked back.

"We'll see how quick you change your mind when you see your precious sweet-boy brother skinned alive as you watch!"

"Let go of me!" Emma cried, trying to unfasten the woman's rigid skeleton fingers away from her. However, Decara squeezed her grip even tighter, shaking the girl intolerably. "I said let go of me, witch!" Emma screamed while twisting herself around the floating prison.

One more, Lukie barked out, "Kick it, *kick it—good!*"

Unfortunately, Emma could not pry away from Decara's fingers, let alone manage to kick at her. However, she did keep striking at

Decara's hands, spinning and pulling away until at last she broke free. Emma fell backward and felt her naked feet scrape against the blossoms beneath her. They felt slimy and scaly. Now instead of glorious voices of melodic song, their vocalizing drastically changed to a demonic chant of screams, evil and foreboding. The once beautiful, fragrant singing blossoms had suddenly turned into a pile of foul-smelling squirming black worms! The room filled with more desperate pleas from the white seal and added threats from the walrus and Lukie, along with deranged grunts and giggles from Oreguss.

Still, it was Decara's voice that shook the very walls of the ship. "Go ahead, you pathetic fool! See what it is like to be sick again! See what it is like to watch your brother be sliced up into tiny pieces!" she screamed with her face pressed up to Emma's. "See what it is like to die! And you will! Oh, I promise that! YOU WILL DIE!"

Just then, and not having any idea how she was able to, Emma forcefully slapped her aunt across the face. In that same instant, her bubble exploded, expelling itself all over Decara, as well as herself. Instantly, Emma fell to the floor, the peculiar gooey substance that made up the dome dripping from every part of her and the once breathtaking garment of royal blue and diamond sparkles. All at once, the room went deadly silent, the only sound coming from Emma's gasp while trying to catch her breath, the horrible burning in her throat having returned. She tried to back away from Decara, who was now directly on top of her, her aunt's hair a mangled hanging gooey mess, her gummy face a mask of raw insanity, her black eyes bulging from their sockets, the slimy dripping bubble substance still melting down her pale face.

"Quick!" Miracle called from across the room. "Run! Get away from her! Run, Emma! Run!"

Regrettably, Emma could not run. Decara was only inches away from her when she saw those terrible eyes of hers burst into two balls of blazing fire. "Oh, you will pay for that! Innocence or no innocence, you will pay!" Decara hissed, lunging at Emma with both of her bony hands outstretched, ready to shred her niece's beautiful face. All Emma could do was to scream. And just as Decara's hands came down over her, a loud sound exploded in the room followed by a sudden shrill—a shrill that sounded stunned and jarred, a shrill most certainly caught off guard. It was an angry, startled screech, this time belonging to *Decara!* Emma had been saved from her aunt's evil grasp, but by whom? A loud most distinguishable voice inundated the room, its owner smacking the wicked woman hard across the back of the head. Decara flipped sideways, falling away from Emma, crashing to the floor as the assailant screamed, "Back off—jerk-ass!"

"Mum!" Miracle yelped, unable to grasp the unthinkable. "You're alive!" he yelped again in utter astonishment. It was at that very moment that the room became pervaded with another one of Decara's disturbing shrieks, for Mum's next smack sent the witch into a wall then back down to the floor. As Emma stood up, she quickly backed away as far as she was able, watching the unimaginable sight play on before her eyes.

Attacking the witch was downright fun for the mad seal, even more fun than when she smacked that stupid Jillith seal over the cliff, even better than rolling over that insufferable penguin. Yes, it was especially jolly catching Decara off guard the way she did. The Mad Mum was thoroughly delighted that neither the witch nor her flunky servant ever anticipated her perfectly sly and out-of-the-blue assault. Slapping the witch on the side of her head with one of her flippers proved to be a real crack-up for the seal, but the absolute crowning moment of merriment came when Mum followed up her smack with a complete backflip in the air, hitting Oreguss in the head, taking him down with a striking thud. The way he came down on the witch, one would think Decara would have been surely reduced to a pancake of a woman. However, unfortunately, Decara's resilience proved to be too powerful; and in a state of premeditated murder, she quickly kicked Oreguss off. Still, it did not matter. In seconds, the mad seal was at it again, this time with another round of her favorite game Clap-Clap, this time played out real fast across the witch's face. Happily, the mad harpie squealed in delicious delight, persistently smacking about the head of Decara, treating it just like a ball.

It's strange what could go through a mad seal's mind at a time like this. Because all the while she witch-smacked Decara, she could not help but revel in the fact that she had finally escaped from that irritable and hateful tight-fitting porthole. Well, it was not exactly escaping; it was more like being wonderfully liberated, and it was marvelous to be free again! True, she did manage to sleep away most of the time while plugged up inside the preposterous opening, but the sudden crash-landing the ill-considered ship made from way up yonder had initially ticked her off. After all, she was sleeping, and what kind of touchdown was that anyway? Why, she had once seen a blind albatross make a better landing. Still, if it wasn't for such an unsuitable and most irregular return to the island, she might still be there. The entire side of the *Tiamat* had fallen away into the icy sea upon its unsuitable drop out of the sky, but Mum, naturally, would take all the credit of such cunning escapism.

Using her black magic, Decara swept herself up off the floor in a blazing light. Standing, she immediately went for the mad beast. However, Mum anticipated her move; and with a twist of her backside, the harp hurled Decara across the room, slamming the woman into another one of the still remaining walls. "I said BUG OFF, bozo!" Mum snapped.

In a voice of maniacal outrage, Decara called out to her servant. As Oreguss picked himself off the floor, his head in a pounding spin, he dizzily approached the mad beast. He felt his ears go numb as he too was swatted like a pesky housefly. Losing his balance, this time, Oreguss fell headfirst into the gold-framed mirror used to capture Emma's beautiful reflection. The mirror exploded into a million chips of glass as he went crashing through it.

"Kick it, Mum!" Lukie shouted from his bubble jail. "Kick it good!"

Although Mum was not able to kick the witch, she did, however, manage to get one more smack in, along with a belly dive, landing right on top of the shrieking Decara's back. *"Yippy-ki-aye, love-us!"* Mum yelled, bucking and bouncing, all the while breaking wind with every bounce.

As if feeling the crunch itself, the *Tiamat* suddenly began to shake, moaning in what sounded like absolute agony. Then the walls started to tremble. With ravaging spasms, they contorted and shook until they began to collapse. The wall next to Lukie and Poo-Coo was the first to crumble. Then the wall nearest Miracle buckled and fell. Finally, the wall behind Emma dropped backward, crashing into the twisted and already destroyed corridor behind it. Instantly, both floating jails fell to the floor, erupting with a burst of the same gooey gore, exploding and looking just like the bubbly domain the three-headed serpent had once slithered. Lukie and Poo-Coo flip-flopped into Miracle, all of them covered with the sticky remains of the burst domes, but they were free! They were slimy and gummy, but they at last were free! Having seen this, Mum, who was still sitting on top of the squirming Decara, smiled an enormous grin as several monumental snot bubbles burst out both sides of her nostrils.

"Lovie-loves," she asked, cheerfully addressing her comrades. "Don't you think this would be a good time to bugger off from this crummy joint? I'm just sayin' . . ." Mum chirped happily, buck-riding the twitching, witch beneath her.

"Mum!" Miracle shouted, excitedly wriggling his gooey self up to her. "Oh, Mum, am I ever glad to see you! You saved us all!"

"*Love-ya*," Mum rejoiced while surveying his sticky fur. "A bit peaked, aren't we?"

"Hurry, Mum, let's get out of here!"

"You all go and wriggle along, I'll be there directly . . . Not quite finished with the witch just yet," she said, giggling and jiggling her many rolls of blubber, bouncing about while from beneath, Decara sparked as if on fire.

"Listen, crazy seal," the injured Poo-Coo howled. "You must come with us now! What's left of this terrible ship is falling apart! We've all got to get out of here before the whole place caves in!"

The mad seal nonchalantly looked down at Decara. All that was visible of the dark woman were bits and pieces of her robe; she was no longer struggling to free herself. In fact, Decara was no longer there; she had vanished. Nonetheless, that did not matter to Lukie. Directly, he wriggled his little gooey self up to the folds of Decara's clothing; and not wasting a moment, he lifted his back end, extended his sticky flipper, and kicked hard at the twisted and gummy material. "That's for biting me," he snapped. "'Cause it was no fun—*neither!*"

Miracle pressed himself to Emma. "She tried to kill you!" he said with eyes that burned with fear and passion.

Emma cleared away the returned burning in her throat and wiped away a drooling string of hair that dribbled more of what remained of the gooey fluid. "Hurry!" she cried as another round of violent shakes and quakes rattled the disabled *Tiamat.* "We haven't a moment to lose!"

"Quick, Mum, let's get out of here!" the white seal begged.

Again, the lunatic harpie dropped her drooling face to look at the flattened cloak on which she sat. She bilked her hindquarters, lowered her head, and sniffed the place where she last saw the witch. Realizing that the vile woman had indeed escaped, she sighed, smacked her lips a few times, answering, "Oh, botherdash, very well, *Love-ya,* if you say so!" And with a tug of her enormous self, she pushed away from Decara's squashed apparel.

Emma shouted, "This way!" pointing toward what remained of the ship, its broken and battered threshold giving a full view of the seal nursery only a few hundred feet away. They would have to cross over a few disconcerting ice floes, but Emma knew that if they were careful, they would make it. Although each creature was large and bulky, they now moved like the wind, all but Mum. She nonchalantly wriggled onward, occasionally stopping to scratch at herself like a dog with fleas, wiping her flippers across her absurd snout where more erupting snot bubbles persistently seemed to leak out.

WICKED SPELL

Through twisted corridors they fled. Half-standing walls wailed and screamed, and the *Tiamat* shook with total outrage; it nearly collapsed the rest of itself onto the fleeing creatures who, at last, found the way out. They were free! Well, almost all were free.

Mum continued lackadaisically wriggling behind, still enjoying her own world of madness and wonder. Emma made it out first, then Miracle. Little Lukie followed as Poo-Coo made his way to meet up with the others where the first of the floes led to the nursery. However, in their wild attempt at leaving the dreadful ship, they all lost track of Mum. Having also lost track of Decara, they could not possibly know that the witch never actually left the *Tiamat*.

Reappearing, Decara ferociously charged toward the place that Oreguss had fallen into—the once grand and gold-framed mirror. Viciously pushing, aside an already out-of-joint Oreguss, she threw him forcibly into the existing half-crumbled wall before her. With a maniacal sweep of her hand, she bent over the serrated heap of splintered glass and snatched up one of the larger shards, the biggest one—the one that would serve her evil purpose. Not waiting for her servant to finish picking himself up off the floor, she hurled her vile curse toward the mad seal that was just making her way off the ship.

"You have made your last mistake, psychotic slug!" Decara shrieked, squeezing tightly the broken shard. It cut into her, making her palm bleed before sparking as if it might burst into flames. Aiming the bloodstained shard toward the remaining pieces of shattered glass, she hurled it down into the shining rubble. It exploded with a hiss, and when the blinding glare faded, the broken glass suddenly sprouted wings—ghoulish bat wings! Each sliver were about two inches long, nearly three hundred in all, each one sharp and jagged—alive, appearing as icy devil bats, their lurid mirrorlike features reflecting blasts of light. In a bombardment of flickering glare, the winged beasts flew toward the mad seal in a crazed swarm.

At first, Mum was hardly aware of the small sharply pointed things. Thinking it was just a case of the itches again, she stopped and proceeded to relieve herself with a quick scurry of her back flipper, but this time the itch did not dissipate. If anything, it got worse—much worse! In only a matter of moments, the massive swarm covered her. Mum felt her skin begin to burn and bleed.

It hurt badly. She tried to swat at the nasty cloud of sharp-edged things, but they sliced and cut at her brutally with every beat of their glaring appendages. Having had enough, she began wriggling toward the existing floes, the swirling swarm following close behind. The intense wind outside inadvertently aided Mum by, blowing the mirrory bats off course, but just temporarily. In no time at all, the glazed monstrosities had once again gained their momentum and were heading right back toward her.

Mum wriggled faster and faster, but all too soon the glassy legion consumed her. Again, she tried to swat at them, but there was just too many of them. Unable to see where she was going, the fleeing harpie blindly scurried onward, swatting her flippers crazily at the swarm. Soon the feeling in her limbs began to numb. Even her weary mind of disillusionment would become null and void. Still, there would be one thing she would be aware of before the switch in her head shut off. For what would be considered a fleeting instant, she would be conscious of screaming when she unexpectedly fell over an unusually steep mountain of scarlet-colored snow, where she unsparingly plunged harshly into a deep and frozen dark hole, right before her spine struck a large and rocky boulder of ice.

Mum no longer felt any pain.

The horrible mass of thronging mirror bats had abruptly flown off, returning back to the crumbling *Tiamat*. They shattered to the floor, once again becoming inanimate shards of bloody broken mirror.

The howling wind had quickly died down, and even the particles of falling moon, now reduced to tiny specks of gray and red, had grown unexcited in their weary travels from outer space. They no longer sounded quite as aggressive as they hit upon the lips of the icy hole that stretched way above where Mum lay lifeless.

Every blood-stained debris of fallout listened with devilish satisfaction, knowing fully that they had assisted the dark powers and, in return, were given a brief moment to rest and gloat over their savage victory, each droplet basking in the smell of death that now came from the hole in the earth. And as they remained unremitting in their listening, no sound came from the dark cavity they spirited around. Excited, the gathering essence of evil pulsated, breathing in what was the maturing stench of death . . . and they were grinning.

HELL HATH NO FURY
LIKE A WOMAN SCORNED

The way Decara looked at the moon while whisking inhumanely through the icy red-painted snow chilled even the unfeeling heart of Oreguss. He tried to keep up with the dark woman who hurried toward the hole she had witnessed the crazed seal fall into. That wretched pissant worm had harassed her for the last time! This time she would make certain that the annoying thing was finally dead! She continued to drip of the exploding bubble jails, along with other nasty excretions the wretched mindless seal had expelled upon her. Wiping her face, trying to remove the stench and slime, she continued dashing to the place that would serve as Mum's final resting place. Oreguss tried to keep up with her wild pace but was unable. She was already looking down into the deep hole when he eventually reached her.

Decara never turned her face from the icy opening. She merely stared down at it, sniffing the air just like a beast, making certain over and over again that the thing that she had caused to become mad, who had destroyed her lover, was indeed dead! Slowly, she lowered herself toward the hole, knowing that the lifeless seal lay fifty feet or more below. Again, she sniffed the air. It was then that Oreguss noticed a most sinister grimace, a frightening grimace even for Decara; suddenly tear itself over the mouth of the dark woman. Like a thick, slippery nightcrawler, it moved insidiously across the saturated and deranged features of his mistress, splitting itself across her wet lips like a scary jack-o'-lantern.

Oreguss found himself taking a few steps away from Decara, feeling the goose bumps eat away at his thick, furry arms, making all the hairs stand up straight. She came toward him with a slow stride, carrying the demented grimace with her. He felt his backside press up against an unnoticed wall of ice. Unable to move, he nervously watched the vile woman come nearer. How he hated when she pulled this creepy stuff! He suddenly felt his knees quiver and his heart quicken as his eyes met up with hers. For the first time in a long time, he was afraid. There was no reason for him to be, but he was afraid—very afraid, but why? After all, his mistress should have been tickled pink! That stupid, mad seal was finally dead! Still, why were his knees still shaking? It was those eyes! Or was it that she no longer had any eyes?

The place that once held her eyes were open sockets, empty and dark like two black holes, two shadows that held no skin. He could actually see right through them, clear straight out the back of her head as if she were a ghost, but that wasn't all. The way the flesh around her cheeks and forehead wavered was as if a bizarre and intense heat was leaking out both of those ghostly black gaps, indicating that whatever had taken away her eyes was still burning. He could hear and smell it sizzle as she opened her mouth, exposing her white shining teeth. Suddenly, without cause, Decara hurled herself away from her servant, casting her empty stare up toward the still falling moon. Again, she smiled, evilly laughing to herself. With a cruel twist to her lips, she hissed like a snake. She hissed and giggled to herself again and again. Yes, her time had finally come! With her body straight as an arrow and her arms stretched out from her sides, she took on the shape of a cross. Jerking her head toward the red glowing seal nursery, she, who remained smiling sinisterly, fell forward.

Plummeting down into the frozen hole that had swallowed up Mum, Decara let herself fall freely. She would not crash upon the perilous bottom as did the mindless imbecilic harpie that lay wasted below her. No, in just a quick breath of a demonic gasp, she was able to change herself into the same hollowness as her vacant eyes—a formless darkness with no substance or true form. Duplicating the blackened pits of obscurity, Decara had transformed into a black and malignant dark shadow, a shadow that began to grow and grow, spreading itself in every direction. Blowing out like a foreboding storm cloud filled with rain and viperous lightning bolts she went, the assisting wind hastily coming to her aid, upholding her, the shadowy form of Decara billowing in the skies, covering up all of Sealssong like wet dirt upon a freshly dug grave.

BROKEN HEART

Emma was the first to notice that Mum had not continued on with them.

Both Poo-Coo and Little Lukie had already ventured onto the floes by the time Miracle realized that Emma was not with him.

Miracle suddenly turned and spotted her. Emma was just standing there with her back toward him, about twenty feet away, just staring out into the hazy red glow before her. In a hurried struggle through the red slush, the white seal quickly wriggled to meet up with her. "Why did you stop? What is it?" he asked in an out-of-breath bark.

Emma remained silent, the tiny particles of what remained of the moon settling on her flat and matted sticky blond hair. The wind was beginning to rise again. A watery diffused light mixed up with reds and oranges danced aimlessly over the stained banks of ice and snow that lay before her.

"Emma," Miracle whispered in a panicked voice. "What has happened, what are you looking at?"

At last Emma came alive. Turning her face to the white seal, he saw that she was crying. "We lost her. We lost Mum," she said.

It was as if an explosion had suddenly burst inside his heart. A sharp pain to his head accompanied the eruption inside him, striking the tragic realization home with a gnashing jab. *"Mum!"* the seal squealed. "Mum, oh no!"

Once more Emma turned from Miracle and looked out into the hilly slopes of tarnished snow. "She didn't make it," she murmured, feeling the unbearable shame melt over her.

"No. You're mistaken!" Miracle insisted. "She's with the others. I know she is! I watched her leave!"

Emma shook her head. "Something bad has happened."

"No! You're wrong, Emma, I said she's with the others!"

Emma felt her tears magnify and burn at her iridescent eyes. She put her fingers to her lips, pressing against them as she spoke through her trembling hands. "I thought she was right behind me," she wept.

"She was! She's waiting for us at the floes! We just didn't see her. She can move fast! I know. I've seen her barrel across the ice many times!" The seal refused to believe anything else. "Come on, we're wasting time!" he called, turning quickly, wriggling back toward the floes.

"Wait!" Emma called after him, but the seal was already halfway there when a sudden echo of exploding gunshot thundered over them. By the time she reached the floes, she could see by the dismal look of unthinkable dread that shadowed his face that he realized the poor mad seal was not waiting there.

"Where is she?" a frantic Miracle barked. "Where is she!" he shouted again, interrogating the walrus and the already terrified and shaking Lukie.

"Miracle—" Emma cried, trying to appeal to his refusal to accept the obvious, but she failed miserably as the seal continued to bark out in grave denial.

"No!" he interrupted. "Where is she? What happened to her, where is Mum!"

Poo-Coo answered this time. "I thought she was with you!"

"Does it look like she is with me!" snapped the white seal, his heart smashing mercilessly against his breath.

Lukie started to cry and shake violently while he floated inside the slush of the slow-moving ice floe. "She wasn't with me—*neither!*" He wailed, scared and confused.

More gunshots rumbled loudly overhead, this time sounding closer than before. "Bro, we've got to get out of here!" warned the tusk-damaged walrus. "The man-beasts, they are almost here!"

Before the morbid picture of a mutilated and destroyed Mum could even begin to dissolve from the pang inside his mind, Miracle dove off the ridge of the floe and into the freezing water. Tearing off at full speed, he cut through the slush of the glowing red sea, riding on a small wave he created. As the panicked seal made squiggled V-shaped ripples in the water, he felt the sting of the wound he had sustained from the apish Oreguss burn, just like it was on fire. It hurt, but not half as much as the unforgiving regret of losing the mad seal he had come to love and cherish these past fleeting years.

Half crippled inside the flow of the waters, Miracle swung out his neck, turning it around and around, looking out in all directions for any signs of the missing seal. "Mum!" he pathetically cried out, pressing through the ice and slosh. As his burning flippers slapped the sea, a multitude of thronging bubbles inundated the waters. Up they came like sputtering clouds of ooze tickling his body with a chilling shudder. More sordid thoughts of a dying Mum stabbed at his mind all the while the bubbles surrounded him. Perhaps these sudden globs of effervescence were only the aftermath created by parasitic fish or turbid discharges coerced out from the changing pressures rising up miles below the open floes. Then again they could have well been gasps of suffocating breath or even gouts of blood. Miracle would speculate no further. He would hear Emma's frantic calling voice but for an instant before it was snuffed out by the sudden compression of the sea.

Down into the icy waters he dove, his searching eyes darting rebelliously against the revealing absence of the mad creature he so desperately sought after. Defiant, he plunged even deeper, opening his mouth, tasting the water for any telltale sign. There was none.

Once more he opened his jaws, spewing a gargled muffle that called out the mad seal's name. Over and over again he throttled out his frantic call to the lost seal whose demise his heart and mind would not accept.

As the sea darkened into a dismal almost blackish green color and the once vivacious bubbles began to dissipate, Miracle experienced the pressures of the sea crush against his throbbing skull. Painfully, its grip suffered in comparison to the gaining heaviness of defeat pressing against his weary heart. As far as he could see, the mad seal was nowhere to be found. There were only endless shadows of despondent shades of blackish greens and even more voids of uninhabited nothingness left—that and the gnawing realization that she was gone. With a stringent thrust upward, he began to swim back to the open floes that flickered sinisterly above him. Not until he broke through the surface with the blind concentration of his despairing search still fresh on his shaken mind did he realize that Emma's voice was still calling to him. She had not once stopped her appeal and was crying out his name when another extraordinary and impressive thunder of firearms overrode her outcry.

Boom!—sounded the clamor of the hunter's killing machines!

It was not long before Emma and Miracle once again found each other. "She isn't there!" gagged the inconsolable seal.

Emma nodded nervously. "The hunters, they'll be here any moment!" she tried to explain through a distorted voice covered up with shakes and shivers, the tears and the burning cough having returned violently.

"And leave Mum?" barked the hyperventilating white seal, madly doggy-paddling against the stinging floes.

Boom! Boom! Boom! Three shots in a row split the air, each one louder and more vicious than the other.

Both Poo-Coo and Lukie had already begun to swim away from Emma and the white seal. "They're here!" Lukie squealed in a high-pitched hysterical voice, all the while wriggling back and forth inside the slushy waters.

"Quick!" the walrus howled. "If we cut through to that narrow strip of water, we could hide inside the caves of that old glacier. Once there, we can go down deep! With any luck, they won't find us!"

Emma turned to look at the icy monster that glistened red in the distance. Squinting, her tear-frozen eyes, she tried to get a better look at it. The sight of the glacier frightened her. Its twisted formation reminded her of a gnarled tree, distorted and weathered from age; and although its pursuit would undoubtedly be dangerous, once inside its concealed caverns, they might just elude the savage seal hunters. As she turned around to find the white seal, she could not help but watch the terrified Little Lukie. He was slapping at the water, looking as though he might drown before ever making it to the ancient ice rampart. Turning away, Emma suddenly spotted Miracle hoist himself out of the floe and back onto the red slushy island. Grabbing its slippery sides, she also pulled herself out with one forceful press. "We must leave this place," she said, shivering uncontrollably.

"I've got to find her!" the white seal barked, never turning around to look at her.

Boom!

This BOOM proved to be the loudest and the most dangerous. This one split the ice only inches between the girl and the writhing seal. With the sudden siege of the shaking ground, Emma fell down, knocking Miracle deep into the slushy ice. In a burst of uncontained emotion, she clutched tightly to the seal. All she could do was bury her face in his wet fur. The shock of her fall startled Miracle back to some semblance of rationality, for he remained still and hushed while the booming sounds stopped for a moment. He could feel Emma's heart beat wildly against his chest. It actually sounded louder than the powerful BOOM's the terrible hunters made.

After taking in a sudden gasp of breath, Emma spoke, her head pressed against the face of the white seal as she lay on top of him, shivering. "It is okay, Miracle," she said tearfully. "I understand. It's okay."

The white seal tried to catch his breath before he spoke. "Why didn't I wait for her? How could I have ever left her for one moment? She needed me, and I left her," he wailed. "I left her!"

"No," Emma begged. "It all happened so quickly. No one is to blame."

Miracle shook his head in remorse.

"Listen to me," Emma begged, her body shaking so much he could barely understand her when she said, "It wasn't your fault, Miracle."

"I'll never forgive myself, never, ever!"

"Please don't cry," she wept while sitting up. Taking the seal to her, she embraced him, allowing him to fill her arms. "Shhh . . ." Emma soothed with a shaking voice, all the while feeling the bitter torments of the cold consume her. "You mustn't do this. She wouldn't want you to."

Shamefully, the brokenhearted seal closed his eyes, the dreaded realization finally flooding over him like a breaking wave. "Oh, Mum . . . ," he wept in a muffled voice against the folds of Emma's steady embrace. "My poor Mum . . . forgive me . . . *Forgive me.*"

Miracle cradled himself inside Emma's arms and his tears seemed to go on forever, but again more gunshots came and both the girl and the seal knew that they had run out of time again. "Come," instructed Emma, struggling to stand up. "It's time to go!"

Resisting the dizziness wanting to pull her back down to the ice, she waited for the seal to pull himself up from the snow. He shook his wet coat, turned his gaze back toward the opposite direction of the floes, and looked out one last time to the place he last saw Mum. Lowering his heavy head, he closed his eyes, forever remembering her, leaving her with a prayer and a large part of his heart. A large single tear trickled off the side of his cheek and ran down the curve of his snout. He turned, preparing to follow the young girl before him.

The gunshots continued to blast all around them, but they didn't seem to notice. They were still grieving the loss of their dear friend, and not even the blasphemous yammers of the man-beasts or the shouts of their firearms could deter them now.

The white seal continued to struggle through the ice and snow, trying to keep up with Emma, wondering how the world could end and fall apart; and yet somehow it just didn't matter—not when your heart was broken.

THE LAST CLAP-CLAP

Mulgrew was the only one to see Mum fall into the icy pit.

It happened so quickly, yet the penguin could not help but witness the blur of flying, shining things swarming over the mad seal before she tumbled into the deep crater. From his position in the seashell cave, he was situated high enough that he could see the fascinating flight of mirrored flashes attack the crazy beast. Filled with a morbid curiosity and against the tenacious opposition of Crumpels's boisterous disapproval over the mere consideration of his leave from the cave, the feisty penguin defiantly shot across the ice away from the walrus and the two man-beasts he was told to guard. With an unintended comical swish to his tiny behind, the curious scurrying bird wiggled through the snow and ice, heading straight for the place he last saw the deranged seal.

It took Mulgrew a while to reach the spot, but his surprising persistence in the matter saw him through the bleeding heavens and still crumbling moon. Out of breath, the penguin neared the dark and shadowed opening in the earth, its wide and open mouth twisting with an oval gasp. He cautiously moved forward, looking both ways before proceeding, making sure he was alone. He could still hear Crumpels's annoying screams of outrage for his abandonment of his post when he dared draw closer to the spot where Mum disappeared. Then the bird took a deep swallow, steeping nervously onto the lip of the crusty ledge. The stupid seal had tumbled in headfirst, as he recalled.

Again, the penguin looked around, sniffing the air deeply before he dared go near. Then gathering up all his courage, he slowly moved further onto the icy ledge, his webbed feet sinking through the crust. Timidly, he crouched down into a squat and stretched out his neck, trying to see into the frozen pit. It was so dark that he was unable to see anything. Mistakenly but determined, the bird continued to stretch out his neck into the black shadows below, this time nearly falling in himself. The smashing sound of fear that his heart made deafened him. Among the drumming vibrations ringing inside his throbbing penguin skull, he heard something coming from inside the hole. Could the mad thing still be alive?

Quickly, he retracted his head, holding on to a queer smirk. "It's impossible," he said aloud. "No one could survive such a fall, no one, not even that slime-drooling hump-pig!" Mulgrew shook his head, insisting on listening again. Nervously, the tiny bird cleared his throat, rubbed his puny wings together, and began to make tiny clicking noises, his webbed feet once again breaking through the thin crust. Making sure he was extra careful, he grasped the sides of the ledge, leaning over, hearing the sound once more. The sound was faint but intensely real and distinct, nonetheless sounding like the moans and slurs of a drunken sot. It was at that moment the penguin recognized the distorted mumbling. After all, he had been unsparingly subjected to its senselessness so many times before!

"Mum!" called the penguin through a raspy voice, but no reply came. Moving a wee bit closer to the twisted mouth of the pit, Mulgrew called out again, trying to contain the shrill his throat was making. "Hey, bonehead, are you okay?" he asked, listening with all his might. Again, no sound echoed from within the dark shadows of the icy hole he warily crouched over. "Answer me, you clumsy hump-pig!"

Although no longer as intense as it had been, the shower of the moon rubble continued, sending his probing thoughts into hundreds of possibilities. The world was coming to an end, and there he was, sitting in front of a big hole in the ground, looking for a creature that was either dead or wasn't even there. Perhaps he imagined the whole thing. Come to think of it, his recollection of the queer and bizarre happening was already becoming hazy. Surely, he had been mistaken. After all, pieces of mirror, be they glass or ice, could never fly, nor have wings; it was preposterous! Just like the ridiculous makings of that stupid hump-pig seal! What had she ever done for him anyway? NOTHING! Nothing, except plague him again and again, making his life a living hell! Why should he care if she was alive or dead, if she was there or wasn't there! She was an idiotic, asinine, irrational, dangerous hump-pig and just one big sloppy mess and a pain in the penguin butt! She should have never been allowed to crawl on any part of the earth; she was that dastardly—she was! She was a menace to herself and everyone around her! Some man-beast hunter should have put her out of her miserable existence long ago! She was a stupid simpleton, an embarrassment to the entire species! Why, it was her fault that he was there now in this desolate place! And yet, and quite disturbed by this notion, if she was all of these things, *and she was*, why was he crouched over the icy hole looking down into its black and measureless mouth trying to find her?

"I must be as crazy as she is!" retorted the penguin as he shook his head, preparing to turn away, when suddenly he heard another sound from inside the shaded ice hole. It was a terrible and desolate noise, like the roaring of fantastic seas colliding against shallow caves. Mulgrew quickly retracted his tiny head from the edge of the hole as the sound continued. Surely, this could not be the preposterous hump-pig! This sound was much more intense and more serious than any sound she could ever produce. Frightened, yet more intrigued than anything else, he continued to listen as the rumbling noise intensified into an alarming blast before suddenly dying down into a murmuring of uncontrolled sobbing. More of the sky fell on the penguin. Still, he would dare listen for an unusually long time before deciding to do the unthinkable. He was actually going to crawl down in the hole! Could he truly be considering such a ludicrous action? He must have been hit in the head too many times by the moon! Still, there was a probing need to find out what exactly happened to the irritating beast that made his life so miserable these past godforsaken days. He would not ponder this decision long or he would surely abandon the entire unbelievable and absurd idea.

Mulgrew cleared his throat and closed his eyes, saying some kind of quick prayer as once more, the strong notion to analyze why he was doing what he was about to do came over him like a plowing punch to the belly. Unbelievably, and quite surprised himself, he dismissed his abandonment, realizing that if he did not go into that scary pit at that very second, he would never have another chance; he would most certainly change his mind.

"Mulgrew!" he called to himself. "You really are as crazy as she is!" He kept squawking while looking down into the pit. "Still, if I don't go down and they find out about it, they'll never let up! I'll be branded a coward for sure forever! No, for once in your life, even if it's over this stupid, fat, clapping, stinky, drooling moron, be brave, old bird! I'll show them that Mulgrew is no lily-livered pansy! Besides, if she's alive, this cliff, or whatever it is, can't be all that deep," reasoned the penguin. If he stretched himself out, he could carefully edge himself down an inch at a time. He would do this until he would at last find the bottom, that's if there was a bottom to this spooky hole.

"Of course there is! That nitwit seal is probably playing that stupid Clap-Clap game of hers right now. I swear if she's not dead when I get there she'll wish she was, stupid hump-pig! Can't believe she's making me do this! Well, I'm sure it isn't as steep as it looks," he again tried to convince himself, his voice suddenly picking up a nervous shrill. Unfortunately, the bird's calculations were way off, and the hole was indeed not only deep but way wider than he assumed. With a most disturbing holler and a high-pitched scream, Mulgrew dropped into the pit.

As he continued to scream out in absolute undisciplined hysterics, his tiny penguin body ricocheted mercilessly from side to side against the slippery walls. Then suddenly and most abruptly, perhaps too abruptly, and with the wind knocked clear out of his gasping lungs, the banged-about penguin came to discover that there was indeed a bottom to this nasty, butt-kicking pitfall. Mulgrew never remembered his backside sting and ache as much as it did at that moment. If it were not for the sound of the voice he next heard, he would have certainly bawled from the sheer pain of it.

"*Are you the Docta?*" the voice asked.

Mulgrew could barely see the seal at first for it was somewhat dark inside that hole, but as his eyes began to adjust to the shadows, he was able to see that he had landed on top of Mum's big cushioned belly. "Hump-pig, it *is* you! You're alive!" he chirped.

As the mad seal tried to sit up, she merely opened her mouth wide as if to scream. Although she did not cry out, if he listened extremely carefully, Mulgrew could hear it. It was the near-silent caresses of the flowing tears that brushed against her once silly-looking face, now anything but silly as she stared lifelessly straight up into the nothingness, her body covered with deep and bloody cuts and scrapes made visible by the existing light coming from the falling heavens above.

Regaining most of his breath, the tiny penguin continued to look down toward Mum, this time with eyes that were no longer filled with contempt. "What have you gotten yourself into this time? What has happened here?" he asked with a gasp, his eyes suddenly taking in her sliced-up form, its sight downright shocking him.

"I cannot move. My back is broken," said the mad creature with a smile so brave it startled the penguin. Aside from the terrible cuts she had sustained, Mulgrew was also shocked by what he heard. Had such rationality actually come from the demented seal? Not once had she ever made any sense to him. Not once had she, as far as he was concerned, ever relinquished any kind of sound statement; if she did, he had never paid any mind to it. She was such a stupid, crazed hump-pig not worth the bother.

However, when he once again looked upon her broken body hearing that horrible, desolate cry she made, sounding like a fantastic sea upon broken hollow caves, all the embitterment and resentment he had hatefully collected from the very beginning miraculously began to dissolve. Hearing the heartbreaking cries of the lacerated harpie he had once despised, he lowered his head in surprising shame and remorse. "Wow," he lamented, his voice in disarray. "They really messed you up, didn't they, kid?"

Mum tried once again to roll over, but even her madness could not pretend away what had happened to her. She knew it in her heart of hearts that she would never swim or move upon the earth ever again. She would soon die inside that dreadful hole, and there wasn't anything anyone could do for her.

Mulgrew gazed upon her with sad eyes, only to find the mad seal smiling again, trying to move her flippers together so she could play Clap-Clap; but the way her spine was damaged, she would never again move, let alone rejoice in the madness of her most cherished pastime. Slowly, he crawled over toward the seal's face, half standing on her bosom, lowering his head despairingly. "I'm very sorry, Mum," he managed to whisper.

"That's okay, pinhead, it's not your fault," the mad harpie replied, her smile still gracing her bruised-up snout, not sounding mad this time. The penguin watched her courageous smile fill her face as she spoke to him. "It's a bit sorry down here, being dark and all . . . kind of glad you dropped in."

"No problem," the penguin answered rubbing the sting out of his hurting buttocks, "thought you might need help."

"Oh, you heard the crying," Mum suspected. "Sorry about that, I promise not to do that again. I'm not such a scare-baby, you see. I'm usually quite—*Hot*, you know."

"I know," he agreed. "You're a lot of things, but a scare-baby, is not one of them."

Mum belched, and then smiled some more.

The penguin steadied his webbed feet between one of Mum's many folds, careful not to touch the wounds while sitting properly on top of her chest. He could see her eyes clearly from this spot. As her massive bosom heaved upward, he quietly sat there moving up and down, never once taking his eyes from the face of the paralyzed seal. "It's okay. I won't leave," he said in a small voice, his own words surprising him, riding the gripping flow of her breath. "Besides, I got nowhere else to go. Anything's better than hanging out with that stupid walrus anyway; the world's coming to an end, so there you go."

Mum kept right on smiling. "Yes, it does look a bit peaked up there, I say," she said, her nose a mass of mucus, her mouth bleeding and foaming a little on each side. "You surprise me, little bird. After all that has happened between us, you came for me."

Mulgrew gave her a quick smirk. "Now, now, don't get all mushy on me, I had to."

Mum closed her eyes, drenching her bloated cheeks with more tears this time. "It's funny, isn't it, birdie? About life, I mean. Sometimes the ones you least expect will be the ones to bring you comfort in the end."

The penguin scrunched up his beak, saying, "Now let's not get the wrong idea here. It's not that I like you or anything, it's just that . . . well . . ." He cleared his throat. "Well, I guess there were times if I must admit that I wasn't exactly, well . . . exactly nice to you either. In any case, someone had to come down here and check on you, you crazy loon. Besides, I was the only one around, so—anyway, it doesn't matter anymore. I'm here now, so let's just leave it at that, shall we?"

The dying harpie courageously kept on smiling, the tears washing over her snout, struggling to move her flippers together but quite unable to do so in any capacity. The penguin, very much out of character, went on to look compassionately at the seal, rising and falling there upon her chest. "Truth is, I had to come, not just for you, but for me too," Mulgrew astonishingly confessed, clearing his throat all over again, looking into the glazed eyes of the mad creature who could not move her head to look at him, her eyes permanently fixed upward. "I had to find you," he told her. "Despite the end of our world, you and me, and the deep blue sea, I knew that I had to find you."

Mum chuckled. "You sound like Crumpels with all, that rhyming hullabaloo."

"I'm trying to tell you something. Now will you let me finish?" Mulgrew snapped, waiting a few moments before he started up again. "No matter how much a pain in the butt you were, and let me tell you YOU WERE! I couldn't just leave you here, not without knowing . . . well, seeing if you were okay."

He sighed. "Well, the thing of it is," the penguin said, all keyed up, suddenly standing, frustrated as he continued, "like it or not, somehow you managed to become a part of all our lives despite yourself! And well, . . ." He ashamedly looked down at the dying harp's heaving bosom, determined to sit properly. "Family should never turn away one of its own. No matter what, we all come from the same place, at least that's what the big Captain Kishk insists on professing. And that's what you are . . . despite you and me and the whole goshdarn crumbling world, you are family."

The bird sighed again, sounding more at peace with himself that time. "So be that as it may, on behalf of the family, as I know they would have me do this, I am staying right here with you, you crazy babbling loon!"

Just then, a large snot bubble burst across the lips of the seal, her enormous smile swallowing it up. The only sensation she could experience besides her full and heavy heart was the tickling kisses her tears made as they rolled off her cheeks. "Thanks, little bird," Mum said with a faint whimper, her burning eyes lingering in their everlasting stare. "Sorry that I stunk on you." The penguin just rolled his eyes before staring down at her, all the while moving up and down. Suddenly, Mum's smile ran away as she confessed, "It's still with me, you know, the madness. It remains with me, even now. I am dying, and I can still feel the madness!" She began to cry in utter anguish.

"It's all right!" chirped the penguin. "It's all right! It doesn't matter anymore. Feel whatever it is you have to feel! Scream your bloody head off if you like!"

"If I did, it would be because I'm bloody angry . . . and yet so afraid," Mum confessed.

"Yeah, I know," replied the bird. "Me too, but I'm not going to leave you no matter what, so you might as well scream all ya like. Won't bother me none." He suddenly turned his head toward the falling skies above before returning his gaze to Mum. This time, it was filled with a peculiar, sincere wonder. "Does it hurt?"

Mum barely shook her head. "I cannot feel anything. Like I said, my spine has snapped," she told the bird before unexpectedly laughing. "Broken like an old crusty seashell." She then tried to clear the blood building up in her throat, asking, "Mulgrew, will you do one more thing for me?"

Without hesitation, the penguin nodded his head. "What is it?"

"Will you lie with me and look up at the falling sky? It's quite lovely, you know . . . yet, so lonely watching it all by me self, it is. All alone with no one to—*love ya, love, love.*"

At first the penguin was taken aback, but then unbelievably, Mulgrew grabbed for a small smirk to cover his beak. "Sure, why the heck not," he told her, uncoiling, careful not to drop off her chest. With his head nearly touching her chin, he laid back and looked up through the gaping hole in the earth's frozen crust, watching as the moon and the stars trickled through the heavens, falling upon the earth.

"I promised I wouldn't cry, tweedy-twit," wept the seal, "but just knowing that I will never again feel the coolness of the sea or ever play Clap-Clap again makes me sadder than I can imagine. My madness, it makes me even unhappier. It disgraces me, even now."

"Now, now, it is okay, just look up at the falling stars."

"Is he all right?"

"Who?"

"*Love-ya*—of course!"

"Yes, not to worry, I'm sure Miracle is fine. Now just watch the skies, there is some pretty nifty stuff happening up there, you know."

Mum tried to move again but only winced out in pain, blood oozing from the sides of her mouth, the tears saturating and burning her wounded cheeks.

Shaking his head, rolling up his eyes again, wondering how he could even contemplate such a task, Mulgrew slowly raised himself up. Reaching over to one side of the seal, nearly falling off, he firmly took hold of one of her inert flippers; and reaching over, stretching out as far as he possibly could, he took hold of the other. Grasping them both within his own frail flipper wings, he somehow brought her two lifeless flippers together before slumping backward, returning his gaze back up into the falling heavens. Remaining with the seal's flippers pressed inside his own, as if in prayer, he quietly and slowly began to pull both flippers apart and then carefully brought them back together, the tips barely touching. He repeated this over and over again, each time to be just a little faster than the last until he was once again making it possible for the paralyzed seal to play as she had done so many times before.

The penguin and the seal would exchange no further words. They would quietly lie there in teary wonder, watching a small piece of the sky burst across the heavens while the rhythm of Mum's breath softened and Mulgrew floated effortlessly upon her chest, holding her flippers, moving them back and forth in innocent playfulness, neither one of them afraid anymore. Neither one remembering their differences, but only aware of the way their hearts beamed expectantly as if they were young again; and together, playing Clap-Clap was as right and natural as the magical bliss of the sea, their home, a place they would almost certainly never again return.

Ancient Glacier

Big Petie had once again found Little Lukie surpassing all odds, eventually meeting up with the others. It was a short but joyous reunion, for the constant sounds of the hunters' guns quickly reminded them that there was not much time for celebrating.

The water felt colder than Emma had ever remembered; however, in a little while, she would not feel anything—she was already numb and turning a dull blue color. Although she continued to hold on to the white seal, she could no longer feel her fingers. From time to time, she was not sure if she was actually gripping the moving creature she rode upon. Miracle kept talking to her, making sure she was all right, but the cold was so severe that she was unable to speak. Petie and Lukie swam next to the white seal, their shining dog-shaped heads moving through the waters, each looking on with terror-filled eyes that remained fixed to the mighty glacier towering before them. Poo-Coo was nearly at the front of the ice formation, when the dreaded sounds of more gunshots split the frosty air. Emma clutched blindly to the wet and freezing fur of Miracle, her head falling backward, forcing her to look straight into the red-painted skies. More than half of the moon had been eaten away; the small part that remained curiously reminded her of the Cheshire cat's smile in *Alice in Wonderland*, but, of course, the storybook's crescent-shaped grin had never dripped with such a dreaded blood color.

She closed her eyes tightly and felt them freeze against her lashes. When she opened them, she could still see and feel the snowy fallout from the chaotic heavens, and the way the universe swirled above her made her shiver with nausea. The planets that could only be seen as distant stars—Mars, Jupiter, and Venus—were now as close as the moon was to the earth. It was as if each planet had suddenly fallen from their high places, their trajectory close, rotating dangerously near one another. Suddenly, Mars seemed to be even closer to earth than the Cheshire cat moon with its blood-filled grin. The red glowing planet hung there like a broken yo-yo, its string hopelessly tangled up in some cluster of dying stars. Emma shut her eyes again, trying to remember fleeting moments of unremembered fear, but the panic-filled voice of the white seal who continued to uphold her would quickly end her faded recollection.

"We're almost there!" Miracle shouted, his voice heightening with chills and freezing rawness.

"Hurry up!" Lukie barked, both he and Big Petie nearing the towering glacier. The seals leapt as they had never leapt before. Up and down they splashed in a neurotic sea dance, accelerating, dashing along. "The man-beasts are coming! The man-beasts are coming!" Lukie shrieked.

By the time Miracle and Emma reached the mountainous ridge, Emma was shivering so badly she could hardly move. Her teeth chattered and assaulted her mouth ruefully, and her lips had turned a blackish blue color. More gunshots rocked the air, and once again Lukie screamed out. "They're here! They're here!" And from the nearness of the gunfire, the terrified seal was surely correct in his assumption.

"Quick, Emma," Miracle pleaded. "You must climb onto the ridge, hurry!"

Emma nodded her frozen head, and hearing the crack that her skin made when she moved caused her to shudder all the more. Somehow finding the strength, she pulled herself from the seal and pathetically fell upon the icy base of the glacier as if dead, her eyes closed. Miracle hastily joined her. Sensing that the girl had given all that she was able, he instinctively opened his jaws and fastened them around the stiff and frozen parts of her blue robe. With the height of fear pulsating through his veins, Miracle rigorously pulled Emma along, hurrying backward toward the entrance of the cavern. Another gunshot gutted the air! Lukie gave out another one of his strident screams just before he dove into the breach of the glacier, its opening only a few feet from the rimming seam of stiff waters that tenaciously licked at its stern foundation like a dog to an open wound.

Miracle lost his grip twice as he wildly dragged Emma's cold and exhausted body along, the blue resistant robe made hard by the harsh elements nearly the same color as her chilled skin. The white seal regained his hold on the girl, twisting the frozen material of the gown around his jaws, persistent in his backward and frantic race toward the entrance of a small tunnel, where, with any luck, would lead them to lower places somewhere inside the gigantic glacier. He could hear Lukie's ongoing screams as he neared the entrance. A blast of gunpowder from the exploding weapons of the zombielike men splintered over the side of the glacier, showering a massive dose of ice and snow over the hurrying and out-of-breath seal. With a flip of his head, he wiggled crazily toward the lifeless legs of Emma. Taking her frozen blue-colored feet into his mouth, he began dragging her further into the cave.

Emma's eyes suddenly fluttered, and she became conscious. She reached out her numb fingers, pulling and clawing at the sides of the icy hole, trying to help the seal along, both falling into a deep shaft, one of the many chambers belonging to this ancient ice giant. Emma could not feel her backside when she hit the bottom or she would have cried out in pain. Everything was numb, all except her thoughts. They were still terribly raw and feeling every part of fear and uncertainty snarling and growling all around her like some monstrous beast. Before Miracle could speak with her, Emma was suddenly aware of the howl coming from the walrus. In a wild voice, Poo-Coo called out to them. "This way!" he called, waiting for the rest to join him at the next level of descent.

Lukie and Big Petie were already at the second icy tunnel requiring them to crawl into, when more gunshots shattered the endless walls of the icy maze. Seeing that she was once again able, Miracle looked on as Emma turned herself around and began to crawl toward the place where the walrus and the two seals were frantically waiting. She pulled herself along as her stiff and frozen robe crunched and scraped the narrow space inside. Miracle tried to push at her backside, giving her added momentum while they hurriedly wormed along the stretch of the icy surface.

"You're almost there!" Petie cheered as Lukie unexpectedly and skittishly wet the icy floor beneath him. Too nervous to move, the soiled seal sat in his pool of acrid excitement until Miracle and Emma finally joined them.

"Hurry," shouted the walrus. "We must descend even lower so that we can beat these savages! They are more cunning than I ever thought possible! Quick," Poo-Coo instructed, "the girl first!" Too exhausted to argue, Emma nodded and reached inside the irregular and bumpy lip of the hole she would have to crawl into. It was totally pitch-dark and foreboding, but she had no other choice but to enter; she could hear the gunshots of the hunters approaching even then. Miracle gave her as much of his strength as possible and waited for her to begin to crawl inside. He quickly followed, then Big Petie, but when the walrus asked Lukie to enter, the suddenly embarrassed seal responded with a mere "After you."

"Dude, look, if you're worried about your little accident—don't bother. If you don't get into that hole right now, your mucky pee puddle won't be the only thing splattered all over the floor! Now get in there!" shouted the aggravated walrus.

"All right, all right!" snapped the harrowed seal. "I'm going! I'm going!" Lukie barked, leaping into the hole. However, before scurrying on his way, Little Lukie quickly turned himself halfway around and finished off by telling the walrus, "There's no need to get all snotty about the whole thing—*neither!*"

"Will you just move it!" Poo-Coo shouted with a sharp growl, swatting the head of the soiled-up seal with a quick smack of his flipper, pushing Lukie down into the twisted cavern of the elongated tunnel.

It seemed as if this particular passage went on forever. Emma was not sure if she possibly could go any further. If it weren't for the help that the seals gave her, she would have never made it. Down they all went, winding and twisting within the tight confines of the tunnel, two by two, Miracle and Emma, Petie and Lukie, and finally Poo-Coo, remaining in constant awareness of the relentless and pursuing man-beasts always just a gunshot behind them.

Through the long hallway of glass they crawled, its dark and translucent runway smooth and clean as if having just been polished, making their quest for sanctuary in the submerged caves all the more difficult. Still, each one remained constant in their pursuit. A cold blast of icy wind had found its way beneath the open caverns and twisting corridors. The eerie moans and groans it made while passing over Emma and the others sounded like screaming ghosts, wild and filled with more menace, making for another reason to squirm through the winding drawn-out tunnel all the faster. When Miracle and Emma reached the end of the passage, they each made semiturns on the ice, waiting for the others to reach them. From the very rear of the connected chain, Poo-Coo motioned with his head, indicating for them to yet once again descend to lower levels.

"This should be the place," the walrus said.

"What will we find there?" the white seal asked.

"Great blue caverns! Once inside, it will be very hard for the humans to find us there. The passageways below us are very tight. There are many of them, hundreds, maybe even thousands. It's like a maze down there, I know. This is not the first time I was inside one of these giant behemoths."

"How far are we from these blue caves?" Miracle questioned his voice breathy and weak.

"They should not be far now, but we must go deeper still, bro!"

"Listen," Petie exclaimed.

An unusual silence prevailed along the eerie cries of the whistling wind that was still following them. "What? I don't hear anything *neither!*" Little Lukie retorted nervously.

"That's just it," Petie said. "No man-beast and their noisy fire blasts."

"Do you think we lost them?" a terrified Lukie asked.

The walrus quickly spoke up. "I doubt it. Come; take any of the passageways ahead. Any of them should lead us down into the caverns. Now hurry!"

"How do you know so much about these caverns?" nervously asked Lukie, feeling as if he was about to wet himself again.

"I already told you, bro. You've seen one giant ice cube, you've seen them all. These vestige titans are all alike," spouted Poo-Coo, his broken tooth seriously hurting, however never saying a word about it to anyone.

Miracle quickly looked at the nearest opening and then looked back at Emma. Drowsing sickly before him, she tried to give him a faint smile, letting him know that she was ready to follow. The white seal returned a smile and gently rubbed his wet and icy head against her blue-colored cheek. Then quickly turning he began to squish and squeeze himself into the tight-fitting hole found in the side of the tunnel. Emma followed. Thinking she was stuck and having no more strength left to tug and push, Petie pressed his head up against her backside, popping her inside with a wet swish. Lukie also managed to get through the tiny porthole, but the walrus would not be that fortunate.

Miracle called out to him from inside the passageway, "Poo-Coo, what's wrong?"

"Dude, you'll have to go on without me. I will never fit . . . thought as much."

"But we can't go on without you! We need you! Please try!"

The walrus, knowing this moment was a definite possibility because of his size, remained silent for a moment. "No. I will have to find you below."

"Please, Poo-Coo, try. You simply must come with us!"

"I'm afraid not, my bro, don't worry, I will find you. I promise. There are hundreds of openings inside this old relic. I'll find one that will accommodate me, now hurry, we haven't much time!"

At that very moment, and with a terrifying jolt, another shot shattered through the whistling hallway. "Oh no!" screamed Lukie.

"Good luck, my friends!" were the last words Miracle and the others heard from the walrus before another gunshot cracked the air. With a jerk and a tremble, the white seal began to hurriedly crawl through the icy tubing. The walrus was right; these tunnels were much more confined. He could no longer turn and see if Emma was behind him. All he could do was pray that she would still be there when he was able to turn around again.

All at once, the close-fitting runway turned exceptionally dark.

Just as he proceeded to call back to Emma, everything below him suddenly caved in and down he fell into what seemed to be an incredibly long shaft. Thinking he would never hit bottom, he suddenly felt the cold splash of frigid water prove otherwise, its blast stabbing all over him. Miracle sprang open his eyes, and the blue-gray color of the sea burst about him. Instantly, another splash exploded in front of him. It was Emma. He watched her and her frozen blue robe descend into the water. As her garment turned downy again, wavering in effortless levitation imitating the graceful dance of a jellyfish, her arms and hair, as well as the many extensions of her robe, wafted ghostlike within the shadows of the moving blue-gray waters. Slowly, she began to sink to the bottom, her eyes closed as she began to disappear into the murkiness. In a flash, Miracle had her robe between his jaws. Higher and higher he pulled her while muted splashing sounds erupted all around him, millions of effervescent bubbles egging him onward. He finally broke the seal of the waters with a surging gasp. Emma immediately followed, her hair exploding in endless disarray like a freshly popped bottle of champagne. Its wet, sticky mass pasted itself heavily over the twitching snout and eyes of the seal, temporarily blinding him. However, when Miracle washed her golden locks away, her lovely face came into view once more. With her eyes still fixed shut and her mouth opened slightly, she appeared to be sleeping, but the seal knew otherwise. He had to get her out of the water and fast before it was too late, if it wasn't already.

Petie and Lukie were expressly at Miracle's side, helping him along, surrounding the unconscious girl in the flowing blue gown, each pulling her toward the shallow part of this newly discovered cavern. When at last they were out of the water, the seals dragged Emma onto the ice. Petie and Lukie immediately shook themselves dry like wet dogs, each one doing so as far from the lifeless girl as would allow. Miracle never left her side. Lowering the stone near Emma's lips, Miracle waited for Emma to open her eyes, but she never did. Allowing her tiny head to fall into the cushion of his furry chest, he waited as Petie and Lukie situated her inanimate body comfortably around his.

"Is she dead?" Lukie squeaked.

"Emma, *Emma!*" cried Miracle.

Suddenly, she came to life as an overflow of seawater poured from her blue lips. She coughed and spit up more of the cold and salty essence of the sea but never opened her eyes. With a heaving chest, she raised her head for a moment and then let it fall limply back down into the softness of the seal.

"Poor thing," Lukie lamented.

"What's going to happen to her?" Petie asked, all the while keeping his weary eyes on her moving chest, secretly hoping that it would keep on working that way. Nevertheless, from the way she looked, Petie was no longer sure she would make it. She had turned an almost entirely bluish gray color by then, and her lips began to change into the color of white coral. Her frail hands were bruised, and they appeared to be bloodless. If it were not for the bluish color in her skin, she could have easily passed for a ghost.

"What's going to happen to us?" Lukie questioned, turning from the girl, looking around the endless caverns of twisted formations of ice and water. The large pool in the middle, as well as the massive walls surrounding it, were all painted a deep and penetrating blue color, making them, especially Emma, appear even more ghostly. Illumination from somewhere above and beyond made the place come alive with thousands of different prisms of light, all of them blue and perforating. An icy breathing murmur shifted between the rocky walls of ice. The hanging ceiling of the berg shimmered and swam with the same etching shafts of dancing blue-gray radiance painted over everything, catching the light like a stained-glass window in some ascending cathedral. Streams of glowing water were still cascading down its sides, and there were peculiar and unremitting cracking noises escaping from the many fractures protruding from surfaces where breaks and extreme cleaves remained, left from the long-forgotten years belonging to this hundred-thousand-ton giant.

Lukie surprisingly ventured out to the very edge of the surrounding pool. Carefully and extremely slowly, he wriggled there. Placing his wiggling nose on the water, he sniffed and then raised his head back to meet with the incredible grandeur of the secret place they had come upon. The awesomeness of its magnitude with its alluring blue colors of reflecting light seemed to frighten the seal. He quickly found his way back to Miracle, Petie, and the blue girl who still remained lifeless. "Will she be all right?" he asked, sounding as though he was about to cry.

Miracle did not answer directly. Not sure what answer to give, he swallowed hard. Then daring to defy any uncertainties, he quickly told the seal, "Yes yes, she will be!"

"She is so blue. I may not know much about man-beasts, but I don't think they're supposed to be that color *neither*," Lukie lamented.

Miracle fought the tears back, explaining, "She's going to be all right!" he protested. "She has to be!" He placed his weary head against her tiny face, pressing it softly against her closed eyes.

Looking fearfully sad, Petie sighed, gazing away from the girl and into the massive canyon of melting waters and the blue exhibits of reflected lights, merging and bouncing just about everywhere. "I wonder if the others are safe," he said in a small and worried voice while Lukie nodded, fighting off a sudden shiver as he wondered along.

Miracle remained silent; his head still pressed against Emma's while the image of his mother painted a watery portrait of her face upon his mind's eye. He wondered if she too was lying still as was Emma and if anyone was there to protect and remain with her just as he remained with Emma. More tears filled up his black and shining eyes, the thousand reflections of the blue shimmers dancing significantly within his gaze. He wondered of Nikki, Bellgar, and their child, Promise; of Poo-Coo, Crumpels, and the ridiculous penguin; of Emma's brother and the man-beast that came with him. He thought of the diabolical witch and her evil servant. He thought of his dear friend Kishk and where he was at that precise moment. He thought of the horrible seal hunters who could find them at any moment inside this most mysterious and secluded world of blue splendor, hidden deep inside the giant monster of ice created long before any of them came into existence. He continued to remember all the mother seals and their pups, wondering if they had escaped the vicious hunters and their explosive weapons—that and the end of the world, and then he thought of Mum. He could not help but feel his heart break again. Surely his heart must have had a thousand lives, for it had died a thousand times before and was yet still able to perish for the one thousand and one time. More guilt and remorse refilled itself over the white seal as he lifted his wearied head from Emma's blue face. He looked frantically to see her shallow breath move her chest up and down. Seeing that it did, he let out a momentary sigh of relief and once again returned his eyes back toward Emma's dormant features. She still looked as if she was asleep, but she was exceptionally blue, almost purple now. That's when Miracle thought of the purple angels she so often spoke of and how they came once before to help her.

Suddenly, turning away from Emma, he looked out into the blue reflections of light, calling out imploringly, "Please, if you can hear me, help us. Whatever purple angels are or where they come from, I do not know, but I do know Emma believes in you, and I believe in Emma, so you just have to be real. Please, if you can hear me—please help her—please help her now!"

A strange surge of wind suddenly appeared out of nowhere. It stirred up the water, chasing the blue reflections of light in a multitude of endless directions. Then everything got unusually quiet again.

The only sound remaining was the trickling and gurgling slurps the cascading waters made as it continued to rain over the icy walls of the breathing glacier. Lukie and Petie were looking at each other with questioning eyes when the extreme quiet came over the place. "Who are you talking to?" Lukie asked while the waters gurgled and the blue reflections danced over his inquisitive face.

Miracle remained silent for a moment, still looking out, still watching, still waiting. Sadly, only more of the same sputtering and babbling of the cave answered him.

"Who are you looking for?" asked Petie with eyes the size of giant seashells.

Miracle continued his silence just a bit longer before answering in a whisper, "The purple angels."

A queer expression suddenly melted over Lukie, drawing closer, wondering, *"The purple angels?"*

"Yes," Miracle answered, his tired and burning eyes still hopefully gazing out into the dancing blue lights of the cave.

Lukie and Petie looked at one another again and then slowly wriggled away from Miracle and the girl, heading for the edge of the pool that glistened and shone profusely. Both listened carefully and searched for something, anything, which possibly might be what the white seal called purple angels, whatever that may have turned out to be. However, just as it had done all along, the only semblance of some kind of presence was the moving shadows and the same blue chaotic, rhythmic lights. This: and the same perpetual trickling noise that the glacier made, and that was all.

Again, Lukie breathed the air, this time harder and longer, saying in a plaintive voice, "Nope, I don't think they're here—*neither.*"

Petie also sniffed hard, searching through the mesmerizing flicker of shimmering light reflections. He then placed a rather discouraged frown upon his snout, most disappointed that the purple angels, what or whoever they were, never bothered to show up.

"Guess you're right." Petie sighed. "There's nobody out there."

The seal's discouraging words cut into Miracle's heart like a sword. Still, he continued to look out into the glitter of the waters before him. Although painful and disheartened, he knew that the bulls were right. There was no one there—no one.

With a definite defeat to their slow and unsteady wriggle, both seals returned to Miracle and the unconscious shivering and purple-colored Emma. For the first time in a long time, even though Lukie, Petie, and Emma remained beside him, the white seal felt eerily afraid, very frustrated, and worst of all, very much alone. Miracle began to lick at Emma's cold face, hoping to revive her, but all that he managed to create was even more shivers for the girl.

"Please don't die," whispered the white seal, staring woefully at his dear companion, her tiny body quivering with disturbing spasms of hypothermia, her eyes fixed shut.

The sight of the once-vibrant stone about his neck suddenly caught his eye. The shade of the stone had nearly turned a deep charcoal black, its colorless futility filling the seal with even more despair. Suddenly, everything seemed to be hopeless. Overwhelmed with fear and defeat, Miracle quickly closed his eyes, sinking into the shivers of the dying purple girl. He tried to keep her trembling body as still and as warm as possible while Petie and Lukie returned to the edge of the pool, searching once again for the curious purple angels that would never show up.

WHEN ALL THE LIGHTS WENT OUT

Kishk watched more of the sky fall apart. The changing colors in the surges of unusual dark green clouds told him that this dreadful night was about ready to explode. Whatever was about to happen was about to happen, and soon!

Directly, an even greater darkness began to overtake the island, making it nearly impossible to see. The whale grew most worried, not because the sky was still falling apart. Not because it was growing increasingly dark and ominous, not because the world was about to end, but because he could no longer hear any kind of sound coming from the other creatures around him. In fact, he could no longer see any of them, including the recently discovered chanters. For this reason and for the sudden realization that he no longer knew the whereabouts of Miracle and the others, his heart fluttered with considerable uneasiness. All that remained visible were the heavens, and he did not like what was happening up yonder, not one bit, and would have wished to remain uninformed about its progress just the same. Nonetheless, there were still shafts of unknown spilling light of green and reds, making it possible to watch its alarming furtherance. The way the hanging planets hung there swaying before him, all colored and bathed in the approaching darkness of the universe, made him feel light-headed and faint. Then the whale felt the sea begin to tremble.

Perhaps this is the end, thought the chanter, feeling forlornness consume him. Never had he felt so alone and afraid. He turned himself around inside the turbulent pull of the sea, not knowing where to look, not knowing where he was. He was suddenly lost! It was as if Sealssong had suddenly vanished and he was somewhere out in the middle of nowhere. Even the falling sky began to evaporate inside a shroud of empty darkness. He quickly turned about inside the raging waters, again calling out for the other blue chanters who were there with him only moments before. Still, he could see or hear nothing, their glorious voices vanquished. For in its place, a great void of gloominess replaced their optimistic song with a sonnet of off-key despondencies. Again, Kishk called out to the sea, praying she would answer him; but only utter and absolute silence acknowledged his summons. Before everything went pitch-black, Kishk heard the entire planet scream out as if in pain—then go deathly quiet.

*   *   *

Crumpels was still grumbling and complaining about Mulgrew's sudden and most unsuitable behavior in the matter of his irresponsible abandonment. She angrily griped inside that seashell of a cave, continuing her watch dutifully in the midst of making sure that everything was all right with the humans; they had not stirred since the dreadful penguin left her to fend for herself, and this worried her. Checking them promptly, she made sure that they were still alive and breathing, when suddenly she noticed that it was getting most suspiciously darker than she thought the night was supposed to get. So she decided to investigate.

In the moments that followed, the walrus felt panic swell inside her throat while approaching the opening of the secluded cave. The contorted and fearful expression on her face was only a few inches from the threshold when the sky looked as though it had dropped right out of the heavens, turning everything totally pitch-black. Then she felt something twist itself around her neck and proceed to squeeze the breath out of her.

*   *   *

Miracle's head jolted from Emma's limp shoulders when all the lights went out. Little Lukie shrieked as Big Petie scrambled about in the darkness, trying to locate the screaming seal, only able to find him by the high-pitched yelps that Lukie kept hurling out. Claiming his companion, Petie blindly escorted Lukie back up the icy slope. Fumbling about, both seals eventually found Miracle and the dying Emma. "What's going on?" Petie barked, flopping one of his flippers over Lukie's mouth just before the screaming seal started up again. "Where did all the lights go?"

Miracle did not answer. Merely raising himself from the cold surface he occupied, careful not to disturb the lifeless form of Emma, the white seal stretched out his neck, furthering it out into the darkness. "Everything is so dark; there is no light at all—anywhere!"

Lukie quickly pulled his head away from Petie's flipper, crying out in an even higher-pitched scream, "I want to go home!" The terrified harp's thunderstruck howl ricocheted into the cave, bouncing and echoing everywhere for a long time before it eventually surrendered to the prevailing dead silence.

"Listen," Miracle said in a hushed, but forceful tone.

"What?" Lukie whimpered, secretly sullying the icy floor beneath him. "I don't hear nothin' *neither!* It's as quiet as a graveyard!"

"That's just it!" Miracle answered. "It's as though everything just stopped!"

"I'm so scared!" Lukie wailed.

"It isn't going to help to scream!" Petie warned. "Something has happened out there, something frightening!"

Miracle quietly crunched back down into the unconscious Emma. He listened for her heartbeat. It was extremely weak, but she was still alive. Her shivers had temporarily lessened because her body was no longer convulsing against his the way it had been. "The whole world is still," Miracle said in a small voice.

"Miracle," Petie uttered, blindly pushing himself nearer to the white seal and the man-beast he protected. "I'm scared too."

Suddenly, Lukie popped out from the middle of the Big Petie and Miracle seal sandwich he had squirmed into. "What was that?" he yipped with a terrified gulp, his eyes widening with absolute fear.

Miracle listened carefully, but only the supreme emptiness of soundlessness intensified over the pitch-black cave. Even the trickling of water cascading over the icy walls had been muted. "What is it, Lukie?" Miracle asked, shuddering inside the darkness.

"Didn't you hear it?"

"Hear what?"

"That noise!"

"What noise?"

"Shhh," Lukie interrupted with alarming compulsion. "There it is again!"

Miracle heard nothing. About to break the silence with additional exasperation, all at once and quite clearly, he heard it!

"There!" Lukie exclaimed, furrowing his seal brow while he uncontrollably wet the ice again, "told ya so!"

Again, the sound came.

"I guess you didn't hear that *neither!*" a terrified Lukie squealed. "What is that?"

Petie nervously stretched out his neck into the surrounding darkness. "Sounded close!"

"Yep," Lukie nervously retorted, finishing off with another acrid squirt.

Miracle cocked his head in the blindness of the shadows. "It sounded like a cry or whimper. Perhaps someone needs our help."

"Or maybe someone has come to help us!" hastened Petie.

"Shhh," Lukie hushed. "There it is again!"

This time the sound was stronger, and this time it could most certainly be identified as a whimper. "I was right," Miracle said. "Someone is crying. Someone is hurt!"

Again, the whimper came this time with a voice. "Help me," it called.

In grilling silence, they sat as if having suddenly been struck mute until Miracle broke the groping speechlessness. "Who is it?"

"Help me, please help me!" the voice begged.

Lukie suddenly blurted out, "Don't talk to it!"

"Don't be silly, someone needs our help," the white seal said, raising himself from the huddled circle that they had all formed. "Where are you? I can't see anything. Please tell me how I can find you."

Petie spoke out before the voice could answer. "Maybe Lukie is right. What if it's a ghost or something?"

Miracle did a double take toward Petie's frightened voice. "Why, Big Petie, I'm surprised. I might expect that from Lukie, but not from you."

Lukie became infuriated. "Hey, wait a minute!"

"Hush now!" Miracle warned as the voice once again spoke out into the absolute dark shadows.

Once again, they could all hear the voice speak. "I've been wounded by the man-beasts. Please don't let me die alone, not like this!" The plea sounded desperate as it hauntingly echoed about them.

"Hey, wait a minute *again!* I know that voice!" Lukie animatedly declared.

"Come to think of it," agreed Petie. "It does sound familiar."

Miracle slowly nodded his head inside the darkness. "You know, you're right. There is something very familiar about it."

"Please help me," cried the voice.

A sharp tingle struck Miracle's heart, the sudden recognition of what was calling out from the darkness becoming abundantly clear to him. Just as he was about to say the name, something equally strange and surprising happened. All the lights came back on again. Lukie screamed, and so did Petie.

Marco Rosato

A returned deluge of blue flickering lights descended over the cave, wild in dance; millions of fractions of splintered rays of shimmer washed plentifully over everything. "What's going on?" Petie barked while Lukie urinated uncontrollably, and Miracle looked down to the unconscious and dying Emma. He watched the scintillating lights swarm all over her, making her look like a beautiful apparition from heavenly places. Again, he checked her breathing. She was still alive, but he knew they were rapidly running out of time; they were always running out of time, and it was maddening. No matter what the cost, he could not just sit there and watch her die. He had to do something, but what?

The familiar voice sounded again. "Please help me!"

"Don't let it in *neither!*" Lukie begged.

"I have to," Miracle explained.

"But you don't realize who it is!"

Miracle nodded affirmatively. "Yes, I do. It's Jillith."

"Jillith!" Petie exclaimed. "What's that dastardly thing doing here?"

"She's back from the dead, I tell you!" Lukie squealed. "She's come to kill us!"

"She'll do nothing of the sort," Miracle said, gently leaving Emma. He looked back at the unconscious girl with a grating sadness that dulled his eyes. How he hated to leave her but for a moment. Knowing it could not be helped, he began to wriggle toward the side of the cave where the cries and whimpers of the injured Jillith were emanating.

"I'm warning you," Lukie pleaded. "Don't let it in!"

Miracle apprehensively continued to wriggle through water and ice toward the voice. "Jillith, is that you?"

"Yes!" confirmed the voice. "I followed you! The man-beasts tried to kill me! They thought they had, but they failed. Oh, Miracle, I have been so wrong about everything!"

The white seal thought for a moment, nearing the wall from where Jillith waited. "How can you even expect me to trust you? You have done unspeakable things. Terrible things! You betrayed us all!"

The voice of Jillith began to cry. "I know I will have to pay for what I did in some way, but surely you can find compassion for me now. I'm wounded. I'm dying, Miracle."

Miracle did not answer her.

"Please," Jillith begged. "They'll be back soon! Don't let them find me! They will find you too and do unthinkable things to us all!"

"You mean the witch?" Miracle barked.

"Yes! She hates all seals! She used me to find you, to hurt you! She tricked me! She tricked us all!"

"Don't believe it!" Lukie screamed. "And don't let it in! She's lying! She's lying!"

"No," Jillith begged. "You must believe me! Please, I'm hurt real bad. Don't leave me like this. Please have mercy, have mercy!"

"Don't listen to it!" a panicked Lukie insisted.

Torn between his doubts, Miracle knew he could not allow the seal hunters to kill Jillith. True, what she did was unthinkable and cruel, but in his heart of hearts, he could not allow her to be left to the murderous ways of man. He would help the dying seal.

"Don't do it! Don't do it!" Lukie cautioned one last time before he buried his head inside the numerous rolls of Big Petie's extensive blubbery chest.

The particular place that Jillith had found turned out to be a fortunate spot. Miracle could almost see her shadowy form on the other side of the icy wall. If he started to dig, he could break through to reach her. Quickly, the white seal went to work. Crouching down as close as he could near the thin wall of ice, his little flippers began to hurriedly scrape against its gaunt surface. In just a short time, he had dug an opening straight through to the other side. He could see the form of the injured Jillith plainly. "Can you crawl through?" he asked, all out of breath.

Jillith shook her head. "I don't think so."

Miracle nodded. "Very well, I'll come for you. I think I can pull you inside without too much trouble."

The ailing Jillith slowly raised her head, saying, "Thank you, thank you, dear friend."

Miracle crouched down again and began to crawl through the tiny opening he had created. He was at Jillith's side in only a matter of moments. Looking into her burning eyes, he said, "Don't worry, it is going to be all right. I'll try to get you inside without hurting you."

Jillith offered him a weak smile along with one of her flippers to aid the seal in getting a better grip on her so he could slip her into the passageway without too much difficulty. "We're almost there," Miracle said, tugging and pulling the damaged harp along. "Just a little bit further," huffed and puffed an out-of-breath Miracle. Both seals came through the freshly dug passageway, then, once again, everything turned to black. This did not occur because the lights had been switched off again. This happened because the suddenly smashing weight of Jillith's bashing flipper against the back of his skull, crushing his snout into the wet ice and snow beneath him, made it so!

Miracle tried to push his head out from under the cutting chips of ice, but Jillith was still slapping and punching at him with all her might, making it impossible to get any kind of leverage away from the blackness suffocating him. The evil, lying and treacherous Jillith laughed wickedly, pushing the seal's head down deeper into the ice. "Stupid, gullible little wimp, you *are* a fool!" She laughed madly.

Despite the packed-tight pressure of ice and snow caked in his nose, coupled with the excruciating throbbing pain drumming inside his head, Miracle could hear Lukie's wild, insane screams cutting through the air like piercing arrows. How could he have ever trusted Jillith? He should have known better! Why, even Lukie had more sense than he.

Oh, why didn't I listen to Lukie? He shamefully thought, trying to breathe through the smothering hold. *WHY?* Then strangely, Miracle abruptly stopped his struggling and just remained still, half buried in the slushy ice of the glacier. His direct instinct would prove to be valid, for just as he did this, he felt the abrasive assault of Jillith leave him. He could, however, still hear Lukie's wild screams. When the mad and echoing yelps and barks of Petie suddenly joined in splattering themselves over the resounding walls, Miracle's blood froze. Both screaming bulls sounded as if they were being flogged, or worse! With a wild thrust, he pulled his saturated head from the ice and snow. What he saw made his stomach flip with nausea and made him feel faint in the head.

Before him a mere twenty or so feet away stood Decara!

She was dressed entirely in black. A long and lengthy robe, that of which seemed to crack and sizzle with electric discharges, squirmed out from every part of her. Her black and shining hair remained undone and worn long over her thin shoulders, utterly disappearing into the black shadows of her massive robe. Her eyes were wild, like two burning embers. Her flesh was ghostly white, making the pulsating veins in her forehead more defined and intrusive. Her mouth was drawn back into a snarl, and there was a strange and irritating humming noise buzzing all around while a peculiar surge of howling wind consumed her, making the flowing black like tentacles of her discursive robe take flight about her. The humming grew, piercing and reverberating, further making Miracle feel sick and nauseous with terror. The ultimate cause for the sick spasms taking place in his stomach was not because of any of the previous mentioned. This great feeling of absolute sickness came from what the terrible woman was holding across her arms.

It was Emma!

The lifeless and precious form of his dear friend was sprawled out, hanging limp and twisted like a broken doll within the skeleton clutches of the witch! He immediately tried to go to Emma, but a sudden and most painful slam from both of Jillith's flippers sent the white seal crashing back into the ice. Having no intention of staying down for the count this time, Miracle quickly pulled up his head, shaking the ice and snow from his throbbing snout. He tried to snap at Jillith, but was unable. Instead, he once again looked at the figure of the witch and the unconscious body of Emma. He noticed that neither bulls were anywhere in sight. All that he could see was the evil witch, Jillith, Emma, and that monstrous and enormous black cloak billowing wickedly about like the shredded, torn-up, out-of-control sails on a doomed vessel in the middle of a horrible storm. Again, he tried to go to Emma, and again the determined and cruel Jillith smashed him down.

"Just don't give up, do ya, freak?" she scoffed with a heartless grin. Persistently, Miracle tried to get up, and persistently Jillith was pressing her mammoth weight directly on his spine. He felt as if it was about to snap. Somehow managing to raise his torso far enough to look directly at the witch, he howled out a wrathful bark, but this time, both the witch and Emma were gone!

He suddenly heard muffled laughter coming from the corner of the cave. The white seal would feel another flip of his stomach and he gasped when once again, he saw the lifeless form of Emma! However, this time she was no longer with the witch. Emma had changed hands and was now inside the hairy and gripping paws of her servant. Oreguss laughed and made his scarce yellow teeth chomp up and down, making ugly and distorted faces toward the seal. Mad with contempt, Miracle shook with uncontrolled anger. The way Oreguss carelessly and deliberately dangled Emma in front of him like a dead trophy that he had fished out of the sea made Miracle try to lunge at him, but he was again stopped, but not by Jillith. This time the situation would prove to be quite different. This time it was the witch who would stop him.

JILLITH SHADOWS

With her enormous black robe billowing ferociously about her stately white face, Decara looked at Miracle the way a large and hungry reptile looks at a small rodent right before it gobbles it up whole. Her black hair blew wildly in front of her face, snapping viciously against her flapping garment, becoming one with it. Lowering her reptilian features toward the white seal, she pinned his spine further into the ice with her boot, sinking down into him, never allowing their eyes to leave each other.

Miracle jerked and pulled, but to no avail. "Let go of me!" he cried.

Decara sighed like a weakening wave retreating, slurping up the white foam about her red lips. "Well, well, well, what have we got here?" she hissed, kneeling over him.

Miracle recoiled from the nearness of her breath, feeling the repulsion squirm over him when suddenly their noses touched. "I'm not afraid of you!" he snapped, terrified as she covered him with the swoop of her dark robe.

"My, such bravery," Decara teased. "Why, I am just aquiver with goose bumps from just the touch of those sassy seal muscles of yours, how electrifying!"

"Get away from me, witch!"

"Now calm down, Hercules, I'm about to set you free, but you mustn't scurry your little self off into the pretty pink sunset just yet," she said with considerable exaggeration, batting her eyes, taunting him further.

"I won't leave, and you know I won't, not as long as you have Emma!"

Decara smiled seductively, slowly shrinking away, removing her boot from the white seal, freeing him. Miracle immediately shook away the ice and snow, twisting his head around and around in every direction, looking for Emma. However, the place was empty, except for the reflecting blue lights. All that remained now was himself, Jillith, and Decara.

"Where is she?" he demanded, wriggling directly up to Decara, getting half tangled up in the fury of her furling robe still rampant in the wind.

"Hmmm . . . you know," smugly stated the evil woman, this time directing her words over to the betraying Jillith seal, her glowing red eyes remaining on Miracle all the while she spoke. "I used to think his fascination for my niece was just a queer passing fancy—absurd, but harmless. Haah-haa," she laughed. "Imagine, a seal in love with a human, how innovative, how charming, how enthralling, how utterly and perfectly—sick and unnatural! It's revolting!" she spat.

Miracle wriggled up even closer to Decara, and raising his chin with defiance, he barked, "Stop it, you horrible woman! Emma is my friend even if she is a human, and there isn't anything I wouldn't do for her, but you wouldn't know about such things, would you? You wouldn't know how kind she is or how brave or how wonderful her heart is."

In a cruel and exaggerated attempt at humiliating the seal further, Decara put both of her hands over her ears and proceeded to make a ridiculous clown face that stretched itself out into grotesqueness. Then babbling out in a daft voice, pretending that she just could not possibly withstand another moment of his brash chastisement, she dementedly pleaded with a disturbing whisper, "*Ple-eeease* stop."

"You're just incapable of understanding anything about love or kindness! You'll never understand how she put all our lives before her own, how she fought the hunters, or how much I—" he stopped.

Unable to hold back, Jillith chimed in, saying, "Oh, I think he's going to cry!" she mocked, enjoying her chance to humiliate the seal once again.

"How touching," Decara ridiculed while staring evilly at the stone about his neck, wanting to rip it from him knowing she was unable. "The ridiculous white worm really believes he's in love with her. He loves her. *He loves her!*" she bellowed in sickening delight, clapping her hands together, pretending she was a seal, making degrading barking sounds while continuing to blow in the wind. She insidiously went on. "Doesn't that precious sappy sentiment just make you want to tippy-tippy-toe through the seashells, flinging about your flapping flippers in gay and delicious delight?"

"Go on with your jokes, witch," surrendered the seal. "Your heart has long since melted away and has become even icier than this old glacier."

A strange thick and worming smile squiggled across Decara's red lips, nearly eating away the rest of her pale face. "Is that so?" she said with an alarming softness. "Well, maybe it is, but let me tell you something else that is so. This game is over! And guess what? You lose—slug!"

The white seal stood steadfast before her. "At least I can feel and I can love. Can you?" Miracle barked rebelliously. "No matter, besides," he growled, "I already told you. I'm no longer afraid of you, so you could just stop all this madness."

Decara suddenly lost her face-eating smile and quickly replaced it with a snarling sneer. *"Madness?* You haven't seen anything yet, slippery slug! Just you wait, you will be very afraid, and soon!"

Miracle turned to look at the treacherous Jillith. His expression looked both sad and disgusted.

Jillith made a grunt that resembled a snicker. "What?" She chuckled nonchalantly. "I've been following you for days. She promised me eternal life if I helped her find you. Now I couldn't turn down such a quaint proposal, could I, freak-O?"

"How could you turn on us all *again?*"

"She found me after that disgusting, mad seal thought she destroyed me," Jillith confessed, snickering some more. "Decara restored me and promised me things . . . things your puny mind could never imagine."

"And for that you sold us out. You're worse than she is!"

Decara quickly interjected with a curious and comical retort. "Oh, I know what you mean," an excited Decara said. "There's nothing I hate more than a stool pigeon seal, don't you agree?" she playfully asked Miracle. Just then the snickering Jillith suddenly lost her snicker as the wildly blowing witch approached her. "After all," Decara went on to say, turning toward Jillith, remaining true to her comic-sounding tone, "if you can't trust a seal, who, in this entire wicky-wacky world can you trust, isn't that so, precious pet?"

The way the witch looked at Jillith suddenly made her blood sour. The betraying seal felt her heart skip several beats; it continued on with an even more upsetting and wildly impulsive jump as the evil woman steadily approached her. Decara's wild robe, with its wind-flapping tentacles reaching out toward her, made Jillith feel like a fly caught in a spider's web. Regrettably, just like the fly, she was doomed and would never escape from the restraint of the web or the bite of the spider. Nervously, the apprehensive seal swallowed down a throbbing lump in her throat, still surveying the witch's approach. Impetuously, Jillith wanted to flee from the cave, but she was unable to move. She could only stare on in terror just like the ill-fated fly. Despite the enormous jack-o'-lantern smile on Decara's face, Jillith sensed disaster about to occur.

"Is something wrong?" the black shining seal nervously asked with a ghost of a smile.

Her eyes somehow fixed in a partial crisscross, looking crazed, Decara carried along her demented wide and unnatural grimace.

She outstretched her arms, and while the robing panels flogged themselves savagely about her face and shoulders, she taunted in a quick whispered voice, "Come, let me kiss you, my precious deceiver. Let me repay you for all that you have done. Let me ingratiate you and your impeccable disloyalty, for without your adept treason, I would have never found this ever so convenient hiding place of theirs. And as you are aware, time is of the essence, my precious pet, is it not?"

Jillith nodded reassuringly. "Yes, and I did it all for you."

"Yes, oh yes-*sss*," Decara hissed upon reaching her. "Of course, you did. Being promised eternal life had absolutely nothing to do with it, did it, my illustrious deceiver?"

Suddenly, the wind stopped and a disturbing quiet flooded over the cave.

Miracle looked on at Decara, unsure as to what it was she was about to do, but like the treacherous Jillith, he too knew it was not going to be pretty.

"Have I offended you in any way, Your Excellency?" the groveling and now terribly frightened Jillith asked, backing away until her backside crunched up against a slab of protruding ice, allowing her to go no further.

"Why, no," Decara moaned, her eyes wild, her hair a mass of disorder, and her insane and hideous grimace stretched out into a monster's face. "I have come to give you exactly what I promised you—eternal life!"

A vexed sigh quickly came to Jillith as she returned a grateful smile, the feeling of extreme uneasiness still inundating itself over the black seal's entire being.

"After all," Decara commanded, "I could not have possibly done it without you. However, still, you see—unfortunately, for you, that is—there is one itsy-bitsy, teensy-weensy problem," she said in a creepy childlike voice.

"Problem?" Jillith uttered feeling her heart kick up in tempo.

"Yes," Decara said, hanging on to her playful voice, still wrapped inside her monster mask grimace. "You see, my precious stoolie, here's the deal. Despite your outstanding disloyalty to this group of spineless slugs, I'm afraid, dear precious, *precious* pet, I despise all seals. And no matter how you dice and slice it up, honey—*you're still one!*" she growled.

Jillith did not have time to scream; it happened that fast. Decara's hand fell down hard upon the black seal's head, and a massive burst of light exploded throughout the cave. Decara's evil laughter resounded about the icy walls while the stunned seal erupted into a blinding form of blazing light. Feeling afraid, the white seal quickly took cover behind a stocky clump of ice. Stretching out his head, he watched with bated breath as Jillith was transformed into a million flickering lights, some shadowed with growing darkness, others left dark blue, her burning quivers forever caught between the bouncing lights within the ancient glacier.

Jillith's embodiment of shadows and light continued to explode throughout the blue cave. From the very tip of the glacier down against its declining walls into the many slush pools of shadowy trails, the traitorous seal's image flooded the ice and water. She was everywhere! Thousands and thousands of her trapped reflections dripped form every crevasse; her distorted face splattering endlessly, for her contorted expression had been hideously and infinitely caught inside millions of different shades of gloom, each one holding a million excruciating and torturous punishments of agony. Each one represented the prison she would occupy with no chance of ever escaping. She was merely a reflection and would unceasingly feel the dispersion of incarceration, there in the shadowing of the cave, forever trapped, forced to remember her treachery, recalling her betrayal, eternally snared within specks of light and shadow. Unlike the maggots inside the tomb, these fiendish torments would, for all time, eat at her—never becoming full, forever ravenous!

In a frightful chorus of echoing howls, Jillith's dark counterparts crawled and scratched feverishly at the icy walls, her haunting wails shaking the cave with dread. "You can't do this to me! You can't! You can't!" she screamed and would go on screaming infinitely. Here, Jillith would spend her eternal life, not quite as promised, but instead agonizing in constant remorse for her unthinkable sedition. She had indeed become the new resident ghost of the ancient glacier, a mere silhouette, only it would not just be the icy walls of this ancient relic that she would haunt. No, the essence of her existence would be for one purpose and one purpose alone—to haunt herself. Forever alone in the shadows, this would be Decara's appreciation and gift for such alliance.

The unceasing and terrifying screams that the scattered about Jillith images made sent immeasurable amounts of shivers down Miracle's back. Even the ongoing cackles of Decara's evil laughter paled in comparison to Jillith's ghastly shrieks of despair, but oh, how the witch did laugh. She laughed and laughed with wicked delight, dancing crazily inside the cavern, displacing the swarming Jillith facades in every direction, pushing bits and pieces of the doomed seal's reflected face beneath her happy feet, kicking at the slush, retaining her latest monstrosity. Twirling her mighty robe about, she continued to scatter the tortured reflections, dancing and singing all the while: *"Tippy-tippy toe! See all the worms upon the snow! Tippy-tippy toe! To hell you all will finally go!"* Finding wicked delight in her own mad antics, Decara started maniacally laughing again. Then from the center of the glacier, as if the ancient giant had had all it was about to endure, the walls of the blue cave began to shake and crumble. With a quick jump, Miracle dodged and tried to take cover, only barely escaping a part of the icy ceiling as it came crashing down around him. The bitter coldness of the pulverized ice chilled his blood, but Decara's mad laughter chilled him even greater.

As the glacier rumbled and the tormented Jillith pictures screamed on and on in agony, the awful humming returned, along with the peculiar and sudden force of the wind that seemed to accompany the witch, always making her entrances and exits just a bit more theatrical. The murmuring sound intensified, antagonizing the many shrieking fragments of the trapped Jillith, as well as the trembling glacier, with absolute madness. All at once, the white seal felt the entire glacier plunge into the sea with a deafening CRUNCH! Infected by the terror, Miracle screamed out, but the gushing surge of waters quickly silenced him. Inside the sea, he could hear the thundering glacier buckle and snap, sounding as if it were dying, sounding as if at any moment it would crumble into millions of piece—and then it did just that. However, the white seal would not be conscious to experience the entire death of the mammoth iceberg. For right before its final descent, Miracle felt the sharp nails and the piercing skeleton grasp of the witch's hand about his neck. He could still hear the witch laughing as the entire insides of the timeworn monument collapsed, taking all the fluttering and still screaming Jillith shadows with it.

And once more, there was darkness.

IT'S ALIVE

The *Tiamat* was not always alive. Before it became possessed to a certain degree, it seemed to be much like any other stately ship, for as once before told, the *Tiamat* remained regarded as being one of the quintessential sealing vessels of all time. Controlled exclusively by Decara's unique enterprises, it sailed for the exportation of seal skin, operating much like any other hunting vessel. Its exterior, however, being a grandiose paragon of ultimate craftsmanship, was considered by many as being too elaborate and eccentric, especially since it would often be involved in rigorous and often dangerous regions of ice and snow. For most, such remote seas that would mar and damage such a vessel was seriously questioned. Nonetheless, the *Tiamat* was constructed precisely and detailed exclusively by Decara and her companion. It would be a ship not to be reckoned with, its only purpose to battle such difficult passageways for the gain of slaughtering and skinning the baby harp seals of Sealssong and, of course, the stealing of seal tears and the ever-constant pursuit of finding the purple stone that held the magic tear. No, the *Tiamat* was never just an ordinary vessel, and now something else had come to replace the standard mechanics of once such a magnificent ship.

Now smashed and crippled upon the shores of Sealssong, the *Tiamat* no longer remained magnificent and unscathed, and yet it continued to remain alive. Its pulsating core, vile and corrupt, oozing with unspeakable evil, went right on corrupting down into the splinters of the once-grand vessel. Lying half covered with broken ice and severed pieces of itself, now a mere reminisce of its former self, its crumbled form appeared upon the shore like a fatally wounded sea monster. Cocked to one side of the icy shoreline, most of its internal parts forever remained smashed beyond recognition, as well as much of the upper deck. It was difficult to recognize it as once ever being a ship, its bow wiped away by the impact sustained when dropped out of the sky, the bowsprit destroyed, leaving little of the ship left at all. Still, the entity that allowed this vessel to breathe had certainly not left; it could never leave—not yet.

It fought for breath like a fish after having been caught, the tearing hook still embedded securely between its shredded jaws. Even as it lay there in shambles, from what remained of the splintered starboard came a wheezing sound. There was also a thumping noise resounding like a heartbeat, a faint one, but a pulse determined not to fade. The very entity of the *Tiamat* would not give up now. Not when it was so close to returning whole, however not as it had lived these past many months, for the thing that fueled the existence of this vile ship had once belonged to the world of the living. It once walked up rocky shores and icy paths of countless places. It ate, drank, and slept. It possessed dreams and schemes and had needs. It lusted, hated, and at times it was doubtful; but most of all, it loved to kill. Yes, this it knew how to do exceptionally well. It fed off the land and took from it, never replenishing it, always sucking every last bit of breath from it, and never, but never having any remorse for doing so. It experimented and tortured the basic creatures of the sea and learned of a dark and powerful deception—the cunning of man's thirst for power and domination over life itself. It was here in that descent into the darkness where it learned of the black forces of the universe, that of which in time, it would harness and eventually control, or so it would believe. For it was once a man with a demonic secret power. Still, even with such vanquished control, it could not elude the power of death that came to it from a mother seal whose pup it had destroyed. It would never contemplate that this seal had a name or that it possessed real emotions. It would, however, forever remember how its mistress took away the seal's mind, replacing it with madness. Unfortunately for it, that is, not even the witch could bring the thing that now resided within the broken walls of the once mighty *Tiamat* back to its human state—not yet.

It remembered its former existence. It remembered all these things as it lay there in ruin upon the red glowing shores of Sealssong. It recalled how the dark sorceress could not bear to lose it to sudden death and how she worked her dark magic to lodge its essence into the boards and walls and halls and every corridor, every inch of the ship she had named *Tiamat*, vowing that one day they would again be reunited.

How it had longed for this moment—the Night of Screams, the awaited night that it would once again be resurrected into human form to reclaim the hand of its beloved.

No matter what little remained, the *Tiamat* would not die, for it had already done this, remembering upon a time it walked and ate and slept, and killed, and had seduced the woman it now waited for so that she would release him. She would come soon, just as she promised. She would come to eradicate what remained of innocence from this wretched planet once and for all, and the thing that now possessed the once magnificent *Tiamat* would become man once more! It would walk with its bride-to-be, not only as the infamous Dr. Adrias, but also as a lord of eternal night, just as the dark master and she had promised. Soon, both, itself and its adored sorceress would rule the blackened universe, and nothing would stop them ever again.

The *Tiamat* took another deep breath, thinking to itself, *your lover is here, my rapturous Decara. Come to me . . . Come to me . . . I am waiting.*

THE LAST NIGHT ON PLANET EARTH

The screams of the seals being either killed or hunted filled the night sky, each cry, each scream, every call of desolation mixing with the falling blood-soaked moon, its form rapidly deteriorating from above. Hundreds of different swirling mini universes consisting of fantastic cosmic colors and unimaginable hues fizzed and sparked during their fall upon the earth. There were whirling clouds of vapors illuminated with insurmountable blinking lights of blues and dark reds, purples, and greens, all of which danced around the dangling planets approaching the earth, now appearing so close one could almost touch them. Light poured around them, amplifying their magnificence, ushering in billions of shafts of radiance. They shone down upon the planet, creating a definitive spotlight for what would most assuredly be remembered as the greatest show on earth!

The lights in the nursery, the very nucleus of the happening, suddenly were snatched away, indicating that the performance was about to begin. Then all the lights on earth and the entire universe went out. All that could be seen from the heavens was a tiny flickering glare, like a candle in the dark. With a potent inhaled breath, the whole universe waited, the entire cosmos gathering in awe of the colossal event. They had all come to witness the demise of mankind—and the end of the world.

*   *   *

From somewhere inside the shattered *Tiamat*, there came a clattering sound. Suddenly, through a ripped-away part of the ship Oreguss appeared. The hairy brute popped his head out from beneath the shambles, chomping his scattered yellow and broken stubby teeth together. He snorted and chuckled and jumped out from the rubble. Quickly turning around, he reached back into the same hole he had just crawled out of; Oreguss began to pull something large from the wreckage. He growled and grunted, determined to pull the thing from the *Tiamat*. Louder and louder he growled, cursing at the heavy thing he dragged from beneath its incredible weight, testing his strength near maximum. Fortunately, Oreguss possessed the brawn of ten men. His furry muscles twisted and bulged as his hulking arms pulled at the thing. Little by little, bit by bit, although struggling with its considerable weight, he revealed the thing, finally bringing it out of the wreckage. He let its massiveness slam hard against the already broken deck. This time, Oreguss nearly sent the thing crashing right back from where it came. He swiped at his forehead with the insides of his furry arms. Scratching feverishly at his exposed and hanging belly, he sat down on top of the thing, trying to catch his breath.

"Get off of it, you fool!" Decara shrieked again. "And bring it to me *now!*"

Oreguss jumped from the black and shining altar, still huffing and puffing from the strenuous workout that the intricately carved and polished ebony slab gave him. Taking a deep breath, he once more scratched at his big hairy belly before taking hold of the sacrificial altar. He proceeded to drag it off the broken vessel, onto the frozen ground, and over to where Decara was ever so impatiently waiting. The ice beneath split and cracked when the portable altar crashed down onto it. A wide and unending line of zigzagging spider webs spread wildly through the ice as Oreguss continued to haul the demonic piece of furniture over icy banks and frozen foothills of petrified snow. Almost losing it over to one of the gaping ice floes, he frantically embedded his feet into the ground and started grunting like a wild animal, attempting to rescue it from oblivion. Feeling Decara's exasperation burn a hole against the back side of his head, he scrambled to get his balance, once again taking charge over the accursed altar with its carved grotesque faces and symbols, all etched and smeared deep and permanently over its ebullient finish of evil. However, in his endeavor of pushing the extravagant thing over a rather steep incline, Oreguss once again lost his grip as well as on the altar! Unattended, it slid quickly over the icy hill, gaining momentum while heading directly toward Decara. Jumping into the air, he lunged at the racing slab and latched on to it, dragging his oversized feet along the ice, nearly shredding his boots to pieces.

Decara did not move a muscle. She merely leered at the approaching calamity with more exasperation, her look telling Oreguss he'd soon wish he'd never been born should the altar touch a morsel of her being. Unfortunately, it did just that. A small corner of the base had run itself over her big toe. Holding in a scream, Decara bit down the pain, chocking on it, glaring viciously at Oreguss while she pulled her toe out from under the heavy slab with nothing less than restrained intolerance, a horrid expression stamped across her face. Wanting to kill the clumsy oaf, Decara's eyes bulged from their sockets. She glared at him, hating him for embarrassing her that way, for the entire universe was still watching her and she had to remember that no matter how much she wanted to kill him.

Forced to retain a grip over her outrage, she quickly retracted her bulging and seething eyes, softening their aggravated glare into a less formidable sight, turning her gaze toward the heavens. She quickly gave up a quaint smile, a smile that didn't fool anyone. Still, she kept right on smiling, turning to face the black altar, her toe screaming from inside her red seal skin boot. Decara attempted not to limp while walking, rearranging her hair, dusting off the moon droppings, fixing the hood of her coat, straightening out its massive train, most of it remaining frozen and half submerged in open floes. With a slight push of her hand, she watched the altar slide directly into the green and vaporous hole in the ground. While sliding into the opening, it merely floated there, bewitched, defying all of gravity, defying all who were watching. Then she turned to Oreguss. Trying not to let anyone but her clumsy servant see the fury of her bulging eyes, she privately flashed him another jolt of her crazed, fuming, and infuriated looks. Totally incensed by his asinine bungling, still wishing to kill him and would have if the whole universe wasn't watching, she coyly smiled while leering at him hatefully. The look was most disturbing.

"Bring me the beast!" she viscously yelled.

Repetitively nodding with an unnerved expression smudged all over his face, Oreguss took off like an arrow, heading straight toward the *Tiamat* once again. Decara watched her servant crawl back down the ripped-open hole in the ship before turning to face the floating black altar. She smiled evilly. Spreading her arms out while running her bony fingers over the carved features of the disembodied heads that clustered throughout the demonic table, she watched with a callow expression, when suddenly, the eyes of the carved heads sprang open! The entire altar was alive with movement. The heads crawled across the black surface like slugs entwining themselves in the dirt, their gruesome squirm moving between the engraved devil symbols. Just then, Decara hurled around, hearing the distinct cry of the sacrificial white seal echoing prominently throughout the eerie-glowing nursery.

"Let go of me!" Miracle shouted, squirming and fighting to free himself from the squeezing paws of Oreguss.

"Bring it to me!" ordered Decara, holding to her sinister grimace, carefully watching her hulking servant walk across the smashed-up deck of her soon-to-be reincarnated lover.

Miracle tried to break free from Oreguss' tight and agonizing clutches, but he was quickly defeated when Oreguss squeezed his mammoth fingers around his throat, clenching the seal's back flippers with unnecessary and grueling force. Miracle's cheeks filled with air from the sudden constriction and found that he was unable to utter a single sound. His breathing severely impaired, he felt himself growing faint. Decara waited anxiously her red, satin fingers outstretched endlessly before her. She scratched and grabbed insanely at the air unable to; contain herself wanting to feel the white beast within her grasp. Even before Oreguss reached her, Decara went flying toward him, savagely grabbing the seal from his robust hold. Miracle winced out loud from Decara's scratching pull. Feeling the surfacing blood sting against the raw wounds she had just inflicted on him, the frightened seal looked up toward the devil woman who now leered at him with a look so terrifying it took away the rest of his breath. She smiled so incredibly malevolently, staring down at him, stroking the side of his head, petting his white fur as she half cradled him in her arms, his backside spilling outside her twisted grasp. Her face was right next to his, and Miracle could smell the foulness in her icy breath when she stuck out her tongue and licked his nose. Miracle cringed and drew back, pushing himself further away from her ghastly embrace.

"*Mmmm,*" hummed Decara licking her lips as if she had sampled something appetizing, "the, taste of pure innocence—how yummy!" She purred while finishing off another slurp around her moist red lips. "Not much of it left in the world now—aye, slug? And soon there will be none. None at all!" she tormented, using a demented singsong voice.

Frozen within her evil clutches, Miracle stared up at the vile woman, petrified and yet amazed at her viciousness, the smell from her sour breath making him nauseous. Suddenly Decara squeezed him tightly, making his eyes bulge. "You can't imagine just how much I've been looking forward to this. How proud you must be. After all, none of this would be possible without you!" she said, struggling to keep just part of him in her aching arms. "In a way, you are the prince of Sealssong, aren't you, my precious undersized pet? And such a royal and noble guest as renowned as yourself, should have a special place of honor venerating his magnificence, don't you agree, my little sacrificial worm?" Taking him to her bosom, she began to sway the white seal back and forth, imitating a mother's gestures while rocking her child to sleep. "Come, my precious worm, it's time to go night-night."

Miracle could hardly breathe; she was squeezing him so tightly against her chest he thought he would suffocate. His heart beat uncontrollably, and yet even then his only thoughts were of Emma and how he would never see her again. He tried to pull away from the witch, but he was helpless. Unable to see where she was taking him, he felt his bottom scrape the ice as Decara haphazardly dragged him along, her seal skin boots sinking through the crust as she savagely trekked onward. He tried to snap at her, but he was unable; her pressing hands were tight around his throat, making it impossible. Some relief finally came when he felt her loosen her vile grip, allowing the cold air to refill his aching lungs. She looked down at him one final time. Her eyes were just beginning to turn a pink color when she smiled at him playfully, picked him up before slamming him down on the black altar, her face changing over to a ghoulish scowl.

Miracle gasped and was about to scream when he suddenly felt himself strapped in tight. The restraints were not of this earth—they were straight from the mouths of demonic faces coming from hell itself. Infesting the unholy altar, a hundred long ebony-colored tongues devilishly snaked out from each of the carved heads, pinning the seal down, wrapping themselves around him over and over again, stretching and anchoring him firmly. This time Miracle screamed. He screamed loud! Unable to move, the wooden tongues squeezed the breath from him like a boa constrictor, keeping him ever so snug to the devil's table with no way of ever unfastening their splintery hold. He barked out with a desperate yelp. That was when Decara suddenly pushed her face directly in front of his, just before he started to yelp again.

Unable to contain herself, Decara immediately exploded with sheer delight, filling the cold air with more bloodcurdling insufferable laughter. "I told you that you would be afraid. Didn't I, worm?" She started to shriek again, engaging in a deranged impromptu dance around the black altar. Abruptly stopping in mid twirl, she flew crazily over to the front of the slab and stuck her face, harshly into Miracle's snout. Again Miracle cringed away in disgust, feeling the cold wooden slab against his back, the clenching of the horrible tongues constricting all the more. Unable to look anywhere else, the white seal stared into the alabaster face of Decara. Her twisted grimace cut into her features like the same Halloween jack-o'-lantern as before, but the wildness in her eyes was of a far greater dread. They burned like fire now and seemed to boil with molten lava that actually made his seal nose blister.

"Are you ready to die, worm?" she hissed.

Miracle did not yelp out this time. He merely looked deeper into those terrifying eyes, so afraid of what he might see and yet not daring to take away his gaze. He suddenly thought of Mum, realizing that the horrible man-beast before him far surpassed any real madness from which Mum had ever suffered. Decara was utterly and completely insane, and no magnitude of reasoning would be remotely feasible. He was going to die, of this he was certain. He did not know how, but he had a strong suspicion he was about to find out. Then for some reason, perhaps just the remembering of Mum, a sudden calmness came over him as he continued to look up at Decara's curled-up jack-o'-lantern grin. "It won't work, Decara! I won't be afraid of you! I won't!"

"Oh, we're back to that again!" she scoffed.

"It's true," Miracle answered. "Do what you have to do, just get it over with!"

"Oh my, another splash of bravery before he starts to cry all over again, how gallant!" she raved.

"When you took Sealssong away, you took away everything!"

"You mean when I took away your precious Emma, don't you?" Decara ranted, looking at the white seal for a few more moments before thoroughly scrutinizing his face and letting out another one of her bellowing cackles. "Come, come now, do you really think she's dead?"

Miracle merely stared at Decara with suspicious eyes. He did not answer.

"Oh dear, oh me, why, it simply isn't so!" she cried, sounding demented again. "Your precious Emma is alive and well and is just dying to see you!"

"You're lying!" Miracle barked.

Decara smashed her face back into Miracle's, bending the tip of his blistered nose back. "Au contraire, fatuous worm, how else could I watch her slit your throat?" she sneered, rubbing her depraved smile over his quivering snout.

"You insane monster, what have you done to her?"

"What do you think?" Decara spit sarcastically.

"I want to see her!"

"And see her you shall!" she promised, holding to her mad grimace, slowly backing away from the malignant black altar. "For the last time, you shall see her!" With this, Decara hurled herself further still from the black table. Raising her arms toward the buzzing skies, she trekked through the snow and stood before a large mountain of ice. It towered high above, disappearing into the whirlwind of the spinning universes and hanging planets that continuously glared down from above. Miracle struggled against the harsh entrapment of the demonic tongues, thinking that he did not remember seeing that particular iceberg the witch now stood in front of moments before. It just suddenly appeared there. He watched as she threw back her head and screamed out a slew of incantations, finally calling out to her dark lord: *"Libat! Dibble-Patchious Bay! Open the gate of desecration! Open, I say!"*

Miracle froze and could only look on in fear while the mighty tower of ice began to shake and crumble hearing the evil woman proceed with her lurid spell. What happened next made the white seal shiver further with additional dread. The entire iceberg began to melt. In chunks, the gigantic structure fell apart, most of it having turned to seawater by the time it hit the icy ground. Thawing into a tremendous wave, it crashed upon the island directly before Decara. However, it never faltered her stand upon the ice; and while it foamed and exploded against the icy domain, it broke, just as a wave does upon the sand, only it did not return to the sea. This swelling of water was immediately sucked up by the boundless gaping hole, enraptured with the strange swirling green mist and the hellish night light. In a matter of moments, the hole eagerly drank up the wave, and there displayed clearly above the white seal stood Emma!

She was indeed alive! She was glowing with beauty. She was dressed grander and more radiant than a princess, and she was holding a large pointed dagger in her left hand, its glistening tip aimed directly at his heart.

THE DEVIL'S TABLE

At first, Miracle believed that the witch was causing him to hallucinate. He took several double takes before accepting the fact that standing there before him was actually the human girl he had come to cherish. It was Emma, there could be no doubt. The same delicate and lovely face that had long since etched itself to his heart was only a short distance away, staring at him; and yet there was something very different about the girl—frightening, menacing. None of it made any sense. Her curly blond hair, although no longer free to frame her dainty features, was pulled back harshly up into a spinning bun that sat twisted and twirled tight atop her head. Once again, her clothes were also different. Her blue and frozen robe had been exchanged for a red one. There was a long red cape attached to it made entirely out of seal pelts, and it came with a satiny stand-up collar that rested flat against the slender swanlike shape of her neck. Her absolute attire, as was Decara's, consisted of the murdered children of Sealssong, each pelt soaked in its own blood just to give it that extra royal polish, again, compliments of Oreguss' morbid handiwork.

Aside from the shining silver dagger that Emma was clutching to, what truly frightened the seal right from the moment when she suddenly appeared out of nowhere were Emma's eyes. Once a stunning blue, they now remained clouded with a dull gray color void of their familiar iridescent vibrancy. Something was seriously wrong with her; for he knew what looked back at him from the face of the treasured girl he would die for had been replaced with something that was most assuredly not Emma! He began to squirm frantically within the clutches of the wooden devil tongues, feeling them press him deeper into the black altar. He was about to scream out to Emma when suddenly the witch stood in front of him. Raising her arms into the air, she pierced her scarlet-clad fingers far into the glow of the hellish green light bursting about her. The earth trembled, and a cold wind blew boisterously, sounding like a million wild wolves howling. The tremendous glare from the green light that came from below hurt Miracle's eyes, almost as much as the cutting particles of ice and snow that blew and scraped over him. He shut his eyes trying to escape the burning assault. It would take a few moments, but when the seal opened his eyes, he would come to find that the entire scenery had been altered yet again! Emma would still be there, but what remained of the recently conjured-up iceberg had split open. Apparently, not all of it had melted, for it now appeared to be perfectly dissected into two separate sections, opening like a magnificent locket, its towering sides disappearing into the watchful shadows of the night.

Deep within the gutted iceberg located to the extreme left side, two magnificent and fantastic-looking thrones had been chiseled out of ice, each looking as though a giant could sit upon them and still have room to spare. The arms of the imposing chairs extended outward, each measuring well over ten feet. A thousand different symbols and shapes imitating the same engraving written all over the black altar were also carved deeply and throughout the icy sculptures. However, the most overwhelming thing about the spectacular thrones was the size of their backs. Their endless icy posteriors seemed to grow higher and higher, shooting straight up and over the split-open face of the iceberg, cutting off and vanishing right into the black universe. Although both thrones were of fantastic proportions, the first one, the one Decara eventually came to sit upon, was most intimidating, far superior in size, consequently and quite assuredly ruling the definitive throne of all thrones. She sat quietly upon the extraordinary royal seat, glaring toward her niece, tapping her skeleton fingers against the icy arms of the chair. She sent an evil grimace to her niece, just watching the girl stare on with a cold, vacant gaze toward the white seal who remained tied to the devil's table before her. Slowly, Emma tilted her head sideways then back again, looking at the white seal as if trying to remember.

"Emma, what has she done to you?" Miracle cried.

From her frosted throne, Decara put her satiny-clad fingers up to her cold ruby-red lips, merely laughing devilishly, hissing and fizzing, thoroughly enjoying the scene playing before her. Once more, the bewitched Emma looked at the white seal with vacant eyes, her tiny fingers wrapped around the silver dagger, her mind desperate to remember.

The white seal took another penetrating look at Emma's face. He immediately noticed that her lips had been painted up with a deep red color, making her appear more like the witch. It made him shudder all the more. "Emma!" he barked. "You must fight whatever it is she is doing to you! Emma, please!"

With further questioning tilts of her head, Emma looked away from the dagger, staring at the seal for a long time. Then slowly, her clouded eyes moved toward the silver dagger in her hand. She looked upon its long chiseled handle and shining blade and studied the strange-looking engraved dragon embellished all over it. Suddenly she opened her hand, allowing the dagger to drop to the ground.

Not missing a beat, Decara flew up from the chair, outstretching her arms, her skeleton fingers pointing to the dagger. "Pick it up!" she wickedly shrieked. Feeling faint, the dazed Emma quickly put her hands to her throbbing forehead, trying to steady herself. Once more, she looked at the white seal. She watched his blurred image spin before her. It appeared as if it was speaking to her, but she could no longer understand the sounds it made. She could no longer remember who it was or who she was. More dizziness engulfed her as she heard the witch call out to her for the second time. "Emma! Pick up the dagger and simply kill the beast. This is not brain surgery, woman!"

Emma merely looked down at the seal, her expression a washed-out palate of nothingness. "Pick it up, I say!" Decara howled. Turning from the black altar, Emma did just what Decara instructed her to do. It was as if she no longer could think for herself. Still, somewhere inside, although exceedingly vague, she could almost hear a familiar awareness. She would not have time to listen further, for once again Decara's loud and monstrous voice shook the ice for the third time. "Emma! Pick up the dagger!" she screeched from her ice throne. With a quiet and lethargic turn, Emma knelt down. She made tiny squeaking sounds on the crust of the snow as she tried to steady herself. Then mentally making an image of the discarded weapon, not bearing to look at it again, she closed her eyes and snatched it hastily from the ice.

Surprisingly, Decara said, "Come here!"

Dazed and unresisting, Emma began to trek through the snow toward the ice thrones. As if drugged into semi-consciousness, she approached her aunt, her red seal cape scraping along after her, brushing clean the tops of snowy slopes while walking onward. Upon reaching Decara, Emma faced the witch. Decara's image, like the seal's, was blurred and almost unrecognizable. The muscles in her stomach tightened, and she felt nausea break out inside her. The swirling of images had gotten worse, and she felt she would lose consciousness again.

Abruptly, Decara sprang from her seat harshly slapping Emma across the face. "Don't, you ever disobey me again! Now . . ." she growled in a lower register, " . . . be seated."

Nearly collapsing onto the massive arm of the throne prepared just for her, Emma quickly fell into the incredibly vast chair. Dwarfed inside its colossal seat, she slumped against the giant outstretched arms of the throne, her dagger digging into one of the many demonic symbols inscribed upon its icy sheath.

"Leave her alone!" Miracle shouted from the devil's table. "You've bewitched her! You're making her do this! You're not fooling anyone, witch lady! I know what you did to her!"

Decara offered him a wicked smile. "Oh? And what is that, precious worm?"

"You've poisoned her mind! You've put her under one of your evil horrible spells!"

Decara laughed. "You don't approve of our new Emma?" she said, turning to look at her disoriented niece. "Why, I think she is perfectly exquisite! She has shed her ludicrous childlike ways and has become a woman!" She continued smiling crudely. "A beautiful, sensual woman, no longer that sniveling brat you would have her as. Emma has come of age. She belongs to me now!"

Before Miracle could bark out his revulsion, another voice suddenly broke through the cold windless air. "She'll never belong to you, Decara, never!"

Miracle immediately recognized the voice. It belonged to Emma's brother—Kenyan. The white seal fought the wooden devil tongues and hurriedly cast his look toward the second part of the sliced iceberg. What he saw there made him shudder all over again. The other side had also been gutted out to make room for the gathered prisoners that Decara ghoulishly collected in particular honor for this monumental event. Closest to the place where the second portion of the glacier remained divided was Oreguss. He continued to jump up and down moronically, chomping his jaws together, banging his hairy fists against the side of the icy wall he stood before. Next was Kenyan. There he was, once again chained and bound to the same icy wall Oreguss continued to beat against. Heavy chains were clasped around both his wrists as the remainder of weighted links disappeared deep into the thick and icy skin of the cut-open iceberg. Miracle watched as the boy unrelentingly fought against the hold of the chains, screaming out threats of hatred toward the witch. There beside him incarcerated in the same way stood the other man-beast, the one that was called a captain. Was this the same man who had once commanded the vile ship? It was hard to believe that now. Although amazingly still alive, his thin and frail body hung like a dead jellyfish within the confines of the heavy shackles he wore. His one eye remained covered, the other, although unmasked, was just as black and bruised a hundred times over as the black patch he wore. His blond hair was long and filthy, much of it frozen to one side of his face, some intertwined within his scraggly beard, much having been torn away by hungry rats. He stared out with one single bloodshot eye from his icy prison with a surging madness, still unable to understand the nightmare playing on and on before him.

Following next beside Thorne was Crumpels, Poo-Coo, Big Petie, and Little Lukie. Instantly Miracle's heart leaped when he saw them gathered there in such a dreadful manner. They each had a heavy steel collar around their neck, which, like the others, had heavy chains attached to it, the remaining links buried deep inside the giant icy jail. Crumpels was crying profusely, rambling incessantly, incoherently spouting out rhymes, while Poo-Coo, as did Kenyan, stubbornly fought against the thick chains holding them. Big Petie merely shivered with fright, still holding to questioning eyes that were as big as seashells, while Little Lukie squirted the icy floor with more acrid bursts of excitement, screaming in a high-pitched yelp the entire time.

As Miracle's eyes scanned further still, he looked for the impish penguin, but he was not there. What he saw next made him gasp. It was his mother! She had been placed further away from the others, up upon a higher shelf of the iceberg as if to be seated in an honored place, there in that ghastly theater of parading terrors. He fought against the vile pull of the devil tongues, pulling himself up, going as far as possible so that he could look upon Arayna.

"Mother!" he called out to her. Arayna looked toward her son with eyes of enduring compassion, her seal tears making her large eyes shine like the stars once did. Instinctively, she attempted to go to him, pulling inadvertently at the mighty bolted collar clenched tight around her neck, the same heavy chains holding her there, swallowed up inside the icy stomach of the dissected glacier. She fell partially back from the cruel pull, helpless, her glistening eyes never leaving Miracle, tears running down both sides of her cheeks.

"Mama—" Miracle cried, feeling his heart crumble with inconsolable grief, but the continued shouts of Kenyan jolted the seal and his eyes were once again on the boy.

"Do you hear me, witch? She'll never be a part of you!" Kenyan swore, still pulling wild like at the biting chains around his wrists.

Decara merely laughed, leisurely rising from her ice throne. Walking over and standing before her niece, she slowly moved her wavering hands in front of Emma's vacant eyes. "Stand up, woman!" she commanded. Emma obeyed, holding on to the dagger with one hand while, steadying herself with the other. "Look at her!" Decara shouted. "Just look at her!" She once more glared at Kenyan before looking over to the altar where the white seal was strapped tight. "Have you ever seen her look more vibrant, more beautiful, and more alive before?"

"What are you talking about?" Kenyan raved. "That's not Emma! What have you done to her?"

Emma remained stationary, merely standing there, her mind swimming in a mist of swirling vapors and spinning lights. Again, Decara smiled sinisterly, this time turning away from her niece, moving toward the boy instead. "On the contrary, I have once again made her well. She is no longer plagued with the nuisance of her illness."

"You witch!" Kenyan spit. "You stripped her of herself! You've taken away her spirit! You've turned her into some kind of a zombie!"

Decara drew closer to the boy, bringing her wicked grimace with her. She clucked her tongue, shaking her head at him, saying, "I return your sister, take away all her maladies and yours, I may add, and this is the thanks I get? Why, she would be dead if it were not for me!" She was now close enough to Kenyan to brush her scarlet fingers over his lips.

Recoiling in disgust, Kenyan twisted his head away, pulling on the heavy chains, backing away from her. "Don't touch me! Don't, you ever touch me again!"

"Come, come . . . ," Decara fussed. "Aren't you a tad bit curious as to why you are feeling so chipper yourself, precious, sweet boy?"

"What are you talking about?"

Decara widened her grotesque grimace, curling it around her pale face. "Why, I think it should be obvious, even to you. I want you most alert for what you are about to witness, my pathetic Prince Charming."

"Stop with the games, witch, say what you mean!"

Decara began to giggle before breaking into more maniacal laughter. "Oh, you are a fool! Poor, misguided, big, tough, precious, sweet boy," she spit then stopped laughing, rushing forcefully up to his face, grabbing it tightly between her skeleton fingers, tearing away some skin in the process as she squeezed her grip roughly about his chin, forcing him to look directly at her.

"You're so cocksure of yourself, aren't you, pismire punk? Do you think you just miraculously gained back your health, just like that?" She twisted her fingers around his chin even tighter, drawing more blood. "Or did you think that Emma's precious little purple angels sprinkled some fairy dust over you, taking away all your nasty and painful little boo-boos?" With a thrusting shove, she sent the boy crashing into the icy wall behind him. "You burned-out degenerate! I returned your health just as I did your sister's! But don't get the wrong idea, cutesy-poo, nothing personal; you're just the mere pawn I've used over and over again, making sure your sister does exactly as she is told, just as she will now!"

"You will never get her to kill the white seal—never!"

Flashing her white teeth around the drooling coils of her red grimace, Decara giggled some more with added amusement. "We will see, sweet, pretty boy!"

"She'll never do it, I tell you!"

"Oh, she'll do it; she'll do it, all right!" Decara drew even closer toward the boy, both her skeleton arms outstretched before him. Kenyan slammed his backside into the gouged-out glacier, unable to avoid her touch. She abusively pulled at the hanging blond hair covering his forehead, saying, "What part of this aren't we getting, sweet boy? Seriously, what did you think?" She cackled. "Did you think I kept you around for company whilst you comforted me in my pathetic lonesomeness?" She started cackling most dementedly backing away from the boy, exploding with more deranged laughter. "She'll do whatever I say not to see me crush you! I make the rules, sweet boy, so I can do what I want! She'll kill the seal, take the tear, and I shall claim the earth, and there isn't anything you or any of your slimy slug friends can do about it! I want it all, and I shall have it all, and your sister is going to help me get it all!"

Then with a cruel grin, she turned, returning to her throne. "Yes . . . Yes . . . Yes . . . She just loves her precious brother. Why, there isn't anything in this whole wide world she wouldn't do for him," Decara vexed. "She would sacrifice herself rather than see him die an excruciating death, and it would be excruciating, that I do promise you, precious, sweet boy!"

Resisting the chains, wanting to lunge at the witch, Kenyan fell backward, no match for their powerful restriction. "She won't do it! You'll see! You'll never get her to do it no matter what!"

Decara flashed him one last wicked grimace before seating herself properly back upon her icy throne. "We'll see," she said, situating herself with the utmost poise and exalted esteem before turning and looking at her niece.

"The time has come. Dare not disappoint me again, child! You know what it is you must do!" Then Decara instinctively looked up into the bleak heavens. She had not bothered to check the status of the falling moon. It was nearly gone from the sky now. She had mistakenly taken too much time with her taunting and theatrical exhibition of torment over the beasts of the sea and the boy and did not have as much time left as she would have hoped. However, if things went as planned, she would still make the fatal deadline. Nevertheless, this sudden realization made her jump from her icy seat with agitated panic. "Take the damn dagger to the altar! Do as I tell you! Kill the seal! Do it now and do it quickly, or I will shred your brother before your lifeless eyes! This I swear! Now go, woman!"

Emma merely stared at her aunt as if she had no idea what she was saying.

Annoyed at her niece's interference, Decara screamed, "Well, go on!"

"Don't listen to her!" Kenyan shouted with arrogant defiance.

With a wild and exaggerated turn of her head, Decara glared at the boy, her eyes glowing red, her mouth twisting into a mad snarl. "I have had just about enough of you!" she hissed. With an angry wave of her hand, Kenyan's mouth suddenly disappeared. It had completely vanished from his face as if it was never there in the first place. Smooth skin covered up what once were his lips and mouth. Unable to speak or even utter a single sound, he looked on with raw terror toward his possessed sister. Decara chuckled, impressed by her cruel artistry, and then once more returned her stare to Emma. "Take the dagger over to the table! Destroy the white beast, remove the stone, and come and take your place with me!"

A very dazed and disoriented Emma swayed to and fro between the confines of the massive throne she stood before. Standing there with eyes that could no longer see anything but shadows and flickers of swirling lights, she felt the cold sting of the dagger bite into her palm. Closing her eyes, fighting off the disturbing swells of dizziness and bewilderment, she slowly left the ice throne and proceeded toward the devil's table that held prisoner the pure one—the one she knew she must destroy.

KILL THE SLUG!

Seeing Emma walk toward the altar, Decara left her throne. With seething red eyes fixed sharply upon her niece, she began to move toward the disheveled, but very much alive, *Tiamat* where it was carefully watching, still waiting, counting every moment as it had from the very beginning.

Finding her way over to the desolate vessel, Decara relinquished her stare upon Emma, unreservedly giving her undivided attention to the broken ship before her. As previously displayed, she blatantly outstretched her arms, wrapping them tightly around the splintered boards of the lingering *Tiamat*, holding it, remembering the once human face of her lover, saying, "The time has come, my darling. We will soon be together forever!" Lowering her reptilian-like neck, she kissed the shredded and splintery surface of the disabled vessel, embracing it, kissing it once more. She whispered something against its cold slabs of wooden remains, and immediately the heartbeat of the *Tiamat* trembled. It pulsated, almost as if it was about to burst, its sudden jolt of excitement brought on by Decara and the eminent lack of time slipping mercilessly away before them.

Decara jolted her eyes away from the wreckage, casting them up toward the eaten-away moon. Again, the *Tiamat*'s heartbeat began to palpitate with even greater significance. Her long and bony fingers immediately went to its splintered exterior. She rubbed against it softly, trying to soothe its restlessness. Then, casting her glance up toward the deteriorating skies, she moved toward Emma, who was now directly facing the altar.

Emma looked down at the black table before her. The furry white thing that remained attached to its surface swirled sickeningly, before her eyes its shape hopelessly lost within the many other gripping twists of black and white flashes bursting before her. She felt as if she was dying again, but this time it was worse—much worse! It felt as if her insides were being stripped off and discarded piece by piece, and soon there would be nothing of her former self left, only an empty shell with no substance. Then an even more terrorizing realization shot through her. Consumed by some strange and bizarre awareness, she began to suspect what was happening. She was being changed, turned into something inhuman, something unearthly, something frightening and haunting. She was becoming a ghost. A thing with no form—a phantom monstrosity! Just like the ghoulish sentinels that had guarded the vault holding the diamond seal tears, she would soon cease to be, having only eternal damnation to feed upon.

The silver dagger in her hand suddenly sparked the moment Decara joined her. Standing directly behind her niece, Decara spoke. "That's it, take away the innocence from the wretched worm, woman!" she exclaimed, her hands reaching out and curling around Emma's tiny waist. "There is no one left on this planet that believes in this outdated, gutless farce anymore. Well, all except for"—she couldn't help but snicker—"the sniveling seals of Sealssong, and soon they and their happy home will no longer exist!" Coiling, her arm further around her niece's waist with a tighter squeeze, Decara's hand slithered over Emma's stomach until it finally came upon Emma's hand, the hand holding the silver dagger. Clasping it, Decara fused with the bewitched girl. "There are no children who believe in this innocence anymore. And even the ones who do soon discard it. Like the contrived and deceptive disease it is, they have come to recognize it, learning to reject and despise it before they've shed their short pants and dirty pinafores." She started to laugh again.

It was as if for the first time, Emma heard the white spinning wormlike blur before her speak. "Don't listen, Emma! Don't listen to her! You still have this innocence, you still have the gift, don't listen to her lies!" the seal shouted while the whole time, the wooden devil tongues made an even tighter grip around him.

"Shut up, worm! Prepare to die, seal scum!" Decara hissed.

Emma suddenly began to feel extremely faint; however, the twirling spins and flashing lights hemorrhaging before her had lessened their flow, and she could see the white thing before her more clearly. She blinked her eyes hard, trying to bring it into a sharper focus, but the still bleeding flares and blazes were not about to surrender. She then felt Decara's hand suddenly grip her own with a powerful wrench; it felt as if she had broken the delicate bones in her hand.

Just then, the ripped-apart boards of the *Tiamat* began to tremble with violent spasms. The entire broken structure rumbled with disturbing moans and groans that pierced the frigid air. It bucked and shook with uncontrolled jerks, bending painfully within the crippling hold of the icy shores. Millions of invisible insect-like creatures began crawling within the tattered wood of the vessel. The clicking sound they made as they dragged themselves along the wooden fibers sounded like a billion termites feasting. As the crunching groans and moans increased, a veritable explosion sounded, tearing a massive hole in the middle of the already torn-away ship. A hundred thousand parts of shredded planks and twisted pieces of itself flew through the air, disappearing into the black firmament. From the rubble came a heaving and choking grunt.

With one tremendous thrust, the broken vessel regurgitated and spewed up the accursed haunted vault, hurling it across the ice. It was damaged and crushed, but the vault still possessed more diamonds. The once-intimidating cryptic vault fell to its side. Instantly the door dropped off like the jaw of a decaying skeleton, breaking clean of its corrupted hinges, ushering dozens of burlap sacks to pour out, their tie strings coming undone, every single diamondiferous seal tear spilling everywhere, covering the ground where Emma stood.

A loud and breathy moan cut through the air before stilling, then in a whispered voice, the morbid sentries warned—*"Take heed! The moon is nearly gone! You have little time left! Be forewarned! There will be no other omen, for we must return to nothingness . . . For our greed now consumes us just as you have commanded! There will be no further warning . . . Beware! For we are nothing! Nothing! Noth—"* A wild and horrific parade of screams followed as the ghoulish sentinels of the vault squeezed what remained of their ghostly skeleton heads through the splintered and torn-away openings in the vessel. In one final shriek of despair, the decapitated things opened their mangled mouths, and with one slurping and disgustingly squishing noise, they swallowed themselves up and vanished!

The horrible screams seemed to jolt Emma from her trance. She fell forward, nearly falling upon the black altar. Decara quickly snatched her back, pinning her securely to herself. With her eyes wild and flaring red, the evil woman looked up once again toward the blackened skies, the moon nearly invisible now. All at once, Decara's face drained to bone white, almost transparent. The beating pulse of the *Tiamat* grew more restless, almost frantic when Decara removed her stare from the hanging heavens in order to look back toward the crippled ship. She suddenly appeared extremely tense, just like the mangled *Tiamat*, most unsure and terribly frenzied. Not pausing another moment, Decara screamed out to Emma, squeezing her hand even tighter, snapping the bones in Emma's thumb and forefinger while raising both of their arms toward the black skies, taking Emma's broken fingers with her. *"Enough!"* Decara screeched. "Kill the damn worm; kill it before I kill you!"

Again, Emma's concentration became interrupted by the vibrating sounds the furry wormlike thing was making. "Emma! Look at me! Try to remember—Try to remember!" Miracle pleaded, the demonic wooden tongues squeezing him the hardest yet, taking his breath from him.

Staring at the white blurry worm Emma was still unable to understand it, her hand raised high by the direct supervision and harsh assistance of the witch standing behind her. Clutching her niece's broken fingers together in one mutilated squash; Decara pushed the silver dagger deep into Emma's hand, cutting the girl's skin, wedging it there so it would not drop. Then crushing her niece's fingers over the engraved body of the dragon that covered most of the dagger, Decara opened her grip with a springing jolt before pulling her hand away, screaming, "Kill it, kill it—*now!*"

Emma stood there with the knife firmly embedded in her hand, blood dripping from the wound, just looking down at the blurry and obscure-looking worm, unable to remember, unable to disobey, knowing only that the horrible worm must die!

Decara watched with crazy eyes as Emma solely held on to the dagger, raising it over the seal, ready to strike, but then suddenly stopping when her naked feet came upon thousands of spilled-over diamond chips covering the icy floor beneath her. She gasped. Gazing down, she wavered to and fro, her hand clasped tight around the dagger. She continued to stare at the glittering marvel, her mind swimming with more flashing lights and twirling images, images she could not make out or understand. Miracle called out to her once again, but when he barked out her name for the second time, the evil devil tongues suddenly recoiled from him like rats from a sinking ship. With one jerking spring, they disappeared, returning back into the thick etches of the black altar, all except the tongues that curled around his neck. They would remain, making sure he could not leave. He tried to call out to Emma, but the tongues were choking him and he could scarcely breathe.

Abruptly, Emma was aware of the sound of approaching footsteps.

Louder and louder they grew, as did the sudden wind that came out of nowhere. Catching sight of moving shadows made up of blurry faces and dark and shifting shapes, she waited, the footsteps finally coming to a halt. The hunters had returned. Still consumed by Decara's power, the zombie men stood around the devil's black altar, their empty eyes staring through dark sockets, having come to witness the destruction of the sacrificial slug. Slowly, Emma turned to look at the men. Their obscure images were vague, but she could still see that they were unyieldingly clutching to their weapons, just as she was clutching the silver dagger that was now pointed directly at the exposed chest of the white worm. More tangles of ghastly visions clawed at her, bringing her to the very edge of madness.

"For the last time, woman, kill the bloody damn worm!" Decara ordered from the blurred shadows.

Emma closed her eyes, trying to resist the insanity of the witch's spell, but was unable. With shaking hands and a tremulous heart, she clutched her weapon even tighter and prepared to drive it straight through the heart of the white worm.

With a trembling hand, she brought the dagger down!

TIME IS OF THE ESSENCE

Something made her stop.

Just as the tip of the dagger pierced the skin above where Miracle's heart beat, she froze. There was a scream, not just any scream. Its plea came from a voice that was hauntingly familiar, but who? Who was it? She turned around, her vision confused and swirling. Again, the screaming voice called out. "Emma! Please don't kill my child! Listen to your heart, not the witch! Your heart is pure and innocent! I still believe in you! Don't harm my son!" cried the mother of the white seal. "You promised! You promised!"

Miracle tried to look toward his mother, but the strangling tongues made it nearly impossible. He felt the superficial wound from his chest begin to ooze blood. It did not appear to be serious, but the way that the blood kept covering him, he began to panic. Emma shook her head in defiance, clutching down on the dagger, feeling as if she was about to faint when she saw all the blood.

Arayna called out to her once again. "Emma, don't! In the name of all that is sacred, please stop and think what you are about to do!" With this, the despairing mother harp threw her head back and howled forth a cutting cry of pure anguish. Utterly startled by Arayna's piercing outcry, Emma suddenly felt the evil spell jolt inside her as if startled as well. Taking advantage of its momentary stupor, she struggled to free herself further from its foul grip, turning hurriedly toward Arayna. She gasped; it was as if the dagger had suddenly pierced her own heart. Then she heard the imploring song radiating from the mother of the doomed seal fill the air. Arayna's song was so heartfelt; it assaulted every part of Emma, making her feel dizzy and nauseous, bringing about a biting sting flush against her cheeks. Finding herself returning her gaze upon the fuzzy white form beneath her, she looked down at it wearily, its black eyes shining with teary wonder. It was apparent that the snow-white creature could hear the lamenting seal song just as she did. Decara began to shriek out more commands, but Emma was now oblivious to them, for the howls of Arayna's beseeching aria had broken over her like a wave, its impact refreshing her, its pureness breaking the spell! A cold wind quickly blasted over Emma. She felt her knees weaken while she painfully continued gazing down toward the white seal of Sealssong, her memory now perfectly restored!

"Emma!" cried Miracle through a choked whisper, tears cascading from his glorious black and shining eyes, the suffocating devil tongues wrapped snugly around his throat. "Remember, we are in this together to the very end!"

Emma continued staring down at him with heart-wrenching recall. The bleeding in his chest had subsided; however, she realized that it was she who had done such a horrific act. Her heart broke before him, and yet through it all, she found that her heart was once again renewed and free from Decara's wicked influence, for there was her Miracle and he was alive! She started to cry, knowing that she had once again found him. However, when she saw him lying there, disabled, she gasped.

"Miracle!" she cried, her voice a teary sea of more gasps and gurgles. Ashamedly aware of the silver dagger in her hand, she threw it from her sight, casting it off toward the towering ice thrones beyond. In a falling heap, Emma collapsed upon the devil's table, clutching the white seal, sobbing, holding him to her broken heart. "Forgive me!" she pleaded, embracing her cherished companion. "Forgive me!" Then without so much as suspecting such a possibility, she was abruptly grasped from behind and hurled from the black altar.

"Pick up the dagger!" a seething Decara demanded her eyes redder and filled with the sheer fires of hell!

Combating her breathlessness, Emma felt herself fall to the icy ground, losing her footing upon the ice. From the red sea of overflowing seal gown that covered the ice and the seal tears she sat upon, Emma looked up toward the witch with eyes of utter contempt. "No!" she growled.

Decara flew at her like a savage animal. Grabbing her niece in her skeleton hold, she pulled Emma up from the shining floor, shaking her about like a rag doll before slapping her hard across the face. "You go over there, pick up that dagger, and kill that wretched beast!"

"Never!" Emma screamed feeling the burn from her assault sting at her viciously.

Decara looked at Emma as though she would actually kill her. Swinging back her red and satiny-clad hand, she harshly struck Emma across the face again, this time sending her back to the ice and the glittering seal tears. "All right, girlie, I'm through fooling around! I've been patient long enough! I've given you every opportunity to find your place with me, but no more, no more! Now you will suffer for your stubborn brattish insolence!"

In a whirling twirl, Decara furled out her lavish seal coat, snapping it sharply in the cold air. In a complete rage, she stormed over toward the mouth-less Kenyan who had been watching mutely with eyes more wild than hers. Decara grabbed him sternly by the neck, slamming him hard into the gouged-out glacier. No groan came from the brutal impact for there was no way he could make a sound. However, Decara was about to change all that again. "I'm warning you," she hissed, directing her venomous bite over to Emma. "Pick up the dagger!"

Emma tried to pull herself up from the ice but suddenly felt a familiar dizziness overcome her. Dazed with nausea and an attack of unforeseen chilling cold, she looked out toward her brother. His disfigurement made her gasp in horror, but the way Decara slammed him about made her cry out in further torment. "Stop it!" she begged. "Stop hurting him!"

Decara quickly turned on her familiar demented jack-o'-lantern smile, motioning to her servant to come to her; and looking out into the crowd of zombie seal hunters, she spotted what she was looking for. One of the men was carrying a large steel blade, a perfect weapon to both kill and scalp seals at the same time. This was exactly what she had in mind for the precious, sweet boy.

In only moments, the oafish Oreguss was at Decara's side; still chomping his yellow broken teeth up and down, hardly able to contain himself from hearing what his deranged mistress would have him do next. Pointing to the hunter, Decara screamed out in an insane blast, "Bring me his sword!"

Oreguss began to jump up and down in playful bliss upon hearing her cruel command. Excitedly nodding his head, the burly servant dashed over to the bewitched seal hunter, grabbing the sword from his grasp with one swift swipe. With childlike glee, Oreguss raced up to Decara, delivering the sharp blade. She snatched it from him with a powerful hand, wildly casting her glare toward Emma, her eyes smoldering with hatred. Then looking toward the mouth-less Kenyan, she widened her grimace. "Sweet boy, I shall now return your voice. I want your sister to hear every precious scream of yours as your flesh is ripped off piece by piece, sliver by sliver!"

With a wave of her bony fingers, Kenyan's face became restored. A loud and earsplitting scream already in progress tore out from his mouth. Emma's blood-chilling scream amply joined in with her brother's as she picked herself up from the ground and began running toward him. Sadly, it was already too late. Decara had raised the sword and had cut into Kenyan's right shoulder. Emma heard him scream out in agony, but the wicked woman had just begun. "One slice — or two?" Decara evilly bantered.

Turning, running, and flinging herself onto the witch, Emma pulled them both to the ground. "This stops now, Decara!" she screamed, wrestling with the dark woman, forcing her aunt's shoulders to the cold slab of icy carpet. "Do you hear me? No more, no more, *witch!*" Oreguss was quick to retrieve the young girl from his mistress with one brutal yank. Emma winced out in pain hanging there before Decara, her legs kicking at the air, partially digging into

Oreguss' gut while he vehemently clutched the back of her red seal attire, suspending her in midair.

Appalled and utterly embarrassed, Decara realized that the entire underworld of darkness was carefully watching every move she made. Nonetheless, she had to play it safe and remain calm no matter how much she wanted to disembowel every creature surrounding her. She began to laugh precariously, rising from the icy ground. Reclaiming the sword while dusting herself off nonchalantly she, sadistically watched the boy squirm with pain. Throwing her head back, preparing to sound off with more laughter; Decara suddenly noticed the moon again. She was indeed running out of time. Now crazed with a streak of visible panic, she delivered another powerful blow, slicing into the boy's other shoulder.

"Kenyan," Emma screamed from her strained suspension in the air, "don't say another word, she'll kill you!"

"That's the idea, brat!" Decara answered with a ghastly sneer, slithering up to her restrained niece who remained crammed between Oreguss' massive fingers. Emma tried to kick at her, but Decara was quick. Grabbing hold of Emma's feet, Decara squeezed them tightly, pulling on them, drawing herself even closer. "Can you feel the cold, little miss innocence? Can you? I'm sure by now you can because, my little ungrateful pismire, the sickness that I had taken from you is slowly returning. Soon you will know that familiar sensation of illness, but this time, it will be far more agonizing than before! I'll make you feel every inch of your body as it rots away right before your eyes!"

Again, Emma tried to kick Decara, but her aunt's skeleton vise was unbreakable.

Kenyan had doubled over with pain from the cuts of the sword. His blood began to turn red the small part of ice he stood upon defiantly shouting, "Don't listen to her!"

"Smell that?" Decara asked, closing her eyes breathing in the air, "the sweet, smell of death!"

All at once, Emma was not only aware of her brother's pleas, but the cries and wails of the entire congregation of incarcerated sea life suddenly saturated her with hurdling urgency. "Kick it, kick it good!" screamed Lukie.

"Smack the witch, smack the witch!" Big Petie protested.

"Let us free, boop-boop-dee-dee!" wailed Crumpels, spitting out more neurotic rhymes and panicked-stricken gasps! Poo-Coo maintained his attempts of breaking free from the chains but was not remotely able to budge the links embedded deep within the icy structure. The weak and confused Captain Thorne watched on with a single eye that remained transfixed in madness. The chains that had weighed him down from the start coiled around his legs and arms like dead snakes as he lay there motionless on the cold floor of ice, still trying desperately to accept the nightmare before him. Arayna merely stared onward with tearful eyes, no longer howling, terror gripping her mind, and sheer anguish consuming her heart.

Looking toward her brother, Emma cried out again. She watched him collapse to the ground, his shirt saturated in blood. "Please, in the name of heaven, stop this! Stop this," she sobbed.

Decara threw Emma's tiny feet from her clutches, crashing them hard into Oreguss' bulging gut, and taking her niece's face in both her elongated hands, she mashed Emma's face together, squishing her nose and lips into a lumpy ball of flesh. "Heaven has nothing to do with this, you asinine mutant! You're the only one who can stop this now! Kill the worm, bring me the tear, and I will let your brother live! Refuse and I swear I'll kill him right here and now!" she shrieked.

Again, a prostrate Kenyan called out to his sister, his voice rattling with flowing noises, his breath crushed with pants and laborious inhales. "Emma! Don't listen to her! Please! Don't listen to her! Don't—"

"What is it to be, girlie girl? Make your choice!"

In that moment, the dark skies had utterly eaten away the moon, and what remained was difficult to see. The *Tiamat*, who had been ever mindful of the decaying moon, suddenly began to rumble and shake with uneasy apprehension, splintering into a hundred million slivers of itself, imitating a snake shedding its skin. Only it would not be able to renew itself like the serpent. The heinous heartbeat it manifested now grew more savage and crazed, crazed by the urgency at hand, Decara seized Emma from Oreguss and threw her down again into the icy carpet of seal tears. "All, right then, now you will pay for your insolence!" Emma, as did the rest, watched with beating hearts and bated breath as Decara suddenly pushed the heavy sword into Oreguss' hand. "Remove the boy's head!" she ranted.

"No!" Emma screamed out, trying to go to her brother, but Decara knocked her down again, tripping her, pinning her further into the icy seal tears as Oreguss smiled, dashing off toward the boy all happy and excited about cutting off his head. Reaching him, Oreguss found that the boy was a perfect target, for the scrawny kid had already collapsed to the ground, exposing the delicate details of his soon-to-be-lopped-off noggin.

"No! No!" Emma begged.

Forcing close Emma's gaping mouth, Decara pressed against her niece's lips with the tip of her boot. "Shut up and do as you are told and save your precious, sweet boy!" Decara hissed. "Just agree to pick up the dagger and destroy the worm!"

Emma felt the madness gush itself over her, making her want to scream out again. "No! Please! Don't hurt him! Please!" she pathetically wept.

Oreguss, already having had the sword three-quarters down, ready to slice off the boy's head, jumped when he heard Decara's voice blast out "Stop!" Coming to an abrupt halt, Oreguss obeyed, knowing he could not afford to upset his maniacal mistress further, not now when she was on the brink of utter madness. Rolling his eyes in disgust and disappointment, the bearish bald man loomed over the boy, waiting for his next instruction, his fingers itchy to finish off the deed. Decara pulled her boot away from Emma's bruised and red face, leering at her with eyes more wild and desperate than Emma had ever remembered. "Then you will do it? You will kill the worm?"

Her eyes filling up, flowing over with tears, Emma lowered her head, alluding to her surrender.

"Fine, fine, good girl," Decara shrieked.

"No!" Kenyan insisted, his head now under the pressure of Oreguss' heavy boot, the hulking man pushing the boy's head further into the snow. "Don't do it no matter what . . . *Don't do it,*" Kenyan gagged, feeling, himself slipping into unconsciousness.

With both of her hands covering her face, Emma continued to weep despondently. Unable to move, she felt the pull of Decara once again. Bringing, her to her feet, the evil woman commanded, "Now kill the beast and save your precious, sweet boy!" Her head lowered in devastating shame, Emma slowly walked over to the silver dagger, its shining blade still gleaming blood. Bending down, nearly collapsing, she snatched the dagger into her hand and then stood upright. The wind began to kick up again. This time it returned in full fury. It howled around her brutishly as she made her way wearily over to the hole in the earth, where the circling green devil mist upheld the black altar confining the condemned white seal.

By now, the ruthlessness of the winds had thoroughly undone Emma's hair, leaving it a mass of unruly golden locks snapping crudely about her delicate tear-streaked face. She looked down at the silver dagger in her hand, feeling it burn into her skin. Slowly, she stepped onto the swirling mist of green vapors, the wind continuing with its determined assault, sweeping the demonic fog all over her while her hair flogged against her face. The ghoulish mist seductively coiled around her shoulders and neck, crawling over her feet, its hot and foul breath upholding her as it did the devil's table. Tearfully, she looked down upon the white seal. Unable to hold back any further, Emma began to sob uncontrollably.

Screaming savage winds howled about everywhere, when Emma suddenly dared to look upon the other seals and walruses watching her. This confrontation ripped at her soul with such bereavement that it painfully stole her breath. Each face looked back at her with such sadness, with such displacing loss that she wished to take the dagger to herself. The lost and forlorn features of the harp seals and walruses were unbearable, but when Emma's eyes came upon Arayna, she began to shake with grief. The mother of the white seal stood erect and steadfast, her eyes never leaving Emma's, filled with both remorse and fear and yet pity. Yes, above all else, there was pity within those tear-infested shining black eyes, pity that still regarded Emma with sincerity and an uncanny honor. Emma watched Arayna as the progression of her seal tears streamed down her lovely careworn face. Not able to look on any further, in agonizing and complete degradation, Emma turned her burning eyes away from Arayna and the others. She heard Kenyan calling out to her as she once again looked upon the white seal. "Emma! Don't do it! Please . . . ," her brother's voice pathetically pleaded before abruptly being cutoff when Oreguss stepped hard on his head, smashing it down deep into the ice.

"Raise the sword!" Decara violently told her hairy henchman. "If she refuses — KILL HIM!"

A wide smile broke out across Oreguss' face, his eyes bulging with newfound joy; and raising the heavy sword, he towered it over the boy's neck, just waiting for her to give the word.

Emma looked at her brother, trembling. "Kenyan," she sadly whispered in a desperate voice, placing both of her shaking hands across her quivering mouth, the dagger resting coldly against her lips. Feeling the dagger sear into her flesh, she pulled it away from her face and closed her eyes tightly before opening them. Once more, she looked down at the white seal. She watched Miracle look up at her, his face a pure and misty cloud of gentleness as it had always been from the very beginning, his black unlit stone covered up by the strapping tongues of the evil table.

"Emma—" Miracle struggled to say through the choking restraints. "I understand. It's okay . . ." His eyes teared over, his furry mouth giving her a brave smile.

More rumbling of the *Tiamat* startled Decara, causing her to growl just like a trapped animal. She had returned to her ice throne. All crunched up, looking piteously small inside its massive domain, her rigid spine pressed tight against the endless backrest of her chair. Her legs brought up toward her heaving chest, the trailing black robe covering up her queenly seat, her long fingers stiff, scratching deep into the icy arms of the throne that dared to tower into the heavens, she neurotically looked on with uneasy madness. She was no longer aware or cared that the heavens and the realms of hell were watching. Her only concern now focused on her niece. "You have only a few more seconds, girlie!" Her mood worsened with mounting apprehension. "Come on, princess," Decara hysterically shrieked with the force of a raging tempest, "Kill the damned thing!"

Emma's tears fell upon the seal, her spirit breaking from both shame and sorrow. She then looked back to her brother, her wrenching heart breaking all over again. Turning back to look at Miracle, she covered her eyes, said a silent pray, and raised the dagger, preparing to drive the blade straight through her own heart. Naturally, Oreguss was there to stop her. Seizing her by the arm, he forced the dagger into her palm, making it bleed again. "Uh-uh, ahhh," he grumbled while pointing at the incarcerated white seal. "Kill!" he commanded.

"I cannot!" Emma wailed, throwing the dagger away from her where it landed on a random pile of crystallized seal tears. Falling down into a broken heap, Emma grabbed on to Miracle, sobbing uncontrollably, "I can't! I can't do it!"

Just then, a sudden stillness engulfed Sealssong. It momentarily took away the wind and everyone's breath as the dagger glistened in the mysterious light. Decara immediately stood up from the ice throne, her face distorted into a mask of raw insanity. "You stupid little fool!" she screamed in a numbing roar, sounding as if she had just severed her vocal cords and was still choking on them. Raking the air with her arms, she ferociously stormed toward Emma, the gushing wind bringing the last traces of the bleeding moon upon the earth. Hurling herself toward her niece, Decara suddenly froze in her tracks, her sewn-together seal dress sharply snapping in the wind, her hair a mass of wild black tentacles, her eyes bulging with depraved madness. For the first time ever, Decara appeared to be frightened; and what was to follow, she had every right to be. She had at last run out of time!

MORNING HAS BROKEN

At that very moment, a single ray of light broke through the black universe, settling directly upon the slumped-over Emma and the white seal, both still floating inside the green mist.

The first ray of the morning sun had somehow found its way.

Out from the *Tiamat*, the red goblins returned, violent and shaken into a crazed swarm. They screamed out in torment, becoming sucked into the diabolical hole suspending the devil's table. Their descent back to hell shook the island like an earthquake. In an unholy gush, sounding like hundreds of freight trains colliding, the gulped-down demons flooded over Emma and Miracle, each monstrosity draining into the opening like rain down a sewer pipe.

All at once, Miracle felt the wooden tongues pull apart with a cutting and abrasive sting, each relinquishing their grip as the accursed altar also descended back into the pit, the green mist and the hellish nightlight from below, following. Holding securely to the white seal, Emma pulled Miracle off the table, saving him just in time from the fatal desertion into the darkness, hurling herself and the seal back onto the island. With a deplorable thud, they fell into the multitudes of seal tears, scattering them about mercilessly. Hundreds of millions of flashing green lights began to shoot through the icy cracks of the seal nursery, shaking it with such a magnitude, breaking the ice apart. Decara was the first to fall to the cold ground. She heard the throbbing heartbeat of the *Tiamat* then its horrific scream of despairing anguish. Emma's refusal to kill the seal had sealed the evil woman's fate and her lost lover. Because of this, there would be no second chance.

The diabolically crazed woman screamed in unbridled contempt, her madness utterly consuming her. Turning to Oreguss, she screeched out her command. "Kill him, kill, the boy!" Having returned to Kenyan, Oreguss felt the earth begin to wind down from its outlandish rocking, giving him time to get a sure foot upon the ice again. Kenyan fought off Oreguss as best as he could, but he remained weak from the loss of blood, and the wounds he sustained made it impossible for him to do anything. Besides, the resilience of the chains he wore left little room for any real combat. As before, he felt himself go down hard, the crushing weight of Oreguss pinning him into the ice, holding him there so he could finally remove his head with one quick chop! Up went the blade! Emma screamed and then Lukie followed, once again squirting the place with yellow excitement.

Kenyan closed his eyes. Unable to move and waiting to die, he heard the swish of the sword cut through the air with a deathly whooshing noise! Had his head been cut off? It must have been. Funny, it didn't hurt as he thought it might. Come to think of it, it didn't hurt at all! Kenyan did not have time to think again because he suddenly became inundated with cold seawater, and the way it washed over him, burning the open wounds on his body, made him realize that he was indeed still alive! The way the earth was cracking and splitting, he knew it just had to be the end of the world. Unable to stand, Oreguss toppled over him, hitting his head on the ridge of the gouged-out glacier before falling to the ground in a massive slump.

As the sea washed over the nursery, the entire island continued to splinter and break, sending hundreds of ice floes out into the swelling of the tide. It rose over the crumbling glacier, breaking over it and all of its trapped occupants. Kenyan felt the chains he wore tear away from the ice and slip easily off of him. It happened the same way with the others. They were all, at last, finally free!

The rushing surge did not last long, and in a short while, it returned to the better part of the sea. This happening occurred long enough for Kenyan to see exactly what was at the core of such a monumental disturbance.

Another wall of rising seawater rose and surrounded the island. Then there was an even more intense eruption in the water as an immense shape, the color of dark blue coral, broke the surface. It came from the east, smashing the shoreline into smithereens—then came another, then another, the third incredible creature coming from the west. The chanters had returned!

The whales glided over the ice, riding the enormous wave, revealing, themselves. The fourth leviathan came out of nowhere, this particular chanter in full smile, exposing its colossal head momentarily; it belonged to Kishk! Immediately, the chanters surrounded the nursery, each meeting in midair with only one intention—that of putting an end to Decara and her monstrous plan! At any cost, the chanters knew that the witch must die!

Kishk continued to ride the enormous wave, hoping to meet up with his comrades already encased within the watery embrace of the climbing sea. It was then that the fantastic quartet of chanting whales began their emphatic song, for it was the whale Kishk who would initiate the memorable note that would set off the voices of the three other leviathans. Up, rose Kishk, accidentally swiping off part of the island with his tail, taking it with him as the tide swallowed him up, his massive rear catapulting him to the highest part of the sky where all four giant wonders eventually met. As the blue chanters ascended, they found their aquatic wings—their song in full glory. Moving swiftly toward the center of the nursery hundreds of feet in the air, their magnificent bodies formed a star as they drew closer to one another, elevated high above Sealssong, there among the clouds. More rays of sunshine had begun to break through the obscure sky when Decara looked directly upward. She saw the four mighty tides swiftly engulfing the island, the towering wave mounting, holding within its translucent sparkle the incomparable giants of the sea. The four singing whales soared like prehistoric birds between the aqueous partitions of the surging ocean, a million shafts of sunlight breaking through the gushing windows of the sea, igniting the recently dark nursery with brilliance never before seen!

Decara stared on with true terror, helplessly watching as the blue whales ate up the sky, each towering unimaginably above her. Fleetingly patches of sky shone through the chanters as they dominated the heavens. In only a matter of moments, they would crush the life out of the witch. She had to stop them! Although she had failed miserably, she could still feel her powers pulsate within her boiling veins; she had no intentions of surrendering now! If anything, Decara's wrath suddenly spawned and mutated into an even more diabolical insanity, lunacy that took her to the deepest part of pure madness that of which she would never recover. Abandoning all self-control, she flew out into the middle of the island, throwing out her skeleton arms. She scratched up toward the cavalcade of chanting mammals looming dangerously overhead while the sky grew black, the four whales meeting directly above her. Each of their fantastic heads gently touched then bowed to one another, each preparing for their descent upon the soon-to-be-crushed Decara, the tremendous surge of seawater upholding them, bowing gracefully along with them.

Beneath the passing shadows of the four giants, Decara spewed out her final curse. "Dibble-Dabble-Dastard-Niff, Curse the sea and make her stiff!" Two magnificent flashes of red blazes burst through her eyes like bolts of lightning. The exploding effulgence hit against the outstretched tips of her fingers, shooting up directly toward the soaring chanters. Upon impact, the luminous blow stopped the whales, literally freezing them. With loud crackling sounds, the water solidified. Decara's evil spell worked just as she intended. The swelling wave had frozen over, sealing the four colossal beasts inside.

Since the wave was in the process of breaking, it now hung down from the sky, fantastically arched and bent immobilized in its fatal curtsy, curved and turning, aimed directly at the dark, evil woman. The mighty wave and its four gallant warriors had nearly succeeded in destroying her. In fact, the wave had almost touched Decara's nose when it eventually and fully turned rock solid in its unbelievable descent from the sky.

Possessing eyes that would remain wild and swimming in a sea of constant fire, Decara, defiant, stared up at the petrified wave. She could clearly see the four trapped whales within, their frozen bodies looming dangerously over her. She studied them in exaggerated awe, looking as if she had discovered the remains of prehistoric creatures frozen for millions of years. Because the solid wave was so close, she reached out and touched the tip of its obstructed crest, snapping her index finger against it hard, breaking off a piece. Instantly, she burst into mad hysterical laughter. With the rushing sensation of yet even more madness, she turned from the mammoth swell hulking only inches away and began to go after her accursed niece and the loathsome white seal. She had nothing to lose now. Her madness thoroughly engulfing her, Decara continued cackling uncontrollably, for all hell was about to break loose!

Another shaft of sunlight snuck out from the rocky incline of the frozen whales. The streaming light made visible exactly what she hoped to see: Emma and the white seal together, both swiftly moving toward the others, every one of them in a state of absolute panic since the dramatic appearance of the four whales. As Decara stormed toward them, she suddenly heard a most harrowing sound. It was a bloodcurdling scream utterly soaked in sheer torment, rattling of impending death. For in that moment, from some obscure place in the heavens, another shaft of sunlight had prevailed and had come to settle upon the disarrayed shambles of what remained of the *Tiamat.* Decara listened to it scream. She ran to it, the familiar voice of her lover filling the wind with excruciating cries of her torturous failure. Nearing, she listened to the broken vessel scream again when another shaft of sunlight stole through the sky, hitting the ship. Like acid to flesh, the vessel screamed out even louder, more of its bloodcurdling howls savagely assaulting her. She tried to go to it, but it was impossible. All at once, the once magnificent and powerful *Tiamat* exploded into flames, but not just ordinary flames. These were fires that had lit up the very place where damned souls were made to suffer without end. They burned with a green flame, eating away everything it touched. Decara covered her face as the *Tiamat* quickly burned, its last dying screams echoing before her. "Decara—Why? *D-e-car-aaaaaa!*"

Once again, she tried to go to it, but the devil's fire torched at her hand; it was already too late. Right before her eyes, the *Tiamat* began to melt into a thick, syrupy green muck, dissolving quickly into the ice and slushy water. It bubbled and hissed, dissipating into the frozen sea, the green flames boiling the remainder of its thick, gooey self into more green muck. Twisting and flipping on the ice, Decara helplessly watched her lover fizzle and pop into smoldering obscurity, knowing that she had failed him irreparably, allowing for his final demise.

"No!" she shrieked. *"No-oooooooo!"* She felt a sting from another sudden streak of sunlight. It burned her flesh like fire. Running from its searing touch, she screamed for Oreguss. Still feeling somewhat disoriented from his fall, he shook his head, hitting the side of his temples, trying to knock sense back to him. "Get me that filthy worm!" she screamed, brutally pushing past the speculating seal hunters daring to stand in her way.

Arayna watched the evil Oreguss swiftly approach. Kenyan and even the weak and sickly Captain Thorne had gathered next to the seals and walruses, all of them nestling together, not knowing what to expect next. "Leave us alone!" Arayna warned, striking at Oreguss' leg, but he merely kicked at her, shoving her hard into the belly of the walrus with the broken tooth. Both Arayna and Poo-Coo crashed into the crumbled parts of the iceberg as the others screamed on in terror. Oreguss grabbed Miracle and dragged him over to Decara, where she was wrathfully waiting in the shadows. She was foaming at the mouth, incensed, utterly out of her mind, and filled with uncontrolled hatred. She would now have her revenge, for she would not perish without destroying every living thing in Sealssong, however, not before she killed the white worm who had stolen her reign of terror. He would be the first to die! Grabbing the dagger from the icy floor that glittered in seal tears, she squeezed onto it, her scarlet-clad fingers making a tight fist around its silver handle. Oreguss threw the struggling Miracle down on the ice in front of her. Emma flew to Miracle's side, but Decara seized her by the hair, discarding her aside with one powerful blow.

"Stop it, stop it!" Emma screamed, but Decara was past the point of hearing her pleas.

"You think you won, girlie girl? Well, think again! Say goodbye to your precious Miracle because only a real miracle can save him now!"

Emma screamed out, trying to go to him once more. Oreguss was there to stop her, of course, but wasn't quick enough this time. Emma slipped through his hairy grasp, latching on to Decara's flowing seal dress. Enraged, Decara's eyes flared a devilish orange color while Emma held on, trying to take the dagger from her hand. Rigidly, Decara's fingers squeezed tighter, and with her last blow to the girl, she plunged the knife directly into her niece's heart. With startled eyes and open mouth, Emma looked down at her chest long enough to watch Decara pull away the dagger. Then putting her trembling fingers to her bleeding heart, Emma looked at Miracle; and while holding to the saddest gaze, she fell to the ground—dead.

CRASHING LEVIATHANS

Miracle was howling and growling at Oreguss with unrestrained loathing, snapping at his leg, and did not see what had just taken place. He did, however, see Emma fall and instantly tried to go to her, but Oreguss' boot pushed him down into the ice, leaving Decara clear access to drive the bloody dagger through the seal's chest. Turning to Miracle, the mad woman monstrously leered down at him. Her eyes were of sheer hatred, sending a massive chill down his spine, but even then, all he could think of was Emma.

Preparing to slit Miracle's throat, Decara placed the blade beneath his chin, attempting to pull the stone away, but he continued to viciously snap at her, his teeth cutting into her flesh. Nonetheless, she was not giving up. Forcing the blade further into his skin, she prepared to make the fatal slice. "It's all over, worm!" Decara foamed. "You wanted to be with your precious Emma, well, join her now—in hell, because that's where I'm sending you both!" As the blade cut into his hide, another ray of sunlight peeked out from behind the towering wave looming overhead. It streaked across her fingers, burning them, causing her to drop the dagger. She screamed out in absolute agony, looking upon her satin-covered hands. They were smoldering. Something felt terribly wrong. Immediately she removed the glove and looked at her hand. What remained there now was no longer flesh—it had turned to ice! Slowly, and with unbridled shock mounting in those hellish eyes of hers, Decara raised her icy stump, bringing it close to her face. Looking at it carefully, she gave out a most ghastly shriek equaling the deranged and bloodcurdling wails of the recently destroyed *Tiamat*. Frantic, she psychotically tried to remove the other glove, breaking off what was once her pinky finger in the process. It fell to the ground like glass, shattering. Howling out in mad torment, she manically continued, monstrously determined to view her other fingers, the newly acquired deformity making it impossible.

"Help me, you, fool!" she yowled, waiting for Oreguss to assist her further in this all-consuming nightmare. In a few moments, he was at her side. "Remove the glove, idiot!" she wailed. Obeying, Oreguss quickly did what she asked. Relieved, Decara frenetically surveyed her remaining human hand and arm. There was still time—for the flesh yet remained there! She would not admit defeat.

Immediately and while it was still possible, the consummated insane woman retrieved the dagger from the ground, still determined to kill the seal. This time, the shaft of sunlight had grown, and with a blazing yawn, it stretched out further over the evil woman. She immediately fell to her knees as if struck by lightning. She began scraping along the ice with her temporarily human hand, clawing, continuing to somehow hold to the dagger. The screams she made now were loud, sporadic, throttling with a miserable and hideous lunacy. Slithering above the ice, a complete mad thing, she unceasingly screamed out breathy short spurts, her throat making inhuman sounds of ghastliness. She was about to die for her unbelievable mistake, her arrogant transgression finally taking her down. Still, she would not succumb without first taking down the filthy white slug. One way or another, he too was about to die! Dragging what remained of her skin-covered skeleton toward Miracle, the seal's body now pinned under Oreguss' boot she ruefully gazed up toward the hairy brute. Shockingly, when Oreguss saw what was happening to her, even he had to step away, releasing Miracle, deserting her, leaving her dead on her own.

Holding to the dagger, Decara tried once more to stab Miracle, but by now, he had already wriggled away from her. He, as did Oreguss, merely stared on as another shot of sunlight paralyzed her, turning her other hand and arm into a gnarled semblance of icy clumps, both upper limbs now long mangled icicles. Attempting to leave her knees, she pushed herself up, but to her terror, her deformed legs shattered into piles of icy chips, becoming much like the multitudes of seal tears splattered about her. With crazed determination and unbearable misery, Decara managed to get upright partially; however, as more and more rays of sunshine fell across her, the rest of her torso began to stiffen and turn to ice. Finding it impossible to move, she felt the heavy weight of her metamorphosis. Savagely, she stared out at the congregation of seals and walruses, her eyes meeting up with Kenyan's, who had already retrieved his dead sister. He glared back at what remained of her and then lowered his head, losing himself over to Emma.

More sunshine began to strike down at her. Decara howled out like a demented beast before abruptly losing her voice. She could no longer make a sound. She tried to scream but found that she was unable, for her throat became filled with raw arctic frost and her face was rapidly turning into a solid mass of lumpy ice, having no semblance of a face at all. Every strand of hair had been stripped from her head, having fallen to the ground, her slimy scalp folding off like skinned seal hide, its warmth still wavering in the chill, crumpled and dissolving into the multitudes of seal tears on which it fell. Most of her mouth and nose appeared to be wiped away, and all that remained were two bulging eyes of sheer madness now discolored, having turned a pale whitish blue.

Another shaft of sunlight directly joined the others, intensifying their shine upon her and all of Sealssong, dissolving the shadows, scaring away their morbid forms; and in that moment, Decara turned into a grotesque and twisted collection of icy revulsion. Screaming in silent madness, she experienced her insides churn with bitter cold, her blood congealing into a thick and solid, petrified ooze that would soon consume her entirely. Even the seal coat she wore had fused into her icy remains, becoming one with it. The last thing she could remotely move before she entirely stiffened was her head. Tilting it up, it froze permanently, then like the rest of her hideous self, it continued to solidify into a monstrous transparency of quintessential horror.

Decara heard herself scream again, her howls confined solely within her demented mind. Hellishly icebound, unable to stir, she stared upward, her features grotesque and smeared her sight, leaving her as the morphing ice began to fuse itself into her frozen sockets. However, before blindness would totally consume her, she would remain helplessly sighted, watching in agonizing outrage as the incredible wave towering directly above her suddenly started to move! Unbounded, the solidified water holding the four giants began to thaw. She watched in unspeakable terror as a single drop of the thawing wave landed precisely where her smooth alabaster cheek once was. It slowly trickled down what would be considered her chin, instantly freezing with the rest of her.

As her brain began to turn to slush and rocky ice, the last thing Decara would ever see and remember was the way that the mighty wall of ocean suddenly began to fall around her. However, heretofore, just a mere stretch away, she was able to see Kishk's large violet eyes spring open before one final and significant crack in the ice split through the dissolving wave. The melting tide zigzagged with a tremendous determination, spitting out like tongues of lightning, conceding a colossal break to slash its way to the very tip of itself. Straight up it shot, cutting its way into the sky, cracking open the thawing ice like the shell of an egg. Then as if the world suddenly became restored to a familiar existence of normalcy, the faithful piece of ocean broke and exploded into a rushing tidal wave. And right before the witch shattered into a hundred billion pieces of tiny chips of ice, Decara watched the four gigantic whales crash down on her, breaking her, snapping off her head first, then blasting what remained of her pulverized and twisted form far out into the cold and frosty ocean.

Oreguss tried to jump onto an existing floe with the desperate hopes of escaping his mutilated mistress's fate; however, the dropping whales proved to be too much even for the massive bearish brute. For with one swift gulp, Kishk gobbled up Oreguss, chomping up and down on him several times before crashing down onto the trembling waters of Sealssong. The remaining blue whales followed with the rest of the moving tidal wave, scattering parts of the seal nursery and its occupants in every possible direction with one massive and explosive blur.

WHOOO-WHOOO! THE WITCH IS DEAD!

Decara had failed and now she was dead, of this there was no doubt.

For every creature in the sea and land, every tree, every mountain, every bird in the sky, the wind, the snow, the ice, the rain, the earth itself, all universally released a sigh of relief as the witch's icy remains were blown off into oblivion.

From this favorable deed came a sudden blinding flash of light. Multitudes of scattered seal tears shot up into the skies. Spraying into the forming pink and yellow clouds, they began whistling from the velocity of their climactic ride. Their piping music quickly turned into high squeals, sounding like the voices of innocent children at play, their angelic tones ringing out against the crashing sounds the water made striking the nursery. Having hurled the seals into the raging sea, the waves poured over the land, drenching miles of icy terrain. The walruses, both swimming at top speed against the mammoth swells, somehow managed to reunite just as the last of the mountainous tides bowed out of the sky, turning much of Sealssong into a frothy twinkle of a blurry star.

Down deep into the waters the whales plunged, bringing most of the split-away shoreline and a sizeable portion of the nursery with them. It would seem that it would take some time for the moving mass to still, but eventually the waters calmed and the streaming shafts of sunlight began to show themselves again.

They filtered down from the clouds, sparkling through the raining seal tears now returning to earth; however, this time, the tears would not return to the snow and ice as they had left. They preferred changing into soft and flowing snow-white rose petals before wafting down to what remained of the nursery. In a dreamy, sleepy fall, the transformed tears, ablaze with wonder, descended, their childlike voices singing out happily as they floated downward.

Just then, Kishk resurfaced from the sea. With a tremendous splash, his gigantic head cut deep through the water, his violet eyes wide and wondering. The three other chanters followed immediately. No longer filled with their intrepid whale song, they listened to the whimsical fallout serenade them with childlike splendor, the petals unceasingly showering upon them. In just a short while, the chanters became covered in billowing rose petals, appearing more like colossal snowmen than whales. No one spoke. They only continued to look around in awe while more of the cracked island bobbed within the moving waters, some of its remains slowly floating to the surface, other portions forever remaining below. Some of the nearby islands, unfortunately, became lost in the great explosion; still, there was a substantial section of the nursery left. The excited waters lapped at the shattered rookery as it floated there in the middle of the sea, the pink and yellow reflections of the filtering sunlight cascading upon it like a fine mist, the fluttering rose petals cushioning its surface.

This remaining part of the nursery was now the focal point for all to seek out its bobbing grounds, patiently waiting for the return of the seals and those who were taken from the ice. In a frantic search, Kishk looked out among the mist of the descending petals. Squinting, his eyes as if trying to see through a snowstorm, the whale spotted Crumpels and Poo-Coo, both swimming toward him.

"This way!" he shouted. Immediately, Poo-Coo signaled to Kishk with his flipper. Crumpels deliriously tried to keep up with her son, having been knocked silly from the incompatible ruckus brought on by the four massive chanters now waiting their approach. She exasperatingly snorted repeatedly in the water, continuing to beat her flippers against the current. Lumbering, she struggled with the pace, maintaining her sad focus on Poo-Coo's broken tusk, the sunlight glaring off it like a beacon. Kishk carefully watched both tooth walkers arrive and waited for Poo-Coo to catch his breath before he spoke. "We must go to the island and wait for the others," he explained.

With a quick nod of heads, the walruses and the chanters swam into place, honoring the single-file convoy that they were now a part of, Kishk leading the way. The flowing white petals continued to keep everyone dressed up in gigantic snowmen suits as they glided up to the nursery. Kishk and the other chanters remained near the borders, each one of their enormous frames encircling the ice with no room to spare while the walruses slumped onto the broken seams of what was to be left of this particular nursery. They immediately saw Little Lukie and Big Petie making their way toward them, Big Petie barking, "You're alive!"

Crumpels nodded her head, happy to see the two harried bulls surround her. Immediately, they all began to rub noses affectionately. "The witch," asked Poo-Coo, "she is dead?"

"Yes!" rejoiced Big Petie. "And so is that horrible, hairy hooligan of hers, both of them killed by the whales when they plopped out of the sky!"

"And the girl," asked Poo-Coo, "where is she?"

Lukie began to shake, whimpering, Petie's eyes filling with sadness, both remaining silent. Poo-Coo continued staring intensely at the seals, fully realizing what their silence meant. "Will you take us to her?"

Petie slowly lifted his pathetic gaze and nodded. Lukie, still unable to speak, continued with his lamenting whimpering, nervously wiping at his saturated snout with his flipper, wriggling away with his companion, the walruses close behind.

A gentle breeze began to suddenly wash itself over the island as the pink and yellow clouds bowed out gracefully, giving way to the dawning sky of pale blue, the falling planets no longer visible, having returned to their proper stations in the universe. Crumpels turned and began plowing through the fallen petals. Believing she heard the promising calls of stray birds, she listened with a full heart while rumbling along tirelessly trying to keep up with everyone else. Soon, the sweet songs of the birds filled the air, their calls merging delicately with the glittering beams of sunshine growing more abundant with each passing moment. However, what awaited her, no amount of sunshine or display of joyful song could possibly ease such sad tidings. With heads bowed, there upon a raised glade of snow, now covered in soft white rose petals, as was the rest of Sealssong, Crumpels, her son, and the two grieving seals looked upon Emma.

She was lying as if asleep upon the petals, her tiny body barely crushing them. Both of her arms remained folded over her chest as if in prayer, and her cheeks were blushed with pink just as if she had been tenderly kissed there, repeatedly. Her golden hair had fallen against her placid face and had just begun to stir in the wind when they came upon her. Initially, they did not utter a sound, but only looked at the careworn face of Kenyan who sorrowfully knelt beside his sister. He stared down at Emma, his heart breaking, his eyes saturated and rimmed red with grief, his wounds still bleeding, burning. Running his fingers lightly over her forehead, he gazed at her lying there, still and quiet, the falling rose petals ever present in their respected vigil.

Lukie broke the unbearable stillness with a few loud sniffles, wiping at his snout with his quivering flipper. "She's dead," he told softly, feeling his eyes well up all over again.

"Oh no!" cried Crumpels, turning her massive face, burying it deep within the folds of her son's chest.

"The witch, she killed her!" Lukie cried, wiping away more tears from his heavily drenched muzzle. "And we can't find Miracle—*neither!*"

"Did he make it out all right?" Poo-Coo asked over the sobbing sounds his mother and Lukie were making.

Petie shook his head. "We're not sure."

The walrus and the seals turned to once again look upon the lifeless girl and the broken boy remaining near her side. It was at this time that the whales came to notice the seal hunters, those surviving the fatal impact upon the island, as well as Decara's evil spell. The men remained in separate clusters, floating in semiconscious states around the premises of the nursery. Some had already gone into hypothermia, floating in the freezing floes with only their heads sticking out of the water, their eyes closed and frozen over. Others found aid from the numerous broken slabs of icebergs scattered endlessly about them. Having climbed upon them, most of the men drifted along, clutching to the frozen rafts most dazed and near death.

Upon seeing this, Kishk instructed the other three chanters to leave the borders in order to claim each man with the intent of taking him from the fatal waters and bringing them upon the island. Despite their incredible differences, Kishk could not be responsible for any further deaths, not even these terrible man-beasts; Oreguss' death was enough. Without hesitation, the whales went to work. One by one, they took each unconscious and semiconscious man in their gigantic mouths, careful not to chew on them or in any way hurt them. The men gave no intentions of refusing their help, for they were near complete exhaustion and could not begin to put up a fight, even if they were able. There were seventeen swilers who had weathered the disastrous ruin of the nursery by the time all four whales had safely succeeded in returning them upon solid ground. Each man was placed with the utmost care upon the billowing piles of snowy rose petals that continued to fall from the pale blue morning sky.

As the last man was brought safely to the portion of the nursery, Kishk turned away and slowly cast his eyes up toward the clearing firmament. There, he saw the returning stages of the fading moon. It had not been destroyed after all, for with the crushing failure of Decara and all her evil powers, the Night of Screams was forever banished; and because of this, all the heavens began to return to their rightful places. It was as if time had been reversed, and upon the next moonlit night, it would once again glow in all its familiar mystic charm and wonder as if never having undergone such traumatic alterations. Kishk would not have time to further witness the moon take its temporary leave from the heavens, for he soon became aware of more disturbances in the waters. Turning his violet eyes, he came upon more returning survivors. He smiled with joy as he saw Bellgar and the blind Nikki swimming side by side, their child, Promise, nestled between them both, his tiny face full of wonder while sailing upon both parents' shoulders.

Bellgar reached the island first, Nikki near his side, having followed his navigation the entire time. Their pup quickly jumped off their backs onto the ice and quickly dove into the endless sea of rose petals spread out as far as the eye could see. Feeling the need to play Clap-Clap among the soft and silky snuggle of their touch, the young pup flipped over to his side in playful delight. However, soon, Promise felt the air sharpen with a distinct sadness he could literally smell. The young pup sniffed hard at the air. Lowering his head, feeling ashamed, he quickly wriggled off toward his mother and father, this time not daring to leave their side. The blind Nikki quickly took Promise into her embrace and then felt panic seize her. She too sniffed at the air. Immediately she could smell the multitudes of man-beasts surrounding them.

"Bellgar!" she growled. "They're here! The murdering humans, they are everywhere! We must leave! We must leave at once!" Nikki cried, clinging desperately to her child, the unconformity of blindness crushing her.

Having been aware of the men from the moment they returned, Bellgar looked at them with little concern. Most appeared dead or incredibly sick in their crumbled state upon the ice. It was clear that they would pose no immediate danger. "It's all right," he told his blind mate. "They cannot harm us, I promise."

Nikki shook her head in panic. "They will kill us all!" She shuddered.

Bellgar bent over, placing his snout directly before Nikki's. He licked at her nose affectionately, saying, "No, I'm sure no harm will come to us. We have been spared and have been returned to Sealssong for a reason. Surely you have felt this just as I have."

An unexpected calm came over Nikki as she once again sniffed the air, stiffening. Yes, she too had sensed it. It was there all around her. Things were no longer the same. It had all been changed, but to what degree she could not be certain. As quickly as it had seized her, the feeling of immediate and impending doom left, taking the last traces of the fully restored moon from the sky. Making sure that Promise remained ever close, she began to follow the sound of her mate. He would lead them through the snowy rose petals and the isles of seal hunters who now stared upon them in silent awe. Nikki stood inches away from Bellgar as they passed the seventeen men. She continuously inhaled deep the air, feeling for her child with every wriggle she took. In a short while, she felt Bellgar stop. "What is it?" she nervously asked.

Bellgar did not immediately answer. It took a while to acclimate to what was playing out before him. There he came upon the lifeless Emma and her injured brother. Circled around the girl in respected genuflection, he saw the figures of the walruses and the two bulls. Then he saw another man-beast with a covering over his eye.

Captain Thorne had found his way to the boy and dead girl but was unable to assist in any way. The entire ordeal had proved to be too much for the once-staunch captain of the former infamous *Tiamat*. He now lay wearied, not far from the lifeless form of Emma, lifeless himself, slumped over to one side, staring out with a vacant look burning in his bloodshot eye once holding the cobalt color of a vibrant sky. Bellgar wriggled just a bit farther, hoping to get a closer look. His heart quickened and he swallowed hard, feeling the saliva throb against the back of his throat. Bellgar gasped.

"What has happened?" Nikki pleaded.

He turned and looked at the brother of the girl that had come to save the world, then lowering his head, Bellgar turned to his mate. "She doesn't seem to be breathing. She appears to be . . . I believe that she . . . she is dead."

Nikki's sightless eyes instantly filled with tears, and she quickly buried her snout into her mate. "Come," Bellgar said. "We must go to them."

Nikki continued to weep, feeling Bellgar draw away from her.

"It's, okay, Mama," a now talking Promise quickly vowed with a brave smile. "I'll take you there." He extended his tiny flipper, offering it over to her. Feeling his gentle touch, Nikki half smiled, wiping away at her teary cheeks, sniffling up more emotion, nodding her head, allowing her child to escort her toward the gathering where the deceased Emma remained prostrate.

SADNESS AT SEALSSONG

Something moved in the water.

The sudden uneasiness in the sea made all four of the surrounding chanters turn away from the downcast gathering. Kishk, once again, would be the first to see who it was. It was Miracle. The head of the white seal broke through the frosty pallet of the moving ocean, when with a forceful intake of breath, he refilled his pounding lungs. He coughed repeatedly, shaking himself; he nearly drowned in the aftermath of the falling whales having been hurled from the island, rendered semiconscious from the blow. Nonetheless, Miracle fought diligently to return to the nursery to once again be reunited with Emma.

None of the whales dared to speak or even remotely make a motion to chant the slightest melody while Miracle struggled in the water, his stone fixed around his still bleeding throat. The watchful whale's large and expressive eyes saddened seeing the seal fight to breathe. Then in one universal gesture, they separated, giving Miracle an open path to the nursery. It was soon after that Miracle began to feel the excruciating grip in his lungs ease up, and in that moment, he looked to find the face of Kishk.

The whale was a considerable distance away by then, but he could still see the valiant witch crusher's violet orbs twinkling. Miracle's eyes widened, and he smiled despondently. Returning a faint almost nonexistent smile, Kishk's expression melted over with a distinct mournfulness. Immediately sensing that something was terribly wrong, Miracle turned from the whale and began swimming directly toward the remains of the island. The falling rose petals were beginning to diminish in their angelic journey from the skies when he raised his head feeling them wash over his face, some of them sticking to him, others floating in slow motion into the sea. He sensed the air turn warm. A sudden breeze whisked over him, blowing the petals in endless disarray. Transforming into what look like flurrying butterflies, they escorted him through their velvety curtain of white flutter.

Approaching the broken-up floes, he pulled himself up onto the fractured portion of the shattered nursery, licking at his wounds, shaking off water and the hundreds of white rose petals that covered him. Within moments, he could smell the humans on the island panicking just as Nikki had when she first became aware of their presence. Nervously, he continued passing them, studying their faces slowly and cautiously advancing. Sniffing the air, he wondered if the seal hunters were, in fact, dead; they appeared to be. However, when he saw the small movements they made when looking at him, he knew otherwise. It was not long before, as did Bellgar, he believed that the humans no longer posed any real threat. In fact, if anything, he felt sorry for them. They looked so pathetic and worn-out. With this affirmation, he knew what he so desperately needed to believe. At last, the vile and evil Decara was dead! She had to be! He had seen the whales snap her into a million pieces just before he felt himself being thrown clean off the island himself.

Sealssong was at last free from the witch! At last! At last!

This revelation was almost too wondrous to comprehend! With a faster stride to his wriggle, Miracle hurriedly passed up more of the seventeen speculating seal hunters, each one crumpled over, lying in their own mountain of billowing rose petals. It did not take long, however, for him to reach the gathering. Stopping for a moment, he tilted his head and, without any further thought, excitedly called out for Emma. When he did this, the drawn-out and sad faces of Poo-Coo, Nikki, Promise, Big Petie, Little Lukie, and finally his mother instantly confronted him. Arayna had only just arrived. She too had been tossed significantly from the blast, injuring both flippers. Hurt and seemingly left to die, she remembered hearing the childlike voices of the floating rose petals as they came down upon her. Each innocent voice called to her, telling her that everything was all right and that all she need do was to follow their song, and she did. Somehow, some way, she was once again reunited with the others, but when she found that Miracle was not there, her heart panicked, but it did not truly break until she looked upon the still and quiet face of the young girl lying before her. Still not aware of her son's presence, exhausted, injured, and confused, Arayna remained in her quiet reverie, pathetically limping closer to Emma, her eyes welling up with flooding emotion.

"Oh no," she cried in a heart-wrenching whisper. Then lowering her face before the girl's partially exposed bare feet, for they, as much of the rest of her, remained significantly blanketed in soft rose petals, Arayna looked down with eyes that burned with unspeakable grief. Placing her beautiful seal face upon the delicate ankles of the brave girl who had sacrificed herself in order to save her son and the world, she began to weep.

At that moment, Arayna heard Miracle excitedly barking, "Mother, you are safe!"

Going to her son directly, she embraced him, and cried "Miracle, you are hurt!"

"I'll be okay . . . the bleeding has nearly stopped. I am so happy to see you, Mama! Are you all right?"

Arayna tried to offer him a smile, but failed miserably.

Seeing the tears in his mother's eyes, he froze. "What's wrong?" he begged, feeling the panic thicken in his throat. "Why are you crying? What has—" The white seal suddenly stopped speaking, not daring to move another inch.

Arayna looked at her son, eternally grateful for his return; but sadly, her observance was imitating the same desolate expression of everyone else who gathered there. Wanting to desperately spare him from such grief, she stopped herself, knowing that she was helpless in protecting him from this mournful tragedy. Again, Arayna lowered her head before painfully placing a flipper upon her son's shoulder;

she turned away, unable to watch the sorrow on his face when he would come upon his dear and cherished companion.

Miracle stared at his mother for a long time before he found the strength to look at the mound of white rose petals outstretched before him. Slowly he began to wriggle himself toward the roses, his body trembling from the intense dread he felt. Still, he pressed onward. In respected reverence, the walruses and the seals, as did the others, carefully moved away from the pillowy bed they mourned before allowing Miracle to find his way. Only a few stray rose petals were floating down from the sky when Miracle finally reached Emma. Her hair remained sporadically covered in the white wonder, the occasional wind stirring it around, revealing portions of her body as it blew about displaying the lovely way her face seemed to glow in the streams of golden sunlight tenderly kissing her brow.

He gazed at Emma, as if in a trance.

Not understanding, unable to accept what had happened, Miracle's palpitating body wriggled even closer. Moving past the wounded brother of his beloved friend, he pressed next to Emma. Respectful of his return, Kenyan allowed the seal to view his sister. Carefully picking, himself up from the spot he knelt upon, hurting, bleeding, and fighting to remain conscious, Kenyan turned and sat despondently on a small block of ice not far from where his sister had been placed. As Miracle's eyes came upon Emma's face, he could not help but remember the first time he laid eyes on her. She was as beautiful as she was then. He could see those wondrously blue iridescent eyes shining at him, her tiny mouth raised in the same adoring smile she had given him so many times before. He could hear the music of her laughter tickle at his nose, and the magic of her heartbeat within his own. If there was such a thing as true love, no matter how indifferent, he knew without a doubt just how much he loved her. "Emma . . . ," Miracle whispered, his snout drawing close to her angelic face. "Emma . . . ," he repeated, this time calling out with a happy voice, "I am here! Wake up. We don't have to be afraid anymore!"

Suddenly, Emma's eyes flickered and opened.

"Emma! You're all right! I knew you would be safe! No one could ever break us apart, could they?" Miracle exclaimed through happy eyes that swam in teary wonder.

Emma looked up toward the white seal, offering him the most enchanting smile he had ever seen. "My Miracle," she said in a voice so small, so delicate, he could hardly hear her.

"Decara is dead!" he cried. "We are free now! Free! She can never hurt us again!" He looked upon her radiant face, the rose petals blowing about her in the swirling wind. However, when the squalling flow of petals settled, he was returned to the unbearable hardship of his reality. Once more he would look upon the still and motionless Emma, her eyes closed, and her breath without movement. She had never spoken, for it was only in his mind's eye that such an image could be possible. For what lay before him would never speak again. Then the ultimate and most insufferable pain he had ever known sliced through his heart, the tears flooding over him with such incredible magnitude. His eyes painfully burned as he looked upon her beautiful face, her image blurring from the swelling of his tears.

"Don't go," he begged with unbearable sorrow, lowering his trembling face, placing it despairingly into her folded fingers. Emma's hands came undone, one falling limply across his head. Miracle looked up to her and began rubbing his head over her cold palms as if she was once again stroking the soft fur upon his cheek. "Stay here with me . . . Don't leave me here alone . . . Stay with me . . . ," he wept, all the while moving Emma's lifeless hand upon the back of his trembling head.

Unable to watch such heartache, Arayna lumbered to Miracle's side. "She is gone, my son," she lamented, once again touching upon his shoulder with her injured flipper. Miracle only buried his head deeper into the rose petals surrounding Emma's breathless chest. "Come," his mother said once again, extending her flipper, attempting to steer her son from the dead girl.

Miracle quickly pulled away, crying, "No! Don't touch her! Don't hurt her anymore!"

Startled, Arayna began to tremble with a stabbing pain that pierced her soul. Wiping at her eyes with her aching flippers, she covered her mouth, blocking out the mournful cry about to reveal itself.

"I won't leave her here all alone. She's so small and fragile," Miracle wept. "She doesn't like the cold, it isn't good for her."

Seeing that the situation was becoming unbearable, Poo-Coo immediately went to Arayna. "It's all right," he told her. "Come; give him a few minutes alone." Closing tight her tear-drenched eyes, the helpless Arayna nodded, allowing the walrus to escort her away from her son.

From the snowy pillow of roses, Miracle raised his head, needing to look upon Emma once more; her face blurred again within his burning sea of tears. He stared at her for a long time, remembering, forever loving her. And raising his flipper up to her quiet face, he gently stroked it. He sadly gazed down at her, his muzzle only inches away, his tears washing over them both before splashing onto the petals adorning her.

"My wonderful Emma . . . what did she do to you? My Emma, my beautiful Emma . . ." Closing his eyes, he placed his head under her chin and began to sob; feeling the last of what little remained of his heart shatter inside his heaving chest. His cries were inconsolable and full of such heart-wrenching anguish, causing all that were there to reverently bow their heads and mourn along with the white seal that had dared to love a human girl.

THE SACRIFICE

As the saddened congregation wept, the white seal could feel the warm rays of the sun light upon his head.

Unexpectedly, the stone around Miracle's neck wavered before him, gently brushing over the dead girl's lips.

Yielding, he bowed his head, looking at Emma as well as the treasured tear that had once held miraculous powers. Immediately, he knew what he must do. Although the tear had long since worked its magic, perhaps there was one more drop of wonder left, one last way to bring back Emma even if it meant his own death.

He would remove the stone!

Adoringly, he gazed down at the dead girl, watching his tears fall then flow across and down her cheeks. Courageously he gave his heart to her for the last time, saying, "This is for Emma . . . for her courage . . . for her purity of heart . . . for finding me and bringing me home." He bowed his head, overwhelmed with such heartfelt emotions, feelings he never thought he was capable of ever experiencing. Rubbing his wet nose softly against her cheek and closing his teary eyes, he bent, nearing her forehead and kissing her as gently as a seal ever possibly could.

Looking down at her just one more time, he gave her his last smile, whispering to her softly, "I love you, Emma." Lower his head, he wept; and before anyone could stop him, he stretched out his injured neck, raised both flippers toward his throat, and pulled the stone up and over his head, sacrificing himself.

He heard the others gasp, each calling out to him in heart-stopping shock. Regrettably, it was already too late. As quickly as he had removed the tear, Miracle had already placed the seashell necklace firmly around the neck of the lifeless Emma. Arayna screamed out and then fainted straight to the ground. Poo-Coo tried to go to Miracle as all the seals and walruses barked and howled with wild alarm, but what the grieving seal had done remained unchanging. There was nothing anyone could do now. In a matter of moments, just as promised by Mum, the covenant of the sacred tear appeared in the wind, murmuring, *"The power of the stone is great when worn, but when removed—death is reborn!"*

Miracle felt his insides twist, squeezing the breath clean out of him. His eyes widened with an intense sensation of displacement, as if he were falling from someplace millions of miles above the earth. His heart quickened, and everything began to swirl around him. Still, he would not remove his eyes from his cherished Emma unremittingly, hopeful that before he died, the magic of the tear would find pity upon the girl and once again return her life.

Sorrowfully, this he would not see. For in the fleeting instant of a breaking wave, the white seal fell upon the girl's breathless body. In his fatal collapse, the hundreds of white rose petals covering Emma suddenly flew into the air. In endless flight, they circled and fluttered around the bodies of the dying seal and the dead girl.

Miracle's final breath was loud and enduring, its lasting resilience continuing for several moments before it died off into a low moaning drawn-out sigh.

Miracle was dead.

THE MIRACLE

The entire earth began to tremble and the sky grew dark. It turned night again.

The ice shook, and the skies swirled chaotically, grabbing waves of stars, pulling them from the heavens. The water rose and began to freeze over while more of the mighty glaciers returned. Rising, crashing through the surface, exploding, drenching the icy grounds, claiming their rightful place in the sea, the massive giants winked at the passing clouds, upholding to their excited climb. The pure sweetness of rose petals permeated the air, and from some obscure place in the universe, perhaps enticed by all the wonderment, a giant night rainbow emerged, painting itself across the moving firmament. Despite this extravagant marvel, all became lost to its magnificence, for every seal, every walrus, and every creature that lived upon Sealssong howled and yelped while becoming tossed about helplessly. Kishk and the other three whales attempted to maintain their stay in the raging ocean, the multitudes of blasting hummocks persisting in lancing the water from every possible angle. As if it could rumble and shake with no greater fervor, the entire seal nursery erupted with an even more ferocious quake!

Little Lukie was squealing madly against the roar of the fantastic happenings, as were Crumpels and Big Petie. Poo-Coo was still attending to the unconscious Arayna while Kenyan tried to remain standing on the ground, attempting to go to his sister. However, the more he tried, the more he continued to fall, sliding pathetically into the fields of scattered rose petals that bounced right along next to him. In complete pandemonium, some of the men made a real effort fleeing from the presumably doomed island, but the surging waters and the blasting towers of ice proceeded to surround them, managing to stop them.

As the seals screamed and the sea violently went off some more, Kenyan endured, determined to reach Emma. Finally, securing a foothold on the ice, he stepped forward. Then all at once, from beneath the ground supporting the dead seal and his sister, he felt a powerful punch snap at his feet; the impact was fantastic! It shattered the ice in several directions like a pane of glass. Happening in a split second, Kenyan helplessly watched as the bodies of Miracle and Emma became inundated with a massive explosion of frothy chaos. A large gaping hole quickly appeared, spreading out over the crumbling nursery as an intense purple light shot up from the heart of the sea. In blinding splendor, it ruptured forth, engulfing and then swallowing Emma and the seal, saturating its stunning radiance over everyone and everything!

Again the earth, shook, this time one notch greater. The sound the nursery made was deafening, as if the very fiber of itself became ripped apart. *"Promise—!"* Nikki screamed feeling her child become savagely torn away from her side while the mighty earthquake rocked on with seemingly no intentions of stopping.

"Maaaaa! Maaaa!" yelped the pup, terrified, falling backward into the dancing throngs of the bursting ice floes. Bellgar quickly dashed for his son, deplorably slipping and sliding just as if he had never been on the ice before. Finally, grasping Promise between his

shaking jaws, he took hold of the pup and returned to the frantic pleas of his mate.

"Bellgar—is he all right!" Nikki hysterically cried, blindly searching and scooping up her baby with both flippers, pressing him closer to her heart.

"I'm all right, Mama!" Promise tearfully told her while shaking pitifully.

"What is happening?" Bellgar roared, petrified as he looked at the erupting waters and the unbelievable sights going on above them. The stars had fallen from their designated places in the universe and began to spin out of control, heading straight for the earth!

Every beast in Sealssong and upon the earth cried out in utter hysteria, each panicked voice ringing out into the swirling chaos dropping down from every place above. "This truly must be the end of our world!" Bellgar cried, gathering up his family, bringing them closely into a huddled circle, preparing for their demise. Again the earth shook and the heavens exploded into beams of fantastic lights appearing much like the brilliance that took away Miracle and the human girl.

More flashing blazes erupted from the core of the icy sea, water and light becoming one. Every drop that burst forth came with an intense iridescent glow of purple. Blasting, the water rose, spilling itself quickly over the island, once more flooding the grounds, washing the white rose petals back into the moving sea. The water overpowered Nikki and her child, pulling them forcibly to the icy ground. Engulfed, they tried to cling to each other, their eyes and mouths filling with the gushing flow, choking them as it spun them around. Promise tried to cry out to his mother but was unable at first, but as the water began to drain away, Nikki's out-of-breath and panicked pup finally called out to her, bawling. "Mama, are we going to die? Is it really the end of the world?" he whimpered out of breath.

"It must be!" his father howled, finding his way over to his mate and his trembling son. However, as the earth insisted upon quaking and the sky persisted falling, Nikki raised her head from the waters that continued to wash over her. Lifting her burning eyes to both her child and mate, she suddenly cried out, "No! It can't be the end of our world for the darkness has left me!" she wept, touching her eyes with her trembling flippers, now able to behold her family clearly, her sight returned! She sobbed zealously. Reaching out her trembling flipper, she desperately watched Bellgar wriggle closer toward her.

Then turning to gaze upon her child, Nikki wept uncontrollably but joyfully. "I can see you, baby! I am no longer blind. I can see again! I can see you! *I can see you!*" she wailed, grasping her son into her passionate embrace.

"*Mama!*" Promise squealed, throwing his tiny flippers around his mother while Bellgar fought to find his place with his family again, a sighted and teary-eyed Nikki longingly watching as he came to her, hugging her close. Being able to look upon his face again made her weep with such unthinkable fullness, and while holding her child's tiny head in her trembling grip, Nikki began kissing Promise over and over again, the tears spilling from her eyes as the healing waters unceasingly washed over her and her family. Bellgar tightly embraced Nikki and then gazed upon her face. He could clearly see that her eyes had indeed regained their magnificent shine of glistening black. They twinkled brilliantly as before, like two glittering onyx stones shining in endless praise, the miracle of sight making Nikki both weep and laugh in absolute enthrallment. It was like nothing any of them ever experienced! Completely taken over by the wonderworking magic of the divine healing, Bellgar started barking and laughing, smacking his flippers together just, like a pup. He even cried. Filled with such bliss, he could no longer contain himself; it was all so wonderful, so remarkably magical, a miracle to end all miracles! And with their out-loud buoyant laughter filling their hearts, their joyful tears drenching their snouts, the happy seal family began to roll about, performing as newborn pups in the newly fallen snow, the earth still shaking inside the warm cleansing of the rippling sea.

Kenyan as well found himself thrown into the surging waters. In fact, he suffered the strongest blow, being that he was the closest to the initial impact. Having witnessed the dead seal and his lost sister plunge into the sea, the blinding light that appeared immediately pushed at him like a powerful hand toppling him backward. Just before he went down, he saw Captain Thorne being torn away from the ice and thrown into the torrential waters as well, for no one could escape its mighty rush. Surrendering himself over to its unyielding force, Kenyan instantly felt the miraculous drench of the sea upon him, as did everyone in Sealssong. The water only choked at him for a moment, and it was not long before he realized that he was breathing effortlessly under its spraying pressure. Like a weightless stream of unbroken light, he twirled around within its splendor, feeling the wounds that ravaged his body begin to tingle until his whole being became filled with tickling chills, making him laugh, creating blasting mouthfuls of dancing bubbles all about his smiling face.

Feeling the deluge of bursting bubbles over their bodies as well, Big Petie and Little Lukie squealed inside the flow, all fear leaving them, each perfectly rejuvenated with a passion of absolute wonder. They swam around Captain Thorne and all the hunters swallowed up by the rushing sea. Playfully tickling the men's bare feet with their rear flippers, Petie and Lukie watched the men buckle over with startling gagging giggles, their pure streams of laughter replenishing the water with even more spirited laughter.

Crumpels found herself riding upon a huge wave. She found it necessary to burst forth with boisterous ecstasy as the wave took her directly toward Kishk and the other chanters who remained lying on their backs, each forming a complete circle. It was incredible to see the blue giants rise, drifting in the swelling tide, the singing behemoths vibrantly breaking out into harmonious song. Crumpels could not help but sing along, utterly off-key naturally. Still, she sang out sourly, her irritating voice ringing with giggles and snorts while the wave broke directly over her and the harmonizing quartet. Despite the crashing tide, the whales continued to sing out in blissful song, inundating the sea with musical zest while buoying on their backsides.

Poo-Coo and Arayna found themselves in a fast-turning whirlpool. They squealed out with high-pitched laughter, spinning in the waters that tickled around them with frolicsome speediness. In dizzy delight, both tried to catch their breath, but their incessant rejoicing would not allow for it. Continuing in their spin, they laughed like children in the sparkling swirl of a happy dream. At that precise moment, Arayna felt her injured flippers heal, and when she looked upon Poo-Coo, she could see that his broken tusk was also made whole again.

The stars were glowing with an intense brightness when abruptly; they exploded, transforming the entire sky into a starlight mist of golden streamers covering every inch of Sealssong. "Boop-boop-oh my, you should look at the sky!" Crumpels barked happily, trying to rescind the sounds of the singing whales. "It has all shiny lights on it!"

Upon seeing this, Kishk and his three comrades flipped over onto their enormous bellies and instantly escalated into an even grander song of whale-istic bliss! Up they all rose in the swell of the sea, crashing through it, sounding like tremendous cymbals, finishing off the most profound symphony ever written, each soaring beast looking out into the glitter of the twinkling sky, a glorious sky—a sky with all shiny lights on it!

GUARDIAN OF THE PURPLE ANGELS

Soon the waters became calm and the whirlpools dissolved; and each creature, be it seal, walrus, or man-beast, found themselves back upon the nursery, all of them short of breath, exhausted, but fully alive, restored and quite able to watch the next wonderment fully display itself in ultimate brilliance.

What happened next nearly took the rest of the island back into the ocean. From the place that claimed Miracle and Emma, insurmountable amounts of seawater spewed forth, ushering the return of the incredible purple light. It ruptured, shooting straight into the sky. Ablaze with electrifying brilliance, the beam of light quickly took the form of a sensational waterspout, its fantastic funnel filling up with half the sea, its vibrant purple hue dominating everything. It spun in a perfect horizontal line, never faltering, ever constant in its unbending stance. From the island, every pair of eyes gazed up toward it, stunned at its breathtaking size, overwhelmed and fascinated as to its origin and what its next move would hold.

Arayna and Poo-Coo had lost the temporary giggles, so did the seals, walruses, the hunters, as well as Kenyan, and a revitalized Captain Thorne. With his long blond hair thick and vibrant, his beard full and coarse, his skin clear and unblemished from rat bites, his body virile and strong, Captain Thorne removed his eye patch and looked straight into the sky with both eyes this time, his cobalt baby blues dazzling with marvel. In fact, all who now gazed from the ice wore an expression of staggering awe, captivated in a dazed trance of disbelief.

More powerful eruptions of water blasted up into the swirling purple waterspout, making it spin even faster, standing tall and soaring, sweeping all the clouds away with one quick whoosh, occupying much of the sparkling heavens. As it danced about, it slowly began to curve toward the nursery, its massive form bending into a definite nosedive. Again, the seals and walruses screamed out, the men scattering as Kenyan and the captain took cover behind a tall slab of ice and snow. Down it came crashing, showering insuperable quantities of water over the four whales and the already flooded nursery. As it hit, a deafening chorus of sounds came upon the earth, sounds of ancient music and voices not belonging to this world but of another. An enormously rushing noise of slurping air reverberated; its origin coming from the sheer breath of the sea! She quickly inhaled, sucking up the energy needed, to, transfix herself once again to the land of the living.

The mighty whooshing strains of gulps soon became joined by moving unnatural forms. At first, appearing misshapen and gluelike, the incited globs of water crisscrossed each other and then partially separated, resembling two gigantic bookends. Almost, instantaneously, the awe-inspiring translucency morphed into two water-filled dolphins, the heavy sound of gurgling filling the air. Both silver dolphins opened wide their magnificent glowing eyes of vibrant pink, then in a low-pitched drone and singsong voice of unearthly reason, they spoke without ever opening their liquefied lips.

"We are the messengers of truth. One voice, one mind, we bring you tidings of dreams . . . and whispers of promise." The liquid dolphins flickered with even more light, their glowing eyes igniting further, and as she had appeared before from the very center of the revolving pillar of water connecting them, the Kellis emerged and stood between the two silver-looking mammals like a strange and curious statue in a magical fountain.

Engulfed within its watery boundaries, the fantastic creature smiled. From purple spinning funnels of misty swirls, she and the dolphins levitated mere inches above the breathing ocean. She looked angelically upon the awestruck congregation facing her. Her, inhuman high singing voice echoing out in glorious song her huge purple saucerlike eyes gleaming in the twilight of the flowing sea. Her half-human, half-mammal face and body fluctuated in the spinning pillars, perpetually washing over her. In dreamlike floatation, she continued to smile through translucent features, floating above the sea, the resplendent crown of watery spines gracing her head slowly beginning to glow. The columns of her gossamer headpiece pulsated before turning into a dazzling light, causing the tips of the aqueous spikes to immediately flair like a burning candelabrum. At that precise moment, the great fireball returned permanently to its rightful place in the heavens. Then the creature with the incredibly enormous purple eyes dominating most of her peculiar oval face nodded, outstretching her arm. It wavered in the watery column with a vague familiarity, changing from human form into a mammal-like semblance as the rays from the streaming shafts of sunlight broke through the watery existence she swam.

With her curious webbed hand floating outward, she revealed a shining object within her alien grasp. It was the precise stone that had once graced the white seal, the stone the Mad Mum stole from Decara. The same stone encasing the tear that Miracle gave his life for so that the human girl might once again live, and as it had done many times before, the tear began to spark with the brightest purple hue yet imagined!

The Kellis allowed the gem to hover above her translucent fingers, staring upon it smilingly. All the small seashells once attached vanished, revealing only the stone and the pulsating tear within. The same low monotone hum underscored her song as her words vocalized through both connected beings made of seawater.

"I am Kellis, the first to be slain. I am the daughter of truth," she sang in unearthly vibrations, her words radiating through the immobile mouths of the liquefied dolphins. With a quick swish of her hand, she snatched the stone and held it tightly, its purple glow showing clearly through her shimmering transparency. "I hold the true treasure of innocence. It belongs to the sea and made of the sea! It is our mother's tear—and is most powerful. For as I have already foretold, when once returned, your world would be reborn," she sang. "From the unthinkable moment it was first taken, there has been much sorrow. Hers was the first tear ever to be shed in your world, a world that comes from the same waters that have existed from the beginning of time—the very same from which I now speak. As are the tears of all mothers, hers is most powerful . . . stolen by the darkness when man first lost its innocence. Its power is most rare and most potent made up of pure and simple love. Its absence has made Our Majesty, the Sea, suffer immensely and all who dwell in her kingdom."

Suddenly, Kellis turned and looked toward Kishk, who was staring at her in absolute amazement just as he did the first time he saw her. The whale gazed at the purple creation, appearing like an infant looking upon his mother for the first time. He smiled in endless adoration as she wavered before him, smiling at him, fluctuating from human images into mammal-like reflections floating before him like a heavenly apparition.

"You have done well, blue giant," the Kellis told him, her song humming along with its high resonance playing clearly via the aid of the water-filled dolphins. "Through the loving sacrifice of the white seal and your courage, you have destroyed this darkness and have broken the ill-fated spell of the tear. For this, we are eternally grateful. Promising to remain in your world until the tear's return has made me most weary, for my home, like the ones who still remain trapped in your world, unseen, existing in the deepest parts of the sea, is far, far away, belonging to places beyond what man is capable of understanding. Unable to return, we have vowed to remain and have waited for this moment."

The Kellis returned her fantastic purple eyes back to the stone in her transparent grasp. "Without it, she has been incomplete, powerless, barren, and vulnerable to man's evil ways. With it, she can once again govern in peace." Holding up the gem toward her water-filled and spiny crown, the stone, as well as her aquatic headpiece, ignited with a blazing white light. "This is the heart of the sea, behold!" she told the crowd. "I thank you, wise and gentle blue giant for this returned treasure. Your world is saved, and innocence shall once more prevail. Guard it well, for it is most precious." Kellis looked upon the now glowing tear, drawing it close to her watery lips before kissing it. Turning her eyes toward the mother of the white seal, Kellis watched as Arayna swam to her on a cloud of mist. With no fear yet, filled with a heavy heart, Arayna moved toward the fantastic being. Drawing next to the whale, her eyes immersed with longing, wanting desperately to know so much more, but realizing that even if she understood, it would never bring her Miracle back.

Before Arayna could possibly utter a sound, Kellis spoke to her. "You have suffered greatly for it was your child who was taken. Perhaps in these words I now offer, you will find comfort. In spite of the being you see before you, I too was once like you—a seal, a harp seal, born unto Sealssong, the first pup ever to be slaughtered by the darkness of man. That was when Our Majesty first shed this sacred tear, your mother, the Sea. It is then that I became what you now observe—a crowned enigma, half earthbound, half celestial, I, the first of the many slain, given the name *Kellis*—guardian of the purple angels—the murdered children of Sealssong."

Arayna remained motionless, staring. "You were truly born a seal?" she asked through a tight throat.

"Yes, the enchantment of the tear changed me into what you see before you, but now I am made free at last, as are the many lost children who have remained here with me these many, many years." All at once, a tiny innocent puplike voice sounded its cry, becoming a part of the Kellis's words and song. "We have remained because of our love for her. We would never abandon our queen." Incredibly large tears came from the Kellis's vast and amazing eyes as she gazed upon the open waters before her. "But now that the tear has been returned, she has been made whole and we can at last leave in peace. For her release is our release. No longer shall we exist in the whitecaps of the waves. We are relinquished, and for this, I give to you this revered gift. Look upon them well, for they shall only be with you for a short time."

Gazing down at the treasure in her hand, Kellis smiled. Slowly, the stone began to open like a locket, and a great brilliance crept out, washing onto the fingers of the wondrous creature; and with the slightest indication of her wavering hand, Kellis, the foremost destroyed baby harp seal and guarding angel of Sealssong, gave the heart of the sea back her scared tear. Blazing with a wondrous brightness, the enchanted tear rolled gracefully from her palm, landing directly into the waters below. Splashing against the waves, the entire ocean lit up, making it possible to see straight to the floor below. Then Kellis waited for her promised gift to unfold before all to see.

The sea erupted, and from the core of this most spectacular expel, a fantastic host of tiny white creatures abruptly spattered up toward the heavens. With bodies appearing as clouds sprouting tiny wings, woven from the foamy white fabric of the sea, hosts of souls belonging to the many slaughtered baby harps filled the skies! Up they rose like a celestial whirlpool of spinning rose petals, for they were indeed the purple angels of Sealssong, the same wonders that protected and saved Emma so many times before. Now, in snow-white shapes of billowy splendor, sprinkled with purple sparkle, they whimsically danced about the skies. They squeaked and giggled playful bursts of laughter, elated with joy for having at last been released. Miracle's selfless act had made it possible for them to leave the earthly waters and at last make their journey to another place far, far away where death could never again claim them, where the skies remained purple, filled with clouds made out of watery twilight. They were going where sicknesses and suffering no longer existed, where man could no longer destroy them, where there was no such thing as greed or hatred. A place where there was only love and a benevolent peace that would embrace them eternally, allowing no harm to ever again come to them. They were going home!

Higher and higher the spinning flock flew, their tiny white gossamer forms making rainbow prisms out of the filtering sunlight, their small wings of foamy sea fluttering like cherubic butterflies, taking them higher still, until they utterly covered up what remained of the sky. Kellis watched, igniting further with a dazzling light show of her own. She smiled contentedly in her fluctuating private sphere, the water-filled dolphins freely copying her triumphant gesture. With a slow curve of her body, she knelt, momentarily becoming level with the sea. Lowering her wavering half-human, half-mammal hand and allowing for her unearthly grasp to break away from her secluded world, she placed a single finger upon the waters. Effervescence of the highest magnitude rumbled the sea, making way for the pièce de résistance of quintessential magic and a magnificent promise fulfilled. Shooting up just like the flowing realms of celestial baby harps, a reawakened Miracle suddenly appeared! Within a gushing spray that washed itself down from the shining sky, the white seal rolled against the frothy cushion of the floating sea. His tiny form was transparent and watery, like the Kellis and the purple angels, his see-through fur glowing with a million purple sparkles. Appearing in the sky like the astonishing angel he was, Miracle tumbled in aimless flight, soon to be joined by another twirling figure.

All at once, from the heart of the misty clouds of bursting seawater—Emma appeared!

Her tiny body was unclothed, and as was Miracle's, she also was transparent and filled with the same watery essence that could be seen from everywhere upon Sealssong. There within the many folds of bending waves and shooting streams she twirled about like a gifted ballerina. Her eyes remained closed as were Miracle's, but the way she commanded the sky and sea with her rhythmic movement, she suggested having performed this dance many times before mastering her poetic and graceful movements long before this moment. For, she was surely a part of the sea, as it was surely a part of her.

In midair, still in slumberous motion, Miracle and Emma touched noses, gently coming together, perfectly their bodies floating in dreamy, watery suspension. That was precisely when the next miracle of miracles happened! Upon that very day, high above the nursery of Sealssong, in front of every creature, every man, seal, and walrus, Emma began to change! Her golden hair suddenly lost its color, quickly turning a pure snow white! Her hands and legs appeared to become more sealike than human, and as her body liquefied, drawing her tiny form further and further into itself, she began to lose her shape against the flow of the moving sea that towered in the sky. Her arms, now obscure, wavered in the floating waters, her fingers folding over, merging into a solid semblance of snowy-white flesh, her legs and toes doing the same. It was not, however, until her face began to change that the true metamorphosis finally allowed itself to be revealed. A tiny black and shiny button nose appeared where Emma's small curled-up nose used to be. Her iridescent blue eyes, now fully open, began to grow in surprising wonder as tiny white lashes swiftly outlined themselves around her eyes, bringing with them many fine snow-white hairs not only confined to just her eyelashes. A multitude of downy white fur would soon cover her face with fluffy disbelief! For this miracle did not play by any given rules. In its infinite wisdom, the powers that be were modifying a mistake remaining to allow much too long.

Magically, Emma became transformed.

With a few more bows of merging water, along with more slivers of bursting sunlight, all aglow with golden arches washing themselves over everything and everyone, there above Sealssong, Kenyan, Arayna, all the others, and right before Miracle himself—Emma turned into a seal!

REBORN

Miracle's eyes flashed open, astounded by the miraculous alteration. Although completely transformed, it was still Emma!

She had physically changed right before his eyes, and yet he could still see it was she, the same lovely girl he had known all along. The same human he had given his life so that she might live, and she was alive in a whole new way! Just as he was! Both transformed—and yet still the same.

Miracle squealed joyfully, mesmerized, gazing into those same wondrous blue eyes of Emma's. She was no longer sick! She was no longer freezing! She was no longer crying! She was no longer dead! Nor was he having also returned, but how? He could not even begin to imagine. He would not even try. All that matter now was that Emma was back! She was not human, but she was alive and she was a seal—a harp seal! Just like him! Unable to hold back the thrill he felt, Miracle squealed out some more, yapping like a newborn.

Emma smiled and blinked her seal eyes, squealing back in midair. Placing her flippers up to her snout, she felt her tingling whiskers and fluffy face and started to giggle with unbridled rapture. It was her silent wish, the same one, which she had made over and over again! Never saying it aloud, it was always with her ever since she could remember—and now it had come true! She was free from the human shell that never quite belonged to her, which never quite fit right, which was always foreign to her. However, this new form was truly familiar and seemed to fit just right! She was free of all sickness! Free of all fears! Her spirit knew no more sorrow, but only joy! A joy that told her that her newly acquired seal heart would eternally beat next to the creature she loved from the moment she first looked upon him. Her Miracle! Unable to share life with him as she would have wanted while in human form, this new reborn embodiment now gave her the gift of sharing a magnificent existence with the white seal that had brought to her for the first time the true meaning of home. She no longer was alone. She no longer was afraid. She was no longer an oddity to be shunned. Instead, a bold spirit free to soar endlessly throughout the universe, eternally grateful for the considerate correction nature had at last amended for her.

When Miracle and Emma once more touched noses way up in the sky, still floating in the flowing waters surrounded by the ever-constant expansion of angelic baby seals above, the touch they encountered this time would be significantly different. For now, both had seal noses and both were exactly the same medium size, every bit of them incredibly adorable. Just the same, these new circumstances remained considerably altered, and that made them both laugh out loud. As if reading each other's thoughts, they slowly extended a flipper, offering it to the other, wanting to make sure it was not all a dream. Their transparent seal fur sparked with purple shimmers when their flippers tenderly pressed against each other. While the miraculous waters sprayed all around them, Emma pushed out her tongue and licked at her lips. Again, it was like pinching herself to see if she was still dreaming. However, when she realized that her lips were indeed no longer human and it was not a dream, she once more began reveling in cheerful delight! She felt like laughing out loud again, and she did! She felt like dancing and singing! She wanted to fly, but when she understood that she *was*, she began laughing even harder. Yes, the heavens were indeed smiling upon her. Having returned a mythical resurrection beyond anything that man could have ever thought possible, there in this magical restoration way up in the sky, surrounded by the familiar purple angels, she knew without a doubt that she too was free!

At last! At last! Bliss!

Emma and Miracle continued to stare at each other in amazement, giggling happily, however, suddenly, they became startled when they began to feel the pull of gravity; and as the water began to return to the awaiting sea, so did they. While in her drop from above, Emma forcibly blinked her iridescent and abnormally

large and blue sparkling seal eyes. Forever to be unlike any other
harp, her eyes would always remain as blue as the most tropical and
mystical of all seas. This would also be Kellis's memorable gift to her.
In moments, they were back in the water. Down they dove in soaring
flight, circling, dancing in watery wonderment as the entire sea and
its congregation sang to them in harmonious praise and honor. She
was swimming effortlessly among them just like a graceful mermaid,
and she was beautiful! She was joyful! She was healed! She was free!
In tearful gratitude, and with a heart that held no boundaries, she
began making flamboyant somersaults within the water, laughing
and squealing like the young seal she was setting the entire sea aglow
with her newfound happiness!

They sailed through the gleaming blue-and-green twilight
of the ocean, its luster growing brighter and brighter as they
began to resurface, their silky white forms tenderly grazing each
other, capturing the sheer core of the sea, taking their queen's
magnificence with them as they spun in golden exhilaration. They
curled around each other, tying off bubbles with their swirls, the
effervesce tickling at their wiggling noses. Then with a sudden rush,
Emma swam to the surface, breaking through the water in bursting
glory! Up she flew into the whistling air, her purple shimmers
exploding in the shafts of sunlight. In a moment, Miracle was at
her side, glowing with all the same kisses of the sun. With another
glorious splash, they plunged back into the ocean, staring at each
other, their eyes ablaze with wonder and their hearts racing with
happiness. For it was real! It was not a dream! This miracle was for
keeps, and they both knew it. With the supreme reality still flooding
over them, they smiled and giggled in teary excitement, ready to
engage in another twirl upon the shimmering storybook dance floor
of the enchanted sea.

Meanwhile, the island became alive with the hustle and bustle
of flapping seal flippers and scraping walrus tusks. For during the
duration of all the miracles taking place, seals from all over the world
had come to the blessed event. They thoroughly surrounded the
waters of Sealssong, the ice and the glaciers, as well as the floating
part of the nursery, shining brightly in the afterglow of the angelic
harps, moving in a fantastic widespread circle across the heavens.

Most of the men that found themselves washed off the island had
once again found their way back, all seventeen of them accounted
for. They crawled and walked across the ice, noticing that some
of their weapons had washed back onto the nursery. Many of the
hundreds and hundreds of seals, as well as the countless newborn

pups accompanying them, studied the men with distrusting eyes as they, in their staggering numbers, engulfed the island and its surrounding waters for many hundreds of miles. None of the seals dared speak, they did, however, continue to suspiciously observe the men pick up their queer-looking weapons. Suddenly, a tiny newborn who did not seem to quite understand decided to investigate. Without her mother's consent, she scurried away, wriggling directly up to one of the men holding a large wooden club. The tiny pup sniffed at the man's bare foot inquisitively before staring up, looking directly into the hunter's eyes. With looming dread, the dark shadow of the club covered her angelic face.

The entire seal assembly gasped, panic filling their veins. As the curious and fearless pup dared move closer still toward the strange creature she had never before seen, she became inundated with a certain fascination over its intention and its reason for being. However, before the mother could reach her curious pup, the man lifted the club toward the flustering skies. Grasping onto its solid base, the seal hunter surveyed his weapon strangely, as if contemplating its purpose. Then saddened with regret, the man suddenly hurled the club from the pup, casting it as far away from the island as possible where the sea instantly swallowed it up. Reaching down, the man knelt next to the small creature, tenderly rubbing the soft lining of her baby seal belly. The daring and playful pup rolled over, permitting the man to tickle her further, giggling with amused excitement. Upon seeing this, in silent togetherness, the rest of the hunters began to clean up the island of its remaining weapons. In gathered spirit, the entire seal congregation watched the men take the strange and vile weapons to the very borders of the island, as one by one they cast the crude instruments out into the sea. All at once, the seals cheered with clapping seal delight, all of them playing Clap-Clap in joyous union.

It was at this time that all four of the whales began emitting trumpetlike sounds from their blowholes while pumping out whopping streams of water, drenching the island and the men with their baptism of accepted fellowship. Not minding a bit for the sea remained warm and invigorating from the moment that the Kellis first appeared, the men rolled over with laughter. The tiny pups joined in the fun, covering them with the furry frolic of festiveness.

Turning to face the many seals of Sealssong, the walruses, the humans, and all the other spellbound creatures watching suddenly turned toward the Kellis. She smiled beautifully, bowing her aquatic head, all the spiny tubes of water bursting forth with a blazing purple light. She would yet leave them with one final thought, again sung through the shine within the liquid bodies of her adjoining dolphins.

"We must leave, as must the rest who have perished long before this day. The porthole to another world is open but for a short time. It will soon close, not opening again until it comes to take each of you home. For now, say your goodbyes to the ones that will follow and to the white seal and the once human girl. Look for them no more, for they will reside within a sea that is not visible to the eye, but only to the heart. If you keep this innocence alive, their song will forever play within these waters, and there shall be peace," the dolphins told in whimsical squeaks of song. With this final confirmation, Kellis stood upright, her enormous eyes to the skies, her arms wide and open. As her limbs stretched, they soon came upon the silver dolphins, each form merging with one another; and in the twinkling of that moment, the dolphins dissolved.

Standing alone, Kellis offered her final smile before igniting into a rush of flashing lights before returning back into the sea, astonishingly losing all traces of her strange aquatic mysteriousness. For just as the waters washed over her, she reverted back to the small baby seal she once was, the innocent smile of contentment filling her tiny face as she joyfully plunged back into the shimmer of the moving sea, its foamy aftermath bubbling over her before she vanished from sight.

TOGETHER AGAIN

The sky and the sea seemed to meet each other, the horizon somehow reaching up to kiss the sky, a sky it had fallen in love with once upon a time when the world was young.

Arayna had been struggling to swim back to the borders of the nursery ever since her encounter with the Kellis. She passed masses of seals, heavily inundating the waters and the island. In her attempts to reach the nursery, she was able to witness her son's return, as well as the transformation of the human girl she had come to accept and truly love. Filled with more emotions than she could carry, Arayna began to tremble. Swimming as fast as she possible could, overwhelmed with a desperate rush to at last find her way upon the ice once more, she fled. When she arrived, pulling herself up onto the nursery, in her hurry, she lost her balance, falling hard upon the ice, landing in a dreadful skid. Scattered about the massive numbers of huddled seals filling the grounds to their full capacity, Arayna cried out in alarm as the crowd fell in around her.

"Spread out, spread out, let the lady through!" she heard a deep voice shout. Upon hearing this, the crushing horde of seals began to break apart, some diving in to the open sea. Arayna quickly turned herself around and looked upon the one responsible for her rescue. It was the blond human man, Captain Thorne. Slowly, he reached down and helped Arayna maintain a better grip on the ice. She looked up at him, trying to catch her breath, no longer afraid but with eyes melting into a quiet of deep appreciation. "Thank you," she said softly as Kenyan ran toward them both.

"Is it true? Did you see it? Is it really true? Is it possible?" Kenyan kept crying out.

Captain Thorne turned toward the excited boy, putting out his hand in a gesture for him to remain calm. "There, there, son, it's all right now," Thorne vowed. "After what I have seen and heard today, talking seals, falling whales, shattered witches, purple angels, I say anything is possible!"

"But she turned into a seal!" Kenyan hysterically shouted. "She turned into a seal right before my eyes! Emma! She turned into a seal! A seal! She turned into *a seal!*"

Arayna smiled. "Yes, I know."

"And that doesn't bother anyone?" the frantic boy ranted.

"Why should it?" Arayna answered, wriggling closer to Kenyan, her eyes sparkling. "Her love for my son somehow found a way."

"But she's a seal! Do you understand what I am saying? My sister is a freaking seal!"

Suddenly, there was another voice. It was Poo-Coo, and Crumpels was not far behind him. "Dude, perhaps," Poo-Coo said, "it was nature's way of correcting itself, always thought she was way too cool to be human, nothing personal, bro."

"Move over, move over, goodness me! Boop-boop-dee-dee! Did you see! Did you see!" Crumpels barked while hectically barreling toward them. "Did you see it? Did you see it?"

"Yes," Kenyan lethargically responded, still in a state of complete shock. "But I don't believe it! How could she just change into a seal like that?"

"No no no, dear, not that. Did you see my baby's tooth? It's all fixed up, deary-dear!" Crumpels exclaimed, holding up Poo-Coo's massive head, revealing that the miraculous waters had wonderfully mended his once-broken tusk. "Boop-boop-dee-Poo-Coo—tusks as good as new-whooo!"

Despondently, Kenyan looked down toward Poo-Coo just as the walrus opened wide his mouth, exaggerating his ridiculous smile. *"Neeee!"* Poo-Coo teased, making a preposterous sound that only a demented smile could sound like.

Shaking his head with more despondency, Kenyan felt the need to sit down. He quickly plopped himself onto the nearest pile of ice, his head pathetically falling into his hands while looking out toward the edges of the island where a massive gathering was taking place.

"They're coming! They're coming!" another voice shouted in frenzied excitement. It was Little Lukie. Big Petie followed closely behind him. Pushing through the tight-fitting crowd, Lukie screamed, "Let me through, everybody! Listen up! Emma and Miracle, they're meeting up with Kishk! They're all coming toward the island! They'll be here any minute now! Hurry, I don't think they have much time to stay *neither!* Hurry up! Hurry up!"

"I must go to them," Arayna said, preparing to once more battle through the squeezing crowds of gawking seals.

"Wait," Poo-Coo blasted. "Let me lead the way! I'll clear out this annoying clinging vine of nosy busybodies!" Then with a mighty walrus roar, the large rumbling tooth walker with the mended new tooth began to push aside the many seal spectators that crammed before them. "Make way for the mother! Make way for the mother!" he blasted, plowing through the crowd.

As Arayna turned to follow the walrus, she suddenly stopped before slowly wriggling to the place where the despairing Kenyan sat just staring out into the sea, shock covering up his pale face. "Come," Arayna said, pressing her snout gently against his knee. "We must go to them now, and we must be brave, my son."

Kenyan turned to the seal before him as if in a drugged semiconsciousness. "You don't understand, my sister is . . . she's no longer my sister . . . I don't know what she is, but she is not my sister!"

"Oh, but she is! You must believe that."

Kenyan turned away from Arayna, his eyes burning, growing with emotions that both frightened and unsettled him. "I don't know what I believe anymore."

"Listen to me," Arayna begged, trying desperately to meet up with his deliberate evasion that no longer welcomed her probing eyes. "Emma is still your sister. Everything that she was before, she is still, only she is somewhat packaged differently, that's all."

"That's all? *That's all!* That's putting it rather mildly, don't you think?"

"You see, your sister ceased being human the moment Decara plunged that knife into her heart," Arayna tried to explain. "But she never stopped being, Emma. The true essence of Emma continues to exist in a mysterious way, one that we might not be able to completely understand. It is her wanting that has made this possible. A special kind of longing that has lived within her for some time, I would imagine."

"No! I can't accept that."

"Don't you see? She was never complete as a human girl. She never truly belonged to your world or to mine. But now, by some wondrous miracle, she does belong, and she has been set free. You, above all else, must know this in your heart and rejoice in this."

Kenyan turned and finally looked straight into Arayna's large eyes. He watched his reflection swim within the teary pools she reflected before him. Drawing closer, he said, "But your son is lost as well. He is dead. How can you rejoice in that?"

Arayna slowly shook her head. "Your sister and my child are not dead. They are reborn."

Looking at the seal, Kenyan's eyes continued to burn with a sad, confused yearning, his mind consumed with so many inconceivable thoughts. "I don't understand anything anymore. None of this seems possible."

"But it is all possible," Arayna reminded him. "After what has happened here today, can there be any doubt? It is only through our blind faith that any of this could ever make sense."

Once more, Kenyan felt the tears begin to sting. "We'll never see them again, will we?"

Arayna sighed and wiped at her eyes with a trembling flipper. "No . . . I suppose not," she answered, the tears freely running down her lovely seal face. "At least, not in this world, but we will all meet again, another day, another time."

Kenyan stood up, leaving the pile of icy rocks he had been sitting on; his stomach felt nauseous and he remained queasy. He looked out toward the sea, and he could see the whale Kishk nearing the borders and felt his heart begin to pound against his chest. "I don't know what to say to her."

Arayna merely smiled. "Your heart will tell you what you must say. Come, they will not be with us for much longer."

As Arayna turned to start her way toward the icy borders of the nursery, Kenyan called out to her. "Where will they go now?" he asked through eyes of teary wonder.

Again, Arayna smiled contentedly. "Home," she offered, her eyes flooding over as she took off in a quick wriggle. Grabbing on to a deep breath, Kenyan tried to gather up whatever wits that had yet somehow remained; and in a dazed and unresisting manner, he began walking toward the place where he would for the last time see his sister.

VOICES FROM THE SKY

Poo-Coo was with his mother and the two bulls, already having made it to the very seams of the island when Little Lukie noticed Nikki, Promise, and Bellgar.

They were all eagerly making their way down a steep slope directly across from where he was waiting with the others. "Over here!" Lukie barked to the excited family. The sighted Nikki and Promise immediately splashed onto a small secluded ice floe that connected itself to the island and then waited for Bellgar before they all wriggled toward the others. "Hurry up," Lukie squealed. "They're coming! They're coming, and you don't want to miss them *neither!*"

In a short while, Nikki and her family found themselves squeezing and pushing their way past the multitudes of chortling seals already gathered there. Finally, after some more pushing and further squeezing, the three seals were once more reunited with the familiar faces that would forever remain a part of their lives. Nikki smiled at them, and her eyes became alive with such gratefulness for being able to look once more upon the precious faces of her treasured friends. With abundant gratitude, she embraced them all.

It was not long before all eyes came upon the blue whale.

Kishk swam toward the broken nursery, the transformed Emma and Miracle closely following him, both swimming side by side. Making their way toward the others, the expanding collection of seal angels above continued to flutter within the passionate kiss of the horizon, reminding them that their time was growing short. Undaunted in silent procession, the two resurrected harps followed the chanter. Emma undulated through the water, nestled ever so close to Miracle, keeping one eye on the soaring purple angels in the living sky above, all of them appearing like tiny butterflies in a beautiful meadow. She could smell their heavenly scent emanating all around, perfuming the gentle breeze with the fragrance of rose blossoms. Aware of the same pleasant scent, Miracle adoringly gazed upon her, sweet seal snout momentarily resting his head above hers. "The purple angels?" he softly said.

"Yes," she answered.

"Guess we are one of them now." Then becoming somewhat pensive, Miracle asked, "You're not afraid, are you, Emma?"

Emma sighed, holding to a kind smile, gently shaking her fluffy head before nestling it safely below Miracle's chin. "No, I could never be afraid, not as long as I have you," she purred. "Besides, I could never fear the purple angels, how could I? They're taking us home."

The giant Kishk, who remained complacent since the miraculous goings-on took place, carried on in his silent procession toward the excited nursery. Suddenly, he opened wide his violet eyes and shouted, "Look!"

Emma and Miracle felt the blast from the whale's blowhole splash over them as they approached the lip of the icy ridge, now just a short distance away from them. "It's Mulgrew!" Kishk trumpeted. "And you'll never guess who he's got with him!"

"*MUM!*" Miracle and Emma thrillingly barked, their voices becoming one. "And she's alive!" they cried in teary bliss.

From the entrance of the island, all could see the odd and once believed deceased couple make their way toward the congested nursery, the cleansing waters having cured them, just as it had restored the others. Mum was lying on her back and blowing kisses, moving along in the water like a merry tugboat while Mulgrew sat proudly upon her belly for all to see. With his tiny bird legs folded beneath, he was happily playing Clap-Clap, both laughing with manic jubilation. Mum immediately spotted Miracle. She sat up abruptly, dropping the tiny penguin off her enormous belly, sending him splashing headfirst into the water. Surprisingly, the feisty Mulgrew no longer seemed to mind. He just kept right on laughing, paddling himself back toward Mum, zooming onto her head just sitting there imitating her old bonnet. Arranging him the way she knew a bonnet should sit, Mum fiddled with the penguin until she situated him properly; and feeling most fashionable, she smiled at the crowd. "*She's hot!*" Mum bellowed, referring to the penguin, her eyes batting in the most preposterous flutter imagined.

"*She's hot?*" Mulgrew protested, holding to a simpering grin.

"Oh, get over it, Mille!"

Immediately, both penguin and seal broke into hysterics, laughing on and on, each waving most happily toward Miracle and Emma. *"Love-ya,"* Mum ecstatically bellowed. "Lookie here! I can play Clap-Clap again!" She proceeded to flap her flippers about madly, nearly knocking the bird clear off her head again.

Miracle's eyes were wide with joy, and as he gazed upon his beloved Mum, words could not describe the happiness his heart now realized. Bringing both of his flippers over his tiny muzzle, he felt the tears fill his eyes.

Seeing Miracle weep, Emma spoke. "Guess even angels can cry," she told him, wiping a flipper over her own spectacular eyes.

Mum continued to shout toward the two angelic creatures, this time addressing Emma, belting heartily, "Hey, Emma, you never looked so good!" She quickly began smacking the water with her flippers, laughing out loud in a crazy fashion.

Mulgrew suddenly became confused. "Are you telling me that—that's Emma? The bird lady?" squeaked a flabbergasted Mulgrew. "Go on—no way!"

"Way! Who else do you suppose?" Mum smugly sang.

The penguin grinned, temporarily refraining from the happy seal game. *"Mmm—mmm—mmm!* Well, I'll be a man-beast's hairy uncle! How'd she do that?"

"Spunk, that's how! *Spunk!* Always knew that kid wasn't human!" Mum boasted. Reaching the nursery, Mum helped Mulgrew to the ice before turning to rest her back on its icy ridge. While still facing out toward the whale and the two approaching seals, she reached backward, digging her nails into the ice. Grabbing on to the penguin, she plopped him back on top of her head, and with a mighty whoosh, she pulled herself and the penguin onto the island, crushing a bunch of unfortunate flippers belonging to various seals still daring not move out of her way.

"Bugger off, bloody dimwits!" she snapped, wriggling and sashaying herself into the crowd. "And lookie again, *Love-ya . . ."* Mum bellowed while watching the whale and the angelic harps near, " . . . not only am I healed in body, I'm no longer mad—Go figure!" she squealed out, sounding as if she were indeed still mad. Then gazing up toward the bird that remained sitting on her head appearing like a plump, fuzzy hat, she asked, *"Are you the Docta?"* Mulgrew, who was now hanging over her forehead, staring upside down right into her ridiculous face, suddenly looked a trifle worried. "Just kidding!" the silly Mum squealed again, sounding as mad as ever. Suddenly losing her balance upon the ice, she sent herself and the penguin back into the water with a gigantic splash, but it didn't matter. In no time at all, both rolled over each other, the water covering them as more crazy laughter echoed about while Kishk and the two transformed seals floated next to them.

Kishk smiled at Mulgrew with eyes that told just how happy he was to see him. The penguin smiled back, fully returning the sentiment; and once again, jumping upon the belly of the once mad harpie, Mulgrew stood erect, touching the cap of his bird head, saluting his tiny flipper toward the blue chanter. "Permission to come aboard, Captain Sir!" stated the penguin still in respected salute.

Kishk gaily offered a wide and endless grin. "Permission granted."

For a moment, the bird looked somewhat befuddled when he looked toward Mum then back toward the blue chanter's massive face. "Oh, it's, okay if Mum comes, isn't it? I mean, I just thought we could always use an extra pair of flippers on board."

Overwhelmed with added glee, Kishk's smile widened further. "Why, Mulgrew, I do believe you have grown a true sailor's heart," the whale said, chuckling and looking toward Mum, who was blowing kisses at him. "Madame, it, would be an honor to have you join us," Kishk told her, bowing his gigantic head, allowing both to come aboard.

Mum actually blushed. "Ah, my lovely!" she exclaimed, flipping her flipper down in a gosh-golly kind of way, graciously accepting, allowing Mulgrew to scamper aboard first. Then turning around, he extended his tiny flipper over to the seal that quickly took it, pulling him toward herself, giving him a wet and sloppy bumper seal of a kiss. Plopping him hard upon the top of her head, she rumbled up the whale's face.

By now, the other three chanters had surrounded the island just in time to see the two transformed seals make their way up to the ridge of the broken nursery. Miracle and Emma looked toward all their cherished friends with eyes filled with love and gratitude, and just as Miracle was about to say something, the purple angels did a strange and wondrous thing. It would be one last visit to the world from which they were about to depart. They again would warn Emma and Miracle as to the seriousness of their parting in as well as achieving something exceptional in their undertaking. In a fluttering rush, the spirits of the deceased baby harps came blowing back down to Sealssong just like twirling autumn leaves.

Seeing the splendor that was occurring, Mum felt her heart leap in her bosom. From her privileged place upon the whale, she immediately recognized one of the flying angels. It was her, very own Sasha! Mum cried out to her pup with open flippers, watching her baby angel with the foamy wings fly over to her, just as graceful and as beautiful as a butterfly, kissing her like new spring blossoms opening for the first time.

Hundreds of more angels did the same to many of the other mothers, each one finding their own, one last time. In multitudes of sprinkled glitter, they came to find their mamas, their joyous smiling faces indicating their happiness. The selected mothers became overwhelmed with sheer emotion, rumbling, bursting through the ice and snow, each trying to catch their children now appearing as if they were once again fluttering rose petals. If only to hold them once more, they reached out to the heavens, their aching flippers desperate to unite with their babies; and but for a brief moment, they would. In a flash of this granted miracle, a portion of the children, found themselves, nestled deep within their mother's remembered embrace, their youthful voices innocently singing to their mamas, all cradled between loving flippers and joyous hearts.

Mum, who wept with sheer joy, remained holding her child so tightly; never wanting to release her, she soon came to realize that this gift would not last. Unable to stop her pup, Sasha, as did the others, once more became air-bound, their angelic seal wings glowing with foamy wonder, each waving a tender goodbye to the maternal hearts that would forever remain with them. As the purple creations whisked out toward the shimmering horizon before soaring back up into the sky, they sang out to Emma and Miracle, telling them that they must follow, their calling tone more serious and unsettling. The porthole to the next world would continue to shrink, and their time upon the earth was nearly over.

A sudden undercurrent engulfed the two procrastinating seal cherubs below. It began pulling them farther and farther away from Sealssong, back toward the horizon that was anxiously waiting for them. However, the seals were not yet ready to join them—not yet. Emma, as did Miracle, looked toward the horizon, each asking for just a little more time; and not waiting for an answer, both seals once again began swimming toward the nursery. "They're still calling us," Emma cried, looking toward Miracle, her huge iridescent eyes glowing with worry and anxiousness. Miracle nodded, feeling the growing tension picking up the pace, now racing through the water, Emma at his side.

Once again, the nursery clearly came into view. There before them were the creatures they loved. How was it possible that they had to now leave them? Gliding next to Miracle, Emma could not help but marvel at the way the water washed over her slippery seal body. She could no longer feel any remote coldness. It was as if she were bathing in warm bathwater as all remembrances of previous freezing sensations became forever erased from her recall. She kept looking down at herself, still in amazement over the flippers that had replaced her arms and hands, the entire experience still leaving her in a hazy, dreamlike fascination. Not knowing where to keep her focus, she continuously studied herself before gazing back up to the sky where she could see the baby seals with the wings made out of flowing foamy seawater. Again, she looked back to the island, knowing they would soon reach it, if only time and the shrinking portal would allow.

Suddenly, and most clearly, Emma became aware that the purple angels were calling out to them, this time with even more urgency. She quickly turned her glance to the horizon, watching it grow smaller and smaller, seeing the entrance to the next world steadily seal itself shut. As happy and elated as she was in her new existence, she regretted one thing—time. Even now, in her new existence, it quickly evaded her, leaving very little duration to spend with the ones now watching with bated breath and examining eyes from the very borders of Sealssong.

Refusing to heed the critical call, they were once again at the nursery ready to say their final goodbyes.

THE BEAUTIFUL MERMAID

Emma searched for her brother.

Slicing through the water, she skirted the borders desperately to find him there. Suddenly, she seemed misplaced. Even Miracle became lost to her, and yet all that mattered now was finding Kenyan. Overcome with an unnerving panic, she cut through the sea, the ever-persistent calls of the purple angels haunting her every move, telepathically communicating that soon she would become total spirit and that she could no longer remain. Frightened and yet determined to find her brother, she chose again to ignore the warning. Consumed in sheer fearfulness, she began barking out his name. Then all at once, she saw him! He was slowly approaching a part of the island away from the intimate faces of the seals and walruses all waiting to say their goodbyes. However, as difficult as it would be to leave those familiar visions consisting of whiskers and tusks and funny little bird heads, nothing would sadden her more than having to say goodbye to the boy she would forever love, the boy who would for always be her beloved brother, Kenyan.

Aware that Emma had finally found her sibling, Miracle continued watching her from afar as she made her way to a tiny segregated portion of the nursery not far from the others. It was then that he became aware of the crowd that was also carefully watching him. Crumpels was the first to break the silence. Both she and Poo-Coo rumbled toward the edge of the ice. She felt her heart sink into her spongy bosom, her eyes covered in walrus tears. "It's so hard to say goodbye! Boop-boop-dee-cry! Oh, how I will miss you, my little White Puff. Take care of each other in that special world you must go to wherever, that is, and please don't forget us," she wailed, quickly pushing her head into the folds of her son, crying, pathetically shaking up and down, all the while Poo-Coo tried to offer his own farewell.

"I'm proud of you, bro," Poo-Coo praised, raising his flipper toward his own massive chest. "You have taught me to be a warrior of the heart, and for that, I will always be grateful. You truly are the prince of the sea, Miracle. I will miss you greatly, dear brother." With this, he bowed his head in reverent honor before turning away with teary eyes, placing his flippers around his inconsolable mother.

Within the confines of the surrounding ice floes, Nikki and her family were watching with heavy hearts, Big Petie and Little Lukie wriggling out even further to the extreme edge of the nursery, fixing themselves between Mum and Mulgrew, who were now on the ice again having joined the others, all of them shadowing the ice. Not so far away, Kenyan continued his dazed and sluggish slope toward the end of the island, carefully moving through the crowds of seals who respectfully moved aside, making way for the boy whose sister helped save Sealssong. Making his final approach to the edge of the icy lip, his weary and disoriented stare fell upon the seal treading water before him. It was Emma. Her blue iridescent eyes were glowing out to him, appearing as a strange, heavenly glow. It was snowing, but he did not notice.

Emma kept her eyes fixed upon her brother with such yearning it made her tremble. She watched Kenyan teeter-totter in his stance, looking as though he might collapse just staring disconcertedly at her aquatic form. Although she seemed a bizarre enigma, despite her alien appearance, he was able to recognize those magnificent eyes of hers. Feeling dizziness swarm around him, he slowly knelt, watching Emma swim up to the incline of ice. From where he stood, the crusty ridge was several feet away from the water, but he would not let his stabbing apprehensions deter him any further. Uneasily, yet decidedly, he sprawled out on top of the ice, his chest partially hanging over the edge, then as nervous as he was, he carefully reached out to her.

Emma neared the ice, remaining in the water, going as far as she dare go. She moved her head toward his reaching fingers and then felt him quickly pull away when his trembling touch experienced her wet fur. Kenyan bolted up and then sat quietly there, dumbfounded, looking toward Emma, his eyes swimming in a fearful, yet surprisingly tranquil wonderment quite foreign to him. He abruptly gazed down at his shaking hand, studying the watery droplets he brought with him after touching Emma's permanent new seal coat. Closing his eyes, he could not help but tremble. When he decidedly opened his eyes, he realized that Emma's expression appeared sad. Treading water in a sea that gently kissed the borders of the nursery, her eyes swam in their own pool of tears. Then she spoke to him. "It's all right, I understand," she said kindly.

Kenyan looked at his sister with burning eyes. "No, no you don't!" he stung. With a sharp yet *"wanting desperately to understand"* expression plainly branded on his face, he began to crawl toward Emma's whiskered snout. Before doing so, his hand momentarily touched the waters. He quickly discovered that it, as were the falling snowflakes, remained warm and inviting. Daring to continue, he proceeded stretching out his hand, relentlessly trying to steady his shaking fingers. Emma closed her eyes, allowing her brother's touch, his fingers brushing against her tear-soaked cheek. "It's really you, isn't it?" he asked with a heavy voice.

Emma smiled, her stunning blue eyes swimming in tears. "Yes, it's Emma, your Emma, as I will always remain," she told him cradling his hand against her snout and furry shoulder.

This time, he did not pull away. "Does it hurt?" he asked, voluntarily scratching the top of her furry white head. "I mean, dying . . . and becoming a—seal."

Emma tearfully studied him before she spoke. "It hurt not to be one . . . as strange as that may sound," she confessed, exposing her spectacular seal smile. "It was kind of like slipping into an elegant dress made out of magical sparkles, just like being a fairy princess or a beautiful mermaid."

"But . . . but you're . . . a-a . . . well, you're not a princess or a mermaid, Emma, that's for sure!"

"Oh, but I am, Kenyan," Emma sang, looking tenderly at her brother. "You must believe this . . . a beautiful princess mermaid, for that is how my heart feels."

Kenyan stared at her intensely, his hand carefully coming off her head before heedfully touching her snout and tiny black button nose. "This is really happening, isn't it? You are truly in there, aren't you?" he again asked, needing desperately to understand.

Emma nodded affectionately.

"And . . . you are happy?" he asked, removing his hand carefully, drawing away his wide and questioning eyes, never daring to leave her for a moment.

"Yes," she answered in a delicate voice. "More than I can tell you."

"No more sickness, no more pain?"

Emma shook her head, smiling all the while.

All at once, the imploring calls of the angel seals blared over Sealssong. "You have to leave now, don't you?" he asked, not wanting her to see him cry, but no longer able to restrain himself.

Emma suddenly came out of the water and onto the ice. Wriggling before her brother, her magnificent eyes shining in full glory, her tears making her eyes glisten like sparkling sapphires, she tenderly said, "I'll miss you so." She wept, her voice breaking up with sorrow.

Kenyan stared at her, his lower lip quivering, his face shaded in anguish.

Emma's muzzle bravely drew closer. Then in a soft voice, she whispered, "I love you, Kenyan, with every part of my heart . . . for always."

His eyes, brimming over with painful emotion, Kenyan fell toward his sister, his arms reaching around her as he embraced her. "Oh, Emma, Emma, my brave and wonderful Emma . . ." He wept as his face became buried within her snow-white fur, continuing to weep, rocking her back and forth in his arms.

Emma melted in his embrace, hoping it to never end, but soon the sounds of the imploring angel seals were once again making their desperate plea. Heaven was indeed closing its doors. "I must go," she told him.

Kenyan slowly pulled away, trying to maintain himself as best as he possibly could, nodding as if he finally understood. "You know something, little sister?" he said, sniffing up, his runny nose touching gently against Emma's precious seal face. "You were always a mermaid. You just never knew it." Wiping his eyes, he leaned forward and kissed Emma on her furry head. "It's okay," he begged. "I think I understand. Go now." He hugged her one last time. "They're waiting for you."

Emma lovingly gazed at her brother, studying his face as if to forever hold it in her aching heart. Then with all the grace of a true princess, Emma kissed Kenyan on the lips and gave him her final smile before she turned and dove back into the sea. She would once more turn to look at him through blurry eyes of emotion but would not utter another word, for nothing she could ever say would equal what she now felt.

"Be happy, little mermaid," Kenyan told her, watching through his water-filled eyes. Turning, Emma immediately headed toward the place Miracle was waiting. It was then that Kenyan heard crunching footsteps coming from behind him. Directly turning around, he saw Captain Thorne. The Captain was smiling a most contented smile, as if all the questions he had ever pondered had suddenly been revealed to him. Slowly, he approached the boy, looked at him, stood quietly beside him, and turned his eyes to the mystical sea and all that was taking place there. Neither said a word, neither of them aware that it was still snowing.

FINAL GOODBYES

Miracle was still in the emotional embrace with his treasured friends when Emma came swimming toward him. His tiny form was floating in the water, still facing toward the crowd that gathered there.

Little Lukie was in the middle of a crying fit by the time Emma finally made her way over to them. "It's just not fair—*neither!*" Lukie wailed. "Why must you go away?"

Miracle tried to explain. "It's all right, Lukie, you'll see me again one day, you'll see."

Big Petie quickly added. "Are you really dead?"

Miracle thought for a moment, then nodded a questionable nod. "I think so."

"That is dreadful!" Lukie shrilled. "I hate this! I don't think my heart could stand any more grief *neither!* Wait for me, Miracle, I'm coming with you!"

Miracle swam closer toward the distressed seal. "Be brave, Lukie, just as you have always been. What would Big Petie do if anything ever happened to you? He's your dearest and best friend, and he needs you as everyone here does."

Lukie just continued to cry.

Petie, Nikki, Bellgar, and Promise came forth upon the ice, each one prepared on giving their last farewell. "We all want to thank you, Miracle and Emma," Petie said his tears flowing down his plump cheeks, "for saving me and Lukie, and the rest of the world. We'll never forget what you did for us."

Nikki was next. Her vibrant eyes looked upon the seal as if she were looking at him for the first time instead of the last. As the memory of moments together playing as pups swiftly filled her mind, she adoringly gazed upon her dear friend, offering an enduring smile. In that moment, in her mind's eye, she could still see them both taking their first magical swim together, recalling everything as if it were yesterday, remembering loving him as she would never love another, as she did now, and would for always. "I'm not going to say goodbye because, well . . . it just would not be proficient of me, would it?" she said, trying to laugh through her tears. "Until, we meet again, mon amour."

Miracle merely stared at her, wondering how things might have turned out should she have remained with him that not so long ago, however, content in knowing, despite all the odds, they were now at the precise spot they belonged. Her unique place in his heart would remain with him long after this moment—just as first loves often do. Wanting desperately to hold him, Nikki painfully fought the desire. "You will always be my—" She suddenly felt she could not finish. Her emotions were seriously rising in her throat, cutting off her voice. Still determined, she valiantly muddled through as best as she knew how. "Bless you . . ." she wept, struggling to finish off her words, " . . . for everything." Then Nikki quickly kissed Miracle on the cheek before returning her grieving face into the waiting protection of her mate's chest.

Nikki's child, Promise, and Bellgar were next to say goodbye. Promise quickly jumped into his father's flippers and waited to be lowered so he could easily reach both angelic harps. Touching Miracle's nose, Promise rubbed it affectionately and smiled before directing his words over to Emma. However, in his anxiousness, he fell into the water. Emma was quick to intercede, taking the pup into her embrace.

"Thank you," Promise told her, "for finding me and giving me a papa and mama to love." Quickly kissing her on the snout, the pup waited for his father to fetch him from Emma's tender hug, which he did. Immediately returning his son back over to his mother, Bellgar stretched over the side of the icy nursery and placed a single flipper on Miracle's shoulder.

"To thank you, Miracle, well, just would not be enough, so I want you to know that I will take your mother into my family where she will always be cared for, she will never want for anything, or ever again be alone. This I promise, my brother."

Miracle's eyes widened and spilled over with thankful tears. Feeling Emma nearing, her head gently nestled next to him, her flipper tenderly touching against his. They were listening to the chorus of weeping and sniffling sounds surrounding them when Mum suddenly rumbled forward. Nearly tossing off the penguin that sat on her head as well as almost toppling herself over the icy ridge in the process, just about falling on top of Miracle, she sniffed at her runny snout. "What's everybody crying for? For goodness, love-ya-love sake, you'd think they were dead, for crying out love!"

"*They are!*" Mulgrew immediately interjected.

"Oh, botherdash," Mum grumbled, realizing the bird was right, grabbing his head, bending him into a half circle while proceeding to blow her wet nose inside him like a handkerchief. "Codswallop, I'm not going to cry! Nope! And do you know why? Because they will always live right here," she barked, placing her flipper against her heart. Despite her brave attempt, the tears began flowing abundantly. Picking up both seals from the water, she snatched them into her hefty bossom, giving them dozens of kisses mixed with gobs of seal drool. However, unforeseen, they both abruptly slipped right through her tight embrace. Like the seal cherubs warned, they were quickly becoming more spiritlike and becoming less tangible, for Mum's flippers could no longer sustain their ghostly forms of misty haze. "Blimey! You both feel just like the slippery insides of a pearl oyster, I say."

"What is happening?" Miracle called out to Mum.

"It's all right, *Love-ya,*" Mum granted. "Not to worry, you are becoming spirit, a true angel, if you will, and as hard as it may be, it is time to go. Now you and Emma be good little seals, *Love-ya,* and I'll see you on the other side, sooner than you think, I would imagine." Sniffing loudly while wiping more tears away right before belching, she violently sneezed, blowing snot bubbles all over Mulgrew who had just cleaned himself and was just about to say his goodbye. The penguin stood in the gooey muck with a queer expression on his little beak, grinning and saluting the seals, flipping the remainder of Mum's snotty goo out into the sea, sending it clear through the ghostly seals' transparent forms.

"My best to you both," Mulgrew pledged, looking at their lucid figures. "Our gratitude and deepest thanks are yours." He remained staunch upon the ice, diligently standing at attention, honoring them both with a steadfast penguin salute.

Kishk slowly moved in, taking a vast portion of the sea with him as he came upon Miracle and Emma. Both of their forms were quickly fading, but the whale could still make out their shapes. "Time has always been our greatest adversary, hasn't it, little ones?" announced the blue chanter, his violet eyes glistening. "I want you to know that I, as well as my fellow chanters, will make sure everyone is transported to where they belong. We will take care of every last creature and man-beast here, it is my solemn promise," Kishk vowed.

"Thank you," Miracle replied, eternally grateful.

At that moment, the three remaining chanters immediately joined Kishk, each one singing out to the valiant seals their proud song of righteousness and glory. Emma and Miracle listened on with respected hearts, honored by their incredible voices and noble gratitude; however, as their song rang throughout the land, Emma looked upon herself once more. This time it was not to admire her furry white coat or the way her flippers moved so gracefully in the water; it was something far more pressing. She was able to see right through herself! She quickly looked at Miracle and then at herself again. Miracle was just as transparent as she was! In a nervous and quick turn, she bolted her gaze toward the horizon. It was nearly sealed! Unsure of the repercussions should it close before they entered, made her shudder. She could clearly hear the now desperate pleas of the purple angels calling to them—and she shuddered some more.

SEALED WITH A KISS!

Realizing that the white seal had not yet said goodbye to his mother in spite of the desperate warning calls from above, Kishk and the other chanters hurriedly began to move away from Miracle, allowing him to view Arayna. She had found her way over to the same segregated part of the island from where Kenyan and Captain Thorne had been watching. Filled with more heartfelt feelings than she could manage, she felt as if she would succumb to uncontrolled weakness. Seeing this, Kenyan steadily assisted the mother of the white seal, helping her toward the ledge of the nursery, her irritated eyes saturating and dripping with heavy emotions. Miracle could see his mother standing in front of him. He felt his heart sink, unsure if he could go through with it, but knowing that he must. The time had come to say goodbye.

Carefully, he swam to the edge and looked up into his mother's beautiful eyes. How they shone just like the very heavens as he had always remembered them. Arayna tenderly looked down at her son but did not say a word. Bowing her head, she waited for Miracle to come to her. As he came upon the ice, he placed his head next to hers, both melancholy and brimming with heartache. That was when things became dire. All at once, he realized that he could no longer experience her tenderness for he was dissolving, becoming even more spiritlike than before, and her lovely seal face, no longer touchable, floated through his as if they were both passing clouds.

"*Mama . . . ,*" Miracle cried, sounding like a pup again, suddenly afraid, not daring to leave her side while she looked at him with teary eyes and a mother's breaking heart.

"My baby, my beautiful, beautiful baby," she wept, trying to feel his precious face with her own, painfully reminded of the time when she remained imprisoned inside that mesh cage, unable to feel him. Having overcome that moment, she shook her head disbelievingly, grief-stricken for having been once again confronted with such heartrending sorrow. Her heart felt as if it would shatter when her snout went straight through him, as if he was no longer there; but he was there, and she knew instinctively that she must forever remember this granted moment. She closed her tear-drenched eyes as did Miracle, and both affectionately began rubbing noses as if they could still feel each other.

Arayna's face continued to float in a misty vapor of whiteness while embracing her son with her mind and with her heart. Then Miracle heard his mother begin to sing to him. It was her beautiful seal lullaby, the same song that had played inside him for as long as he could remember. He listened, smiling as she sang her face angelic and covered in a mysterious glow. Suddenly, the dire circumstance grew even direr. Miracle tried to remain on the ice, but could no longer. He was fully spirit now, and the ice could no longer hold him. Like the breeze on the water, he floated before her. "Mama!"

he called out in a heartfelt whimper. Fighting the impairing haze, Arayna found that she could barely see him, his smoky shape wafting in the sea. By some remaining unknown miracle, she was, however, able to make out the glow of his eyes; and with her face still floating in heavenly mist, she reached out to him. "My baby," she wept.

Once more, Miracle tearfully went to her, wanting desperately to kiss his mother goodbye, but he would not be permitted; he had remained too long, and yet their longing would find a way. Overwhelmed with insurmountable emotions, Arayna placed a flipper against her lips, kissing it gently before slowly offering her final goodbye. Miracle moved forward and extended his tiny ghostlike flipper toward hers. Raising it, he held it there, merging into a dreamy embrace. The two seal flippers drifted in the white glow, wavering back and forth, blending into a misty haze of vaporous shimmers. Miracle was weeping, barely able to speak when he gazed at his mother. Finding his voice, he tenderly whispered, "I love you, Mama, with all my heart."

With these spoken words, Arayna watched his little face and eyes disappear altogether, and yet she continued to hold out her trembling flipper, unable to take it away, her tears blinding her vision. All at once, Miracle felt himself being pulled backward, Emma not far from his side. Arayna's flipper was still reaching out to him when Miracle and Emma became taken toward the glowing horizon, their hearts suddenly wheeling in absolute wonder. As this strange sensation washed over them, their transparent bodies began to change into what looked like sketchy outlines, each appearing as drawings resembling the charcoal pictures Emma once created, once upon a time when she was human.

While the stringent grip of the living ocean pulled at the angelic couple, they began jumping in and out of the water, imitating skipping stones, squeaking and splashing while tumbling out toward the horizon in frolicking rapture. The nursery continued to watch in awe, and each spectator there suddenly saw the celestial couple's purple silhouettes shine against the borders of the glowing horizon. As both seals looked back to Sealssong, they instantly became drawn from the sea and into the sky. They rose in and out of moving vapors filled with starry swirls, thousands of baby seals surrounding them like a mighty wind filled with endless snowflakes. In a continuous twirl, the heavenly host of seal angels danced around them, pulling them toward the shimmering horizon, happy and most relieved to at last have them in their eager grasp.

A heavyhearted Arayna watched the horizon while Kenyan walked up beside her, the captain still at his side. The encompassing seal kingdom, the walruses, and the majestic sea herself continued to revel in what glistened before them. Then the same men who had spent most of their adult life in pursuit of destroying the snow-white children of Sealssong surprisingly did a peculiar and unexpected thing. They each knelt down on one knee as if in prayer, and looking out to the horizon, as did the rest, they watched the last miracle take place. With a sudden flash, Emma and Miracle ignited into a golden light, and from the heart of this wondrous glow, a distinctive gift was granted to the once human girl and the white seal—just the blessing needed to enter the new world awaiting them. *The gift of wings!*

Right there before all to see, Miracle's and Emma's forms exploded into bright lights; and with the swish of a falling star radiating from their dazzling bodies, two magnificent wings made of foamy brilliance spanned forth. In one incredible sweep, they each stretched their resplendent wings, blanketing half of the heavens with their glorious spread! In that moment of awe, Arayna remembered Apollo, her life mate, yearning for him now, watching, as their son prepared to leave her world. With this passing vision of longing, she hoped that Miracle would at last come to know his father in that great somewhere he was about to become a part of, finding comfort that one day she would find them both there waiting for her. She felt the tears burn against her skin, recalling a time she no longer could cry, happy that she could once again know this emotion. For she knew now that tears were mere reminders that somewhere within all of us, even the hardest heart could still know and remember this special gift of innocence with which we are all born.

With a jolting tug back to reality, or what would be considered unreality, Arayna became aware of Kenyan standing beside her. She slowly turned toward him as the boy reached out his hand and gently settled it upon her shoulder. Looking up with teary eyes, she smiled and nestled her head into his touch, feeling it warm against her furry tear-stained cheek. Kenyan fondly looked down at her, smiling through his own tears, drawing Arayna close to him. It was at that moment Kenyan felt the strong hand of Captain Thorne slowly come down upon his head. The handsome captain playfully ruffled Kenyan's wavy blond hair, offering his own brilliant smile to both the boy and the mother of the white seal before returning his incredible blue eyes to the sky, each remaining in a heartfelt embrace.

As all the seals raised their flippers and the penguins cheered, and as the dolphins and birds squealed and sang out, while the sea swelled and danced in fantastic surges of blissful magnitude, the whales chanted forth a blending chorus of unequaled song, each man continuing to kneel, looking toward the horizon. They nestled side by side in harmonious unity, each hand and flipper joined together for the first time, all waving to the two soaring purple angels with the mighty wings of dazzle—man and beast at last united in reverent peace. And before the gleaming curtain of the netherworld finally closed, the two soaring harps glanced back one last time upon the sparkling terrain below them. With its snow and ice castles all aglow, they caressed the memory of Sealssong and the ones they would for always remember and love. Returning their eyes to one another, Miracle and Emma smiled, gently rubbing seal noses before kissing; and with true love's kiss, they further opened their magnificent wings, covering up the entire sky before blowing into the horizon like the gust of a momentous whirlwind, taking all the purple angels and the falling snow with them.

Every gaze remained fixed upon the place where the sky and water continued in their eternal courtship, right there in the heart of a place called Sealssong. And on that day, before the sea and all who watched, the skies abruptly turned into a canvas of shining jewels—*seal tears*, but joyful tears! Yes, sketched, resembling one of Emma's aesthetic drawings in that star-filled firmament forever remained the twinkling configuration of the kissing silhouettes of two winged seals—Miracle and Emma, eternally preserved for all to see.

Wondrously, from that glorious moment on, whoever chose to look up into the skies upon those clear and starry-lit nights, not only in Sealssong but all over the world, they would find them there. Glistening just like the magnificent seal tears, a reminder, to us all, of the precious gift of innocence and the time when magic was possible. When a tiny seal and a young girl brought back a miracle that remained long forgotten, and through their love conquered darkness, returned the light, and saved the world.

CPSIA information can be obtained at www.ICGtesting.com
Printed in the USA
BVOW07s0632030813

327578BV00001B/4/P